STEPHEN KING

AND

PETER STRAUB

BLACK HOUSE

HODDER & STOUGHTON

First published in Great Britain in 2001 by HarperCollins Publishers

First Hodder & Stoughton paperback edition of *Black House* published in 2026

4

A CIP catalogue record for this title is available from the British Library

Paperback ISBN 978 1 399 76476 6
ebook ISBN 978 1 409 10388 2

Typeset in Bembo Std by Palimpsest Book Production Limited, Falkirk, Stirlingshire

Printed and bound in Great Britain by Clays Ltd, Elcograf S.p.A.

Hodder & Stoughton policy is to use papers that are natural, renewable and recyclable products and made from wood grown in sustainable forests. The logging and manufacturing processes are expected to conform to the environmental regulations of the country of origin.

Hodder & Stoughton Limited
Carmelite House
50 Victoria Embankment
London EC4Y 0DZ

The authorised representative in the EEA is Hachette Ireland, 8 Castlecourt Centre, Dublin 15, D15 XTP3, Ireland (email: info@hbgi.ie)

www.hodder.co.uk

BLACK HOUSE

'One of the most brilliant and chilling thrillers of modern times . . . a thrill-a-minute ghost train ride of a novel, filled with astonishingly vivid characters. Reading it is like holding on to a live electric wire. You may want to put it down, but you find that you can't' – *Daily Mail*

'Fabulous . . . the ultimate in storytelling by two masters of the craft' – *Independent on Sunday*

'There's so much here to revel in, from expertly executed sequences of terror, awe or passion – the novel is a deep reservoir of genuine emotion – to some of the most wonderful characters to spring from a page in years, to a story whose energy is so high and craft so accomplished that most readers will wish it ran twice its great length' – *Publishers Weekly*

'A masterpiece of modern terror . . . a knock-out twist' – *Irish Independent*

'A virtuoso performance' – *TLS*

'An intelligent . . . suspenseful page-turner . . . It's a relief to find popular fiction that is as unpretentious yet rich in literary allusion and human detail as *Black House*' – *Wall Street Journal*

'Jack's saga overflows with dark wit, sly literary references, suspense, and heartache. What elevates *Black House* beyond ordinary horror novels is the richness of its cast' – *New York Times Book Review*

PRAISE FOR THE TALISMAN

'Chilling horror story or fantastic journey though a strange world . . . this book works like . . . well, like magic' – *Mirror*

'A classic . . . a journey to rival the greatest adventure stories ever told . . . rare and dazzling' – *New York Daily News*

'Extraordinary . . . makes your hair stand on end' – *Washington Post*

'Gripping . . . immensely satisfying' – *Los Angeles Times*

Stephen King and Peter Straub are co-authors of *The Talisman*, *Black House* and *Other Worlds Than These: A Talisman novel.*

STEPHEN KING is the author of more than seventy books, all of them worldwide bestsellers. Among his bestselling fiction titles are *Fairy Tale*, *Never Flinch* and *The Dark Tower* series.

Many of King's titles are the basis for major motion pictures, TV series and streamed events, including *The Green Mile*, *IT* and *The Shawshank Redemption*, which is IMDb's top-rated movie of all time.

King is the recipient of *The Sunday Times* Award for Literary Excellence 2022, the 2020 Audio Publishers Association Lifetime Achievement Award, the 2018 PEN America Literary Service Award, the 2014 National Medal of Arts, and the 2003 National Book Foundation Medal for Distinguished Contribution to American Letters. He lives in Maine, with his wife, novelist Tabitha King.

PETER STRAUB authored numerous bestselling novels, including *Ghost Story*, *A Dark Matter*, *Floating Dragon* and *Koko*. He also published short fiction, poetry and a graphic novel. For the Library of America, he edited the volume *H.P. Lovecraft: Tales* and the anthology *American Fantastic Tales.*

A prolific Grand Master of Horror, he received numerous literary honours including the British Fantasy Award; the Bram Stoker Award; the World Fantasy Award, and the International Horror Guild Award. He was also the recipient of several lifetime achievement awards. He passed away in 2022.

By Stephen King and published by Hodder & Stoughton

NOVELS:

Carrie
'Salem's Lot
The Shining
The Stand
The Dead Zone
Firestarter
Cujo
Cycle of the Werewolf
Christine
Pet Sematary
IT
The Talisman (with Peter Straub)
The Eyes of the Dragon
Misery
The Tommyknockers
The Dark Half
Needful Things
Gerald's Game
Dolores Claiborne
Insomnia
Rose Madder
Desperation
Bag of Bones
The Girl Who Loved Tom Gordon
Dreamcatcher
Black House (with Peter Straub)
From a Buick 8
Cell
Lisey's Story
Duma Key
Under the Dome
11.22.63
Doctor Sleep
Mr Mercedes
Revival
Finders Keepers
End of Watch
Gwendy's Button Box
(with Richard Chizmar)
Sleeping Beauties (with Owen King)
The Outsider
Elevation
The Institute
Billy Summers
Gwendy's Final Task
(with Richard Chizmar)
Fairy Tale
Holly
Never Flinch
The Life of Chuck

The Dark Tower

The Dark Tower I: The Gunslinger
The Dark Tower II:
The Drawing of the Three
The Dark Tower III: The Waste Lands
The Dark Tower IV: Wizard and Glass
The Dark Tower V: Wolves of the Calla
The Dark Tower VI: Song of Susannah
The Dark Tower VII: The Dark Tower
The Wind through the Keyhole:
A Dark Tower Novel

As Richard Bachman

Thinner
The Running Man
The Bachman Books
The Regulators
Blaze

STORY COLLECTIONS:

Night Shift
Different Seasons
Skeleton Crew
Four Past Midnight
Nightmares and Dreamscapes
Hearts in Atlantis
Everything's Eventual
Just After Sunset
Stephen King Goes to the Movies
Full Dark, No Stars
The Bazaar of Bad Dreams
If It Bleeds
You Like It Darker

NON-FICTION:

Danse Macabre
On Writing (A Memoir of the Craft)

By Peter Straub and published by Hodder & Stoughton

Ghost Story
The Talisman (with Stephen King)
The Hellfire Club
Black House (with Stephen King)
A Dark Matter

For David Gernert and Ralph Vicinanza

Grateful acknowledgment is made to the following for permission to reprint copyrighted material:

I CAN'T GET STARTED, by Ira Gershwin and Vernon Duke
© 1935 (Renewed) Ira Gershwin Music and Chappell & Co.
All Rights o/b/o Ira Gershwin Music administered
by WB Music Corp.
All Rights Reserved. Used by permission.
WARNER BROS. PUBLICATIONS U.S. INC.,
Miami, FL 33014

QUEEN OF THE WORLD, by Gary Louris, Tim O'Reagan,
Bob Ezrin © 2000 Warner-Tamerlane Publishing Corp. (BMI),
Absinthe Music (BMI) & Under-Cut-Music Publ. Co. (PRS).
All Rights o/b/o Absinthe Music administered
by Warner-Tamerlane Publishing Corp.
All Rights Reserved. Used by permission.
WARNER BROS. PUBLICATIONS U.S. INC.,
Miami, FL 33014

WHEN THE RED, RED ROBIN COMES
BOB, BOB BOBBIN' ALONG
Written by Harry Woods
© 1926, renewed
All rights controlled by Callicoon Music.
Used by permission. All rights reserved.

You take me to a place I never go,
You send me kisses made of gold,
I'll place a crown upon your curls,
All hail the Queen of the World!

– The Jayhawks

Right Here and Now . . .

Part One

WELCOME TO COULEE COUNTRY

1

Right here and now, as an old friend used to say, we are in the fluid present, where clear-sightedness never guarantees perfect vision. *Here:* about two hundred feet, the height of a gliding eagle, above Wisconsin's far western edge, where the vagaries of the Mississippi River declare a natural border. *Now:* an early Friday morning in mid-July a few years into both a new century and a new millennium, their wayward courses so hidden that a blind man has a better chance of seeing what lies ahead than you or I. Right here and now, the hour is just past six a.m., and the sun stands low in the cloudless eastern sky, a fat, confident yellow-white ball advancing as ever for the first time toward the future and leaving in its wake the steadily accumulating past, which darkens as it recedes, making blind men of us all.

Below, the early sun touches the river's wide, soft ripples with molten highlights. Sunlight glints from the tracks of the Burlington Northern Santa Fe Railroad running between the riverbank and the backs of the shabby two-story houses along County Road Oo, known as Nailhouse Row, the lowest point of the comfortable-looking little town extending uphill and eastward beneath us. At this moment in the Coulee Country, life seems to be holding its breath. The motionless air around us carries such remarkable purity and sweetness that you might imagine a man could smell a radish pulled out of the ground a mile away.

Moving toward the sun, we glide away from the river and over the shining tracks, the backyards and roofs of Nailhouse Row, then a line of Harley-Davidson motorcycles tilted on their kickstands. These unprepossessing little houses were built, early in the century recently vanished, for the metal pourers, mold makers, and crate men employed by the Pederson Nail factory. On the grounds that working stiffs would be unlikely to complain about the flaws in their subsidized accommodations, they were constructed as cheaply as possible. (Pederson Nail, which had suffered multiple hemorrhages during the fifties, finally bled to death in 1963.) The waiting Harleys suggest that the factory hands have been replaced by a motorcycle gang. The uniformly ferocious appearance of the Harleys' owners, wild-haired, bushy-bearded, swag-bellied men sporting earrings, black leather jackets, and less than the full complement of teeth, would seem to support this assumption. Like most assumptions, this one embodies an uneasy half-truth.

The current residents of Nailhouse Row, whom suspicious locals dubbed the Thunder Five soon after they took over the houses along the river, cannot so easily be categorized. They have skilled jobs in the Kingsland Brewing Company, located just out of town to the south and one block east of the Mississippi. If we look to our right, we can see 'the world's largest six-pack,' storage tanks painted over with gigantic Kingsland Old-Time Lager labels. The men who live on

Nailhouse Row met one another on the Urbana-Champaign campus of the University of Illinois, where all but one were undergraduates majoring in English or philosophy. (The exception was a resident in surgery at the UI-UC university hospital.) They get an ironic pleasure from being called the Thunder Five: the name strikes them as sweetly cartoonish. What they call themselves is 'the Hegelian Scum.' These gentlemen form an interesting crew, and we will make their acquaintance later on. For now, we have time only to note the hand-painted posters taped to the fronts of several houses, two lamp poles, and a couple of abandoned buildings. The posters say: FISHERMAN, YOU BETTER PRAY TO YOUR STINKING GOD WE DON'T CATCH YOU FIRST! REMEMBER AMY!

From Nailhouse Row, Chase Street runs steeply uphill between listing buildings with worn, unpainted facades the color of fog: the old Nelson Hotel, where a few impoverished residents lie sleeping, a blank-faced tavern, a tired shoe store displaying Red Wing workboots behind its filmy picture window, a few other dim buildings that bear no indication of their function and seem oddly dreamlike and vaporous. These structures have the air of failed resurrections, of having been rescued from the dark westward territory although they were still dead. In a way, that is precisely what happened to them. An ocher horizontal stripe, ten feet above the sidewalk on the facade of the Nelson Hotel and two feet from the rising ground on the opposed, ashen faces of the last two buildings, represents the high-water mark left behind by the flood of 1965, when the Mississippi rolled over its banks, drowned the railroad tracks and Nailhouse Row, and mounted nearly to the top of Chase Street.

Where Chase rises above the flood line and levels out,

it widens and undergoes a transformation into the main street of French Landing, the town beneath us. The Agincourt Theater, the Taproom Bar & Grille, the First Farmer State Bank, the Samuel Stutz Photography Studio (which does a steady business in graduation photos, wedding pictures, and children's portraits) and shops, not the ghostly relics of shops, line its blunt sidewalks: Benton's Rexall drugstore, Reliable Hardware, Saturday Night Video, Regal Clothing, Schmitt's Allsorts Emporium, stores selling electronic equipment, magazines and greeting cards, toys, and athletic clothing featuring the logos of the Brewers, the Twins, the Packers, the Vikings, and the University of Wisconsin. After a few blocks, the name of the street changes to Lyall Road, and the buildings separate and shrink into one-story wooden structures fronted with signs advertising insurance offices and travel agencies; after that, the street becomes a highway that glides eastward past a 7-Eleven, the Reinhold T. Grauerhammer VFW Hall, a big farm-implement dealership known locally as Goltz's, and into a landscape of flat, unbroken fields. If we rise another hundred feet into the immaculate air and scan what lies beneath and ahead, we see kettle moraines, coulees, blunted hills furry with pines, loam-rich valleys invisible from ground level until you have come upon them, meandering rivers, miles-long patchwork fields, and little towns – one of them, Centralia, no more than a scattering of buildings around the intersection of two narrow highways, 35 and 93.

Directly below us, French Landing looks as though it had been evacuated in the middle of the night. No one moves along the sidewalks or bends to insert a key into one of the locks of the shop fronts along Chase Street. The angled spaces before the shops are empty of the cars and pickup trucks that will begin to appear, first by ones and twos, then in a mannerly little stream, an hour or two later. No lights burn behind the windows in the commercial buildings or the unpretentious houses lining the surrounding streets. A block north of Chase on Sumner Street, four matching red-brick buildings of two stories each house, in west–east order, the French Landing Public Library; the offices of Patrick J. Skarda, MD, the local general practitioner, and Bell & Holland, a two-man law firm now run by Garland Bell and Julius Holland, the sons of its founders; the Heartfield & Son Funeral Home, now owned by a vast, funereal empire centered in St Louis; and the French Landing Post Office.

Separated from these by a wide driveway into a good-sized parking lot at the rear, the building at the end of the block, where Sumner intersects with Third Street, is also of red brick and two stories high but longer than its immediate neighbors. Unpainted iron bars block the rear second-floor windows, and two of the four vehicles in the parking lot are patrol cars with light bars across their tops and the letters FLPD on their sides. The presence of police cars and barred windows seems incongruous in this rural fastness – what sort of crime can happen here? Nothing serious, surely; surely nothing worse than a little shoplifting, drunken driving, and an occasional bar fight.

As if in testimony to the peacefulness and regularity of small-town life, a red van with the words LA RIVIERE HERALD on its side panels drifts slowly down Third Street, pausing at nearly all of the mailbox stands for its driver to insert copies of the day's newspaper, wrapped in a blue plastic bag, into gray metal cylinders bearing the same words. When the van turns onto Sumner, where the buildings have mail slots instead of boxes, the route man simply throws the wrapped papers at the front doors. Blue parcels thwack against the doors of the police station, the funeral home, and the office buildings. The post office does not get a paper.

What do you know, lights *are* burning behind the front downstairs windows of the police station. The door opens. A tall, dark-haired young man in a pale blue short-sleeved uniform shirt, a Sam Browne belt, and navy trousers steps outside. The wide belt and the gold badge on Bobby Dulac's chest gleam in the fresh sunlight, and everything he is wearing, including the 9mm pistol strapped to his hip, seems as newly made as Bobby Dulac himself. He watches the red van turn left onto Second Street, and frowns at the rolled newspaper. He nudges it with the tip of a black, highly polished shoe, bending over just far enough to suggest that he is trying to read the headlines through the plastic. Evidently this technique does not work all that well. Still frowning, Bobby tilts all the way over and picks up the newspaper with unexpected delicacy, the way a mother cat picks up a kitten in need of relocation. Holding it a little distance away from his body, he gives a quick glance up and down Sumner Street, about-faces smartly, and steps back into the station. We, who in our curiosity have been steadily descending toward the interesting spectacle presented by Officer Dulac, go inside behind him.

A gray corridor leads past a blank door and a bulletin board with very little on it to two sets of metal stairs, one going down to a small locker room, shower stalls, and a firing range, the other upward to an interrogation room and two facing rows of cells, none presently occupied. Somewhere near, a radio talk show is playing at a level that seems too loud for a peaceful morning.

Bobby Dulac opens the unmarked door and enters, with us on his shiny heels, the ready room he has just left. A rank of filing cabinets stands against the wall to our right, beside them a beat-up wooden table on which sit neat stacks of papers in folders and a transistor radio, the source of the discordant noise. From the nearby studio of KDCU-AM, Your Talk Voice in the Coulee Country, the entertainingly rabid George Rathbun has settled into *Badger Barrage*, his popular morning broadcast. Good old George sounds too loud for the occasion no matter how low you dial the volume; the guy is just flat-out *noisy* – that's part of his appeal.

Set in the middle of the wall directly opposite us is a closed door with a dark pebble-glass window on which has been painted DALE GILBERTSON, CHIEF OF POLICE. Dale will not be in for another half hour or so.

Two metal desks sit at right angles to each other in the corner to our left, and from the one that faces us, Tom Lund, a fair-haired officer of roughly his partner's age but without his appearance of having been struck gleaming from the mint five minutes before, regards the bag tweezed between two fingers of Bobby Dulac's right hand.

'All right,' Lund says. 'Okay. The latest installment.'

'You thought maybe the Thunder Five was paying us another social call? Here. I don't want to read the damn thing.'

Not deigning to look at the newspaper, Bobby sends the new day's issue of the *La Riviere Herald* sailing in a flat, fast arc across ten feet of wooden floor with an athletic snap of his wrist, spins rightward, takes a long stride, and positions himself in front of the wooden table a moment before Tom Lund fields his throw. Bobby glares at the two names and various details scrawled on the long chalkboard hanging on the wall behind the table. He is not pleased, Bobby Dulac;

he looks as though he might burst out of his uniform through the sheer force of his anger.

Fat and happy in the KDCU studio, George Rathbun yells, 'Caller, gimme a break, willya, and get your prescription fixed! Are we talking about the same game here? Caller—'

'Maybe Wendell got some sense and decided to lay off,' Tom Lund says.

'*Wendell*,' Bobby says. Because Lund can see only the sleek, dark back of his head, the little sneering thing he does with his lip wastes motion, but he does it anyway.

'Caller, let me ask you this one question, and in all sincerity, I want you to be honest with me. Did you actually *see* last night's game?'

'I didn't know *Wendell* was a big buddy of yours,' Bobby says. 'I didn't know you ever got as far south as La Riviere. Here I was thinking your idea of a big night out was a pitcher of beer and trying to break one hundred at the Arden Bowl-A-Drome, and now I find out you hang out with newspaper reporters in college towns. Probably get down and dirty with the Wisconsin Rat, too, that guy on KWLA. Do you pick up a lot of punk babes that way?'

The caller says he missed the first inning on account of he had to pick up his kid after a special counseling session at Mount Hebron, but he sure saw everything after that.

'Did I say Wendell Green was a friend of mine?' asks Tom Lund. Over Bobby's left shoulder he can see the first of the names on the chalkboard. His gaze helplessly focuses on it. 'It's just, I met him after the Kinderling case, and the guy didn't seem so bad. Actually, I kind of liked him. *Actually*, I wound up feeling sorry for him. He wanted to do an interview with Hollywood, and Hollywood turned him down flat.'

Well, naturally he saw the extra innings, the hapless caller says, that's how he knows Pokey Reese was safe.

'And as for the Wisconsin Rat, I wouldn't know him if I saw him, and I think that so-called music he plays sounds like the worst bunch of crap I ever heard in my life. How did that scrawny pasty-face creep get a radio show in the first place? On the *college station*? What does that tell you about our wonderful UW–La Riviere, Bobby? What does it say about our whole society? Oh, I forgot, you like that shit.'

'No, I like 311 and Korn, and you're so out of it you can't tell the difference between Jonathan Davis and Dee Dee Ramone, but forget about that, all right?' Slowly, Bobby Dulac turns around and smiles at his partner. 'Stop stalling.' His smile is none too pleasant.

'*I'm* stalling?' Tom Lund widens his eyes in a parody of wounded innocence. 'Gee, was it me who fired the paper across the room? No, I guess not.'

'If you never laid eyes on the Wisconsin Rat, how come you know what he looks like?'

'Same way I know he has funny-colored hair and a pierced nose. Same way I know he wears a beat-to-shit black leather jacket day in, day out, rain or shine.'

Bobby waited.

'By the way he sounds. People's voices are full of *information*. A guy says, Looks like it'll turn out to be a nice day, he tells you his whole life story. Want to know something else about Rat Boy? He hasn't been to the dentist in six, seven years. His teeth look like shit.'

From within KDCU's ugly cement-block structure next to the brewery on Peninsula Drive, via the radio Dale Gilbertson donated to the station house long before either Tom Lund or Bobby Dulac first put on their uniforms, comes good old dependable George Rathbun's patented bellow of genial outrage, a passionate, inclusive uproar that for a hundred miles around causes breakfasting farmers to smile across their tables at their wives and passing truckers to laugh out loud:

'I swear, caller, and this goes for my last caller, too, and every single one of you out there, I love you *dearly*, that is the honest truth, I love you like my momma loved her *turnip patch*, but sometimes you people DRIVE ME CRAZY! Oh, boy. *Top of the eleventh inning, two outs!* Six–seven, *Reds!* Men on second and third. Batter lines to short center field, Reese takes off from third, good throw to the plate, clean tag, *clean tag*. A BLIND MAN COULDA MADE THAT CALL!'

'Hey, I thought it was a good tag, and I only heard it on the radio,' says Tom Lund.

Both men are stalling, and they know it.

'In fact,' shouts the hands-down most popular Talk Voice of the Coulee Country, 'let me go out on a *limb* here, boys and girls, let me make the following *recommendation*, okay? Let's replace every umpire at Miller Park, hey, every umpire in the *National League*, with BLIND MEN! You know what, my friends? I *guarantee* a sixty to seventy percent *improvement* in the accuracy of their calls. GIVE THE JOB TO THOSE WHO CAN HANDLE IT – THE BLIND!'

Mirth suffuses Tom Lund's bland face. That George Rathbun, man, he's a hoot. Bobby says, 'Come on, okay?'

Grinning, Lund pulls the folded newspaper out of its wrapper and flattens it on his desk. His face hardens; without altering its shape, his grin turns stony. 'Oh, no. Oh, hell.'

'What?'

Lund utters a shapeless groan and shakes his head.

'Jesus. I don't even want to know.' Bobby rams his hands into his pockets, then pulls himself perfectly upright, jerks his right hand free, and clamps it over his eyes. 'I'm a blind guy, all right? Make me an umpire – I don't wanna be a cop anymore.'

Lund says nothing.

'It's a headline? Like a banner headline? How bad is it?' Bobby pulls his hand away from his eyes and holds it suspended in midair.

'Well,' Lund tells him, 'it looks like Wendell didn't get some sense, after all, and he sure as hell didn't decide to lay off. I can't believe I said I liked the dipshit.'

'Wake up,' Bobby says. 'Nobody ever told you law enforcement officers and journalists are on opposite sides of the fence?'

Tom Lund's ample torso tilts over his desk. A thick lateral crease like a scar divides his forehead, and his stolid cheeks burn crimson. He aims a finger at Bobby Dulac. 'This is one thing that really *gets* me about you, Bobby. How long have you been here? Five, six months? Dale hired me four years ago, and when him and Hollywood put the cuffs on Mr Thornberg *Kinderling*, which was the biggest case in this county for maybe thirty years, I can't claim any credit, but at least I pulled my weight. I helped put some of the pieces together.'

'One of the pieces,' Bobby says.

'I reminded Dale about the girl bartender at the Taproom, and Dale told Hollywood, and Hollywood talked to the girl, and that was a big, big piece. It helped get him. So don't you talk to me that way.'

Bobby Dulac assumes a look of completely hypothetical contrition. 'Sorry, Tom. I guess I'm kind of wound up and beat to shit at the same time.' What he thinks is: *So you got a couple years on me and you once gave Dale this crappy little bit of information, so what, I'm a better cop than you'll ever be. How heroic were you last night, anyhow?*

At 11:15 the previous night, Armand 'Beezer' St Pierre and his fellow travelers in the Thunder Five had roared up from Nailhouse Row to surge into the police station and demand of its three occupants, each of whom had worked an eighteen-hour shift, exact details of the progress they were making on the issue that most concerned them all. What the hell was going on here? What about the third one, huh, what about Irma Freneau? Had they found her yet? Did these clowns have *anything*, or were they still just blowing smoke? You need help? Beezer roared. Then deputize us, we'll give you all the goddamn help you need and then some. A giant named Mouse had strolled smirking up to Bobby Dulac and kept on strolling, jumbo belly to six-pack belly, until Bobby was backed up against a filing cabinet, whereupon the giant Mouse had mysteriously inquired, in a cloud of beer and marijuana, whether Bobby had ever dipped into the works of a gentleman named Jacques Derrida. When Bobby replied that he had never heard of the gentleman, Mouse said, 'No shit, Sherlock,' and stepped aside to glare at the names on the chalkboard. Half an hour later, Beezer, Mouse, and their companions were sent away unsatisfied, undeputized, but pacified, and Dale Gilbertson said he had to go home and get some sleep, but Tom ought to remain, just in case. The regular night men had both found excuses not to come in. Bobby said he would stay, too, no problem, Chief, which is why we find these two men in the station so early in the morning.

'Give it to me,' says Bobby Dulac.

Lund picks up the paper, turns it around, and holds it out for Bobby to see: FISHERMAN STILL AT LARGE IN FRENCH LANDING AREA, reads the headline over an article that takes up three columns on the top left-hand side of the front page.

The columns of type have been printed against a background of pale blue, and a black border separates them from the remainder of the page. Beneath the head, in smaller print, runs the line *Identity of Psycho Killer Baffles Police*. Underneath the subhead, a line in even smaller print attributes the article to *Wendell Green, with the support of the editorial staff*.

'The Fisherman,' Bobby says. 'Right from the start, your *friend* has his thumb up his butt. The Fisherman, the Fisherman, the Fisherman. If I all of a sudden turned into a fifty-foot ape and started stomping on buildings, would you call me King Kong?' Lund lowers the newspaper and smiles. 'Okay,' Bobby allows, 'bad example. Say I held up a couple banks. Would you call me John Dillinger?'

'Well,' says Lund, smiling even more broadly, 'they say Dillinger's tool was so humongous, they put it in a jar in the Smithsonian. So . . .'

'Read me the first sentence,' Bobby says.

Tom Lund looks down and reads: '"As the police in French Landing fail to discover any leads to the identity of the fiendish double murderer and sex criminal this reporter has dubbed 'the Fisherman,' the grim specters of fear, despair, and suspicion run increasingly rampant through the streets of that little town, and from there out into the farms and villages throughout French County, darkening by their touch every portion of the Coulee Country."'

'Just what we need,' Bobby says. 'Jee-*zus!*' And in an instant has crossed the room and is leaning over Tom Lund's shoulder, reading the *Herald*'s front page with his hand resting on the butt of his Glock, as if ready to drill a hole in the article right here and now.

'"Our traditions of trust and good neighborliness, our habit of extending warmth and generosity to all [writes

Wendell Green, editorializing like crazy], are eroding daily under the corrosive onslaught of these dread emotions. Fear, despair, and suspicion are poisonous to the soul of communities large and small, for they turn neighbor against neighbor and make a mockery of civility.

'"Two children have been foully murdered and their remains partially consumed. Now a third child has disappeared. Eight-year-old Amy St Pierre and seven-year-old Johnny Irkenham fell victim to the passions of a monster in human form. Neither will know the happiness of adolescence or the satisfactions of adulthood. Their grieving parents will never know the grandchildren they would have cherished. The parents of Amy and Johnny's playmates shelter their children within the safety of their own homes, as do parents whose children never knew the deceased. As a result, summer playgroups and other programs for young children have been canceled in virtually every township and municipality in French County.

'"With the disappearance of ten-year-old Irma Freneau seven days after the death of Amy St Pierre and only three after that of Johnny Irkenham, public patience has grown dangerously thin. As this correspondent has already reported, Merlin Graasheimer, fifty-two, an unemployed farm laborer of no fixed abode, was set upon and beaten by an unidentified group of men in a Grainger side street late Tuesday evening. Another such episode occurred in the early hours of Thursday morning, when Elvar Praetorious, thirty-six, a Swedish tourist traveling alone, was assaulted by three men, again unidentified, while asleep in La Riviere's Leif Eriksson Park. Graasheimer and Praetorious required only routine medical attention, but future incidents of vigilantism will almost certainly end more seriously."'

Tom Lund looks down at the next paragraph, which

describes the Freneau girl's abrupt disappearance from a Chase Street sidewalk, and pushes himself away from his desk.

Bobby Dulac reads silently for a time, then says, 'You gotta hear this shit, Tom. This is how he winds up:

'"When will the Fisherman strike again?

'"For he will strike again, my friends, make no mistake.

'"And when will French Landing's chief of police, Dale Gilbertson, do his duty and rescue the citizens of this county from the obscene savagery of the Fisherman and the understandable violence produced by his own inaction?"'

Bobby Dulac stamps to the middle of the room. His color has heightened. He inhales, then exhales a magnificent quantity of oxygen. 'How about the next time the Fisherman *strikes*,' Bobby says, 'how about he goes right up Wendell Green's flabby rear end?'

'I'm with you,' says Tom Lund. 'Can you believe that shinola? "Understandable violence"? He's telling people it's okay to mess with anyone who looks suspicious!'

Bobby levels an index finger at Lund. 'I personally am going to nail this guy. That *is* a promise. I'll bring him down, alive or dead.' In case Lund may have missed the point, he repeats, 'Personally.'

Wisely choosing not to speak the words that first come to his mind, Tom Lund nods his head. The finger is still pointing. He says, 'If you want some help with that, maybe you should talk to Hollywood. Dale didn't have no luck, but could be you'd do better.'

Bobby waves this notion away. 'No need. Dale and me . . . and you, too, of course, we got it covered. But I personally am going to get this guy. That is a guarantee.' He pauses for a second. 'Besides, Hollywood retired when he moved here, or did you forget?'

'Hollywood's too young to retire,' Lund says. 'Even in cop years, the guy is practically a baby. So you must be the next thing to a fetus.'

And on their cackle of shared laughter, we float away and out of the ready room and back into the sky, where we glide one block farther north, to Queen Street.

Moving a few blocks east we find, beneath us, a low, rambling structure branching out from a central hub that occupies, with its wide, rising breadth of lawn dotted here and there with tall oaks and maples, the whole of a block lined with bushy hedges in need of a good trim. Obviously an institution of some kind, the structure at first resembles a progressive elementary school in which the various wings represent classrooms without walls, the square central hub the dining room and administrative offices. When we drift downward, we hear George Rathbun's genial bellow rising toward us from several windows. The big glass front door swings open, and a trim woman in cat's-eye glasses comes out into the bright morning, holding a poster in one hand and a roll of tape in the other. She immediately turns around and, with quick, efficient gestures, fixes the poster to the door. Sunlight reflects from a smoky gemstone the size of a hazelnut on the third finger of her right hand.

While she takes a moment to admire her work, we can peer over her crisp shoulder and see that the poster announces, in a cheerful burst of hand-drawn balloons, that TODAY IS STRAWBERRY FEST!!!; when the woman walks back inside, we take in the presence, in the portion of the entry visible just beneath the giddy poster, of two or three folded wheelchairs. Beyond the wheelchairs, the woman, whose chestnut hair has been pinned back into an architectural whorl, strides on her high-heeled pumps through a pleasant lobby with blond wooden chairs and matching tables strewn artfully with magazines, marches past a kind of unmanned guardpost or reception desk before a handsome fieldstone wall, and vanishes, with the trace of a skip, through a burnished door marked WILLIAM MAXTON, DIRECTOR.

What kind of school is this? Why is it open for business, why is it putting on festivals, in the middle of July?

We could call it a graduate school, for those who reside here have graduated from every stage of their existences but the last, which they live out, day after day, under the careless stewardship of Mr William 'Chipper' Maxton, Director. This is the Maxton Elder Care Facility, once – in a more innocent time, and before the cosmetic renovations done in the mid-eighties – known as the Maxton Nursing Home, which was owned and managed by its founder, Herbert Maxton, Chipper's father. Herbert was a decent if wishy-washy man who, it is safe to say, would be appalled by some of the things the sole fruit of his loins gets up to. Chipper never wanted to take over 'the family playpen,' as he calls it, with its freight of 'gummers,' 'zombies,' 'bed wetters,' and 'droolies,' and after getting an accounting degree at UW-La Riviere (with hard-earned minors in promiscuity, gambling, and beer drinking), our boy accepted a position with the Madison, Wisconsin, office of the Internal Revenue Service, largely for the purpose of learning how to steal from the government undetected. Five years with the IRS taught him much that was useful, but when his subsequent career as a freelancer failed to match his ambitions, he yielded to his father's increasingly frail entreaties and threw in his lot with the undead and the droolies. With a certain grim relish, Chipper acknowledged that despite a woeful shortage of glamour, his father's business would at least provide him with the opportunity to steal from the clients and the government alike.

Let us flow in through the big glass doors, cross the handsome lobby (noting, as we do so, the mingled odors of air freshener and ammonia that pervade even the public areas of all such institutions), pass through the door bearing Chipper's name, and find out what that well-arranged young woman is doing here so early.

Beyond Chipper's door lies a windowless cubicle equipped with a desk, a coatrack, and a small bookshelf crowded with computer printouts, pamphlets, and flyers. A door stands open beside the desk. Through the opening, we see a much larger office, paneled in the same burnished wood as the director's door and containing leather chairs, a glass-topped coffee table, and an oatmeal-colored sofa. At its far end looms a vast desk untidily heaped with papers and so deeply polished it seems nearly to glow.

Our young woman, whose name is Rebecca Vilas, sits perched on the edge of this desk, her legs crossed in a particularly architectural fashion. One knee folds over the other, and the calves form two nicely molded, roughly parallel lines running down to the triangular tips of the black high-heeled pumps, one of which points to four o'clock and the other to six. Rebecca Vilas, we gather, has arranged herself to be seen, has struck a pose intended to be appreciated, though certainly not by us. Behind the cat's-eye glasses, her eyes look skeptical and amused, but we cannot see what has aroused these emotions. We assume that she is Chipper's secretary, and this assumption, too, expresses only half of the truth: as the ease and irony of her attitude imply, Ms Vilas's duties have long extended beyond the purely secretarial. (We might speculate about the source of that nice ring she is wearing; as long as our minds are in the gutter, we will be right on the money.)

We float through the open door, follow the direction of Rebecca's increasingly impatient gaze, and find ourselves staring at the sturdy, khaki-clad rump of her kneeling employer, who has thrust his head and shoulders into a good-sized safe, in which we glimpse stacks of record books and a number of manila envelopes apparently stuffed with currency. A few bills flop out of these envelopes as Chipper pulls them from the safe.

'You did the sign, the poster thing?' he asks without turning around.

'Aye, aye,' says Rebecca Vilas. 'And a splendid day it is we shall be havin' for the great occasion, too, as is only roight and proper.' Her Irish accent is surprisingly good, if a bit generic. She has never been anywhere more exotic than Atlantic City, where Chipper used his frequent-flier miles to escort her for five enchanted days two years before. She learned the accent from old movies.

'I hate Strawberry Fest,' Chipper says, dredging the last of the envelopes from the safe. 'The zombies' wives and children mill around all afternoon, cranking them up so we have to sedate them into comas just to get some peace. And if you want to know the truth, I *hate* balloons.' He dumps the money onto the carpet and begins to sort the bills into stacks of various denominations.

'Only Oi was wonderin', in me simple country manner,' says Rebecca, 'why Oi should be requested to appear at the crack o' dawn on the grand day.'

'Know what else I hate? The whole music thing. Singing zombies and that stupid deejay. Symphonic Stan with his big-band records, whoo boy, talk about thrills.'

'I assume,' Rebecca says, dropping the stage-Irish accent, 'you want me to do something with that money before the action begins.'

'Time for another journey to Miller.' An account under a fictitious name in the State Provident Bank in Miller, forty miles away, receives regular deposits of cash skimmed from patients' funds intended to pay for extra goods and services. Chipper turns around on his knees with his hands full of money and looks up at Rebecca. He sinks back down to his heels and lets his hands fall into his lap. 'Boy, do you have great legs. Legs like that, you ought to be famous.'

'I thought you'd never notice,' Rebecca says.

Chipper Maxton is forty-two years old. He has good teeth, all his hair, a wide, sincere face, and narrow brown eyes that always look a little damp. He also has two kids, Trey, nine, and Ashley, seven and recently diagnosed with ADD, a matter Chipper figures is going to cost him maybe two thousand a year in pills alone. And of course he has a wife, his life's partner, Marion, thirty-nine years of age, five foot five, and somewhere in the neighborhood of 190 pounds. In addition to these blessings, as of last night Chipper owes his bookie $13,000, the result of an unwise investment in the Brewers game George Rathbun is still bellowing about. He has noticed, oh, yes he has, Chipper has noticed Ms Vilas's splendidly cantilevered legs.

'Before you go over there,' he says, 'I was thinking we could kind of stretch out on the sofa and fool around.'

'Ah,' Rebecca says. 'Fool around how, exactly?'

'Gobble, gobble, gobble,' Chipper says, grinning like a satyr.

'You romantic devil, you,' says Rebecca, a remark that utterly escapes her employer. Chipper thinks he actually is being romantic.

She slides elegantly down from her perch, and Chipper pushes himself inelegantly upright and closes the safe door with his foot. Eyes shining damply, he takes a couple of thuggish, strutting strides across the carpet, wraps one arm around Rebecca Vilas's slender waist and with the other slides the fat manila envelopes onto the desk. He is yanking at his belt even before he begins to pull Rebecca toward the sofa.

'So can I see him?' says clever Rebecca, who understands exactly how to turn her lover's brains to porridge . . .

. . . and before Chipper obliges her, we do the sensible thing and float out into the lobby, which is still empty. A corridor to the left of the reception desk takes us to two large, blond, glass-inset doors marked DAISY and BLUEBELL, the names of the wings to which they give entrance. Far down the gray length of Bluebell, a man in baggy coveralls dribbles ash from his cigarette onto the tiles over which he is dragging, with exquisite slowness, a filthy mop. We move into Daisy.

The functional parts of Maxton's are a great deal less attractive than the public areas. Numbered doors line both sides of the corridor. Hand-lettered cards in plastic holders beneath the numerals give the names of the residents. Four doors along, a desk at which a burly male attendant in an unclean white uniform sits dozing upright faces the entrances to the men's and women's bathrooms – at Maxton's, only the most expensive rooms, those on the other side of the lobby, in Asphodel, provide anything but a sink. Dirty mop-swirls harden and dry all up and down the tiled floor, which stretches out before us to improbable length. Here, too, the walls and air seem the same shade of gray. If we look closely at the edges of the hallway, at the juncture of the walls and the ceiling, we see spiderwebs, old stains, accumulations of grime. Pine-Sol, ammonia, urine, and worse scent the atmosphere. As an elderly lady in Bluebell wing likes to say, when you live with a bunch of people who are old and incontinent, you never get far from the smell of caca.

The rooms themselves vary according to the conditions and capacities of their inhabitants. Since nearly everyone is asleep, we can glance into a few of these quarters. Here in D10, a single room two doors past the dozing aide, old Alice Weathers lies (snoring gently, dreaming of dancing in perfect partnership with Fred Astaire across a white marble floor) surrounded by so much of her former life that she must navigate past the chairs and end tables to maneuver from the door to her bed. Alice still possesses even more of her wits than she does her old furniture, and she cleans her room herself, immaculately. Next door in D12, two old farmers named Thorvaldson and Jesperson, who have not spoken to each other in years, sleep, separated by a thin curtain, in a bright clutter of family photographs and grandchildren's drawings.

Farther down the hallway, D18 presents a spectacle completely opposite to the clean, crowded jumble of D10, just as its inhabitant, a man known as Charles Burnside, could be considered the polar opposite of Alice Weathers. In D18, there are no end tables, hutches, overstuffed chairs, gilded mirrors, lamps, woven rugs, or velvet curtains: this barren room contains only a metal bed, a plastic chair, and a chest of drawers. No photographs of children and grandchildren stand atop the chest, and no crayon drawings of blocky houses and stick figures decorate the walls. Mr Burnside has no interest in housekeeping, and a thin layer of dust covers the floor, the windowsill, and the chest's bare top. D18 is bereft of history, empty of personality; it seems as brutal and soulless as a prison cell. A powerful smell of excrement contaminates the air.

For all the entertainment offered by Chipper Maxton and all the charm of Alice Weathers, it is Charles Burnside, 'Burny,' we have most come to see.

2

Chipper's background we know. Alice arrived at Maxton's from a big house on Gale Street, the old part of Gale Street, where she outlived two husbands, raised five sons, and taught piano to four generations of French Landing children, none of whom ever became professional pianists but who all remember her fondly and think of her with affection. Alice came to this place as most people do, in a car driven by one of her children and with a mixture of reluctance and surrender. She had become too old to live alone in the big house in the old section of Gale Street; she had two grown, married sons who were kind enough, but she could not tolerate adding to their cares. Alice Weathers had spent her entire life in French Landing, and she had no desire to live anywhere else; in a way, she had always known that she would end her days in Maxton's, which though not at all luxurious was agreeable enough. On the day her son Martin had driven her over to inspect the place, she had realized that she knew at least half the people there.

Unlike Alice, Charles Burnside, the tall, skinny old man lying covered by a sheet before us in his metal bed, is not in full possession of his wits, nor is he dreaming of Fred Astaire. The veiny expanse of his bald, narrow head curves down to eyebrows like tangles of gray wire, beneath which, on either side of the fleshy hook of his nose, two narrow eyes shine at his north-facing window and the expanse of woods beyond Maxton's. Alone of all the residents of Daisy wing, Burny is not asleep. His eyes gleam, and his lips are wormed into a bizarre smile – but these details mean nothing, for Charles Burnside's mind may be as empty as his room. Burny has suffered from Alzheimer's disease for many years, and what looks like an aggressive form of pleasure could be no more than physical satisfaction of a very basic kind. If we had failed to guess that he was the origin of the stench in this room, the stains rising into the sheet that covers him make it clear. He has just evacuated, massively, into his bed, and the very least we can say about his response to the situation is that he does not mind a bit; no sir, shame is not a part of this picture.

But if – unlike delightful Alice – Burny no longer has a firm grasp on all of his marbles, neither is he a typical Alzheimer's patient. He might spend a day or two mumbling into his oatmeal like the rest of Chipper's zombies, then revitalize himself and join the living again. When not undead, he usually manages to get down the hall to the bathroom as necessary, and he spends hours either sneaking off on his own or patrolling the grounds, being unpleasant – in fact, offensive – to all and sundry. Restored from zombiehood, he is sly, secretive, rude, caustic, stubborn, foul-tongued, mean-spirited, and resentful, in other words – in the world according to Chipper – a blood brother to the other old men who reside at Maxton's. Some of the nurses, aides, and attendants doubt that Burny really does have Alzheimer's. They think he is faking it, opting out, lying low, deliberately making them work harder while he rests up and gathers his strength for yet another episode of unpleasantness. We can hardly blame them for their suspicion. If Burny has not been misdiagnosed, he is probably the only advanced Alzheimer's patient in the world to experience prolonged spells of remission.

In 1996, his seventy-eighth year, the man known as Charles Burnside arrived at Maxton's in an ambulance from La Riviere General Hospital, not in a vehicle driven by a helpful relative. He had appeared in the emergency room one morning, carrying two heavy suitcases filled with dirty clothing and loudly demanding medical attention. His demands were not coherent, but they were clear. He claimed to have walked a considerable distance to reach the hospital, and he wanted the hospital to take care of him. The distance varied from telling to telling – ten miles, fifteen miles, twenty-five. He either had or had not spent some nights sleeping in fields or by the side of the road. His general condition and the way he smelled suggested that he had been wandering the countryside and sleeping rough for perhaps a week. If he had once had a wallet, he had lost it on his journey. La Riviere General cleaned him up, fed him, gave him a bed, and tried to extract a history. Most of his statements trailed off into disjointed babble, but in the absence of any documents, at least these facts seemed reliable: Burnside had been a carpenter, framer, and plasterer in the area for many years, working for himself and general contractors. An aunt who lived in the town of Blair had given him a room.

He had walked the eighteen miles from Blair to La Riviere, then? No, he had started his walk somewhere else, he could not remember where, but it was ten miles away, no, twenty-five miles away, some town, and the people in that town were no-good jackass asswipes. *What was the name of his aunt?* Althea Burnside. *What were her address and telephone number?* No idea, couldn't remember. *Did his aunt have a job of any kind?* Yes, she was a full-time jackass asswipe. *But she had permitted him to live in her house?* Who? Permitted what? Charles Burnside needed no one's permission, he did what he damn well wanted. *Had his aunt ordered him out of her house?* Who are you talking about, you jackass asshole?

The admitting MD entered an initial diagnosis of Alzheimer's disease, pending the results of various tests, and the social worker got on the telephone and requested the address and telephone number of an Althea Burnside currently residing in Blair. The telephone company reported no listing for a person of that name in Blair, nor was she listed in Ettrick, Cochrane, Fountain, Sparta, Onalaska, Arden, La Riviere, or any other of the towns and cities within a fifty-mile radius. Widening her net, the social worker consulted the Records Office and the departments of Social Security, Motor Vehicle License, and Taxation for information about Althea and Charles Burnside. Of the two Altheas that popped up out of the system, one owned a diner in Butternut, far to the north of the state, and the other was a black woman who worked in a Milwaukee day-care center. Neither had any connection to the man in La Riviere General. The Charles Burnsides located by the records search were not the social worker's Charles Burnside. Althea seemed not to exist. Charles, it seemed, was one of those elusive people who go through life without ever paying taxes, registering to vote, applying for a Social Security card, opening a bank account, joining the armed forces, getting a driver's license, or spending a couple of seasons at the state farm.

Another round of telephone calls resulted in the elusive Charles Burnside's classification as a ward of the county and his admission to the Maxton Elder Care Facility until accommodation could be found at the state hospital in Whitehall.

The ambulance conveyed Burnside to Maxton's at the expense of the generous public, and grumpy Chipper slammed him into Daisy wing. Six weeks later, a bed opened up in a ward at the state hospital. Chipper received the telephone call a few minutes after the day's mail brought him a check, drawn by an Althea Burnside on a bank in De Pere, for Charles Burnside's maintenance at his facility. Althea Burnside's address was a De Pere post office box. When the state hospital called, Chipper announced that in the spirit of civic duty he would be happy to continue Mr Burnside's status at Maxton Elder Care. The old fellow had just become his favorite patient. Without putting Chipper through any of the usual shenanigans, Burny had doubled his contribution to the income stream.

For the next six years, the old man slid relentlessly into the darkness of Alzheimer's. If he was faking, he gave a brilliant performance. Down he went, through the descending way stations of incontinence, incoherence, frequent outbursts of anger, loss of memory, loss of the ability to feed himself, loss of personality. He dwindled into infancy, then into vacuity, and spent his days strapped into a wheelchair. Chipper mourned the inevitable loss of a uniquely cooperative patient. Then, in the summer of the year before these events, the amazing resuscitation occurred. Animation returned to Burny's slack face, and he began to utter vehement nonsense syllables. *Abbalah! Gorg! Munshun! Gorg!* He wanted to feed himself, he wanted to exercise his legs, to stagger around and reacquaint himself with his surroundings. Within a week, he was using English words to insist on wearing his own clothes and going to the bathroom by himself. He put on weight, gained strength, once again became a nuisance. Now, often in the same day, he passes back and forth between late-stage Alzheimer's lifelessness and a guarded, gleaming surliness so healthy in a man of eighty-five it might be called robust. Burny is like a man who went to Lourdes and experienced a cure but left before it was complete. For Chipper, a miracle is a miracle. As long as the old creep stays alive, who cares if he is wandering the grounds or drooping against the restraining strap in his wheelchair?

We move closer. We try to ignore the stench. We want to see what we can glean from the face of this curious fellow. It was never a pretty face, and now the skin is gray and the cheeks are sunken potholes. Prominent blue veins wind over the gray scalp, spotted as a plover's egg. The rubbery-looking nose hooks slightly to the right, which adds to the impression of slyness and concealment. The wormy lips curl in a disquieting smile – the smile of an arsonist contemplating a burning building – that may after all be merely a grimace.

Here is a true American loner, an internal vagrant, a creature of shabby rooms and cheap diners, of aimless journeys resentfully taken, a collector of wounds and injuries lovingly fingered and refingered. Here is a spy with no cause higher than himself. Burny's real name is Carl Bierstone, and under this name he conducted, in Chicago, from his mid-twenties until the age of forty-six, a secret rampage, an unofficial war, during which he committed wretched deeds for the sake of the pleasures they afforded him. Carl Bierstone is Burny's great secret, for he cannot allow anyone to know that this former incarnation, this earlier self, still lives inside his skin. Carl Bierstone's awful pleasures, his foul toys, are also Burny's, and he must keep them hidden in the darkness, where only he can find them.

So is that the answer to Chipper's miracle? That Carl Bierstone found a way to creep out through a seam in Burny's zombiedom and assume control of the foundering ship? The human soul contains an infinity of rooms, after all, some of them vast, some no bigger than a broom closet, some locked, some few imbued with a radiant light. We bow closer to the veiny scalp, the wandering nose, the wire-brush eyebrows; we lean deeper into the stink to examine those interesting eyes. They are like black neon; they glitter like moonlight on a sodden riverbank. All in all, they look unsettlingly gleeful, but not particularly human. Not much help here.

Burny's lips move: he is still smiling, if you can call that rictus a smile, but he has begun to whisper. What is he saying?

. . . dey are gowering in their bloody holes and govering their eyes, dey are whimbering in derror, my boor loss babbies . . . No, no, dat won't help, will it? Ah, zee de engynes, yezz, oh dose beeyoodiful beeyoodiful engynes, whad a zight, the beeyoodiful engynes againzt de vire, how they churrn, how dey churrn and burrn . . . I zee a hole, yez yez dere id iz oho zo brighd around de etches zo folded back . . .

Carl Bierstone may be reporting in, but his babble is not of much help. Let us follow the direction of Burny's mud-glitter gaze in hopes that it might give us a hint as to what has so excited the old boy. Aroused, too, as we observe from the shape beneath the sheet. He and Chipper seem to be in sync here, since both are standing at the ready, except that instead of the benefit of Rebecca Vilas's expert attentions, Burny's only stimulation is the view through his window.

The view hardly measures up to Ms Vilas. Head slightly elevated upon a pillow, Charles Burnside looks raptly out over a brief expanse of lawn to a row of maple trees at the beginning of an extensive woods. Farther back tower the great, leafy heads of oaks. A few birch trunks shine candle-like in the inner darkness. From the height of the oaks and the variety of the trees, we know that we are regarding a remnant of the great climax forest that once blanketed this entire part of the country. Like all of the ancient forest's traces, the woods extending north and east from Maxton's speak of profound mysteries in a voice nearly too deep to be heard. Beneath its green canopy, time and serenity embrace bloodshed and death; violence roils on unseen, constantly, absorbed into every aspect of a hushed landscape that never pauses but moves with glacial lack of haste. The spangled, yielding floor covers millions of scattered bones in layer upon layer; all that grows and thrives here thrives on rot. Worlds within worlds churn, and great, systematic universes hum side by side, each ignorantly bringing abundance and catastrophe upon its unguessed-at neighbors.

Does Burny contemplate these woods, is he enlivened by what he sees in them? Or, for that matter, is he in fact still asleep, and does Carl Bierstone caper behind Charles Burnside's peculiar eyes?

Burny whispers, *Fogzes down fogzhulls, radz in radhulls, hyenaz over embdy stomachs wail, oho aha dis iz mozt-mozt gladzome my frenz, more an more de liddle wunz drudge drudge drudge oho on bledding foodzies . . .*

Let's blow this pop stand, okay?

Let's sail away from old Burny's ugly mouth – enough is enough. Let us seek the fresh air and fly north, over the woods. Foxes down foxholes and rats in ratholes may be wailing, true, that's how it works, but we are not about to find any starving hyenas in western Wisconsin. Hyenas are always hungry anyhow. No one feels sorry for them, either. You'd have to be a real bleeding heart to pity a creature that does nothing but skulk around the periphery of other species until the moment when, grinning and chuckling, it can plunder their leftovers. Out we go, right through the roof.

East of Maxton's, the woods carpet the ground for something like a mile or two before a narrow dirt road curves in from Highway 35 like a careless parting in a thick head of hair. The woods continue for another hundred yards or so, then yield to a thirty-year-old housing development consisting of two streets. Basketball hoops, backyard swing sets, tricycles, bicycles, and vehicles by Fisher-Price clutter the driveways of the modest houses on Schubert and Gale. The children who will make use of them lie abed, dreaming of cotton candy, puppy dogs, home runs, excursions to distant territories, and other delightful infinitudes; also asleep are their anxious parents, doomed to become even more so after reading Wendell Green's contribution to the front page of the day's *Herald*.

Something catches our eye – that narrow dirt road curving into the woods from Highway 35's straightaway. More a lane than an actual road, its air of privacy seems at odds with its apparent uselessness. The lane loops off into the woods and, three-fourths of a mile later, comes to an end. What is its point, what is it for? From our height above the earth, the track resembles a faint line sketched by a No. 4 pencil – you practically need an eagle's eye to see it at all – but someone went to considerable effort to draw this line through the woods. Trees had to be cut and cleared, stumps to be pried from the ground. If one man did it, the work would have taken months of sweaty, muscle-straining labor. The result of all that inhuman effort has the remarkable property of *concealing* itself, of evading the eye, so that it fades away if attention wanders, and must be located again. We might think of dwarfs and secret dwarf mines, the path to a dragon's hidden cache of gold – a treasure so safeguarded that access to it has been camouflaged by a magic spell. No, dwarf mines, dragon treasures, and magic spells are too childish, but when we drop down for a closer examination, we see that a weathered NO TRESPASSING sign stands at the beginning of the lane, proof that something is being guarded, even if it is merely privacy.

Having noticed the sign, we look again at the end of the lane. In the darkness under the trees down there, one area seems murkier than the rest. Even as it shrinks back into the gloom, this area possesses an unnatural solidity that distinguishes it from the surrounding trees. Aha oho, we say to ourselves in an echo of Burny's gibberish, what have we here, a wall of some kind? It seems that featureless. When we reach the midpoint in the curve of the lane, a triangular section of darkness all but obscured by the treetops abruptly defines itself as a peaked roof. Not until we are nearly upon it does the entire structure move into definition as a three-story wooden house, oddly shambling in structure, with a sagging front porch. This house has clearly stood empty for a long time, and after taking in its eccentricity, the first thing we notice is its inhospitability to new tenants. A second NO TRESPASSING sign, leaning sideways at an improbable angle against a newel post, merely underlines the impression given by the building itself.

The peaked roof covers only the central section. To the left, a two-story extension retreats back into the woods. On the right, the building sprouts additions like outsized sheds, more like growths than afterthoughts. In both senses of the word, the building looks unbalanced: an off-kilter mind conceived it, then relentlessly brought it into off-center being. The intractable result deflects inquiry and resists interpretation. An odd, monolithic invulnerability emanates from the bricks and boards, despite the damage done by time and weather. Obviously built in search of seclusion, if not isolation, the house seems still to demand them.

Oddest of all, from our vantage point the house appears to have been painted a uniform black – not only the boards, but every inch of the exterior, the porch, the trim, the rain gutters, even the windows. Black, from top to bottom. And that cannot be possible; in this guileless, good-hearted corner of the world, not even the most crazily misanthropic builder would turn his house into its own shadow. We float down to just above ground level and move nearer along the narrow lane . . .

When we come close enough for reliable judgment, which is uncomfortably close, we find that misanthropy can go further than we had supposed. The house is not black now, but it used to be. What it has faded into makes us feel that we might have been too critical about the original color. The house has become the leaden gray-black of thunderheads and dismal seas and the hulls of wrecked ships. Black would be preferable to this utter lifelessness.

We may be certain that very few of the adults who live in the nearby development, or any adults in French Landing or the surrounding towns, have defied the admonition on 35 and ventured up the narrow lane. Almost none so much as notice the sign anymore; none of them know of the existence of the black house. We can be just as certain, however, that a number of their children have explored the lane, and that some of those children wandered far enough to come upon the house. They would have seen it in a way their parents could not, and what they saw would have sent them racing back toward the highway.

The black house seems as out of place in western Wisconsin as a skyscraper or a moated palace. In fact, the black house would be an anomaly anywhere in our world, except perhaps as a 'Haunted Mansion,' a 'Castle of Terrors,' in an amusement park, where its capacity to repel ticket buyers would put it out of business within a week. Yet in one specific way it might remind us of the dim buildings along the ascent of Chase Street into respectability from the riverbank and Nailhouse Row. The shabby Nelson Hotel, the obscure tavern, the shoe store, and the others, marked with the horizontal stripe drawn by the river's grease pencil, share the same eerie, dreamlike, half-unreal flavor that saturates the black house.

At this moment in our progress – and through everything that follows – we would do well to remember that this strange flavor of the dreamlike and slightly unnatural is characteristic of borderlands. It can be detected in every seam between one specific territory and another, however significant or insignificant the border in question. Borderlands places are different from other places; they are *borderish*.

Say you happen to be driving for the first time through a semirural section of Oostler County in your home state, on your way to visit a recently divorced friend of the opposite sex who has abruptly and, you think, unwisely decamped to a small town in adjacent Orelost County. On the passenger seat beside you, atop a picnic basket containing two bottles of a superior white Bordeaux held tightly in place by various gourmet goodies in exquisite little containers, lies a map carefully folded to expose the relevant area. You may not know your exact location, but you are on the right road and making good time.

Gradually, the landscape alters. The road veers around a nonexistent berm, then begins winding through inexplicable curves; on either side, the trees slouch; beneath their twisted boughs, the intermittent houses grow smaller and seedier. Ahead, a three-legged dog squirms through a hedge and barrels snarling toward your right front tire. A crone wearing a teensy straw hat and what appears to be a shroud glances up red-eyed from a listing porch swing. Two front yards along, a little girl costumed in dirty pink gauze and a foil crown flaps a glittery, star-headed wand over a heap of burning tires. Then a rectangular placard bearing the legend WELCOME TO ORELOST COUNTY glides into view. Soon the trees improve their posture and the road straightens out. Released from anxieties barely noticed until they were gone, you nudge the accelerator and hasten toward your needy friend.

Borderlands taste of unruliness and distortion. The grotesque, the unpredictable, and the lawless take root in them and luxuriate. The central borderlands flavor is of *slippage.* And while we are in a setting of wondrous natural beauty, we have also been traveling over a natural borderland, delineated by a great river and defined by other, lesser rivers, wide glacial moraines, limestone cliffs, and valleys that remain invisible, like the black house, until you turn the right corner and meet them face to face.

Have you ever seen a furious old wreck in worn-out clothes who pushes an empty shopping cart down deserted streets and rants about a 'fushing feef'? Sometimes he wears a baseball cap, sometimes a pair of sunglasses with one cracked lens.

Have you ever moved frightened into a doorway and watched a soldierly man with a zigzag lightning-bolt scar on one side of his face storm into a drunken mob and discover, lying spread-eagled in death on the ground, a boy, his head smashed and his pockets turned out? Have you seen the anger and the pity blaze in that man's mutilated face?

These are signs of *slippage.*

Another lies concealed below us on the outskirts of French Landing, and despite the terror and heartbreak that surround this sign, we have no choice but to stand in witness before it. By our witness, we shall do it honor, to the measure of our individual capabilities; by being witnessed, by offering its testimony to our mute gaze, it will repay us in measure far greater.

We are back in midair, and spread out – we could say, *spread-eagled* out – beneath us French County sprawls like a topographical map. The morning sunlight, stronger now, glows on green rectangular fields and dazzles off the lightning rods rising from the tops of barns. The roads look clean. Molten pools of light shine from the tops of the few cars drifting toward town along the edges of the fields. Holsteins nudge pasture gates, ready for the confinement of their stanchions and the morning's date with the milking machine.

At a safe distance from the black house, which has already given us an excellent example of slippage, we are gliding eastward, crossing the long straight ribbon of Eleventh Street and beginning a journey into a transitional area of scattered houses and small businesses before Highway 35 cuts through actual farmland. The 7-Eleven slips by, and the VFW hall, where the flagpole will not display Old Glory for another forty-five minutes. In one of the houses set back from the road, a woman named Wanda Kinderling, the wife of Thornberg Kinderling, a wicked and foolish man serving a life sentence in a California prison, awakens, eyes the level of the vodka in the bottle on her bedside table, and decides to postpone breakfast for another hour. Fifty yards along, gleaming tractors in military rows face the giant steel-and-glass bubble of Ted Goltz's farm-implement dealership, French County Farm Equipment, where a decent, troubled husband and father named Fred Marshall, whom we shall be meeting before long, will soon report for work.

Beyond the showy glass bubble and the asphalt sea of Goltz's parking lot, a half mile of stony, long-neglected field eventually degenerates into bare earth and spindly weeds. At the end of a long, overgrown turn-in, what seems to be a pile of rotting lumber stands between an old shed and an antique gas pump. This is our destination. We glide toward the earth.

The heap of lumber resolves into a leaning, dilapidated structure on the verge of collapse. An old tin Coca-Cola sign pocked with bullet holes tilts against the front of the building. Beer cans and the milkweed of old cigarette filters litter the scrubby ground. From within comes the steady, somnolent buzz of a great many flies. We wish to retreat into the cleansing air and depart. The black house was pretty bad; in fact, it was terrible, but this . . . this is going to be worse.

One secondary definition of *slippage* is: the feeling that things in general have just gotten, or very shortly will get, worse.

The ruined boxcar-shaped shack before us used to house a comically ill-run and unsanitary establishment called Ed's Eats & Dawgs. From behind an eternally messy counter, a chortling 350-pound mass of blubber named Ed Gilbertson once served up greasy, overdone hamburgers, baloney-and-mayonnaise sandwiches ornamented with black thumbprints, and oozing ice-cream cones to a small, undiscriminating clientele, mostly local children who arrived on bicycles. Now long deceased, Ed was one of the numerous uncles of French Landing's chief of police, Dale Gilbertson, and a good-hearted slob and dimwit of great local renown. His cook's apron was of an indescribable filthiness; the state of his hands and fingernails would have brought any visiting health inspector to the verge of nausea; his utensils might as well have been cleaned by cats. Immediately behind the counter, tubs of melting ice cream cooked in the heat from the crusted griddle. Overhead, limp flypaper ribbons hung invisible within the fur of a thousand fly corpses. The unlovely truth is that for decades Ed's Eats permitted generation upon generation of microbes and germs to multiply unchecked, swarming from floor, counter, and griddle – not hesitating to colonize Ed himself! – to spatula, fork, and the unwashed ice-cream scoop, thence into the horrible food, finally into the mouths and guts of the kids who ate that stuff, plus those of the occasional mother.

Remarkably, no one ever died from eating at Ed's, and after a long-overdue heart attack felled its proprietor one day when he mounted a stool for the purpose of finally tacking up a dozen new strips of flypaper, nobody had the heart to raze his little shack and clear away the rubble. For twenty-five years, under the shelter of darkness its rotting shell has welcomed romantic teenage couples, as well as gatherings of boys and girls in need of a secluded place to investigate for the first time in recorded history, or so it seemed to them, the liberation of drunkenness.

The rapt buzzing of the flies tells us that whatever we might be about to witness within this ruin will be neither a pair of spent young lovers nor a few silly, passed-out kids. That soft, greedy uproar, inaudible from the road, declares the presence of ultimate things. We could say that it represents a kind of portal.

We enter. Mild sunlight filtering in through gaps in the eastern wall and the battered roof paints luminous streaks across the gritty floor. Feathers, dust, eddy and stir over animal tracks and the dim impressions left by many long-gone shoes. Threadbare army-surplus blankets speckled with mold lie crumpled against the wall to our left; a few feet away, discarded beer cans and flattened cigarette ends surround a kerosene-burning hurricane lamp with a cracked glass housing. The sunlight lays warm stripes over crisp footprints advancing in a wide curve around the remains of Ed's appalling counter and into the vacancy formerly occupied by the stove, a sink, and a rank of storage shelves. There, in what once was Ed's sacred domain, the footprints vanish. Some ferocious activity has scattered the dust and grit, and something that is not an old army blanket, though we wish it were, lies disarrayed against the rear wall, half in, half out of a dark, irregular pool of tacky liquid. Delirious flies hover and settle upon the dark pool. In the far corner, a rust-colored mongrel with quill-like hair gets its teeth into the knuckle of meat and bone protruding from the white object held between its front paws. The white object is a running shoe, a sneaker. A New Balance sneaker, to be exact. To be more exact, a child's New Balance sneaker, size 5.

We want to invoke our capacity for flight and get the hell out of here. We want to float through the unresisting roof, to regain the harmless air, but we cannot, we must bear witness. An ugly dog is chewing on a child's severed foot while making every effort to extract the foot from the white New Balance sneaker. The mongrel's scrawny back arches down and extends, the quilled shoulders and narrow head drop, the bony front legs rigidly clamp the prize, tug tug tug, but the sneaker's laces are tied – too bad for the mutt.

As for the something that is not an old army-surplus blanket, beyond a swirl of dusty tracks and furrows, at the floor's far edge, its pale form lies flattened and face-up on the floor, its top half extending out of the dark pool. One arm stretches limply out into the grit; the other props upright against the wall. The fingers of both hands curl palmward. Blunt, strawberry-blond hair flops back from the small face. If the eyes and mouth display any recognizable expression, it is that of mild surprise. This is an accident of structure; it means nothing, for the configuration of this child's face caused her to look faintly surprised even while she was asleep. Bruises like ink stains and eraser smudges lie upon her cheekbones, her temple, her neck. A white T-shirt bearing the logo of the Milwaukee Brewers and smeared with dirt and dried blood covers her torso from neck to navel. The lower half of her body, pale as smoke except where drizzled with blood, lengthens into the dark pool, where the ecstatic flies hover and settle. Her bare, slender left leg incorporates a scabby knee and concludes with the uptick of a bloodstained New Balance sneaker, size 5, laces double-knotted, toe pointed to the ceiling. Where the partner to this leg should be is a vacancy, for her right hip ends, abruptly, at a ragged stump.

We are in the presence of the Fisherman's third victim, ten-year-old Irma Freneau. The shock waves aroused by her disappearance yesterday afternoon from the sidewalk outside the video store will increase in force and number after Dale Gilbertson comes upon her body, a little over a day from now.

The Fisherman gathered her up on Chase Street and transported her – we cannot say how – up the length of Chase Street and Lyall Road, past the 7-Eleven and the VFW hall, past the house where Wanda Kinderling seethes and drinks, past the shiny glass spaceship of Goltz's, and across the border between town and farmland.

She was alive when the Fisherman moved her through the doorway next to the pockmarked Coca-Cola sign. She must have struggled, she must have screamed. The Fisherman brought her to the rear wall and silenced her with blows to the face. Very likely, he strangled her. He lowered her body to the floor and arranged her limbs. Except for the white New Balance sneakers, he removed all the clothing from her waist down, underwear, jeans, shorts, whatever Irma had been wearing when he abducted her. After that, the Fisherman amputated her right leg. Using some sort of long, heavy-bladed knife, and without the assistance of cleaver or saw, he parted flesh and bone until he had managed to detach the leg from the rest of the body. Then, perhaps with no more than two or three downward chops to the ankle, he severed the foot. He tossed it, still contained within the white sneaker, aside. Irma's foot was not important to the Fisherman – all he wanted was her leg.

Here, my friends, we have true *slippage.*

Irma Freneau's small, inert body seems to flatten out as if it intends to melt through the rotting floorboards. The drunken flies sing on. The dog keeps trying to yank the whole of its juicy prize out of the sneaker. Were we to bring simpleminded Ed Gilbertson back to life and stand him beside us, he would sink to his knees and weep. We, on the other hand . . .

We are not here to weep. Not like Ed, anyhow, in horrified shame and disbelief. A tremendous mystery has inhabited this hovel, and its effects and traces hover everywhere about us. We have come to observe, register, and record the impressions, the afterimages, left in the comet trail of the mystery. It speaks from their details, therefore it lingers in its own wake, therefore it surrounds us. A deep, deep gravity flows outward from the scene, and this gravity humbles us. Humility is our best, most accurate first response. Without it, we would miss the point; the great mystery would escape us, and we would go on deaf and blind, ignorant as pigs. Let us not go on like pigs. We must honor this scene – the flies, the dog worrying the severed foot, the poor, pale body of Irma Freneau, the magnitude of what befell Irma Freneau – by acknowledging our littleness. In comparison, we are no more than vapors.

A fat bee wanders in through the empty window frame in the side wall six feet from Irma's body and makes a slow, exploratory circuit around the rear of the shack. Suspended beneath its blurred wings, the bee looks nearly too heavy for flight, but it proceeds with easy, unhurried deliberation, moving well above the bloody floor in a wide curve. The flies, the mongrel, and Irma pay it no attention.

For us, though, the bee, which continues to drift contentedly about the rear of the horror chamber, has ceased to be a welcome distraction and has been absorbed into the surrounding mystery. It is a detail within the scene, and it, too, commands our humility and speaks. The weighty, burrowing rumble of its wings seems to define the exact center of the undulating sound waves, higher in pitch, produced by the greedy flies: Like a singer at a microphone in front of a chorus, the bee controls the aural background. The sound gathers and comes to a serious point. When the bee ambles into a shaft of yellow light streaming through the eastern wall, its stripes glow black and gold, the wings coalesce into a fan, and the insect becomes an intricate, airborne wonder. The slaughtered girl flattens into the bloody floorboards. Our humility, our sense of littleness, our appreciation of the gravity deeply embedded in this scene grant us the sense of forces and powers beyond our understanding, of a kind of grandeur always present and at work but perceptible only during moments like this.

We have been honored, but the honor is unbearable. The speaking bee circles back to the window and passes into another world, and, following his lead, we move on, out the window, into the sun, and into the upper air.

Smells of shit and urine at Maxton Elder Care; the fragile, slick feel of *slippage* at the off-kilter house north of Highway 35; the sound of the flies and the sight of the blood at the former Ed's Eats. Ag! Yuck! Is there no place here in French Landing, we may ask, where there is something nice under the skin? Where what we see is what we get, so to speak?

The short answer: no. French Landing should be marked

with big road signs at every point of ingress: WARNING! SLIPPAGE IN PROGRESS! PASS AT YOUR OWN RISK!

The magic at work here is Fishermagic. It has rendered 'nice' at least temporarily obsolete. But we can go someplace nice-*er*, and if we can we probably should, because we need a break. We may not be able to escape *slippage*, but we can at least visit where no one shits the bed or bleeds on the floor (at least not yet).

So the bee goes its way and we go ours; ours takes us southwest, over more woods exhaling their fragrance of life and oxygen – there is no air like this air, at least not in this world – and then back to the works of man again.

This section of town is called Libertyville, so named by the French Landing Town Council in 1976. You won't believe this, but big-bellied Ed Gilbertson, the Hot Dog King himself, was a member of that bicentennial band of town fathers; those were strange days, pretty mama, strange days indeed. Not as strange as these, however; in French Landing, these are the Fisherdays, the slippery slippage days.

The streets of Libertyville have names that adults find colorful and children find painful. Some of the latter have been known to call this area of town Faggotyville. Let us descend now, down through the sweet morning air (it's warming up already; this will be a Strawberry Fest kind of day for sure). We cruise silently over Camelot Street, past the intersection of Camelot and Avalon, and travel on down Avalon to Maid Marian Way. From Maid Marian we progress to – is it any surprise? – Robin Hood Lane.

Here, at No. 16, a sweet little Cape Cod honey of a home that looks just right for The Decent Hardworking Family On Its Way Up, we find a kitchen window open. There is the smell of coffee and toast, a wonderful combined odor that denies slippage (if only we did not know better; if only we had not seen the dog at work, eating a foot out of a sneaker as a child might eat the hot dog right out of its bun), and we follow the aroma in. It's nice to be invisible, isn't it? To watch in our godlike silence. If only what our godlike eyes saw was just a little less goddamn upsetting! But that is by the way. We're in it now, for better or for worse, and we had better get on about our business. Daylight's a-wasting, as they say in this part of the world.

Here in the kitchen of No. 16 is Fred Marshall, whose picture currently graces the Salesman of the Month easel in the showroom of French County Farm Equipment. Fred has also been named Employee of the Year three years out of the last four (two years ago Ted Goltz gave the award to Otto Eisman, just to break the monotony), and when he is on the job no one radiates more charm, personality, or all around *niceness*. You wanted nice? Ladies and gentlemen, presenting Fred Marshall!

Only now his confident smile is not in evidence, and his hair, always carefully combed on the job, hasn't yet seen the brush. He's wearing Nike shorts and a tee with cutoff sleeves instead of his usual pressed khakis and sport shirt. On the counter is the Marshall copy of the *La Riviere Herald*, open to an inside page.

Fred has his share of problems just lately – or, rather, his wife, Judy, has problems, and what's hers is his, so said the minister when he joined them in holy wedlock – and what he's reading isn't making him feel any better. Far from it. It's a sidebar to the lead story on the front page, and of course the author is everyone's favorite muckraker, Wendell 'FISHERMAN STILL AT LARGE' Green.

The sidebar is your basic recap of the first two murders (*Gruesome and Gruesomer* is how Fred thinks of them), and as he reads, Fred bends first his left leg up behind him and then his right, stretching those all-important thigh muscles and preparing for his morning run. What could be more antislippage than a morning run? What could be *nicer*? What could possibly spoil such a lovely start to such a beautiful Wisconsin day?

Well, how about this:

Johnny Irkenham's dreams were simple enough, according to his grief-stricken father. [*Grief-stricken father*, Fred thinks, stretching and imagining his son asleep upstairs. *Dear God, save me from ever being a grief-stricken father.* Not knowing, of course, how soon he must assume this role.] *'Johnny wanted to be an astronaut,' George Irkenham said, a smile briefly lighting his exhausted face. 'When he wasn't putting out fires for the French Landing FD or fighting crime with the Justice League of America, that is.'*

These innocent dreams ended in a nightmare we cannot imagine. [*But I'm sure you'll try*, Fred thinks, now beginning his toe raises.] *Earlier this week, his dismembered body was discovered by Spencer Hovdahl of Centralia. Hovdahl, a First Farmer State Bank loan officer, was inspecting an abandoned French Landing farm owned by John Ellison, who lives in a neighboring county, with an eye to initiating repossession proceedings. 'I didn't want to be there in the first place,' Hovdahl told this reporter. 'If there's anything I hate, it's the repo stuff.* [Knowing Spence Hovdahl as he does, Fred very much doubts if 'stuff' was the word he used.] *I wanted to be there even less after I went into the henhouse. It's all rickety and falling down, and I would have stayed out except for the sound of the bees. I thought there might be a hive in there. Bees are an interest of mine, and I was curious. God help me, I was curious. I hope I'll never be curious again.'*

What he found in the henhouse was the body of seven-year-old

John Wesley Irkenham. The corpse had been dismembered, the pieces hung from the henhouse's decaying rafters by chains. Although Police Chief Dale Gilbertson would neither confirm nor deny it, reliable police sources in La Riviere say that the thighs, torso, and buttocks had been bitten—

Okay, that's enough for Fred, everybody out of the pool. He sweeps the newspaper closed and shoves it all the way down the counter to the Mr Coffee. By God, they never put stuff like that in the paper when *he* was a kid. And why the Fisherman, for heaven's sake? Why did they have to tag every monster with a catchy nickname, turn a guy like whoever did this into the Celebrity Sicko of the Month?

Of course, nothing like this had ever happened when he was Tyler's age, but the principle . . . the goddamned *principle* of the matter . . .

Fred finishes his toe raises, reminding himself to have a talk with Tyler. It will be harder than their little talk about why his thing sometimes gets hard, but it absolutely must be done. *Buddy system*, Fred will say. *You've got to stick with your buddies now, Ty. No more rambling around on your own for a while, okay?*

Yet the idea of Ty actually being murdered seems remote to Fred; it is the stuff of TV docudramas or maybe a Wes Craven movie. Call it *Scream 4: The Fisherman*. In fact, wasn't there a movie sort of like that? A guy in a fisherman's slicker wandering around and killing teenagers with a hook? Maybe, but not little kids, not *babies* like Amy St Pierre and Johnny Irkenham. Jesus, the world was disintegrating right in front of him.

Body parts hanging from chains in a crumbling henhouse, that is the part which haunts him. Can that really be? Can it be *here*, right here and now in Tom Sawyer–Becky Thatcher country?

Well, let it go. It's time to run.

But maybe the paper kind of got lost this morning, Fred thinks, picking it up from the counter and folding it until it looks like a thick paperback book (but part of the headline accuses him even SO: FISHERMAN STILL AT L). *Maybe the paper just kind of, I don't know, migrated straight to the old garbage can beside the house.*

Yes, good idea. Because Judy has been strange lately, and Wendell Green's pulsating stories about the Fisherman are not helping. (*Thighs and torso bitten*, Fred thinks as he glides through the early-morning-quiet house toward the door, *and while you're at it, waiter, have them cut me a nice rare chunk of butt.*) She reads the press accounts obsessively, making no comment, but Fred doesn't like the way her eyes jump around, or some of the other tics she's picked up: the obsessive touching of her tongue to her upper lip, for instance . . . and sometimes, this in the last two or three days, he has seen her tongue reach all the way up and pet at her philtrum just below her nose, a feat he would have thought impossible if he had not seen it again last night, during the local news. She goes to bed earlier and earlier, and sometimes she talks in her sleep – strange, slurry words that don't sound like English. Sometimes when Fred speaks to her, she doesn't respond, simply stares off into space, eyes wide, lips moving slightly, hands kneading together (cuts and scratches have begun to show up on the backs of them, even though she keeps her nails cropped sensibly short).

Ty has noticed his mother's encroaching oddities, too. On Saturday, while father and son were having lunch together – Judy was upstairs taking one of her long naps, another new wrinkle – the boy suddenly asked, right out of a blue clear sky, 'What's wrong with Mom?'

'Ty, nothing's wrong with—'

'There *is*! Tommy Erbter says she's a Coke short of a Happy Meal these days.'

And had he almost reached across the tomato soup and toasted-cheese sandwiches and clouted his son? His only child? Good old Ty, who was nothing but concerned? God help him, he had.

Outside the door, at the head of the concrete path leading down to the street, Fred begins to jog slowly in place, taking deep breath after deep breath, depositing the oxygen he will soon withdraw. It is usually the best part of his day (assuming he and Judy don't make love, that is, and lately there has been precious little of that). He likes the feeling – the *knowledge* – that his path might be the beginning of the road to anywhere, that he could start out here in the Libertyville section of French Landing and wind up in New York . . . San Francisco . . . Bombay . . . the mountain passes of Nepal. Every step outside one's own door invites the world (perhaps even the universe), and this is something Fred Marshall intuitively understands. He sells John Deere tractors and Case cultivators, yes, all *right*, already, but he is not devoid of imagination. When he and Judy were students at UW–Madison, their first dates were at the coffeehouse just off campus, an espresso-jazz-and-poetry haven called the Chocolate Watchband. It would not be entirely unfair to say that they had fallen in love to the sound of angry drunks declaiming the works of Allen Ginsberg and Gary Snyder into the Chocolate Watchband's cheap but exquisitely loud sound system.

Fred draws one more deep breath and begins to run. Down Robin Hood Lane to Maid Marian Way, where he gives Deke Purvis a wave. Deke, in his robe and slippers, is just picking Wendell Green's daily dose of doom up off his own stoop. Then he wheels onto Avalon Street, picking it up a little now, showing his heels to the morning.

He cannot outrun his worries, however.

Judy, Judy, Judy, he thinks in the voice of Cary Grant (a little joke that has long since worn thin with the love of his life).

There is the gibberish when she sleeps. There's the way her eyes dart hither and yon. And let's not forget the time (just three days ago) when he followed her into the kitchen and she wasn't there – she'd turned out to be *behind* him, coming down the stairs, and *how* she had done that seems less important to him than *why* she had done it, gone sneaking up the back stairs and then come tromping down the front ones (because that is what she must have done; it's the only solution he can think of). There's the constant tapping and petting she does with her tongue. Fred knows what it all adds up to: Judy has been acting like a woman in terror. This has been going on since *before* the murder of Amy St Pierre, so it can't be the Fisherman, or not *entirely* the Fisherman.

And there is a larger issue. Before the last couple of weeks, Fred would have told you that his wife doesn't have a fearful bone in her body. She might be just five foot two ('Why, you're no bigger than a minute' was his grandmother's comment when she first met Fred's intended), but Judy has the heart of a lion, of a Viking warrior. This isn't bullshit, or hype, or poetic license; it is the simple truth as Fred sees it, and it is the contrast between what he has always known and what he sees now that scares him the most.

From Avalon he races onto Camelot, crossing the intersection without looking for traffic, going much faster than usual, almost sprinting instead of jogging. He is remembering something that happened about a month after they started going out.

It was the Chocolate Watchband they had gone to, as usual, only this time during the afternoon, to listen to a jazz quartet that had actually been pretty good. Not that they had listened very much, as Fred now recalls it; mostly he had talked to Judy about how little he liked being in the College of Agricultural and Life Sciences (Moo U, the Letters and Science snooties called it), and how little he liked the unspoken family assumption that when he graduated he would come on back home and help Phil run the family farm in French Landing. The idea of spending his life in harness with Phil gave Fred a severe case of the glooms.

What do you want, then? Judy had asked. Holding his hand on the table, a candle burning inside a jelly glass, the combo onstage working a sweet little number called 'I'll Be There for You.'

I don't know, he'd said, *but I tell you what, Jude, I should be in Business Admin, not Moo U. I'm a hell of a lot better at selling than at planting.*

Then why don't you switch?

Because my family thinks—

Your family isn't going to have to live your life, Fred – you are.

Talk is cheap, he remembers thinking, but then something had happened on the way back to campus, something so amazing and out of his understanding of how life was supposed to work that it fills him with wonder even now, some thirteen years later.

Still talking about his future and their future together (*I could be a farm wife*, Judy had said, *but only if my husband really wants to be a farmer*). Deep into that. Letting their feet carry them along without much interest in exactly where they were. And then, at the intersection of State Street and Gorham, a scream of brakes and a hearty metallic bang had interrupted the conversation. Fred and Judy had looked around and seen a Dodge pickup that had just tangled bumpers with an elderly Ford station wagon.

Getting out of the wagon, which had pretty clearly run the stop sign at the end of Gorham Street, was a middle-aged man in a middle-aged brown suit. He looked scared as well as shaken up, and Fred thought there was good reason for that; the man advancing toward him from the pickup truck was young, heavyset (Fred particularly remembered the belly bulging over the waist of his jeans), and carrying a tire iron. *You goddamn careless asshole!* Young and Heavyset cried. *Look what you done to my truck! This my dad's truck, you goddamn asshole!*

Middle-Aged Suit backing up, eyes wide, hands raised, Fred watching fascinated from in front of Rickman's Hardware, thinking *Oh no, mister, bad idea. You don't back away from a guy like this, you go* toward *him, even as mad as he is. You're provoking him – can't you see that you're provoking him?* So fascinated he didn't realize that Judy's hand was no longer in his, listening with a kind of sick foreknowledge as Mr Middle-Aged Suit, still backing up, blathered about how he was sorry . . . entirely his fault, wasn't looking, wasn't thinking . . . insurance papers . . . State Farm . . . draw a diagram . . . get a policeman to take statements . . .

And all the time Young and Heavyset was advancing, thwocking the end of the tire iron into the palm of his hand, not listening. This wasn't about insurance or compensation; this was about how Mr Middle-Aged Suit had scared the shit out of him while he was just driving along and minding his own business and listening to Johnny Paycheck sing 'Take This Job and Shove It.' Young and Heavyset intended to take a little payback paycheck of his own for getting the shit scared out of him and all jounced around behind the wheel . . . *had* to take a little, because the other man's smell was inciting him, that piss-yellow smell of fear and innate defenselessness. It was a case of rabbit and farmyard dog, and all at once the rabbit was clean out of backing room; Mr Middle-Aged Suit was pressed against the side of his station wagon, and in a moment the tire iron was going to start swinging and the blood was going to start flying.

Except there *was* no blood and not a single swing, because all at once Judy DeLois was there, no bigger than a minute but standing between them, looking fearlessly up into Young and Heavyset's burning face.

Fred blinked, wondering how in the name of God she'd gotten there so damned fast. (Much later he would feel the same way when he followed her into the kitchen, only to hear the steady thump of her feet descending the front stairs.) And then? Then Judy slapped Young and Heavyset's arm! *Whack*, right on the meaty bicep she slapped him, leaving a white palm print on the sunburned freckled flesh below the sleeve of the guy's torn blue T-shirt. Fred saw it but couldn't believe it.

Quit it! Judy shouted up into Young and Heavyset's surprised, beginning-to-be-bewildered face. *Put it down, quit it! Don't be dumb! You want to go to jail over seven hundred dollars' worth of bodywork? Put it down! Get it together, big boy! Put . . . that . . . thing . . . DOWN!*

There'd been one second when Fred was quite sure Young and Heavyset was going to bring the tire iron down anyway, and right on his pretty little girlfriend's head. But Judy never flinched; her eyes never left the eyes of the young man with the tire iron, who towered at least a foot over her and must have outweighed her by a couple of hundred pounds. There was certainly no pissy yellow fear smell coming off her that day; her tongue did no nervous patting at her upper lip or her philtrum; her blazing eyes were steadfast.

And, after another moment, Young and Heavyset put the tire iron down.

Fred wasn't aware that a crowd had gathered until he heard the spontaneous applause from perhaps thirty onlookers. He joined in, never more proud of her than he was at that moment. And for the first time, Judy looked startled. She hung in there, though, startled or not. She got the two of them together, tugging Mr Middle-Aged Suit forward by one arm, and actually hectored them into shaking hands. By the time the cops arrived, Young and Heavyset and Mr Middle-Aged Suit were sitting side by side on the curb, studying each other's insurance papers. Case closed.

Fred and Judy walked on toward the campus, holding hands again. For two blocks Fred didn't speak. Was he in awe of her? He supposes now that he was. At last he said: *That was amazing.*

She gave him an uncomfortable little look, an uncomfortable little smile. *No it wasn't,* she said. *If you want to call it something, call it good citizenship. I could see that guy getting ready to send himself to jail. I didn't want that to happen. Or the other guy to be hurt.*

Yet she said that last almost as an afterthought, and Fred for the first time sensed not only her courage but her unflinching Viking's heart. She was on the side of Young and Heavyset because . . . well, because the other fellow had been afraid.

Weren't you worried, though? he asked her. He had still been so stunned by what he'd seen that it hadn't crossed his mind – yet – to think he should be a little ashamed; after all, it was his girlfriend who'd stepped in instead of him, and that wasn't the Gospel According to Hollywood. *Weren't you afraid that in the heat of the moment the guy with the tire iron would take a swing at you?*

Judy's eyes had grown puzzled. *It never crossed my mind,* she said.

★

Camelot eventually debouches into Chase Street, where there is a pleasant little gleam of the Mississippi on clear days like this one, but Fred doesn't go that far. He turns at the top of Liberty Heights and starts back the way he came, his shirt now soaked with sweat. Usually the run makes him feel better, but not today, at least not yet. The fearless Judy of that afternoon on the corner of State and Gorham is so unlike the shifty-eyed, sometimes disconnected Judy who now lives in his house – the nap-taking, hand-wringing Judy – that Fred has actually spoken to Pat Skarda about it. Yesterday, this was, when the doc was in Goltz's, looking at riding lawn mowers.

Fred had shown him a couple, a Deere and a Honda, inquired after his family, and then asked (casually, he hoped), *Hey, Doc, tell me something – do you think it's possible for a person to just go crazy? Without any warning, like?*

Skarda had given him a sharper look than Fred had really liked. *Are we talking about an adult or an adolescent, Fred?*

Well, we're not talking about anyone, *actually*. Big, hearty laugh – unconvincing to Fred's own ears, and judging from Pat Skarda's look, not very convincing to him, either. *Not anyone* real, *anyway. But as a hypothetical case, let's say an adult.*

Skarda had thought about it, then shook his head. *There are few absolutes in medicine, even fewer in* psychiatric *medicine. That said, I have to tell you that I think it's very unlikely for a person to 'just go crazy.' It may be a fairly rapid process, but it is a process. We hear people say 'So-and-so snapped,' but that's rarely the case. Mental dysfunction – neurotic or psychotic behavior – takes time to develop, and there are usually signs. How's your mom these days, Fred?*

Mom? Oh hey, she's fine. Right in the pink.

And Judy?

It had taken him a moment to get a smile started, but

once he did, he managed a big one. Big and guileless. *Judy? She's in the pink, too, Doc. Of course she is. Steady as she goes.*

Sure. Steady as she goes. Just showing a few *signs*, that was all.

Maybe they'll pass, he thinks. Those good old endorphins are finally kicking in, and all at once this seems plausible. Optimism is a more normal state for Fred, who does not believe in *slippage*, and a little smile breaks on his face – the day's first. *Maybe the signs will pass. Maybe whatever's wrong with her will blow out as fast as it blew in. Maybe it's even, you know, a menstrual thing. Like PMS.*

God, if that was all it was, what a *relief*! In the meantime, there's Ty to think about. He has to have a talk with Tyler about the buddy system, because while Fred doesn't believe what Wendell Green is apparently trying to insinuate, that the ghost of a fabulous turn-of-the-century cannibal and all-around boogerman named Albert Fish has for some reason turned up here in Coulee Country, *someone* is certainly out there, and this someone has murdered two little children and done unspeakable (at least unless you're Wendell Green, it seems) things to the bodies.

Thighs, torso, and buttocks bitten, Fred thinks, and runs faster, although now he's getting a stitch in his side. Yet this bears repeating: he does not believe that these horrors can actually touch his son, nor does he see how they can have caused Judy's condition, since her oddities started while Amy St Pierre was still alive, Johnny Irkenham too, both of them presumably playing happily in their respective backyards.

Maybe this, maybe that . . . but enough of Fred and his worries, all right? Let us rise from the environs of his troubled head and precede him back to No. 16, Robin Hood Lane – let's go directly to the source of his troubles.

★

The upstairs window of the connubial bedroom is open, and the screen is certainly no problem; we strain ourselves right through, entering with the breeze and the first sounds of the awakening day.

The sounds of French Landing awakening do not awaken Judy Marshall. Nope, she has been starey-eyed since three, conning the shadows for she doesn't know what, fleeing dreams too horrible to remember. Yet she does remember *some* things, little as she wants to.

'Saw the eye again,' she remarks to the empty room. Her tongue comes out and with no Fred around to watch her (she knows he's watching, she is beset but not *stupid*), it does not just pet at her philtrum but *slathers* it in a great big wipe, like a dog licking its chops after a bowl of scraps. 'It's a red eye. *His* eye. Eye of the King.'

She looks up at the shadows of the trees outside. They dance on the ceiling, making shapes and faces, shapes and faces.

'Eye of the King,' she repeats, and now it starts with the hands: kneading and twisting and squeezing and digging. 'Abbalah! Foxes down foxholes! Abbalah-doon, the Crimson King! Rats in their ratholes! Abbalah Munshun! The King is in his Tower, eating bread and honey! The Breakers in the basement, making all the money!'

She shakes her head from side to side. Oh, these voices, out of the darkness they come, and sometimes she awakens with a vision burning behind her eyes, a vision of a vast slaty tower standing in a field of roses. A field of blood. Then the talking begins, the speaking in tongues, testification, words she can't understand let alone control, a mixed stream of English and gibberish.

'Trudge, trudge, trudge,' she says. 'The little ones are

trudging on their bleeding footsies . . . oh for Christ's sake, won't this ever stop?'

Her tongue yawns out and licks across the tip of her nose; for a moment her nostrils are plugged with her own spit, and her head roars

– *Abbalah, Abbalah-doon, Can-tah Abbalah* –

with those terrible foreign words, those terrible impacted images of the Tower and the burning caves beneath, caves through which little ones trudge on bleeding feet. Her mind strains with them, and there is only one thing that will make them stop, only one way to get relief.

Judy Marshall sits up. On the table beside her there is a lamp, a copy of the latest John Grisham novel, a little pad of paper (a birthday present from Ty, each sheet headed HERE'S ANOTHER GREAT IDEA I HAD!), and a ballpoint pen with LA RIVIERE SHERATON printed on the side.

Judy seizes the pen and scribbles on the pad.

No Abbalah no Abbalah-doon no Tower no Breakers no Crimson King only dreams these are just my dreams

It is enough, but pens are also roads to anywhere, and before she can divorce the tip of this one from the birthday pad, it writes one more line:

The Black House is the doorway to Abbalah the entrance to hell Sheol Munshun all these worlds and spirits

No more! Good merciful God, no more! And the worst thing: What if it all begins to make sense?

She throws the pen back on the table, where it rolls to the base of the lamp and lies still. Then she tears the page from the pad, crumples it, and sticks it in her mouth. She chews furiously, not tearing it but at least mashing it sodden, then swallows. There is an awful moment when it sticks in her throat, but then it goes down. Words and worlds recede and Judy falls back against the pillows, exhausted. Her face is pale and sweaty, her eyes huge with unshed tears, but the moving shadows on the ceiling no longer look like faces to her – the faces of trudging children, of rats in their ratholes, foxes in foxholes, eye of the King, Abbalah-Abbalah-doon! Now they are just the shadows of the trees again. She is Judy DeLois Marshall, wife of Fred, mother of Ty. This is Libertyville, this is French Landing, this is French County, this is Wisconsin, this is America, this is the Northern Hemisphere, this is the world, and there is no other world than this. Let it be so.

Ah, let it be so.

Her eyes close, and as she finally slips back to sleep we slip across the room to the door, but just before we get there, Judy Marshall says one other thing – says it as she crosses over the border and into sleep.

'Burnside is not your name. Where is your hole?'

The bedroom door is closed and so we use the keyhole, passing through it like a sigh. Down the hall we go, past pictures of Judy's family and Fred's, including one photo of the Marshall family farm where Fred and Judy spent a horrible but blessedly short period not long after their marriage. Want some good advice? Don't talk to Judy Marshall about Fred's brother, Phil. Just don't get her started, as George Rathbun would undoubtedly say.

No keyhole in the door at the end of the hall and so we slide underneath like a telegram and into a room we immediately know is a boy's room: we can tell from the mingled smells of dirty athletic socks and neat's-foot oil. It's small, this room, but it seems bigger than Fred and Judy's down the hall, very likely because the odor of anxiety is missing. On the walls are pictures of Shaquille O'Neal, Jeromy Burnitz, last year's Milwaukee Bucks team . . . and Tyler Marshall's idol, Mark

McGwire. McGwire plays for the Cards, and the Cards are the enemy, but hell, it's not as if the Milwaukee Brewers are actually competition for anything. The Brew Crew were doormats in the American League, and they are likewise doormats in the National. And McGwire . . . well, he's a hero, isn't he? He's strong, he's modest, and he can hit the baseball a country mile. Even Tyler's dad, who roots strictly for Wisconsin teams, thinks McGwire is something special. 'The greatest hitter in the history of the game,' he called him after the seventy-home-run season, and Tyler, although little more than an infant in that fabled year, has never forgotten this.

Also on the wall of this little boy who will soon be the Fisherman's fourth victim (yes, there has already been a third, as we have seen), holding pride of place directly over his bed, is a travel poster showing a great dark castle at the end of a long and misty meadow. At the bottom of the poster, which he has Scotch-taped to the wall (his mom absolutely forbids pushpins), it says COME BACK TO THE AULD SOD in big green letters. Ty is considering taking the poster down long enough to cut this part off. He doesn't like the poster because he has any interest in Ireland; to him the picture whispers of somewhere else, somewhere Entirely Else. It is like a photograph of some splendid mythical kingdom where there might be unicorns in the forests and dragons in the caves. Never mind Ireland; never mind Harry Potter, either. Hogwarts is fine enough for summer afternoons, but this is a castle in the Kingdom of Entirely Else. It's the first thing Tyler Marshall sees in the morning, the last thing he sees at night, and that's just the way he likes it.

He lies curled on his side in his underwear shorts, a human comma with tousled dark blond hair and a thumb that is close to his mouth, really just an inch or so away from being sucked. He is dreaming – we can see his eyeballs moving back and forth behind his closed lids. His lips move . . . he's whispering something . . . Abbalah? Is he whispering his mother's word? Surely not, but . . .

We lean closer to listen, but before we can hear anything, a circuit in Tyler's jazzy red clock-radio goes hot, and all at once the voice of George Rathbun fills the room, calling Tyler hence from whatever dreams have been playing themselves out under that tousled thatch.

'Fans, you gotta listen to me now, how many times have I told you this? If you don't know Henreid Brothers Furniture of French Landing and Centralia, then you don't know furniture. That's right, I'm talking Henreid Brothers, home of the Colonial Blowout. Living-room sets dining-room sets bedroom sets, famous names you know and trust like La-Z-Boy, Breton Woods and Moosehead, EVEN A BLIND MAN CAN SEE THAT HENREID BROTHERS MEANS QUALITY!'

Ty Marshall is laughing even before he's got both eyes fully open. He loves George Rathbun; George is absolutely fly.

And now, without even changing gears from the commercial: 'You guys are all ready for the Brewer Bash, ain'tcha? Sent me those postcards with your name, address, and *el teléfono* on 'em? Hope so, because the contest closed at midnight. If you missed out . . . so solly, Cholly!'

Ty closes his eyes again and mouths the same word over three times: *Shit, shit, shit.* He *did* forget to enter, and now he can only hope that his dad (who knows how forgetful his son can be) remembered and entered the contest for him.

'Grand prize?' George is saying. 'ONLY the chance for you or the fav-o-rite young person of your acquaintance to be the Brew Crew's batboy or batgirl for the entire Cincinnati series. ONLY the chance to win an aut-o-graphed Richie

Sexson bat, the LUMBER that holds the LIGHTNING! Not to mention fifty free seats on the first-base side with me, George Rathbun, Coulee Country's Traveling College of Baseball Knowledge. BUT WHY AM I TELLING YOU THIS? If you missed out, you're too late. Case closed, game over, zip up your fly! Oh, I know why I brought it up – to make sure you tune in next Friday to see if I speak YOUR NAME over the radio!'

Ty groans. There are only two chances that George will speak his name over the radio: slim and none. Not that he cared so much about being a batboy, dressed in a baggy Brewers uni and running around in front of all those people at Miller Park, but to own Richie Sexson's *own bat*, the lumber with the lightning . . . how boss would that've been?

Tyler rolls out of bed, sniffs the armpits of yesterday's T-shirt, tosses it aside, gets another out of the drawer. His dad sometimes asks him why he sets his alarm so *early* – it's summer vacation, after all – and Tyler can't seem to make him understand that every day is important, especially those filled with warmth and sunlight and no particular responsibilities. It's as if there's some little voice deep inside him, warning him not to waste a minute, not a single one, because time is short.

What George Rathbun says next drives the remaining sleep-fog from Tyler's brain – it's like a dash of cold water. 'Say there, Coulee, want to talk about the Fisherman?'

Tyler stops what he's doing, an odd little chill running up his back and then down his arms. The Fisherman. Some crazy guy killing kids . . . and *eating* them? Well, he's heard that rumor, mostly from the bigger kids down at the baseball field or at the French Landing Rec Center, but who would do something so gross? Cannibalism, ack!

George's voice drops. 'Now I'm going to tell you a little secret, so listen close to your Uncle George.' Tyler sits on his bed, holding his sneakers by the laces and listening closely to his Uncle George, as bidden. It seems odd to hear George Rathbun talking about a subject so . . . so *unsporty*, but Tyler trusts him. Didn't George Rathbun predict that the Badgers would go to at least the Elite Eight two years ago, when everyone else said they'd get blown out in the first round of the Big Dance? Yeah, he did. Case closed, game over, zip up your fly.

George's voice drops further, to what is almost a confidential whisper. 'The original Fisherman, boys and girls, Albert Fish, has been dead and gone for sixty-seven years, and s'far's I know, he never got much west of New Jersey. *Furthermore*, he was probably a DAMYANKEE FAN! SO COOL IT, COULEE COUNTRY! JUST CAAAALM DOWN!'

Tyler relaxes, smiling, and starts putting on his sneakers. Calm down, you got that right. The day is new, and yeah, okay, his mom's been a little on the Tinky Winky side lately, but she'll pull out of it.

Let us leave on this optimistic note – make like an amoeba and split, as the redoubtable George Rathbun might say. And speaking of George, that ubiquitous voice of the Coulee Country morning, should we not seek him out? Not a bad idea. Let us do so immediately.

3

Out Tyler's window we go, away from Libertyville, flying southwest on a diagonal, not lingering now but really flapping those old wings, flying with a purpose. We're headed toward the heliograph flash of early-morning sun on the Father of Waters, also toward the world's largest six-pack. Between it and County Road Oo (we can call it Nailhouse Row if we want; we're practically honorary citizens of French Landing now) is a radio tower, the warning beacon on top now invisible in the bright sunshine of this newborn July day. We smell grass and trees and warming earth, and as we draw closer to the tower, we also smell the yeasty, fecund aroma of beer.

Next to the radio tower, in the industrial park on the east side of Peninsula Drive, is a little cinder-block building with a parking lot just big enough for half a dozen cars and the Coulee patrol van, an aging Ford Econoline painted candy-apple pink. As the day winds down and afternoon wears into evening, the cylindrical shadows of the six-pack will fall first over the sign on the balding lawn facing the drive, then the building, then the parking lot. KDCU-AM, this sign reads, YOUR TALK VOICE IN COULEE COUNTRY. Spray-painted across it, in a pink that almost matches the patrol van, is a fervent declaration: TROY LUVS MARYANN! YES! Later on, Howie Soule, the U-Crew engineer, will clean this off (probably during the Rush Limbaugh show, which is satellite fed and totally automated), but for now it stays, telling us all we need to know about small-town luv in middle America. Looks like we found something nice after all.

Coming out of the station's side door as we arrive is a slender man dressed in pleated khaki Dockers, a tieless white shirt of Egyptian cotton buttoned all the way to the neck, and maroon braces (they are as slim as he is, those braces, and far too cool to be called suspenders; suspenders are vulgar things worn by such creatures as Chipper Maxton and Sonny Heartfield, down at the funeral home). This silver-haired fellow is also wearing a *very* sharp straw fedora, antique but beautifully kept. The maroon hatband matches his braces. Aviator-style sunglasses cover his eyes. He takes a position on the grass to the left of the door, beneath a battered speaker that is amping KDCU's current broadcast: the local news. This will be followed by the Chicago farm report, which gives him ten minutes before he has to settle in behind the mike again.

We watch in growing puzzlement as he produces a pack of American Spirit cigarettes from his shirt pocket and fires one up with a gold lighter. Surely this elegant fellow in the braces, Dockers, and Bass Weejuns cannot be George Rathbun. In our minds we have already built up a picture of George, and it is one of a fellow very different from this. In our mind's eye we see a guy with a huge belly hanging over the white belt of his checked pants (all those ballpark bratwursts), a brick-red complexion (all those ballpark beers, not to mention all that bellowing at the dastardly umps), and a squat, broad neck (perfect for housing those asbestos vocal cords). The

George Rathbun of our imagination – and all of Coulee Country's, it almost goes without saying – is a pop-eyed, broad-assed, wild-haired, leather-lunged, Rolaids-popping, Chevy-driving, Republican-voting heart attack waiting to happen, a churning urn of sports trivia, mad enthusiasms, crazy prejudices, and high cholesterol.

This fellow is not that fellow. This fellow moves like a dancer. This fellow is iced tea on a hot day, cool as the king of spades.

But say, that's the joke of it, isn't it? Uh-huh. The joke of the fat deejay with the skinny voice, only turned inside out. In a very real sense, George Rathbun does not exist at all. He is a hobby in action, a fiction in the flesh, and only one of the slim man's multiple personalities. The people at KDCU know his real name and think they're in on the joke (the punch line of course being George's trademark line, the even-a-blind-man thing), but they don't know the half of it. Nor is this a metaphorical statement. They know exactly one-third of it, because the man in the Dockers and the straw fedora is actually four people.

In any case, George Rathbun has been the saving of KDCU, the last surviving AM station in a predatory FM market. For five mornings a week, week in and week out, he has been a drive-time bonanza. The U-Crew (as they call themselves) love him just about to death.

Above him, the loudspeaker cackles on: '– still no leads, according to Chief Dale Gilbertson, who has called *Herald* reporter Wendell Green "an out-of-town fearmonger who is more interested in selling papers than in how we do things in French Landing."

'Meanwhile, in Arden, a house fire has taken the lives of an elderly farmer and his wife. Horst P. Lepplemier and his wife, Gertrude, both eighty-two . . .'

'Horst P. Lepplemier,' says the slim man, drawing on his cigarette with what appears to be great enjoyment. 'Try saying that one ten times fast, you moke.'

Behind him and to his right, the door opens again, and although the smoker is still standing directly beneath the speaker, he hears the door perfectly well. The eyes behind the aviator shades have been dead his whole life, but his hearing is exquisite.

The newcomer is pasty-faced and comes blinking into the morning sun like a baby mole that has just been turned out of its burrow by the blade of a passing plow. His head has been shaved except for the Mohawk strip up the center of his skull and the pigtail that starts just above the nape of his neck and hangs to his shoulder blades. The Mohawk has been dyed bright red; the 'tail is electric blue. Dangling from one earlobe is a lightning-bolt earring that looks suspiciously like the Nazi SS insignia. He is wearing a torn black T-shirt with a logo that reads SNIVELLING SHITS '97: THE WE GET HARD FOR JESUS TOUR. In one hand this colorful fellow has a CD jewel box.

'Hello, Morris,' says the slim man in the fedora, still without turning.

Morris pulls in a little gasp, and in his surprise looks like the nice Jewish boy that he actually is. Morris Rosen is the U-Crew's summer intern from the Oshkosh branch of UW. 'Man, I love that unpaid grunt labor!' station manager Tom Wiggins has been heard to say, usually while rubbing his hands together fiendishly. Never has a checkbook been guarded so righteously as the Wigger guards the KDCU checkbook. He is like Smaug the Dragon reclining on his heaps of gold (not that there are heaps of anything in the 'DCU accounts; it bears repeating to say that, as an AM talker, the station is lucky just to be alive).

Morris's look of surprise – it might be fair to call it *uneasy* surprise – dissolves into a smile. 'Wow, Mr Leyden! Good grab! What a pair of ears!'

Then he frowns. Even if Mr Leyden – who's standing directly beneath the outside honker, can't forget that – heard *someone* come out, how in God's name did he know *which* someone it was?

'How'd you know it was me?' he asks.

'Only two people around here smell like marijuana in the morning,' Henry Leyden says. 'One of them follows his morning smoke with Scope; the other – that's you, Morris – just lets her rip.'

'Wow,' Morris says respectfully. 'That is totally bitchrod.'

'I *am* totally bitchrod,' Henry agrees. He speaks softly and thoughtfully. 'It's a tough job, but somebody has to do it. In regard to your morning rendezvous with the undeniably tasty Thai stick, may I offer an Appalachian aphorism?'

'Go, dude.' This is Morris's first real discussion with Henry Leyden, who is every bit the head Morris has been told to expect. Every bit and more. It is no longer so hard to believe that he could have another identity . . . a *secret* identity, like Bruce Wayne. But still . . . this is just so *pimp*.

'What we do in our childhood forms as a habit,' Henry says in the same soft, totally un–George Rathbun voice. 'That is my advice to you, Morris.'

'Yeah, totally,' Morris says. He has no clue what Mr Leyden is talking about. But he slowly, shyly, extends the CD jewel box in his hand. For a moment, when Henry makes no move to take it, Morris feels crushed, all at once seven years old again and trying to wow his always-too-busy father with a picture he has spent all afternoon drawing in his room. Then he thinks, *He's* blind, *dickweed. He may be able to smell pot on your breath and he may have ears like a bat, but how's he supposed to know you're holding out a fucking CD?*

Hesitantly, a bit frightened by his own temerity, Morris takes Henry's wrist. He feels the man start a little, but then Leyden allows his hand to be guided to the slender box.

'Ah, a CD,' Henry says. 'And what is it, pray tell?'

'You gotta play the seventh track tonight on your show,' Morris says. *'Please.'*

For the first time, Henry looks alarmed. He takes a drag on his cigarette, then drops it (without even looking – of course, ha ha) into the sand-filled plastic bucket by the door.

'What show could you possibly mean?' he asks.

Instead of answering directly, Morris makes a rapid little smacking noise with his lips, the sound of a small but voracious carnivore eating something tasty. And, to make things worse, he follows it with the Wisconsin Rat's trademark line, as well known to the folks in Morris's age group as George Rathbun's hoarse 'Even a blind man' cry is known to their elders: 'Chew it up, eat it up, wash it down, *it aaallll comes out the same place!*'

He doesn't do it very well, but there's no question *who* he's doing: the one and only Wisconsin Rat, whose evening drive-time program on KWLA-FM is famous in Coulee Country (except the word we probably want is 'infamous'). KWLA is the tiny college FM station in La Riviere, hardly more than a smudge on the wallpaper of Wisconsin radio, but the Rat's audience is huge.

And if anyone found out that the comfortable Brew Crew–rooting, Republican-voting, AM-broadcasting George Rathbun was also the Rat – who had once narrated a gleeful on-air evacuation of his bowels onto a Backstreet Boys CD – there could be trouble. Quite serious, possibly, resounding well beyond the tight-knit little radio community.

'What in God's name would ever make you think that I'm the Wisconsin Rat, Morris?' Henry asks. 'I barely know who you're talking about. Who put such a weird idea in your head?'

'An informed source,' Morris says craftily.

He won't give Howie Soule up, not even if they pull out his fingernails with red-hot tongs. Besides, Howie only found out by accident: went into the station crapper one day after Henry left and discovered that Henry's wallet had fallen out of his back pocket while he was sitting on the throne. You'd have thought a fellow whose other senses were so obviously tightwired would have sensed the absence, but probably Henry's mind had been on other things – he was obviously a heavy dude who undoubtedly spent his days getting through some heavy thoughts. In any case, there was a KWLA ID card in Henry's wallet (which Howie had thumbed through 'in the spirit of friendly curiosity,' as he put it), and on the line marked NAME, someone had stamped a little inkpad drawing of a rat. Case closed, game over, zip up your fly.

'I have never in my life so much as stepped through the door of KWLA,' Henry says, and this is the absolute truth. He makes the Wisconsin Rat tapes (among others) in his studio at home, then sends them in to the station from the downtown Mail Boxes Etc., where he rents under the name of Joe Strummer. The card with the rat stamped on it was more in the nature of an invitation from the KWLA staff than anything else, one he's never taken up . . . but he kept the card.

'Have you become anyone else's informed source, Morris?'

'Huh?'

'Have you told anyone that you think I'm the Wisconsin Rat?'

'No! Course not!' Which, as we all know, is what people always *say*. Luckily for Henry, in this case it happens to be true. So far, at least, but the day is still young.

'And you won't, will you? Because rumors have a way of taking root. Just like certain bad habits.' Henry mimes puffing, pulling in smoke.

'I know how to keep my mouth shut,' Morris declares, with perhaps misplaced pride.

'I hope so. Because if you bruited this about, I'd have to kill you.'

Bruited, Morris thinks. *Oh man, this guy is complete.*

'Kill me, yeah,' Morris says, laughing.

'And eat you,' Henry says. *He* is not laughing; not even smiling.

'Yeah, right.' Morris laughs again, but this time the laugh sounds strangely forced to his own ears. 'Like you're Hannibal Lecture.'

'No, like I'm the Fisherman,' Henry says. He slowly turns his aviator sunglasses toward Morris. The sun reflects off them, for a moment turning them into rufous eyes of fire. Morris takes a step back without even realizing that he has done so. 'Albert Fish liked to start with the ass, did you know that?'

'N—'

'Yes indeed. He claimed that a good piece of young ass was as sweet as a veal cutlet. His exact words. Written in a letter to the mother of one of his victims.'

'Far out,' Morris says. His voice sounds faint to his own ears, the voice of a plump little pig denying entrance to the big bad wolf. 'But I'm not exactly, like, worried that you're the Fisherman.'

'No? Why not?'

'Man, you're *blind*, for one thing!'

Henry says nothing, only stares at the now vastly uneasy Morris with his fiery glass eyes. And Morris thinks: *But* is *he blind? He gets around pretty good for a blind guy . . . and the way he tabbed me as soon as I came out here, how weird was that?*

'I'll keep quiet,' he says. 'Honest to God.'

'That's all I want,' Henry says mildly. 'Now that we've got that straight, what exactly have you brought me?' He holds up the CD – but not as if he's *looking* at it, Morris observes with vast relief.

'It's, um, this Racine group. Dirtysperm? And they've got this cover of "Where Did Our Love Go"? The old Supremes thing? Only they do it at like a hundred and fifty beats a minute? It's fuckin' hilarious. I mean, it destroys the whole pop thing, man, *blitzes* it!'

'Dirtysperm,' Henry says. 'Didn't they used to be Jane Wyatt's Clit?'

Morris looks at Henry with awe that could easily become love. 'Dirtysperm's lead guitarist, like, *formed* JWC, man. Then him and the bass guy had this political falling-out, something about Dean Kissinger and Henry Acheson, and Ucky Ducky – he's the guitarist – went off to form Dirtysperm.'

'"Where Did Our Love Go"?' Henry muses, then hands the CD back. And, as if he sees the way Morris's face falls: 'I can't be seen with something like that – use your head. Stick it in my locker.'

Morris's gloom disappears and he breaks into a sunny smile. 'Yeah, okay! You got it, Mr Leyden!'

'And don't let anyone see you doing it. Especially not Howie Soule. Howie's a bit of a snoop. You'd do well not to emulate him.'

'No way, baby!' Still smiling, delighted at how all this has gone, Morris reaches for the door handle.

'And Morris?'

'Yeah?'

'Since you know my secret, perhaps you'd better call me Henry.'

'Henry! Yeah!' Is this the best morning of the summer for Morris Rosen? You better believe it.

'And something else.'

'Yeah? *Henry?*' Morris dares imagine a day when they will progress to Hank and Morrie.

'Keep your mouth shut about the Rat.'

'I already told you—'

'Yes, and I believe you. But temptation comes creeping, Morris; temptation comes creeping like a thief in the night, or like a killer in search of prey. If you give in to temptation, I'll know. I'll smell it on your skin like bad cologne. Do you believe me?'

'Uh . . . yeah.' And he does. Later, when he has time to kick back and reflect, Morris will think what a ridiculous idea that is, but yes, at the time, he believes it. Believes *him*. It's like being hypnotized.

'Very good. Now off you go. I want Ace Hardware, Zaglat Chevy, and Mr Tastee Ribs all cued up for the first seg.'

'Gotcha.'

'Also, last night's game—'

'Wickman striking out the side in the eighth? That was pimp. Totally, like, un-Brewers.'

'No, I think we want the Mark Loretta home run in the fifth. Loretta doesn't hit many, and the fans like him. I can't think why. Even a blind man can see he has no range, especially from deep in the hole. Go on, son. Put the CD in my locker, and if I see the Rat, I'll give it to him. I'm sure he'll give it a spin.'

'The track—'

'Seven, seven, rhymes with heaven. I won't forget and neither will he. Go on, now.'

Morris gives him a final grateful look and goes back inside. Henry Leyden, alias George Rathbun, alias the Wisconsin Rat, also alias Henry Shake (we'll get to that one, but not now; the hour draweth late), lights another cigarette and drags deep. He won't have time to finish it; the farm report is already in full flight (hog bellies up, wheat futures down, and the corn as high as an elephant's eye), but he needs a couple of drags just now to steady himself. A long, long day stretches out ahead of him, ending with the Strawberry Fest Hop at Maxton Elder Care, that house of antiquarian horrors. God save him from the clutches of William 'Chipper' Maxton, he has often thought. Given a choice between ending his days at MEC and burning his face off with a blowtorch, he would reach for the blowtorch every time. Later, if he's not totally exhausted, perhaps his friend from up the road will come over and they can begin the long-promised reading of *Bleak House*. That would be a treat.

How long, he wonders, can Morris Rosen hold on to his momentous secret? Well, Henry supposes he will find that out. He likes the Rat too much to give him up unless he absolutely has to; that much is an undeniable fact.

'Dean Kissinger,' he murmurs. 'Henry Acheson. Ucky Ducky. God save us.'

He takes another drag on his cigarette, then drops it into the bucket of sand. It is time to go back inside, time to replay last night's Mark Loretta home run, time to start taking more calls from the Coulee Country's dedicated sports fans.

And time for us to be off. Seven o'clock has rung from the Lutheran church steeple.

★

In French Landing, things are getting into high gear. No one lies abed long in this part of the world, and we must speed along to the end of our tour. Things are going to start happening soon, and they may happen fast. Still, we have done well, and we have only one more stop to make before arriving at our final destination.

We rise on the warm summer updrafts and hover for a moment by the KDCU tower (we are close enough to hear the tik-tik-tik of the beacon and the low, rather sinister hum of electricity), looking north and taking our bearings. Eight miles upriver is the town of Great Bluff, named for the limestone outcropping that rises there. The outcropping is reputed to be haunted, because in 1888 a chief of the Fox Indian tribe (Far Eyes was his name) assembled all his warriors, shamans, squaws, and children and told them to leap to their deaths, thereby escaping some hideous fate he had glimpsed in his dreams. Far Eyes's followers, like Jim Jones's, did as they were bidden.

We won't go that far upriver, however; we have enough ghosts to deal with right here in French Landing. Let us instead fly over Nailhouse Row once more (the Harleys are gone; Beezer St Pierre has led the Thunder Five off to their day's work at the brewery), over Queen Street and Maxton Elder Care (Burny's down there, still looking out his window – ugh), to Bluff Street. This is almost the countryside again. Even now, in the twenty-first century, the towns in Coulee Country give up quickly to the woods and the fields.

Herman Street is a left turn from Bluff Street, in an area that is not quite town and not quite city. Here, in a sturdy brick house sitting at the end of a half-mile meadow as yet undiscovered by the developers (even here there are a few developers, unknowing agents of *slippage*), lives Dale Gilbertson with his wife, Sarah, and his six-year-old son, David.

We can't stay long, but let us at least drift in through the kitchen window for a moment. It's open, after all, and there is room for us to perch right here on the counter, between the Silex and the toaster. Sitting at the kitchen table, reading the newspaper and shoveling Special K into his mouth without tasting it (he has forgotten both the sugar and the sliced banana in his distress at seeing yet another Wendell Green byline on the front page of the *Herald*), is Chief Gilbertson himself. This morning he is without doubt the unhappiest man in French Landing. We will meet his only competition for that booby prize soon, but for the moment, let us stick with Dale.

The Fisherman, he thinks mournfully, his reflections on this subject very similar to those of Bobby Dulac and Tom Lund. *Why didn't you name him something a little more turn-of-the-century, you troublesome scribbling fuck? Something a little bit local? Dahmerboy, maybe, that'd be good.*

Ah, but Dale knows why. The similarities between Albert Fish, who did his work in New York, and their boy here in French Landing are just too good – too *tasty* – to be ignored. Fish strangled his victims, as both Amy St Pierre and Johnny Irkenham were apparently strangled; Fish dined on his victims, as both the girl and the boy were apparently dined upon; both Fish and the current fellow showed an especial liking for the . . . well, for the posterior regions of the anatomy.

Dale looks at his cereal, then drops his spoon into the mush and pushes the bowl away with the side of his hand.

And the letters. Can't forget the letters.

Dale glances down at his briefcase, crouched at the side of his chair like a faithful dog. The file is in there, and it draws him like a rotted, achy tooth draws the tongue. Maybe he can keep his *hands* off it, at least while he's here at home, where he plays toss with his son and makes love to his wife, but keeping his *mind* off it . . . that's a whole 'nother thing, as they also say in these parts.

Albert Fish wrote a long and horribly explicit letter to the mother of Grace Budd, the victim who finally earned the old cannibal a trip to the electric chair. ('What a thrill electrocution will be!' Fish reputedly told his jailers. 'The only one I haven't tried!') The current doer has written similar letters, one addressed to Helen Irkenham, the other to Amy's father, the awful (but genuinely grief-stricken, in Dale's estimation) Armand 'Beezer' St Pierre. It would be good if Dale could believe these letters were written by some troublemaker not otherwise connected to the murders, but both contain information that has been withheld from the press, information that presumably only the killer could know.

Dale at last gives in to temptation (how well Henry Leyden would understand) and hauls up his briefcase. He opens it and puts a thick file where his cereal bowl lately rested. He returns the briefcase to its place by his chair, then opens the file (it is marked ST PIERRE/IRKENHAM rather than FISHERMAN). He leafs past heartbreaking school photos of two smiling, gap-toothed children, past state medical examiner reports too horrible to read and crime-scene photos too horrible to look at (ah, but he must look at them, again and again he must look at them – the blood-slicked chains, the flies, the open eyes). There are also various transcripts, the longest being the interview with Spencer Hovdahl, who found the Irkenham boy and who was, very briefly, considered a suspect.

Next come Xerox copies of three letters. One had been sent to George and Helen Irkenham (addressed to Helen alone, if it made any difference). One went to Armand 'Beezer'

St Pierre (addressed just that way, too, nickname and all). The third had been sent to the mother of Grace Budd, of New York City, following the murder of her daughter in the late spring of 1928.

Dale lays the three of them out, side by side.

Grace sat in my lap and kissed me. I made up my mind to eat her. So Fish had written to Mrs Budd.

Amy sat in my lap and hugged me. I made up my mind to eat her. So had Beezer St Pierre's correspondent written, and was it any wonder the man had threatened to burn the French Landing police station to the ground? Dale doesn't like the son of a bitch, but has to admit he might feel the same way in Beezer's shoes.

I went upstairs and stripped all my clothes off. I knew if I did not I would get her blood on them. Fish, to Mrs Budd.

I went around back of the hen-house and stripped all my cloes off. New if I did not I would get his blood on them. Anonymous, to Helen Irkenham. And here was a question: How could a mother receive a letter like that and retain her sanity? Was that possible? Dale thought not. Helen answered questions coherently, had even offered him tea the last time he was out there, but she had a glassy, poleaxed look in her eye that suggested she was running entirely on instruments.

Three letters, two new, one almost seventy-five years old. And yet all three are so similar. The St Pierre letter and the Irkenham letter had been hand-printed by someone who was left-handed, according to the state experts. The paper was plain white Hammermill mimeo, available in every Office Depot and Staples in America. The pen used had probably been a Bic – now, *there* was a lead.

Fish to Mrs Budd, back in '28: *I did* not *fuck her tho I could of had I wished. She died a* virgin.

Anonymous to Beezer St Pierre: *I did NOT fuck her tho I could of had I wished. She died a VIRGIN.*

Anonymous to Helen Irkenham: *This may comfort you I did NOT fuck him tho I could of had I wished. He died a VIRGIN.*

Dale's out of his depth here and knows it, but he hopes he isn't a complete fool. This doer, although he did not sign his letters with the old cannibal's name, clearly *wanted* the connection to be made. He had done everything but leave a few dead trout at the dumping sites.

Sighing bitterly, Dale puts the letters back into the file, the file back into the briefcase.

'Dale? Honey?' Sarah's sleepy voice, from the head of the stairs.

Dale gives the guilty jump of a man who has almost been caught doing something nasty and latches his briefcase. 'I'm in the kitchen,' he calls back. No need to worry about waking Davey; he sleeps like the dead until at least seven-thirty every morning.

'Going in late?'

'Uh-huh.' He often goes in late, then makes up for it by working until seven or eight or even nine in the evening. Wendell Green hasn't made a big deal of *that* . . . at least not so far, but give him time. Talk about your cannibals!

'Give the flowers a drink before you go, would you? It's been so dry.'

'You bet.' Watering Sarah's flowers is a chore Dale likes. He gets some of his best thinking done with the garden hose in his hand.

A pause from upstairs . . . but he hasn't heard her slippers shuffling back toward the bedroom. He waits. And at last: 'You okay, hon?'

'Fine,' he calls back, pumping what he hopes will be the right degree of heartiness into his voice.

'Because you were still tossing around when I dropped off.'

'No, I'm fine.'

'Do you know what Davey asked me last night while I was washing his hair?'

Dale rolls his eyes. He hates these long-distance conversations. Sarah seems to love them. He gets up and pours himself another cup of coffee. 'No, what?'

'He asked, "Is Daddy going to lose his job?"'

Dale pauses with the cup halfway to his lips. 'What did you say?'

'I said no. Of course.'

'Then you said the right thing.'

He waits, but there is no more. Having injected him with one more dram of poisonous worry – David's fragile psyche, as well as what a certain party might do to the boy, should David be so unlucky as to run afoul of him – Sarah shuffles back to their room and, presumably, to the shower beyond.

Dale goes back to the table, sips his coffee, then puts his hand to his forehead and closes his eyes. In this moment we can see precisely how frightened and miserable he is. Dale is just forty-two and a man of abstemious habits, but in the cruel morning light coming through the window by which we entered, he looks, for the moment, anyway, a sickly sixty.

He *is* concerned about his job, knows that if the fellow who killed Amy and Johnny keeps it up, he will almost certainly be turned out of office the following year. He is also concerned about Davey . . . although Davey isn't his chief concern, for, like Fred Marshall, he cannot actually conceive that the Fisherman could take his and Sarah's own child. No, it is the *other* children of French Landing he is more worried about, possibly the children of Centralia and Arden as well.

His worst fear is that he is simply not good enough to catch the son of a bitch. That he will kill a third, a fourth, perhaps an eleventh and twelfth.

God knows he has requested help. And gotten it . . . sort of. There are two State Police detectives assigned to the case, and the FBI guy from Madison keeps checking in (on an informal basis, though; the FBI is not officially part of the investigation). Even his outside help has a surreal quality for Dale, one that has been partially caused by an odd coincidence of their names. The FBI guy is Agent John P. Redding. The state detectives are Perry Brown and Jeffrey Black. So he has Brown, Black, and Redding on his team. The Color Posse, Sarah calls them. All three making it clear that they are strictly working support, at least for the time being. Making it clear that Dale Gilbertson is the man standing on ground zero.

Christ, but I wish Jack would sign on to help me with this, Dale thinks. *I'd deputize him in a second, just like in one of those corny old Western movies.*

Yes indeed. In a second.

When Jack had first come to French Landing, almost four years ago, Dale hadn't known what to make of the man his officers immediately dubbed Hollywood. By the time the two of them had nailed Thornberg Kinderling – yes, inoffensive little Thornberg Kinderling, hard to believe but absolutely true – he knew *exactly* what to make of him. The guy was the finest natural detective Dale had ever met in his life.

The only *natural detective, that's what you mean.*

Yes, all right. The *only* one. And although they had shared the collar (at the LA newcomer's absolute insistence), it had been Jack's detective work that had turned the trick. He was almost like one of those storybook detectives . . . Hercule Poirot, Ellery Queen, one of those. Except that Jack didn't exactly deduct, nor did he go around tapping his temple and talking about his 'little gray cells.' He . . .

'He listens,' Dale mutters, and gets up. He heads for the back door, then returns for his briefcase. He'll put it in the back seat of his cruiser before he waters the flower beds. He doesn't want those awful pictures in his house any longer than strictly necessary.

He listens.

Like the way he'd listened to Janna Massengale, the bartender at the Taproom. Dale had had no idea why Jack was spending so much time with the little chippy; it had even crossed his mind that Mr Los Angeles Linen Slacks was trying to hustle her into bed so he could go back home and tell all his friends on Rodeo Drive that he'd gotten himself a little piece of the cheese up there in Wisconsin, where the air was rare and the legs were long and strong. But that hadn't been it at all. He had been *listening*, and finally she had told him what he needed to hear.

Yeah, shurr, people get funny ticks when they're drinking, Janna had said. *There's this one guy who starts doing this after a couple of belts.* She had pinched her nostrils together with the tips of her fingers . . . only with her hand turned around so the palm pointed out.

Jack, still smiling easily, still sipping a club soda: *Always with the palm out? Like this?* And mimicked the gesture.

Janna, smiling, half in love: *That's it, doll – you're a quick study.*

Jack: *Sometimes, I guess. What's this fella's name, darlin'?*

Janna: *Kinderling. Thornberg Kinderling.* She giggled. *Only, after a drink or two – once he's started up with that pinchy thing – he wants everyone to call him Thorny.*

Jack, still with his own smile: *And does he drink Bombay gin, darlin'? One ice cube, little trace of bitters?*

Janna's smile starting to fade, now looking at him as if he might be some kind of wizard: *How'd you know that?*

But how he knew it didn't matter, because that was really the whole package, done up in a neat bow. Case closed, game over, zip up your fly.

Eventually, Jack had flown back to Los Angeles with Thornberg Kinderling in custody – Thornberg Kinderling, just an inoffensive, bespectacled farm-insurance salesman from Centralia, wouldn't say boo to a goose, wouldn't say shit if he had a mouthful, wouldn't dare ask your mamma for a drink of water on a hot day, but he had killed two prostitutes in the City of Angels. No strangulation for Thorny; he had done his work with a Buck knife, which Dale himself had eventually traced to Lapham Sporting Goods, the nasty little trading post a door down from the Sand Bar, Centralia's grungiest drinking establishment.

By then DNA testing had nailed Kinderling's ass to the barn door, but Jack had been glad to have the provenance of the murder weapon anyway. He had called Dale personally to thank him, and Dale, who'd never been west of Denver in his life, had been almost absurdly touched by the courtesy. Jack had said several times during the course of the investigation that you could never have enough evidence when the doer was a genuine bad guy, and Thorny Kinderling had turned out to be about as bad as you could want. He'd gone the insanity route, of course, and Dale – who had privately hoped he might be called upon to testify – was delighted when the jury rejected the plea and sentenced him to consecutive life terms.

And what made all that happen? What had been the first cause? Why, a man listening. That was all. Listening to a lady bartender who was used to having her breasts stared at while her words most commonly went in one ear of the man doing the staring and out the other. And who had Hollywood Jack listened to before he had listened to Janna Massengale? Some Sunset Strip hooker, it seemed . . . or more likely a whole bunch of them. (*What would you call that, anyway?* Dale wonders absently as he goes out to the garage to get his trusty hose. *A shimmy of streetwalkers? A strut of hookers?*) None of them could have picked Thornberg Kinderling out of a lineup, because the Thornberg who visited LA surely hadn't looked much like the Thornberg who traveled around to the farm-supply companies in the Coulee and over in Minnesota. LA Thorny had worn a wig, contacts instead of specs, and a little false mustache.

'The most brilliant thing was the skin darkener,' Jack had said. 'Just a little, just enough to make him look like a native.'

'Dramatics all four years at French Landing High School,' Dale had replied grimly. 'I looked it up. The little bastard played Don Juan his junior year, do you believe it?'

A lot of sly little changes (too many for a jury to swallow an insanity plea, it seemed), but Thorny had forgotten that one revelatory little signature, that trick of pinching his nostrils together with the palm of his hand turned outward. Some prostitute had remembered it, though, and when she mentioned it – only in passing, Dale has no doubt, just as Janna Massengale did – Jack heard it.

Because he listened.

Called to thank me for tracing the knife, and again to tell me how the jury came back, Dale thinks, *but that second time he wanted something, too. And I knew what it was. Even before he opened his mouth I knew.*

Because, while he is no genius detective like his friend from the Golden State, Dale had not missed the younger man's unexpected, immediate response to the landscape of western Wisconsin. Jack had fallen in love with the Coulee Country, and Dale would have wagered a good sum that it had been love at first look. It had been impossible to mistake the expression on his face as they drove from French Landing to Centralia, from Centralia to Arden, from Arden to Miller: wonder, pleasure, almost a kind of rapture. To Dale, Jack had looked like a man who has come to a place he has never been before only to discover he is back home.

'Man, I can't get over this,' he'd said once to Dale. The two of them had been riding in Dale's old Caprice cruiser, the one that just wouldn't stay aligned (and sometimes the horn stuck, which could be embarrassing). 'Do you realize how lucky you are to live here, Dale? It must be one of the most beautiful places in the world.'

Dale, who had lived in the Coulee his entire life, had not disagreed.

Toward the end of their final conversation concerning Thornberg Kinderling, Jack had reminded Dale of how he'd once asked (not quite kidding, not quite serious, either) for Dale to let him know if a nice little place ever came on the market in Dale's part of the world, something out of town. And Dale had known at once from Jack's tone – the almost anxious drop in his voice – that the kidding was over.

'So you owe me,' Dale murmurs, shouldering the hose. 'You *owe* me, you bastard.'

Of course he has asked Jack to lend an unofficial hand with the Fisherman investigation, but Jack has refused . . . almost with a kind of fear. *I'm retired*, he'd said brusquely. *If you don't know what that word means, Dale, we can look it up in the dictionary together.*

But it's ridiculous, isn't it? Of course it is. How can a man not yet thirty-five be retired? Especially one who is so infernally good at the job?

'You *owe* me, baby,' he says again, now walking along the side of the house toward the bib faucet. The sky above is cloudless; the well-watered lawn is green; there is nary a sign of *slippage*, not out here on Herman Street. Yet perhaps there is, and perhaps we feel it. A kind of discordant hum, like the sound of all those lethal volts coursing through the steel struts of the KDCU tower.

But we have stayed here too long. We must take wing again and proceed to our final destination of this early morning. We don't know everything yet, but we know three important things: first, that French Landing is a town in terrible distress; second, that a few people (Judy Marshall, for one; Charles Burnside, for another) understand on some deep level that the town's ills go far beyond the depredations of a single sick pedophile-murderer; third, that we have met no one capable of consciously recognizing the force – the slippage – that has now come to bear on this quiet town hard by Tom and Huck's river. Each person we've met is, in his own way, as blind as Henry Leyden. This is as true of the folks we haven't so far encountered – Beezer St Pierre, Wendell Green, the Color Posse – as it is of those we have.

Our hearts groan for a hero. And while we may not find one (this is the twenty-first century, after all, the days not of d'Artagnan and Jack Aubrey but of George W. Bush and Dirtysperm), we can perhaps find a man who *was* a hero once upon a time. Let us therefore search out an old friend, one we last glimpsed a thousand and more miles east of here, on the shore of the steady Atlantic. Years have passed and they have in some ways lessened the boy who was; he has forgotten much and has spent a good part of his adult life maintaining that state of amnesia. But he is French Landing's only hope, so let us take wing and fly almost due east, back over the woods and fields and gentle hills.

Mostly, we see miles of unbroken farmland: regimental corn fields, luxuriant hay fields, fat yellow swaths of alfalfa. Dusty, narrow drives lead to white farmhouses and their arrays of tall barns, granaries, cylindrical cement-block silos, and long metal equipment sheds. Men in denim jackets are moving along the well-worn paths between the houses and the barns. We can already smell the sunlight. Its odor, richly compacted of butter, yeast, earth, growth, and decay, will intensify as the sun ascends and the light grows stronger.

Below us, Highway 93 intersects Highway 35 at the center of tiny Centralia. The empty parking lot behind the Sand Bar awaits the noisy arrival of the Thunder Five, who customarily spend their Saturday afternoons, evenings, and nights in the enjoyment of the Sand Bar's pool tables, hamburgers, and pitchers of that ambrosia to the creation of which they have devoted their eccentric lives, Kingsland Brewing Company's finest product and a beer that can hold up its creamy head among anything made in a specialty microbrewery or a Belgian monastery, Kingsland Ale. If Beezer St Pierre, Mouse, and company say it is the greatest beer in the world, why should we doubt them? Not only do they know much more about beer than we do, they called upon every bit of the knowledge, skill, expertise, and seat-of-the-pants inspiration at their disposal to make Kingsland Ale a benchmark of the brewer's art. In fact, they moved to French Landing because the brewery, which they had selected after careful deliberation, was willing to work with them.

To invoke Kingsland Ale is to wish for a good-sized mouthful of the stuff, but we put temptation behind us; 7:30 a.m. is far too early for drinking anything but fruit juice, coffee, and milk (except for the likes of Wanda Kinderling, and Wanda thinks of beer, even Kingsland Ale, as a dietary supplement to Aristocrat vodka); and we are in search of our old friend and the closest we can come to a hero, whom we last saw as a boy on the shore of the Atlantic Ocean. We are not about to waste time; we are on the move, right here and now. The miles fly past beneath us, and along Highway 93 the fields narrow as the hills rise up on both sides.

For all our haste, we must *take this in*, we must *see where we are.*

4

Three years ago, our old friend traveled down this stretch of 93 in the passenger seat of Dale Gilbertson's old Caprice, his heart going crazy in his chest, his throat constricting, and his mouth dry, as friendly Dale, in those days little more than a small-town cop whom he had impressed beyond rational measure simply by doing his job more or less as well as he could, piloted him toward a farmhouse and five acres left Dale by his deceased father. 'The nice little place' could be purchased for next to nothing, since Dale's cousins did not particularly want it and it had no value to anyone else. Dale had been holding on to the property for sentimental reasons, but he had no particular interest in it, either. Dale had scarcely known what to do with a second house, apart from spending a great deal of time keeping it up, a task he had found oddly enjoyable but did not at all mind turning over to someone else. And at this point in their relationship, Dale was so in awe of our friend that, far from resenting the prospect of this man occupying his father's old house, he considered it an honor.

As for the man in the passenger seat, he was too caught up in his response to the landscape – too caught up *by* the landscape – to be embarrassed by Dale's awe. Under ordinary circumstances, our friend would have urged his admirer into a quiet bar, bought him a beer and said, 'Look, I know you were impressed by what I did, but after all, Dale, I'm just another cop, like you. That's all. And in all honesty, I'm a lot luckier than I deserve to be.' (It would be the truth, too: ever since we last saw him, our friend has been blessed, if it is a blessing, with such extravagantly good luck that he no longer dares to play cards or bet on sporting events. When you win almost all the time, winning tastes like spoiled grape juice.) But these were not ordinary circumstances, and in the swarm of emotion that had been threatening to undo him since they left Centralia on the flat straightaway of Highway 93, Dale's adulation barely registered. This short drive to a place he had never seen before felt like a long-delayed journey home: everything he saw seemed charged with remembered meaning, a part of him, essential. Everything seemed sacred. He knew he was going to buy the nice little place, no matter what it looked like or how much it cost, not that price could in any way have been an obstacle. He was going to buy it, that was all. Dale's heroworship affected him only to the extent that he realized he would be forced to keep his admirer from undercharging him. In the meantime, he struggled against the tears that wanted to fill his eyes.

From above, we see the glacial valleys dividing the landscape to the right of 93 like the imprint of a giant's fingers. He saw only the sudden narrow roads that split off the highway and slipped into mingled sunshine and darkness. Each road said, *Nearly there*. The highway said, *This is the way*. Gazing down, we can observe a roadside parking area, two gasoline pumps, and a long gray roof bearing the fading legend ROY'S STORE; when he looked to his right and saw, past the gas pumps, the wooden stairs rising to a wide, inviting porch and the store's entrance, he felt as though he had already mounted those stairs a hundred times before and gone inside to pick up bread, milk, beer, cold cuts, work gloves, a screwdriver, a bag of tenpenny nails, whatever he needed from the practical cornucopia crowded onto the shelves, as after that day he would do, a hundred times and more.

Fifty yards down the highway the blue-gray sliver of Tamarack Creek comes winding into Norway Valley. When Dale's car rolled across the rusting little metal bridge, the bridge said, *This is it!*, and the casually but expensively dressed man in the passenger seat, who looked as though all he knew of farmland had been learned through the windows next to first-class seats on transcontinental flights and in fact was incapable of telling wheat from hay, felt his heart shiver. On the other side of the bridge, a road sign read NORWAY VALLEY ROAD.

'This is it,' said Dale, and made the right turn into the valley. Our friend covered his mouth with his hand, stifling whatever sounds his shivering heart might cause him to utter.

Here and there, wildflowers bloomed and nodded on the roadside, some of them audacious and bright, others half-hidden in a blanket of vibrant green. 'Driving up this road always makes me feel good,' Dale said.

'No wonder,' our friend managed to say.

Most of what Dale said failed to penetrate the whirlwind of emotion roaring through his passenger's mind and body. That's the old Lund farm – cousins of my mother. The one-room schoolhouse where my great-grandmother taught used to be right over there, only they tore it down way back. This here is Duane Updahl's place, he's no relation, thank goodness. Buzz blur mumble. Blur mumble buzz. They once again drove over Tamarack Creek, its glittering blue-gray water laughing and calling out, *Here we are!* Around a bend in the road they went, and a wealth of luxuriant wildflowers leaned carousing toward the car. In their midst, the blind, attentive faces of tiger lilies tilted to meet our friend's face. A ripple of feeling distinct from the whirlwind, quieter but no less potent, brought dazzled tears to the surface of his eyes.

Tiger lilies, why? Tiger lilies meant nothing to him. He used the pretense of a yawn to wipe his eyes and hoped that Dale had not noticed.

'Here we are,' Dale said, having noticed or not, and swerved into a long, overgrown drive, hedged with wildflowers and tall grasses, which appeared to lead nowhere except into a great expanse of meadow and banks of waist-high flowers. Beyond the meadow, striped fields sloped upward to the wooded hillside. 'You'll see my dad's old place in a second. The meadow goes with the house, and my cousins Randy and Kent own the field.'

Our friend could not see the white two-story farmhouse that stands at the end of the last curve of the drive until the moment Dale Gilbertson swung halfway into the curve, and he did not speak until Dale had pulled up in front of the house, switched off the engine, and both men had left the car. Here was 'the nice little place,' sturdy, newly painted, lovingly maintained, modest yet beautiful in its proportions, removed from the road, removed from the world, at the edge of a green and yellow meadow profuse with flowers.

'My God, Dale,' he said, 'it's perfection.'

Here we will find our former traveling companion, who in his own boyhood knew a boy named Richard Sloat and, once, too briefly, knew yet another whose name was, simply, Wolf. In this sturdy, comely, removed white farmhouse we will find our old friend, who once in his boyhood journeyed cross-country from ocean to ocean in pursuit of a certain crucial thing, a necessary object, a great talisman, and who, despite horrendous obstacles and fearful perils, succeeded in finding the object of his search and used it wisely and well. Who, we could say, accomplished a number of miracles, heroically. And who remembers none of this. Here, making breakfast for himself in his kitchen while listening to George Rathbun on KDCU, we at last find the former Los Angeles County lieutenant of police, Homicide Division, Jack Sawyer.

Our Jack. Jacky-boy, as his mother, the late Lily Cavanaugh Sawyer, used to say.

He had followed Dale through the empty house, upstairs and down, into the basement, dutifully admiring the new furnace and water heater Gilbertson had installed the year before his father's death, the quality of the repairs he had made since then, the shining grain of the wooden floors, the thickness of the insulation in the attic, the solidity of the windows, the many craftsmanlike touches that met his eye.

'Yeah, I did a lot of work on the place,' Dale told him. 'It was pretty shipshape to begin with, but I like working with my hands. After a while it turned into sort of a hobby. Whenever I had a couple of hours free, weekends and such, I got in the habit of driving over here and puttering around. I don't know, maybe it helped me feel like I was staying in touch with my dad. He was a really good guy, my dad. He wanted me to be a farmer, but when I said I was thinking of getting into law enforcement, he supported me straight down the line. Know what he said? "Go into farming halfhearted, it'll kick you in the tail sunrise to sundown. You'd wind up feeling no better than a mule. Your mom and I didn't bring you into this world to turn you into a mule."'

'What did she think?' Jack had asked.

'My mom came from a long line of farmers,' Dale had said. 'She thought I might find out that being a mule wasn't so bad after all. By the time she passed away, which was four years before my dad, she'd gotten used to my being a cop. Let's go out the kitchen door and take a gander at the meadow, okay?'

While they were standing outside and taking their gander, Jack had asked Dale how much he wanted for the house. Dale, who had been waiting for this question, had knocked five thousand off the most he and Sarah had ever thought he could get. Who was he kidding? Dale had wanted Jack Sawyer to buy the house where he had grown up – he'd wanted Jack to live near him for at least a couple of weeks during the year. And if Jack did not buy the place, no one else would.

'Are you serious?' Jack had asked.

More dismayed than he wished to admit, Dale had said, 'Sounds like a fair deal to me.'

'It isn't fair to *you*,' Jack had said. 'I'm not going to let you give this place away just because you like me. Raise the asking price, or I walk.'

'You big-city hotshots sure know how to negotiate. All right, make it three thousand more.'

'Five,' Jack said. 'Or I'm outta here.'

'Done. But you're breaking my heart.'

'I hope this is the last time I buy property off one of you low-down Norwegians,' Jack said.

He had purchased the house long-distance, sending a down payment from LA, exchanging signatures by fax, no mortgage, cash up front. Whatever Jack Sawyer's background might have been, Dale had thought, it was a lot wealthier than the usual police officer's. Some weeks later, Jack had reappeared at the center of a self-created tornado, arranging for the telephone to be connected and the electricity billed in his name, scooping up what looked like half the contents of Roy's Store, zipping off to Arden and La Riviere to buy a new bed, linens, tableware, cast-iron pots and pans and a set of French knives, a compact microwave and a giant television, and a stack of sound equipment so sleek, black, and resplendent that Dale, who had been invited over for a companionable drink, figured it must have cost more than his own annual salary. Much else, besides, had Jack reeled in, some of the much else consisting of items Dale had been surprised to learn could be obtained in French County, Wisconsin. Why would anyone need a sixty-five-dollar corkscrew called a WineMaster? Who was this guy, what kind of family had produced him?

He'd noticed a bag bearing an unfamiliar logo filled with compact discs – at fifteen, sixteen dollars a pop, he was looking at a couple hundred dollars' worth of CDs. Whatever else might have been true of Jack Sawyer, he was into music in a big way. Curious, Dale bent down, pulled out a handful of jewel boxes, and regarded images of people, generally black, generally with instruments pressed to or in their mouths. Clifford Brown, Lester Young, Tommy Flanagan, Paul Desmond. 'I never heard of these guys,' he said. 'What is this, jazz, I guess?'

'You guess right,' Jack said. 'Could I ask you to help me move furniture around and hang pictures, stuff like that, in a month or two? I'm going to have a lot of stuff shipped here.'

'Anytime.' A splendid idea bloomed in Dale's mind. 'Hey, you have to meet my uncle Henry! He's even a neighbor of yours, lives about a quarter mile down the road. He was married to my aunt Rhoda, my father's sister, who died three years ago. Henry's like an encyclopedia of weird music.'

Jack did not take up the assumption that jazz was weird.

Maybe it was. Anyhow, it probably sounded weird to Dale. 'I wouldn't have thought farmers had much time to listen to music.'

Dale opened his mouth and uttered a bray of laughter. 'Henry isn't a farmer. Henry . . .' Grinning, Dale raised his hands, palms up and fingers spread, and looked into the middle distance, searching for the right phrase. 'He's like the *reverse* of a farmer. When you get back, I'll introduce you to him. You're going to be crazy about the guy.'

Six weeks later, Jack returned to greet the moving van and tell the men where to put the furniture and other things he had shipped; a few days afterward, when he had unpacked most of the boxes, he telephoned Dale and asked if he was still willing to give him a hand. It was 5:00 on a day so slow that Tom Lund had fallen asleep at his desk, and Dale drove over without even bothering to change out of his uniform.

His first response, after Jack had shaken his hand and ushered him in, was undiluted shock. Having taken a single step past the doorway, Dale froze in his tracks, unable to move any farther. Two or three seconds passed before he realized that it was a *good* shock, a shock of pleasure. His old house had been transformed: it was as if Jack Sawyer had tricked him and opened the familiar front door upon the interior of another house altogether. The sweep from the living room into the kitchen looked nothing like either the space he remembered from childhood or the clean, bare progression of the recent past. Jack had decorated the house with the wave of a wand, it seemed to Dale, in the process somehow turning it into he hardly knew what – a villa on the Riviera, a Park Avenue apartment. (Dale had never been to New York or the south of France.) Then it struck him that, instead of transforming the old place into something it was not, Jack had simply seen more in it than Dale ever had. The leather sofas and chairs, the glowing rugs, the wide tables and discreet lamps, had come from another world but fit in perfectly, as if they had been made specifically for this house. Everything he saw beckoned him in, and he found that he could move again.

'Wow,' he said. 'Did I ever sell this place to the right guy.'

'I'm glad you like it,' Jack said. 'I have to admit, I do, too. It looks even better than I expected.'

'What am I supposed to do? The place is already organized.'

'We're going to hang some pictures,' Jack said. '*Then* it'll be organized.'

Dale supposed Jack was talking about family photographs. He did not understand why anyone would need help to hang up a bunch of framed photos, but if Jack wanted his assistance, he would assist. Besides that, the pictures would tell him a considerable amount about Jack's family, still a subject of great interest to him. However, when Jack led him to a stack of flat wooden crates leaning against the kitchen counter, Dale once again got the feeling that he was out of his depth here, that he had entered an unknown world. The crates had been made by hand; they were serious objects built to provide industrial-strength protection. Some of them were five or six feet tall and nearly as wide. These monsters did not have pictures of Mom and Dad inside them. He and Jack had to pry up the corners and loosen the nails along the edges before they could get the crates open. It took a surprising amount of effort to lever the tops off the crates. Dale regretted not stopping at his house long enough to take off his uniform, which was damp with sweat by the time he and Jack had pulled from their cocoons five heavy, rectangular objects thickly swaddled in layers of tissue. Many crates remained.

An hour later, they carried the empty crates down to the

basement and came back upstairs to have a beer. Then they sliced open the layers of tissue, exposing paintings and graphics in a variety of frames, including a few that looked as if the artist had nailed them together himself out of barn siding. Jack's pictures occupied a category Dale vaguely thought of as 'modern art.' He did not grasp what some of these things were supposed to be about, although he actually liked almost all of them, especially a couple of landscapes. He knew that he had never heard of the artists, but their names, he thought, would be recognized by the kind of people who lived in big cities and hung out in museums and galleries. All this art – all of these images large and small now lined up on the kitchen floor – stunned him, not altogether pleasantly. He really had entered another world, and he knew none of its landmarks. Then he remembered that he and Jack Sawyer were going to hang these pictures on the walls of his parents' old house. Immediately, unexpected warmth flooded into this notion and filled it to the brim. Why shouldn't adjoining worlds mingle now and then? And wasn't this other world Jack's?

'All right,' he said. 'I wish Henry, that uncle I was telling you about? Who lives right down the road? I wish he could see this stuff. Henry, he'd know how to appreciate it.'

'Why won't he be able to see them? I'll invite him over.'

'Didn't I say?' Dale asked. 'Henry's blind.'

Paintings went up on the living-room walls, ascended the stairwell, moved into the bedrooms. Jack put up a couple of small pictures in the upstairs bathroom and the little half bath on the ground floor. Dale's arms began to ache from holding the frames while Jack marked the places where the nails would go in. After the first three paintings, he had removed his necktie and rolled up his sleeves, and he could feel sweat trickling out of his hair and sliding down his face. His unbuttoned collar had soaked through. Jack Sawyer had worked as hard or harder than he, but looked as if he had done nothing more strenuous than think about dinner.

'You're like an art collector, huh?' Dale said. 'Did it take a long time to get all these paintings?'

'I don't know enough to be a collector,' Jack said. 'My father picked up most of this work back in the fifties and sixties. My mother bought a few things, too, when she saw something that turned her on. Like that little Fairfield Porter over there, with the front porch and a lawn and the flowers.'

The little Fairfield Porter, which name Dale assumed to be that of its painter, had appealed to him as soon as he and Jack had pulled it out of its crate. You could hang a picture like that in your own living room. You could almost step into a picture like that. The funny thing was, Dale thought, if you hung it in your living room, most of the people who came in would never really notice it at all.

Jack had said something about being glad to get the paintings out of storage. 'So,' Dale said, 'your mom and dad *gave* them to you?'

'I inherited them after my mother's death,' Jack said. 'My father died when I was a kid.'

'Oh, darn, I'm sorry,' Dale said, snapped abruptly out of the world into which Mr Fairfield Porter had welcomed him. 'Had to be tough on you, losing your dad so young.' He thought Jack had given him the explanation for the aura of apartness and isolation that seemed always to envelop him. A second before Jack could respond, Dale told himself he was bullshitting. He had no idea how someone wound up being like Jack Sawyer.

'Yeah,' Jack said. 'Fortunately, my mother was even tougher.'

Dale seized his opportunity with both hands. 'What did your folks do? Were you brought up in California?'

'Born and raised in Los Angeles,' Jack said. 'My parents were in the entertainment industry, but don't hold that against them. They were great people.'

Jack did not invite him to stay for supper – that was what stuck with Dale. Over the hour and a half it took them to hang the rest of the pictures, Jack Sawyer remained friendly and good-humored, but Dale, who was not a cop for nothing, sensed something evasive and adamant in his friend's affability: a door had opened a tiny crack, then slammed shut. The phrase 'great people' had placed Jack's parents out of bounds. When the two men broke for another beer, Dale noticed a pair of bags from a Centralia grocery next to the microwave. It was then nearly 8:00, at least two hours past French County's suppertime. Jack might reasonably have assumed that Dale had already eaten, were his uniform not evidence to the contrary.

He tossed Jack a softball about the hardest case he had ever solved and sidled up to the counter. The marbled red tips of two sirloin steaks protruded from the nearest bag. His stomach emitted a reverberant clamor. Jack ignored the thunder roll and said, 'Thornberg Kinderling was right up there with anything I handled in LA. I was really grateful for your help.' Dale got the picture. Here was another locked door. This one had declined to open by as much as a crack. History was not spoken here; the past had been nailed shut.

They finished their beers and installed the last of the pictures. Over the next few hours, they spoke of a hundred things, but always within the boundaries Jack Sawyer had established. Dale was sure that his question about Jack's parents had shortened the evening, but why should that be true? What was the guy hiding? And from whom was he hiding it? After their work was done, Jack thanked him warmly and walked him outside to his car, thereby cutting off any hope of a last-minute reprieve. Case closed, game over, zip up your fly, in the words of the immortal George Rathbun. While they stood in the fragrant darkness beneath the millions of stars arrayed above them, Jack sighed with pleasure and said, 'I hope you know how grateful I am. Honestly, I'm sorry I have to go back to LA. Would you *look* at how beautiful this is?'

Driving back to French Landing, his the only headlights on the long stretch of Highway 93, Dale wondered if Jack's parents had been involved in some aspect of the entertainment business embarrassing to their adult son, like pornography. Maybe Dad directed skin flicks, and Mom starred in them. The people who made dirty movies probably raked in the dough, especially if they kept it in the family. Before his odometer ticked off another tenth of a mile, the memory of the little Fairfield Porter turned Dale's satisfaction to dust. No woman who earned her keep having on-camera sex with strangers would spend actual money on a painting like that.

Let us enter Jack Sawyer's kitchen. The morning's *Herald* lies unfolded on the dining table; a black frying pan recently sprayed with Pam heats atop the circle of blue flames from the gas stove's front left-hand burner. A tall, fit, distracted-looking man wearing an old USC sweatshirt, jeans, and Italian loafers the color of molasses is swirling a whisk around the interior of a stainless steel bowl containing a large number of raw eggs.

Looking at him as he frowns at a vacant section of air well above the shiny bowl, we observe that the beautiful twelve-year-old boy last seen in a fourth-floor room of a deserted New Hampshire hotel has aged into a man whose good looks contribute only the smallest portion to what makes him interesting. For that Jack Sawyer *is* interesting declares itself instantly. Even when troubled to distraction by some private concern, some *enigma*, we might as well say in the face of that contemplative frown, Jack Sawyer cannot help but radiate a persuasive authority. Just by looking at him, you know that he is one of those persons to whom others turn when they feel stumped, threatened, or thwarted by circumstance. Intelligence, resolve, and dependability have shaped the cast of his features so deeply that their attractiveness is irrelevant to their meaning. This man never pauses to admire himself in mirrors – vanity plays no part in his character. It makes perfect sense that he should have been a rising star in the Los Angeles Police Department, that his file bulged with commendations, and that he had been selected for several FBI-sponsored programs and training courses designed to aid the progress of rising stars. (A number of Jack's colleagues and superiors had privately concluded that he would become the police commissioner of a city like San Diego or Seattle around the time he turned forty and, ten to fifteen years later, if all went well, step up to San Francisco or New York.)

More strikingly, Jack's age seems no more relevant than his attractiveness: he has the air of having passed through lifetimes before this one, of having gone places and seen things beyond the scope of most other people. No wonder Dale Gilbertson admires him; no wonder Dale yearns for Jack's assistance. In his place, we would want it, too, but our luck would be no better than his. This man has *retired*, he is out of the game, sorry, damn shame and all that, but a man's gotta whisk eggs when he's gotta have omelettes, as John Wayne said to Dean Martin in *Rio Bravo*.

'And as my momma told me,' Jack says out loud to himself, 'she said, "Sonny boy," said she, "when the Duke *spoke* up, everdangbody *lissened* up, lessen he was a-grindin' one of his numerous political axes," yes, she did, them were her same exack words, just as she said 'em to me.' A half second later, he adds, 'On that fine morning in Beverly Hills,' and finally takes in what he is doing.

What we have here is a spectacularly lonely man. Loneliness has been Jack Sawyer's familiar for so long that he takes it for granted, but what you can't fix eventually turns into wallpaper, all right? Plenty of things, such as cerebral palsy and Lou Gehrig's disease, to name but two, are worse than loneliness. Loneliness is just part of the program, that's all. Even Dale noticed this aspect of his friend's character, and despite his many virtues, our chief of police cannot be described as a particularly pyschological human being.

Jack glances at the clock above the stove and sees he has another forty-five minutes before he must drive to French Landing and pick up Henry Leyden at the end of his shift. That's good; he has plenty of time, he's keeping it together, the subtext to which is *Everything is all right, and nothing's wrong with me, thank you very much.*

When Jack woke up this morning, a small voice in his head announced *I am a coppiceman.* Like hell I am, he thought, and told the voice to leave him alone. The little voice could go to hell. He had given up on the coppiceman business, he had walked away from the homicide trade . . .

. . . the lights of a carousel reflected on the bald head of a black man lying dead on the Santa Monica Pier . . .

No. Don't go there. Just . . . just don't, that's all.

Jack should not have been in Santa Monica, anyhow. Santa Monica had its own coppicemen. As far as he knew, they were a swell bunch of guys, though perhaps not quite up to the standard set by that ace boy, whizbang, and youngest-ever lieutenant of LAPD's Homicide Division, himself. The only reason the ace boy and whizbang had been on their turf in the first place was that he had just broken up with this extremely nice, or at least moderately nice, resident of Malibu, Ms Brooke Greer, a screenwriter greatly esteemed within her genre, the action adventure–romantic comedy, also a person of remarkable wit, insight, and bodily charm, and as he sped homeward down the handsome stretch of the Pacific Coast Highway below the Malibu Canyon exit he yielded to an uncharacteristically edgy spell of gloom.

A few seconds after swinging up the California Incline into Santa Monica, he saw the bright ring of the Ferris wheel revolving above the strings of lights and the lively crowd on the pier. A tawdry enchantment, or an enchanted tawdriness, spoke to him from the heart of this scene. On a whim, Jack parked his car and walked down to the array of brilliant lights glowing in the darkness. The last time he had visited the Santa Monica Pier, he had been an excited six-year-old boy pulling on Lily Cavanaugh Sawyer's hand like a dog straining at a leash.

What happened was accidental. It was too meaningless to be called coincidence. Coincidence brings together two previously unrelated elements of a larger story. Here nothing connected, and there was no larger story.

He came to the pier's gaudy entrance and noticed that, after all, the Ferris wheel was not revolving. A circle of stationary lights hung over empty gondolas. For a moment, the giant machine looked like an alien invader, cleverly disguised and biding its time until it could do the maximum amount of damage. Jack could almost hear it purring to itself. *Right*, he thought, *an evil Ferris wheel – get a grip. You're shaken up more than you want to admit.* Then he looked back down at the scene before him, and finally took in that his fantasy of the pier had hidden a real-life evil rendered far too familiar by his profession. He had stumbled onto the initial stages of a homicide investigation.

Some of the brilliant lights he had seen flashed not from the Ferris wheel but from the tops of Santa Monica patrol cars. Out on the pier, four uniforms were discouraging a crowd of civilians from breaching the circle of crime-scene tape around a brightly illuminated carousel. Jack told himself to leave it alone. He had no role here. Besides that, the carousel aroused some smoky, indistinct feeling, an entire set of unwelcome feelings, in him. The carousel was creepier than the stalled Ferris wheel. Carousels had always spooked him, hadn't they? Painted midget horses frozen into place with their teeth bared and steel poles rammed through their guts – sadistic kitsch.

Walk away, Jack told himself. *Your girlfriend dumped you and you're in a rotten mood.*

And as for carousels . . .

The abrupt descent of a mental lead curtain ended the debate about carousels. Feeling as though pushed from within, Jack stepped onto the pier and began moving through the crowd. He was half conscious of taking the most unprofessional action of his career.

When he had pushed his way to the front of the crowd, he ducked under the tape and flashed his badge at a baby-faced cop who tried to order him back. Somewhere nearby, a guitarist began playing a blues melody Jack could almost identify; the title swam to the surface of his mind, then dove out of sight. The infant cop gave him a puzzled look and walked away to consult one of the detectives standing over a long shape Jack did not quite feel like looking at just then. The music annoyed him. It annoyed him a lot. In fact, it bugged the hell out of him. His irritation was out of proportion to its cause, but what kind of idiot thought homicides needed a sound track?

A painted horse reared, frozen in the garish light.

Jack's stomach tightened, and deep in his chest something fierce and insistent, something at all costs not to be named, flexed itself and threw out its arms. Or extended its wings. The terrible something wished to break free and make itself known. Briefly, Jack feared he would have to throw up. The passing of this sensation bought him a moment of uncomfortable clarity.

Voluntarily, idly, he had walked into craziness, and now he was crazy. You could put it no other way. Marching toward him with an expression nicely combining disbelief and fury was a detective named Angelo Leone, before his expedient transfer to Santa Monica a colleague of Jack's distinguished by his gross appetites, his capacity for violence and corruption, his contempt for all civilians regardless of color, race, creed, or social status, and, to be fair, his fearlessness and utter loyalty to all police officers who went with the program and did the same things he did, which meant anything they could get away with. Angelo Leone's disdain for Jack Sawyer, who had not gone with the program, had equaled his resentment at the younger man's success. In a few seconds, this brutal caveman would be in his face. Instead of trying to figure out how to explain himself to the caveman, he was obsessing about carousels and guitars, attending to the details of going crazy. He had no way of explaining himself. Explanation was impossible. The internal necessity that had pushed him into this position hummed on, but Jack could hardly speak to Angelo Leone of internal necessities. Nor could he offer a rational explanation to his captain, if Leone filed a complaint.

Well, you see, it was like someone else was pulling my strings, like another person was doing the driving . . .

The first words out of Angelo Leone's fleshy mouth rescued him from disaster.

– Don't tell me you're here for a reason, you ambitious little prick.

A piratical career like Leone's inevitably exposed the pirate to the danger of an official investigation. A strategic sidestep to a neighboring force offered little protection from the covert archaeological digs police officials mounted into records and reputations when the press gave them no other choice. Every decade or two, do-gooders, whistle-blowers, whiners, snitches, pissed-off civilians, and cops too stupid to accept the time-honored program got together, rammed a cherry bomb up the press's collective anus, and set off an orgy of bloodletting. Leone's essential, guilt-inspired paranoia had instantly suggested to him that LA Homicide's ace boy might be gilding his résumé.

As Jack had known it would, his claim of having been pulled toward the scene like a fire horse to a fire magnified Leone's suspicions.

– Okay, you *happened* to walk into my investigation. Fine. Now listen to me. If I *happen* to hear your name in some connection I don't like anytime during the next six months, make that ever, you'll be pissing through a tube for the rest of your life. Now get the fuck out of here and let me do my job.

– I'm gone, Angelo.

Leone's partner started to come forward across the gleaming pier. Leone grimaced and waved him back. Without intending to do so, without thinking about it, Jack let his eyes drift past the detective and down to the corpse in front of the carousel. Far more powerfully than it had the first time, the ferocious creature at the center of his chest flexed itself, unfurled, and extended its wings, its arms, its talons, whatever they were, and by means of a tremendous upward surge attempted to rip free of its moorings.

The wings, the arms, the talons crushed Jack's lungs. Hideous claws splayed through his stomach.

There is one act a homicide detective, especially a homicide lieutenant, must never commit, and it is this: confronted with a dead body, he must not puke. Jack struggled to remain on the respectable side of the Forbidden. Bile seared the back of his throat, and he closed his eyes. A constellation of glowing dots wavered across his eyelids. The creature, molten and foul, battered against its restraints.

Lights reflected on the scalp of a bald, black man lying dead beside a carousel . . .

Not you. No, not you. Knock all you like, but you can't come in.

The wings, arms, talons retracted; the creature dwindled to a dozing speck. Having succeeded in avoiding the Forbidden Act, Jack found himself capable of opening his eyes. He had no idea how much time had passed. Angelo Leone's corrugated forehead, murky eyes, and carnivorous mouth heaved into view and, from a distance of six inches, occupied all the available space.

– What are we doing here? Reviewing our situation?

– I wish that idiot would put his guitar back in its case.

And that was one of the oddest turns of the evening.

– Guitar? I don't hear no guitar.

Neither, Jack realized, did he.

Wouldn't any rational person attempt to put such an episode out of mind? To throw this garbage overboard? You couldn't *do* anything with it, you couldn't *use* it, so why hold on to it? The incident on the pier meant nothing. It connected to nothing beyond itself, and it led to nothing. It was literally inconsequential, for it had had no consequences. After his lover had sandbagged him Jack had lost his bearings, suffered a momentary aberration, and trespassed upon another jurisdiction's crime scene. It was no more than an embarrassing mistake.

Fifty-six days and eleven hours later, the ace boy slipped into his captain's office, laid down his shield and his gun, and announced, much to the captain's astonishment, his immediate retirement. Knowing nothing of the confrontation with Detective Leone on the Santa Monica Pier, the captain did not inquire as to the possible influence upon his lieutenant's decision of a stalled carousel and a dead black man; if he had, Jack would have told him he was being ridiculous.

Don't go there, he advises himself, and does an excellent job of not going there. He receives a few involuntary flashes, no more, strobe-lit snapshots of a wooden pony's rearing head, of Angelo Leone's distempered mug, also of one other thing, the object occupying the dead center of the scene in every sense, that which above all must not be witnessed . . . the instant these imagistic lightning bolts appear, he *sends them away*. It feels like a magical performance. He is doing magic, good magic. He knows perfectly well that these feats of image banishment represent a form of self-protection, and if the motives behind his need for this protective magic remain unclear, the need is motive enough. When you gotta have an omelette, you gotta whisk eggs, to quote that unimpeachable authority, Duke Wayne.

Jack Sawyer has more on his mind than the irrelevancies suggested by a dream voice's having uttered the word 'policeman' in baby talk. These matters, too, he wishes he could *send away* by the execution of a magic trick, but the wretched matters refuse banishment; they zoom about him like a tribe of wasps.

All in all, he is not doing so well, our Jack. He is marking time and staring at the eggs, which no longer look quite right, though he could not say why. The eggs resist interpretation. The eggs are the least of it. In the periphery of his vision, the banner across the front page of the *La Riviere Herald* seems to rise off the sheet of newsprint and float toward him. FISHERMAN STILL AT LARGE IN . . . Nope, that's enough; he turns away with the terrible knowledge of having brought on this Fisherman business by himself. How about IN STATEN ISLAND OR IN BROOKLYN, where the real Albert Fish, a tormented piece of work if there ever was one, found two of his victims?

This stuff is making him sick. Two dead kids, the Freneau girl missing and probably dead, body parts eaten, a lunatic who plagiarized from Albert Fish . . . Dale insisted on assaulting him with information. The details enter his system like a contaminant. The more he learns – and for a man who truly wished to be out of the loop, Jack has learned an amazing amount – the more the poisons swim through his bloodstream, distorting his perceptions. He had come to Norway Valley in flight from a world that had abruptly turned unreliable and rubbery, as if liquefying under thermal pressure. During his last month in Los Angeles, the thermal pressure had become intolerable. Grotesque possibilities leered from darkened windows and the gaps between buildings, threatening to take form. On days off, the sensation of dishwater greasing his lungs made him gasp for breath and fight against nausea, so he worked without stopping, in the process solving more cases than ever before. (His diagnosis was that the work was getting to him, but we can hardly blame the captain for his astonishment at the ace boy's resignation.)

He had escaped to this obscure pocket of the countryside, this shelter, this haven at the edge of a yellow meadow, removed from the world of threat and madness, removed by nearly twenty miles from French Landing, removed a good distance even from Norway Valley Road. However, the layers of removal had failed to do their job. What he was trying to escape riots around him again, here in his redoubt. If he let himself succumb to self-centered fantasy, he would have to conclude that what he had fled had spent the last three years sniffing his trail and had finally succeeded in tracking him down.

In California, the rigors of his task had overwhelmed him; now the disorders of western Wisconsin must be kept at arm's length. Sometimes, late at night, he awakens to the echo of the little, poisoned voice wailing, *No more coppiceman, I won't, too close, too close.* What was too close, Jack Sawyer refuses to consider; the echo proves that he must avoid any further contamination.

Bad news for Dale, he knows, and he regrets both his inability to join the investigation and to explain his refusal to his friend. Dale's ass is on the line, no two ways about it. He is a good chief of police, more than good enough for French Landing, but he misjudged the politics and let the staties set him up. With every appearance of respect for local authority, state detectives Brown and Black had bowed low, stepped aside, and permitted Dale Gilbertson, who thought they were doing him a favor, to slip a noose around his neck. Too bad, but Dale has just figured out that he is standing on a trapdoor with a black bag over his face. If the Fisherman murders one more kid . . . Well, Jack Sawyer sends his most profound regrets. He can't perform a miracle right now, sorry. Jack has more pressing matters on his mind.

Red feathers, for example. Small ones. Little red feathers are much on Jack's mind, and have been, despite his efforts to magic them away, since a month before the murders started. One morning as he emerged from his bedroom and began to go down to fix breakfast, a single red feather, a plume smaller than a baby's finger, *seemed to* float out of the slanted ceiling at the top of the stairs. In its wake, two or three others came drifting toward him. An oval section of plaster two inches across *seemed to* blink and open like an eye, and the eye released a tight, fat column of feathers that zoomed out of the ceiling as if propelled through a straw. A feather explosion, a feather hurricane, battered his chest, his raised arms, his head.

But this . . .

This never happened.

Something else happened, and it took him a minute or two to figure it out. A wayward brain neuron misfired. A mental receptor lapped up the wrong chemical, or lapped up too much of the right chemical. The switches that nightly triggered the image conduits responded to a false signal and produced a *waking dream*. The waking dream resembled an hallucination, but hallucinations were experienced by wet-brain alcoholics, drug takers, and crazy people, specifically paranoid schizophrenics, with whom Jack had dealt on many an occasion during his life as a coppiceman. Jack fit into none of those categories, including the last. He knew he was not a paranoid schizophrenic or any other variety of madman. If you thought Jack Sawyer was crazy, *you* were. He has complete, at least 99 percent complete, faith in his sanity.

Since he is not delusional, the feathers must have flown toward him in a waking dream. The only other explanation involves reality, and the feathers had no connection to reality. What kind of world would this be, if such things could happen to us?

Abruptly George Rathbun bellows, 'It *pains* me to say this, truly it does, for *I love* our dear old Brew Crew, you know I do, but there come times when *love* must grit its teeth and face a *painful* reality – for example, take the sorrowful state of our pitching staff. Bud Selig, oh *BUUD*, this is *Houston* calling. Could you *please* return to earth immediately? A *blind man* could throw more strikes than that aggregation of WIMPS, LOSERS, AND AIRHEADS!'

Good old Henry. Henry has George Rathbun down so perfectly you can see the sweat stains under his armpits. But the best of Henry's inventions – in Jack's opinion – has to be that embodiment of hipster cool, the laid-back, authoritative Henry Shake ('the Sheik, the Shake, the Shook of Araby'), who can, if in the mood, tell you the color of the socks worn by Lester Young on the day he recorded 'Shoe Shine Boy' and 'Lady Be Good' and describe the interiors of two dozen famous but mostly long-departed jazz clubs.

. . . and before we get into the very cool, very beautiful, very simpático music whispered one Sunday at the Village Vanguard by the Bill Evans Trio, we might pay our respects to the third, inner eye. Let us honor the inner eye, the eye of imagination. It is late on a hot July afternoon in Greenwich Village, New York City. On sundazzled Seventh Avenue South, we stroll into the shade of the Vanguard's marquee, open a white door, and proceed down a long, narrow flight of stairs to a roomy underground cave. The musicians climb onto the stand. Bill Evans slides onto the piano bench and nods at the audience. Scott LaFaro hugs his bass. Paul Motian picks up his brushes. Evans lowers his head way, way down and drops his hands on the keyboard. For those of us who are privileged to be there, nothing will ever be the same again.

'My Foolish Heart' by the Bill Evans Trio, live at the Village Vanguard, the twenty-fifth of June, 1961. I am your host, Henry Shake – the Sheik, the Shake, the Shook of Araby.

Smiling, Jack pours the beaten eggs into the frying pan, twice swirls them with a fork, and marginally reduces the gas flame. It occurs to him that he has neglected to make coffee. Nuts to coffee. Coffee is the last thing he needs; he can drink orange juice. A glance at the toaster suggests that he has also neglected to prepare the morning's toast. Does he require toast, is toast essential? Consider the butter, consider slabs of cholesterol waiting to corrupt his arteries. The omelette is risky enough; in fact, he has the feeling he cracked way too many eggs. Now Jack cannot remember why he wanted to make an omelette in the first place. He rarely eats omelettes. In fact, he tends to buy eggs out of a sense of duty aroused by the two rows of egg-sized depressions near the top of his refrigerator door. If people were not supposed to buy eggs, why would refrigerators come with egg holders?

He nudges a spatula under the edges of the hardening but still runny eggs, tilts the pan to slide them around, scrapes in the mushrooms and scallions, and folds the result in half. All right. Okay. Looks good. A luxurious forty minutes of freedom stretches out before him. In spite of everything, he seems to be functioning pretty well. Control is not an issue here.

Unfolded on the kitchen table, the *La Riviere Herald* catches Jack's eye. He has forgotten about the newspaper. The newspaper has not forgotten him, however, and demands its proper share of attention. FISHERMAN STILL AT LARGE IN, and so on. ARCTIC CIRCLE would be nice, but no, he moves nearer to the table and sees that the Fisherman remains a stubbornly local problem. From beneath the headline, Wendell Green's name leaps up and lodges in his eye like a pebble. Wendell Green is an all-around, comprehensive pest, an ongoing irritant. After reading the first two paragraphs of Green's article, Jack groans and clamps a hand over his eyes.

I'm a blind man, make me an umpire!

Wendell Green has the confidence of a small-town athletic

hero who never left home. Tall, expansive, with a crinkly mat of red-blond hair and a senatorial waistline, Green swaggers through the bars, the courthouses, the public arenas of La Riviere and its surrounding communities, distributing wised-up charm. Wendell Green is a reporter who knows how to act like one, an old-fashioned print journalist, the *Herald*'s great ornament.

At their first encounter, the great ornament struck Jack as a third-rate phony, and he has seen no reason to change his mind since then. He distrusts Wendell Green. In Jack's opinion, the reporter's gregarious facade conceals a limitless capacity for treachery. Green is a blowhard posturing in front of a mirror, but a canny blowhard, and such creatures will do anything to gain their own ends.

After Thornberg Kinderling's arrest, Green requested an interview. Jack turned him down, as he declined the three invitations that followed his removal to Norway Valley Road. His refusals had not deterred the reporter from staging occasional 'accidental' meetings.

The day after the discovery of Amy St Pierre's body, Jack emerged from a Chase Street dry cleaner's shop with a box of freshly laundered shirts under his arm, began walking toward his car, and felt a hand close on his elbow. He looked back and beheld, contorted into a leer of spurious delight, the florid public mask of Wendell Green.

– Hey, hey, Holly—A bad-boy smirk. I *mean*, Lieutenant Sawyer. Hey, I'm glad I ran into you. This is where you have your shirts done? They do a good job?

– If you leave out the part about the buttons.

– Good one. You're a funny guy, Lieutenant. Let me give you a tip. Reliable, on Third Street in La Riviere? They live up to their name. No smashee, no breakee. Want your shirts done right, go to a Chink every time. Sam Lee, try him out, Lieutenant.

– I'm not a lieutenant anymore, Wendell. Call me Jack or Mr Sawyer. Call me Hollywood, I don't care. And now—

He walked toward his car, and Wendell Green walked beside him.

– Any chance of a few words, Lieutenant? Sorry, Jack? Chief Gilbertson is a close friend of yours, I know, and this tragic case, little girl, apparently mutilated, terrible things, can you offer us your expertise, step in, give us the benefit of your thoughts?

– You want to know my thoughts?

– Anything you can tell me, buddy.

Pure, irresponsible malice inspired Jack to extend an arm over Green's shoulders and say:

– Wendell, old buddy, check out a guy named Albert Fish. It was back in the twenties.

– Fisch?

– F-i-s-h. From an old-line WASP New York family. An amazing case. Look it up.

Until that moment, Jack had been barely conscious of remembering the outrages committed by the bizarre Mr Albert Fish. Butchers more up-to-date – Ted Bundy, John Wayne Gacy, and Jeffrey Dahmer – had eclipsed Albert Fish, not to mention exotics like Edmund Emil Kemper III, who, after committing eight murders, decapitated his mother, propped her head on his mantel, and used it as a dartboard. (By way of explanation, Edmund III said, 'This seemed appropriate.') Yet the name of Albert Fish, an obscure back number, had surfaced in Jack's mind, and into Wendell Green's ready ear he had uttered it.

What had gotten *into* him? Well, that was the question, wasn't it?

Whoops, the omelette. Jack grabs a plate from a cabinet, silverware from a drawer, jumps to the stove, turns off the burner, and slides the mess in the pan onto his plate. He sits down and opens the *Herald* to page 5, where he reads about Milly Kuby's nearly winning third place at the big statewide spelling bee, but for the substitution of an *i* for an *a* in *opopanax*, the kind of thing that is supposed to be in a local paper. How can you expect a kid to spell *opopanax* correctly, anyhow?

Jack takes two or three bites of his omelette before the peculiar taste in his mouth distracts him from the monstrous unfairness done to Milly Kuby. The funny taste is like half-burned garbage. He spits the food out of his mouth and sees a wad of gray mush and raw, half-chewed vegetables. The uneaten part of his breakfast does not look any more appetizing. He did not cook this omelette; he ruined it.

He drops his head and groans. A shudder like a loose electrical wire travels here and there through his body, throwing off sparks that singe his throat, his lungs, his suddenly palpitating organs. *Opopanax*, he thinks. *I'm falling apart. Right here and now. Forget I said that. The savage opopanax has gripped me in its claws, shaken me with the fearful opopanax of its opopanax arms, and intends to throw me into the turbulent Opopanax River, where I shall meet my opopanax.*

'What is happening to me?' he says aloud. The shrill sound of his voice scares him.

Opopanax tears sting his opopanax eyes, and he gets groaning up off his opopanax, dumps the swill into the garbage disposal, rinses the plate, and decides that it is damn well time to start making sense around here. Opopanax me no opopanaxes. Everybody makes mistakes. Jack examines the door of the refrigerator, trying to remember if he still has an egg or two in there. Sure he does: a whole bunch of eggs, about nine or ten, had nearly filled the entire row of egg-shaped depressions at the top of the door. He could not have squandered all of them; he wasn't that out of it.

Jack closes his fingers around the edge of the refrigerator door. Entirely unbidden, the vision of lights reflected on a black man's bald head.

Not you.

The person being addressed is not present; the person being addressed is scarcely a person at all.

No, no, not you.

The door swings open under the pressure of his fingers; the refrigerator light illuminates the laden shelves. Jack Sawyer regards the egg holders. They appear to be empty. A closer look reveals, nested within the rounded depression at the end of the first row, the presence of a small, egg-shaped object colored a pale and delicate shade of blue: a nostalgic, tender blue, quite possibly the half-remembered blue of a summer sky observed in early afternoon by a small boy lying face-up on the quarter acre of grass located behind a nice residential property on Roxbury Drive in Beverly Hills, California. Whoever owns this residential property, boy, you can put your money on one thing: they're in the entertainment business.

Jack knows the name of this precise shade of blue due to an extended consideration of color samples undertaken in the company of Claire Evinrude, MD, an oncologist of lovely and brisk dispatch, during the period when they were planning to repaint their then-shared bungalow in the Hollywood Hills. Claire, Dr Evinrude, had marked this color for the master bedroom; he, recently returned from a big-deal, absurdly selective VICAP course of instruction at Quantico, Virginia, and newly promoted to the rank of lieutenant, had dismissed it as, um, well, maybe a little cold.

Jack, have you ever seen an actual robin's egg? Dr Evinrude inquired. Do you have any idea how beautiful they are? Dr Evinrude's gray eyes enlarged as she grasped her mental scalpel.

Jack inserts two fingers into the egg receptacle and lifts from it the small, egg-shaped object the color of a robin's egg. What do you know, this is a robin's egg. An 'actual,' in the words of Dr Claire Evinrude, robin's egg, hatched from the body of a robin, sometimes called a robin red-breast. He deposits the egg in the palm of his left hand. There it sits, this pale blue oblate the size of a pecan. The capacity for thought seems to have left him. What the hell did he do, *buy* a robin's egg? Sorry, no, this relationship isn't working, the opopanax is out of whack, Roy's Store doesn't sell robin's eggs, I'm gone.

Slowly, stiffly, awkward as a zombie, Jack progresses across the kitchen floor and reaches the sink. He extends his left hand over the maw at the sink's center and releases the robin's egg. Down into the garbage disposal it drops, irretrievably. His right hand switches the machine into action, with the usual noisy results. Growl, grind, snarl, a monster is enjoying a nice little snack. Grrr. The live electrical wire shudders within him, shedding sparks as it twitches, but he has become zombiefied and barely registers the internal shocks. All in all, taking everything into consideration, what Jack Sawyer feels most like doing at this moment . . .

When the red, red . . .

For some reason, he has not called his mother in a long, long while. He cannot think why he has not, and it is about time he did. Robin me no red robins. The voice of Lily Cavanaugh Sawyer, the Queen of the B's, once his only companion in a rapture-flooded, transcendent, rigorously forgotten New Hampshire hotel room, is precisely the voice Jack needs to hear right about now. Lily Cavanaugh is the one person in the world to whom he can spill the ridiculous mess in which he finds himself. Despite the dim, unwelcome awareness of trespassing beyond the borders of strict rationality and therefore bringing further into question his own uncertain sanity, he moves down the kitchen counter, picks up his cell phone, and punches in the number of the nice residential property on Roxbury Drive, Beverly Hills, California.

The telephone in his old house rings five times, six times, seven. A man picks up and, in an angry, slightly drunken, sleep-distorted voice, says, 'Kimberley . . . whatever the hell this is about . . . for your sake . . . I hope it's really, really important.'

Jack hits END and snaps his phone shut. Oh God oh hell oh damn. It is just past five a.m. in Beverly Hills, or Westwood, or Hancock Park, or wherever that number now reaches. He forgot his mother was dead. Oh hell oh damn oh God, can you beat that?

Jack's grief, which has been sharpening itself underground, once again rises up to stab him, as if for the first time, bang, dead-center in the heart. At the same time the idea that even for a second he could have *forgotten that his mother was dead* strikes him, God knows why, as hugely and irresistibly funny. How ridiculous can you get? The goofy stick has whapped him on the back of the head, and without knowing if he is going to burst into sobs or shouts of laughter, Jack experiences a brief wave of dizziness and leans heavily against the kitchen counter.

Jive-ass turkey, he remembers his mother saying. Lily had been describing her late husband's recently deceased partner in the days after her suspicious accountants discovered that the partner, Morgan Sloat, had been diverting into his own pockets three-fourths of the income from Sawyer & Sloat's astonishingly vast real estate holdings. Every year since Phil Sawyer's death in a so-called hunting accident, Sloat had stolen millions of dollars, many millions, from his late partner's family. Lily diverted the flow back into the proper channels and sold half the company to its new partners, in the process guaranteeing her son a tremendous financial bonanza, not to mention the annual bonanza that produces the interest Jack's private foundation funnels off to noble causes. Lily had called Sloat things far more colorful than *jive-ass turkey*, but that is the term her voice utters in his inner ear.

Way back in May, Jack tells himself, he probably came across that robin's egg on an absentminded stroll through the meadow and put it in the refrigerator for safekeeping. To keep it safe. Because, after all, it was of a delicate shade of blue, a beautiful blue, to quote Dr Evinrude. So long had he kept it safe that he'd forgotten all about it. Which, he gratefully recognizes, is why the waking dream presented him with an explosion of red feathers!

Everything happens for a reason, concealed though the reason may be; loosen up and relax long enough to stop being a jive-ass turkey, and the reason might come out of hiding.

Jack bends over the sink and, for the sake of refreshment internal and external, immerses his face in a double handful of cold water. For the moment, the cleansing shock washes away the ruined breakfast, the ridiculous telephone call, and the corrosive image flashes. It is time to strap on his skates and get going. In twenty-five minutes, Jack Sawyer's best friend and only confidant will, with his customary aura of rotary perception, emerge through the front door of KDCU-AM's cinder-block building and, applying his golden lighter's flame to the tip of a cigarette, glide down the walkway to Peninsula Drive. Should rotary perception inform him that Jack Sawyer's pickup awaits, Henry Leyden will unerringly locate the handle and climb in. This exhibition of blind-man cool is too dazzling to miss.

And miss it he does not, for in spite of the morning's difficulties, which from the balanced, mature perspective granted by his journey through the lovely countryside eventually seem trivial, Jack's pickup pulls in front of the Peninsula Drive end of KDCU-AM's walkway at 7:55, a good five minutes before his friend is to stroll out into the sunlight. Henry will be good for him: just the *sight* of Henry will be like a dose of soul tonic. Surely Jack cannot be the first man (or woman) in the history of the world who momentarily lost his (or her) grip under stress and kind of halfway forgot that his (or her) mother had shuffled off the old mortal coil and departed for a higher sphere. Stressed-out mortals turned naturally to their mothers for comfort and reassurance. The impulse is coded into our DNA. When he hears the story, Henry will chuckle and advise him to tighten his wig.

On second thought, why cloud Henry's sky with a story so absurd? The same applies to the robin's egg, especially since Jack has not spoken to Henry about his waking dream of a feather eruption, and he does not feel like getting involved in a lot of pointless backtracking. Live in the present; let the past stretch out in its grave; keep your chin high and walk around the mud puddles. Don't look to your friends for therapy.

He switches on the radio and hits the button for KWLA-FM, the UW–La Riviere station, home to both the Wisconsin Rat and Henry the Sheik the Shake the Shook. What pours glittering from the cab's hidden speakers raises the hairs on his arms: Glenn Gould, inner eye luminously open, blazing through something by Bach, he could not say exactly what. But Glenn Gould, but Bach, for sure. One of the Partitas, maybe.

A CD jewel box in one hand, Henry Leyden strolls through the humble doorway at the side of the station, enters the sunlight, and without hesitation begins to glide down the flagged walkway, the rubber soles of his Hershey-brown suede loafers striking the center of each successive flagstone.

Henry . . . Henry is a vision.

Today, Jack observes, Henry comes attired in one of his Malaysian teak forest owner ensembles, a handsome collarless shirt, shimmering braces, and an heirloom straw fedora creased to a fare-thee-well. Had Jack not been so welcomed into Henry's life, he would not have known that his friend's capacity for flawless wardrobe assemblage depended upon the profound organization of his enormous walk-in closet long ago established by Rhoda Gilbertson Leyden, Henry's deceased wife: Rhoda had arranged every article of her husband's clothing by season, style, and color. Item by item, Henry memorized the entire system. Although blind since birth, therefore incapable of distinguishing between matching and mismatching shades, Henry never errs.

Henry extracts from his shirt pocket a gold lighter and a yellow pack of American Spirits, fires up, exhales a radiant cloud brightened by sunlight to the color of milk, and continues his unwavering progress down the flagstones.

The pink, back-slanting capitals of TROY LUVS MARYANN! YES! sprayed across the sign on the bare lawn suggest that 1) Troy spends a lot of time listening to KDCU-AM, and 2) Maryann loves him back. Good for Troy, good for Maryann. Jack applauds love's announcement, even in pink spray paint, and wishes the lovers happiness and good fortune. It occurs to him that if at this present stage of his existence he could be said to love anyone, that person would have to be Henry Leyden. Not in the sense that Troy luvs Maryann, or vice versa, but he luvs him all the same, a matter that has never been as clear as it is this moment.

Henry traverses the last of the flagstones and approaches the curb. A single stride brings him to the door of the pickup; his hand closes on the recessed metal bar; he opens the door, steps up, and slides in. His head tilts, cocking his right ear to the music. The dark lenses of his aviator glasses shine.

'How can you do that?' Jack asks. 'This time, the music helped, but you don't need music.'

'I can do that because I am totally, totally bitchrod,' Henry says. 'I learned that lovely word from our pothead intern, Morris Rosen, who kindly applied it to me. Morris thinks I am God, but he must have something on the ball, because he figured out that George Rathbun and the Wisconsin Rat are one and the same. I hope the kid keeps his mouth shut.'

'I do, too,' Jack says, 'but I'm not going to let you change the subject. How can you always open the door right away? How do you find the handle without groping for it?'

Henry sighs. 'The handle tells me where it is. Obviously. All I have to do is listen to it.'

'The door handle makes a *sound*?'

'Not like your high-tech radio and *The Goldberg Variations*, no. More like a vibration. The sound of a sound. The sound *inside* a sound. Isn't Daniel Barenboim a great piano player? Man, listen to that – every note, a different coloration. Makes you want to kiss the lid of his Steinway, baby. Imagine the muscles in his hands.'

'That's Barenboim?'

'Well, who else could it be?' Slowly, Henry turns his head to Jack. An irritating smile raises the corners of his mouth. 'Ah. I see, yes. Knowing you as I do, you poor schmuck, I see you imagined you were listening to Glenn Gould.'

'I did not,' Jack says.

'Please.'

'Maybe for a minute I wondered if it was Gould, but—'

'Don't, don't, don't. Don't even try. Your voice gives you away. There's a little, whiny topspin on every word; it's so pathetic. Are we going to drive back to Norway Valley, or would you like to sit here and keep lying to me? I want to tell you something on the way home.'

He holds up the CD. 'Let's put you out of your misery. The pothead gave this to me – Dirtysperm doing an old Supremes ditty. Me, I *loathe* that sort of thing, but it might be perfect for the Wisconsin Rat. Cue up track seven.'

The pianist no longer sounds anything like Glenn Gould, and the music seems to have slowed to half its former velocity. Jack puts himself out of his misery and inserts the CD into the opening beneath the radio. He pushes a button, then another. At an insanely fast tempo, the screeches of madmen subjected to unspeakable tortures come blasting out of the speakers. Jack rocks backward into the seat, jolted. 'My God, Henry,' he says, and reaches for the volume control.

'Don't dare touch that dial,' Henry says. 'If this crap doesn't make your ears bleed, it isn't doing its job.'

'Ears,' Jack knows, is jazz-speak for the capacity to hear what is going on in music as it unfurls across the air. A musician with good ears soon memorizes the songs and arrangements he is asked to play, picks up or already knows the harmonic movement underlying the theme, and follows the transformations and substitutions to that pattern introduced by his fellow musicians. Whether or not he can accurately read notes written on a staff, a musician with *great* ears learns melodies and arrangements the first time he hears them, grasps harmonic intricacies through flawless intuition, and immediately identifies the notes and key signatures registered by taxi horns, elevator bells, and mewing cats. Such people inhabit a world defined by the particularities of individual sounds, and Henry Leyden is one of them. As far as Jack is concerned, Henry's ears are Olympian, in a class by themselves.

It was Henry's ears that gave him access to Jack's great secret, the role his mother, Lily Cavanaugh Sawyer, 'Lily Cavanaugh,' had occupied in life, and he is the only person ever to discover it. Shortly after Dale introduced them, Jack and Henry Leyden entered into an easy, companionable friendship surprising to both. Each the answer to the other's loneliness, they spent two or three nights of every week having dinner together, listening to music, and talking about whatever came into their well-stocked minds. Either Jack drove down the road to Henry's eccentric house, or he picked Henry up and drove him back to his place. After something like six or seven months, Jack wondered if his friend might enjoy spending an hour or so listening to him read aloud from books agreed upon by both parties. Henry replied, *Ivey-divey, my man, what a beautiful idea. How about starting with some whacked-out crime novels?* They began with Chester Himes and Charles Willeford, changed gear with a batch of contemporary novels, floated through S. J. Perelman and James Thurber, and ventured emboldened into fictional mansions erected by Ford Madox Ford and Vladimir Nabokov. (Marcel Proust lies somewhere ahead, they understand, but Proust can wait; at present they are to embark upon *Bleak House*.)

One night after Jack had finished the evening's installment of Ford's *The Good Soldier*, Henry cleared his throat and said, Dale said you told him your parents were in the entertainment industry. In show business.

– That's right.

– I don't want to pry, but would you mind if I asked you some questions? If you feel like answering, just say yes or no.

Already alarmed, Jack said, What's this about, Henry?

– I want to see if I'm right about something.

– Okay. Ask.

– Thank you. Were your parents in different aspects of the industry?

– Um.

– Was one of them in the business end of things, and the other a performer?

– Um.

– Was your mother an actress?

– Uh-huh.

A famous actress, in a way. She never really got the respect she deserved, but she made a ton of movies all through the fifties and into the mid-sixties, and at the end of her career she won an Oscar for Best Supporting Actress.

– Henry, Jack said. Where did you—

– Clam up. I intend to relish this moment. Your mother was Lily Cavanaugh. That's wonderful. Lily Cavanaugh was always so much more talented than most people gave her credit for. Every time out, she brought those roles she played, those girls, those tough little waitresses and dames with guns in their handbags, up to a new level. Beautiful, smart, gutsy, no pretensions, just lock in and inhabit the part. She was about a hundred times better than anyone else around her.

– Henry . . .

– Some of those movies had nice sound tracks, too. *Lost Summer*, Johnny Mandel? Out of sight.

– Henry, how did—

–You told me; how else could I know? These little things your voice does, that's how. You slide over the tops of your *r*'s, and you hit the rest of your consonants in a kind of cadence, and that cadence runs through your sentences.

– A cadence?

– Bet your ass, junior. An underlying rhythm, like your own personal drummer. All through *The Good Soldier* I kept trying to remember where I'd heard it before. Faded in, faded back out. A couple of days ago, I nailed it. Lily Cavanaugh. You can't blame me for wanting to see if I was right, can you?

– Blame you? Jack said. I'm too stunned to blame anybody, but give me a couple of minutes.

–Your secret's safe. When people see you, you don't want their first thought to be, Hey, there's Lily Cavanaugh's son. Makes sense to me.

Henry Leyden has great ears, all right.

As the pickup rolls through French Landing the din filling the cab makes conversation impossible. Dirtysperm is burning a hole through the marzipan center of 'Where Did Our Love Go' and in the process committing hideous atrocities upon those cute little Supremes. Henry, who claims to loathe this kind of thing, slouches in his seat, knees up on the dash, hands steepled below his chin, grinning with pleasure. The shops on Chase Street have opened for business, and half a dozen cars jut at an angle from parking spaces.

Four boys astride bicycles swerve off the sidewalk before Schmitt's Allsorts and into the road twenty feet in front of the moving pickup. Jack hits his brakes; the boys come to an abrupt halt and line up side by side, waiting for him to pass. Jack trolls forward. Henry straightens up, checks his mysterious sensors, and drops back into position. All is well with Henry. The boys, however, do not know what to make of the uproar growing ever louder as the pickup approaches. They stare at Jack's windshield in bafflement tinged with distaste, the way their great-grandfathers once stared at the Siamese twins and the Alligator Man in the freak show at the back of the fairground. Everybody knows that the drivers of pickup trucks listen to only two kinds of music, heavy metal or country, so what's with *this* creep?

As Jack drives past the boys, the first, a scowling heavyweight with the inflamed face of a schoolyard bully, displays an upraised second finger. The next two continue the imitations of their great-grandfathers having a hot night out in 1921 and gape, idiotically, mouths slack and open. The fourth boy, whose dark blond hair beneath a Brewers cap, bright eyes, and general air of innocence make him the nicest-looking of the group, gazes directly into Jack's face and gives him a sweet, tentative smile. This is Tyler Marshall, out for a spin – though he is completely unaware of it – into no-man's-land.

The boys glide into the background, and Jack glances into the mirror to see them pedaling furiously up the street, Sluggo in front, the smallest, most appealing one in the rear, already falling behind.

'A sidewalk panel of experts has reported in on the Dirtysperm,' Jack says. 'Four kids on bikes.' Since he can scarcely make out his words, he does not think Henry will be able to hear them at all.

Henry, it seems, has heard him perfectly, and he responds with a question that disappears into the uproar. Having a reasonably good idea of what it must have been, Jack answers it anyhow. 'One firm negative, two undecideds tending toward negative, and one cautious positive.' Henry nods.

Violent marzipan-destruction crashes and thuds to a

conclusion on Eleventh Street. As if a haze has blown from the cab, as if the windshield has been freshly washed, the air seems clearer, the colors more vibrant. 'Interesting,' Henry says. He reaches unerringly for the EJECT button, extracts the disc from the holder, and slips it into its case. 'That was very revealing, don't you think? Raw, self-centered hatred should never be dismissed automatically. Morris Rosen was right. It's perfect for the Wisconsin Rat.'

'Hey, I think they could be bigger than Glenn Miller.'

'That reminds me,' Henry says. 'You'll never guess what I'm doing later. I have a gig! Chipper Maxton, actually his second in command, this Rebecca Vilas woman, who I am sure is as gorgeous as she sounds, hired me to put on a record hop as the slam-bang climax to Maxton's big Strawberry Fest. Well, not me – an old, long-neglected persona of mine, Symphonic Stan, the Big-Band Man.'

'Do you need a ride?'

'I do not. The wondrous Miss Vilas has attended to my needs, in the form of a car with a comfy back seat for my turntable and a trunk spacious enough for the speakers and record cartons, which she will be sending. But thanks anyhow.'

'Symphonic Stan?' Jack said.

'A knocked-out, all-frantic, all-zoot-suit embodiment of the big-band era, and a charming, mellifluous gentleman besides. For the residents of Maxton's, an evocation of their salad days and a joy to behold.'

'Do you actually own a zoot suit?'

Magnificently inexpressive, Henry's face swings toward him.

'Sorry. I don't know what came over me. To change the subject, what you said, I mean what George Rathbun said, about the Fisherman this morning probably did a lot of good. I was glad to hear that.'

Henry opens his mouth and summons George Rathbun in all his avuncular glory. '"*The original Fisherman, boys and girls, Albert Fish, has been dead and gone for sixty-seven years.*"' It is uncanny, hearing the voice of that charged-up fat man leap from Henry Leyden's slender throat. In his own voice, Henry says, 'I hope it did some good. After I read your buddy Wendell Green's nonsense in the paper this morning, I thought George had to say *something*.'

Henry Leyden enjoys using terms like *I read, I was reading, I saw, I was looking at*. He knows these phrases disconcert his auditors. And he called Wendell Green 'your buddy' because Henry is the only person to whom Jack has ever admitted that he alerted the reporter to the crimes of Albert Fish. Now Jack wishes he had confessed to no one. Glad-handing Wendell Green is not his buddy.

'Having been of some assistance to the press,' Henry says, 'you might reasonably be thought in a position to do the same for our boys in blue. Forgive me, Jack, but you opened the door, and I'll only say this once. Dale is my nephew, after all.'

'I don't believe you're doing this to me,' Jack says.

'Doing what, speaking my mind? Dale *is* my nephew, remember? He could use your expertise, and he is very much of the opinion that you owe him a favor. Hasn't it occurred to you that you could help him stay in his job? Or that if you love French Landing and Norway Valley as much as you say, you owe these folks a little of your time and talent?'

'Hasn't it occurred to you, Henry, that I'm retired?' Jack says through gritted teeth. 'That investigating homicides is the last thing, I mean, the *last* thing in the world I want to do?'

'Of course it has,' Henry says. 'But – and again I hope you'll forgive me, Jack – here you are, the person I know you are, with the skills you have, which are certainly far beyond

Dale's and probably well beyond all these other guys', and I can't help wondering what the hell your problem is.'

'I don't have a *problem*,' Jack says. 'I'm a civilian.'

'You're the boss. We might as well listen to the rest of the Barenboim.' Henry runs his fingers over the console and pushes the button for the tuner.

For the next fifteen minutes, the only voice to be heard in the pickup's cab is that of a Steinway concert grand meditating upon *The Goldberg Variations* in the Teatro Colón, Buenos Aires. A splendid voice it is, too, Jack thinks, and you'd have to be an ignoramus to mistake it for Glenn Gould. A person capable of making that mistake probably couldn't hear the vibration-like inner sound produced by a General Motors door handle.

When they turn right off Highway 93 onto Norway Valley Road, Henry says, 'Stop sulking. I shouldn't have called you a schmuck. And I shouldn't have accused you of having a problem, because I'm the one with the problem.'

'You?' Jack looks at him, startled. Long experience has immediately suggested that Henry is about to ask for some kind of unofficial investigative help. Henry is facing the windshield, giving nothing away. 'What kind of problem can *you* have? Did your socks get out of order? Oh – are you having trouble with one of the stations?'

'That, I could deal with.' Henry pauses, and the pause stretches into a lengthy silence. 'What I was going to say is, I feel like I'm losing my mind. I think I'm going sort of crazy.'

'Come on.' Jack eases up on the gas pedal and cuts his speed in half. Has Henry witnessed a feather explosion? Of course he hasn't; Henry cannot see anything. And his own feather explosion was merely a waking dream.

Henry quivers like a tuning fork. He is still facing the windshield.

'Tell me what's going on,' Jack says. 'I'm starting to worry about you.'

Henry opens his mouth to a crack that might accommodate a communion wafer, then closes it again. Another tremor runs through him.

'Hmm,' he says. 'This is harder than I thought.' Astonishingly, his dry, measured voice, the true voice of Henry Leyden, wobbles with a wide, helpless vibrato.

Jack slows the pickup to a crawl, begins to say something, and decides to wait.

'I hear my wife,' Henry says. 'At night, when I'm lying in bed. Around three, four in the morning. Rhoda's footsteps are moving around in the kitchen, they're coming up the stairs. I must be losing my mind.'

'How often does this happen?'

'How many times? I don't know, exactly. Three or four.'

'Do you get up and look for her? Call out her name?'

Henry's voice again sails up and down on the vibrato trampoline. 'I've done both those things. Because I was sure I heard her. Her *footsteps*, her way of walking, her *tread*. Rhoda's been gone for six years now. Pretty funny, huh? I'd think it was funny, if I didn't think I was going bats.'

'You call out her name,' Jack says. 'And you get out of bed and go downstairs.'

'Like a lunatic, like a madman. "Rhoda? Is that you, Rhoda?" Last night, I went all around the house. "Rhoda? Rhoda?" You'd think I was expecting her to answer.' Henry pays no attention to the tears that leak from beneath his aviator glasses and slip down his cheeks. 'And I was, that's the problem.'

'No one else was in the house,' Jack says. 'No signs of disturbance. Nothing misplaced or missing, or anything like that.'

'Not as far as I saw. Everything was still where it should have been. Right where I left it.' He raises a hand and wipes his face.

The entrance to Jack's looping driveway slides past on the right side of the cab.

'I'll tell you what I think,' Jack says, picturing Henry wandering through his darkened house. 'Six years ago, you went through all the grief business that happens when someone you love dies and leaves you, the denial, the bargaining, the anger, the pain, whatever, acceptance, that whole range of emotions, but afterward you still missed Rhoda. No one ever says you keep on missing the dead people you loved, but you do.'

'Now, that's profound,' Henry says. 'And comforting, too.'

'Don't interrupt. Weirdness happens. Believe me, I know what I'm talking about. Your mind rebels. It distorts the evidence, it gives false testimony. Who knows why? It just does.'

'In other words, you go batshit,' Henry says. 'I believe that is where we came in.'

'What I mean,' Jack says, 'is that people can have waking dreams. That's what is happening to you. It's nothing to worry about. All right, here's your drive, you're home.'

He turns into the grassy entrance and rolls up to the white farmhouse in which Henry and Rhoda Leyden had spent the fifteen lively years between their marriage and the discovery of Rhoda's liver cancer. For nearly two years after her death, Henry went wandering through his house every evening, turning on the lights.

'Waking dreams? Where'd you get that one?'

'Waking dreams aren't uncommon,' Jack says. 'Especially in people who never get enough sleep, like you.' *Or like me*, he silently adds. 'I'm not making this up, Henry. I've had one or two myself. One, anyhow.'

'Waking dreams,' Henry says in a different, considering tone of voice. 'Ivey-divey.'

'Think about it. We live in a rational world. People do not return from the dead. Everything happens for a reason, and the *reasons* are always rational. It's a matter of chemistry or coincidence. If they weren't rational, we'd never figure anything out, and we'd never know what was going on.'

'Even a blind man can see that,' Henry says. 'Thanks. Words to live by.' He gets out of the cab and closes the door. He moves away, steps back, and leans in through the window. 'Do you want to start on *Bleak House* tonight? I should get home about eight-thirty, something like that.'

'I'll turn up around nine.'

By way of parting, Henry says, 'Ding-dong.' He turns away, walks to his doorstep, and disappears into his house, which is of course unlocked. Around here, only parents lock their doors, and even that's a new development.

Jack reverses the pickup, swings down the drive and onto Norway Valley Road. He feels as though he has done a doubly good deed, for by helping Henry he has also helped himself. It's nice, how things turn out sometimes.

When he turns into his own long driveway, a peculiar rattle comes from the ashtray beneath his dashboard. He hears it again at the last curve, just before his house comes into view. The sound is not so much a rattle as a small, dull clunk. A button, a coin – something like that. He rolls to a stop at the side of his house, turns off the engine, and opens his door. On an afterthought, he reaches over and pulls out the ashtray.

What Jack finds nestled in the grooves at the bottom of the sliding tray, a tiny robin's egg, a robin's egg the size of an almond M&M, expels all the air from his body.

The little egg is so blue a blind man could see it.

Jack's trembling fingers pluck the egg from the ashtray. Staring at it, he leaves the cab and closes the door. Still staring at the egg, he finally remembers to breathe. His hand revolves on his wrist and releases the egg, which falls in a straight line to the grass. Deliberately, he lifts his foot and smashes it down onto the obscene blue speck. Without looking back, he pockets his keys and moves toward the dubious safety of his house.

Part Two

THE TAKING OF TYLER MARSHALL

5

We glimpsed a janitor on our whirlwind early-morning tour of Maxton Elder Care – do you happen to remember him? Baggy overalls? A wee bit thick in the gut? Dangling cigarette in spite of the NO SMOKING! LUNGS AT WORK! signs that have been posted every twenty feet or so along the patient corridors? A mop that looks like a clot of dead spiders? No? Don't apologize. It's easy enough to overlook Pete Wexler, a onetime nondescript youth (final grade average at French Landing High School: 79) who passed through a nondescript young manhood and has now reached the edge of what he expects to be a nondescript middle age. His only hobby is administering the occasional secret, savage pinch to the moldy oldies who fill his days with their grunts, nonsensical questions, and smells of gas and piss. The Alzheimer's assholes are the worst. He has been known to stub out the occasional cigarette on their scrawny backs or buttocks. He likes their strangled cries when the heat hits and the pain cores in. This small and ugly torture has a double-barreled effect: it wakes them up a little and satisfies something in him. Brightens his days, somehow. Refreshes the old outlook. Besides, who are they going to tell?

And oh God, there goes the worst of them now, shuffling slowly down the corridor of Daisy. Charles Burnside's mouth is agape, as is the back of his johnny. Pete has a better view of Burnside's scrawny, shit-smeared buttocks than he ever wanted. The chocolate stains go all the way down to the backs of his knees, by God. He's headed for the bathroom, but it's just a leetle bit late. A certain brown horse – call him Morning Thunder – has already bolted from its stall and no doubt galloped across Burny's sheets.

Thank God cleaning 'em up isn't my job, Pete thinks, and smirks around his cigarette. *Over to you, Butch.*

But the desk up there by the little boys' and girls' rooms is for the time being unattended. Butch Yerxa is going to miss the charming sight of Burny's dirty ass sailing by. Butch has apparently stepped out for a smoke, although Pete has told the idiot a hundred times that all those NO SMOKING signs mean nothing – Chipper Maxton could care less about who smoked where (or where the smokes were butted out, for that matter). The signs are just there to keep good old Drooler Manor in compliance with certain tiresome state laws.

Pete's smirk widens, and at that moment he looks a good deal like his son Ebbie, Tyler Marshall's sometime friend (it was Ebbie Wexler, in fact, who just gave Jack and Henry the finger). Pete is wondering whether he should go out and tell Butch he's got a little cleanup job in D18 – plus D18's occupant, of course – or if he should just let Butch discover Burny's latest mess on his own. Perhaps Burny will go back to his room and do a little fingerpainting, kind of spread the joy around. That would be good, but it would also be good to see Butch's face fall when Pete tells him—

'Pete.'

Oh no. Sandbagged by the bitch. She's a fine-looking

bitch, but a bitch is still a bitch. Pete stands where he is for a moment, thinking that maybe if he ignores her, she'll go away.

Vain hope.

'Pete.'

He turns. There is Rebecca Vilas, current squeeze of the big cheese. Today she is wearing a light red dress, perhaps in honor of Strawberry Fest!, and black high-heeled pumps, probably in honor of her own fine gams. Pete briefly imagines those fine gams wrapped around him, those high heels crossed at the small of his back and pointing like clock hands, then sees the cardboard box she's holding in her arms. Work for him, no doubt. Pete also notes the glinting ring on her finger, some sort of gemstone the size of a goddamn robin's egg, although considerably paler. He wonders, not for the first time, just what a woman does to earn a ring like that.

She stands there, tapping her foot, letting him have his look. Behind him, Charles Burnside continues his slow, tottery progress toward the men's. You'd think, looking at that old wreck with his scrawny legs and flyaway milkweed hair, that his running days were long behind him. But you'd be wrong. Terribly wrong.

'Miz Vilas?' Pete says at last.

'Common room, Pete. On the double. And how many times have you been told not to smoke in the patient wings?'

Before he can reply, she turns with a sexy little flirt of the skirt and starts off toward the Maxton common room, where that afternoon's Strawberry Fest! dance will be held.

Sighing, Pete props his mop against the wall and follows her.

Charles Burnside is now alone at the head of the Daisy corridor. The vacancy leaves his eyes and is replaced with a brilliant and feral gleam of intelligence. All at once he looks younger. All at once Burny the human shit machine is gone. In his place is Carl Bierstone, who reaped the young in Chicago with such savage efficiency.

Carl . . . and something else. Something not human.

He – *it* – grins.

On the unattended desk is a pile of paper weighed down with a round stone the size of a coffee cup. Written on the stone in small black letters is BUTCH'S PET ROCK.

Burny picks up Butch Yerxa's pet rock and walks briskly toward the men's room, still grinning.

In the common room, the tables have been arranged around the walls and covered with red paper cloths. Later, Pete will add small red lights (battery powered; no candles for the droolers, gosh, no). On the walls, great big cardboard strawberries have been taped up everywhere, some looking rather battered – they have been put up and taken down every July since Herbert Maxton opened this place at the end of the swingin' sixties. The linoleum floor is open and bare.

This afternoon and early evening, the moldy oldies who are still ambulatory and of a mind to do so will shuffle around out there to the big-band sounds of the thirties and forties, clinging to each other during the slow numbers and probably dampening their Depends with excitement at the end of the jitterbugs. (Three years ago a moldy oldie named Irving Christie had a minor heart attack after doing a particularly strenuous lindyhop to 'Don't Sit Under the Apple Tree with Anyone Else but Me.') Oh yes, the Strawberry Fest Hop is always exciting.

Rebecca has all by herself pushed together three wooden flats and covered them with a white cloth, creating the basis for Symphonic Stan's podium. In the corner stands a brilliantly chromed microphone with a large round head, a genuine antique from the thirties that saw service at the Cotton Club. It is one of Henry Leyden's prize possessions. Beside it is the tall, narrow carton in which it arrived yesterday. On the podium, beneath a beam decorated with red and white crepe and more cardboard strawberries, is a stepladder. Seeing it, Pete feels a moment's possessive jealousy. Rebecca Vilas has been in his closet. Trespassing bitch! If she stole any of his weed, by God—

Rebecca sets her carton down on the podium with an audible grunt, then straightens up. She brushes a lock of silky chestnut hair off one flushed cheek. It's only mid-morning, but the day is going to be a genuine Coulee Country scorcher. Air-condition your underwear and double up on the deodorant, folks, as George Rathbun has been known to bellow.

'Oi thought you'd never come, me foine bucko,' Rebecca says.

'Well, I'm here,' Pete says sullenly. 'Looks like you're doing fine without me.' He pauses, then adds: '*Foine.*' For Pete, this is quite a witticism. He walks forward and peers into the carton, which, like the one by the mike, is stamped PROPERTY OF HENRY LEYDEN. Inside the box is a small spotlight with an electrical cord wrapped around it, and a circular pink gel that is meant to turn the light the color of candy canes and sugar strawberries.

'What's this shit?' Pete asks.

Rebecca gives him a brilliant, dangerous smile. Even to a relatively dull fellow like Pete, the message of that smile is clear: you're on the edge of the gator pool, buddy; how many more steps do you want to take?

'Light,' she says. 'L-I-G-H-T. Hangs up there, on that

hook. H-O-O-K. It's something the deejay insists on. Says it gets him in the mood. M-O-O—'

'What happened to Weenie Erickson?' Pete grumbles. 'There was none of this shit with Weenie. He played the goddamn records for two hours, had a few out of his hip flask, then shut it down.'

'He moved,' Rebecca says indifferently. 'Racine, I think.'

'Well—' Pete is looking up, studying the beam with its intertwined fluffs of red and white crepe. 'I don't see no hook, Miz Vilas.'

'Christ on a bicycle,' she says, and mounts the stepladder. 'Here. Are you blind?'

Pete, most definitely not blind, has rarely been so grateful for his sighted state. From his position below her, he's got a clear view of her thighs, the red lace froth of her panties, and the twin curves of her buttocks, now nicely tensed as she stands on the fifth step of the ladder.

She looks down at him, sees the stunned look on his face, notes the direction of his sight line. Her expression softens a bit. As her dear mother so wisely observed, some men are just fools for a flash of panty.

'Pete. Earth to Pete.'

'Uh?' He looks up at her, mouth agape, a dot of spittle on his lower lip.

'There is no hook of any kind on my underwear, I'm sure of that as of few things in life. But if you will direct your gaze upward . . . to my hand instead of my ass . . .'

He looks up, face still dazed, and sees one red-tipped nail (Rebecca is a through-and-through vision in strawberry red today, no doubt about it) tapping a hook that just gleams out of the crepe, like a fisherman's hook gleaming murderously out of a gaudy lure.

'Hook,' she says. 'Attach gel to light, attach light to hook. Light becomes warm pink spotlight, as per deejay's explicit instructions. You get-um message, Kemo sabe?'

'Uh . . . yeah . . .'

'Then, if I may coin a phrase, will you please get it up?'

She comes down the ladder, deciding Pete Wexler has gotten the biggest free show he can reasonably expect for one lousy chore. And Pete, who has already achieved one erection, pulls Symphonic Stan's pink pinspot out of its box and prepares to achieve another. As he mounts the stepladder, his crotch rises past Rebecca's face. She notes the bulge there and gnaws the inside of one cheek to suppress a smile. Men are fools, all right. *Lovable* fools, some of them, but fools, all the same. It's just that some fools can afford rings and trips and midnight suppers at Milwaukee nightspots, and some fools cannot.

With some fools, the best you can get them to do is put up a lousy light.

'Wait up, you guys!' Ty Marshall calls. 'Ebbie! Ronnie! T.J.! Wait *up*!'

Over his shoulder, Ebbie Wexler (who really *does* look like Nancy's not-too-bright boyfriend, Sluggo) calls back: 'Catch us, slowpoke!'

'Yeah!' Ronnie Metzger yells. 'Catch us, po-sloke!' Ronnie, a kid with a lot of hours in the speech-therapy room ahead of him, looks back over his own shoulder, almost crashes his bike into a parking meter, and just manages to swerve around it. Then they are fleeing, the three of them filling the sidewalk with their bikes (God help the pedestrian headed the other way), their racing shadows fleeing beside them.

Tyler considers a final catch-up dash, then decides his

legs are just too tired. His mother and father say that he *will* catch up in time, that he's just small for his age, but brother, Ty has his doubts. And he has had increasing doubts about Ebbie, Ronnie, and T.J., too. Are they really worth keeping up *with*? (If Judy Marshall knew of these doubts, she would stand and applaud – she has wondered for the last two years when her bright and thoughtful son will finally tire of hanging out with such a bunch of losers . . . what she calls 'low-raters.')

'Suck an elf,' Ty says disconsolately – he has picked up this harmless vulgarity from Sci-Fi Channel reruns of a mini-series called *The 10th Kingdom* – and dismounts his bike. There's no real reason to speed after them, anyway; he knows where he'll find them, in the parking lot of the 7-Eleven, drinking Slurpees and trading Magic cards. This is another problem Tyler is having with his friends. These days he'd much rather trade baseball cards. Ebbie, Ronnie, and T.J. could care less about the Cardinals, the Indians, the Red Sox, and the Brew Crew. Ebbie has gone so far as to say that baseball is gay, a comment Ty considers stupid (almost pitiable) rather than outrageous.

He walks his bike slowly up the sidewalk, catching his breath. Here is the intersection of Chase and Queen streets. Ebbie calls Queen Street Queer Street. Of course. No surprise there. And isn't that a big part of the problem? Tyler is a boy who likes surprises; Ebbie Wexler is a boy who doesn't. Which makes their opposite reactions to the music pouring out of the pickup a little earlier that morning perfectly predictable.

Tyler pauses at the corner, looking down Queen Street. There are shaggy hedges on both sides. Above those on the right rise a number of interconnected red roofs. The old folks' home. Beside the main gate, some sort of sign has been placed. Curious, Tyler remounts his bike and rides slowly down the sidewalk for a look. The longest branches of the hedge beside him whisper against the handlebar of his bike.

The sign turns out to be a great big strawberry. TODAY IS STRAWBERRY FEST!!! is written below it. What, Ty Marshall wonders, is a Strawberry Fest? A party, something strictly for old folks? It's a question, but not a very interesting one. After mulling it over for a few seconds, he turns his bike and prepares to ride back down to Chase Street.

Charles Burnside enters the men's room at the head of the Daisy corridor, still grinning and clutching Butch's pet rock. To his right is a line of sinks with a mirror over each one – they are the sort of metal mirrors one finds in the toilets of lower-class bars and saloons. In one of these, Burny sees his own grinning reflection. In another, the one closest the window, he sees a small boy in a Milwaukee Brewers T-shirt. The boy is standing astride his bike, just outside the gate, reading the Strawberry Fest! sign.

Burny begins to drool. There is nothing discreet about it, either. Burny drools like a wolf in a fairy tale, white curds of foamy spit leaking from the corners of his mouth and flowing over the slack, liver-colored roll of his lower lip. The drool runs down his chin like a stream of soapsuds. He wipes at it absently with the back of one gnarled hand and shakes it to the floor in a splatter, never taking his eyes from the mirror. The boy in the mirror is not one of this creature's poor lost babies – Ty Marshall has lived in French Landing his whole life and knows exactly where he is – but he *could* be. He could very easily become lost, and wind up in a certain room. A certain cell. Or trudging toward a strange horizon on burning, bleeding footsies.

Especially if Burny has his way. He will have to move

fast, but as we have already noted, Charles Burnside can, with the proper motivation, move very fast indeed.

'Gorg,' he says to the mirror. He speaks this nonsense word in a perfectly clear, perfectly flat midwestern accent. 'Come, Gorg.'

And without waiting to see what comes next – he *knows* what comes next – Burny turns and walks toward the line of four toilet stalls. He steps into the second from the left and closes the door.

Tyler has just remounted his bike when the hedge rustles ten feet from the Strawberry Fest! sign. A large black crow shrugs its way out of the greenery and onto the Queen Street sidewalk. It regards the boy with a lively, intelligent eye. It stands with its black legs spread, opens its beak, and speaks. 'Gorg!'

Tyler looks at it, beginning to smile, not sure he heard this but ready to be delighted (at ten, he's always ready to be delighted, always primed to believe the unbelievable). 'What? Did you say something?'

The crow flutters its glossy wings and cocks its head in a way that renders the ugly almost charming.

'Gorg! Ty!'

The boy laughs. It said his name! The crow said his name!

He dismounts his bike, puts it on the kickstand, and takes a couple of steps toward the crow. Thoughts of Amy St Pierre and Johnny Irkenham are – unfortunately – the furthest things from his mind.

He thinks the crow will surely fly away when he steps toward it, but it only flutters its wings a little and takes a slide-step toward the bushy darkness of the hedge.

'Did you say my name?'

'Gorg! Ty! Abbalah!'

For a moment Ty's smile falters. That last word is almost familiar to him, and the associations, although faint, are not exactly pleasant. It makes him think of his mother, for some reason. Then the crow says his name again; surely it is saying *Ty*.

Tyler takes another step away from Queen Street and toward the black bird. The crow takes a corresponding step, sidling closer still to the bulk of the hedge. There is no one on the street; this part of French Landing is dreaming in the morning sunshine. Ty takes another step toward his doom, and all the worlds tremble.

Ebbie, Ronnie, and T.J. come swaggering out of the 7-Eleven, where the raghead behind the counter has just served them blueberry Slurpees (*raghead* is just one of many pejorative terms Ebbie has picked up from his dad). They also have fresh packs of Magic cards, two packs each.

Ebbie, his lips already smeared blue, turns to T.J. 'Go on downstreet and get the slowpoke.'

T.J. looks injured. 'Why me?'

'Because Ronnie bought the cards, dumbwit. Go on, hurry up.'

'Why do we need him, Ebbie?' Ronnie asks. He leans against the bike rack, noshing on the cold, sweet chips of ice.

'Because I say so,' Ebbie replies loftily. The fact is, Tyler Marshall usually has money on Fridays. In fact, Tyler has money almost every day. His parents are loaded. Ebbie, who is being raised (if you can call it that) by a single father who has a crappy janitor's job, has already conceived a vague hate for Tyler on this account; the first humiliations aren't far away, and the first beatings will follow soon after. But now all he wants is more Magic cards, a third pack for each of them. The fact that Tyler doesn't even *like* Magic that much will only make getting him to pony up that much sweeter.

But first they have to get the little slowpoke up here. Or the little po-sloke, as mush-mouthed Ronnie calls him. Ebbie likes that, and thinks he will start using it. Po-sloke. A good word. Makes fun of Ty and Ronnie at the same time. Two for the price of one.

'Go on, T.J. Unless you want an Indian burn.'

T.J. doesn't. Ebbie Wexler's Indian burns hurt like a mad bastard. He gives a theatrical sigh, backs his bike out of the rack, mounts it, and rides back down the mild slope of the hill, holding a handlebar in one hand and his Slurpee in the other. He expects to see Ty right away, probably walking his bike because he's *just . . . so . . . tiyyy-urd*, but Ty doesn't seem to be on Chase Street at all – what's up with that?

T.J. pedals a little faster.

In the men's room, we are now looking at the line of toilet stalls. The door of the one second from the left is closed. The other three stand ajar on their chrome hinges. Beneath the closed door, we see a pair of gnarled, veiny ankles rising from a pair of filthy slippers.

A voice cries out with surprising strength. It is a young man's voice, hoarse, hungry, and angry. It echoes flatly back from the tile walls: '*Abbalah! Abbalah-doon! Munshun gorg!*'

Suddenly the toilets flush. Not just the one in the closed cubicle but all of them. Across the room the urinals also flush, their chromed handles dipping in perfect synchronicity. Water runs down their curved porcelain surfaces.

When we look back from the urinals to the toilets, we see that the dirty slippers – and the feet that were in them

– are gone. And for the first time we have actually *heard* the sound of slippage, a kind of hot exhale, the sort of sound one hears escaping one's lungs when waking from a nightmare at two in the morning.

Ladies and gentlemen, Charles Burnside has left the building.

The crow has backed right up against the hedge now. Still it regards Tyler with its bright, eerie eyes. Tyler steps toward it, feeling hypnotized.

'Say my name again,' he breathes. 'Say my name again and you can go.'

'*Ty!*' the crow croaks obligingly, then gives its wings a little shake and slips into the hedge. For a moment Tyler can still see it, a mixture of shiny black in the shiny green, and then it's gone.

'Holy crow!' Tyler says. He realizes what he's said and gives a small, shaky laugh. Did it happen? It did, didn't it?

He leans closer to where the crow reentered the hedge, thinking if it shed a feather he will take it for a souvenir, and when he does, a scrawny white arm shoots out through the green and seizes him unerringly by the neck. Tyler has time to give a single terrified squawk, and then he is dragged through the hedge. One of his sneakers is pulled off by the short, stiff branches. From the far side there is a single guttural, greedy cry – it might have been '*Boy!*' – and then a thud, the sound of a pet rock coming down on a small boy's head, perhaps. Then there's nothing but the distant drone of a lawn mower and the closer drone of a bee.

The bee is bumbling around the flowers on the far side of the hedge, the Maxton side. There is nothing else to be seen over there but green grass, and closer to the building, the tables where the elderly inhabitants will, at noon, sit down to the Strawberry Fest Picnic.

Tyler Marshall is gone.

T. J. Renniker coasts to a stop at the corner of Chase and Queen. His Slurpee is dripping dark blue juice over his wrist, but he barely notices. Halfway down Queen Street he sees Ty's bike, leaning neatly over on its kickstand, but no Ty.

Moving slowly – he has a bad feeling about this, somehow – T.J. rides over to the bike. At some point he becomes aware that what was a Slurpee has now dissolved into a soggy cup of melting goop. He tosses it into the gutter.

It's Ty's ride, all right. No mistaking that red twenty-inch Schwinn with the ape-hanger handlebars and the green Milwaukee Bucks decal on the side. The bike, and—

Lying on its side by the hedge that creates a border between the world of the old folks and the world of regular people, the *real* people, T.J. sees a single Reebok sneaker. Scattered around it are a number of shiny green leaves. One feather protrudes from the sneaker.

The boy stares at this sneaker with wide eyes. T.J. may not be as smart as Tyler, but he's a few watts brighter than Ebbie Wexler, and it's easy enough for him to imagine Tyler being dragged through the hedge, leaving his bike behind . . . and one sneaker . . . one lonely, overturned sneaker . . .

'Ty?' he calls. 'Are you jokin' around? Because if you are, you better stop. I'll tell Ebbie to give you the biggest Indian burn you ever had.'

No answer. Ty isn't joking around. T.J. somehow knows it.

Thoughts of Amy St Pierre and Johnny Irkenham suddenly explode in T.J.'s mind. He hears (or imagines he hears) stealthy footsteps behind the hedge: the Fisherman, having secured dinner, has come back for dessert!

T.J. tries to scream and cannot. His throat has shrunk down to a pinhole. Instead of screaming, he hunches himself over the handlebars of his bike and begins pedaling. He swerves off the sidewalk and into the street, wanting to get away from the dark bulk of that hedge just as fast as he can. When he leaves the curb, the front tire of his Huffy bike squashes through the remains of his Slurpee. As he pedals toward Chase Street, bent over his handle-bars like a Grand Prix racer, he leaves a dark and shiny track on the pavement. It looks like blood. Somewhere nearby, a crow caws. It sounds like laughter.

16 Robin Hood Lane: we've been here before, as the chorus girl said to the archbishop. Peek through the kitchen window and we see Judy Marshall, asleep in the rocking chair in the corner. There's a book in her lap, the John Grisham novel we last saw on her bedside table. Sitting beside her on the floor is half a cup of cold coffee. Judy managed to read ten pages before dozing off. We shouldn't blame Mr Grisham's narrative skills; Judy had a hard night last night, and it's not the first. It's been over two months since she last got more than two hours of sleep in one stretch. Fred knows something is wrong with his wife, but has no idea how deep it runs. If he did, he would be a lot more than frightened. Soon, God help him, he is going to have a better picture of her mental state.

Now she begins to moan thickly, and to turn her head from side to side. Those nonsense words begin to issue from her again. Most of them are too sleep-fuzzy to understand, but we catch *abbalah* and *gorg*.

Her eyes suddenly flash open. They are a brilliant, royal

blue in the morning light, which fills the kitchen with summer's dusty gold.

'*Ty!*' she gasps, and her feet give a convulsive waking jerk. She looks at the clock over the stove. It is twelve minutes past nine, and everything seems twisted, as it so often does when we sleep deeply but not well or long. She has sucked some miserable, not-quite-a-nightmare dream after her like mucusy strings of afterbirth: men with fedora hats pulled down so as to shadow their faces, walking on long R. Crumb legs that ended in big round-toed R. Crumb shoes, sinister keep on truckin' sharpies who moved too fast against a city background – Milwaukee? Chicago? – and in front of a baleful orange sky. The dream's sound track was the Benny Goodman band playing 'King Porter Stomp,' the one her father had always played when he was getting a little shot, and the feeling of the dream had been a terrible darkwood mix of terror and grief: awful things had happened, but the worst was waiting.

There's none of the relief people usually feel upon waking from bad dreams – the relief she herself had felt when she had been younger and . . . and . . .

'And sane,' she says in a croaky, just-woke-up voice. '"King Porter Stomp." Think of that.' To her it had always sounded like the music you heard in the old cartoons, the ones where mice in white gloves ran in and out of ratholes with dizzying, feverish speed. Once, when her father was dancing her around to that one, she had felt something hard poking against her. Something in his pants. After that, when he put on his dance music, she tried to be somewhere else.

'Quit it,' she says in the same croaky voice. It's a crow's voice, and it occurs to her that there was a crow in her dream. Sure, you bet. The Crow Gorg.

'Gorg means death,' she says, and licks her dry upper

lip without realizing it. Her tongue comes out even farther, and on the return swipe the tip licks across her nostrils, warm and wet and somehow comforting. 'Over there, *gorg* means death. Over there in the—'

Faraway is the word she doesn't say. Before she can, she sees something on the kitchen table that wasn't there before. It's a wicker box. A sound is coming from it, some low sleepy sound.

Distress worms into her lower belly, making her bowels feel loose and watery. She knows what a box like that is called: a creel. It's a fisherman's creel.

There is a fisherman in French Landing these days. A bad fisherman.

'Ty?' she calls, but of course there is no answer. The house is empty except for her. Fred is at work, and Ty will be out playing – you bet. It's half-past July, the heart of summer vacation, and Ty will be rolling around the town, doing all the Ray Bradbury–August Derleth things boys do when they've got the whole endless summer day to do them in. But he won't be alone; Fred has talked with him about buddying up until the Fisherman is caught, at *least* until then, and so has she. Judy has no great liking for the Wexler kid (the Metzger or Renniker kids, either), but there's safety in numbers. Ty probably isn't having any great cultural awakenings this summer, but at least—

'At least he's safe,' she says in her croaky Crow Gorg voice. Yet the box that has appeared on the kitchen table during her nap seems to deny that, to negate the whole concept of safety. Where did it come from? And what is the white thing on top of it?

'A note,' she says, and gets up. She crosses the short length of floor between the rocker and the table like someone still in a dream. The note is a piece of paper, folded over. Written across the half she can see is Sweet Judy Blue Eyes. In college, just before meeting Fred, she had a boyfriend who used to call her that. She asked him to stop – it was annoying, sappy – and when he kept forgetting (on purpose, she suspected), she dropped him like a rock. Now here it is again, that stupid nickname, mocking her.

Judy turns on the sink tap without taking her eyes from the note, fills her cupped hand with cold water, and drinks. A few drops fall on Sweet Judy Blue Eyes and the name smears at once. Written in fountain-pen ink? How antique! Who writes with a fountain pen these days?

She reaches for the note, then draws back. The sound from inside the box is louder now. It's a humming sound. It—

'It's flies,' she says. Her throat has been refreshed by the water and her voice isn't so croaky, but to herself, Judy still sounds like the Crow Gorg. 'You know the sound of flies.'

Get the note.

Don't want to.

Yes, but you NEED to! Now get it! What happened to your GUTS, you little chickenshit?

Good question. *Fucking* good question. Judy's tongue comes out, slathers her upper lip and philtrum. Then she takes the note and unfolds it.

> Sorry there is only one 'kiddie-knee'
> (kindney). The other I fryed and ate.
> It was very good!
>
> The Fisherman

The nerves in Judy Marshall's fingers, palms, wrists, and forearms suddenly shut down. The color drops so completely from her face that the blue veins in her cheeks become visible.

It's surely a miracle that she doesn't pass out. The note drops from her fingers and goes seesawing to the floor. Shrieking her son's name over and over again, she throws back the lid of the fisherman's creel.

Inside are shiny red coils of intestine, crawling with flies. There are the wrinkled sacs of lungs and the fist-sized pump that was a child's heart. There is the thick purple pad of a liver . . . and one kidney. This mess of guts is crawling with flies and all the world is gorg, is gorg, is gorg.

In the sunny stillness of her kitchen Judy Marshall now begins to howl, and it is the sound of madness finally broken free of its flimsy cage, madness unbound.

Butch Yerxa intended to go in after a single smoke – there's always a lot to do on Strawberry Fest! days (although kind-hearted Butch doesn't hate the little artificial holiday the way Pete Wexler does). Then Petra English, an orderly from Asphodel, wandered over and they started talking motorcycles, and before you know it twenty minutes have passed.

He tells Petra he has to go, she tells him to keep the shiny side up and the rubber side down, and Butch slips back in through the door to an unpleasant surprise. There is Charles Burnside, starkers, standing beside the desk with his hand on the rock Butch uses as a paperweight. (His son made it in camp last year – painted the words on it, anyway – and Butch thinks it's cute as hell.) Butch has nothing against the residents – certainly he would give Pete Wexler a pasting if he knew about the thing with the cigarettes, never mind just reporting him – but he doesn't like them touching his things. Especially this guy, who is fairly nasty when he has his few wits about him. Which he does now. Butch can see it in his eyes. The real Charles Burnside has come up for air, perhaps in honor of Strawberry Fest!

And speaking of strawberries, Burny has apparently been into them already. There are traces of red on his lips and tucked into the deep folds at the corners of his mouth.

Butch barely looks at this, though. There are other stains on Burny. Brown ones.

'Want to take your hand off that, Charles?' he asks.

'Off what?' Burny asks, then adds: 'Asswipe.'

Butch doesn't want to say *Off my pet rock*, that sounds stupid. 'Off my paperweight.'

Burny looks down at the rock, which he has just replaced (there was a little blood and hair on it when he emerged from the toilet stall, but cleanup is what bathroom sinks are for). He drops his hand from it and just stands there. 'Clean me up, bozo. I shit myself.'

'So I see. But first tell me if you've gone and spread your crap around the kitchen. And I know you've been down there, so don't lie.'

'Warshed my hands first,' Burny says, and shows them. They are gnarled, but pink and clean for all that. Even the nails are clean. He certainly has washed them. He then adds: 'Jackoff.'

'Come on down to the bathroom with me,' Butch says. 'The jackoff asswipe will get you cleaned up.'

Burny snorts, but comes willingly enough.

'You ready for the dance this afternoon?' Butch asks him, just to be saying something. 'Got your dancing shoes all polished, big boy?'

Burny, who can surprise you sometimes when he's actually home, smiles, showing a few yellow teeth. Like his lips, they are stained with red. 'Yowza, I'm ready to rock,' he says.

★

Although Ebbie's face doesn't show it, he listens with growing unease to T.J.'s story about Tyler Marshall's abandoned bike and sneaker. Ronnie's face, on the other hand, shows *plenty* of unease.

'So what're we gonna do, Ebbie?' T.J. asks when he's done. He's finally getting his breath back from his rapid pedal up the hill.

'What do you mean, what're we gonna do?' Ebbie says. 'Same things we were gonna do anyway, go downstreet, see what we can find for returnable bottles. Go down the park and trade Magics.'

'But . . . but what if—'

'Shut your yap,' Ebbie says. He knows what two words T.J. is about to say, and he doesn't want to hear them. His dad says it's bad luck to toss a hat on the bed, and Ebbie never does it. If that's bad luck, mentioning some freako killer's name has got to be twice as bad.

But then that idiot Ronnie Metzger goes and says it anyway . . . sort of. 'But Ebbie, what if it's the Misherfun? What if Ty got grabbed by the—'

'Shut the fuck up!' Ebbie says, and draws back his fist as if to hit the damn mushmouth.

At that moment the raghead clerk pops out of the 7-Eleven like a turbaned jack out of his box. 'I want none of that talk here!' he cries. 'You go now, do your filthy-talk another place! Or I call police!'

Ebbie starts to pedal slowly away, in a direction that will take him farther from Queer Street (under his breath he mutters *dune coon*, another charming term he has learned from his father), and the other two boys follow him. When they have put a block between them and the 7-Eleven, Ebbie stops and faces the other two, both his gut and his jaw jutting.

'He rode off on his own half an hour ago,' he says.

'*Huh?*' says T.J.

'Who did what?' says Ronnie.

'Ty Marshall. If anyone asks, he rode off on his own half an hour ago. When we were . . . ummm . . .' Ebbie casts his mind back, something that's hard for him because he has had so little practice. In ordinary circumstances, the present is all Ebbie Wexler needs.

'When we were looking in the window of the Allsorts?' T.J. asks timidly, hoping he isn't buying himself one of Ebbie's ferocious Indian burns.

Ebbie looks at him blankly for a moment, then smiles. T.J. relaxes. Ronnie Metzger only goes on looking bewildered. With a baseball bat in his hands or a pair of hockey skates on his feet, Ronnie is prince of all he surveys. The rest of the time he's pretty much at sea.

'That's right,' Ebbie says, 'yeah. We was lookin' in the window of Schmitt's, then that truck came along, the one playin' the punk-ass music, and then Ty said he hadda split.'

'Where'd he have to go?' T.J. asks.

Ebbie isn't bright, but he is possessed of what might be termed 'low cunning.' He knows instinctively that the best story is a *short* story – the less there is, the smaller the chance that someone will trip you up with an inconsistency. 'He didn't tell us that. He just said he hadda go.'

'He didn't go anywhere,' Ronnie says. 'He just got behind because he's a . . .' He pauses, arranging the word, and this time it comes out right. 'Slowpoke.'

'You never mind that,' Ebbie says. 'What if the . . . what if *that guy* got him, you dummocks? You want people sayin' it was because he couldn't keep up? That he got killed or somethin' because we left him behind? You want people sayin' it was our fault?'

'Gee,' Ronnie says. 'You don't really think the Misherfun – *Fisherman* – got Ty, do you?'

'I don't know and I don't care,' Ebbie says, 'but I don't mind it that he's gone. He was startin' to piss me off.'

'Oh.' Ronnie contrives to look both vacant and satisfied. *What a dummocks he is*, Ebbie marvels. *What a total and complete dummocks*. And if you didn't believe it, just think of how Ronnie, who's as strong as a horse, allows Ebbie to give him Indian burn after Indian burn. A day will probably come when Ronnie realizes he doesn't have to put up with that anymore, and on that day he may well pound Ebbie into the ground like a human tent peg, but Ebbie doesn't worry about such things; he's even worse at casting his mind forward than he is at casting it back.

'Ronnie,' Ebbie says.

'What?'

'Where were we when Tyler took off?'

'Um . . . Schmitt's Allsorts?'

'Right. And where'd he go?'

'Didn't say.'

Ebbie sees that for Ronnie this is already becoming the truth and is satisfied. He turns to T.J. 'You got it?'

'I got it.'

'Then let's go.'

They pedal off. The dummocks pulls a little ahead of Ebbie and T.J. as they roll along the tree-lined street, and Ebbie allows this. He swings his bike a little closer to T.J.'s and says: 'You see anything else back there? Anybody? Like a guy?'

T.J. shakes his head. 'Just his bike and his sneaker.' He pauses, remembering as hard as he can. 'There were some leaves scattered around. From the hedge. And I think there might have been a feather. Like a crow feather?'

Ebbie dismisses this. He is grappling with the question

of whether or not the Fisherman has actually come close to him this morning, close enough to snatch one of his buddies. There is a bloodthirsty part of him that likes the idea, that relishes the thought of some shadowy, no-face monster killing the increasingly annoying Ty Marshall and eating him for lunch. There is also a childish part of him that is terrified of the boogeyman (this part will be in charge tonight as he lies awake in his room, looking at shadows that seem to take form and slink ever closer around his bed). And there is the older-than-his-years part of him, which has taken instinctive and immediate measures to avoid the eye of authority, should Tyler's disappearance turn into what Ebbie's father calls 'a fuckarow.'

But mostly, as with Dale Gilbertson and Ty's father, Fred, there is a continent of fundamental disbelief inside of Ebbie Wexler. He simply cannot believe that anything *final* has happened to Tyler. Not even after Amy St Pierre and Johnny Irkenham, who was carved into pieces and hung up in an old henhouse. These are kids of whom Ebbie has heard on the evening news, fictions from the Land of TV. He didn't know Amy or Johnny, so they could have died, just as make-believe people were always dying in the movies and on TV. Ty is different. Ty was just here. He talked to Ebbie, Ebbie talked to him. In Ebbie's mind, this equals immortality. Or *should*. If Ty could be snatched by the Fisherman, any kid could be snatched. Including him. Hence, like Dale and Fred, he just doesn't believe it. His most secret and fundamental heart, the part of him that assures the rest of him that everything is fine on Planet Ebbie, denies the Fisherman and all his works.

T.J. says: 'Ebbie, do you think—'

'Nah,' Ebbie says. 'He'll turn up. Come on, let's go to the park. We can look for cans and bottles later.'

★

Fred Marshall has left his sport coat and tie in his office, rolled up his sleeves, and is helping Rod Tisbury unpack a new Hiler rototiller. It's the first of the new Hiler line, and it's a beaut.

'I've been waiting for a gadget like this twenty years or more,' Rod says. He expertly inserts the wide end of his crowbar at the top of the big crate, and one of the wooden sides falls to the concrete floor of the maintenance garage with a flat clap. Rod is Goltz's chief mechanic, and out here in maintenance he is king. 'It's gonna work for the small farmer; it's gonna work for the town gardener, as well. If you can't sell a dozen of these by fall, you're not doing your job.'

'I'll sell twenty by the end of August,' Fred says with perfect confidence. All his worries have been temporarily swept away by this splendid little green machine, which can do a hell of a lot more than rototill; there are a number of sexy attachments that snap in and out as easily as the lining in a fall jacket. He wants to start it up, listen to it run. That two-cylinder engine looks pretty sweet.

'Fred?'

He looks around impatiently. It's Ina Gaitskill, Ted Goltz's secretary and the dealership receptionist. 'What?'

'You've got a call on line one.' She points across the floor – alive with clanging machinery and the noisy whir of pneumatic screwdrivers loosening bolts on an old Case tractor – to the phone on the wall, where several lights are blinking.

'Can you take a message, Ina? I was going to help Rod get a battery in this little beast and then—'

'I think you should take the call. It's a woman named Enid Purvis. A neighbor of yours?'

For a moment Fred blanks, and then his salesman's mind, which stores up names compulsively, comes to his rescue. Enid

Purvis. Wife of Deke. Corner of Robin Hood and Maid Marian. He saw Deke just this morning. They waved to each other.

At the same time, he becomes aware that Ina's eyes are too big and her normally generous mouth is too small. She looks worried.

'What is it?' Fred asks. 'Ina, what is it?'

'I don't know.' Then, reluctantly: 'Something about your wife.'

'Better take it, hoss,' Rod says, but Fred is already crossing the oil-stained concrete floor to the phone.

He arrives home ten minutes after leaving Goltz's, peeling out of the employees' parking lot and laying rubber like a teenager. The worst part had been Enid Purvis's calm and careful delivery, how hard she'd been trying not to sound frightened.

She had been walking Potsie past the Marshall house, she said, when she heard Judy scream. Not once, but twice. Of course Enid had done what any good neighbor would, God bless her: gone up to the door, rapped, then pushed open the letter slot and called through it. If there had been no answer, she told Fred, she probably would have phoned the police. She wouldn't even have gone back home to do it; she would have crossed the street to the Plotskys' house and called from there. But—

'I'm all right,' Judy had called back, and then she had laughed. The laugh was shrill, ending in a tittery gasp. Enid had found this laugh somehow even more upsetting than the screams. 'It was all a dream. Even Ty was a dream.'

'Did you cut yourself, dear?' Enid had called through the letter slot. 'Did you fall down?'

'There was no creel,' Judy had called back. She might have said *keel*, but Enid was quite sure it was *creel*. 'I dreamed that, too.' Then, Enid reluctantly told Fred, Judy Marshall had begun crying. It had been very upsetting, listening to that sound come to her through the letter slot. It had even made the dog whine.

Enid had called through one more time, asking if she could come in and make sure Judy wasn't hurt.

'Go away!' Judy had called back. In the midst of her crying, she'd laughed again – an angry, distracted laugh. 'You're a dream, too. This whole world is a dream.' Then there had been the sound of shattering glass, as if she had struck a coffee mug or water tumbler and knocked it to the floor. Or thrown it at the wall.

'I didn't call the police, because she sounded all right,' Enid told Fred (Fred standing with the phone jammed up against one ear and his hand plastered over the other to cut out all the yammering mechanical sounds, which he ordinarily enjoys and which at that moment seemed to go into his head like chrome spikes). '*Physically* all right, anyway. But Fred . . . I think you ought to go home and check on her.'

All of Judy's recent oddities went through his mind in a whirl. So did Pat Skarda's words. *Mental dysfunction . . . We hear people say 'So-and-so snapped,' but there are usually signs . . .*

And he has *seen* the signs, hasn't he?

Seen them and done nothing.

Fred parks his car, a sensible Ford Explorer, in the driveway and hurries up the steps, already calling his wife's name. There is no answer. Even when he has stepped through the front door (he pushes it open so hard the brass letter slot gives a nonsensical little clack), there is no answer. The air-conditioned interior of the house feels too cold on his skin and he realizes he's sweating.

'Judy? Jude?'

Still no answer. He hurries down the hall to the kitchen,

where he is most apt to find her if he comes home for something in the middle of the day.

The kitchen is sun-washed and empty. The table and the counter are clean; the appliances gleam; two coffee cups have been placed in the dish drainer, winking sun from their freshly washed surfaces. More sun winks from a heap of broken glass in the corner. Fred sees a flower decal on one piece and realizes it was the vase on the windowsill.

'Judy?' he calls again. He can feel the blood hammering in his throat and at his temples.

She doesn't answer him, but he hears her upstairs, beginning to sing.

'Rock-a-bye baby . . . on the treetop . . . when the wind blows . . .'

Fred recognizes it, and instead of feeling relieved at the sound of her voice, his flesh goes even colder. She used to sing it to Tyler when their son was little. Ty's lullabye. Fred hasn't heard that particular ditty come out of her mouth in years.

He goes back down the hall to the stairs, now seeing what he missed on his first trip. The Andrew Wyeth print, *Christina's World*, has been taken down and set against the baseboard heater. The wallpaper below the picture hook has been scraped away in several places, revealing the plasterboard beneath. Fred, colder than ever, knows that Judy did this. It isn't intuition, exactly; not deduction, either. Call it the telepathy of the long married.

Floating down from above, beautiful and on-key yet at the same time perfectly empty: '. . . *the cradle will rock. When the bough breaks, the cradle will fall* . . .'

Fred is up the stairs two at a time, calling her name.

The upper hall is a scary mess. This is where they have hung the gallery of their past: Fred and Judy outside Madison

Shoes, a blues club they sometimes went to when there was nothing interesting going on at the Chocolate Watchband; Fred and Judy dancing the first dance at their wedding reception while their folks happily looked on; Judy in a hospital bed, exhausted but smiling, holding the wrapped bundle that was Ty; the photo of the Marshall family farm that she always sniffed at; more.

Most of these framed photographs have been taken down. Some, like the one of the farm, have been *thrown* down. Glass litters the hall in sparkling sprays. And she has been at the wallpaper behind half a dozen. In the spot where the picture of Judy and Ty in the hospital had hung, the paper has been torn almost completely away, and he can see where she scraped at the wallboard beneath. Some of the scratches are dappled with drying spots of blood.

'Judy! *Judy!*'

Tyler's door stands open. Fred sprints the length of the upstairs hall with glass crunching under his loafers.

'*. . . and down will come Tyler, cradle and all.*'

'Judy! Ju—'

He stands in the door, all words temporarily knocked out of him.

Ty's room looks like the aftermath of a rough search in a detective movie. The drawers have been yanked out of his bureau and lie everywhere, most overturned. The bureau itself has been pulled away from the wall. Summer clothes are spread hell to breakfast – jeans and T-shirts and underwear and white athletic socks. The closet door is open and more clothes have been struck from the hangers; that same spousal telepathy tells him she tore Ty's slacks and button-up shirts down so she could make sure nothing was behind them. The coat of Tyler's only suit hangs askew from the closet's doorknob. His posters have been pulled from the walls; Mark McGwire has been torn in half. In every case but one she has left the wallpaper behind the posters alone, but the one exception is a beaut. Behind the rectangle where the poster of the castle hung (COME BACK TO THE AULD SOD), the wallpaper has been almost entirely stripped away. There are more streaks of blood on the wallboard beneath.

Judy Marshall sits on the bare mattress of her son's bed. The sheets are heaped in the corner, along with the pillow. The bed itself has been yanked away from the wall. Judy's head is down. He can't see her face – her hair is screening it – but she's wearing shorts and he can see dapples and streaks of blood on her tanned thighs. Her hands are clasped below her knees, out of sight, and Fred is glad. He doesn't want to see how badly she has hurt herself until he has to. His heart is hammering in his chest, his nervous system is redlining with adrenaline overload, and his mouth tastes like a burnt fuse.

She begins to sing the chorus of Ty's lullabye again and he can't stand it. 'Judy, no,' he says, going to her through the strewn minefield that was, only last night when he came in to give Ty a good-night kiss, a reasonably neat little boy's room. 'Stop, honey, it's okay.'

For a wonder, she does stop. She raises her head, and when he sees the terrified look in her eyes, he loses what little breath he has left. It's more than terror. It's *emptiness*, as if something inside her has slipped aside and exposed a black hole.

'Ty's gone,' she says simply. 'I looked behind all the pictures I could . . . I was sure he'd be behind that one, if he was anywhere he'd be behind that one . . .'

She points toward the place where the Ireland travel poster hung, and he sees that four of the nails on her left hand have been ripped partly or completely away. His stomach does a flip-flop. Her fingers look as if they have been dipped in red ink. *If only it was ink*, Fred thinks. *If only.*

'. . . but of course it's just a picture. They're all just pictures. I see that now.' She pauses, then cries: 'Abbalah! Munshun! Abbalah-gorg, Abbalah-doon!' Her tongue comes out – comes out to an impossible, cartoonish length – and swipes spittishly across her nose. Fred sees it but cannot believe it. This is like coming into a horror movie halfway through the show, discovering it's real, and not knowing what to do. What *is* he supposed to do? When you discover that the woman you love has gone mad – had a break with reality, at the very least – what are you supposed to *do*? How the hell do you deal with it?

But he loves her, has loved her from the first week he knew her, helplessly and completely and without the slightest regret ever after, and now love guides him. He sits down next to her on the bed, puts his arm around her, and simply holds her. He can feel her trembling from the inside out. Her body thrums like a wire.

'I love you,' he says, surprised at his voice. It's amazing that seeming calmness can issue from such a crazy cauldron of confusion and fear. 'I love you and everything is going to be all right.'

She looks up at him and something comes back into her eyes. Fred cannot call it sanity (no matter how much he would like to), but it is at least some sort of marginal awareness. She knows where she is and who is with her. For a moment he sees gratitude in her eyes. Then her face cramps in a fresh agony of grief and she begins to weep. It is an exhausted, lost sound that wrenches at him. Nerves, heart, and mind, it wrenches at him.

'Ty's gone,' Judy says. 'Gorg fascinated him and the abbalah took him. Abbalah-doon!' The tears course down her cheeks.

When she raises her hands to wipe them away, her fingers leave appalling streaks of blood.

Even though he's sure Tyler is fine (certainly *Fred* has had no premonitions today, unless we count his rosy sales prediction about the new Hiler roto), he feels a shudder course through him at the sight of those streaks, and it is not Judy's condition that causes it but what she's just said: *Ty's gone.* Ty is with his friends; he told Fred just last night that he, Ronnie, T.J., and the less-than-pleasant Wexler boy intended to spend the day 'goofing off.' If the other three boys go somewhere Ty doesn't want to be, he has promised to come directly home. All the bases seem to be covered, yet . . . is there not such a thing as mother's intuition? *Well,* he thinks, *maybe on the Fox Network.*

He picks Judy up in his arms and is appalled all over again, this time by how light she is. *She's lost maybe twenty pounds since the last time I picked her up like this,* he thinks. *At least ten. How could I not have noticed?* But he knows. Preoccupation with work was part of it; a stubborn refusal to let go of the idea that things were basically all right was the rest of it. *Well,* he thinks, carrying her out the door (her arms have crept tiredly up and locked themselves around his neck), *I'm over* that *little misconception.* And he actually believes this, in spite of his continued blind confidence in his son's safety.

Judy hasn't toured their bedroom during her rampage, and to Fred it looks like a cool oasis of sanity. Judy apparently feels the same way. She gives a tired sigh, and her arms drop away from her husband's neck. Her tongue comes out, but this time it gives only a feeble little lick at her upper lip. Fred bends and puts her down on the bed. She holds up her hands, looks at them.

'I cut myself . . . scraped myself . . .'

'Yes,' he says. 'I'm going to get something for them.'

'How . . .?'

He sits beside her for a moment. Her head has sunk into the soft double thickness of her pillows, and her eyelids are drooping. He thinks that, beyond the puzzlement in them, he can still see that terrifying blankness. He hopes he is wrong.

'Don't you remember?' he asks her gently.

'No . . . did I fall down?'

Fred chooses not to answer. He is starting to think again. Not much, he's not capable of much just yet, but a little. 'Honey, what's a gorg? What's an abbalah? Is it a person?'

'Don't . . . know . . . Ty . . .'

'Ty's fine,' he says.

'No . . .'

'*Yes*,' he insists. Perhaps he's insisting to both of the people in this pretty, tastefully decorated bedroom. 'Honey-bunch, you just lie there. I want to get a couple of things.'

Her eyes drift closed. He thinks she will sleep, but her lids struggle slowly back up to half-mast.

'Lie right there,' he says. 'No getting up and wandering around. There's been enough of that. You scared poor Enid Purvis out of a year's life. You promise?'

'Promise . . .' Her eyelids drift back down.

Fred goes into the adjoining bathroom, ears alert for any movement behind him. He has never seen anyone in his life who looks more bolt-shot than Judy does right now, but mad people are clever, and despite his prodigious capacity for denial in some areas, Fred can no longer fool himself about his wife's current mental state. Mad? Actually stark raving mad? Probably not. But off the rails, certainly. *Temporarily* off the rails, he amends as he opens the medicine cabinet.

He takes the bottle of Mercurochrome, then scans the prescription bottles on the shelf above. There aren't many. He grabs the one on the far left. Sonata, French Landing Pharmacy, one capsule at bedtime, do not use more than four nights in a row, prescribing physician Patrick J. Skarda, MD.

Fred can't see the entire bed in the medicine-cabinet mirror, but he can see the foot of it . . . and one of Judy's feet, as well. Still on the bed. Good, good. He shakes out one of the Sonatas, then dumps their toothbrushes out of the glass – he has no intention of going all the way downstairs for a clean glass, does not want to leave her alone that long.

He fills the glass, then goes back into the bedroom with the water, the pill, and the bottle of Mercurochrome. Her eyes are shut. She is breathing so slowly that he has to put one hand on her chest to make sure she's breathing at all.

He looks at the sleeping pill, debates, then gives her a shake. 'Judy! Jude! Wake up a little, hon. Just long enough to take a pill, okay?'

She doesn't even mutter, and Fred sets the Sonata aside. It won't be necessary after all. He feels some faint optimism at how fast she's fallen asleep and how deep she has gone. It's as if some vile sac has popped, discharged its poison, left her weak and tired but possibly okay again. Could that be? Fred doesn't know, but he's positive that she isn't just shamming sleep. All of Judy's current woes began with insomnia, and the insomnia has been the one constant throughout. Although she's only been exhibiting distressing symptoms for a couple of months – talking to herself and doing that odd and rather disgusting thing with her tongue, to mention only a couple of items – she hasn't been sleeping well since January. Hence the Sonata. Now it seems that she has finally tipped over. And is it too much to hope that when she wakes from a normal sleep she'll be her old normal self again? That her worries about her son's safety during the summer of the Fisherman have forced her to some sort of climax? Maybe, maybe not . . . but at least it has given Fred some time to think about what he should do next, and he had better use it well. One thing seems to him beyond argument: if Ty is here when his mother wakes up, Ty is going to have a much happier mother. The immediate question is how to locate Tyler as soon as possible.

His first thought is to call the homes of Ty's friends. It would be easy; those numbers are posted on the fridge, printed in Judy's neat back-slanting hand, along with the numbers of the fire department, the police department (including Dale Gilbertson's private number; he's an old friend), and French Landing Rescue. But it takes Fred only a moment to realize what a bad idea this is. Ebbie's mother is dead and his father is an unpleasant moron – Fred met him just once, and once is more than enough. Fred doesn't much like his wife labeling some people 'low-raters' (*Who do you think you are*, he asked her once, *Queen of the doggone Realm?*), but in the case of Pete Wexler, the shoe fits. He won't have any idea of where the boys are today and won't care.

Mrs Metzger and Ellen Renniker might, but having once been a boy on summer vacation himself – the whole world laid at your feet and at least two thousand places to go – Fred doubts it like hell. There's a chance the boys might be eating lunch (it's getting to be that time) at the Metzgers' or Rennikers', but is that slight chance worth scaring the hell out of two women? Because the killer will be the first thing they think of, just as sure as God made little fishes . . . and fishermen to catch 'em.

Once more sitting on the bed beside his wife, Fred feels his first real tingle of apprehension on his son's behalf and dismisses it brusquely. This is no time to give in to the heebie-jeebies. He has to remember that his wife's mental problems and his son's safety are not linked – except in her mind. His job is to present Ty, front and center and all squared away, thus proving her fears groundless.

Fred looks at the clock on his side of the bed and sees that it's quarter past eleven. *How the time flies when you're having fun*, he thinks. Beside him, Judy utters a single gaspy snore. It's a small sound, really quite lady-like, but Fred jumps anyway. How she scared him when he first saw her in Ty's room! He's still scared.

Ty and his friends may come here for lunch. Judy says they often do because the Metzgers don't have much to eat and Mrs Renniker usually serves what the boys call 'goop,' a mystery dish consisting of noodles and some gray meat. Judy makes them Campbell's soup and baloney sandwiches, stuff they like. But Ty has money enough to treat them all to McDonald's out by the little mall on the north side, or they could go into Sonny's Cruisin' Restaurant, a cheap diner with a cheesy fifties ambience. And Ty isn't averse to treating. He's a generous boy.

'I'll wait until lunch,' he murmurs, completely unaware that he is talking as well as thinking. Certainly he doesn't disturb Judy; she has gone deep. 'Then—'

Then what? He doesn't know, exactly.

He goes downstairs, kicks the Mr Coffee back into gear, and calls work. He asks Ina to tell Ted Goltz he'll be out the rest of the day – Judy's sick. The flu, he tells her. Throwing up and everything. He runs down a list of people he was expecting to see that day and tells her to speak to Otto Eisman about handling them. Otto will be on that like white on rice.

An idea occurs to him while he's talking to her, and when he's done, he calls the Metzgers' and Rennikers' after all. At the Metzgers' he gets an answering machine and hangs up without leaving a message. Ellen Renniker, however, picks up on the second ring. Sounding casual and cheerful – it comes naturally, he's a hell of a salesman – he asks her to have Ty call home if the boys show up there for lunch. Fred says he has something to tell his son, making it sound like something good. Ellen says she will, but adds that T.J. had four or five dollars burning a hole in his jeans when he left the house that morning, and she doesn't expect to see him until suppertime.

Fred goes back upstairs and checks on Judy. She hasn't moved so much as a finger, and he supposes that's good.

No. There's nothing good about any of this.

Instead of receding now that the situation has stabilized – sort of – his fear seems to be intensifying. Telling himself that Ty is with his friends no longer seems to help. The sunny, silent house is creeping him out. He realizes he no longer wants Ty front and center simply for his wife's sake. Where would the boys go? Is there any one place—?

Of course there is. Where they can get Magic cards. That stupid, incomprehensible game they play.

Fred Marshall hurries back downstairs, grabs the phone book, hunts through the Yellow Pages, and calls the 7-Eleven. Like most of French Landing, Fred is in the 7-Eleven four or five times a week – a can of soda here, a carton of orange juice there – and he recognizes the lilt of the Indian day clerk's voice. He comes up with the man's name at once: Rajan Patel. It's that old salesman's trick of keeping as many names as possible in the active file. It sure helps here. When Fred calls the man Mr Patel, the day clerk immediately becomes friendly, perfectly willing to help. Unfortunately, there isn't much help he can give. Lots of boys in. They are buying Magic cards, also Pokémon and baseball cards. Some are trading these cards outside. He *does* recall three that came in that morning on bikes, he says. They bought Slurpees as well as cards, and then argued about something outside. (Rajan Patel doesn't mention the cursing, although this is chiefly why he remembers these boys.) After a little while, he says, they went on their way.

Fred is drinking coffee without even remembering when he poured it. Fresh threads of unease are spinning spider-silky webs in his head. Three boys. *Three.*

It means nothing, you know that, don't you? he tells himself. He *does* know it, and at the same time he *doesn't* know it. He can't even believe he's caught a little of Judy's freakiness, like a cold germ. This is just . . . well . . . freakiness for freakiness's sake.

He asks Patel to describe the kids and isn't too surprised when Patel can't. He thinks one of them was a bit of a fat boy, but he's not even sure of that. 'Sorry, but I see so many,' he says. Fred tells him he understands. He does, too, only all the understanding in the world won't ease his mind.

Three boys. Not four but three.

Lunchtime has come, but Fred is not the least bit hungry. The spooky, sunny silence maintains itself. The spiderwebs continue to spin.

Not four but three.

If it was Ty's bunch that Mr Patel saw, the fattish boy was certainly Ebbie Wexler. The question is, who were the other two? And which one was missing? Which one had been stupid enough to go off on his own?

Ty's gone. Gorg fascinated him and the abbalah took him.

Crazy talk, no doubt about it . . . but Fred's arms nevertheless break out in a lush of goose bumps. He puts his coffee mug down with a bang. He'll clean up the broken glass, that's what he'll do. That's the next step, no doubt about it.

The *actual* next step, the *logical* next step, whispers through his mind as he climbs the stairs, and he immediately pushes it away. He's sure the cops are just lately overwhelmed with queries from hysterical parents who have lost track of their kids for an hour or so. The last time he saw Dale Gilbertson, the poor guy looked careworn and grim. Fred doesn't want to be marked down as part of the problem instead of part of the solution. Still . . .

Not four but three.

He gets the dustpan and broom out of the little utility closet next to the laundry room and begins sweeping up broken glass. When he's done he checks on Judy, sees she's still sleeping (more deeply than ever, from the look of her), and goes down to Ty's room. If Ty saw it like this, he'd be upset. He'd think his mom was a lot more than a Coke short of a Happy Meal.

You don't have to worry about that, his mind whispers. *He won't be seeing his room, not tonight, not ever. Gorg fascinated him and the abbalah took him.*

'Stop it,' Fred tells himself. 'Stop being an old woman.'

But the house is too empty, too silent, and Fred Marshall is afraid.

Setting Tyler's room to rights takes longer than Fred ever would have expected; his wife went through it like a whirlwind. How can such a little woman have such strength in her? Is it the strength of the mad? Perhaps, but Judy doesn't *need* the strength of the mad. When she sets her mind to something, she is a formidable engine.

By the time he's finished cleaning up, almost two hours have passed and the only obvious scar is the scratched-out rectangle of wallpaper where the Irish travel poster hung. Sitting on Ty's remade bed, Fred finds that the longer he looks at that spot, the less he can stand the white wallboard, peering through as brazenly as a broken bone through outraged skin. He has washed away the streaks of blood, but can do nothing about the scratch marks she made with her nails.

Yes I can, he thinks. *Yes I can, too.*

Ty's dresser is mahogany, a piece of furniture that came to them from the estate of some distant relative on Judy's side. Moving it really isn't a one-man job, and under the circumstances, that suits Fred just fine. He slides a rug remnant under it to keep from marking up the floor, then pulls it across the room. Once it's been placed against the far wall, it covers most of the scratched area. With the bald spot out of sight, Fred feels better. Saner. Ty hasn't come home for lunch, but Fred didn't really expect he would. He'll be home by four, at the latest. Home for supper. Take it to the bank.

Fred strolls back to the master bedroom, massaging the small of his back as he walks. Judy *still* hasn't moved, and once again he puts an anxious hand on her chest. Her breathing is slow, but steady as she goes. *That's* all right. He lies down beside her on the bed, goes to loosen his tie, and laughs when he feels his open collar. Coat and tie, both back at Goltz's. Well, it's been a crazy day. For the time being it's just good to lie here in the air-conditioned cool, easing his aching back. Moving that dresser was a bitch, but he's glad he did it. Certainly there's no chance he'll drop off; he's far too upset. Besides, napping in the middle of the day has never been his thing.

So thinking, Fred falls asleep.

Beside him, in her own sleep, Judy begins to whisper. Gorg . . . abbalah . . . the Crimson King. And a woman's name.

The name is Sophie.

6

In the ready room of the French Landing PD, the phone on the desk rings. Bobby Dulac has been mining for nose-gold. Now he squashes his latest treasure on the sole of his shoe and picks up the phone.

'*Yell*-o, Police Department, Officer Dulac speaking, how can I help you?'

'Hey, Bobby. It's Danny Tcheda.'

Bobby feels a prink of unease. Danny Tcheda – last name pronounced *Cheetah* – is one of French Landing's fourteen full-time RMP cops. He's currently on duty, and ordinary procedure dictates that duty cops radio in – that's what the R in RMP stands for, after all. The only exception to the rule has to do with the Fisherman. Dale has mandated that patrol officers call in on a landline if they think they have a situation involving the killer. Too many people have their ears on out there, doubtless including Wendell 'Pisshead' Green.

'Danny, what's up?'

'Maybe nothing, maybe something not so good. I got a bike and a sneaker in the trunk of my car. I found 'em over on Queen Street. Near Maxton Elder Care?'

Bobby draws a pad toward him and begins to jot. The tickle of unease has become a sinking feeling.

'Nothing wrong with the bike,' Danny continues, 'just sitting there on its kickstand, but combined with the sneaker . . .'

'Yeah, yeah, I see your point, Danny, but you never should have fooled with what could be evidence of a crime.' *Please God don't let it be evidence of a crime*, Bobby Dulac is thinking. *Please God don't let it be another one.*

Irma Freneau's mother has just been in to see Dale, and while there was no screaming or shouting, she came out with tears on her cheeks and looking like death on the half shell. They can't still be sure the little girl has become the Fisherman's third victim, but—

'Bobby, I *had* to,' Danny is saying. 'I'm ridin' solo, I didn't want to put this out on the air, I hadda find a phone. If I'd left the bike there, someone *else* coulda monkeyed with it. Hell, stolen it. This is a good bike, Schwinn three-speed. Better'n the one my kid's got, tell you that.'

'What's your twenty?'

'7-Eleven, up the hill on 35. What I did was mark the location of the bike and the sneaker with chalk X's on the sidewalk. I handled them with gloves and put the sneaker in an evidence bag.' Danny is sounding more and more anxious. Bobby knows how he must feel, sympathizes with the choices Danny had to make. Riding solo is a bitch, but French Landing is already supporting as many cops – full-time and part-time – as the budget will bear. Unless, of course, this Fisherman business gets totally out of control; in that case, the town fathers will no doubt discover a bit more elastic in the budget.

Maybe it's already out of control, Bobby thinks.

'Okay, Danny. Okay. See your point.' *Whether or not* Dale *sees it is a whole 'nother thing*, Bobby thinks.

Danny lowers his voice. 'No one needs to know I broke the chain of evidence, do they? I mean, if the subject ever came up. In court, or something.'

'I guess that's up to Dale.' *Oh God*, Bobby thinks. A new problem has just occurred to him. All calls that come in on this phone are automatically taped. Bobby decides the taping machinery is about to have a malfunction, retroactive to about two o'clock in the afternoon.

'And you want to know the other thing?' Danny is asking. 'The *big* thing? I didn't want people to see it. A bike standing all by itself that way, you don't have to be Sherlock Fucking Holmes to draw a certain conclusion. And folks're getting close to the panic line, especially after that goddamned irresponsible story in the paper this morning. I didn't want to call from Maxton's for the same reason.'

'I'm gonna put you on hold. You better talk to Dale.'

In a vastly unhappy voice, Danny says: 'Oh boy.'

In Dale Gilbertson's office there is a bulletin board dominated by enlarged photographs of Amy St Pierre and Johnny Irkenham. A third photo will be added soon, he fears – that of Irma Freneau. Beneath the two current photos, Dale sits at his desk, smoking a Marlboro 100. He's got the fan on. It will, he hopes, blow the smoke away. Sarah would just about kill him if she knew he was smoking again, but dear Jesus Christ, he needs *something*.

His interview with Tansy Freneau had been short and nothing short of purgatorial. Tansy is a juicer, a regular patron of the Sand Bar, and during their interview the smell of coffee brandy was so strong it almost seemed to be coming out of her pores (another excuse for the fan). Half drunk, she had been, and Dale was glad. It kept her calm, at least. It didn't put any sparkle in her dead eyes, coffee brandy was no good for that, but she had been calm. Hideously, she had even said 'Thank you for helping me, sir' before leaving.

Tansy's ex – Irma's father – lives across the state in Green Bay ('Green Bay is the devil's town,' Dale's father used to say, God knows why), where he works in a garage and, according to Tansy, supports several bars with names like the End Zone and the Fifty-Yard Line. Until today, there has been some reason to believe – at least to hope – that Richard 'Cubby' Freneau snatched his daughter. An e-mail from the Green Bay Police Department has put paid to that little idea. Cubby Freneau is living with a woman who has two kids of her own, and he was in jail – D&D – the day Irma disappeared. There is still no body, and Tansy hasn't received a letter from the Fisherman, but—

The door opens. Bobby Dulac sticks his head in. Dale mashes his cigarette out on the inside lip of the wastebasket, burning the back of his hand with sparks in the process.

'Gosh 'n' fishes, Bobby, do you know how to *knock*?'

'Sorry, Chief.' Bobby looks at the smoke ribboning up from the wastebasket with neither surprise nor interest. 'Danny Tcheda's on the phone. I think you better take it.'

'What's it about?' But he knows. Why else would it be the phone?

Bobby only repeats, not without sympathy, 'I think you better take it.'

The car sent by Rebecca Vilas delivers Henry to Maxton Elder Care at three-thirty, ninety minutes before the Strawberry Fest! dance is scheduled to begin. The idea is for the old folks to work up an appetite on the floor, then troop down to the caff – suitably decorated for the occasion – for a glamorously late (seven-thirty is *quite* late for Maxton's) dinner. With wine, for those who drink it.

A resentful Pete Wexler has been drafted by Rebecca Vilas to bring in the deejay's shit (Pete thinks of Henry as 'the blind record-hopper'). Said shit consists of two speakers (very large), one turntable (light, but awkward as a motherfucker to carry), one preamp (very heavy), assorted wires (all tangled up, but that's the blind record-hopper's problem), and four boxes of actual records, which went out of style about a hundred years ago. Pete guesses that the blind record-hopper never heard a CD in his whole life.

The last item is a suit bag on a hanger. Pete has peeked in and ascertained that the suit is white.

'Hang it in there, please,' Henry says, pointing with unerring accuracy toward the supply closet that has been designated his dressing room.

'Okay,' Pete says. 'What exactly is it, if you don't mind me asking?'

Henry smiles. He knows perfectly well that Pete has already had a peep. He heard the plastic bag rattling and the zipper chinking in a duet that only occurs when someone pulls the bag away from the hanger at the neck. 'Inside that bag, my friend, Symphonic Stan, the Big-Band Man, is just waiting for me to put him on and bring him to life.'

'Oh, uh-huh,' Pete says, not knowing if he has been answered or not. All he's really sure of is that those records were almost as heavy as the preamp. Someone should really give the blind record-hopper some information about CDs, the next great leap forward.

'You asked me one; may I ask you one?'

'Be my guest,' Pete says.

'There appears to have been a police presence at Maxton

Elder Care this afternoon,' the blind record-hopper says. 'They're gone now, but they were here when I arrived. What's that about? There hasn't been a robbery or an assault among the geriatrics, I hope?'

Pete stops in his tracks beneath a large cardboard strawberry, holding the suit bag and looking at the blind record-hopper with an amazement Henry can almost touch. 'How'd you know the cops were here?'

Henry puts a finger to the side of his nose and tips his head to one side. He replies in a hoarse, conspiratorial whisper. 'Smelled something blue.'

Pete looks puzzled, debates whether or not to inquire further, and decides not to. Resuming his march toward the supply closet–dressing room, he says: 'They're playing it cagey, but I think they're looking for another lost kid.'

The look of amused curiosity fades from Henry's face. 'Good Christ,' he says.

'They came and went in a hurry. No kids here, Mr . . . uh, Leyden?'

'Leyden,' Henry confirms.

'A kid in this place would stand out like a rose in a patch of poison ivy, if you know what I mean.'

Henry doesn't consider old folks in any way analogous to poison ivy, but he does indeed get Mr Wexler's drift. 'What made them think—?'

'Someone found sumpin' on the sidewalk,' Pete says. He points out the window, then realizes the blind guy can't see him pointing. *Duh*, as Ebbie would say. He lowers his hand. 'If a kid got snatched, someone probably came along in a car and snatched him. No kidnappers in here, I can tell you that much.' Pete laughs at the very idea of a Maxton moldy oldie snatching any kid big enough to ride a bike. The kid would probably break the guy over his knee like a dry stick.

'No,' Henry says soberly, 'that hardly seems likely, does it?'

'But I guess the cops got to dot all the *t*'s and cross all the *i*'s.' He pauses. 'That's just a little joke of mine.'

Henry smiles politely, thinking that with some people, Alzheimer's disease might be an actual improvement. 'When you hang my suit up, Mr Wexler, would you be so good as to give it a gentle shake? Just to banish any incipient wrinkles?'

'Okay. Want me to take it out of the bag forya?'

'Thanks, that won't be necessary.'

Pete goes into the supply closet, hangs up the suit bag, and gives it a little shake. *Incipient*, just what the hell does *that* mean? There's a rudiment of a library here at Maxton's; maybe he'll look it up in the dictionary. It pays to increase your word power, as it says in the *Reader's Digest*, although Pete doubts it will pay him much in this job.

When he goes back out to the common room, the blind record-hopper – Mr Leyden, Symphonic Stan, whoever the hell he is – has begun unraveling wires and plugging them in with a speed and accuracy Pete finds a trifle unnerving.

Poor old Fred Marshall is having a terrible dream. *Knowing* it's a dream should make it less horrible but somehow doesn't. He's in a rowboat with Judy, out on a lake. Judy is sitting in the bow. They are fishing. *He* is, at least; Judy is just holding her pole. Her face is an expressionless blank. Her skin is waxy. Her eyes have a stunned, hammered look. He labors with increasing desperation to make contact with her, trying one conversational gambit after another. None work. To make what is, under the circumstances, a fairly apt metaphor, she spits every lure. He sees that her empty eyes appear fixed on the creel sitting between them in the bottom of the boat. Blood is oozing through the wickerwork in fat red dribbles.

It's nothing, just fishblood, he tries to assure her, but she makes no reply. In fact, Fred isn't so sure himself. He's thinking he ought to take a look inside the creel, just to be sure, when his pole gives a tremendous jerk – if not for quick reflexes, he would have lost it over the side. He's hooked a big one!

Fred reels it in, the fish on the other end of the line fighting him for every foot. Then, when he finally gets it near the boat, he realizes he has no net. *Hell with it*, he thinks, *go for broke*. He whips the pole backward, just *daring* the line to snap, and the fish – biggest goddamned lake trout you'd ever hope to see – flies out of the water and through the air in a gleaming, fin-flipping arc. It lands in the bottom of the boat (beside the oozing creel, in fact) and begins thrashing. It also begins to make gruesome choking noises. Fred has never heard a fish make noises like that. He bends forward and is horrified to see that the trout has Tyler's face. His son has somehow become a weretrout, and now he's dying in the bottom of the boat. Strangling.

Fred grabs at it, wanting to remove the hook and throw it back while there's still time, but the terrible choking thing keeps slipping through his fingers, leaving only a shiny slime of scales behind. It would be tough to get the hook out, in any case. The Ty-fish has swallowed it whole, and the barbed tip is actually protruding from one of the gills, just below the point where the human face melts away. Ty's choking becomes louder, harsher, infinitely more horrible—

★

Fred sits up with a low cry, feeling as if he's choking himself. For a moment he's completely adrift as to place and time – lost in the slippage, we might say – and then he realizes he's in his own bedroom, sitting up on his side of the bed he shares with Judy.

He notices that the light in here is much dimmer, because the sun has moved to the other side of the house. *My God*, he thinks, *how long have I been asleep? How could I—*

Oh, but here is another thing: that hideous choking sound has followed him out of his dream. It's louder than ever. It will wake Judy, scare her—

Judy is no longer on the bed, though.

'Jude? *Judy?*'

She's sitting in the corner. Her eyes are wide and blank, just as they were in his dream. A corsage of crumpled paper is protruding from her mouth. Her throat is grotesquely swelled, looks to Fred like a sausage that has been grilled until the casing is ready to pop.

More paper, he thinks. *Christ, she's choking on it.*

Fred rolls himself across the bed, falls off, and lands on his knees like a gymnast doing a trick. He reaches for her. She makes no move to evade him. There's that, at least. And although she's choking, he still sees no expression in her eyes. They are dusty zeros.

Fred yanks the corsage of paper from her mouth. There's another behind it. Fred reaches between her teeth, tweezes this second ball of paper between the first two fingers of his right hand (thinking *Please don't bite me, Judy, please don't*), and pulls it out, too. There's a third ball of paper behind this one, way at the back of her mouth. He gets hold of this one as well, and extracts it. Although it's crumpled, he can see the printed words GREAT IDEA, and knows what she's swallowed: sheets of paper from the notepad Ty gave her for her birthday.

She's still choking. Her skin is turning slate.

Fred grabs her by her upper arms and pulls her up. She comes easily, but when he relaxes his hold her knees bend and she starts to go back down. She's turned into Raggedy Ann. The choking sound continues. Her sausage throat—

'Help me, Judy! Help me, you bitch!'

Unaware of what he is saying. He yanks her hard – as hard as he yanked the fishing pole in his dream – and spins her around like a ballerina when she comes up on her toes. Then he seizes her in a bear hug, his wrists brushing the undersides of her breasts, her bottom tight against his crotch, the kind of position he would find extremely sexy if his wife didn't happen to be choking to death.

He pops his thumb up between her breasts like a hitch-hiker, then says the magic word as he pulls sharply upward and backward. The magic word is *Heimlich*, and it works. Two more wads of paper fly from Judy's mouth, propelled by a jet of vomit that is little more than bile – her intake of food over the last twelve hours amounts to three cups of coffee and a cranberry muffin.

She gives a gasp, coughs twice, then begins to breathe more or less normally.

He puts her on the bed . . . drops her on the bed. His lower back is spasming wildly, and it's really no wonder; first Ty's dresser, now this.

'Well, what did you think you were doing?' he asks her loudly. 'What in the name of Christ did you think you were *doing*?'

He realizes that he has raised one hand over Judy's upturned face as if to strike her. Part of him *wants* to strike her. He loves her, but at this moment he also hates her. He has imagined plenty of bad things over the years they've been married – Judy getting cancer, Judy paralyzed in an accident, Judy first taking a lover and then demanding a divorce – but he has never imagined Judy going chickenshit on him, and isn't that what this amounts to?

'What did you think you were *doing*?'

She looks at him without fear . . . but without anything else, either. Her eyes are dead. Her husband lowers his hand, thinking: *I'd cut it off before I hit you. I might be pissed at you, I* am *pissed at you, but I'd cut it off before I did that.*

Judy rolls over, face-down on the coverlet, her hair spread around her head in a corona.

'Judy?'

Nothing. She just lies there.

Fred looks at her for a moment, then uncrumples one of the slimy balls of paper with which she has tried to strangle herself. It is covered with tangles of scribbled words. Gorg, abbalah, eeleelee, munshun, bas, lum, opopanax: these mean nothing to him. Others – drudge, asswipe, black, red, Chicago, and Ty – are actual words but have no context. Printed up one side of the sheet is IF YOU'VE GOT PRINCE ALBERT IN A CAN, HOW CAN YOU EVER GET HIM OUT? Up the other, like a teletype stuck in repeat mode, is this: BLACK HOUSE CRIMSON KING BLACK HOUSE CRIMSON KING BLACK

If you waste time looking for sense in this, you're as crazy as she is, Fred thinks. *You can't waste time—*

Time.

He looks at the clock on his side of the bed and cannot believe its news: 4:17 p.m. Is that possible? He looks at his watch and sees that it is.

Knowing it's foolish, knowing he would have heard his

son come in even if in a deep sleep, Fred strides to the door on big nerveless legs. *'Ty!'* he yells. *'Hey, Ty! TYLER!'*

Waiting for an answer that will not come, Fred realizes that everything in his life has changed, quite possibly forever. People tell you this can happen – *in the blink of an eye*, they say, *before you know it*, they say – but you don't believe it. Then a wind comes.

Go down to Ty's room? Check? Be sure?

Ty isn't there – Fred knows this – but he does it just the same. The room is empty, as he knew it would be. And it looks oddly distorted, almost sinister, with the dresser now on the other side.

Judy. You left her alone, you idiot. She'll be chewing paper again by now, they're clever, mad people are clever—

Fred dashes back down to the master bedroom and exhales a sigh of relief when he sees Judy lying just as he left her, face-down, hair spread around her head. He discovers that his worries about his mad wife are now secondary to his worries about his missing son.

He'll be home by four, at the latest . . . take it to the bank. So he had thought. But four has come and gone. A strong wind has arisen and blown the bank away. Fred walks to his side of the bed and sits down beside his wife's splayed right leg. He picks up the phone and punches in a number. It's an easy number, only three digits.

'*Yell*-o, Police Department, Officer Dulac speaking, you've dialed 911, do you have an emergency?'

'Officer Dulac, this is Fred Marshall. I'd like to speak to Dale, if he's still there.' Fred is pretty sure Dale is. He works late most nights, especially since—

He pushes the rest away, but inside his head the wind blows harder. Louder.

'Gee, Mr Marshall, he's here, but he's in a meeting and I don't think I can—'

'Get him.'

'Mr Marshall, you're not hearing me. He's in with two guys from the WSP and one from the FBI. If you could just tell me—'

Fred closes his eyes. It's interesting, isn't it? Something interesting here. He called in on the 911 line, but the idiot on the other end seems to have forgotten that. Why? Because it's someone he knows. It's good old Fred Marshall, bought a Deere lawn tractor from him just the year before last. Must have dialed 911 because it was easier than looking up the regular number. Because *no one Bobby knows* can actually have an emergency.

Fred remembers having a similar idea himself that morning – a different Fred Marshall, one who believed that the Fisherman could never touch his son. Not *his* son.

Ty's gone. Gorg fascinated him and the abbalah took him.

'Hello? Mr Marshall? Fred? Are you still—'

'Listen to me,' Fred says, his eyes still closed. Down at Goltz's, he would be calling the man on the other end Bobby by now, but Goltz's has never seemed so far away; Goltz's is in the star-system Opopanax, on Planet Abbalah. 'Listen to me carefully. Write it down if you have to. My wife has gone mad and my son is missing. Do you understand those things? Wife mad. Son missing. *Now put me through to the chief!*'

But Bobby Dulac doesn't, not right away. He has made a deduction. A more diplomatic police officer (Jack Sawyer as he was in his salad days, for instance) would have kept said deduction to himself, but Bobby can't do that. Bobby has hooked a big one.

'Mr Marshall? Fred? Your son doesn't own a Schwinn,

does he? Three-speed Schwinn, red? Got a novelty license plate that reads . . . uh . . . BIG MAC?'

Fred cannot answer. For several long and terrible moments he cannot even draw a breath. Between his ears, the wind blows both louder and harder. Now it's a hurricane.

Gorg fascinated him . . . the abbalah took him.

At last, just when it seems he will begin to strangle himself, his chest unlocks and he takes in a huge, tearing breath. '*PUT CHIEF GILBERTSON ON! DO IT NOW, YOU MOTHERFUCKER!*'

Although he shrieks this at the top of his lungs, the woman lying face-down on the coverlet beside him never moves. There is a click. He's on hold. Not for long, but it's long enough for him to see the scratched, bald place on his missing son's bedroom wall, the swelled column of his mad wife's throat, and blood dribbling through the creel in his dream. His back spasms cruelly, and Fred welcomes the pain. It's like getting a telegram from the real world.

Then Dale is on the phone, Dale is asking him what's wrong, and Fred Marshall begins to cry.

7

God may know where Henry Leyden found that astounding suit, but we certainly do not. A costume shop? No, it is too elegant to be a costume; this is the real thing, not an imitation. But what sort of real thing is it? The wide lapels sweep down to an inch below the waist, and the twin flaps of the swallowtail reach nearly to the ankles of the billowing, pleated trousers, which seem, beneath the snowfield expanse of the double-breasted waistcoat, to ride nearly at the level of the sternum. On Henry's feet, white, high-button spats adorn white patent-leather shoes; about his neck, a stiff, high collar turns its pointed peaks over a wide, flowing, white satin bow tie, perfectly knotted. The total effect is of old-fashioned diplomatic finery harmoniously wedded to a zoot suit: the raffishness of the ensemble outweighs its formality, but the dignity of the swallowtail and the waistcoat contribute to the whole a regal quality of a specific kind, the regality often seen in African American entertainers and musicians.

Escorting Henry to the common room while surly Pete Wexler comes along behind, pushing a handcart loaded with boxes of records, Rebecca Vilas dimly remembers having seen

Duke Ellington wearing a white cutaway like this in a clip from some old film . . . or was it Cab Calloway? She recalls an upraised eyebrow, a glittering smile, a seductive face, an upright figure posed before a band, but little more. (If alive, either Mr Ellington or Mr Calloway could have informed Rebecca that Henry's outfit, including the 'high-drape' pants with a 'reet pleat,' terms not in her vocabulary, had undoubtedly been handmade by one of four specific tailors located in the black neighborhoods of New York, Washington, DC, Philadelphia, or Los Angeles, masters of their trade during the thirties and forties, underground tailors, men now alas as dead as their celebrated clients. Henry Leyden knows exactly who tailored his outfit, where it came from, and how it fell into his hands, but when it comes to persons such as Rebecca Vilas, Henry imparts no more information than is already likely to be known.) In the corridor leading to the common room, the white cutaway appears to shine from within, an impression only increased by Henry's oversized, daddy-cool dark glasses with bamboo frames, in which what may be tiny sapphires wink at the corners of the bows.

Is there maybe some shop that sells Spiffy Clothes of Great 1930s Bandleaders? Does some museum inherit this stuff and auction it off? Rebecca cannot contain her curiosity a moment longer. 'Mr Leyden, where did you get that beautiful outfit?'

From the rear and taking care to sound as though he is muttering to himself, Pete Wexler opines that obtaining an outfit like that probably requires chasing a person of an ethnicity beginning with the letter *n* for at least a couple of miles.

Henry ignores Pete and smiles. 'It's all a matter of knowing where to look.'

'Guess you never heard of CDs,' Pete says. 'They're like this big new breakthrough.'

'Shut up and tote them bales, me bucko,' says Ms Vilas. 'We're almost there.'

'Rebecca, my dear, if I may,' Henry says. 'Mr Wexler has every right to grouse. After all, there's no way he could know that I own about three thousand CDs, is there? And if the man who originally owned these clothes can be called a nigger, I'd be proud to call myself one, too. That would be an *incredible* honor. I wish I could claim it.'

Henry has come to a halt. Each, in a different way, shocked by his use of the forbidden word, Pete and Rebecca have also stopped moving.

'And,' Henry says, 'we owe respect to those who assist us in the performance of our duties. I asked Mr Wexler to shake out my suit when he hung it up, and he very kindly obliged me.'

'Yeah,' Pete says. 'Plus I also hung up your light and put your turntable and speakers and shit right where you want 'em.'

'Thank you very much, Mr Wexler,' Henry says. 'I appreciate your efforts in my behalf.'

'Well, shit,' Pete says, 'I was only doing my job, you know? But anything you want after you're done, I'll give you a hand.'

Without benefit of a flash of panties or a glimpse of ass, Pete Wexler has been completely disarmed. Rebecca finds this amazing. All in all, sightless or not, Henry Leyden, it comes to her, is far and away the coolest human being she has ever been privileged to encounter in her entire twenty-six years on the face of the earth. Never mind his clothes – where did *guys* like this come from?

'Do you really think some little boy vanished from the sidewalk out in front of here this afternoon?' Henry asks.

'What?' Rebecca asks.

'Seems like it to me,' Pete says.

'What?' Rebecca asks again, this time to Pete Wexler, not Henry. 'What are you saying?'

'Well, he ast me, and I tol' him,' Pete says. 'That's all.'

Simmering dangerously, Rebecca takes a stride toward him. 'This happened on *our* sidewalk? Another kid, in front of *our building*? And you didn't say anything to me or Mr Maxton?'

'There wasn't nothin' to say,' Pete offers in self-defense.

'Maybe you could tell us what actually happened,' Henry says.

'Sure. What happened was, I went outside for a smoke, see?' This is less than strictly truthful. Faced with the choice of walking ten yards to the Daisy corridor men's room to flush his cigarette down a toilet or walking ten feet to the entrance and pitching it into the parking lot, Pete had sensibly elected outdoor disposal. 'So I get outside and that's when I saw it. This police car, parked right out there. So I walked up to the hedge, and there's this cop, a young guy, I think his name is Cheetah, or something like that, and he's loadin' this bike, like a kid's bike, into his trunk. And something else, too, only I couldn't see what it was except it was small. And after he did that, he got a piece a chalk outta his glove compartment and he came back and made like X marks on the sidewalk.'

'Did you talk to him?' Rebecca asks. 'Did you ask him what he was doing?'

'Miz Vilas, I don't talk to cops unless it's like you got no other choice, know what I mean? Cheetah, he never even saw me. The guy wouldn't of said nothing anyhow. He had this expression on his face – it was like, Jeez, I hope I get to the crapper before I drop a load in my pants, that kind of expression.'

'Then he just drove away?'

'Just like that. Twenty minutes later, two other cops showed up.'

Rebecca raises both hands, closes her eyes, and presses her fingertips to her forehead, giving Pete Wexler an excellent opportunity, of which he does not fail to take full advantage, to admire the shape of her breasts underneath her blouse. It may not be as great as the view from the bottom of the ladder, but it'll do, all right, yes it will. As far as Ebbie's dad is concerned, a sight like Rebecca Vilas's Hottentots pushing out against her dress is like a good fire on a cold night. They are bigger than you'd expect on a slender little thing like her, and you know what? When the arms go up, the Hottentots go up, too! Hey, if he had known she was going to put on a show like this, he would have told her about Cheetah and the bicycle as soon as it happened.

'All right, okay,' she says, still flattening the tips of her fingers against her head. She lifts her chin, raising her arms another few inches, and frowns in concentration, for a moment looking like a figure on a plinth.

Hoo-ray and hallelujah, Pete thinks. *There's a bright side to everything. If another little snotnose gets grabbed off the sidewalk tomorrow morning, it won't be soon enough for me.*

Rebecca says, 'Okay, okay, okay,' opens her eyes, and lowers her arms. Pete Wexler is staring firmly at a point over her shoulder, his face blank with a false innocence she immediately comprehends. Good God, what a caveman. 'It's not as bad as I thought. In the first place, all you saw was a policeman picking up a bike. Maybe it was stolen. Maybe some other kid borrowed the bike, dumped it, and ran away. The cop could have been looking for it. Or the kid who *owned* the bike could have been hit by a car or something. And even if the worst did happen, I don't see any way that it could hurt us. Maxton's isn't responsible for whatever goes on outside the grounds.'

She turns to Henry, who looks as though he wishes he were a hundred miles away. 'Sorry, I know that sounded awfully cold. I'm as distressed about this Fisherman business as everyone else, what with those two poor kids and the missing girl. We're all so upset we can hardly think straight. But I'd hate to see *us* dragged into the mess, don't you see?'

'I see perfectly,' Henry says. 'Being one of those blind men George Rathbun is always yelling about.'

'Hah!' Pete Wexler barks.

'And you agree with me, don't you?'

'I'm a gentleman, I agree with everybody,' Henry says. 'I agree with Pete that another child may well have been abducted by our local monster. Officer Cheetah, or whatever his name is, sounded too anxious to be just picking up a lost bicycle. And I agree with you that Maxton's cannot be blamed for anything that happened.'

'Good,' Rebecca says.

'Unless, of course, someone here is involved in the murders of these children.'

'But that's impossible!' Rebecca says. 'Most of our male clients can't even remember their own names.'

'A ten-year-old girl could take most of these feebs,' Pete says. 'Even the ones who don't have old-timer's disease walk around covered in their own . . . you know.'

'You're forgetting about the staff,' Henry says.

'Oh, now,' Rebecca says, momentarily rendered nearly wordless. 'Come on. That's . . . that's a totally irresponsible thing to say.'

'True. It is. But if this goes on, nobody will be above suspicion. That's my point.'

Pete Wexler feels a sudden chill – if the town clowns start grilling Maxton's residents, his private amusements might come to light, and wouldn't Wendell Green have a field day with that stuff? A gleaming new idea comes to him, and he brings it forth, hoping to impress Miz Vilas. 'You know what? The cops should talk to that California guy, the big-time detective who nailed that Kinderling asshole two-three years ago. He lives around here somewhere, don't he? Someone like that, he's the guy we need on this. The cops here, they're way outta their depth. That guy, he's like a whaddayacallit, a goddamn *resource*.'

'Odd you should say that,' Henry says. 'I couldn't agree with you more. It is about time Jack Sawyer did his thing. I'll work on him again.'

'You know him?' Rebecca asks.

'Oh, yes,' Henry says. 'That I do. But isn't it about time for me to do my own thing?'

'Soon. They're all still outside.'

Rebecca leads him down the rest of the corridor and into the common room, where all three of them move across to the big platform. Henry's microphone stands beside a table mounted with his speakers and turntable. With unnerving accuracy, Henry says, 'Lot of space in here.'

'You can tell that?' she asks.

'Piece of cake,' Henry says. 'We must be getting close now.'

'It's right in front of you. Do you need any help?'

Henry extends one foot and taps the side of the flat. He glides a hand down the edge of the table, locates the mike stand, says, 'Not at the moment, darlin',' and steps neatly up onto the platform. Guided by touch, he moves to the back of the table and locates the turntable. 'All is copacetic,' he says. 'Pete, would you please put the record boxes on the table? The one on top goes *here*, and the other one right next to it.'

'What's he like, your friend Jack?' Rebecca asks.

'An orphan of the storm. A pussycat, but an extremely *difficult* pussycat. I have to say, he can be a real pain in the bunghole.'

Crowd noises, a buzz of conversation interlaced with children's voices and songs thumped out on an old upright piano, have been audible through the windows since they entered the room, and when Pete has placed the record boxes on the table, he says, 'I better get out there, 'cuz Chipper's probly lookin' for me. Gonna be a shitload of cleanup once they come inside.'

Pete shambles out, rolling the handcart before him. Rebecca asks if there is anything more Henry would like her to do for him.

'The overhead lights are on, aren't they? Please turn them off, and wait for the first wave to come in. Then switch on the pink spot, and prepare to jitterbug your heart out.'

'You want me to turn off the lights?'

'You'll see.'

Rebecca moves back across to the door, turns off the overhead lights, and does see, just as Henry had promised. A soft, dim illumination from the rank of windows hovers in the air, replacing the former brightness and harshness with a vague mellow haze, as if the room lay behind a scrim. That pink spotlight is going to look pretty good in here, Rebecca thinks.

Outside on the lawn, the predance wingding is winding down. Lots of old men and women are busily polishing off their strawberry shortcakes and soda pop at the picnic tables, and the piano-playing gent in the straw boater and red sleeve garters comes to the end of 'Heart and Soul,' *ba bump ba bump ba ba bump bump bump*, no finesse but plenty of volume, closes the lid of the upright, and stands up to a scattering of applause. Grandchildren who had earlier complained about having to come to the great fest dodge through the tables and wheelchairs, evading their parents' glances and hoping to wheedle a last balloon from the balloon lady in the clown suit and frizzy red wig, oh joy unbounded.

Alice Weathers applauds the piano player, as well she might: forty years ago, he reluctantly absorbed the rudiments of pianism at her hands just well enough to pick up a few bucks at occasions like this, when not obliged to perform his usual function, that of selling sweatshirts and baseball caps on Chase Street. Charles Burnside, who, having been scrubbed clean by good-hearted Butch Yerxa, decked himself out in an old white shirt and a pair of loose, filthy trousers, stands slightly apart from the throng in the shade of a large oak, not applauding but sneering. The unbuttoned collar of the shirt droops around his ropy neck. Now and then he wipes his mouth or picks his teeth with a ragged thumbnail, but mainly he does not move at all. He looks as though someone plunked him down by the side of a road and drove off. Whenever the careering grandkids swerve near Burny, they instantly veer away, as if repelled by a force field.

Between Alice and Burny, three-fourths of the residents of Maxton's belly up to the tables, stump around on their walkers, sit beneath the trees, occupy their wheelchairs, hobble here and there – yakking, dozing, chuckling, farting, dabbing at fresh strawberry-colored stains on their clothing, staring at their relatives, staring at their trembling hands, staring at nothing. Half a dozen of the most vacant among them wear conical party hats of hard, flat red and hard, flat blue, the shades of enforced gaiety. The women from the kitchen have begun to circulate through the tables with big black garbage bags, for soon they must retire to their domain to prepare the evening's great feast of potato salad, mashed potatoes, creamed potatoes, baked beans, Jell-O salad, marshmallow salad, and whipped-cream salad, plus of course more mighty strawberry shortcake!

The undisputed and hereditary sovereign of this realm, Chipper Maxton, whose disposition generally resembles that of a skunk trapped in a muddy hole, has spent the previous ninety minutes ambling about smiling and shaking hands, and he has had enough. 'Pete,' he growls, 'what the hell took you so long? Start racking up the folding chairs, okay? And help shift these people into the common room. Let's get a goddamn move on here. Wagons west.'

Pete scurries off, and Chipper claps his hands twice, loudly, then raises his outstretched arms. 'Hey, everybody,' he bellows, 'can you truly believe what a gol-durn gorgeous day the good Lord gave us for this beautiful event? Isn't this *something*?'

Half a dozen feeble voices rise in agreement.

'Come on, people, you can do better than that! I want to hear it for this wonderful day, this wonderful time we're all having, and for all the wonderful help and assistance given us by our volunteers and staff!'

A slightly more exuberant clamor rewards his efforts.

'All *right!* Hey, you know what? As George Rathbun would say, even a blind man could see what a great time we're all having. I know I am, and we're not done yet! We got the greatest deejay you ever heard, a fellow called Symphonic Stan, the Big-Band Man, waiting to put on a great, great show in the common room, music and dancing right up to the big Strawberry Fest dinner, and we got him cheap, too – but don't tell him I said that! So, friends and family, it's time to say your good-byes and let your loved ones cut a rug to the golden oldies, just like them, ha ha! Golden oldies one and all, that's all of us here at Maxton's. Even I'm not as young as I used to be, ha ha, so I might take a spin across the floor with some lucky lady.

'Seriously, folks, it's time for us to put on our dancing shoes. Please kiss Dad or Mom, Granddad or Grandma good-bye, and on your way out, you may wish to leave a contribution toward our expenses in the basket on top of Ragtime Willie's piano right over here, ten dollars, five dollars, anything you can spare helps us cover the costs of giving your mom, your dad, a bright, bright day. *We* do it out of love, but half of that love is *your* love.'

And in what may seem to us a surprisingly short amount of time, but does not to Chipper Maxton, who understands that very few people wish to linger in an elder-care facility any longer than they must, the relatives bestow their final hugs and kisses, round up the exhausted kiddies, and file down the paths and over the grass into the parking lot, along the way a good number depositing bills in the basket atop Ragtime Willie's upright piano.

No sooner does this exodus begin than Pete Wexler and Chipper Maxton set about persuading, with all the art available to them, the oldsters back into the building. Chipper says things like, 'Now don't you know how much we all want to see you trip the light fantastic, Mrs Syverson?' while Pete takes the more direct approach of, 'Move along, bud, time to stir your stumps,' but both men employ the techniques of subtle and not-so-subtle nudges, pushes, elbow grasping, and wheelchair rolling to get their doddering charges through the door.

At her post, Rebecca Vilas watches the residents enter the hazy common room, some of them traveling at a rate a touch too brisk for their own good. Henry Leyden stands motionless behind his boxes of LPs. His suit shimmers; his head is merely a dark silhouette before the windows. For once too busy to ogle Rebecca's chest, Pete Wexler moves past with one hand on the elbow of Elmer Jesperson, deposits him eight feet inside the room, and whirls around to locate Thorvald Thorvaldson, Elmer's dearest enemy and fellow inhabitant of D12. Alice Weathers wafts in under her own guidance and folds her hands beneath her chin, waiting for the music to begin. Tall, scrawny, hollow-cheeked, at the center of an empty space that is his alone, Charles Burnside slides through the door and quickly moves a good distance off to the side. When his dead eyes indifferently meet hers, Rebecca shivers. The next pair of eyes to meet hers belongs to Chipper, who pushes Flora Flostad's wheelchair as if it held a crate of oranges and gives her an impatient glare completely at odds with the easy smile on his face. Time is money, you bet, but money is money, too, let's get this show on the road, pronto. The first wave, Henry had told her – is that what they have here, the first wave? She glances across the room, wondering how to ask, and sees that the question has already been answered, for as soon as she looks up, Henry flashes her the okay sign.

Rebecca flips the switch for the pink spot, and nearly everybody in the room, including a number of old parties who had appeared well beyond response of any kind, utters a soft *aaah.* His suit, his shirt, his spats blazing in the cone of light, a transformed Henry Leyden glides and dips toward the microphone as a twelve-inch LP, seemingly magicked out of the air, twirls like a top on the palm of his right hand. His teeth shine; his sleek hair gleams; the sapphires wink from the bows of his enchanted sunglasses. Henry seems almost to be dancing himself, with his sweet, clever sidestepping glide . . . only he is no longer Henry Leyden; no way, Renee, as George Rathbun likes to roar. The suit, the spats, the slicked-back hair, the shades, even the wondrously effective pink spot are mere stage dressing. The real magic here is Henry, that uniquely malleable creature. When he is George Rathbun, he is *all* George. Ditto the Wisconsin Rat; ditto Henry Shake. It has been eighteen months since he took Symphonic Stan from the closet and fit into him like a hand into a glove to dazzle the crowd at a Madison VFW record hop, but the clothes still fit, oh yes, they fit, and he fits within them, a hipster reborn whole into a past he never saw firsthand.

On his extended palm, the spinning LP resembles a solid, unmoving, black beachball.

Whenever Symphonic Stan puts on a hop, he always begins with 'In the Mood.' Although he does not detest Glenn Miller as some jazz aficionados do, over the years he has grown tired of this number. But it always does the job. Even if the customers have no choice but to dance with one foot in the grave and the other on the proverbial banana peel, they *do* dance. Besides, he knows that after Miller was drafted he told the arranger Billy May of his plan to 'come out of this war as some kind of hero,' and, hell, he was as good as his word, wasn't he?

Henry reaches the mike and slips the revolving record onto the platter with a negligent gesture of his right hand. The crowd applauds him with an exhaled *oooh*.

'Welcome, welcome, all you hepcats and hepkitties,' Henry says. The words emerge from the speakers wrapped in the smooth, slightly above-it-all voice of a true broadcaster in 1938 or 1939, one of the men who did live remotes from dance halls and nightclubs located from Boston to Catalina. Honey poured through their throats, these muses of the night, and they never missed a beat. 'Say, tell me this, you gates and gators, can you think of a better way to kick off a swingin' soiree than with Glenn Miller? Come on, brothers and sisters, give me *yeahhh*.'

From the residents of Maxton's – some of whom are already out on the floor, others wheelchair-bound on its edges in various postures of confusion or vacuity – comes a whispery response, less a party cry than the rustle of an autumn wind through bare branches. Symphonic Stan grins like a shark and holds up his hands as if to still a hopped-up multitude, then twirls and spins like a Savoy Ballroom dancer inspired by Chick Webb. His coattails spread like wings, his sparkling feet fly and land and fly again. The moment evaporates, and two black beachballs appear on the deejay's palms, one of them spinning back into its sleeve, the other down to meet the needle.

'All-reety all-righty all-rooty, you hoppin' hens and boppin' bunnies, here comes the Sentimental Gentleman, Mr Tommy Dorsey, so get off your money and grab your honey while vocalist Dick Haymes, the pride of Buenos Aires, Argentina, asks the musical question "How Am I to Know You?" Frank Sinatra hasn't entered the building yet, brethren and sistren, but life is still fine as mmmmmm wine.'

Rebecca Vilas cannot believe what she is seeing. This guy is getting just about everyone out onto the floor, even some of the wheelchair cases, who are dipping and swirling with the best of them. Dolled up in his exotic, astonishing outfit, Symphonic Stan – Henry Leyden, she reminds herself – is corny and breathtaking, absurd and convincing, all at once. He's like . . . some kind of *time capsule*, locked into both his role and what these old people want to hear. He has charmed them back into life, back into whatever youth they had left in them. Unbelievable! No other word will do. People she had written off as shuffling basket cases are blooming right in front of her. As for Symphonic Stan, he's carrying on like an elegant dervish, making her think of words like *suave, polished, urbane, unhinged, sexy, graceful*, words that do not connect except in him. And that thing he does with the records! How is that possible?

She does not realize that she is tapping her foot and swaying in time to the music until Henry puts on Artie Shaw's 'Begin the Beguine,' when she literally begins her own beguine by starting to dance by herself. Henry's hepcat jive-dance, the sight of so many white-haired, blue-haired, and bald-headed people gliding around the floor, Alice Weathers beaming happily in the arms of none other than gloomy Thorvald Thorvaldson, Ada Meyerhoff and 'Tom Tom' Boettcher twirling around each other in their wheelchairs, the sweeping pulse of the music driving everything beneath the molten radiance of Artie Shaw's clarinet, all of these things abruptly, magically coalesce into a vision of earthly beauty that brings tears stinging to her eyes. Smiling, she raises her arms, spins, and finds herself expertly grasped by Tom Tom's twin brother, eighty-six-year-old Hermie Boettcher, the retired geography teacher in A17 formerly considered something of a stick, who without a word fox-trots her right out to the middle of the floor.

'Shame to see a pretty girl dancing all on her lonesome,' Hermie says.

'Hermie, I'd follow you anywhere,' she tells him.

'Let's us get closer to the bandstand,' he says. 'I want a better look at that hotshot in the fancy suit. They say he's blind as a bat, but I don't believe it.'

His hand planted firmly at the base of her spine, his hips swerving in time to Artie Shaw, Hermie guides her to within a foot of the platform, where the Symphonic One is already doing his trick with a new record as he waits for the last bar of the present one. Rebecca could swear that Stan/Henry not only senses her presence before him but actually *winks* at her! But that is truly impossible . . . isn't it?

The Symphonic One twirls the Shaw record into its sleeve, the new one onto the platter, and says, 'Can you say "Vout"? Can you say "Solid"? Now that we're all limbered up, let's get jumpin' and jivin' with Woody Herman and "Wild Root." This tune is dedicated to all you beautiful ladies, especially the lady wearing Calyx.'

Rebecca laughs and says, 'Oh, dear.' He could smell her perfume; he recognized it!

Undaunted by the steamy tempo of 'Wild Root,' Hermie Boettcher slides into a back step, extends his arm, and spins Rebecca around. On the first beat of the next bar, he catches her in his arms and reverses direction, spinning them both toward the far end of the platform, where Alice Weathers stands next to Mr Thorvaldson, gazing up at Symphonic Stan.

'The special lady must be you,' Hermie says. 'Because that perfume of yours is worth a dedication.'

Rebecca asks, 'Where'd you learn to dance like this?'

'My brother and I, we were town boys. Learned how to dance in front of the jukebox at Alouette's, over by Arden.' Rebecca knows Alouette's, on Arden's Main Street, but what was once a soda fountain is now a lunch counter, and the jukebox disappeared around the time Johnny Mathis dropped off the charts. 'You want a good dancer, you find yourself a town boy. Tom Tom, now he was always the slickest dancer around, and you can plunk him in that chair, but you can't take away his rhythm.'

'Mr Stan, yoo-hoo, Mr Stan?' Alice Weathers has tilted her head and cupped her hands around her mouth. 'Do you take requests?'

A voice as flat and hard as the sound of two stones grinding together says, 'I was here first, old woman.'

This implacable rudeness brings Rebecca to a halt. Hermie's right foot comes gently down atop her left, then swiftly moves off, doing her no more injury than a kiss. Towering over Alice, Charles Burnside glares at Thorvald Thorvaldson. Thorvaldson steps back and tugs at Alice's hand.

'Certainly, my dear,' says Stan, bending down. 'Tell me your name and what you'd like to hear.'

'I am Alice Weathers, and—'

'I was here first,' Burny loudly repeats.

Rebecca glances at Hermie, who shakes his head and makes a sour face. Town boy or not, he is as intimidated as Mr Thorvaldson.

'"Moonglow," please. By Benny Goodman.'

'It's my turn, you jackass. I want that Woody Herman number called "Lady Magowan's Nightmare." That one's *good*.'

Hermie leans toward Rebecca's ear. 'Nobody likes that fella, but he gets his own way.'

'Not this time,' Rebecca says. 'Mr Burnside, I want you to—'

Symphonic Stan silences her with a wave of his hand. He turns to face the owner of the remarkably unpleasant voice. 'No can do, mister. The song is called "Lady Magowan's Dream," and I didn't bring that snappy little item with me this afternoon, sorry.'

'Okay, bud, how about "I Can't Get Started," the one Bunny Berigan did?'

'Oh, I *love* that,' Alice says. 'Yes, play "I Can't Get Started."'

'Happy to oblige,' Stan says in Henry Leyden's normal voice. Without bothering to jive around or spin the records on his hands, he simply exchanges the LP on the turntable for one from the first box. He seems oddly wilted as he steps to the mike and says, 'I've flown around the world on a plane, I settled revolutions in Spain. Can't get started. Dedicated to the lovely Alice Blue Gown and the One Who Walks by Night.'

'You're no better'n a monkey on a stick,' says Burny.

The music begins. Rebecca taps Hermie on the arm and moves up alongside Charles Burnside, for whom she has never felt anything but mild revulsion. Now that she has him in focus, her outrage and disgust cause her to say, 'Mr Burnside, you are going to apologize to Alice and to our guest here. You're a crude, obnoxious bully, and after you apologize, I want you to get back into your room, where you belong.'

Her words have no effect. Burnside's shoulders have slumped. He has a wide, sloppy grin on his face, and he is staring empty-eyed at nothing in particular. He looks too far gone to remember his own name, much less Bunny Berigan's. In any case, Alice Weathers has danced away, and Symphonic Stan, back at the far end of the platform and out of the pink spot, appears to be deep in thought. The elderly couples sway back and forth on the dance floor. Off to the side, Hermie Boettcher pantomimes dancing and quizzes her with a look.

'I'm sorry about that,' she says to Stan/Henry.

'No need to apologize. "I Can't Get Started" was my wife's favorite record. I've been thinking about her a lot, the past few days. Sort of took me by surprise.' He runs a hand over his sleek hair and shakes out his arms, visibly getting back into his role.

Rebecca decides to leave him alone. In fact, she wants to leave everyone alone for a little while. Signaling regret and the press of duty to Hermie, she makes her way through the crowd and exits the common room. Somehow, old Burny has beaten her to the corridor. He shuffles absently toward Daisy wing, head drooping, feet scuffing the floor.

'Mr Burnside,' she says, 'your act may fool everyone else, but I want you to know that it doesn't fool me.'

Moving by increments, the old man turns around. First one foot shifts, then a knee, the spavined waist, the second foot, finally the cadaverous trunk. The ugly bloom of Burny's head droops on its thin stalk, offering Rebecca a view of his mottled scalp. His long nose protrudes like a warped rudder. With the same dreadful slowness, his head lifts to reveal muddy eyes and a slack mouth. A flash of sheer vindictiveness rises into the dull eyes, and the dead lips writhe.

Frightened, Rebecca takes an instinctive step backward. Burny's mouth has moved all the way into a horrible grin. Rebecca wants to escape, but anger at having been humiliated by this miserable jerk lets her hold her ground.

'Lady Magowan had a bad, bad nightmare,' Burny informs her. He sounds drugged, or half asleep. 'And Lady Sophie had a nightmare. Only hers was worse.' He giggles. 'The king was in his countinghouse, counting out his honeys. That's what Sophie saw when she fell asleep.' His giggling rises in pitch, and he says something that might be 'Mr Munching.' His lips flap, revealing yellow, irregular teeth, and his sunken face undergoes a subtle change. A new kind of intelligence seems to sharpen his features. 'Does you know Mr Munshun? Mr Munshun and his li'l friend Gorg? Does you know what happened in Chicago?'

'Stop this right now, Mr Burnside.'

'Duz you know uff Fridz Haarman, him who wazz zo loff-ly? Dey called him, dey called him, dey called him "da Vamp, Vamp, Vamp of Hanover," yez dey dud, dud, dud. Evveybuddy, evveybuddy, evveybuddy haz godz nide-marez all da dime, dime, dime, ha ha ho ho.'

'*Stop talking like that!*' Rebecca shouts. '*You're not fooling me!*'

For a moment, the new intelligence flares within Burny's dim eyes. It almost instantly retreats. He licks his lips and says, 'Way-gup, Burn-Burn.'

'Whatever,' Rebecca says. 'Dinner is downstairs at seven, if you want it. Go take a nap or something, will you?'

Burny gives her a peeved, murky look and plops a foot down on the floor, beginning the tedious process that will turn him around again. 'You could write it down. Fritz Haarman. In Hanover.' His mouth twists into a smile of unsettling slyness. 'When the king comes here, maybe we can dance together.'

'No, thanks.' Rebecca turns her back on the old horror and clacks down the hallway on her high heels, uncomfortably aware of his eyes following her.

Rebecca's nice little Coach handbag lies flat on her desk in the windowless vestibule to Chipper's office. Before going in, she pauses to rip off a sheet of notepaper, write down *Fritz Harmann(?)*, *Hanover(?)*, and slip the paper into the bag's central compartment. It might be nothing – it probably is – but who knows? She is furious that she let Burnside frighten her, and if she can find a way to use his nonsense against him, she will do her best to expel him from Maxton's.

'Kiddo, is that you?' Chipper calls out.

'No, it's Lady Magowan and her freakin' nightmare.' She strides into Chipper's office and finds him behind his desk, happily counting out the bills contributed that afternoon by the sons and daughters of his clientele.

'My li'l Becky looks all ticked off,' he says. 'What happened, one of our zombies stomp on your foot?'

'Don't call me Becky.'

'Hey, hey, cheer up. You won't believe how much your silver-tongued boyfriend conned out of the relatives today. A hundred and twenty-six smackers! Free money! Okay, what went wrong, anyhow?'

'Charles Burnside spooked me, that's what. He ought to be in a mental hospital.'

'Are you kidding? That particular zombie is worth his weight in gold. As long as Charles Burnside can draw breath into his body, he will always have a place in my heart.' Grinning, he brandishes a handful of bills. 'And if you have a place in my heart, honey-baby, you'll always have a place at Maxton's.'

The memory of Burnside saying, *The king was in his countinghouse, counting out his honeys* makes her feel unclean. If Chipper were not grinning in that exultant, loose-lipped way, Rebecca supposes, he would not remind her so unpleasantly of his favorite resident. *Evveybuddy haz godz nide-marez all da dime, dime, dime* – that wasn't a bad description of the Fisherman's French Landing. Funny, you wouldn't think Old Burny would take more notice of those murders than Chipper. Rebecca had never heard him mention the Fisherman's crimes, apart from the time he groused that he would not be able to tell anyone he was going fishing until Dale Gilbertson finally got off his big fat butt, and what kind of crappy deal was that?

8

Two telephone calls and another, private matter, one he is doing his best to deny, have conspired to pluck Jack Sawyer from his cocoon in Norway Valley and put him on the road to French Landing, Sumner Street, and the police station. The first call had been from Henry, and Henry, calling from the Maxton cafeteria during one of the Symphonic One's breaks, had insisted on speaking his mind. A child had apparently been abducted from the sidewalk in front of Maxton's earlier that day. Whatever Jack's reasons for staying out of the case, which by the way he had never explained, they didn't count anymore, sorry. This made four children who had been lost to the Fisherman, because Jack didn't really think Irma Freneau was going to walk in her front door anytime soon, did he? Four children!

– No, Henry had said, I didn't hear about it on the radio. It happened this morning.

– From a janitor at Maxton's, Henry had said. He saw a worried-looking cop pick up a bicycle and put it in his trunk.

– All right, Henry had said, maybe I don't *know* for

certain, but I *am* certain. By tonight, Dale will identify the poor kid, and tomorrow his name will be all over the newspaper. And *then* this whole county is going to flip out. Don't you get it? Just knowing you are involved will do a lot to keep people calm. You no longer have the luxury of retirement, Jack. You have to do your part.

Jack had told him he was jumping to conclusions, and that they would talk about it later.

Forty-five minutes later, Dale Gilbertson had called with the news that a boy named Tyler Marshall had vanished from in front of Maxton's sometime that morning, and that Tyler's father, Fred Marshall, was down there right now, in the station, demanding to see Jack Sawyer. Fred was a great guy, a real straight arrow and family man, a solid citizen, a *friend* of Dale's, you could say, but at the moment he was at the end of his rope. Apparently Judy, his wife, had been having some kind of mental problems even before the trouble started, and Tyler's disappearance had driven her off the edge. She talked in gibberish, injured herself, tore the house apart.

– And I kind of know Judy Marshall, Dale had said. Beautiful, beautiful woman, a little thing but tough as all get-out on the inside, both feet on the ground, a great person, a tremendous person, someone you'd think would never lose her grip, no matter what. It seems she thought, knew, whatever, that Tyler had been snatched even before his bicycle turned up. Late this afternoon, she got so bad Fred had to call Dr Skarda and get her over to French County Lutheran in Arden, where they took one look at her and put her in Ward D, the mental wing. So you can imagine what kind of shape Fred's in. He insists on talking to you. *I have no confidence in you*, he said to me.

– Well, Dale had said, if you don't come down here,

Fred Marshall is going to show up at your house, that's what'll happen. I can't put the guy on a leash, and I'm not going to lock him up just to keep him away from you. On top of everything else, we need you here, Jack.

– All right, Dale had said. I know you're not making any promises. But you know what you should do.

Would these conversations have been enough to get him into his pickup and on the road to Sumner Street? Very likely, Jack imagines, which renders the third factor, the secret, barely acknowledged one, inconsequential. It means nothing. A silly attack of nerves, a buildup of anxiety, completely natural under the circumstances. The kind of thing that could happen to anybody. He felt like getting out of the house, so what? No one could accuse him of *escaping*. He was traveling toward, not running away from, that which he most wanted to *escape* – the dark undertow of the Fisherman's crimes. Neither was he committing himself to any deeper involvement. A friend of Dale's and the father of a child apparently missing, this Fred Marshall, insisted on talking to him; fine, let him talk. If half an hour with a retired detective could help Fred Marshall get a handle on his problems, the retired detective was willing to give him the time.

Everything else was merely personal. Waking dreams and robins' eggs messed with your mind, but that was merely personal. It could be outwaited, outwitted, figured out. No rational person took that stuff seriously: like a summer storm, it blew in, it blew out. Now, as he coasted through the green light at Centralia and noted, with a cop's reflexive awareness, the row of Harleys lined up in the Sand Bar's parking lot, he felt himself coming into alignment with the afternoon's difficulties. It made perfect sense that he should have found himself unable – well, let us say unwilling – to open the refrigerator door. Nasty surprises made you think twice. A light in his living room had expired, and when he had gone to the drawer that contained half a dozen new halogen bulbs, he had been unable to open it. In fact, he had not quite been able to open any drawer, cabinet, or closet in his house, which had denied him the capacity to make a cup of tea, change his clothes, prepare lunch, or do anything but leaf half-heartedly through books and watch television. When the flap of the mailbox had threatened to conceal a pyramid of small blue eggs, he had decided to put off collecting the mail until the next day. Anyhow, all he ever got were financial statements, magazines, and junk mail.

Let's not make it sound worse than it was, Jack says to himself. *I* could *have opened every door, drawer, and cabinet in the place, but I didn't* want *to. I wasn't afraid that robins' eggs were going to come spilling out of the refrigerator or the closet – it's just that I didn't want to take the chance of finding one of the blasted things. Show me a psychiatrist who says that's neurotic, and I'll show you a moron who doesn't understand psychology. All the old-timers used to tell me that working homicide messed with your head. Hell, that's why I retired in the first place!*

What was I supposed to do, stay on the force until I ate my gun? You're a smart guy, Henry Leyden, and I love you, but there are some things you don't GET!

All right, he was going to Sumner Street. Everybody was yelling at him to do something, and that's what he was doing. He'd say hello to Dale, greet the boys, sit down with this Fred Marshall, the solid citizen with a missing son, and give him the usual oatmeal about everything possible being done, blah blah, the FBI is working hand in glove with us on this one, and the bureau has the finest investigators in the world. *That* oatmeal. As far as Jack was concerned, his primary duty was to stroke Fred Marshall's fur, as if to soothe the feelings of an injured cat; when Marshall had calmed down, Jack's supposed obligation to the community – an obligation that existed entirely in the minds of others – would be fulfilled, freeing him to go back to the privacy he had earned. If Dale didn't like it, he could take a running jump into the Mississippi; if *Henry* didn't like it, Jack would refuse to read *Bleak House* and force him to listen instead to Lawrence Welk, Vaughn Monroe, or something equally excruciating. Bad Dixieland. Years ago, someone had given Jack a CD called *Fats Manassas & His Muskrat All Stars Stompin' the Ramble*. Thirty seconds of Fats Manassas, and Henry would be begging for mercy.

This image makes Jack feel comfortable enough to prove that his hesitation before cupboards and drawers had been merely a temporary unwillingness, not phobic inability. Even while his attention was elsewhere, as it chiefly was, the shoved-in ashtray below the dash has mocked and taunted him since he first climbed into the pickup. A kind of sinister suggestiveness, an aura of latent malice, surrounds the ashtray's flat little panel.

Does he fear that a small blue egg lurks behind the little panel?

Of course not. Nothing is in there but air and molded black plastic.

In that case, he can pull it out.

The buildings on the outskirts of French Landing glide past the pickup's windows. Jack has reached almost the exact point at which Henry pulled the plug on Dirtysperm. Obviously he can open the ashtray. Nothing could be simpler. You just get your fingers under there and tug. Easiest thing in the world. He extends a hand. Before his fingers touch the panel, he snatches the hand back. Drops of perspiration glide down his forehead and lodge in his eyebrows.

'It isn't a big deal,' he says aloud. 'You got some kind of problem here, Jacky-boy?'

Again, he extends his hand to the ashtray. Abruptly aware that he is paying more attention to the bottom of his dashboard than to the road, he glances up and cuts his speed by half. He refuses to hit his brakes. It's just an ashtray, for God's sake. His fingers meet the panel, then curl under its lip. Jack glances at the road once more. Then, with the decisiveness of a nurse ripping a strip of tape off a patient's hairy abdomen, he yanks out the sliding tray. The lighter attachment, which he had unknowingly dislodged in his driveway that morning, bounces three inches into the air, greatly resembling, to Jack's appalled eye, a flying black-and-silver egg.

He veers off the road, bumps over the weedy shoulder, and heads toward a looming telephone pole. The lighter drops back into the tray with a loud, metallic thwack no egg in the world could have produced. The telephone pole swims closer and nearly fills the windshield. Jack stamps on the brake and jerks to a halt, arousing a flurry of ticks and rattles from the ashtray. If he had not cut his speed before opening the ashtray, he would have driven straight into the pole, which stands about four feet from the hood of the pickup. Jack wipes the sweat off his face and picks up the lighter. 'Shit on a shingle.' He clicks the attachment into its receptacle and collapses backward against the seat. 'No wonder they say smoking can kill you,' he says. The joke is too feeble to amuse him, and for a couple of seconds he does nothing but slump against the seat and regard the sparse traffic on Lyall Road. When his heart rate drops back to something like normal, he reminds himself that he did, after all, open the ashtray.

★

Blond, rumpled Tom Lund has evidently been prepped for his arrival, for when Jack walks past three bicycles lined up next to the door and enters the station, the young officer takes off from behind his desk and rushes forward to whisper that Dale and Fred Marshall are waiting for him in Dale's office, and he will show him right in. They'll be glad to see him, that's for sure. 'I am, too, Lieutenant Sawyer,' Lund adds. 'Boy, I gotta say it. What you got, I think, we need.'

'Call me Jack. I'm not a lieutenant anymore. I'm not even a cop anymore.' Jack had met Tom Lund during the Kinderling investigation, and he had liked the young man's eagerness and dedication. In love with his job, his uniform, and his badge, respectful of his chief and awed by Jack, Lund had uncomplainingly logged hundreds of hours on the telephone, in records offices, and in his car, checking and rechecking the often contradictory details spun off by the collision between a Wisconsin farm-insurance salesman and two Sunset Strip working girls. All the while, Tom Lund had retained the energetic sparkle of a high school quarterback running onto the field for his first game.

He does not look that way anymore, Jack observes. Dark smudges hang beneath his eyes, and the bones in his face are more prominent. More than sleeplessness and exhaustion lie behind Lund's affect: his eyes bear the helplessly startled expression of those who have suffered a great moral shock. The Fisherman has stolen a good part of Tom Lund's youth.

'But I'll see what I can do,' Jack says, offering the promise of a commitment greater than he intends.

'We can sure use anything you can give us,' Lund says. It is too much, too servile, and as Lund turns away and leads him to the office, Jack thinks, *I didn't come here to be your savior.*

The thought instantly makes him feel guilty.

Lund knocks, opens the door to announce Jack, shows him in, and vanishes like a ghost, utterly unnoticed by the two men who rise from their chairs and fasten their eyes upon their visitor's face, one with visible gratitude, the other with an enormous degree of the same emotion mixed with naked need, which makes Jack even more uncomfortable.

Over Dale's garbled introduction, Fred Marshall says, 'Thank you for agreeing to come, thank you so much. That's all I can . . .' His right arm sticks out like a pump handle. When Jack takes his hand, an even greater quantity of feeling floods into Fred Marshall's face. His hand fastens on Jack's and seems almost to *claim* it, as an animal claims its prey. He squeezes, hard, a considerable number of times. His eyes fill. 'I can't . . .' Marshall pulls his hand away and scrubs the tears off his face. Now his eyes look raw and intensely vulnerable. 'Boy oh boy,' he says. 'I'm really glad you're here, Mr Sawyer. Or should I say Lieutenant?'

'Jack is fine. Why don't the two of you fill me in on what happened today?'

Dale points toward a waiting chair; the three men take their places; the painful but essentially simple story of Fred, Judy, and Tyler Marshall begins. Fred speaks first, at some length. In his version of the story, a valiant, lion-hearted woman, a devoted wife and mother, succumbs to baffling, multifaceted transformations and disorders, and develops mysterious symptoms overlooked by her ignorant, stupid, self-centered husband. She blurts out nonsense words; she writes crazy stuff on sheets of notepaper, rams the papers into her mouth, and tries to swallow them. *She sees the tragedy coming in advance, and it unhinges her.* Sounds crazy, but the self-centered husband thinks it's the truth. That is, he *thinks* he thinks it's the truth, because he's been thinking about it since he first talked to Dale, and even though it sounds crazy, it kind of makes sense. Because what other explanation could there be? So that's what he thinks he thinks – that his wife started to lose her mind because she knew that the Fisherman was on the way. Things like that are possible, he guesses. For example, the brave afflicted wife knew that her beautiful wonderful son was missing even before the stupid selfish husband, who went to work exactly as if it were a normal day, told her about the bicycle. That pretty much proved what he was talking about. The beautiful little boy went out with his three friends, but only the three friends came back, and Officer Danny Tcheda found the little son's Schwinn bike and one of his poor sneakers on the sidewalk outside Maxton's.

'Danny Cheetah?' asks Jack, who, like Fred Marshall, is beginning to think he thinks a number of alarming things.

'Tcheda,' says Dale, and spells it for him. Dale tells his own, far shorter version of the story. In Dale Gilbertson's story, a boy goes out for a ride on his bicycle and vanishes, perhaps as a result of abduction, from the sidewalk in front of Maxton's. That is all of the story Dale knows, and he trusts that Jack Sawyer will be able to fill in many of the surrounding blanks.

Jack Sawyer, at whom both of the other men in the room are staring, takes time to adjust to the three thoughts he now thinks he thinks. The first is not so much a thought as a response that embodies a hidden thought: from the moment Fred Marshall clutched his hand and said 'Boy oh boy,' Jack found himself liking the man, an unanticipated turn in the evening's plot. Fred Marshall strikes him as something like the poster boy for small-town life. If you put his picture on billboards advertising French County real estate, you could sell a lot of second homes to people in Milwaukee and

Chicago. Marshall's friendly, good-looking face and slender runner's body are as good as testimonials to responsibility, decency, good manners and good neighborliness, modesty, and a generous heart. The more Fred Marshall accuses himself of selfishness and stupidity, the more Jack likes him. And the more he likes him, the more he sympathizes with his terrible plight, the more he wishes to help the man. Jack had come to the station expecting that he would respond to Dale's friend like a policeman, but his cop reflexes have rusted from disuse. He is responding like a fellow citizen. Cops, as Jack well knows, seldom view the civilians caught up in the backwash of a crime as fellow citizens, certainly never in the early stages of an investigation. (The thought hidden at the center of Jack's response to the man before him is that Fred Marshall, being what he is, cannot harbor suspicions about anyone with whom he is on good terms.)

Jack's second thought is that of both a cop and a fellow citizen, and while he continues his adjustment to the third, which is wholly the product of his rusty yet still accurate cop reflexes, he makes it public. 'The bikes I saw outside belong to Tyler's friends? Is someone questioning them now?'

'Bobby Dulac,' Dale says. 'I talked to them when they came in, but I didn't get anywhere. According to them, they were all together on Chase Street, and Tyler rode off by himself. They claim they didn't see anything. Maybe they didn't.'

'But you think there's more.'

'Honest to God, I do. But I don't know what the dickens it could be, and we have to send them home before their parents get bent out of shape.'

'Who are they, what are their names?'

Fred Marshall wraps his fingers together as if around the handle of an invisible baseball bat. 'Ebbie Wexler, T. J.

Renniker, and Ronnie Metzger. They're the kids Ty's been hanging around with this summer.' An unspoken judgment hovers about this last sentence.

'It sounds like you don't consider them the best possible company for your son.'

'Well, no,' says Fred, caught between his desire to tell the truth and his innate wish to avoid the appearance of unfairness. 'Not if you put it like that. Ebbie seems like kind of a bully, and the other two are maybe a little on the . . . *slow* side? I hope . . . or I was hoping . . . that Ty would realize he could do better and spend his free time with kids who are more on, you know . . .'

'More on his level.'

'Right. The trouble is, my son is sort of small for his age, and Ebbie Wexler is . . . um . . .'

'Heavyset and tall for his age,' Jack says. 'The perfect situation for a bully.'

'You're saying *you* know Ebbie *Wexler?*'

'No, but I saw him this morning. He was with the other two boys and your son.'

Dale jolts upright in his chair, and Fred Marshall drops his invisible bat. 'When was that?' Dale asks. At the same time, Fred Marshall asks, 'Where?'

'Chase Street, about ten past eight. I came in to pick up Henry Leyden and drive him home. When we were on our way out of town, the boys drove their bikes into the road right in front of me. I got a good look at your son, Mr Marshall. He seemed like a great kid.'

Fred Marshall's widening eyes indicate that some kind of hope, some promise, is taking shape before him; Dale relaxes. 'That pretty much matches their story. It would have been right before Ty took off on his own. If he did.'

'Or they took off and left him,' says Ty's father. 'They were faster on their bikes than Ty, and sometimes they, you know . . . they teased him.'

'By racing ahead and leaving him alone,' Jack says. Fred Marshall's glum nod speaks of boyhood humiliations shared with this sympathetic father. Jack remembers the inflamed, hostile face and raised finger of Ebbie Wexler and wonders if and how the boy might be protecting himself. Dale had said that he smelled the presence of falsity in the boys' story, but why would they lie? Whatever their reasons, the lie almost certainly began with Ebbie Wexler. The other two followed orders.

For the moment setting aside the third of his thoughts, Jack says, 'I want to talk to the boys before you send them home. Where are they?'

'The interrogation room, top of the stairs.' Dale aims a finger at the ceiling. 'Tom will take you up.'

With its battleship-gray walls, gray metal table, and single window narrow as a slit in a castle wall, the room at the top of the stairs seems designed to elicit confessions through boredom and despair, and when Tom Lund leads Jack through the door, the four inhabitants of the interrogation room appear to have succumbed to its leaden atmosphere. Bobby Dulac looks sideways, stops drumming a pencil on the tabletop, and says, 'Well, hoo-ray for Hollywood. Dale said you were coming down.' Even Bobby gleams a little less conspicuously in this gloom. 'Did you want to interrogate these here hoodlums, Lieutenant?'

'In a minute, maybe.' Two of the three hoodlums on the far side of the table watch Jack move alongside Bobby Dulac as if fearing he will clap them in a cell. The words 'interrogate' and 'Lieutenant' have had the bracing effect of a cold wind from Canada. Ebbie Wexler squints at Jack, trying to look tough, and the boy beside him, Ronnie Metzger, wriggles in his chair, his eyes like dinner plates. The third boy, T. J. Renniker, has dropped his head atop his crossed arms and appears to be asleep.

'Wake him up,' Jack says. 'I have something to say, and I want you all to hear it.' In fact, he has nothing to say, but he needs these boys to pay attention to him. He already knows that Dale was right. If they are not lying, they are at least holding something back. That's why his abrupt appearance within their dozy scene frightened them. If Jack had been in charge, he would have separated the boys and questioned them individually, but now he must deal with Bobby Dulac's mistake. He has to treat them collectively, to begin with, and he has to work on their fear. He does not want to terrorize the boys, merely to get their hearts pumping a bit faster; after that, he can separate them. The weakest, guiltiest link has already declared himself. Jack feels no compunction about telling lies to get information.

Ronnie Metzger shoves T.J.'s shoulder and says, 'Wake up, bumdell . . . *dumbbell.*'

The sleeping boy moans, lifts his head from the table, begins to stretch out his arms. His eyes fasten on Jack, and blinking and swallowing he snaps into an upright position.

'Welcome back,' Jack says. 'I want to introduce myself and explain what I am doing here. My name is Jack Sawyer, and I am a lieutenant in the Homicide Division of the Los Angeles Police Department. I have an excellent record and a roomful of citations and medals. When I go after a bad guy, I usually wind up arresting him. Three years ago, I came here on a case from Los Angeles. Two weeks later, a man named Thornberg Kinderling was shipped back to LA in chains.

Because I know this area and have worked with its law enforcement officers, the LAPD asked me to assist your local force in its investigation of the Fisherman murders.' He glances down to see if Bobby Dulac is grinning at this nonsense, but Bobby is staring frozen-faced across the table. 'Your friend Tyler Marshall was with you before he disappeared this morning. Did the Fisherman take him? I hate to say it, but I think he did. Maybe we can get Tyler back, and maybe we can't, but if I am going to stop the Fisherman, I need you to tell me exactly what happened, down to the last detail. You have to be completely honest with me, because if you lie or keep anything secret, you will be guilty of obstruction of justice. Obstruction of justice is a serious, serious crime. Officer Dulac, what is the minimum sentence for that crime in the state of Wisconsin?'

'Five years, I'm pretty sure,' Bobby Dulac says.

Ebbie Wexler bites the inside of his cheek; Ronnie Metzger looks away and frowns at the table; T. J. Renniker dully contemplates the narrow window.

Jack sits down beside Bobby Dulac. 'Incidentally, I was the guy in the pickup one of you gave the finger to this morning. I can't say I'm thrilled to see you again.'

Two heads swivel toward Ebbie, who squints ferociously, trying to solve this brand-new problem. 'I did not,' he says, having settled on outright denial. 'Maybe it looked like I did, but I didn't.'

'You're lying, and we haven't even started to talk about Tyler Marshall yet. I'll give you one more chance. Tell me the truth.'

Ebbie smirks. 'I don't go around flipping the bird at people I don't know.'

'Stand up,' Jack says.

Ebbie glances from side to side, but his friends are unable to meet his gaze. He shoves back his chair and stands up, uncertainly.

'Officer Dulac,' Jack says, 'take this boy outside and hold him there.'

Bobby Dulac performs his role perfectly. He uncoils from his chair and keeps his eyes on Ebbie as he glides toward him. He resembles a panther on the way to a sumptuous meal. Ebbie Wexler jumps back and tries to stay Bobby with a raised palm. 'No, don't – I take it back – I did it, okay?'

'Too late,' Jack says. He watches as Bobby grasps the boy's elbow and pulls him toward the door. Red-faced and sweating, Ebbie plants his feet on the floor, and the forward pressure applied to his arm folds him over the bulge of his stomach. He staggers forward, yelping and scattering tears. Bobby Dulac opens the door and hauls him into the bleak second-floor corridor. The door slams shut and cuts off a wail of fear.

The two remaining boys have turned the color of skim milk and seem incapable of movement. 'Don't worry about him,' Jack says. 'He'll be fine. In fifteen, twenty minutes, you'll be free to go home. I didn't think there was any point in talking to someone who lies from the git-go, that's all. Remember: even lousy cops know when they're being lied to, and I am a *great* cop. So this is what we are going to do now. We're going to talk about what happened this morning, about what Tyler was doing, the way you separated from him, where you were, what you did afterward, anyone you might have seen, that kind of thing.' He leans back and flattens his hands on the table. 'Go on, tell me what happened.'

Ronnie and T.J. look at each other. T.J. inserts his right index finger into his mouth and begins to worry the nail with his front teeth. 'Ebbie flipped you,' Ronnie says.

'No kidding. After that.'

'Uh, Ty said he hadda go someplace.'

'He hadda go someplace,' T.J. chimes in.

'Where were you right then?'

'Uh . . . outside the Allsorts Pomorium.'

'*Emporium*,' T.J. says. 'It's not a pomorium, mushhead, it's a *em-por-ee-um*.'

'And?'

'And Ty said—' Ronnie glances at T.J. 'Ty said he hadda go somewhere.'

'Which way did he go, east or west?'

The boys treat this question as though it were asked in a foreign language, by puzzling over it, mutely.

'Toward the river, or away from the river?'

They consult each other again. The question has been asked in English, but no proper answer exists. Finally, Ronnie says, 'I don't know.'

'How about you, T.J.? Do you know?'

T.J. shakes his head.

'Good. That's honest. You don't know because you didn't see him leave, did you? And he didn't really say he had to go somewhere, did he? I bet Ebbie made that up.'

T.J. wriggles, and Ronnie gazes at Jack with wondering awe. He has just revealed himself to be Sherlock Holmes.

'Remember when I drove past in my truck?' They nod in unison. 'Tyler was with you.' They nod again. 'You'd already left the sidewalk in front of the Allsorts Emporium, and you were riding east on Chase Street – away from the river. I saw you in my rearview mirror. Ebbie was pedaling very fast. The two of you could almost keep up with him. Tyler was smaller than the rest of you, and he fell behind. So I *know* he didn't go off on his own. He couldn't keep up.'

Ronnie Metzger wails, 'And he got way, way behind, and the Misherfun came out and grabbed him.' He promptly bursts into tears.

Jack leans forward. 'Did you see it happen? Either one of you?'

'*Noooaa*,' Ronnie sobs. T.J. slowly shakes his head.

'You didn't see anyone talking with Ty, or a car stopping, or him going into a shop, or anything like that?'

The boys utter an incoherent, overlapping babble to the effect that they saw nothing.

'When did you realize he was gone?'

T.J. opens his mouth, then closes it. Ronnie says, 'When we were having the Slurpees.' His face pursed with tension, T.J. nods in agreement.

Two more questions reveal that they had enjoyed the Slurpees at the 7-Eleven, where they also purchased Magic cards, and that it had probably taken them no more than a couple of minutes to notice Tyler Marshall's absence. 'Ebbie said Ty would buy us some more cards,' helpful Ronnie adds.

They have reached the moment for which Jack has been waiting. Whatever the secret may be, it took place soon after the boys came out of the 7-Eleven and saw that Tyler had still not joined them. And the secret is T.J.'s alone. The kid is practically sweating blood, while the memory of the Slurpees and Magic cards has calmed down his friend to a remarkable degree. There is only one more question he wishes to ask the two of them. 'So Ebbie wanted to find Tyler. Did you all get on your bikes and search around, or did Ebbie send just one of you?'

'Huh?' Ronnie says. T.J. drops his chin and crosses his arms on the top of his head, as if to ward off a blow. 'Tyler went somewheres,' Ronnie says. 'We didn't look for him, we went to the park. To trade the Magic cards.'

'I see,' Jack says. 'Ronnie, thank you. You have been very helpful. I'd like you to go outside and stay with Ebbie and Officer Dulac while I have a short conversation with T.J. It shouldn't take more than five minutes, if that.'

'I can go?' At Jack's nod, Ronnie moves hesitantly out of his chair. When he reaches the door, T.J. emits a whimper. Then Ronnie is gone, and T.J. jerks backward into his chair and tries to become as small as possible while staring at Jack with eyes that have become shiny, flat, and perfectly round.

'T.J.,' Jack says, 'you have nothing to worry about, I promise you.' Now that he is alone with the boy who had declared his guilt by falling asleep in the interrogation room, Jack Sawyer wants above all to absolve him of that guilt. He knows T.J.'s secret, and the secret is nothing; it is useless. 'No matter what you tell me, I'm not going to arrest you. That's a promise, too. You're not in any trouble, son. In fact, I'm glad you and your friends could come down here and help us straighten things out.'

He goes on in this vein for another three or four minutes, in the course of which T. J. Renniker, formerly condemned to death by firing squad, gradually comprehends that his pardon has come through and his release from what his buddy Ronnie would call vurance dile is imminent. A little color returns to his face. He returns to his former size, and his eyes lose their horror-stricken glaze.

'Tell me what Ebbie did,' Jack says. 'Just between you and me. I won't tell him anything. Honest. I won't rat you out.'

'He wanted Ty to buy more Magic cards,' T.J. says, feeling his way through unknown territory. 'If Ty was there, he woulda. Ebbie can get kind of mean. So . . . so he told me, go downstreet and get the slowpoke, or I'll give you an Indian burn.'

'You got on your bike and rode back down Chase Street.'

'Uh-huh. I looked, but I didn't see Ty anywheres. I thought I *would*, you know? Because where else could he be?'

'And . . .?' Jack reels in the answer he knows is coming by winding his hand through the air.

'And I still didn't see him. And I got to Queen Street, where the old folks' home is, with the big hedge out front. And, um, I saw his bike there. On the sidewalk in front of the hedge. His sneaker was there, too. And some leaves off the hedge.'

There it is, the worthless secret. Maybe not entirely worthless: it gives them a pretty accurate fix on the time of the boy's disappearance: 8:15, say, or 8:20. The bike lay on the sidewalk next to the sneaker for something like four hours before Danny Tcheda spotted them. Maxton's takes up just about all the land on that section of Queen Street, and no one was showing up for the Strawberry Fest until noon.

T.J. describes being afraid – if the Fisherman pulled Ty into that hedge, maybe he'd come back for more! In answer to Jack's final question, the boy says, 'Ebbie told us to say Ty rode away from in front of the Allsorts, so people wouldn't, like, blame us. In case he was killed. Ty isn't really killed, is he? Kids like *Ty* don't get killed.'

'I hope not,' Jack says.

'Me, too.' T.J. snuffles and wipes his nose on his arm.

'Let's get you on your way home,' Jack says, leaving his chair.

T.J. stands up and begins to move along the side of the table. 'Oh! I just remembered!'

'What?'

'I saw feathers on the sidewalk.'

The floor beneath Jack's feet seems to roll left, then right, like the deck of a ship. He steadies himself by grasping the back of a chair. 'Really.' He takes care to compose himself before turning to the boy. 'What do you mean, feathers?'

'Black ones. Big. They looked like they came off a crow. One was next to the bike, and the other was *in* the sneaker.'

'That's funny,' says Jack, buying time until he ceases to reverberate from the unexpected appearance of feathers in his conversation with T. J. Renniker. That he should respond at all is ridiculous; that he should have felt, even for a second, that he was likely to faint is grotesque. T.J.'s feathers were real crow feathers on a real sidewalk. His were dream feathers, feathers from unreal robins, illusory as everything else in a dream. Jack tells himself a number of helpful things like this, and soon he does feel normal once again, but we should be aware that, for the rest of the night and much of the next day, the word *feathers* floats, surrounded by an aura as charged as an electrical storm, beneath and through his thoughts, now and then surfacing with the sizzling crackle of a lightning bolt.

'It's weird,' T.J. says. 'Like, how did a feather get in his *sneaker*?'

'Maybe the wind blew it there,' Jack says, conveniently ignoring the nonexistence of wind this day. Reassured by the stability of the floor, he waves T.J. into the hallway, then follows him out.

Ebbie Wexler pushes himself off the wall and stamps up alongside Bobby Dulac. Still in character, Bobby might have been carved from a block of marble. Ronnie Metzger sidles away. 'We can send these boys home,' Jack says. 'They've done their duty.'

'T.J., what did you say?' Ebbie asks, glowering.

'He made it clear that you know nothing about your friend's disappearance,' Jack says.

Ebbie relaxes, though not without distributing scowls all around. The final and most malignant scowl is for Jack, who raises his eyebrows. 'I didn't cry,' Ebbie says. 'I was scared, but I didn't cry.'

'You were scared, all right,' Jack says. 'Next time, don't lie to me. You had your chance to help the police, and you blew it.'

Ebbie struggles with this notion and succeeds, at least partially, in absorbing it. 'Okay, but I wasn't really flippin' at you. It was the stupid music.'

'I hated it, too. The guy who was with me insisted on playing it. You know who he was?'

In the face of Ebbie's suspicious glower, Jack says, 'George Rathbun.'

It is like saying 'Superman,' or 'Arnold Schwarzenegger'; Ebbie's suspicion evaporates, and his face transforms. Innocent wonder fills his small, close-set eyes. 'You know George Rathbun?'

'He's one of my best friends,' Jack says, not adding that most of his other best friends are, in a sense, also George Rathbun.

'Cool,' Ebbie says.

In the background, T.J. and Ronnie echo, '*Cool.*'

'George *is* pretty cool,' Jack says. 'I'll tell him you said that. Let's go downstairs and get you kids on your bikes.'

Still wrapped in the glory of having gazed upon the great, the *tremendous* George Rathbun, the boys mount their bicycles, pedal away down Sumner Street, and swerve off onto Second. Bobby Dulac says, 'That was a good trick, what you said about George Rathbun. Sent them away happy.'

'It wasn't a trick.'

So startled that he jostles back into the station house

side by side with Jack, Bobby says, 'George Rathbun is a friend of yours?'

'Yep,' Jack says. 'And sometimes, he can be a real pain in the ass.'

Dale and Fred Marshall look up as Jack enters the office, Dale with a cautious expectancy, Fred Marshall with what Jack sees, heartbreakingly, as hope.

'Well?' Dale says.

(feathers)

'You were right, they were hiding something, but it isn't much.'

Fred Marshall slumps against the back of his chair, letting some of his belief in a future hope leak out of him like air from a punctured tire.

'Not long after they got to the 7-Eleven, the Wexler boy sent T.J. down the street to look for your son,' Jack says. 'When T.J. got to Queen Street, he saw the bike and the sneaker lying on the sidewalk. Of course, they all thought of the Fisherman. Ebbie Wexler figured they might get blamed for leaving him behind, and he came up with the story you heard – that Tyler left them, instead of the other way around.'

'If you saw all four boys around ten past eight, that means Tyler disappeared only a few minutes later. What does this guy do, lurk in hedges?'

'Maybe he does exactly that,' Jack says. 'Did you have people check out that hedge?'

(feathers)

'The staties went over it, through it, and under it. Leaves and dirt, that's what they came up with.'

As if driving a spike with his hand, Fred Marshall bangs his fist down onto the desk. 'My son was gone for four hours before anyone noticed his bike. Now it's almost seven-thirty! He's been missing for most of the day! I shouldn't be sitting here, I should be driving around, looking for him.'

'Everybody is looking for your son, Fred,' Dale says. 'My guys, the staties, even the FBI.'

'I have no faith in them,' Fred says. 'They haven't found Irma Freneau, have they? Why should they find my son? As far as I can see, I've got one chance here.' When he looks at Jack, emotion turns his eyes into lamps. 'That chance is you, Lieutenant. Will you help me?'

Jack's third and most troubling thought, withheld until now and purely that of an experienced policeman, causes him to say, 'I'd like to talk to your wife. If you're planning on visiting her tomorrow, would you mind if I came along?'

Dale blinks and says, 'Maybe we should talk about this.'

'Do you think it would do some good?'

'It might,' Jack says.

'Seeing you might do *her* some good, anyhow,' Fred says. 'Don't you live in Norway Valley? That's on the way to Arden. I can pick you up about nine.'

'Jack,' Dale says.

'See you at nine,' Jack says, ignoring the signals of mingled distress and anger emanating from his friend, also the little voice that whispers (*feather*).

'Amazing,' says Henry Leyden. 'I don't know whether to thank you or congratulate you. Both, I suppose. It's too late in the game to make "bitchrod," like me, but I think you could have a shot at "dope."'

'Don't lose your head. The only reason I went down there was to keep the boy's father from coming to my house.'

'That wasn't the only reason.'

'You're right. I was feeling sort of edgy and hemmed in. I felt like getting out, changing the scenery.'

'But there was also *another* reason.'

'Henry, you are hip-deep in pigshit, do you know that? You want to think I acted out of civic duty, or honor, or compassion, or altruism, or something, but I didn't. I don't like having to say this, but I'm a lot less good-hearted and responsible than you think I am.'

'"Hip-deep in pigshit"? Man, you are absolutely on the money. I have been hip-deep in pigshit, not to mention chest-deep and even *chin*-deep in pigshit, most of my life.'

'Nice of you to admit it.'

'However, you misunderstand me. You're right, I do think you are a good, decent person. I don't just think it, I know it. You're modest, you're compassionate, you're honorable, you're responsible – no matter what you think of yourself right now. But that wasn't what I was talking about.'

'What *did* you mean, then?'

'The other reason you decided to go to the police station is connected to this problem, this concern, whatever it is, that's been bugging you for the past couple of weeks. It's like you've been walking around under a shadow.'

'Huh,' Jack said.

'This problem, this *secret* of yours, takes up half your attention, so you're only half present; the rest of you is somewhere else. Sweetie, don't you think I can tell when you're worried and preoccupied? I might be blind, but I can see.'

'Okay. Let's suppose that something has been on my mind lately. What could that have to do with going to the station house?'

'There are two possibilities. Either you were going off to confront it, or you were fleeing from it.'

Jack does not speak.

'All of which suggests that this problem has to do with your life as a policeman. It could be some old case coming back to haunt you. Maybe a psychotic thug you put in jail was released and is threatening to kill you. Or, hell, I'm completely full of shit and you found out you have liver cancer and a life expectancy of three months.'

'I don't have cancer, at least as far as I know, and no ex-con wants to kill me. All of my old cases, most of them, anyway, are safely asleep in the records warehouse of the LAPD. Of course, something has been bothering me lately, and I should have expected you to see that. But I didn't want to, I don't know, burden you with it until I managed to figure it out for myself.'

'Tell me one thing, will you? Were you going toward it, or running away?'

'There's no answer to that question.'

'We shall see. Isn't the food ready by now? I'm starving, literally *starving*. You cook too slow. I would have been done ten minutes ago.'

'Hold your horses,' Jack says. 'Coming right up. The problem is this crazy kitchen of yours.'

'Most rational kitchen in America. Maybe in the world.'

After ducking out of the police station quickly enough to avoid a useless conversation with Dale, Jack had yielded to impulse and called Henry with the offer of making dinner for both of them. A couple of good steaks, a nice bottle of wine, grilled mushrooms, a big salad. He could pick up everything they needed in French Landing. Jack had cooked for Henry on three or four previous occasions, and Henry had prepared one stupendously bizarre dinner for Jack. (The housekeeper had taken all the herbs and spices off their rack to wash it, and she had put everything back in the wrong place.) What was he doing in French Landing? He'd explain that when he got there. At eight-thirty he had pulled up before Henry's roomy white farmhouse, greeted Henry, and carried the groceries and his copy of *Bleak House* into the kitchen. He had tossed the book to the far end of the table, opened the wine, poured a glass for his host and one for himself, and started cooking. He'd had to spend several minutes reacquainting himself with the eccentricities of Henry's kitchen, in which objects were not located by kind – pans with pans, knives with knives, pots with pots – but according to what sort of meal required their usage. If Henry wanted to whip up a grilled trout and some new potatoes, he had only to open the proper cabinet to find all the necessary utensils. These were arranged in four basic groups (meat, fish, poultry, and vegetables), with many subgroups and subsubgroups within each category. The filing system confounded Jack, who often had to peer into several widely separated realms before coming upon the frying pan or spatula he was looking for. As Jack chopped, wandered the shelves, and cooked, Henry had laid the table in the kitchen with plates and silverware and sat down to quiz his troubled friend.

Now the steaks, rare, are transported to the plates, the mushrooms arrayed around them, and the enormous wooden salad bowl installed on the center of the table. Henry pronounces the meal delicious, takes a sip of his wine, and says, 'If you still won't talk about your trouble, whatever it is, you'd better at least tell me what happened at the station. I suppose there's very little doubt that another child was snatched.'

'Next to none, I'm sorry to say. It's a boy named Tyler Marshall. His father's name is Fred Marshall, and he works out at Goltz's. Do you know him?'

'Been a long time since I bought a combine,' Henry says.

'The first thing that struck me was that Fred Marshall was a very nice guy,' Jack says, and goes on to recount, in great detail and leaving nothing out, the evening's events and revelations, except for one matter, that of his third, his unspoken, thought.

'You actually asked to visit Marshall's wife? In the mental wing at French County Lutheran?'

'Yes, I did,' Jack says. 'I'm going there tomorrow.'

'I don't get it.' Henry eats by hunting the food with his knife, spearing it with his fork, and measuring off a narrow strip of steak. 'Why would you want to see the mother?'

'Because one way or another I think she's involved,' Jack says.

'Oh, come off it. The boy's own mother?'

'I'm not saying she's the Fisherman, because of course she isn't. But according to her husband, Judy Marshall's behavior started to change before Amy St Pierre disappeared. She got worse and worse as the murders went on, and on the day her son vanished, she flipped out completely. Her husband had to have her committed.'

'Wouldn't you say she had an excellent reason to break down?'

'She flipped out *before* anyone told her about her son. Her husband thinks she has ESP! He said she saw the murders in advance, she knew the Fisherman was on the way. And she knew her son was gone before they found the bike – when Fred Marshall came home, he found her tearing at the walls and talking nonsense. Completely out of control.'

'You hear about lots of cases where a mother is suddenly aware of some threat or injury to her child. A pyschic bond. Sounds like mumbo jumbo, but I guess it happens.'

'I don't believe in ESP, and I don't believe in coincidence.'

'So what are you saying?'

'Judy Marshall *knows* something, and whatever she knows is a real showstopper. Fred can't see it – he's much too close – and Dale can't see it, either. You should have heard him talk about her.'

'So what is she supposed to know?'

'I think she may know the doer. I think it has to be someone close to her. Whoever he is, she knows his name, and it's driving her crazy.'

Henry frowns and uses his inchworm technique to entrap another piece of steak. 'So you're going to the hospital to open her up,' he finally says.

'Yes. Basically.'

A mysterious silence follows this statement. Henry quietly whittles away at the meat, chews what he whittles, and washes it down with Jordan cabernet.

'How did your deejay gig go? Was it okay?'

'It was a thing of beauty. All the adorable old swingers cut loose on the dance floor, even the ones in wheelchairs. One guy sort of rubbed me the wrong way. He was rude to a woman named Alice, and he asked me to play "Lady Magowan's Nightmare," which doesn't exist, as you probably know—'

'It's "Lady Magowan's Dream." Woody Herman.'

'Good boy. The thing was, he had this *terrible* voice. It sounded like something out of hell! Anyhow, I didn't have the Woody Herman record, and he asked for the Bunny Berigan "I Can't Get Started." Which happened to be Rhoda's favorite record. What with my goofy ear hallucinations and all, it shook me up. I don't know why.'

For a few minutes they concentrate on their plates.

Jack says, 'What do you think, Henry?'

Henry tilts his head, auditing an inner voice. Scowling,

he sets down his fork. The inner voice continues to demand his attention. He adjusts his shades and faces Jack. 'In spite of everything you say, you still think like a cop.'

Jack bridles at the suspicion that Henry is not paying him a compliment. 'What do you mean by that?'

'Cops see differently than people who aren't cops. When a cop looks at someone, he wonders what he's guilty of. The possibility of innocence never enters his mind. To a longtime cop, a guy who's put in ten years or more, everyone who isn't a cop is guilty. Only most of them haven't been caught yet.'

Henry has described the mind-set of dozens of men Jack once worked with. 'Henry, how do you know about that?'

'I can see it in their eyes,' Henry says. 'That's the way policemen approach the world. You are a policeman.'

Jack blurts out, 'I am a coppiceman.' Appalled, he blushes. 'Sorry, that stupid phrase has been running around and around in my head, and it just popped out.'

'Why don't we clear the dishes and start on *Bleak House*?'

When their few dishes have been stacked beside the sink, Jack takes the book from the far side of the table and follows Henry toward the living room, pausing on the way to glance, as he always does, at his friend's studio. A door with a large glass insert opens into a small, soundproofed chamber bristling with electronic equipment: the microphone and turntable back from Maxton's and reinstalled before Henry's well-padded, swiveling chair; a disc changer and matching digital–analog converter mount, close at hand, beside a mixing board and a massive tape recorder adjacent to the other, larger window, which looks into the kitchen. When Henry had been planning the studio, Rhoda requested the windows, because, she'd said, she wanted to be able to see him at work. There isn't a wire in sight. The entire studio has the disciplined neatness of the captain's quarters on a ship.

'Looks like you're going to work tonight,' Jack says.

'I want to get two more Henry Shakes ready to send, and I'm working on something for a birthday salute to Lester Young and Charlie Parker.'

'Were they born on the same day?'

'Close enough. August twenty-seventh and twenty-ninth. You know, I can't quite tell if you'll want the lights on or not.'

'Let's turn them on,' Jack says.

And so Henry Leyden switches on the two lamps beside the window, and Jack Sawyer moves to the overstuffed chair near the fireplace and turns on the tall lamp at one of its rounded arms and watches as his friend walks unerringly to the light just inside the front door and the ornate fixture alongside his own, his favorite resting place, the Mission-style sofa, clicking first one, then the other into life, then settles down onto the sofa with one leg stretched out along its length. Even, low light pervades the long room and swells into greater brightness around Jack's chair.

'*Bleak House*, by Charles Dickens,' he says. He clears his throat. 'Okay, Henry, we're off to the races.

'London. Michaelmas Term lately over,' he reads, and marches into a world made of soot and mud. Muddy dogs, muddy horses, muddy people, a day without light. Soon he has reached the second paragraph: 'Fog everywhere. Fog up the river, where it flows among green aits and meadows; fog down the river, where it rolls defiled among the tiers of shipping, and the waterside pollutions of a great (and dirty) city. Fog on the Essex marshes, fog on the Kentish heights. Fog creeping into the cabooses of collier-brigs; fog lying out on the yards, and hovering in the rigging of great ships; fog drooping on the gunwales of barges and small boats.'

His voice catches, and his mind temporarily drifts off-focus. What he is reading unhappily reminds him of French Landing, of Sumner Street and Chase Street, of the lights in the window of the Oak Tree Inn, the Thunder Five lurking in Nailhouse Row, and the gray ascent from the river, of Queen Street and Maxton's hedges, the little houses spreading out on grids, all of it choked by unseen fog – which engulfs a battered NO TRESPASSING sign on the highway and swallows the Sand Bar and glides hungry and searching down the valleys.

'Sorry,' he says. 'I was just thinking—'

'I was, too,' Henry says. 'Go on, please.'

But for that brief flicker of an old NO TRESPASSING sign completely unaware of the black house he one day will have to enter, Jack concentrates again on the page and continues reading *Bleak House*. The windows darken as the lamps grow warmer. The case of Jarndyce and Jarndyce grinds through the courts, aided or impeded by attorneys Chizzle, Mizzle, and Drizzle; Lady Dedlock leaves Sir Leicester Dedlock alone at their great estate with its moldy chapel, stagnant river, and 'Ghost's Walk'; Esther Summerson begins to chirp away in the first person. Our friends decide that the appearance of Esther demands a small libation, if they are to get through much more chirping. Henry unfolds from the sofa, sails into the kitchen, and returns with two short, fat glasses one-third filled with Balvenie Doublewood single-malt whiskey, as well as a glass of plain water for the reader. A couple of sips, a few murmurs of appreciation, and Jack resumes. Esther, Esther, Esther, but beneath the water torture of her relentless sunniness the story gathers steam and carries both reader and listener along in its train.

Having come to a convenient stopping point, Jack closes the book and yawns. Henry stands up and stretches. They move to the door, and Henry follows Jack outside beneath a vast night sky brilliantly scattered with stars. 'Tell me one thing,' Henry says.

'Shoot.'

'When you were in the station house, did you really feel like a cop? Or did you feel like you were pretending to be one?'

'Actually, it was kind of surprising,' Jack says. 'In no time at all, I felt like a cop again.'

'Good.'

'Why is that good?'

'Because it means you were running toward that mysterious secret, not away from it.'

Shaking his head and smiling, deliberately not giving Henry the satisfaction of a reply, Jack steps up into his vehicle and says good-bye from the slight but distinct elevation of the driver's seat. The engine coughs and churns, his headlights snap into being, and Jack is on his way home.

9

Not many hours later, Jack finds himself walking down the midway of a deserted amusement park under a gray autumn sky. On either side of him are boarded-over concessions: the Fenway Franks hot dog stand, the Annie Oakley Shooting Gallery, the Pitch-Til-U-Win. Rain has fallen and more is coming; the air is sharp with moisture. Not far away, he can hear the lonely thunder of waves hurling themselves against a deserted shingle of beach. From closer by comes the snappy sound of guitar picking. It should be cheerful, but to Jack it is dread set to music. He shouldn't be here. This is an old place, a dangerous place. He passes a boarded-up ride. A sign out front reads: THE SPEEDY OPOPANAX WILL REOPEN MEMORIAL DAY 1982 – SEE YA THEN!

Opopanax, Jack thinks, only he is no longer Jack; now he's Jacky. He's Jacky-boy, and he and his mother are on the run. From whom? From Sloat, of course. From hustlin', bustlin' Uncle Morgan.

Speedy, Jack thinks, and as if he has given a telepathic cue, a warm, slightly slurry voice begins to sing. '*When the red red robin comes bob bob bobbin' along, / There'll be no more sobbin' when he starts throbbin' his old sweet song . . .*'

No, Jack thinks. *I don't want to see you. I don't want to hear your old sweet song. You can't be here anyway, you're dead. Dead on the Santa Monica Pier. Old bald black man dead in the shadow of a frozen merry-go-round horse.*

Oh, but no. When the old cop logic comes back it takes hold like a tumor, even in dreams, and it doesn't take much of it to realize that this isn't Santa Monica – it's too cold and too old. This is the land of ago, when Jacky and the Queen of the B's fled out of California like the fugitives they had become. And didn't stop running until they got to the other coast, the place where Lily Cavanaugh Sawyer –

No, I don't think of this, I never *think of this*

– had come to die.

'Wake up, wake up you sleepyhead!'

The voice of his old friend.

Friend, my ass. He's the one who put me on the road of trials, the one who came between me and Richard, my real *friend. He's the one who almost got me killed, almost drove me crazy.*

'Wake up, wake up, get out of bed!'

Way-gup, way-gup, way-gup. Time to face the fearsome opopanax. Time to get back to your not-so-sweet used-to-be.

'No,' Jacky whispers, and then the midway ends. Ahead is the carousel, sort of like the one on the Santa Monica Pier and sort of like the one he remembers from . . . well, from ago. It is a hybrid, in other words, a dream specialty, neither here nor there. But there's no mistaking the man who sits beneath one of the frozen rearing horses with his guitar on his knee. Jacky-boy would know that face anywhere, and all the old love rises in his heart. He fights it, but that is a fight few people win, especially not those who have been turned back to the age of twelve.

'Speedy!' he cries.

The old man looks at him and his brown face cracks open in a smile. 'Travelin' Jack!' he says. 'How I have missed you, son.'

'I've missed you, too,' he says. 'But I don't travel anymore. I've settled down in Wisconsin. This . . .' He gestures at his magically restored boy's body, clad in jeans and a T-shirt. 'This is just a dream.'

'Maybe so, maybe not. In any case, you got a mite more traveling to do, Jack. I been telling you that for some time.'

'What do you mean?'

Speedy's grin is sly in the middle, exasperated at the corners. 'Don't play the fool with me, Jacky. Sent you the feathers, didn't I? Sent you a robin's egg, didn't I? Sent you more'n one.'

'Why can't people leave me alone?' Jack asks. His voice is suspiciously close to a whine. Not a pretty sound. 'You . . . Henry . . . Dale . . .'

'Quit on it now,' Speedy says, growing stern. 'Ain't got no more time to ask you nice. The game has gotten rough. Ain't it?'

'Speedy—'

'You got your job and I got mine. Same job, too. Don't you whine at me, Jack, and don't make me chase you no mo'. You're a coppiceman, same as ever was.'

'I'm retired—'

'*Shit* on your retired! The kids he killed, that's bad enough. The kids he *might* kill if he's let to go on, that's worse. But the one he's got . . .' Speedy leans forward, dark eyes blazing in his dark face. 'That boy has got to be brought back, and *soon*. If you can't get him back, you got to kill him yourself, little as I like to think of it. Because he's a Breaker. A powerful one. One more might be all he needs to take it down.'

'Who might need?' Jack asks.

'The Crimson King.'

'And what is it this Crimson King wants to take down?'

Speedy looks at him a moment, then starts to play that perky tune again instead of answering. 'There'll be no more sobbin' when he starts throbbin' his old sweet song . . .'

'Speedy, I *can't*!'

The tune ends in a discordant jangle of strings. Speedy looks at twelve-year-old Jack Sawyer with a coldness that chills the boy inward all the way to the hidden man's heart. And when he speaks again, Speedy Parker's faint southern accent has deepened. It has filled with a contempt that is almost liquid.

'You get busy now, hear me? Y'all quit whinin' and cryin' and slackin' off. Y'all pick up yo' guts from wherever you left 'em and *get busy*!'

Jack steps back. A heavy hand falls on his shoulder and he thinks, *It's Uncle Morgan. Him or maybe Sunlight Gardener. It's 1981 and I've got to do it all over again—*

But that is a boy's thought, and this is a man's dream. Jack Sawyer as he is now thrusts the child's acquiescing despair away. *No, not at all. I deny that. I have put those faces and those places aside. It was hard work, and I won't see it all undone by a few phantom feathers, a few phantom eggs, and one bad dream. Find yourself another boy, Speedy. This one grew up.*

He turns, ready to fight, but no one's there. Lying behind him on the boardwalk, on its side like a dead pony, is a boy's bicycle. There's a license plate on the back reading BIG MAC. Scattered around it are shiny crow's feathers. And now Jack hears another voice, cold and cracked, ugly and unmistakably evil. He knows it's the voice of the thing that touched him.

'That's right, asswipe. Stay out of it. You mess with me and I'll strew your guts from Racine to La Riviere.'

A spinning hole opens in the boardwalk just in front of the bike. It widens like a startled eye. It continues to widen, and Jack dives for it. It's the way back. The way out. The contemptuous voice follows him.

'That's right, jackoff,' it says. 'Run! Run from the abbalah! Run from the King! Run for your miserable fucking life!' The voice dissolves into laughter, and it is the mad sound of that laughter which follows Jack Sawyer down into the darkness between worlds.

Hours later, Jack stands naked at his bedroom window, absently scratching his ass and watching the sky lighten in the east. He's been awake since four. He can't remember much of his dream (his defenses may be bending, but even now they have not quite broken), yet enough of it lingers for him to be sure of one thing: the corpse on the Santa Monica Pier upset him so badly that he quit his job because it reminded him of someone he once knew.

'All of that never happened,' he tells the coming day in a falsely patient voice. 'I had a kind of preadolescent breakdown, brought on by stress. My mother thought she had cancer, she grabbed me, and we ran all the way to the East Coast. All the way to New Hampshire. She thought she was going back to the Great Happy Place to die. Turned out to be mostly vapors, some goddamn actress midlife crisis, but what does a kid know? I was stressed. I had dreams.'

Jack sighs.

'I dreamed I saved my mother's life.'

The phone behind him rings, the sound shrill and broken in the shadowy room.

Jack Sawyer screams.

★

'I woke you up,' Fred Marshall says, and Jack knows at once that this man has been up all night, sitting in his wifeless, sonless home. Looking at photo albums, perhaps, while the TV plays. Knowing he is rubbing salt into the wounds but unable to quit.

'No,' Jack says, 'actually I was—'

He stops. The phone's beside the bed and there's a pad beside the phone. There's a note written on the pad. Jack must have written it, since he's the only one here – ella-fucking-ment'ry, my dear Watson – but it isn't in his handwriting. At some point in his dream, he wrote this note in his dead mother's handwriting.

> *The Tower. The Beams. If the Beams are broken, Jacky-boy, if the Beams are broken and the Tower falls*

There's no more. There is only poor old Fred Marshall, who has discovered how quickly things can go bad in the sunniest midwestern life. Jack's mouth has attempted to say a couple of things while his mind is occupied with this forgery from his subconscious, probably not very sensible things, but that doesn't bother Fred; he simply goes droning along with none of the stops and drops that folks usually employ to indicate the ends of sentences or changes of thought. Fred is just getting it out, unloading, and even in his own distressed state Jack realizes that Fred Marshall of 16 Robin Hood Lane, that sweet little Cape Cod honey of a home, is nearing the edge of his endurance. If things don't turn around for him soon, he won't need to visit his wife in Ward D of French County Lutheran; they'll be roommates.

And it is their proposed visit to Judy of which Fred is speaking, Jack realizes. He quits trying to interrupt and simply listens, frowning down at the note he has written to himself as he does so. Tower and Beams. What kind of beams? Sunbeams? Hornbeams? Raise high the roof beam, carpenters?

'– know I said I'd pick you up at nine but Dr Spiegleman that's her doctor up there Spiegleman his name is he said she had a very bad night with a lot of yelling and screaming and then trying to get up the wallpaper and eat it and maybe a seizure of some kind so they're trying her on a new medication he might have said Pamizene or Patizone I didn't write it down Spiegleman called me fifteen minutes ago I wonder if those guys ever sleep and said we should be able to see her around four he thinks she'll be more stabilized by four and we could see her then so could I pick you up at three or maybe you have –'

'Three would be fine,' Jack says quietly.

'– other stuff to do other plans I'd understand that but I could come by if you don't it's mostly that I don't want to go alone –'

'I'll be waiting for you,' Jack said. 'We'll go in my pickup.'

'– thought maybe I'd hear from Ty or from whoever snatched him like maybe a ransom demand but no one called only Spiegleman he's my wife's doctor up there at –'

'Fred, I'm going to find your boy.'

Jack is appalled at this bald assurance, at the suicidal confidence he hears in his own voice, but it serves at least one purpose: bringing Fred's flood of dead words to an end. There is blessed silence from the other end of the line.

At last, Fred speaks in a trembling whisper. 'Oh, sir. If only I could believe that.'

'I want you to try,' Jack says. 'And maybe we can find your wife's mind while we're at it.'

Maybe both are in the same place, he thinks, but this he does not say.

Liquid sounds come from the other end of the line. Fred has begun to cry.

'Fred.'

'Yes?'

'You're coming to my place at three.'

'Yes.' A mighty sniff; a miserable cry that is mostly choked back. Jack has some comprehension of how empty Fred Marshall's house must feel at this moment, and even that dim understanding is bad enough.

'My place in Norway Valley. Come past Roy's Store, over Tamarack Creek—'

'I know where it is.' A faint edge of impatience has crept into Fred's voice. Jack is very glad to hear it.

'Good. I'll see you.'

'You bet.' Jack hears a ghost of Fred's salesman cheer, and it twists his heart.

'What time?'

'Th-three?' Then, with marginal assurance: 'Three.'

'That's right. We'll take my truck. Maybe have a bite of supper at Gertie's Kitchen on our way back. Good-bye, Fred.'

'Good-bye, sir. And thank you.'

Jack hangs up the phone. Looks a moment longer at his memory's reproduction of his mother's handwriting and wonders what you'd call such a thing in cop-speak. Autoforgery? He snorts, then crumples the note up and starts getting dressed. He will drink a glass of juice, then go out walking for an hour or so. Blow all the bad dreams out of his head. And blow away the sound of Fred Marshall's awful droning voice while he's at it. Then, after a shower, he might or might not call Dale Gilbertson and ask if there have been any developments. If he's really going to get involved in this, there'll be a lot of paperwork to catch up on . . . he'll want to reinterview the parents

. . . take a look at the old folks' home close to where the Marshall kid disappeared . . .

With his mind full of such thoughts (*pleasant* thoughts, actually, although if this had been suggested to him, he would have strenuously denied it), Jack almost stumbles over the box sitting on the welcome mat just outside his front door. It's where Buck Evitz, the postman, leaves packages when he has packages to leave, but it's not gone six-thirty yet, and Buck won't be along in his little blue truck for another three hours.

Jack bends down and cautiously picks the package up. It's the size of a shoe box, covered with brown paper that has been cut raggedly and secured not with tape but with big drools of red sealing wax. In addition to this, there are complicated loops of white string secured with a child's oversized bow. There's a cluster of stamps in the upper corner, ten or a dozen, featuring various birds. (No robins, however; Jack notes this with understandable relief.) There's something not right about those stamps, but at first Jack doesn't see what it is. He's too focused on the address, which is *spectacularly* not right. There's no box number, no RFD number, no zip code. No *name*, not really. The address consists of a single word, scrawled in large capital letters:

J A C K Y

Looking at those bedraggled letters, Jack imagines a fisted hand clutching a Sharpie marker; narrowed eyes; a tongue poked from the corner of some lunatic's mouth. His heartbeat has sped up to double-time. 'I'm not liking this,' he breathes. 'I am *so* not liking this.'

And of course there are perfectly good reasons, coppiceman reasons, not to. It *is* a shoe box; he can feel the edge of the top right through the brown paper, and nutters have been known to put bombs in shoe boxes. He'd be crazy to open it, but he has an idea he *will* open it, just the same. If it blows him sky-high, at least he'll be able to opt out of the Fisherman investigation.

Jack raises the package to listen for ticking, fully aware that ticking bombs are as out-of-date as Betty Boop cartoons. He hears nothing, but he *does* see what's wrong with the stamps, which aren't stamps at all. Someone has carefully cut the front panels from a dozen or so cafeteria sugar packets and taped them to this wrapped shoe box. A grunt of humorless laughter escapes Jack. Some nut sent him this, all right. Some nut in a locked facility, with easier access to sugar packets than to stamps. But how has it gotten *here*? Who left it (with the fake stamps uncanceled) while he was dreaming his confused dreams? And who, in this part of the world, could possibly know him as Jacky? His Jacky days are long gone.

No they ain't, Travelin' Jack, a voice whispers. *Not by half. Time to stop your sobbin' and get bob-bob-bobbin' along, boy. Start by seein' what's in that box.*

Resolutely ignoring his own mental voice, which tells him he's being dangerously stupid, Jack snaps the twine and uses his thumbnail to cut through the sloppy blobs of red wax. Who uses sealing wax in this day and age, anyway? He sets the wrapping paper aside. Something else for the forensics boys, maybe.

It isn't a shoe box but a sneaker box. A New Balance sneaker box, to be exact. Size 5. A child's size. And at that, Jack's heart speeds up to triple-time. He feels beads of cold sweat springing up on his forehead. His gorge and sphincter are both tightening up. This is also familiar. It is how coppicemen get cocked and locked, ready to look at something awful. And this *will* be awful. Jack has no doubt about it, and no doubt about who the package is from.

This is my last chance to back out, he thinks. *After this it's all aboard and heigh-ho for the . . . the wherever.*

But even that is a lie, he realizes. Dale will be looking for him at the police station on Sumner Street by noon. Fred Marshall is coming to Jack's place at three o'clock and they are going to see the Mad Housewife of Robin Hood Lane. The backout point has already come and gone. Jack still isn't sure how it happened, but it looks like he's back in harness. And if Henry Leyden has the temerity to congratulate him on this, Jack thinks, he'll probably kick Henry's blind ass for him.

A voice from his dream whispers up from beneath the floorboards of Jack's consciousness like a whiff of rotten air – *I'll strew your guts from Racine to La Riviere* – but this bothers him less than the madness inherent in the sugar-pack stamps and the laboriously printed letters of his old nickname. He has dealt with crazies before. Not to mention his share of threats.

He sits down on the steps with the sneaker box on his thighs. Beyond him, in the north field, all is still and gray. Bunny Boettcher, son of Tom Tom, came and did the second cutting only a week ago, and now a fine mist hangs above the ankle-high stubble. Above it, the sky has just begun to brighten. Not a single cloud as yet marks its calm no-color. Somewhere a bird calls out. Jack breathes deeply and thinks, *If this is where I go out, I could do worse. A lot worse.*

Then, very carefully, he takes the lid off the box and sets it aside. Nothing explodes. But it looks as if someone has filled the New Balance sneaker box with night. Then he realizes that it's been packed with shiny black crow feathers, and his arms roughen with goose bumps.

He reaches toward them, then hesitates. He wants to

touch those feathers about as much as he'd want to touch the corpse of a half-decayed plague victim, but there's something beneath them. He can see it. Should he get some gloves? There are gloves in the front hall closet—

'Fuck the gloves,' Jack says, and dumps the box onto the brown paper wrapping lying beside him on the porch. There's a flood of feathers, which swirl a bit even in the perfectly still morning air. Then a thump as the object around which the feathers were packed lands on Jack's porch. The smell hits Jack's nose a moment later, an odor like rotting baloney.

Someone has delivered a child's bloodstained sneaker chez Sawyer on Norway Valley Road. Something has gnawed at it pretty briskly, and even more briskly at what's inside it. He sees a lining of bloody white cotton – that would be a sock. And inside the sock, tatters of skin. This is a child's New Balance sneaker with a child's foot inside it, one that has been badly used by some animal.

He sent it, Jack thinks. *The Fisherman.*

Taunting him. Telling him *If you want in, come on in. The water's fine, Jacky-boy, the water is* fine.

Jack gets up. His heart is hammering, the beats now too close together to count. The beads of sweat on his forehead have swelled and broken and gone running down his face like tears, his lips and hands and feet are numb . . . yet he tells himself he is calm. That he has seen worse, much worse, piled up against bridge abutments and freeway underpasses in LA. Nor is this his first severed body part. Once, in 1997, he and his partner Kirby Tessier found a single testicle sitting on top of a toilet tank in the Culver City public library like an ancient soft-boiled egg. So he tells himself he is calm.

He gets up and walks down the porch steps. He walks past the hood of his burgundy-colored Dodge Ram with the world-class sound system inside; he walks past the bird hotel he and Dale put up at the edge of the north field a month or two after Jack moved into this, the most perfect house in the universe. He tells himself he is calm. He tells himself that it's evidence, that's all. Just one more loop in the hangman's noose that the Fisherman will eventually put around his own neck. He tells himself not to think of it as part of a kid, part of a little girl named Irma, but as Exhibit A. He can feel dew wetting his sockless ankles and the cuffs of his pants, knows that any sort of extended stroll through the hay stubble is going to ruin a five-hundred-dollar pair of Gucci loafers. And so what if it does? He's rich well beyond the point of vulgarity; he can have as many shoes as Imelda Marcos, if he wants. The important thing is he's calm. Someone brought him a shoe box with a human foot inside it, laid it on his porch in the dark of night, but he's calm. It's evidence, that's all. And he? He is a coppiceman. Evidence is his meat and drink. He just needs to get a little air, needs to clear his nose of the rotted baloney smell that came puffing out of the box—

Jack makes a strangled gagging, urking sound and begins to hurry on a little faster. There is a sense of approaching climax growing in his mind (*my* calm *mind*, he tells himself). Something is getting ready to break . . . or change . . . or change *back*.

That last idea is particularly alarming and Jack begins to run across the field, knees lifting higher, arms pumping. His passage draws a dark line through the stubble, a diagonal that starts at the driveway and might end anywhere. Canada, maybe. Or the North Pole. White moths, startled out of their dew-heavy morning doze, flutter up in lacy swirls and then slump back into the cut stubble.

He runs faster, away from the chewed and bloody sneaker lying on the porch of the perfect house, away from his own horror. But that sense of coming climax stays with him. Faces begin to rise in his mind, each with its own accompanying snippet of sound track. Faces and voices he has ignored for twenty years or more. When these faces rise or those voices mutter, he has until now told himself the old lie, that once there was a frightened boy who caught his mother's neurotic terror like a cold and made up a story, a grand fantasy with good old Mom-saving Jack Sawyer at its center. None of it was real, and it was forgotten by the time he was sixteen. By then he was calm. Just as he's calm now, running across his north field like a lunatic, leaving that dark track and those clouds of startled moths behind him, but doing it *calmly*.

Narrow face, narrow eyes under a tilted white paper cap: *If you can run me out a keg when I need one, you can have the job.* Smokey Updike, from Oatley, New York, where they drank the beer and then ate the glass. Oatley, where there'd been something in the tunnel outside of town and where Smokey had kept him prisoner. Until—

Prying eyes, false smile, brilliant white suit: *I've met you before, Jack . . . where? Tell me. Confess.* Sunlight Gardener, an Indiana preacher whose name had also been Osmond. Osmond in some other world.

The broad, hairy face and frightened eyes of a boy who wasn't a boy at all: *This is a bad place, Jacky, Wolf knows.* And it was, it was a very bad place. They put him in a box, put good old Wolf in a box, and finally they killed him. Wolf died of a disease called America.

'Wolf!' the running man in the field gasps. 'Wolf, ah, God, I'm sorry!'

Faces and voices, all those faces and voices, rising in front of his eyes, dinning into his ears, demanding to be seen and heard, filling him with that sense of climax, every defense on the verge of being washed away like a breakwater before a tidal wave.

Nausea roars through him and tilts the world. He makes that urking sound again, and this time it fills the back of his throat with a taste he remembers: the taste of cheap, rough wine. And suddenly it's New Hampshire again, Arcadia Funworld again. He and Speedy are standing beside the carousel again, all those frozen horses (*'All carousel horses is named, don't you know that, Jack?'*), and Speedy is holding out a bottle of wine and telling him it's magic juice, one little sip and he'll go over, *flip* over—

'No!' Jack cries, knowing it's already too late. '*I don't want to go over!*'

The world tilts the other way and he falls into the grass on his hands and knees with his eyes squeezed shut. He doesn't need to open them; the richer, deeper smells that suddenly fill his nose tell him everything he needs to know. That, and the sense of coming home after so many dark years when almost every waking motion and decision has in some way been dedicated to canceling (or at least postponing) the arrival of this very moment.

This is Jack Sawyer, ladies and gentlemen, down on his knees in a vast field of sweet grass under a morning sky untainted by a single particle of pollution. He is weeping. He knows what has happened, and he is weeping. His heart bursts with fear and joy.

This is Jack Sawyer twenty years along, grown to be a man, and back in the Territories again at last.

It is the voice of his old friend Richard – sometimes known as Rational Richard – that saves him. Richard as he is now, head of his own law firm (Sloat & Associates, Ltd), not Richard as he was when Jack perhaps knew him best, during long vacation days on Seabrook Island, in South Carolina. The Richard of Seabrook Island had been imaginative, quick-spoken, fast on his feet, mop-topped, skinny as a morning shadow. The current Richard, Corporate Law Richard, is thinning on top, thick in the middle, much in favor of sitting and Bushmills. Also, he has crushed his imagination, so brilliantly playful in those Seabrook Island days, like a troublesome fly. Richard Sloat's life has been one of reduction, Jack has sometimes thought, but one thing has been added (probably in law school): the pompous, sheeplike sound of hesitation, particularly annoying on the phone, which is now Richard's vocal signature. This sound starts with the lips closed, then opens out as Richard's lips spring wide, making him look like an absurd combination of Vienna choirboy and Lord Haw-Haw.

Now, kneeling with his eyes shut in the vast green reach of what used to be his very own north field, smelling the new, deeper smells that he remembers so well and has longed for so fiercely without even realizing it, Jack hears Richard Sloat begin speaking in the middle of his head. What a relief those words are! He knows it's only his own mind mimicking Richard's voice, but it's still wonderful. If Richard were here, Jack thinks he'd embrace his old friend and say, *May you pontificate forever, Richie-boy. Sheep bray and all.*

Rational Richard says: *You realize you're dreaming, Jack, don't you?* . . . ba-haaaa . . . *the stress of opening that package no doubt* . . . ba-haaaa . . . *no doubt caused you to pass out, and that in turn has caused* . . . ba-HAAAA! . . . *the dream you are having now.*

Down on his knees, eyes still closed and hair hanging in his face, Jack says, 'In other words, it's what we used to call—'

Correct! What we used to call . . . ba-haaaa . . . *'Seabrook*

Island stuff.' But Seabrook Island was a long time ago, Jack, so I suggest you open your eyes, get back on your feet, and remind yourself that should you see anything out of the ordinary . . . b'haa! . . . *it's not really there.*

'Not really there,' Jack murmurs. He stands up and opens his eyes.

He knows from the very first look that it *is* really here, but he holds Richard's pompous I-look-thirty-five-but-I'm-really-sixty voice in his head, shielding himself with it. Thus he is able to maintain a precarious balance instead of passing out for real, or – perhaps – cracking up entirely.

Above him, the sky is an infinitely clear dark blue. Around him, the hay and timothy is rib-high instead of ankle-high; there has been no Bunny Boettcher in this part of creation to cut it. In fact, there is no house back the way he came, only a picturesque old barn with a windmill standing off to one side.

Where are the flying men? Jack thinks, looking up into the sky, then shakes his head briskly. No flying men; no two-headed parrots; no werewolves. All that was Seabrook Island stuff, a neurosis he picked up from his mother and even passed on to Richard for a while. It was all nothing but . . . *ba-haaa* . . . bullshit.

He accepts this, knowing at the same time that the real bullshit would be not believing what's all around him. The smell of the grass, now so strong and sweet, mixed with the more flowery smell of clover and the deeper, basso profundo smell of black earth. The endless sound of the crickets in this grass, living their unthinking cricket lives. The fluttering white field moths. The unblemished cheek of the sky, not marked by a single telephone wire or electrical cable or jet contrail.

What strikes Jack most deeply, however, is the perfection of the field around him. There's a matted circle where he fell on his knees, the dew-heavy grass crushed to the ground. But there is no path *leading* to the circle, not a mark of passage through the wet and tender grass. He might have dropped out of the sky. That's impossible, of course, more Seabrook Island stuff, but—

'I *did* sort of fall out of the sky, though,' Jack says in a remarkably steady voice. 'I came here from Wisconsin. I *flipped* here.'

Richard's voice protests this strenuously, exploding in a flurry of *hrrumphs* and *ba-haaas*, but Jack hardly notices. It's just good old Rational Richard, doing his Rational Richard thing inside his head. Richard had lived through stuff like this once before and come out the other side with his mind more or less intact . . . but he'd been twelve. They'd both been twelve that fall, and when you're twelve, the mind and body are more elastic.

Jack has been turning in a slow circle, seeing nothing but open fields (the mist over them now fading to a faint haze in the day's growing warmth) and blue-gray woods beyond them. Now there's something else. To the southwest, there's a dirt road about a mile away. Beyond it, at the horizon or perhaps just beyond, the perfect summer sky is a little stained with smoke.

Not woodstoves, Jack thinks, *not in July, but maybe small manufactories. And . . .*

He hears a whistle – three long blasts made faint with distance. His heart seems to grow large in his chest, and the corners of his mouth stretch up in a kind of helpless grin.

'The Mississippi's that way, by God,' he says, and around him the field moths seem to dance their agreement, lace of the morning. 'That's the Mississippi, or whatever they call it over here. And the whistle, friends and neighbors—'

Two more blasts roll across the making summer day. They are faint with distance, yes, but up close they would be mighty. Jack knows this.

'That's a riverboat. A damn big one. Maybe a paddle wheeler.'

Jack begins to walk toward the road, telling himself that this is all a dream, not believing a bit of that but using it as an acrobat uses his balance pole. After he's gone a hundred yards or so, he turns and looks back. A dark line cuts through the timothy, beginning at the place where he landed and cutting straight to where he is. It is the mark of his passage. The *only* mark of it. Far to the left (in fact almost behind him now) are the barn and the windmill. *That's my house and garage*, Jack thinks. *At least that's what they are in the world of Chevrolets, Mideast warfare, and the* Oprah Winfrey *show*.

He walks on, and has almost reached the road when he realizes there is more than smoke in the southwest. There is a kind of vibration, as well. It beats into his head like the start of a migraine headache. And it's strangely variable. If he stands with his face pointed dead south, that unpleasant pulse is less. Turn east and it's gone. North and it's *almost* gone. Then, as he continues to turn, it comes all the way back to full. Worse than ever now that he's noticed it, the way the buzz of a fly or the knock of a radiator in a hotel room is worse after you really start to notice it.

Jack turns another slow, full circle. South, and the vibration sinks. East, it's gone. North, it's starting to come back. West, it's coming on strong. Southwest and he's locked in like the SEEK button on a car radio. Pow, pow, pow. A black and nasty vibration like a headache, a smell like ancient smoke . . .

'No, no, no, not smoke,' Jack says. He's standing almost up to his chest in summer grass, pants soaked, white moths flittering around his head like a half-assed halo, eyes wide, cheeks once more pale. In this moment he looks twelve again. It is eerie how he has rejoined his younger (and perhaps better) self. 'Not smoke, that smells like . . .'

He suddenly makes that urking sound again. Because the smell – not in his nose but in the center of his head – is rotted baloney. The smell of Irma Freneau's half-rotted, severed foot.

'I'm smelling him,' Jack whispers, knowing it's not a smell he means. He can make that pulse whatever he wants . . . including, he realizes, gone. 'I'm smelling the Fisherman. Either him or . . . I don't know.'

He starts walking, and a hundred yards later he stops again. The pulse in his head is indeed gone. It has faded out the way radio stations do when the day warms and the temperature thickens. It's a relief.

Jack has almost reached the road, which no doubt leads one way to some version of Arden and the other way to versions of Centralia and French Landing, when he hears an irregular drumming sound. He feels it as well, running up his legs like a Gene Krupa backbeat.

He turns to the left, then shouts in mingled surprise and delight. Three enormous brown creatures with long, lolloping ears go leaping past Jack's position, rising above the grass, sinking back into it, then rising above it again. They look like rabbits crossed with kangaroos. Their protruding black eyes stare with comic terror. Across the road they go, their flat feet (white-furred instead of brown) slapping up dust.

'Christ!' Jack says, half-laughing and half-sobbing. He whacks himself in the center of his forehead with the heel of his palm. 'What was that, Richie-boy? Got any comments on *that*?'

Richie, of course, does. He tells Jack that Jack has just suffered an extremely vivid . . . *ba-haaa!* . . . hallucination.

'Of course,' Jack says. 'Giant bunny rabbits. Get me to the nearest AA meeting.' Then, as he steps out onto the road, he looks toward the southwestern horizon again. At the haze of smoke there. A village. And do the residents fear as the shadows of the evening come on? Fear the coming of the night? Fear the creature that is taking their children? Do they need a coppiceman? Of course they do. Of course they—

Something is lying on the road. Jack bends down and picks up a Milwaukee Brewers baseball cap, jarringly out of place in this world of giant hopping range rabbits, but indubitably real. Judging from the plastic adjustment band in the back, it's a child's baseball cap. Jack looks inside, knowing what he'll find, and there it is, carefully inked on the bill: TY MARSHALL. The cap's not as wet as Jack's jeans, which are soaked with morning dew, but it's not dry, either. It has been lying here on the edge of the road, he thinks, since yesterday. The logical assumption would be that Ty's abductor brought Ty this way, but Jack doesn't believe that. Perhaps it is the lingering pulse of vibration that gives rise to a different thought, a different image: the Fisherman, with Ty carefully stashed away, walking out this dirt road. Under his arm is a wrapped shoe box decorated with bogus stamps. On his head is Ty's baseball hat, kind of balancing there because it's really too small for the Fisherman. Still, he doesn't want to change the adjustment band. Doesn't want Jack to mistake it for a man's cap, even for a single second. Because he is teasing Jack, inviting Jack into the game.

'Took the boy in our world,' Jack mutters. 'Escaped with him to *this* world. Stashed him someplace safe, like a spider stashing a fly. Alive? Dead? Alive, I think. Don't know why.

Maybe it's just what I want to believe. Leave it. Then he went to wherever he stashed Irma. Took her foot and brought it to me. Brought it through *this* world, then flipped back to *my* world to leave it on the porch. Lost the hat on the way, maybe? Lost it off his head?'

Jack doesn't think so. Jack thinks this fuck, this skell, this world-hopping dirtbag, left the cap on purpose. Knew that if Jack walked this road he'd find it.

Holding the hat to his chest like a Miller Park fan showing respect to the flag during the national anthem, Jack closes his eyes and concentrates. It's easier than he would have expected, but he supposes some things you never forget – how to peel an orange, how to ride a bike, how to flip back and forth between worlds.

Boy like you don't need no cheap wine, anyhow, he hears his old friend Speedy Parker say, and there's the edge of a laugh in Speedy's voice. At the same time, that sense of vertigo twists through Jack again. A moment later he hears the alarming sound of an oncoming car.

He steps back, opening his eyes as he does so. Catches a glimpse of a tarred road – Norway Valley Road, but—

A horn blares and a dusty old Ford slams by him, the passenger side-view mirror less than nine inches from Jack Sawyer's nose. Warm air, once again filled with the faint but pungent odor of hydrocarbons, surfs over Jack's cheeks and brow, along with some farm kid's indignant voice:

'– hell out of the road, *asssholllе* –'

'Resent being called an asshole by some cow-college graduate,' Jack says in his best Rational Richard voice, and although he adds a pompous *Ba-haaa!* for good measure, his heart is pumping hard. Man, he'd almost flipped back right in front of that guy!

Please, Jack, spare me, Richard said. *You dreamed the whole thing.*

Jack knows better. Although he looks around himself in total amazement, the core of his heart isn't amazed at all, no, not even a little bit. He still has the cap, for one thing – Ty Marshall's Brewers cap. And for another, the bridge across Tamarack Creek is just over the next rise. In the other world, the one where giant rabbits went hopping past you, he has walked maybe a mile. In this one he's come at least *four.*

That's the way it was before, he thinks, *that's the way it was when Jacky was six. When everybody lived in California and nobody lived anywhere else.*

But that's wrong. Somehow wrong.

Jack stands at the side of the road that was dirt a few seconds ago and is tarred now, stands looking down into Ty Marshall's baseball cap and trying to figure out exactly what is wrong and *how* it's wrong, knowing he probably won't be able to turn the trick. All that was a long time ago, and besides, he's worked at burying his admittedly bizarre childhood memories since he was thirteen. More than half his life, in other words. A person can't dedicate that much time to forgetting, then suddenly just snap his fingers and expect—

Jack snaps his fingers. Says to the warming summer morning: 'What happened when Jacky was six?' And answers his own question: 'When Jacky was six, Daddy played the horn.'

What does *that* mean?

'Not Daddy,' Jack says suddenly. 'Not *my* daddy. Dexter Gordon. The *tune* was called "Daddy Played the Horn." Or maybe the album. The LP.' He stands there, shaking his head, then nods. '*Plays.* Daddy Plays. "*Daddy Plays the Horn.*"' And just like that it all comes back. Dexter Gordon playing on the hi-fi. Jacky Sawyer behind the couch, playing with his toy

London taxi, so satisfying because of its weight, which somehow made it seem more real than a toy. His father and Richard's father talking. Phil Sawyer and Morgan Sloat.

Imagine what this guy would be like over there, Uncle Morgan had said, and that had been Jack Sawyer's first hint of the Territories. When Jacky was six, Jacky got the word. And—

'When Jacky was twelve, Jacky actually *went* there,' he says.

Ridiculous! Morgan's son trumpets. *Utterly* . . . ba-haaa! . . . *ridiculous! Next you'll be telling me there really* were *men in the sky!*

But before Jack can tell his mental version of his old pal that or anything else, another car arrives. This one pulls up beside him. Looking suspiciously out of the driver's window (the expression is habitual, Jack has found, and means nothing in itself) is Elvena Morton, Henry Leyden's housekeeper.

'What in the tarnal are you doin' way down here, Jack Sawyer?' she asks.

He gives her a smile. 'Didn't sleep very well, Mrs Morton. Thought I'd take a little walk to clear my head.'

'And do you always go walking through the dews and the damps when you want to clear your head?' she asks, casting her eyes down at his jeans, which are wet to the knee and even a bit beyond. 'Does that help?'

'I guess I got lost in my own thoughts,' he says.

'I guess you did,' she says. 'Get in and I'll give you a lift most of the way back to your place. Unless, that is, you've got a little more head clearing to do.'

Jack has to grin. That's a good one. Reminds him of his late mother, actually. (When asked by her impatient son what was for dinner and when it would be served, Lily Cavanaugh was apt to say, 'Fried farts with onions, wind pudding and air sauce for dessert, come and get it at ha' past a pickle.')

'I guess my head's as clear as I can expect today,' he says, and goes around the front of Mrs Morton's old brown Toyota. There's a brown bag on the passenger seat with leafy stuff poking out of it. Jack moves it to the middle, then sits down.

'I don't know if the early bird gets the worm,' she says, driving on, 'but the early shopper gets the best greens at Roy's, I can tell you that. Also, I like to get there before the layabouts.'

'Layabouts, Mrs Morton?'

She gives him her best suspicious look, eyes cutting to the side, right corner of her mouth quirked down as if at the taste of something sour.

'Take up space at the lunch counter and talk about the Fisherman this and the Fisherman that. Who he might be, *what* he might be – a Swede or a Pole or an Irish – and of course what they'll do to him when he's caught, which he would have been long ago if anyone but that nummie-squarehead Dale Gilbertson was in charge of things. So says they. Easy to take charge when you got your ass cozied down on one of Roy Soderholm's stools, cuppa coffee in one hand and a sinker in the other. So thinks I. Course, half of 'em's also got the unemployment check in their back pockets, but they won't talk about that. My father used to say, "Show me a man who's too good to hay in July and I'll show you a man that won't turn a hand the rest of the year, neither."'

Jack settles in the passenger bucket, knees against the dash, and watches the road unroll. They'll be back in no time. His pants are starting to dry and he feels oddly at peace. The nice thing about Elvena Morton is that you don't have to hold up your end of the conversation, because she is glad to take care of everything. Another Lily-ism occurs to him. Of a very talkative person (Uncle Morgan, for instance), she was apt to say that So-and-so's tongue was 'hung in the middle and running on both ends.'

He grins a little, and raises a casual hand to hide his mouth from Mrs M. She'd ask him what was so funny, and what would he tell her? That he had just been thinking her tongue was hung in the middle? But it's also funny how the thoughts and memories are flooding back. Did he just yesterday try to call his mother, forgetting she was dead? That now seems like something he might have done in a different life. Maybe it *was* a different life. God knows he doesn't seem like the same man who swung his legs out of bed this morning, wearily, and with a feeling best described as doomish. He feels fully alive for the first time since . . . well, since Dale first brought him out this very same road, he supposes, and showed him the nice little place that had once belonged to Dale's father.

Elvena Morton, meanwhile, rolls on.

'Although I also admit that I take any excuse to get out of the house when he starts with the Mad Mongoloid,' she says. The Mad Mongoloid is Mrs Morton's term for Henry's Wisconsin Rat persona. Jack nods understanding, not knowing that before many hours are passed, he will be meeting a fellow nicknamed the Mad Hungarian. Life's little coincidences.

'It's always early in the morning that he takes it into his head to do the Mad Mongoloid, and I've told him, "Henry, if you have to scream like that and say awful things and then play that awful music by kids who never should have been let near a *tuba*, let alone an *electrical guitar*, why do you do it in the morning when you know it spoils you for the whole day?" And it does, he gets a headache four times out of every five he pretends to be the Mad Mongoloid and by afternoon he's lying in his bedroom with an icebag on his poor forehead and not a bite of lunch will he take on those days, neither. Sometimes his supper will be gone when I check the next day – I always leave it in the same place in the refrigerator, unless he tells me he wants to cook himself – but half the time it's still there and even when it's gone I think that sometimes he just tips it down the garbage disposer.'

Jack grunts. It's all he has to do. Her words wash over him and he thinks of how he will put the sneaker in a Baggie, handling it with the fire tongs, and when he turns it over at the police station, the chain of evidence will begin. He's thinking about how he needs to make sure there's nothing else in the sneaker box, and check the wrapping paper. He also wants to check those sugar packets. Maybe there's a restaurant name printed under the bird pictures. It's a longshot, but—

'And *he* says, "Mrs M., I can't help it. Some days I just wake up as the Rat. And although I pay for it later, there's such joy in it while the fit is on me. Such total *joy*." And I asked him, I said, "How can there be joy in music about children wanting to kill their parents and eat fetuses and have sex with animals" – as one of those songs really *was* about, Jack, I heard it clear as day – "and all of that?" I asked him, and he said— Uhhp, here we are.'

They have indeed reached the driveway leading to Henry's house. A quarter of a mile further along is the roof of Jack's own place. His Ram pickup twinkles serenely in the driveway. He can't see his porch, most certainly can't see the horror that lies upon its boards, waiting for someone to clean it up. To clean it up in the name of decency.

'I *could* run you all the way up,' she says. 'Why don't I just do that?'

Jack, thinking of the sneaker and the rotten baloney smell hanging around it, smiles, shakes his head, and quickly opens the passenger door. 'Guess I need to do a little more thinking after all,' he says.

She looks at him with that expression of discontented suspicion which is, Jack suspects, love. She knows that Jack has brightened Henry Leyden's life, and for that alone he believes she loves him. He likes to hope so, anyway. It occurs to him that she never mentioned the baseball cap he's holding, but why would she? In this part of the world, every man's got at least four.

He starts up the road, hair flopping (his days of styled cuts at Chez-Chez on Rodeo Drive are long behind him now – this is the Coulee Country, and when he thinks of it at all, he gets his hair cut by old Herb Roeper down on Chase Street next to the Amvets), his gait as loose and lanky as a boy's. Mrs Morton leans out her window and calls after him. 'Change out of those jeans, Jack! The minute you get back! Don't let them dry on you! That's how arthritis starts!'

He raises a hand without turning and calls back, 'Right!'

Five minutes later, he's walking up his own driveway again. At least temporarily, the fear and depression have been burned out of him. The ecstasy as well, which is a relief. The last thing a coppiceman needs is to go charging through an investigation in a state of ecstasy.

As he sights the box on the porch – and the wrapping paper, and the feathers, and the ever-popular child's sneaker, can't forget that – Jack's mind turns back to Mrs Morton quoting that great sage Henry Leyden.

I can't help it. Some days I just wake up as the Rat. And although I pay for it later, there's such joy in it while the fit is on me. Such total joy.

Total joy. Jack has felt this from time to time as a detective, sometimes while investigating a crime scene, more often while questioning a witness who knows more than he or she is telling . . . and this is something Jack Sawyer almost always knows, something he smells. He supposes carpenters feel that joy when they are carpentering particularly well, sculptors when they're having a good nose or chin day, architects when the lines are landing on their blueprints just right. The only problem is, someone in French Landing (maybe one of the surrounding towns, but Jack is guessing French Landing) gets that feeling of joy by killing children and eating parts of their little bodies.

Someone in French Landing is, more and more frequently, waking up as the Fisherman.

Jack goes into his house by the back door. He stops in the kitchen for the box of large-size Baggies, a couple of wastebasket liners, a dustpan, and the whisk broom. He opens the refrigerator's icemaker compartment and loads about half the cubes into one of the plastic liners – as far as Jack Sawyer is concerned, Irma Freneau's poor foot has reached its maximum state of decay.

He ducks into his study, where he grabs a yellow legal pad, a black marker, and a ballpoint pen. In the living room he gets the shorter set of fire tongs. And by the time he steps back onto the porch, he has pretty much put his secret identity as Jack Sawyer aside.

I am COPPICEMAN, he thinks, smiling. *Defender of the American Way, friend of the lame, the halt, and the dead.*

Then, as he looks down at the sneaker, surrounded by its pitiful little cloud of stink, the smile fades. He feels some of the tremendous mystery we felt when we first came upon Irma in the wreckage of the abandoned restaurant. He will do his absolute best to honor this remnant, just as we did our best to honor the child. He thinks of autopsies he has attended, of the true solemnity that lurks behind the jokes and butcher-shop crudities.

'Irma, is it you?' he asks quietly. 'If it is, you help me, now. Talk to me. This is the time for the dead to help the living.' Without thinking about it, Jack kisses his fingers and blows the kiss down toward the sneaker. He thinks, *I'd like to kill the man – or the thing – that did this. String him up alive and screaming while he filled his pants. Send him out in the stink of his own dirt.*

But such thoughts are not honorable, and he banishes them.

The first Baggie is for the sneaker with the remains of the foot inside it. Use the tongs. Zip it closed. Mark the date on the Baggie with the marker. Note the nature of the evidence on the pad with the ballpoint. Put it in the wastebasket liner with the ice in it.

The second is for the cap. No need for the tongs here; he's already handled the item. He puts it in the Baggie. Zips it closed. Marks the date, notes the nature of the evidence on the pad.

The third bag is for the brown wrapping paper. He holds it up for a moment in the tongs, examining the bogus bird stamps. MANUFACTURED BY DOMINO is printed below each picture, but that's all. No restaurant name, nothing of that sort. Into the Baggie. Zip it closed. Mark the date. Note the nature of the evidence.

He sweeps up the feathers and puts them in a fourth Baggie. There are more feathers in the box. He picks the box up with the tongs, dumps the feathers inside onto the dustpan, and then his heart takes a sudden hard leap in his chest, seeming to knock against the left side of his rib cage like a fist. Something is written on the box's bottom. The same Sharpie marker has been used to make the same straggling letters. And whoever wrote this knew who he was writing *to*. Not the outer Jack Sawyer, or else he – the Fisherman – would have no doubt called him Hollywood.

This message is addressed to the inner man, and to the child who was here before Jack 'Hollywood' Sawyer was ever thought of.

Try Ed's Eats and Dogs, coppiceman.
Your fiend,
THE FISHERMAN.

'Your fiend,' Jack murmurs. 'Yes.' He picks up the box with the tongs and puts it into the second wastebasket liner; he doesn't have any Baggies quite big enough for it. Then he gathers all the evidence beside him in a neat little pile. This stuff always looks the same, at once grisly and prosaic, like the kind of photographs you used to see in those true-crime magazines.

He goes inside and dials Henry's number. He's afraid he'll get Mrs Morton, but it turns out to be Henry instead, thank God. His current fit of Rat-ism has apparently passed, although there's a residue; even over the phone Jack can hear the faint thump and bray of 'electrical guitars.'

He knows Ed's Eats well, Henry says, but why in the world would *Jack* want to know about a place like that? 'It's nothing but a wreck now; Ed Gilbertson died quite a time ago and there are people in French Landing who'd call that a blessing, Jack. The place was a ptomaine palace if ever there was one. A gut-ache waiting to happen. You'd have expected the board of health to shut him down, but Ed knew people. Dale Gilbertson, for one.'

'The two of them related?' Jack asks, and when Henry replies 'Fuck, yeah,' something his friend would never say in the ordinary course of things, Jack understands that while Henry may have avoided a migraine this time, that Rat is still running in his head. Jack has heard similar bits of George Rathbun pop out from time to time, unexpected fat exultations from Henry's slim throat, and there is the way Henry often says good-bye, throwing a *Ding-dong* or *Ivey-divey* over his shoulder: that's just the Sheik, the Shake, the Shook coming up for air.

'Where exactly is it?' Jack asks.

'That's hard to say,' Henry replies. He now sounds a bit testy. 'Out by the farm equipment place . . . Goltz's? As I recall, the driveway's so long you might as well call it an access road. And if there was ever a sign, it's long gone. When Ed Gilbertson sold his last microbe-infested chili dog, Jack, you were probably in the first grade. What's all this about?'

Jack knows that what he's thinking of doing is ridiculous by normal investigatory standards – you don't invite a John Q. to a crime scene, especially not a murder scene – but this is no normal investigation. He has one piece of bagged evidence that he recovered in another world, how's that for abnormal? Of course he can find the long-defunct Ed's Eats; someone at Goltz's will no doubt point him right at it. But—

'The Fisherman just sent me one of Irma Freneau's sneakers,' Jack says. 'With Irma's foot still inside it.'

Henry's initial response is a deep, sharp intake of breath.

'Henry? Are you all right?'

'Yes.' Henry's voice is shocked but steady. 'How terrible for the girl and her mother.' He pauses. 'And for you. For Dale.' Another pause. 'For this town.'

'Yes.'

'Jack, do you want me to take you to Ed's?'

Henry can do that, Jack knows. Easy as pie. Ivey-divey. And let's get real – why did he call Henry in the first place?

'Yes,' he says.

'Have you called the police?'

'No.'

He'll ask me why not, and what will I say? That I don't want Bobby Dulac, Tom Lund, and the rest of them tromping around out there, mixing their scents with the doer's scent, until I get a chance to smell for myself? That I don't trust a mother's son of them not to fuck things up, and that includes Dale himself?

But Henry doesn't ask. 'I'll be standing at the end of my driveway,' he said. 'Just tell me when.'

Jack calculates his remaining chores with the evidence, chores that will end with stowing everything in the lock-box in the bed of his truck. Reminds himself to take his cell phone, which usually does nothing but stand on its little charging device in his study. He'll want to call everything in as soon as he has seen Irma's remains in situ and finished that vital first walk-through. Let Dale and his boys come then. Let them bring along the high school marching band, if they want to. He glances at his watch and sees that it's almost eight o'clock. How did it get so late so early? Distances are shorter in the other place, this he remembers, but does time go faster as well? Or has he simply lost track?

'I'll be there at eight-fifteen,' Jack says. 'And when we get to Ed's Eats, you're going to sit in my truck like a good little boy until I tell you you can get out.'

'Understood, *mon capitaine*.'

'Ding-dong.' Jack hangs up and heads back out to the porch.

Things aren't going to turn out the way Jack hopes. He's not going to get that clear first look and smell. In fact, by this afternoon the situation in French Landing, volatile already, will be on the verge of spinning out of control. Although there are many factors at work here, the chief cause of this latest escalation will be the Mad Hungarian.

There's a dose of good old small-town humor in this nickname, like calling the skinny bank clerk Big Joe or the trifocal-wearing bookstore proprietor Hawkeye. Arnold Hrabowski, at five foot six and one hundred and fifty pounds, is the smallest man on Dale Gilbertson's current roster. In fact, he's the smallest *person* on Dale's current roster, as both Debbi Anderson and Pam Stevens outweigh him and stand taller (at six-one, Debbi could eat scrambled eggs off Arnold Hrabowski's head). The Mad Hungarian is also a fairly inoffensive fellow, the sort of guy who continues to apologize for giving tickets no matter how many times Dale has told him that this is a very bad policy, and who has been known to start interrogations with such unfortunate phrases as *Excuse me, but I was wondering*. As a result, Dale keeps him on desk as much as possible, or downtown, where everyone knows him and most treat him with absent respect. He tours the county grammar schools as Officer Friendly. The little ones, unaware that they are getting their first lessons on the evils of pot from the Mad Hungarian, adore him. When he gives tougher lectures on dope, drink, and reckless driving at the high school, the kids doze or pass notes, although they do think the federally funded DARE car he drives – a low, sleek Pontiac with JUST SAY NO emblazoned on the doors – is way cool. Basically, Officer Hrabowski is about as exciting as a tuna on white, hold the mayo.

But in the seventies, you see, there was this relief pitcher for St Louis and then the Kansas City Royals, a *very* fearsome fellow indeed, and his name was *Al* Hrabosky. He stalked rather than walked in from the bullpen, and before beginning to pitch (usually in the ninth inning with the bases juiced and the game on the line), Al Hrabosky would turn from the plate, lower his head, clench his fists, and pump them once, very hard, psyching himself up. Then he would turn and begin throwing nasty fastballs, many of them within kissing distance of the batters' chins. He was of course called the Mad Hungarian, and even a blind man could see he was the best damn reliever in the majors. And of course Arnold Hrabowski is now known, *must* be known, as the Mad Hungarian. He even tried to grow a Fu Manchu mustache a few years back, like the one the famed reliever wore. But whereas Al Hrabosky's Fu was as fearsome as Zulu warpaint, Arnold's only provoked chuckles – a Fu sprouting on that mild accountant's face, just imagine! – and so he shaved it off.

The Mad Hungarian of French Landing is not a bad fellow; he does his absolute level best, and under normal circumstances his level best is good enough. But these aren't ordinary days in French Landing, these are the slippery slippage days, the abbalah-opopanax days, and he is exactly the sort of officer of whom Jack is afraid. And this morning he is, quite without meaning to, going to make a bad situation very much worse.

The call from the Fisherman comes in to the 911 phone at 8:10 a.m., while Jack is finishing his notes on the yellow legal pad and Henry is strolling down his driveway, smelling the summer morning with great pleasure in spite of the shadow Jack's news has cast over his mind. Unlike some of the officers (Bobby Dulac, for instance), the Mad Hungarian reads the script taped next to the 911 phone word for word.

ARNOLD HRABOWSKI: Hello, this is the French Landing Police Department, Officer Hrabowski speaking. You've dialed 911. Do you have an emergency? [*Unintelligible sound . . . throat-clearing?*]

AH: Hello? This is Officer Hrabowski answering on 911. Do you—

CALLER: Hello, asswipe.

AH: Who is this? Do you have an emergency?

C: You have an emergency. Not me. You.

AH: Who is this, please?

C: Your worst nightmare.

AH: Sir, could I ask you to identify yourself?

C: Abbalah. Abbalah-doon. [*Phonetic.*]

AH: Sir, I don't—

C: I'm the Fisherman.

[*Silence.*]

C: What's wrong? Scared? You ought to be scared.

AH: Sir. Ah, sir. There are penalties for false—

C: There are whips in hell and chains in shayol. [*Caller may be saying 'Sheol.'*]

AH: Sir, if I could have your name—

C: My name is legion. My number is many. I am a rat under the floor of the universe. Robert Frost said that. [*Caller laughs.*]

AH: Sir, if you hold, I can put on my chief—

C: Shut up and listen, asswipe. Your tape running? I hope so. I could shag [*Caller may be saying 'scram' but word is indistinct*] it if I wanted to but I don't want to.

AH: Sir, I—

C: Kiss my scrote, you monkey. I left you one and I'm tired of waiting for you to find her. Try Ed's Eats and Dogs. Might be a little rotten now, but when she was new she was very [*Caller rolls* r's, *turning the word into 'verrry'*] tasty.

AH: Where are you? Who is this? If this is a joke—

C: Tell the coppiceman I said hello.

★

When the call began, the Mad Hungarian's pulse was lubdubbing along at a perfectly normal sixty-eight beats a minute. When it ends at 8:12, Arnold Hrabowski's ticker is in overdrive. His face is pale. Halfway through the call he looked at the Caller ID readout and wrote down the number displayed there with a hand shaking so badly that the numbers jigged up and down over three lines on his pad. When the Fisherman hangs up and he hears the sound of an open line, Hrabowski is so flustered that he tries to dial the callback on the red phone, forgetting that 911 is a one-way street. His fingers strike the smooth plastic front of the phone and he drops it back into the cradle with a frightened curse. He looks at it like something that has bitten him.

Hrabowski grabs the receiver from the black telephone beside 911, starts to punch in the callback, but his fingers betray him and hit two numbers at once. He curses again, and Tom Lund, passing by with a cup of coffee, says, 'What's wrong there, Arnie?'

'Get Dale!' the Mad Hungarian shouts, startling Tom so badly he spills coffee on his fingers. 'Get him out here *now*!'

'What the hell's wrong with y—'

'NOW, goddamnit!'

Tom stares at Hrabowski a moment longer, eyebrows raised, then goes to tell Dale that the Mad Hungarian seems to have really gone mad.

The second time Hrabowski tries, he succeeds in dialing the callback number. It rings. It rings. And it rings some more.

Dale Gilbertson appears with his own cup of coffee. There are dark circles under his eyes, and the lines at the corners of his mouth are a lot more prominent than they used to be.

'Arnie? What's—'

'Play back the last call,' Arnold Hrabowski says. 'I think

it was . . . hello!' He barks this last, sitting forward behind the dispatch desk and shoving papers every which way. 'Hello, who is this?'

Listens.

'It's the police, that's who it is. Officer Hrabowski, FLPD. Now you talk to me. Who is this?'

Dale, meanwhile, has got the earphones on his head and is listening to the most recent call to French Landing 911 with mounting horror. *Oh dear God*, he thinks. His first impulse – the very first – is to call Jack Sawyer and ask for help. To *bawl* for it, like a little kid with his hand caught in a door. Then he tells himself to take hold, that this is his job, like it or not, and he had better take hold and try to do it. Besides, Jack has gone up to Arden with Fred Marshall to see Fred's crazy wife. At least that was the plan.

Cops, meanwhile, are clustering around the dispatch desk: Lund, Tcheda, Stevens. What Dale sees when he looks at them is nothing but big eyes and pale, bewildered faces. And the ones on patrol? The ones currently off duty? No better. With the possible exception of Bobby Dulac, no better. He feels despair as well as horror. Oh, this is a nightmare. A truck with no brakes rolling downhill toward a crowded school playground.

He pulls the earphones off, tearing a small cut by his ear, not feeling it. 'Where'd it come from?' he asks Hrabowski. The Mad Hungarian has hung up the telephone and is just sitting there, stunned. Dale grabs his shoulder and gives it a shake. '*Where'd it come from?*'

'The 7-Eleven,' the Mad Hungarian replies, and Dale hears Danny Tcheda grunt. Not too far from where the Marshall boy's bike disappeared, in other words. 'I just spoke with Mr Rajan Patel, the day clerk. He says the callback number belongs to the pay phone, just outside.'

'Did he see who made the call?'

'No. He was out back, taking a beer delivery.'

'You positive Patel himself didn't—'

'Yeah. He's got an Indian accent. Heavy. The guy on 911 . . . Dale, you heard him. He sounded like *anybody*.'

'What's going on?' Pam Stevens asks. She has a good idea, though; they all do. It's just a question of details. 'What's happened?'

Because it's the quickest way to get them up to speed, Dale replays the call, this time on speaker.

In the stunned silence that follows, Dale says: 'I'm going out to Ed's Eats. Tom, you're coming with me.'

'Yessir!' Tom Lund says. He looks almost ill with excitement.

'Four more cruisers to follow me.' Most of Dale's mind is frozen; this procedural stuff skates giddily on top of the ice. *I'm okay at procedure and organization*, he thinks. *It's just catching the goddamn psycho murderer that's giving me a little trouble.* 'All pairs. Danny, you and Pam in the first. Leave five minutes after Tom and I do. Five minutes by the clock, and no lights or siren. We're going to keep this quiet just as long as we can.'

Danny Tcheda and Pam Stevens look at each other, nod, then look back at Dale. Dale is looking at Arnold 'the Mad Hungarian' Hrabowski. He ticks off three more pairs, ending with Dit Jesperson and Bobby Dulac. Bobby is the only one he really wants out there; the others are just insurance and – God grant it not be necessary – crowd control. All of them are to come at five-minute intervals.

'Let me go out, too,' Arnie Hrabowski pleads. 'Come on, boss, what do you say?'

Dale opens his mouth to say he wants Arnie right where he is, but then he sees the hopeful look in those watery brown eyes. Even in his own deep distress, Dale can't help responding to that, at least a little. For Arnie, police life is too often standing on the sidewalk while the parade goes by.

Some parade, he thinks.

'I tell you what, Arn,' he says. 'When you finish all your other calls, buzz Debbi. If you can get her in here, you can come out to Ed's.'

Arnold nods excitedly, and Dale almost smiles. The Mad Hungarian will have Debbi in here by nine-thirty, he guesses, even if he has to drag her by the hair like Alley Oop. 'Who do I pair with, Dale?'

'Come by yourself,' Dale says. 'In the DARE car, why don't you? But, Arnie, if you leave this desk without relief waiting to drop into the chair the second you leave it, you'll be looking for a new job come tomorrow.'

'Oh, don't worry,' Hrabowski says, and, Hungarian or not, in his excitement he sounds positively Suh-vee-dish. Nor is that surprising, since Centralia, where he grew up, was once known as Swede Town.

'Come on, Tom,' Dale says. 'We'll grab the evidence kit on our—'

'Uh . . . boss?'

'*What*, Arnie?' Meaning, of course, *What now?*

'Should I call those State Police guys, Brown and Black?'

Danny Tcheda and Pam Stevens snicker. Tom smiles. Dale doesn't do either. His heart, already in the cellar, now goes even lower. *Subbasement, ladies and gentlemen – false hopes on your left, lost causes on your right. Last stop, everybody out.*

Perry Brown and Jeff Black. He had forgotten them, how funny. Brown and Black, who would now almost certainly take his case away from him.

'They're still out at the Paradise Motel,' the Mad

Hungarian goes on, 'although I think the FBI guy went back to Milwaukee.'

'I—'

'And County,' the Hungarian plows relentlessly along. 'Don't forget them. You want me to call the ME first, or the evidence wagon?' The evidence wagon is a blue Ford Econoline van, packed with everything from quick-drying plaster for taking tire impressions to a rolling video studio. Stuff the French Landing PD will never have access to.

Dale stands where he is, head lowered, looking dismally at the floor. They are going to take the case away from him. With every word Hrabowski says, that is clearer. And suddenly he wants it for his own. In spite of how he hates it and how it scares him, he wants it with all his heart. The Fisherman is a monster, but he's not a county monster, a state monster, or a Federal Bureau of Investigation monster. The Fisherman is a French Landing monster, *Dale Gilbertson's* monster, and he wants to keep the case for reasons that have nothing to do with personal prestige or even the practical matter of holding on to his job. He wants him because the Fisherman is an offense against everything Dale wants and needs and believes in. Those are things you can't say out loud without sounding corny and stupid, but they are true for all that. He feels a sudden, foolish anger at Jack. If Jack had come on board sooner, maybe—

And if wishes were horses, beggars would ride. He has to notify County, if only to get the medical examiner out at the scene, and he has to notify the State Police, in the persons of Detectives Brown and Black, as well. But not until he has a look at what's out there, in the field beyond Goltz's. At what the Fisherman has left. By God, not until then.

And, perhaps, has one final swing at the bastard.

'Get our guys rolling at five-minute intervals,' he says,

'just as I told you. Then get Debbi in the dispatch chair. Have *her* call State and County.' Arnold Hrabowski's puzzled face makes Dale feel like screaming, but somehow he retains his patience. 'I want some lead time.'

'Oh,' Arnie says, and then, when he actually *does* get it: '*Oh!*'

'And don't tell anyone other than our guys about the call or our response. *Anyone.* You'd likely start a panic. Do you understand?'

'Absolutely, boss,' says the Hungarian.

Dale glances at the clock: 8:26 a.m. 'Come on, Tom,' he says. 'Let's get moving. *Tempus fugit.*'

The Mad Hungarian has never been more efficient, and things fall into place like a dream. Even Debbi Anderson is a good sport about the desk. And yet through it all, the voice on the phone stays with him. Hoarse, raspy, with just a tinge of accent – the kind anyone living in this part of the world might pick up. Nothing unusual about that. Yet it haunts him. Not that the guy called him an asswipe – he's been called much worse by your ordinary Saturday night drunks – but some of the other stuff. *There are whips in hell and chains in shayol. My name is legion.* Stuff like that. And *abbalah.* What was an abbalah? Arnold Hrabowski doesn't know. He only knows that the very sound of it in his head makes him feel bad and scared. It's like a word in a secret book, the kind you might use to conjure up a demon.

When he gets the willies, there's only one person who can take them away, and that's his wife. He knows Dale told him not to tell anybody about what was going down, and he understands the reasons, but surely the chief didn't mean Paula. They have been married twenty years, and Paula isn't like another person at all. She's like the rest of him.

So (more in order to dispel his bad case of the willies than to gossip; let's at least give Arnold that much) the Mad Hungarian makes the terrible mistake of trusting his wife's discretion. He calls Paula and tells her that he spoke to the Fisherman not half an hour ago. Yes, really, the *Fisherman*! He tells her about the body that is supposedly waiting for Dale and Tom Lund out at Ed's Eats. She asks him if he's all right. Her voice is trembling with awe and excitement, and the Mad Hungarian finds this quite satisfying, since he's feeling awed and excited himself. They talk a little more, and when Arnold hangs up, he feels better. The terror of that rough, strangely knowing voice on the phone has receded a little.

Paula Hrabowski is discretion itself, the very soul of discretion. She tells only her two best friends about the call Arnie got from the Fisherman and the body at Ed's Eats, and swears them both to secrecy. Both say they will never tell a soul, and this is why, one hour later, even before the State Police and the county medical and forensics guys have been called, everyone knows that the police have found a slaughterhouse out at Ed's Eats. Half a dozen murdered kids.

Maybe more.

10

As the cruiser with Tom Lund behind the wheel noses down Third Street to Chase – roof-rack lights decorously dark, siren off – Dale takes out his wallet and begins digging through the mess in the back: business cards people have given him, a few dog-eared photographs, little licks of folded-over notebook paper. On one of the latter he finds what he wants.

'Whatcha doin', boss?' Tom asks.

'None of your beeswax. Just drive the car.'

Dale grabs the phone from its spot on the console, grimaces and wipes off the residue of someone's powdered doughnut, then, without much hope, dials the number of Jack Sawyer's cell phone. He starts to smile when the phone is answered on the fourth ring, but the smile metamorphoses into a frown of puzzlement. He knows that voice and should recognize it, but—

'Hello?' says the person who has apparently answered Jack's cell phone. 'Speak now, whoever you are, or forever hold your peace.'

Then Dale knows. Would have known immediately if he had been at home or in his office, but in this context—

'Henry?' he says, knowing he sounds stupid but not able to help it. 'Uncle Henry, is that you?'

Jack is piloting his truck across the Tamarack Bridge when the cell phone in his pants pocket starts its annoying little tweet. He takes it out and taps the back of Henry's hand with it. 'Deal with this,' he says. 'Cell phones give you brain cancer.'

'Which is okay for me but not for you.'

'More or less, yeah.'

'That's what I love about you, Jack,' Henry says, and opens the phone with a nonchalant flick of the wrist. 'Hello?' And, after a pause: 'Speak now, whoever you are, or forever hold your peace.' Jack glances at him, then back at the road. They're coming up on Roy's Store, where the early shopper gets the best greens. 'Yes, Dale. It is indeed your esteemed—' Henry listens, frowning a little bit and smiling a little bit. 'I'm in Jack's truck, with Jack,' he says. 'George Rathbun isn't working this morning because KDCU is covering the Summer Marathon over in La Riv—'

He listens some more, then says: 'If it's a Nokia – which is what it feels like and sounds like – then it's digital rather than analog. Wait.' He looks at Jack. 'Your cell,' he says. 'It's a Nokia?'

'Yes, but why—'

'Because digital phones are supposedly harder to snoop,' Henry says, and goes back to the phone. 'It's a digital, and I'll put him on. I'm sure Jack can explain everything.' Henry hands him the telephone, folds his hands primly in his lap, and looks out the window exactly as he would if surveying the scenery. *And maybe he is,* Jack thinks. *Maybe in some weird fruit-bat way, he really is.*

He pulls over to the shoulder on Highway 93. He doesn't

like the cell phone to begin with – twenty-first-century slave bracelets, he thinks them – but he absolutely *loathes* driving while talking on one. Besides, Irma Freneau isn't going anywhere this morning.

'Dale?' he says.

'Where are you?' Dale asks, and Jack knows at once that the Fisherman has been busy elsewhere, too. *As long as it's not another dead kid*, he thinks. *Not that, not yet, please.* 'How come you're with Henry? Is Fred Marshall there, too?'

Jack tells him about the change in plan, and is about to go on when Dale breaks in.

'Whatever you're doing, I want you to get your ass out to a place called Ed's Eats and Dawgs, near Goltz's. Henry can help you find it. The Fisherman called the station, Jack. He called 911. Told us Irma Freneau's body is out there. Well, not in so many words, but he did say *she*.'

Dale is not quite babbling, but almost. Jack notes this as any good clinician would note the symptoms of a patient.

'I need you, Jack. I really—'

'That's where we were headed anyway,' Jack says quietly, although they are going absolutely nowhere at this moment, just sitting on the shoulder while the occasional car blips past on 93.

'What?'

Hoping that Dale and Henry are right about the virtues of digital technology, Jack tells French Landing's police chief about his morning delivery, aware that Henry, although still looking out the window, is listening sharply. He tells Dale that Ty Marshall's cap was on top of the box with the feathers and Irma's foot inside it.

'Holy . . .' Dale says, sounding out of breath. 'Holy shit.'

'Tell me what you've done,' Jack says, and Dale does. It

sounds pretty good – so far, at least – but Jack doesn't like the part about Arnold Hrabowski. The Mad Hungarian has impressed him as the sort of fellow who will never be able to behave like a real cop, no matter how hard he tries. Back in LA, they used to call the Arnie Hrabowskis of the world Mayberry RFDs.

'Dale, what about the phone at the 7-Eleven?'

'It's a *pay* phone,' Dale says, as if speaking to a child.

'Yes, but there could be fingerprints,' Jack says. 'I mean, there are going to be *billions* of fingerprints, but forensics can isolate the freshest. *Easily*. He might have worn gloves, but maybe not. If he's leaving messages and calling cards as well as writing to the parents, he's gone Stage Two. Killing isn't enough for him anymore. He wants to play you now. Play *with* you. Maybe he even wants to be caught and stopped, like Son of Sam.'

'The phone. Fresh fingerprints on the phone.' Dale sounds badly humiliated, and Jack's heart goes out to him. 'Jack, I can't do this. I'm lost.'

This is something to which Jack chooses not to speak. Instead he says, 'Who've you got who can see to the phone?'

'Dit Jesperson and Bobby Dulac, I guess.'

Bobby, Jack thinks, is entirely too good to waste for long at the 7-Eleven outside town. 'Just have them crisscross the phone with yellow tape and talk to the guy on duty. Then they can come on out to the site.'

'Okay.' Dale hesitates, then asks a question. The defeat in it, the sense of almost complete abrogation, makes Jack sad. 'Anything else?'

'Have you called the State Police? County? Does that FBI guy know? The one who thinks he looks like Tommy Lee Jones?'

Dale snorts. 'Uh . . . actually, I'd decided to sit on notification for a little while.'

'Good,' Jack says, and the savage satisfaction in his voice causes Henry to turn from his blind regard of the countryside and regard his friend instead, eyebrows raised.

Let us rise up again – on wings as eagles, as the Reverend Lance Hovdahl, French Landing's Lutheran pastor, might say – and fly down the black ribbon of Highway 93, back toward town. We reach Route 35 and turn right. Closer and to our right is the overgrown lane that leads not to a dragon's hidden gold or secret dwarf mines but to that peculiarly unpleasant black house. A little farther on, we can see the futuristic dome shape of Goltz's (well . . . it seemed futuristic in the seventies, at least). All our landmarks are in place, including the rubbly, weedy path that shoots off from the main road to the left. This is the track that leads to the remains of Ed Gilbertson's erstwhile palace of guilty pleasures.

Let us flutter onto the telephone line just across from this track. Hot gossip tickles our birdy feet: Paula Hrabowski's friend Myrtle Harrington passing on the news of the dead body (or bodies) at Ed's to Richie Bumstead, who will in turn pass it on to Beezer St Pierre, grieving father and spiritual leader of the Thunder Five. This passage of voices through the wire probably shouldn't please us, but it does. Gossip is no doubt nasty stuff, but it *does* energize the human spirit.

Now, from the west comes the cruiser with Tom Lund at the wheel and Dale Gilbertson in the shotgun seat. And from the east comes Jack's burgundy-colored Ram pickup. They reach the turnoff to Ed's at the same time. Jack motions for Dale to go first, then follows him. We take wing, fly above and then ahead of them. We roost on the rusty Esso gas pump to watch developments.

*

Jack drives slowly down the lane to the half-collapsed building that stands in a scruff of high weeds and goldenrod. He's looking for any sign of passage, and sees only the fresh tracks made by Dale and Tom's police car.

'We've got the place to ourselves,' he informs Henry.

'Yes, but for how long?'

Not very would have been Jack's answer, had he bothered to give one. Instead, he pulls up next to Dale's car and gets out. Henry rolls down his window but stays put, as ordered.

Ed's was once a simple wooden building about the length of a Burlington Northern boxcar and with a boxcar's flat roof. At the south end, you could buy sof'-serve ice cream from one of three windows. At the north end you could get your nasty hot dog or your even nastier order of fish and chips to go. In the middle was a small sit-down restaurant featuring a counter and red-top stools. Now the south end has entirely collapsed, probably from the weight of snow. All the windows have been broken in. There's some graffiti – So-and-so chugs cock, we fucked Patty Jarvis untill she howelled, TROY LUVS MARYANN – but not as much as Jack might have expected. All but one of the stools have been looted. Crickets are conversing in the grass. They're loud, but not as loud as the flies inside the ruined restaurant. There are *lots* of flies in there, a regular fly convention in progress. And—

'Do you smell it?' Dale asks him.

Jack nods. Of course he does. He's smelled it already today, but now it's worse. Because there's more of Irma out here to send up a stink. Much more than what would fit into a single shoe box.

Tom Lund has produced a handkerchief and is mopping his broad, distressed face. It's warm, but not warm enough to account for the sweat streaming off his face and brow. And his skin is pasty.

'Officer Lund,' Jack says.

'Huh!' Tom jumps and looks rather wildly around at Jack.

'You may have to vomit. If you feel you must, do it over there.' Jack points to an overgrown track, even more ancient and ill-defined than the one leading in from the main road. This one seems to meander in the direction of Goltz's.

'I'll be okay,' Tom says.

'I know you will. But if you need to unload, don't do it on what may turn out to be evidence.'

'I want you to start stringing yellow tape around the entire building,' Dale tells his officer. 'Jack? A word?'

Dale puts a hand on Jack's forearm and starts walking back toward the truck. Although he's got a good many things on his mind, Jack notices how strong that hand is. And no tremble in it. Not yet, anyway.

'What is it?' Jack asks impatiently when they're standing near the passenger window of the truck. 'We want a look before the whole world gets here, don't we? Wasn't that the idea, or am I—'

'You need to get the foot, Jack,' Dale says. And then: 'Hello, Uncle Henry, you look spiff.'

'Thanks,' Henry says.

'What are you talking about?' Jack asks. 'That foot is *evidence*.'

Dale nods. 'I think it ought to be evidence found here, though. Unless, of course, you relish the idea of spending twenty-four hours or so answering questions in Madison.'

Jack opens his mouth to tell Dale not to waste what little time they have with arrant idiocies, then closes it again. It suddenly occurs to him how his possession of that foot might look to minor-league smarties like Detectives Brown and Black. Maybe even to a major-league smarty like John Redding of the FBI. Brilliant cop retires at an impossibly young age, and to the impossibly bucolic town of French Landing, Wisconsin. He has plenty of scratch, but the source of income is blurry, to say the least. And oh, look at this, all at once there's a serial killer operating in the neighborhood.

Maybe the brilliant cop has got a loose screw. Maybe he's like those firemen who enjoy the pretty flames so much they get into the arson game themselves. Certainly Dale's Color Posse would have to wonder why the Fisherman would send an early retiree like Jack a victim's body part. *And the hat*, Jack thinks. *Don't forget Ty's baseball cap*.

All at once he knows how Dale felt when Jack told him that the phone at the 7-Eleven had to be cordoned off. *Exactly*.

'Oh man,' he says. 'You're right.' He looks at Tom Lund, industriously running yellow POLICE LINE tape while butterflies dance around his shoulders and the flies continue their drunken buzzing from the shadows of Ed's Eats. 'What about him?'

'Tom will keep his mouth shut,' Dale says, and on that Jack decides to trust him. He wouldn't, had it been the Hungarian.

'I owe you one,' Jack says.

'Yep,' Henry agrees from his place in the passenger seat. 'Even a blind man could see he owes you one.'

'Shut up, Uncle Henry,' Dale says.

'Yes, *mon capitaine*.'

'What about the cap?' Jack asks.

'If we find anything else of Ty Marshall's . . .' Dale pauses, then swallows. 'Or Ty himself, we'll leave it. If not, you keep it for the time being.'

'I think maybe you just saved me a lot of major irritation,'

Jack says, leading Dale to the back of the truck. He opens the stainless steel box behind the cab, which he hasn't bothered to lock for the run out here, and takes out one of the trash-can liners. From inside it comes the slosh of water and the clink of a few remaining ice cubes. 'The next time you get feeling dumb, you might remind yourself of that.'

Dale ignores this completely. 'Ohgod,' he says, making it one word. He's looking at the Baggie that has just emerged from the trash-can liner. There are beads of water clinging to the transparent sides.

'The *smell* of it!' Henry says with undeniable distress. 'Oh, the poor child!'

'You can smell it even through the plastic?' Jack asks.

'Yes indeed. And coming from there.' Henry points at the ruined restaurant and then produces his cigarettes. 'If I'd known, I would have brought a jar of Vicks and an El Producto.'

In any case, there's no need to walk the Baggie with the gruesome artifact inside it past Tom Lund, who has now disappeared behind the ruins with his reel of yellow tape.

'Go on in,' Dale instructs Jack quietly. 'Get a look and take care of the thing in that Baggie if you find . . . you know . . . her. I want to speak to Tom.'

Jack steps through the warped, doorless doorway into the thickening stench. Outside, he can hear Dale instructing Tom to send Pam Stevens and Danny Tcheda back down to the end of the access road as soon as they arrive, where they will serve as passport control.

The interior of Ed's Eats will probably be bright by afternoon, but now it is shadowy, lit mostly by crazed, criss-crossing rays of sun. Galaxies of dust spin lazily through them. Jack steps carefully, wishing he had a flashlight, not wanting to go back and get one from the cruiser until he's taken care of the foot. (He thinks of this as 'redeployment.') There are human tracks through the dust, trash, and drifts of old gray feathers. The tracks are man-sized. Weaving in and out of them are a dog's pawprints. Off to his left, Jack spies a neat little pile of droppings. He steps around the rusty remains of an overturned gas grill and follows both sets of tracks around the filthy counter. Outside, the second French Landing cruiser is rolling up. In here, in this darker world, the sound of the flies has become a soft roar and the stench . . . the *stench* . . .

Jack fishes a handkerchief from his pocket and places it over his nose as he follows the tracks into the kitchen. Here the pawprints multiply and the human footprints disappear completely. Jack thinks grimly of the circle of beaten-down grass he made in the field of that other world, a circle with no path of beaten-down grass leading to it.

Lying against the far wall near a pool of dried blood is what remains of Irma Freneau. The mop of her filthy strawberry-blond hair mercifully obscures her face. Above her on a rusty piece of tin that probably once served as a heat shield for the deep-fat fryers, two words have been written with what Jack feels sure was a black Sharpie marker:

Hello boys

'Ah, *fuck*,' Dale Gilbertson says from almost directly behind him, and Jack nearly screams.

Outside, the snafu starts almost immediately.

Halfway back down the access road, Danny and Pam (not in the least disappointed to have been assigned guard duty once they have actually seen the slumped ruin of Ed's and smelled the aroma drifting from it) nearly have a head-on with an old

International Harvester pickup that is bucketing toward Ed's at a good forty miles an hour. Luckily, Pam swings the cruiser to the right and the driver of the pickup – Teddy Runkleman – swings left. The vehicles miss each other by inches and swerve into the grass on either side of this poor excuse for a road. The pickup's rusty bumper thumps against a small birch.

Pam and Danny get out of their unit, hearts pumping, adrenaline spurting. Four men come spilling out of the pickup's cab like clowns out of the little car in the circus. Mrs Morton would recognize them all as regulars at Roy's Store. Layabouts, she would call them.

'What in the name of God are you *doing*?' Danny Tcheda roars. His hand drops to the butt of his gun and then falls away a bit reluctantly. He's getting a headache.

The men (Runkleman is the only one the officers know by name, although between them they recognize the faces of the other three) are goggle-eyed with excitement.

'How many ja find?' one of them spits. Pam can actually see the spittle spraying out in the morning air, a sight she could have done without. 'How many'd the bastid kill?'

Pam and Danny exchange a single dismayed look. And before they can reply, holy God, here comes an old Chevrolet Bel Air with another four or five men inside it. No, one of them is a woman. They pull up and spill out, also like clowns from the little car.

But we're the real clowns, Pam thinks. *Us.*

Pam and Danny are surrounded by eight semihysterical men and one semihysterical woman, all of them throwing questions.

'Hell, I'm going up there and see for myself!' Teddy Runkleman shouts, almost jubilantly, and Danny realizes the situation is on the verge of spinning out of control. If these fools get the rest of the way up the access road, Dale will first tear him a new asshole and then salt it down.

'*HOLD IT RIGHT THERE, ALL OF YOU!*' he bawls, and actually draws his gun. It's a first for him, and he hates the weight of it in his hand – these are ordinary people, after all, not bad guys – but it gets their attention.

'This is a crime scene,' Pam says, finally able to speak in a normal tone of voice. They mutter and look at one another; worst fears confirmed. She steps to the driver of the Chevrolet. 'Who are you, sir? A Saknessum? You look like a Saknessum.'

'Freddy,' he admits.

'Well, you get back in your vehicle, Freddy Saknessum, and the rest of you who came with him also get in, and you back the hell right out of here. Don't bother trying to turn around, you'll just get stuck.'

'But—' the woman begins. Pam thinks she's a Sanger, a clan of fools if ever there was one.

'Stow it and go,' Pam tells her.

'And you right behind him,' Danny tells Teddy Runkleman. He just hopes to Christ no more will come along, or they'll end up trying to manage a parade in reverse. He doesn't know how the news got out, and at this moment can't afford to care. 'Unless you want a summons for interfering with a police investigation. That can get you five years.' He has no idea if there is such a charge, but it gets them moving even better than the sight of his pistol.

The Chevrolet backs out, rear end wagging from side to side like a dog's tail. Runkleman's pickup goes next, with two of the men standing up in back and peering over the cab, trying to catch sight of the old restaurant's roof, at least. Their curiosity lends them a look of unpleasant vacuity. The PD unit comes last, herding the old car and older truck like a corgi herding sheep, roof-rack lights now pulsing. Pam is forced to ride mostly on the brake, and as she drives she lets loose a low-pitched stream of words her mother never taught her.

'Do you kiss your kids good-night with that mouth?' Danny asks, not without admiration.

'Shut up,' she says. Then: 'You got any aspirin?'

'I was going to ask you the same thing,' Danny says.

They get back out to the main road just in time. Three more vehicles are coming from the direction of French Landing, two from the direction of Centralia and Arden. A siren rises in the warming air. Another cruiser, the third in what was supposed to be an unobtrusive line, is coming along, passing the lookie-loos from town.

'Oh man.' Danny sounds close to tears. 'Oh man, oh man, oh man. It's gonna be a carnival, and I bet the staties *still* don't know. They'll have kittens. *Dale* is gonna have kittens.'

'It'll be all right,' Pam says. 'Calm down. We'll just pull across the road and park. Also stick your gun back in the fucking holster.'

'Yes, Mother.' He stows his piece as Pam swings across the access road, pulling back to let the third cruiser through, then pulling forward again to block the way. 'Yeah, maybe we caught it in time to put a lid on it.'

'Course we did.'

They relax a little. Both of them have forgotten the old stretch of road that runs between Ed's and Goltz's, but there are plenty of folks in town who know about it. Beezer St Pierre and his boys, for instance. And while Wendell Green does not, guys like him always seem able to find the back way. They've got an instinct for it.

11

Beezer's journey began with Myrtle Harrington, the loving wife of Michael Harrington, whispering down the telephone line to Richie Bumstead, on whom she has an industrial-strength crush in spite of his having been married to her second-best friend, Glad, who dropped down dead in her kitchen at the amazing age of thirty-one. For his part, Richie Bumstead has had enough macaroni-tuna casseroles and whisper-voiced phone calls from Myrtle to last him through two more lifetimes, but this is one set of whispers he's glad, even oddly relieved, to listen to, because he drives a truck for the Kingsland Brewing Company and has come to know Beezer St Pierre and the rest of the boys, at least a little bit.

At first, Richie thought the Thunder Five was a bunch of hoodlums, those big guys with scraggly shoulder-length hair and foaming beards roaring through town on their Harleys, but one Friday he happened to be standing alongside the one called Mouse in the pay-window line, and Mouse looked down at him and said something funny about how working for love never made the paycheck look bigger, and they got into a conversation that made Richie Bumstead's head spin.

Two nights later he saw Beezer St Pierre and the one called Doc shooting the breeze in the yard when he came off-shift, and after he got his rig locked down for the night he went over and got into another conversation that made him feel like he'd walked into a combination of a raunchy blues bar and a *Jeopardy!* championship. These guys – Beezer, Mouse, Doc, Sonny, and Kaiser Bill – looked like rockin', stompin', red-eyed violence, but they were *smart*. Beezer, it turned out, was head brewmaster in Kingsland Ale's special-projects division, and the other guys were just under him. They had all gone to *college*. They were interested in making great beer and having a good time, and Richie sort of wished he could get a bike and let it all hang out like them, but a long Saturday afternoon and evening at the Sand Bar proved that the line between a high old time and utter abandon was too fine for him. He didn't have the stamina to put away two pitchers of Kingsland, play a decent game of pool, drink two more pitchers while talking about the influences of Sherwood Anderson and Gertrude Stein on the young Hemingway, get into some serious head-butting, put down another couple of pitchers, emerge clearheaded enough to go barrelassing through the countryside, pick up a couple of experimental Madison girls, smoke a lot of high-grade shit, and romp until dawn. You have to respect people who can do that and still hold down good jobs.

As far as Richie is concerned, he has a *duty* to tell Beezer that the police have finally learned the whereabouts of Irma Freneau's body. That busybody Myrtle said it was a secret Richie has to keep to himself, but he's pretty sure that right after Myrtle gave him the news, she called four or five other people. Those people will call their best friends, and in no time at all half of French Landing is going to be heading over on 35 to be in on the action. Beezer has a better right to be there than most, doesn't he?

Less than thirty seconds after getting rid of Myrtle Harrington, Richie Bumstead looks up Beezer St Pierre in the directory and dials the number.

'Richie, I sure hope you aren't shitting me,' Beezer says.

'He called in, yeah?' Beezer wants Richie to repeat it. 'That worthless piece of shit in the DARE car, the Mad Hungarian? . . . And he said the girl was *where*?'

'Fuck, the whole town is gonna be out there,' Beezer says. 'But thanks, man, thanks a lot. I owe you.' In the instant before the receiver slams down, Richie thinks he hears Beezer start to say something else that gets dissolved in a scalding rush of emotion.

And in the little house on Nailhouse Row, Beezer St Pierre swipes tears into his beard, gently moves the telephone a few inches back on the table, and turns to face Bear Girl, his common-law spouse, his old lady, Amy's mother, whose real name is Susan Osgood, and who is staring up at him from beneath her thick blond bangs, one finger holding her place in a book.

'It's the Freneau girl,' he says. 'I gotta go.'

'Go,' Bear Girl tells him. 'Take the cell phone and call me as soon as you can.'

'Yeah,' he says, and plucks the cell phone from its charger and rams it into a front pocket of his jeans. Instead of moving to the door, he thrusts a hand into the huge red-brown tangle of his beard and absentmindedly combs it with his fingers. His feet are rooted to the floor; his eyes have lost focus. 'The Fisherman called 911,' he says. 'Can you believe this shit? They couldn't find the Freneau girl by themselves, they needed *him* to tell them where to find her body.'

'Listen to me,' Bear Girl says, and gets up and travels the space between them far more quickly than she seems to. She snuggles her compact little body into his massive bulk, and Beezer inhales a chestful of her clean, soothing scent, a combination of soap and fresh bread. 'When you and the boys get out there, it's going to be up to you to keep them in line. So you have to keep *yourself* in line, Beezer. No matter how angry you are, you can't go nuts and start beating on people. Cops especially.'

'I suppose you think I shouldn't go.'

'You have to. I just don't want you to wind up in jail.'

'Hey,' he says, 'I'm a brewer, not a brawler.'

'Don't forget it,' she says, and pats him on the back. 'Are you going to call them?'

'Street telephone.' Beezer walks to the door, bends down to pick up his helmet, and marches out. Sweat slides down his forehead and crawls through his beard. Two strides bring him to his motorcycle. He puts one hand on the saddle, wipes his forehead, and bellows, 'THE FUCKING FISHERMAN TOLD THAT FUCKING HUNGARIAN COP WHERE TO FIND IRMA FRENEAU'S BODY. WHO'S COMING WITH ME?'

On both sides of Nailhouse Row, bearded heads pop out of windows and loud voices shout 'Wait Up!' 'Holy Shit!' and 'Yo!' Four vast men in leather jackets, jeans, and boots come barreling out of four front doors. Beezer almost has to smile – he loves these guys, but sometimes they remind him of cartoon characters. Even before they reach him, he starts explaining about Richie Bumstead and the 911 call, and by the time he finishes, Mouse, Doc, Sonny, and Kaiser Bill are on their bikes and waiting for the signal.

'But this here's the deal,' Beezer says. 'Two things. We're

going out there for Amy and Irma Freneau and Johnny Irkenham, not for ourselves. We want to make sure everything gets done the right way, and we're not gonna bust anybody's head open, not unless they ask for it. You got that?'

The others rumble, mumble, and grumble, apparently in assent. Four tangled beards wag up and down.

'And number two, when we *do* bust open somebody's head, it's gonna be the Fisherman's. Because we have put up with enough crap around here, and now I am pretty damn sure it's our turn to hunt down the fucking bastard who killed my little girl—' Beezer's voice catches in his throat, and he raises his fist before continuing. 'And dumped this other little girl in that fucking shack out on 35. Because I am going to get my hands on that fucking fuckhead, and when I do, I am gonna get RIGHTEOUS on his ass!'

His boys, his crew, his posse shake their fists in the air and bellow. Five motorcycles surge noisily into life. 'We'll take a look at the place from the highway and double back to the road behind Goltz's,' Beezer shouts, and charges down the road and uphill on Chase Street with the others in his slip-stream.

Through the middle of town they roll, Beezer in the lead, Mouse and Sonny practically on his tailpipe, Doc and the Kaiser right behind, their beards flowing in the wind. The thunder of their bikes rattles the windows in Schmitt's Allsorts and sends starlings flapping up from the marquee of the Agincourt Theater. Hanging over the bars of his Harley, Beezer looks a little bit like King Kong getting set to rip apart a jungle gym. Once they get past the 7-Eleven, Kaiser and Doc move up alongside Sonny and Mouse and take up the entire width of the highway. People driving west on 35 look at the figures charging toward them and swerve onto the shoulder;

drivers who see them in their rearview mirrors drift to the side of the road, stick their arms out of their windows, and wave them on.

As they near Centralia, Beezer passes about twice as many cars as really ought to be traveling down a country highway on a weekend morning. The situation is even worse than he figured it would be: Dale Gilbertson is bound to have a couple of cops blocking traffic turning in from 35, but two cops couldn't handle more than ten or twelve ghouls dead set on seeing, really *seeing*, the Fisherman's handiwork. French Landing doesn't have enough cops to keep a lid on all the screwballs homing in on Ed's Eats. Beezer curses, picturing himself losing control, turning a bunch of twisted Fisherman geeks into tent pegs. Losing control is exactly what he cannot afford to do, not if he expects any co-operation from Dale Gilbertson and his flunkies.

Beezer leads his companions around a crapped-out old red Toyota and is visited by an idea so perfect that he forgets to strike unreasoning terror into the beater's driver by looking him in the eye and snarling, 'I make Kingsland Ale, the best beer in the world, you dimwit cur.' He has done this to two drivers this morning, and neither one let him down. The people who earn this treatment by either lousy driving or the possession of a truly ugly vehicle imagine that he is threatening them with some grotesque form of sexual assault, and they freeze like rabbits, they stiffen right up. Jolly good fun, as the citizens of Emerald City sang in *The Wizard of Oz*. The idea that has distracted Beezer from his harmless pleasures possesses the simplicity of most valid inspirations. *The best way to get cooperation is to give it.* He knows exactly how to soften up Dale Gilbertson: the answer is putting on a baseball cap, grabbing its car keys, and heading out the door – the answer lies all around him.

★

One small part of that answer sits behind the wheel of the red Toyota just being overtaken by Beezer and his jolly crew. Wendell Green earned the mock rebuke he failed to receive on both of the conventional grounds. His little car may not have been ugly to begin with, but by now it is so disfigured by multiple dents and scrapes that it resembles a rolling sneer; and Green drives with an unyielding arrogance he thinks of as 'dash.' He zooms through yellow lights, changes lanes recklessly, and tailgates as a means of intimidation. Of course, he blasts his horn at the slightest provocation. Wendell is a menace. The way he handles his car perfectly expresses his character, being inconsiderate, thoughtless, and riddled with grandiosity. At the moment, he is driving even worse than usual, because as he tries to overtake every other vehicle on the road, most of his concentration is focused on the pocket tape recorder he holds up to his mouth and the golden words his equally golden voice pours into the precious machine. (Wendell often regrets the shortsightedness of the local radio stations in devoting so much air time to fools like George Rathbun and Henry Shake, when they could move up to a new level simply by letting him give an ongoing commentary on the news for an hour or so every day.) Ah, the delicious combination of Wendell's words and Wendell's voice – Edward R. Murrow in his heyday never sounded so eloquent, so resonant.

Here is what he is saying: *This morning I joined a virtual caravan of the shocked, the grieving, and the merely curious in a mournful pilgrimage winding eastward along bucolic Highway 35. Not for the first time, this journalist was struck, and struck deeply, by the immense contrast between the loveliness and peace of the Coulee Country's landscape and the ugliness and savagery one deranged human being has wrought in its unsuspecting bosom. New paragraph.*

The news had spread like wildfire. Neighbor called neighbor, friend called friend. According to a morning 911 call to the French Landing police station, the mutilated body of little Irma Freneau lies within the ruins of a former ice-cream parlor and café called Ed's Eats and Dawgs. And who had placed the call? Surely, some dutiful citizen. Not at all, ladies and gentlemen, not at all . . .

Ladies and gentlemen, this is frontline reportage, this is the news being written *while it happens*, a concept that cannot but murmur 'Pulitzer Prize' to an experienced journalist. The scoop had come to Wendell Green by way of his barber, Roy Royal, who heard it from his wife, Tillie Royal, who had been clued in by Myrtle Harrington herself, and Wendell Green has done his duty to his readers: he grabbed his tape recorder and his camera and ran out to his nasty little vehicle without pausing to telephone his editors at the *Herald*. He doesn't need a photographer; he can take all the photographs he needs with that dependable old Nikon F2A on the passenger seat. A seamless blend of words and pictures – a penetrating examination of the new century's most hideous crime – a thoughtful exploration into the nature of evil – a compassionate portrayal of one community's suffering – an unsparing exposé of one police department's ineptitude –

With all this going on in his mind as his mellifluous words drip one by one into the microphone of his upheld cassette recorder, is it any wonder that Wendell Green fails to hear the sound of motorcycles, or to take in the presence of the Thunder Five in any way, until he happens to glance sideways in search of the perfect phrase? Glance sideways he does, and with a spurt of panic observes, no more than two feet to his left, Beezer St Pierre astride his roaring Harley, apparently singing, to judge from his own moving lips

singing

huh?

Can't be, nope. In Wendell's experience, Beezer St Pierre is far more likely to be cursing like a navvy in a waterfront brawl. When, after the death of Amy St Pierre, Wendell, who was merely obeying the ancient rules of his trade, dropped in at 1 Nailhouse Row, and inquired of the grieving father how it felt to know that his daughter had been slaughtered like a pig and partially eaten by a monster in human form, Beezer had gripped the innocent newshound by the throat, unleashed a torrent of obscenities, and concluded by bellowing that if he should ever see Mr Green again, he would tear off his head and use the stump as a sexual orifice.

It is this threat that causes Wendell's moment of panic. He glances into his rearview mirror and sees Beezer's cohorts strung out across the road like an invading army of Goths. In his imagination, they are waving skulls on ropes made of human skin and yelling about what they are going to do to his neck after they rip his head off. Whatever he was about to dictate into the invaluable machine instantly evaporates, along with his daydreams of winning the Pulitzer Prize. His stomach clenches, and sweat bursts from every pore on his broad, ruddy face. His left hand trembles on the wheel, his right shakes the cassette recorder like a castanet. Wendell lifts his foot from the accelerator and slides down on the car seat, turning his head as far to the right as he dares. His basic desire is to curl up in the well beneath the dashboard and pretend to be a fetus. The huge roar of sound behind him grows louder, and his heart leaps in his chest like a fish. Wendell whimpers. A rank of kettledrums batters the air beyond the fragile skin of the car door.

Then the motorcycles swoop past him and race off up the highway. Wendell Green wipes his face. Slowly, he persuades his body to sit up straight. His heart ceases its attempt to escape his chest. The world on the other side of his windshield, which had contracted to the size of a housefly, expands back to its normal size. It occurs to Wendell that he was no more afraid than any normal human being would be, under the circumstances. Self-regard fills him like helium fills a balloon. Most guys he knows would have driven right off the road, he thinks; most guys would have crapped in their pants. What did Wendell Green do? He slowed down a little, that's all. He acted like a gentleman and let the assholes of the Thunder Five drive past him. When it comes to Beezer and his apes, Wendell thinks, being a gentleman is the better part of valor. He picks up speed, watching the bikers race on ahead.

In his hand, the cassette recorder is still running. Wendell raises it to his mouth, licks his lips, and discovers that he has forgotten what he was going to say. Blank tape whirls from spool to spool. 'Damn,' he says, and pushes the OFF button. An inspired phrase, a melodious cadence, has vanished into the ether, perhaps for good. But the situation is far more frustrating than that. It seems to Wendell that a whole series of logical connections has vanished with the lost phrase: he can remember seeing the shape of a vast outline for at least half a dozen penetrating articles that would go beyond the Fisherman to . . . do what? Win him the Pulitzer, for sure, but how? The area in his mind that had given him the immense outline still holds its shape, but the shape is empty. Beezer St Pierre and his goons murdered what now seems the greatest idea Wendell Green ever had, and Wendell has no certainty that he can bring it back to life.

What are these biker freaks doing out here, anyhow?

The question answers itself: some creepy do-gooder thought Beezer ought to know about the Fisherman's 911 call, and now the biker freaks are headed to the ruins of Ed's, just like him. Fortunately, so many other people are going to the same place that Wendell figures he can steer clear of his nemesis. Taking no chances, he drops a couple of cars behind the bikers.

The traffic thickens and slows down; up ahead, the bikers form a single line and zoom up alongside the line crawling toward the dusty old lane to Ed's place. From seventy or eighty yards back, Wendell can see two cops, a man and a woman, trying to wave the rubberneckers along. Every time a fresh car pulls up in front of them, they have to go through the same pantomine of turning its occupants away and pointing down the road. To reinforce the message, a police car is parked sideways across the lane, blocking anyone who should try to get fancy. This spectacle troubles Wendell not at all, for the press has automatic access to such scenes. Journalists are the medium, the aperture, through which otherwise prohibited places and events reach the general public. Wendell Green is the people's representative here, and the most distinguished journalist in western Wisconsin besides.

After he has inched along another thirty feet, he sees that the cops riding herd on the traffic are Danny Tcheda and Pam Stevens, and his complacency wavers. A couple of days ago, both Tcheda and Stevens had responded to his request for information by telling him to go to hell. Pam Stevens is a know-it-all bitch anyhow, a professional ballbreaker. Why else would a reasonably okay-looking dame want to be a cop? Stevens would turn him away from the scene for the sheer hell of it – she'd *enjoy* it! Probably, Wendell realizes, he will have to sneak in somehow. He pictures himself crawling through the fields on his belly and shivers with distaste.

At least he can have the pleasure of watching the cops giving the finger to Beezer and crew. The bikers roar past another half-dozen cars without slowing down, so Wendell supposes they plan on going into a flashy, skidding turn, dodging right by those two dumbbells in blue, and zooming around the patrol car as if it didn't exist. What will the cops do then, Wendell wonders – drag out their guns and try to look fierce? Fire warning shots and hit each other in the foot?

Astonishingly, Beezer and his train of fellow bikers pay no attention to the cars attempting to move into the lane, to Tcheda and Stevens, or to anything else up there. They do not even turn their heads to gape up at the ruined shack, the chief's car, the pickup truck – which Wendell instantly recognizes – and the men standing on the beaten grass, two of whom are Dale Gilbertson and the pickup's owner, Hollywood Jack Sawyer, that snooty LA prick. (The third guy, who is wearing an ice-cream hat, sunglasses, and a spiffy vest, makes no sense at all, at least not to Wendell. He looks like he dropped in from some old Humphrey Bogart movie.) No, they blast on by the whole messy scene with their helmets pointed straight ahead, as if all they have in mind is cruising into Centralia and busting up the fixtures in the Sand Bar. On they go, all five of the bastards, indifferent as a pack of wild dogs. As soon as they hit open road again, the other four move into parallel formation behind Beezer and fan out across the highway. Then, as one, they veer off to the left, send up five great plumes of dust and gravel, and spin into five U-turns. Without breaking stride – without even appearing to slow down – they separate into their one-two-two pattern and come streaking back westward toward the crime scene and French Landing.

I'll be damned, Wendell thinks. *Beezer turned tail and gave up. What a wimp.* The knot of bikers grows larger and larger as it swoops toward him, and soon the amazed Wendell Green makes out Beezer St Pierre's grim face, which beneath its helmet also gets larger and larger as it approaches. 'I never figured you for a quitter,' Wendell says, watching Beezer loom ever nearer. The wind has parted his beard into two equal sections that flare out behind him on both sides of his head. Behind his goggles, Beezer's eyes look as if he is aiming down the barrel of a rifle. The thought that Beezer might turn those hunter's eyes on him makes Wendell's bowels feel dangerously loose. 'Loser,' he says, not very loudly. With an ear-pounding roar, Beezer flashes past the dented Toyota. The rest of the Thunder Five hammer the air, then streak down the road.

This evidence of Beezer's cowardice brightens Wendell's heart as he watches the bikers diminish in his rearview mirror, but a thought he cannot ignore begins to worm its way upward through the synapses of his brain. Wendell may not be the Edward R. Murrow of the present day, but he has been a reporter for nearly thirty years, and he has developed a few instincts. The thought winding through his mental channels sets off a series of wavelike alarms that at last push it into consciousness. Wendell *gets* it – he sees the hidden design; he understands what's going down.

'Well, hot doggy,' he says, and with a wide grin blasts his horn, cranks his wheel to the left, and jolts into a turn with only minimal damage to his fender and that of the car in front of him. 'You sneaky bastard,' he says, nearly chuckling with delight. The Toyota squeezes out of the line of vehicles pointed eastward and drifts over into the westbound lanes. Clanking and farting, it shoots away in pursuit of the crafty bikers.

There will be no crawling through cornfields for Wendell Green: that sneaky bastard Beezer St Pierre knows a back way to Ed's Eats! All our star reporter has to do is hang back far enough to stay out of sight and he gets a free pass into the scene. Beautiful. Ah, the irony: Beezer gives the press a helpful hand – many thanks, you arrogant thug. Wendell hardly supposes that Dale Gilbertson will give him the run of the place, but it will be harder to throw him out than to turn him away. In the time he has, he can ask a few probing questions, snap a few telling photos, and – above all! – soak up enough atmosphere to produce one of his legendary 'color' pieces.

With a cheerful heart, Wendell poodles down the highway at fifty miles per hour, letting the bikers race far ahead of him without ever letting them pass out of sight. The number of cars coming toward him thins out to widely spaced groups of two and three, then to a few single cars, then to nothing. As if they have been waiting to be unobserved, Beezer and his friends swerve across the highway and go blasting up the driveway to Goltz's space-age dome.

Wendell feels an unwelcome trickle of self-doubt, but he is not about to assume that Beezer and his louts have a sudden yearning for tractor hitches and riding lawn mowers. He speeds up, wondering if they have spotted him and are trying to throw him off their trail. As far as he knows, there is nothing up on that rise except the showroom, the maintenance garage, and the parking lot. Damn place looks like a wasteland. Beyond the parking lot . . . what? On one side, he remembers a scrubby field stretching away to the horizon, on the other a bunch of trees, like a forest, only not as thick. He can see the trees from where he is now, running downhill like a windbreak.

Without bothering to signal, he speeds across the oncoming lanes and into Goltz's driveway. The sound of the motorcycles is still audible but growing softer, and Wendell experiences a jolt of fear that they have somehow tricked him and are getting away, jeering at him! At the top of the rise, he zooms around the front of the showroom and drives into the big lot. Two huge yellow tractors stand in front of the equipment garage, but his is the only car in sight. At the far end of the empty lot, a low concrete wall rises to bumper height between the asphalt and the meadow bordered by trees. On the other side of the tree line, the wall ends at the swoop of asphalt drive coming around from the back of the showroom.

Wendell cranks the wheel and speeds toward the far end of the wall. He can still hear the motorcycles, but they sound like a distant swarm of bees. They must be about a half mile away, Wendell thinks, and jumps out of the Toyota. He jams the cassette recorder in a jacket pocket, slings the Nikon on its strap around his neck, and runs around the low wall and into the meadow. Even before he reaches the tree line, he can see the remains of an old macadam road, broken and overgrown, cutting downhill between the trees.

Wendell imagines, overestimating, that Ed's old place is about a mile distant, and he wonders if his car could go the distance on this rough, uneven surface. In some places, the macadam has fissured into tectonic plates; in others, it has crumbled away to black gravel. Sinkholes and weedy rills radiate out from the thick, snaking roots of the trees. A biker could jounce over this mess reasonably well, but Wendell sees that his legs will manage the journey better than his Toyota, so he sets off down the old track through the trees. From what he took in while he was on the highway, he still has plenty of time before the medical examiner and the evidence wagon show up. Even with the help of the famous Hollywood Sawyer, the local cops are mooning around in a daze.

The sound of motorcycles grows louder as Wendell picks

his way along, as if the boys stopped moving in order to talk things over when they came to the far end of the old back road. That's perfect. Wendell hopes they will keep jawing until he has nearly caught up with them; he hopes they are shouting at one another and waving their fists in the air. He wants to see them cranked to the gills on rage and adrenaline, plus God knows what else those savages might have in their saddlebags. Wendell would love to get a photograph of Beezer St Pierre knocking out Dale Gilbertson's front teeth with a well-aimed right, or putting the choke hold on his buddy Sawyer. The photograph Wendell wants most, however, and for the sake of which he is prepared to bribe every cop, county functionary, state official, or innocent by-stander capable of holding out his hand, is a good, clean, dramatic picture of Irma Freneau's naked corpse. Preferably one that leaves no doubt about the Fisherman's depredations, whatever they were. Two would be ideal – one of her face for poignancy, the other a full-body shot for the perverts – but he will settle for the body shot if he has to. An image like that would go around the world, generating millions as it went. The *National Enquirer* alone would fork over, what – two hundred thousand, three? – for a photo of poor little Irma sprawled out in death, mutilations clearly visible. Talk about your gold mines, talk about your Big Kahunas!

When Wendell has covered about a tenth of a mile of the miserable old road, his concentration divided between gloating over all the money little Irma is going to siphon into his pockets and his fears of falling down and twisting his ankle, the uproar caused by the Thunder Five's Harleys abruptly ceases. The resulting silence seems immense, then immediately fills with other, quieter sounds. Wendell can hear his breath struggling in and out, and also some other noise, a combined rattle and thud, from behind him. He whirls around and beholds, far up the ruined road, an ancient pickup lurching toward him.

It's almost funny, the way the truck rocks from side to side as one tire, then another, sinks into an invisible depression or rolls up a tilting section of road surface. That is, it would be funny if these people were not horning in on his private access route to Irma Freneau's body. Whenever the pickup climbs over a particularly muscular-looking length of tree root, the four dark heads in the cab bob like marionettes. Wendell takes a step forward, intending to send these yokels back where they came from. The truck's suspension scrapes against a flat rock, and sparks leap from the undercarriage. That thing must be thirty years old, at least, Wendell thinks – it's one of the few vehicles on the road that looks even worse than his car. When the truck jolts closer to him, he sees that it is an International Harvester. Weeds and twigs decorate the rusty bumper. Does I.H. even make pickups anymore? Wendell holds up his hand like a juror taking the oath, and the truck jounces and dips over another few rutted feet before coming to a halt. Its left side sits noticeably higher than the right. In the darkness cast by the trees, Wendell cannot quite make out the faces peering at him through the windshield, but he has the feeling that at least two of them are familiar.

The man behind the wheel pokes his head out of the driver's window and says, 'Hidey-ho, Mr Bigshot Reporter. They slam the front door in your face, too?' It is Teddy Runkleman, who regularly comes to Wendell's attention while he is going over the day's police reports. The other three people in the cab bray like mules at Teddy's wit. Wendell knows two of them – Freddy Saknessum, part of a low-life clan that oozes in and out of various run-down shacks along the river, and Toots Billinger, a scrawny kid who somehow supports himself by scavenging scrap metal in La Riviere and French Landing. Like Runkleman, Toots has been arrested for a number of third-rate crimes but never convicted of anything. The hard-worn, scruffy woman between Freddy and Toots rings a bell too dim to identify.

'Hello, Teddy,' Wendell says. 'And you, Freddy and Toots. No, after I got a look at the mess out front, I decided to come in the back way.'

'Hey, *Wen*-dell, doncha 'member me?' the woman says, a touch pathetically. 'Doodles Sanger, in case your memory's all shot to hell. I started out with a whole buncha guys in Freddy's Bel Air, and Teddy was with a whole 'nother bunch, but after we got run off by Miss Bitch, the rest of 'em wanted to go back to their barstools.'

Of course he does remember her, although the hardened face before him now only faintly resembles that of the bawdy party girl named Doodles Sanger who served up drinks at the Nelson Hotel a decade ago. Wendell thinks she got fired more for drinking too much on the job than for stealing, but God knows she did both. Back then, Wendell threw a lot of money across the bar at the Nelson Hotel. He tries to remember if he ever hopped in the sack with Doodles.

He plays it safe and says, 'Cripes, Doodles, how the hell could I forget a pretty little thing like you?'

The boys get a big yuck out of this sally. Doodles jabs her elbow into Toots Billinger's vaporous ribs, gives Wendell a pouty little smile, and says, 'Well thank-ee, kind sir.' Yep, he boffed her, all right.

This would be the perfect time to order these morons back to their ratholes, but Wendell is visited by grade-A inspiration. 'How would you charming people like to assist a gentleman of the press and earn fifty bucks in the process?'

'Fifty each, or all together?' asks Teddy Runkleman.

'Come on, all together,' Wendell says.

Doodles leans forward and says, 'Twenty each, all right, big-timer? If we agree to do what you want.'

'Aw, you're breakin' my heart,' Wendell says, and extracts his wallet from his back pocket and removes four twenties, leaving only a ten and three singles to see him through the day. They accept their payment and, in a flash, tuck it away. 'Now this is what I want you to do,' Wendell says, and leans toward the window and the four jack-o'-lantern faces in the cab.

12

A few minutes later, the pickup lurches to a halt between the last of the trees, where the macadam disappears into the weeds and tall grass. The Thunder Five's motorcycles stand tilted in a neat row a few yards ahead and off to his left. Wendell, who has replaced Freddy Saknessum on the seat, gets out and moves a few paces forward, hoping that none of the ripe aroma of dried sweat, unwashed flesh, and stale beer emerging from his fellow passengers has clung to his clothing. Behind him, he hears Freddy jumping down from the back of the truck as the others climb out and shut the doors without making any more than twice as much noise as necessary. All Wendell can see from his position is the colorless, rotting rear wall of Ed's Eats rising from a thick tangle of Queen Anne's lace and tiger lilies. Low voices, one of them Beezer St Pierre's, come to him. Wendell gives the Nikon a quick once-over, removes the lens cap, and cranks a new roll of film into place before moving with slow, quiet steps past the bikes and along the side of the ruined structure.

Soon he is able to see the overgrown access road and the patrol car astride it like a barrier. Down close to the highway, Danny Tcheda and Pam Stevens wrangle with half a dozen men and women who have left their cars strewn like toys behind them. That's not going to work much longer: if Tcheda and Stevens are supposed to be a dam, the dam is about to spring some serious leaks. Good news for Wendell: a maximum amount of confusion would give him a lot more leeway and make for a more colorful story. He wishes he could murmur into his recorder right now.

The inexperience of Chief Gilbertson's force was evident in the futile efforts of Officers Tcheda and Stevens to turn back the numbers of those citizens eager to witness for themselves the latest evidence of the Fisherman's insanity . . . Ah, something, something, then: *but this journalist was able to place himself at the heart of the scene, where he felt proud and humbled to serve as the eyes and ears of his readers . . .*

Wendell hates to lose such splendid stuff, but he cannot be sure he will remember it, and he does not dare to take the risk of being overheard. He moves closer to the front of Ed's Eats.

The humble ears of the public take in the sound of Beezer St Pierre and Dale Gilbertson having a surprisingly amiable conversation directly in front of the building; the humble eyes of the public observe Jack Sawyer walking into view, an empty plastic bag and a baseball cap swinging from the fingers of his right hand. The humble nose of the public reports a truly awful stench that guarantees the presence of a decomposing body in the shabby little structure to the right. Jack is moving a little more quickly than usual, and although it is clear that he is just going to his pickup, he keeps glancing from side to side.

What's going on here? Golden Boy looks more than a little furtive. He's acting like a shoplifter just stuffing the goodies under his coat, and golden boys shouldn't behave that way. Wendell raises his camera and focuses in on his target. There you are, Jack old boy, old fellow, old sport, crisp as a new bill and twice as sharp. Look pretty for the camera, now, and let us see what you've got in your hand, okay? Wendell snaps a picture and watches through his viewfinder as Jack approaches his truck. Golden Boy is going to stash those things in the glove compartment, Wendell thinks, and he doesn't want anyone to see him do it. Too bad, kid, you're on Candid Camera. And too bad for the proud yet humble eyes and ears of French County, because when Jack Sawyer reaches his truck he does not climb in but leans over the side and fiddles around with something, giving our noble journalist a fine view of his back and nothing else. The noble journalist takes a picture anyhow, to establish a sequence with the next photo, in which Jack Sawyer turns away from his truck empty-handed and no longer furtive. He stashed his grubby treasures back there and got them out of sight, but what made them treasures?

Then a lightning bolt strikes Wendell Green. His scalp shivers, and his crinkly hair threatens to straighten out. A great story just became *unbelievably* great. Fiendish Murderer, Mutilated Dead Child, and . . . the Downfall of a Hero! Jack Sawyer walks out of the ruin carrying a plastic bag and a Brewers cap, tries to make sure he is unobserved, and hides the stuff in his truck. He *found* those things in Ed's Eats, and he squirreled them away right under the nose of his friend and admirer Dale Gilbertson. Golden Boy removed *evidence* from *the scene of a crime!* And Wendell has the proof on film, Wendell has the goods on the high-and-mighty Jack Sawyer, Wendell is going to bring him down with one godalmighty huge crash. Man oh man, Wendell feels like dancing, he does, and is unable to restrain himself from executing a clumsy jig with the wonderful camera in his hands and a sloppy grin on his face.

He feels so good, so triumphant, that he almost decides to forget about the four idiots waiting for his signal and just pack it in. But hey, let's not get all warm and fuzzy here. The supermarket tabloids are panting for a nice, gruesome photograph of Irma Freneau's dead body, and Wendell Green is the man to give it to them.

Wendell takes another cautious step toward the front of the ruined building and sees something that stops him cold. Four of the bikers have gone down to the end of the overgrown lane, where they seem to be helping Tcheda and Stevens turn away the people who want to get a good look at all the bodies. Teddy Runkleman heard that the Fisherman stowed at least six, maybe eight half-eaten kids in that shack: the news grew more and more sensational as it filtered through the community. So the cops can use the extra help, but Wendell wishes that Beezer and crew were blowing the lid off things instead of helping to keep it on. He comes to the end of the building and peers around it to see everything that is going on. If he is to get what he wants, he will have to wait for the perfect moment.

A second FLPD car noses in through the vehicles hovering out on 35 and moves up past Tcheda's car to swing onto the weeds and rubble in front of the old store. Two youngish part-time cops named Holtz and Nestler get out and stroll toward Dale Gilbertson, trying hard not to react to the stench that gets more sickening with each step they take. Wendell can see that these lads have even more difficulty concealing their dismay and astonishment at seeing their chief engaged in apparently amiable conversation with Beezer St Pierre, whom they probably suspect of myriad nameless crimes. They are farm boys, UW-River Falls dropouts, who split a single salary and are trying so hard to make the grade as police officers that they tend to see things in rigid black-and-white. Dale calms them down, and Beezer, who could pick each of them up with one hand and smash their skulls like soft-boiled eggs, smiles benignly. In response to what must have been Dale's orders, the new boys trot back down to the highway, on the way casting worshipful glances at Jack Sawyer, the poor saps.

Jack wanders up to Dale for a little confab. Too bad Dale doesn't know that his buddy is concealing evidence, hah! Or, Wendell considers, *does* he know – is he in on it, too? One thing's for sure: it will all come out in the wash, once the *Herald* runs the telltale pictures.

In the meantime, the dude in the straw hat and the sunglasses just stands there with his arms folded across his chest, looking serene and confident, like he has everything so under control that even the smell can't reach him. This guy is obviously a key player, Wendell thinks. He calls the shots. Golden Boy and Dale want to keep him happy; you can see it in their body language. A touch of respect, of deference. If they are covering something up, they're doing it for him. But why? And what the devil is he? The guy is middle-aged, somewhere in his fifties, a generation older than Jack and Dale; he is too stylish to live in the country, so he's from Madison, maybe, or Milwaukee. He is obviously not a cop, and he doesn't look like a businessman, either. This is one self-reliant mother; that comes through loud and clear.

Then another police car breaches the defenses down on 35 and rolls up beside the part-timers'. Golden Boy and Gilbertson walk up to it and greet Bobby Dulac and that other one, the fat boy, Dit Jesperson, but the dude in the hat doesn't even look their way. Now, *that's* cool. He stands there, all by himself, like a general surveying his troops. Wendell watches the mystery man produce a cigarette, light up, and exhale a plume of white smoke. Jack and Dale walk the new arrivals into the old store, and this bird keeps on smoking his cigarette, sublimely detached from everything around him. Through the rotting wall, Wendell can hear Dulac and Jesperson complaining about the smell; then one of them grunts *Uh!* when he sees the body. 'Hello boys?' Dulac says. 'Is this shit for real? *Hello boys?*' The voices give Wendell a good fix on the location of the corpse, way back against the far wall.

Before the three cops and Sawyer begin to shuffle toward the front end of the store, Wendell leans out, aims his camera, and snaps a photograph of the mystery man. To his horror, the Cat in the Hat instantly looks in his direction and says, 'Who took my picture?' Wendell jerks himself back into the protection of the wall, but he knows the guy must have seen him. Those sunglasses were pointed right at him! The guy has ears like a bat – he picked up the noise of the shutter. 'Come on out,' Wendell hears him say. 'There's no point in hiding; I know you're there.'

From his reduced vantage point, Wendell can just see a State Police car, followed by French Landing's DARE Pontiac, barreling up from the congestion at the end of the lane. Things seem to have reached the boiling point down there. Unless Wendell is wrong, he thinks he glimpses one of the bikers pulling a man out through the window of a nice-looking green Olds.

Time to call in the cavalry, for sure. Wendell steps back from the front of the building and waves to the troops. Teddy Runkleman yells, *'Hoo boy!'* Doodles screeches like a cat in heat, and Wendell's four assistants charge past him, making all the noise he could wish for.

13

Danny Tcheda and Pam Stevens already have their hands full with would-be gate-crashers when they hear the sound of motorcycles gunning toward them, and the arrival of the Thunder Five is all they need to make their day really complete. Getting rid of Teddy Runkleman and Freddy Saknessum had been easy enough, but not five minutes later the eastbound lanes of Highway 35 filled up with people who thought they had a perfect right to gawk at all the little corpses that were supposed to be stacked up in the wreckage of Ed's Eats. For every car they finally manage to send away, two more show up in its place. Everybody demands a long explanation of why they, as taxpayers and concerned citizens, should not be allowed to enter a crime scene, especially one so tragic, so poignant, so . . . well, so exciting. Most of them refuse to believe that the only body inside that tumbledown building is Irma Freneau's; three people in a row accuse Danny of abetting a cover-up, and one of them actually uses the word 'Fishergate.' Yikes. In a weird way, lots of these corpse hunters almost think that the local police are protecting the Fisherman!

Some of them finger rosaries while they chew him out.

One lady waves a crucifix in his face and tells him he has a dirty soul and is bound for hell. At least half of the people he turns away are carrying cameras. What kind of person sets off on a Saturday morning to take pictures of dead children? What gets Danny is this: they all think they're perfectly normal. Who's the creep? *He* is.

The husband of an elderly couple from Maid Marian Way says, 'Young man, apparently you are the only person in this county who does not understand that history is happening all around us. Madge and I feel we have the right to a keepsake.'

A keepsake?

Sweaty, out of sorts, and completely fed up, Danny loses his cool. 'Buddy, I agree with you right down the line,' he says. 'If it was up to me, you and your lovely wife would be able to drive away with a bloodstained T-shirt, maybe even a severed finger or two, in your trunk. But what can I say? The chief is a very unreasonable guy.'

Off zooms Maid Marian Way, too shocked to speak. The next guy in line starts yelling the moment Danny leans down to his window. He looks exactly like Danny's image of George Rathbun, but his voice is raspier and slightly higher in pitch. '*Don't think I can't see what you're doing, buster!*' Danny says good, because he's trying to protect a crime scene, and the George Rathbun guy, who is driving an old blue Dodge Caravan minus the front bumper and the right side-view mirror, shouts, '*I been sitting here twenty minutes while you and that dame do doodly-squat! I hope you won't be surprised when you see some VIGILANTE ACTION around here!*'

It is at this tender moment that Danny hears the unmistakable rumble of the Thunder Five charging toward him down the highway. He has not felt right since he found Tyler Marshall's bicycle in front of the old folks' home, and the thought of wrangling with Beezer St Pierre fills his brain with dark oily smoke and whirling red sparks. He lowers his head and stares directly into the eyes of the red-faced George Rathbun look-alike. His voice emerges in a low, dead monotone. 'Sir, if you continue on your present course, I will handcuff you, park you in the back of my car until I am free to leave, and then take you to the station and charge you with everything that comes to mind. That is a promise. Now do yourself a favor and get the hell out of here.'

The man's mouth opens and closes, goldfishlike. Splotches of brighter red appear on his jowly, already flushed face. Danny keeps staring into his eyes, almost hoping for an excuse to truss him in handcuffs and roast him in the back seat of his car. The guy considers his options, and caution wins. He drops his eyes, moves the shift lever to R, and nearly backs into the Miata behind him.

'I don't believe this is happening,' Pam says. 'What dumb so-and-so spilled the beans?'

Like Danny, she is watching Beezer and his friends roar toward them past the row of waiting cars.

'I don't know, but I'd like to ram my nightstick down his throat. And after him, I'm looking for Wendell Green.'

'You won't have to look very far. He's about six cars back in the line.' Pam points to Wendell's traveling sneer.

'Good God,' Danny says. 'Actually, I'm sort of glad to see that miserable blowhard. Now I can tell him exactly what I think of him.' Smiling, he bends down to speak to the teenaged boy at the wheel of the Miata. The boy leaves, and Danny waves off the driver behind him while watching the Thunder Five get closer and closer. He says to Pam, 'At this point, if Beezer climbs up in my face and even *looks* like he wants to get physical, I'm pulling out my roscoe, honest to God.'

'Paperwork, paperwork,' Pam says.

'I really don't give a damn.'

'Well, here we go,' she says, telling him that if he pulls his gun, she will back him up.

Even the drivers trying to argue their way into the lane are taking time out to watch Beezer and the boys. In motion, hair and beards blowing, faces set, they look ready to commit as much mayhem as possible. Danny Tcheda's heart begins to speed, and he feels his sphincter tighten.

But the Thunder Five bikers race past without so much as turning their heads, one after another. Beezer, Mouse, Doc, Sonny, and the Kaiser – there they go, leaving the scene.

'Well, *damn*,' Danny says, unable to decide if he feels relieved or disappointed. The abrupt jolt of dismay he registers when the bikers wheel around in a comprehensive, gravel-spraying U-turn thirty yards up ahead tells him that what he had felt was relief.

'Oh, please, no,' Pam says.

In the waiting automobiles, every head turns as the motorcycles flash by again, returning the way they came. For a couple of seconds, the only sound to be heard is the receding furor of five Harley-Davidson cycles. Danny Tcheda takes off his uniform hat and wipes his forehead. Pam Stevens arches her back and exhales. Then someone blasts his horn, and two other horns join in, and a guy with a graying walrus mustache and a denim shirt is holding up a three-quarter-sized badge in a leather case and explaining that he is the cousin of a county-circuit judge and an honorary member of the La Riviere police force, which basically means he never gets speeding or parking tickets and can go wherever he likes. The mustache spreads out in a big grin. 'So just let me get by, and you can go back to your business, Officer.'

Not letting him get by *is* his business, Danny says, and he is forced to repeat this message several times before he can get on to the next case. After sending away a few more disgruntled citizens, he checks to see how long he must wait before he can tell off Wendell Green. Surely the reporter cannot be more than two or three cars back. As soon as Danny raises his head, horns blast and people start shouting at him. *Let us in! Hey, bud, I pay your salary, remember? I wanna talk to Dale, I wanna talk to Dale!*

A few men have gotten out of their cars. Their fingers are pointing at Danny, their mouths are working, but he cannot make out what they are yelling. A band of pain runs like a red-hot iron bar from behind his left eye to the middle of his brain. Something is wrong; he cannot see Green's ugly red car. Where the hell is it? Damn damn and double damn, Green must have eased out of the line and driven into the field alongside Ed's. Danny snaps around and inspects the field. Angry voices and car horns boil up at his back. No beat-up red Toyota, no Wendell Green. What do you know, the windbag gave up!

A few minutes later the traffic thins out, and Danny and Pam think their job is pretty much over. All four lanes of Highway 35 are empty, their usual condition on a Saturday morning. The one truck that rolls along keeps on rolling, on its way to Centralia.

'Think we ought to go up there?' Pam asks, nodding toward the remains of the store.

'Maybe, in a couple minutes.' Danny is not eager to get within range of that smell. He would be perfectly happy to stay down here until the ME and the evidence wagon come along. What gets into people, anyhow? He would happily surrender two days' pay to be spared the sight of Irma Freneau's poor body.

Then he and Pam hear two distinct sounds at once, and

neither one makes them comfortable. The first is that of a fresh wave of vehicles racing down the highway to their position; the second, the rumble of motorcycles descending upon the scene from somewhere behind the old store.

'Is there a back road to this place?' he asks, incredulous.

Pam shrugs. 'Sounds like it. But look – Dale'll have to deal with Beezer's goons, because we're gonna have our hands full down here.'

'Aw, cripes,' Danny says. Maybe thirty cars and pickups are converging on the end of the little lane, and both he and Pam can see that these people are angrier and more determined than the first bunch. At the far end of the crowd, some men and women are leaving their vehicles on the shoulder and walking toward the two officers. The drivers at the front of the pack are waving their fists and shouting even before they try to turn in. Incredibly, a woman and two teenage kids are holding up a long banner that reads WE WANT THE FISHERMAN! A man in a dusty old Caddy thrusts his arm through the window and displays a handmade placard: GILBERTSON MUST GO.

Danny looks over his shoulder and sees that the Thunder Five must have found a back road, because four of them are standing out in front of Ed's, looking oddly like Secret Service agents, while Beezer St Pierre is deep in discussion with the chief. And what *they* look like, it occurs to Danny, is two heads of state working out a trade agreement. This makes no sense at all, and Danny turns back to the cars, the lunatics with signs, and the men and women working their way toward him and Pam.

A barrel-chested, seventy-one-year-old man with a white goatee, Hoover Dalrymple, plants himself in front of Pam and starts demanding his inalienable rights. Danny remembers his name because Dalrymple initiated a brawl in the bar of the

Nelson Hotel about six months earlier, and now here he is all over again, getting his revenge. 'I will *not* speak to your partner,' he yells, 'and I will *not* listen to anything he says, because your partner has no interest in the rights of the people of this community.'

Danny sends away an orange Subaru driven by a sullen teenage boy in a Black Sabbath T-shirt, then a black Corvette with La Riviere dealer's plates and a strikingly pretty, strikingly foulmouthed young woman. Where do these people come from? He does not recognize anyone except Hoover Dalrymple. Most of the people in front of him now, Danny supposes, were hailed in from out of town.

He has set out to help Pam when a hand closes on his shoulder, and he looks behind him to see Dale Gilbertson side by side with Beezer St Pierre. The four other bikers hover a few feet away. The one called Mouse, who is of course roughly the size of a haystack, catches Dale's eye and grins.

'What are you *doing*?' Danny asks.

'Calm down,' Dale says. 'Mr St Pierre's friends have volunteered to assist our crowd-control efforts, and I think we can use all the help they can give us.'

Out of the side of his eye, Danny glimpses the Neary twins breaking out of the front of the crowd, and he holds up a hand to stop them. 'What do they get out of this?'

'Simple information,' the chief says. 'Okay, boys, get to work.'

Beezer's friends move apart and approach the crowd. The chief moves beside Pam, who first looks at him in amazement, then nods. Mouse snarls at Hoover Dalrymple and says, 'By the power invested in me, I order you to get the fuck out of here, Hoover.' The old man vanishes so quickly he seems to have dematerialized.

The rest of the bikers have the same effect on the angry sightseers. Danny hopes they can maintain their cool in the face of steady abuse: a three-hundred-pound man who looks like a Hells Angel on a knife edge between self-control and mounting fury works wonders on a rebellious crowd. The biker nearest Danny sends Floyd and Frank Neary away just by raising his fist at them. As they melt back to their car, the biker winks at Danny and introduces himself as Kaiser Bill. Beezer's friend enjoys the process of controlling a crowd, and an immense grin threatens to break through his scowl, yet molten anger bubbles underneath, just the same.

'Who are the other guys?' Danny asks.

Kaiser Bill identifies Doc and Sonny, who are dispersing the crowd to Danny's right.

'Why are you guys doing this?'

The Kaiser lowers his head so that his face hangs two inches from Danny's. It is like confronting a bull. Heat and rage pour from the broad features and hairy skin. Danny almost expects to see steam puffing from the man's wide nostrils. One of the pupils is smaller than the other; explosive red wires tangle through the whites. 'Why? We're doing it for *Amy*. Isn't that clear to you, Officer Tcheda?'

'Sorry,' Danny mutters. Of course. He hopes Dale will be able to keep a lid on these monsters. Watching Kaiser Bill rock an ancient Mustang belonging to a fool kid who failed to back up in time, he is extremely happy that the bikers don't have any blunt instruments.

Through the vacant space formerly occupied by the kid's Mustang, a police car rolls toward Danny and the Kaiser. As it makes its way through the crowd, a woman wearing a sleeveless T-shirt and Capri pants bangs her hand against the passenger windows. When the car reaches Danny the two part-timers, Bob Holtz and Paul Nestler, jump out, gape at the Kaiser, and ask if he and Pam need help. 'Go up and talk to the chief,' Danny says, though he should not have to. Holtz and Nestler are nice guys, but they have a lot to learn about chain of command, along with everything else.

About a minute and a half later, Bobby Dulac and Dit Jesperson show up. Danny and Pam wave them through as the bikers charge into the fray and drag chanting citizens off the sides and hoods of their vehicles. Sounds of struggle reach Danny over angry shouts coming from the mob before him. It seems that he has been out here for hours. Thrusting people out of the way with great backswings of his arms, Sonny emerges to stand beside Pam, who is doing her best. Mouse and Doc wade into the clear. A trail of blood leaking from his nose, a red smear darkening his beard at the corner of his mouth, the Kaiser strides up beside Danny.

Just as the crowd begins chanting, 'HELL NO, WE WON'T GO! HELL NO, WE WON'T GO!' Holtz and Nestler return to bolster the line. *Hell no, we won't go?* Danny wonders. *Isn't that supposed to be about Vietnam?*

Only dimly aware of the sound of a police siren, Danny sees Mouse wade into the crowd and knock out the first three people he can reach. Doc settles his hands on the open window of an all-too-familiar Oldsmobile and asks the small, balding driver what the hell he thinks he is doing. 'Doc, leave him alone,' Danny says, but the siren whoops again and drowns out his words.

Although the little man at the wheel of the Olds looks like an ineffectual math teacher or a low-level civic functionary, he possesses the determination of a gladiator. He is the Reverend Lance Hovdahl, Danny's old Sunday school teacher.

'I thought I could help,' the reverend says.

'What with all this racket, I can't really hear you too good. Let me help you get closer,' Doc says. He reaches in through the window as the siren whoops again and a State Police car slides by on the other side.

'Hold it, Doc, STOP!' Danny shouts, seeing the two men in the state car, Brown and Black, craning their necks to stare at the spectacle of a bearded man built like a grizzly bear dragging a Lutheran minister out through the window of his car. Creeping along behind them, another surprise, is Arnold Hrabowski, the Mad Hungarian, goggling through the windshield of his DAREmobile as if terrified by the chaos around him.

The end of the lane is like a war zone now. Danny strides into the screaming mob and shoves a few people aside on his way to Doc and his old Sunday school teacher, who looks shaken but not at all injured. 'Well, Danny, my *goodness*,' the minister says. 'I'm certainly glad to see you here.'

Doc glares at the two of them. 'You know each other?'

'Reverend Hovdahl, this is Doc,' Danny says. 'Doc, this is Reverend Hovdahl, the pastor at Mount Hebron Lutheran.'

'Holy moly,' says Doc, and immediately begins to pat the little man's lapels and tug at the hem of his jacket, as if to pull him into shape. 'Sorry, Reverend, I hope I didn't hurt you none.'

The state cops and the Mad Hungarian manage at last to squeeze out of the crowd. The sound level decreases to a mild hubbub – one way or another, Doc's friends have silenced the loudest members of the opposition.

'Fortunately, the window is wider than I am,' the reverend says.

'Say, maybe I could come over and talk to you someday,' says Doc. 'I've been doing a lot of reading about first-century

Christianity lately. You know, Géza Vermès, John Dominic Crossan, Paula Fredriksen, stuff like that. I'd like to bounce some ideas off you.'

Whatever Reverend Hovdahl intends to say is obliterated by the sudden explosion of noise from the other end of the lane. A woman's voice rises like a banshee's, in an inhuman screeching that shivers the hairs on the nape of Danny's neck. It sounds to him as though escaped lunatics a thousand times more dangerous than the Thunder Five are raving through the landscape. What the devil could have *happened* up there?

'"Hello boys"?' Unable to contain his indignation, Bobby Dulac turns to stare first at Dale, then at Jack. His voice rises, hardens. 'Is this shit for real? "*Hello boys*"?'

Dale coughs into his fist and shrugs. 'He wanted us to find her.'

'Well, of course,' Jack says. 'He told us to come here.'

'Why would he do that, though?' Bobby asks.

'He's proud of his work.' From some dim crossroads in Jack's memory, an ugly voice says, *Stay out of it. You mess with me and I'll strew your guts from Racine to La Riviere.* Whose voice had that been? With no more evidence than his conviction, Jack understands that if he could place that voice, he would put a name to the Fisherman. He cannot; all Jack Sawyer can do at this moment is remember a stink worse than the foul cloud that fills this crumbling building – a hideous smell that came from the southwest of another world. That was the Fisherman, too, or whatever the Fisherman was in that world.

A thought worthy of the former rising star of the LAPD's Homicide Division awakens in his mind, and he says, 'Dale, I think you should let Henry hear that 911 tape.'

'I don't get it. What for?'

'Henry's tuned in to stuff even bats can't hear. Even if he doesn't recognize the voice, he'll learn a hundred times more than what we know now.'

'Well, Uncle Henry never forgets a voice, that's true. Okay, let's get out of here. The ME and the evidence wagon should show up in a couple of minutes.'

Trailing behind the other two men, Jack thinks of Tyler Marshall's Brewers cap and where he found it – that world he has spent more than half his life denying, and his return to which this morning continues to send shocks through his system. The Fisherman left the cap for him in the Territories, the land he had first heard of when Jacky was six – when Jacky was six, and Daddy played the horn. It is all coming back to him, that immense adventure, not because he wishes it, but because it *has to* come back: forces outside himself are picking him up by the scruff of his neck and carrying him forward. Forward into his own past! The Fisherman is proud of his handiwork, yes, the Fisherman is deliberately taunting them – a truth so obvious none of the three men had to speak it aloud – but really the Fisherman is baiting only Jack Sawyer, who alone has seen the Territories. And if *that's* true, as it has to be, then –

– then the Territories and all they contain are involved somehow in these wretched crimes, and he has been thrust into a drama of enormous consequence he cannot possibly grasp right now. *The Tower. The Beam.* He had seen this in his mother's handwriting, something about the Tower falling and the Beams breaking: these things are parts of the puzzle, whatever they mean, as is Jack's gut conviction that Tyler Marshall is still alive, tucked away in some pocket of the other world. The recognition that he can never speak of all this to anyone else, not even Henry Leyden, makes him feel intensely alone.

Jack's thoughts blow away in the noisy chaos that erupts alongside and in front of the shack. It sounds like an Indian attack in a cowboy movie, whooping and yelling and the sound of running feet. A woman sends up a shrill scream eerily like the *blip-blips* of the police siren he had half-noted a few moments ago. Dale mutters 'Jeez,' and breaks into a run, followed by Bobby and Jack.

Outside, what appears to be a half dozen crazy people are racing around in the weedy gravel in front of Ed's. Dit Jesperson and Beezer, still too stunned to react, watch them caper back and forth. The crazy people make an amazing amount of noise. One man yells, 'KILL THE FISHERMAN! KILL THE DIRTY BASTARD!' Another is shouting 'LAW 'N' ORDER 'N' FREE BEER!' A scrawny character in bib overalls picks up 'FREE BEER! WE WANT FREE BEER!' A harpy too old for her tank top and blue jeans skitters around waving her arms and screeching at the top of her lungs. The grins on their faces indicate that these people are engaged in some dimwitted prank. They are having the time of their lives.

Up from the end of the lane comes a State Police car, with the Mad Hungarian's DARE Pontiac right behind it. In the middle of the chaos, Henry Leyden tilts his head and smiles to himself.

When he sees his chief take off after one of the men, fat Dit Jesperson lurches into action and spots Doodles Sanger, against whom he has borne a grudge ever since she turned him down late one night in the Nelson Hotel. Dit recognizes Teddy Runkleman, the tall galoot with the broken nose Dale is chasing; and he knows Freddy Saknessum, but Freddy is undoubtedly too fast for him and, besides, Dit has the feeling that if he put his hands on Freddy Saknessum, about eight hours later he would probably come down with something really nasty. Bobby Dulac is on the skinny guy's case, so Doodles is Dit's target, and he looks forward to pulling her down into the weeds and making her pay for calling him what she did, six years ago in the Nelson's filthy bar. (In front of maybe a dozen of French Landing's most raffish characters, Doodles had compared him to the then chief's smelly, waddling old mongrel, Tubby.)

Dit looks her in the eye, and for a second she stops jumping around to stand flat-footed on the ground and give him a little come-hither gesture with the fingers of both hands. He launches himself at her, but when he gets to where she was, she is six feet off to the right, shifting on her feet like a basketball player. 'Tubby-Tubby,' she says. 'Come and get it, Tub-Tub.' Furious, Dit reaches, misses, and nearly loses his balance. Doodles prances away laughing and mouths the hateful expression. Dit doesn't get it – why doesn't Doodles just break away and take off? It's like she almost wants to get caught, but first she has to run out the clock.

After another serious lunge that misses the target by only an inch or two, Dit Jesperson wipes the sweat off his face and checks out the scene. Bobby Dulac is snapping cuffs on the skinny guy, but Dale and Hollywood Sawyer are faring only a little better than he is. Teddy Runkleman and Freddy Saknessum dodge and bob away from their pursuers, both of them cackling like idiots and shouting their halfwit slogans. Why is low-life scum always so agile? Dit supposes that rodents like Runkleman and Saknessum get more practice in being light on their feet than regular people.

He charges Doodles, who slips past him and goes into a chuckling, high-stepping diddley-bop. Over her shoulder, Dit sees Hollywood finally fake out Saknessum, wrap an arm around his waist, and throw him to the ground.

'You didn't have to get all physical on my ass,' Saknessum says. His eyes shift, and he gives a brief nod. 'Hey, Runks.'

Teddy Runkleman glances at him, and his eyes shift, too. He stops moving. The chief says, 'What, you run out of gas?'

'Party's over,' Runkleman says. 'Hey, we were just funnin', you know?'

'Aw, Runksie, I wanna play some more,' Doodles says, throwing a few hip wiggles into the diddley-bop. In a flash, Beezer St Pierre thrusts his mountainous self between her and Dit. He steps forward, rumbling like a semi going up a steep grade. Doodles tries to dance backward, but Beezer envelops her and carries her toward the chief.

'Beezie, don'cha love me no more?' Doodles asks.

Beezer grunts in disgust and deposits her in front of the chief. The two state cops, Perry Brown and Jeff Black, are hanging back, looking even more disgusted than the biker. If Dit's mental processes were to be transcribed from their shorthand into standard English, the result would be, *He's gotta have something on the ball if he brews that Kingsland Ale, because that is some fine, fine beer. And look at the chief! He's so ready to bust a gut, he can't even see that we're about to lose this case.*

'You were FUNNIN'?' the chief roars. 'What's the MATTER with you idiots? Don't you have any respect for that poor girl in there?'

As the state cops step forward to take charge, Dit sees Beezer go rigid with shock for a moment, then move as inconspicuously as possible away from the group. No one but Dit Jesperson pays any attention to him – the enormous biker has done his bit, and now his part is over. Arnold Hrabowski, who had been more or less concealed behind Brown and Black, shoves his hands in his pockets, hunches his shoulders, and gives Dit a glance of shamefaced apology. Dit doesn't get it: What does the Mad Hungarian have to feel so guilty about? Hell, he just *got* here. Dit looks back at Beezer, who is advancing ponderously toward the side of the shack and – surprise, surprise! – everybody's best pal and favorite reporter, Mr Wendell Green, now appearing a little alarmed. *Guess more than one kind of scum just rose to the surface,* Dit thinks.

Beezer likes women who are smart and levelheaded, like Bear Girl; brainless skanks like Doodles drive him crazy. He reaches out, grabs two handfuls of pasty, rayon-covered flesh, and scoops wriggling Doodles under his arm.

Doodles says, 'Beezie, don'cha love me no more?'

He lowers the dumb mutt to the ground in front of Dale Gilbertson. When Dale finally explodes at these four grown-up juvenile delinquents, Beezer remembers the signal Freddy had given Runksie, and looks over the chief's shoulder at the front of the old store. To the left of the rotting gray entrance, Wendell Green is aiming his camera at the group before him, getting fancy, bending and leaning, stepping to one side and another as he snaps pictures. When he sees Beezer looking at him through his lens, Wendell straightens up and lowers his camera. He has an awkward little smile on his face.

Green must have slithered in through the back way, Beezer imagines, because there's no way the cops down front would give him a pass. Come to think of it, Doodles and the Dodos must have come the same way. He hopes all of them did not learn of the back road by following him, but that's a possibility.

The reporter lets his camera hang from its strap and, keeping his eyes on Beezer, sidles away from the old shanty. The guilty, frightened way he moves reminds Beezer of a hyena's slink toward its carrion. Wendell Green does fear Beezer, and Beezer cannot blame him. Green is lucky that Beezer did not actually rip off his head, instead of merely talking about it. Yet . . . Green's hyenalike crawl strikes Beezer as pretty strange, under the circumstances. He can't be afraid of getting beaten up in front of all these cops, can he?

Green's uneasiness forms a link in Beezer's mind to the communication he had seen pass between Runkleman and Freddy. When their eyes shifted, when they looked away, they were looking at the reporter! *He had set the whole thing up in advance*. Green was using the Dodos as a distraction from whatever he was doing with his camera, of course. Such total sleaziness, such moral ugliness, infuriates Beezer. Galvanized by loathing, he moves quietly away from Dale and the other policemen and walks toward Wendell Green, keeping his eyes locked on the reporter's.

He sees Wendell consider making a break for it, then reject the idea, most likely because he knows he doesn't have a chance of getting away.

When Beezer comes to within ten feet of him, Green says, 'We don't need any trouble here, Mr St Pierre. I'm just doing my job. Surely you can understand that.'

'I understand a lot of things,' Beezer says. 'How much did you pay those clowns?'

'Who? What clowns?' Wendell pretends to notice Doodles and the others for the first time. 'Oh, them? Are they the ones who were making all that ruckus?'

'And why would they go do a thing like that?'

'Because they're animals, I guess.' The expression on Wendell's face communicates a great desire to align himself with Beezer on the side of human beings, as opposed to animals like Runkleman and Saknessum.

Taking care to fix Green's eyes, instead of his camera,

with his own, Beezer moves in closer and says, 'Wendy, you're a real piece of work, you know that?'

Wendell holds up his hands to ward off Beezer. 'Hey, we may have had our differences in the past, but—'

Still looking him in the eye, Beezer folds his right hand around the camera and plants his left on Wendell Green's chest. He jerks the right hand back and gives Green a massive shove with the left. One of two things is going to break, Green's neck or the camera strap, and he does not much care which it is to be.

To a sound like the crack of a whip, the reporter flails backward, barely managing to remain upright. Beezer is pulling the camera out of the case, from which dangle two strips of severed leather. He drops the case and rotates the camera in his big hands.

'Hey, don't do that!' Wendell says, his voice louder than speech but softer than a shout.

'What is it, an old F2A?'

'If you know that, you know it's a classic. Give it back to me.'

'I'm not going to hurt it, I'm going to clean it out.' Beezer snaps open the back of the camera, gets one thick finger under the exposed length of film, and rips out the entire roll. He smiles at the reporter and tosses the film into the weeds. 'See how much better it feels without all that crap in there? This is a nice little machine – you shouldn't fill it with garbage.'

Wendell does not dare show how furious he is. Rubbing the sore spot on the back of his neck, he growls, 'That so-called garbage is my livelihood, you oaf, you moron. Now give me back my camera.'

Beezer casually holds it out before him. 'I didn't quite catch all of that. What did you say?'

His only response a bleak glance, Wendell snatches the camera from Beezer's hand.

When the two state cops finally step forward, Jack feels a mixture of disappointment and relief. What they are going to do is obvious, so let them do it. Perry Brown and Jeff Black will take the Fisherman case away from Dale and run their own investigation. From now on, Dale will be lucky to get random scraps from the state's table. Jack's greatest regret is that Brown and Black should have walked into this madhouse, this circus. They have been waiting for their moment all along – in a sense, waiting for the local guy to prove his incompetence – but what is going on now is a public humiliation for Dale, and Jack wishes it weren't happening. He could not have imagined feeling grateful for the arrival of a biker gang at a crime scene, but that's how bad it is. Beezer St Pierre and his companions kept the crowd away more efficiently than Dale's officers. The question is, how did all those people find out?

Apart from the damage to Dale's reputation and self-esteem, however, Jack has few regrets about the case passing to another jurisdiction. Let Brown and Black scour every basement in French County: Jack has the feeling they won't get any further than the Fisherman permits. To go further, he thinks, you'd have to travel in directions Brown and Black could never understand, visit places they are certain do not exist. Going further means making friends with *opopanax*, and men like Brown and Black distrust anything that even smells like *opopanax*. Which means that, in spite of everything Jack has said to himself since the murder of Amy St Pierre, he will have to catch the Fisherman by himself. Or maybe not entirely by himself. Dale is going to have a lot more time on his hands, after all, and no matter what the State Police do to him, Dale is too wrapped up in this case to walk away from it.

'Chief Gilbertson,' says Perry Brown, 'I believe we have seen enough here. Is this what you call securing an area?'

Dale gives up on Teddy Runkleman and turns in frustration to the state cops, who stand side by side, like storm troopers. In his expression, Jack can see that he knows exactly what is going to happen, and that he hopes it will not be humiliatingly brutal. 'I did everything in my power to make this area secure,' Dale says. 'After the 911 call came in, I talked to my men face to face and ordered them to come out in pairs at reasonable intervals, to keep from arousing any curiosity.'

'Chief, you must have used your radio,' says Jeff Black. 'Because for sure *somebody* was tuned in.'

'I did not use the radio,' Dale says. 'And my people knew better than to spread the news. But you know what, Officer Black? If the Fisherman called us on 911, maybe he also made a couple of anonymous calls to the citizens.'

Teddy Runkleman has been attending to this discussion like a spectator at a tennis final. Perry Brown says, 'Let's handle first things first. What do you intend to do with this man and his friends? Are you going to charge them? The sight of his face is getting on my nerves.'

Dale thinks for a moment, then says, 'I'm not going to charge them. Get out of here, Runkleman.' Teddy moves backward, and Dale says, 'Hold it for a second. How did you get here?'

'The back road,' Teddy says. 'Comes straight down from behind Goltz's. Thunder Five came the same way. So did that big-shot reporter, Mr Green.'

'Wendell Green is here?'

Teddy points to the side of the ruin. Dale glances over

his shoulder, and Jack looks in the same direction and witnesses Beezer St Pierre ripping film from the back of a camera while Wendell Green watches in dismay.

'One more question,' Dale says. 'How did you learn that the Freneau girl's body was out here?'

'They was five or six bodies up at Ed's, is what I heard. My brother Erland called up and told me. He heard it from his girlfriend.'

'Go on, get out of here,' Dale says, and Teddy Runkleman ambles away as if he has been awarded a medal for good citizenship.

'All right,' Perry Brown says. 'Chief Gilbertson, you have reached the end of your leash. As of now, this investigation is to be conducted by Lieutenant Black and myself. I'll want a copy of the 911 tape and copies of all notes and statements taken by you and your officers. Your role *is* to be entirely subordinate to the state's investigation, and to cooperate fully when called upon. You *will* be given updates at the discretion of Lieutenant Black and myself.

'If you ask me, Chief Gilbertson, you are getting far more than you deserve. I have never seen a more disorganized crime scene. You violated the security of this site to an *unbelievable* degree. How many of you walked into the . . . the structure?'

'Three,' Dale says. 'Myself, Officer Dulac, and Lieutenant Sawyer.'

'Lieutenant *Sawyer*,' Brown says. 'Excuse me, has Lieutenant *Sawyer* rejoined the LAPD? Has he become an official member of your department? And if not, why did you give him access to that structure? In fact, what is *Mr* Sawyer doing here in the first place?'

'He's cleared more homicide cases than you and me ever will, no matter how long we live.'

Brown gives Jack an evil glance, and Jeff Black stares straight ahead. Beyond the two state cops, Arnold Hrabowski also glances at Jack Sawyer, though not at all the way Perry Brown did. Arnold's expression is that of a man who deeply wishes to be invisible, and when he finds Jack's eye on him, he quickly glances sideways and shifts on his feet.

Oh, Jack thinks. *Of course, the Mad Mad Mad Mad Mad Hungarian, there you go.*

Perry Brown asks Dale what *Mr* St Pierre and his friends are doing on the scene, and Dale replies that they are assisting with crowd control. Did Dale advise Mr St Pierre that in exchange for this service he would be kept up-to-date on the investigation? It was something like that, yes.

Jack steps back and begins to move sideways along a gentle arc that will bring him to Arnold Hrabowski.

'Incredible,' says Brown. 'Tell me, Chief Gilbertson, did you decide to delay a little bit before passing the news on to Lieutenant Black and myself?'

'I did everything according to procedure,' Dale says. In answer to the next question he says that yes, he has called for the medical examiner and the evidence wagon, which, by the way, he can see coming up the lane right now.

The Mad Hungarian's efforts at self-control succeed only in making him look as though he urgently needs to urinate. When Jack places a hand on his shoulder, he stiffens like a cigar-store Indian.

'Calm down, Arnold,' Jack says, then raises his voice. 'Lieutenant Black, if you're taking over this case, there's some information you should have.'

Brown and Black turn their attention to him.

'The man who made the 911 call used the pay phone at the 7-Eleven store on Highway 35 in French Landing. Dale had the phone taped off, and the owner knows to keep people from handling it. You might get some useful prints from that phone.'

Black scribbles something in his notebook, and Brown says, 'Gentlemen, I think your role is finished here. Chief, use your people to disperse those individuals at the bottom of the lane. By the time the ME and I come out of that structure, I don't want to see a single person down there, including you and your officers. You'll get a call later in the week, if I have any new information.'

Wordlessly, Dale turns away and points Bobby Dulac down the path, where the crowd has dwindled to a few stubborn souls leaning against their cars. Brown and Black shake hands with the medical examiner and confer with the specialists in charge of the evidence wagon.

'Now, Arnold,' Jack says, 'you like being a cop, don't you?'

'Me? I love being a cop.' Arnold cannot quite force himself to meet Jack's eyes. 'And I could be a good one, I know I could, but the chief doesn't have enough faith in me.' He thrusts his trembling hands into his pants pockets.

Jack is torn between feeling pity for this pathetic wanna-be and the impulse to kick him all the way down to the end of the lane. A good cop? Arnold couldn't even be a good scoutmaster. Thanks to him, Dale Gilbertson got a public dressing-down that probably made him feel as though he'd been put in the stocks. 'But you didn't follow orders, did you, Arnold?'

Arnold quivers like a tree struck by lightning. 'What? I didn't do anything.'

'You told someone. Maybe you told a couple of people.'

'No!' Arnold shakes his head violently. 'I just called my

wife, that's all.' He looks imploringly at Jack. 'The Fisherman talked to *me*, he told *me* where he put the girl's body, and I wanted Paula to know. Honest, Holl—Lieutenant Sawyer, I didn't think she'd call anybody, I just wanted to *tell* her.'

'Bad move, Arnold,' Jack says. 'You are going to tell the chief what you did, and you're going to do it right now. Because Dale deserves to know what went wrong, and he shouldn't have to blame himself. You like Dale, don't you?'

'The chief?' Arnold's voice wobbles with respect for his chief. 'Sure I do. He's, he's . . . he's great. But isn't he going to fire me?'

'That's up to him, Arnold,' Jack says. 'If you ask me, you deserve it, but maybe you'll get lucky.'

The Mad Hungarian shuffles off toward Dale. Jack watches their conversation for a second, then walks past them to the side of the old store, where Beezer St Pierre and Wendell Green face each other in unhappy silence.

'Hello, Mr St Pierre,' he says. 'And hello to you, Wendell.'

'I'm lodging a complaint,' Green says. 'I'm covering the biggest story of my life, and this lout spoils a whole roll of film. You can't treat the press that way; we have a *right* to photograph whatever the hell we like.'

'I guess you woulda said you had a right to photograph my daughter's dead body, too.' Beezer glares at Jack. 'This piece of shit paid Teddy and the other lunkheads to go nuts so nobody would notice him sneaking inside there. He took pictures of the girl.'

Wendell jabs a finger at Jack's chest. 'He has no proof of that. But I'll tell you something, Sawyer. I did get pictures of you. You were concealing evidence in the back of your truck, and I got you dead to rights. So think twice before you try to mess with me, because I'll hang you out to dry.'

A dangerous red mist seems to fill Jack's head. 'Were you going to sell photographs of that girl's body?'

'What's it to you?' An ugly smirk widens Wendell Green's mouth. 'You're not exactly lily-white either, are you? Maybe we can do each other some good, huh?'

The red mist darkens and fills Jack's eyes. 'We can do each other some good?'

Standing beside Jack, Beezer St Pierre clenches and unclenches his enormous fists. Beezer, Jack knows, catches his tone perfectly, but the vision of dollar signs has so gripped Wendell Green that he hears Jack's threat as a straightforward question.

'You let me reload my camera and get the pictures I need, and I keep quiet about you.'

Beezer lowers his head and balls his hands again.

'Tell you what. I'm a generous guy – maybe I could even cut you in, say ten percent of my total.'

Jack would prefer to break his nose, but he contents himself with a hard punch to the reporter's stomach. Green clutches his gut and folds in half, then falls to the ground. His face has turned a hectic pink, and he struggles for breath. His eyes register shock and disbelief.

'See, I'm a generous guy, too, Wendell. I probably saved you thousands of dollars in dental work, plus a broken jaw.'

'Don't forget the plastic surgery,' says Beezer, grinding a fist into the palm of the other hand. He looks as if someone just stole his favorite dessert off the dinner table.

Wendell's face has become a reddish shade of purple.

'For your information, Wendell, no matter what you think you saw, I am not concealing evidence. If anything I am *revealing* it, though I hardly expect you to understand.'

Green manages to wheeze in something like a cubic inch of air.

'When your wind starts to come back, get out of here. Crawl, if you have to. Go back to your car and drive away. And for God's sake, make it snappy, or our friend here is likely to put you in a wheelchair for the rest of your life.'

Slowly, Wendell Green gets to his knees, takes another noisy sip of oxygen, and levers himself semi-upright. He waggles one open hand at them, but his meaning is unclear. He could be telling Beezer and Jack to stay away from him, or that he will trouble them no further, or both. His trunk tilted over his belt, his hands pressed to his stomach, Green stumbles around the side of the building.

'I guess I oughta thank you,' Beezer says. 'You let me keep my promise to my old lady. But I have to say, Wendell Green is one guy I'd really like to deconstruct.'

'Man,' Jack says, 'I wasn't sure if I could get in before you did.'

'It's true, my restraint was crumbling.'

Both men smile. 'Beezer St Pierre,' Beezer says, and sticks out a hand.

'Jack Sawyer.' Jack takes his hand and experiences no more than a second of pain.

'Are you gonna let the state guys do all the work, or will you keep going on your own?'

'What do you think?' Jack says.

'If you ever need any help, or you want reinforcements, all you have to do is ask. Because I do want to get this son of a bitch, and I figure you have a better chance of finding him than anyone else.'

On the drive back to Norway Valley, Henry says, 'Oh, Wendell took a picture of the body, all right. When you came out of the building and went to your truck, I heard someone take a couple of pictures, but I thought it might have been Dale. Then I heard it again when you and Dale were inside with Bobby Dulac, and I realized someone was taking a picture of *me*! *Well, now*, I say to myself, *this must be Mr Wendell Green*, and I told him to come out from behind the wall. That's when those people charged out, yelling and screaming. As soon as that happened, I heard Mr Green trot around from the side, go into the building, and shoot a few pictures. Then he sneaked out and stood by the side of the building, which is where your friend Beezer caught up with him and took care of things. Beezer is a remarkable fellow, isn't he?'

'Henry, were you going to *tell* me about this?'

'Of course, but you were running around all over the place, and I knew Wendell Green wasn't going to leave until he was thrown out. I'll never read another word he writes. Never.'

'Same here,' Jack says.

'But you're not giving up on the Fisherman, are you? In spite of what that pompous state cop said.'

'I can't give up now. To tell you the truth, I think those waking dreams I mentioned yesterday were connected to this case.'

'*Ivey-divey*. Now, let's get back to Beezer. Didn't I hear him say he wanted to "deconstruct" Wendell?'

'Yeah, I think so.'

'He must be a fascinating man. I gather from my nephew that the Thunder Five spends Saturday afternoons and evenings in the Sand Bar. Next week, maybe I'll start up Rhoda's old car and drive to Centralia, have a few beers and a nice gab with Mr St Pierre. I'm sure he has interesting taste in music.'

'You want to drive to Centralia?' Jack stares at Henry, whose only concession to the absurdity of this suggestion is a little smile.

'Blind people can drive perfectly well,' Henry says. 'Probably, they can drive better than most sighted people. Ray Charles can, anyhow.'

'Come on, Henry. Why would you think Ray Charles can drive a car?'

'Why, you ask? Because one night in Seattle, this was, oh, forty years ago, back when I had a gig at KIRO, Ray took me out for a spin. Smooth as Lady Godiva's backside. No trouble at all. We stuck to the side roads, of course, but Ray got up to fifty-five, I'm pretty sure.'

'Assuming this really happened, weren't you scared?'

'Scared? Of course not. I was his navigator. I certainly don't think I'd have a problem navigating to Centralia along this sleepy stretch of backcountry highway. The only reason blind people don't drive is that other people won't let them. It's a power issue. They want us to stay marginalized. Beezer St Pierre would understand perfectly.'

'And here I was, thinking I was going to visit the madhouse this afternoon,' Jack says.

14

At the top of the steep hill between Norway Valley and Arden, the zigzag, hairpin turns of Highway 93, now narrowed to two lanes, straighten out for the long, ski-slope descent into the town, and on the eastern side of the highway, the hilltop widens into a grassy plateau. Two weatherbeaten red picnic tables wait for those who choose to stop for a few minutes and appreciate the spectacular view. A patchwork of quilted farms stretches out over fifteen miles of gentle landscape, not quite flat, threaded with streams and country roads. A solid row of bumpy, blue-green hills form the horizon. In the immense sky, sun-washed white clouds hang like fresh laundry.

Fred Marshall steers his Ford Explorer onto the gravel shoulder, comes to a halt, and says, 'Let me show you something.'

When he climbed into the Explorer at his farmhouse, Jack was carrying a slightly worn black leather briefcase, and the case is now lying flat across his knees. Jack's father's initials, P.S.S., for Philip Stevenson Sawyer, are stamped in gold beside the handle at the top of the case. Fred has glanced curiously at the briefcase a couple of times, but has not asked about it, and Jack has volunteered nothing. There will be time for show-and-tell, Jack thinks, after he talks to Judy Marshall. Fred gets out of the car, and Jack slides his father's old briefcase behind his legs and props it against the seat before he follows the other man across the pliant grass. When they reach the first of the picnic tables, Fred gestures toward the landscape. 'We don't have a lot of what you could call tourist attractions around here, but this is pretty good, isn't it?'

'It's very beautiful,' Jack says. 'But I think everything here is beautiful.'

'Judy really likes this view. Whenever we go over to Arden on a decent day, she has to stop here and get out of the car, relax and look around for a while. You know, sort of store up on the important things before getting back into the grind. Me, sometimes I get impatient and think, Come on, you've seen that view a thousand times, I have to get back to work, but I'm a guy, right? So every time we turn in here and sit down for a few minutes, I realize my wife knows more than I do and I should just listen to what she says.'

Jack smiles and sits down at the bench, waiting for the rest of it. Since picking him up, Fred Marshall has spoken only two or three sentences of gratitude, but it is clear that he has chosen this place to get something off his chest.

'I went over to the hospital this morning, and she – well, she's *different*. To look at her, to talk to her, you'd have to say she's in much better shape than yesterday. Even though she's still worried sick about Tyler, it's *different*. Do you think that could be due to the medication? I don't even know what they're giving her.'

'Can you have a normal conversation with her?'

'From time to time, yeah. For instance, this morning she was telling me about a story in yesterday's paper on a little girl from La Riviere who nearly took third place in the statewide spelling bee, except she couldn't spell this crazy word nobody ever heard of. *Popoplax*, or something like that.'

'Opopanax,' Jack says. He sounds like he has a fishbone caught in his throat.

'You saw that story, too? That's interesting, you both picking up on that word. Kind of gave her a kick. She asked the nurses to find out what it meant, and one of them looked it up in a couple of dictionaries. Couldn't find it.'

Jack had found the word in his *Concise Oxford Dictionary*; its literal meaning was unimportant. 'That's probably the definition of *opopanax*,' Jack says. '"1. A word not to be found in the dictionary. 2. A fearful mystery."'

'Hah!' Fred Marshall has been moving nervously around the lookout area, and now he stations himself beside Jack, whose upward glance finds the other man surveying the long panorama. 'Maybe that is what it means.' Fred's eyes remain fixed on the landscape. He is still not quite ready, but he is making progress. 'It was great to see her interested in something like that, a tiny little item in the *Herald* . . .'

He wipes tears from his eyes and takes a step toward the horizon. When he turns around, he looks directly at Jack. 'Uh, before you meet Judy, I want to tell you a few things about her. Trouble is, I don't know how this is going to sound to you. Even to me, it sounds . . . I don't know.'

'Give it a try,' Jack says.

Fred says, 'Okay,' knits his fingers together, and bows his head. Then he looks up again, and his eyes are as vulnerable as a baby's. 'Ahhh . . . I don't know how to put this. Okay, I'll just say it. With part of my brain, I think Judy *knows* something. Anyhow, I want to think that. On the other hand, I don't want to fool myself into believing that just because she seems to be better, she can't be crazy anymore. But I do want to believe that. Boy oh boy, do I ever.'

'Believe that she knows something.' The eerie feeling aroused by *opopanax* diminishes before this validation of his theory.

'Something that isn't even real clear to her,' Fred says. 'But do you remember? She knew Ty was gone even before I told her.'

He gives Jack an anguished look and steps away. He knocks his fists together and stares at the ground. Another internal barrier topples before his need to explain his dilemma.

'Okay, look. This is what you have to understand about Judy. She's a special person. All right, a lot of guys would say their wives are special, but Judy's special in a special way. First of all, she's sort of amazingly beautiful, but that's not even what I'm talking about. And she's tremendously brave, but that's not it, either. It's like she's connected to something the rest of us can't even begin to understand. But can that be real? How crazy is that? Maybe when you're going crazy, at first you put up a big fight and get hysterical, and then you're too crazy to fight anymore and you get all calm and accepting. I have to talk to her doctor, because this is tearing me apart.'

'What kinds of things does she say? Does she explain why she's so much calmer?'

Fred Marshall's eyes burn into Jack's. 'Well, for one thing, Judy seems to think that Ty is still alive, and that you're the only person who can find him.'

'All right,' Jack says, unwilling to say more until after he can speak to Judy. 'Tell me, does Judy ever mention someone she used to know – or a cousin of hers, or an old boyfriend – she thinks might have taken him?' His theory seems less convincing than it had in Henry Leyden's ultrarational, thoroughly bizarre kitchen; Fred Marshall's response weakens it further.

'Not unless he's named the Crimson King, or Gorg, or Abbalah. All I can tell you is, Judy thinks she *sees* something, and even though it makes no sense, I sure as hell hope it's there.'

A sudden vision of the world where he found a boy's Brewers cap pierces Jack Sawyer like a steel-tipped lance. 'And that's where Tyler is.'

'If part of me didn't think that might just *possibly* be true, I'd go out of my mind right here and now,' Fred says. 'Unless I'm already out of my gourd.'

'Let's go talk to your wife,' Jack says.

From the outside, French County Lutheran Hospital resembles a nineteenth-century madhouse in the north of England: dirty red-brick walls with blackened buttresses and lancet arches, a peaked roof with finial-capped pinnacles, swollen turrets, miserly windows, and all of the long facade stippled black with ancient filth. Set within a walled parkland dense with oaks on Arden's western boundary, the enormous building, Gothic without the grandeur, looks punitive, devoid of mercy. Jack half-expects to hear the shrieking organ music from a Vincent Price movie.

They pass through a narrow, peaked wooden door and enter a reassuringly familiar lobby. A bored, uniformed man at a central desk directs visitors to the elevators; stuffed animals and sprays of flowers fill the gift shop's window; bathrobed patients tethered to IV poles occupy randomly placed tables with their families, and other patients perch on the chairs lined against the side walls; two white-coated doctors confer in a corner. Far overhead, two dusty, ornate chandeliers distribute a soft ocher light that momentarily seems to gild the luxurious heads of the lilies arrayed in tall vases beside the entrance of the gift shop.

'Wow, it sure looks better on the inside,' Jack says.

'Most of it does,' Fred says.

They approach the man behind the desk, and Fred says, 'Ward D.' With a mild flicker of interest, the man gives them two rectangular cards stamped VISITOR and waves them through. The elevator clanks down and admits them to a wood-paneled enclosure the size of a broom closet. Fred Marshall pushes the button marked 5, and the elevator shudders upward. The same soft, golden light pervades the comically tiny interior. Ten years ago, an elevator remarkably similar to this, though situated in a grand Paris hotel, had held Jack and a UCLA art-history graduate student named Iliana Tedesco captive for two and a half hours, in the course of which Ms Tedesco announced that their relationship had reached its final destination, thank you, despite her gratitude for what had been at least until that moment a rewarding journey together. After thinking it over, Jack decides not to trouble Fred Marshall with this information.

Better behaved than its French cousin, the elevator trembles to a stop and with only a slight display of resistance slides open its door and releases Jack Sawyer and Fred Marshall to the fifth floor, where the beautiful light seems a touch darker than in both the elevator and the lobby. 'Unfortunately, it's way over on the other side,' Fred tells Jack. An apparently endless corridor yawns like an exercise in perspective off to their left, and Fred points the way with his finger.

They go through two big sets of double doors, past the corridor to Ward B, past two vast rooms lined with curtained cubicles, turn left again at the closed entrance to Gerontology, down a long, long hallway lined with bulletin boards, past the opening to Ward C, then take an abrupt right at the men's and women's bathrooms, pass Ambulatory Ophthalmology and Records Annex, and at last come to a corridor marked WARD D. As they proceed, the light seems progressively to darken, the walls to contract, the windows to shrink. Shadows lurk in the corridor to Ward D, and a small pool of water glimmers on the floor.

'We're in the oldest part of the building now,' Fred says.

'You must want to get Judy out of here as soon as possible.'

'Well, sure, soon as Pat Skarda thinks she's ready. But you'll be surprised; Judy kind of likes it in here. I think it's helping. What she told me was, she feels completely safe, and the ones that can talk, some of them are extremely interesting. It's like being on a cruise, she says.'

Jack laughs in surprise and disbelief, and Fred Marshall touches his shoulder and says, 'Does that mean she's a lot better or a lot worse?'

At the end of the corridor, they emerge directly into a good-sized room that seems to have been preserved unaltered for a hundred years. Dark brown wainscoting rises four feet from the dark brown wooden floor. Far up in the gray wall to their right, two tall, narrow windows framed like paintings admit filtered gray light. A man seated behind a polished wooden counter pushes a button that unlocks a double-sized metal door with a WARD D sign and a small window of reinforced glass. 'You can go in, Mr Marshall, but who is he?'

'His name is Jack Sawyer. He's here with me.'

'Is he either a relative or a medical professional?'

'No, but my wife wants to see him.'

'Wait here a moment.' The attendant disappears through the metal door and locks it behind him with a prisonlike clang. A minute later, the attendant reappears with a nurse whose heavy, lined face, big arms and hands, and thick legs make her look like a man in drag. She introduces herself as Jane Bond, the head nurse of Ward D, a combination of words and circumstances that irresistibly suggest at least a couple of nicknames. The nurse subjects Fred and Jack, then only Jack, to a barrage of questions before she vanishes back behind the great door.

'Ward Bond,' Jack says, unable not to.

'We call her Warden Bond,' says the attendant. 'She's tough, but on the other hand, she's unfair.' He coughs and stares up at the high windows. 'We got this orderly, calls her Double-oh Zero.'

A few minutes later, Head Nurse Warden Bond, Agent OO Zero, swings open the metal door and says, 'You may enter now, but pay attention to what I say.'

At first, the ward resembles a huge airport hangar divided into a section with a row of padded benches, a section with round tables and plastic chairs, and a third section where two long tables are stacked with drawing paper, boxes of crayons, and watercolor sets. In the vast space, these furnishings look like dollhouse furniture. Here and there on the cement floor, painted a smooth, anonymous shade of gray, lie padded rectangular mats; twenty feet above the floor, small, barred windows punctuate the far wall, of red brick long ago given a couple of coats of white paint. In a glass enclosure to the left of the door, a nurse behind a desk looks up from a book. Far down to the right, well past the tables with art supplies, three locked metal doors open into worlds of their own. The sense of being in a hangar gradually yields to a sense of a benign but inflexible imprisonment.

A low hum of voices comes from the twenty to thirty

men and women scattered throughout the enormous room. Only a very few of these men and women are talking to visible companions. They pace in circles, stand frozen in place, lie curled like infants on the mats; they count on their fingers and scribble in notebooks; they twitch, yawn, weep, stare into space and into themselves. Some of them wear green hospital robes, others civilian clothes of all kinds: T-shirts and shorts, sweat suits, running outfits, ordinary shirts and slacks, jerseys and pants. No one wears a belt, and none of the shoes have laces. Two muscular men with close-cropped hair and in brilliant white T-shirts sit at one of the round tables with the air of patient watchdogs. Jack tries to locate Judy Marshall, but he cannot pick her out.

'I asked for your attention, Mr Sawyer.'

'Sorry,' Jack says. 'I wasn't expecting it to be so big.'

'We'd better be big, Mr Sawyer. We serve an expanding population.' She waits for an acknowledgment of her significance, and Jack nods. 'Very well. I'm going to give you some basic ground rules. If you listen to what I say, your visit here will be as pleasant as possible for all of us. Don't stare at the patients, and don't be alarmed by what they say. Don't act as though you find anything they do or say unusual or distressing. Just be polite, and eventually they will leave you alone. If they ask you for things, do as you choose, within reason. But please refrain from giving them money, any sharp objects, or edibles not previously cleared by one of the physicians – some medications interact adversely with certain kinds of food. At some point, an elderly woman named Estelle Packard will probably come up to you and ask if you are her father. Answer however you like, but if you say no, she will go away disappointed, and if you say yes, you'll make her day. Do you have any questions, Mr Sawyer?'

'Where is Judy Marshall?'

'She's on this side, with her back to us on the farthest bench. Can you see her, Mr Marshall?'

'I saw her right away,' Fred says. 'Have there been any changes since this morning?'

'Not as far as I know. Her admitting physician, Dr Spiegleman, will be here in about half an hour, and he might have more information for you. Would you like me to take you and Mr Sawyer to your wife, or would you prefer going by yourself?'

'We'll be fine,' Fred Marshall says. 'How long can we stay?'

'I'm giving you fifteen minutes, twenty max. Judy is still in the eval stage, and I want to keep her stress level at a minimum. She looks pretty peaceful now, but she's also deeply disconnected and, quite frankly, delusional. I wouldn't be surprised by another hysterical episode, and we don't want to prolong her evaluation period by introducing new medication at this point, do we? So please, Mr Marshall, keep the conversation stress-free, light, and positive.'

'You think she's delusional?'

Nurse Bond smiles pityingly. 'In all likelihood, Mr Marshall, your wife has been delusional for years. Oh, she's managed to keep it hidden, but ideations like hers don't spring up overnight, no no. These things take years to construct, and all the time the person can appear to be a normally functioning human being. Then something triggers the psychosis into full-blown expression. In this case, of course, it was your son's disappearance. By the way, I want to extend my sympathies to you at this time. What a terrible thing to have happened.'

'Yes, it was,' says Fred Marshall. 'But Judy started acting strange even before . . .'

'Same thing, I'm afraid. She needed to be comforted, and her delusions – her delusional world – came into plain view, because that world provided exactly the comfort she needed. You must have heard some of it this morning, Mr Marshall. Did your wife mention anything about going to other worlds?'

'Going to other worlds?' Jack asks, startled.

'A fairly typical schizophrenic ideation,' Nurse Bond says. 'More than half the people on this ward have similar fantasies.'

'You think my wife is schizophrenic?'

Nurse Bond looks past Fred to take a comprehensive inventory of the patients in her domain. 'I'm not a psychiatrist, Mr Marshall, but I have had twenty long years of experience in dealing with the mentally ill. On the basis of that experience, I have to tell you, in my opinion your wife manifests the classic symptoms of paranoid schizophrenia. I wish I had better news for you.' She glances back at Fred Marshall. 'Of course, Dr Spiegleman will make the final diagnosis, and he will be able to answer all your questions, explain your treatment options, and so forth.'

The smile she gives Jack seems to congeal the moment it appears. 'I always tell my new visitors it's tougher on the family than it is on the patient. Some of these people, they don't have a care in the world. Really, you almost have to envy them.'

'Sure,' Jack says. 'Who wouldn't?'

'Go on, then,' she says, with a trace of peevishness. 'Enjoy your visit.'

A number of heads turn as they walk slowly across the dusty wooden floor to the nearest row of benches; many pairs of eyes track their progress. Curiosity, indifference, confusion, suspicion, pleasure, and an impersonal anger show in the pallid faces. To Jack, it seems as though every patient on the ward is inching toward them.

A flabby middle-aged man in a bathrobe has begun to cut through the tables, looking as though he fears missing his bus to work. At the end of the nearest bench, a thin old woman with streaming white hair stands up and beseeches Jack with her eyes. Her clasped, upraised hands tremble violently. Jack forces himself not to meet her eyes. When he passes her, she half-croons, half-whispers, 'My ducky-wucky was behind the door, but I didn't know it, and there he was, *in all that water.*'

'Um,' Fred says. 'Judy told me her baby son drowned in the bath.'

Through the side of his eye, Jack has been watching the fuzzy-haired man in the bathrobe rush toward them, open-mouthed. When he and Fred reach the back of Judy Marshall's bench, the man raises one finger, as if signaling the bus to wait for him, and trots forward. Jack watches him approach; nuts to Warden Bond's advice. He's not going to let this lunatic climb all over him, no way. The upraised finger comes to within a foot of Jack's nose, and the man's murky eyes search his face. The eyes retreat; the mouth snaps shut. Instantly, the man whirls around and darts off, his robe flying, his finger still searching out its target.

What was that, Jack wonders. *Wrong bus?*

Judy Marshall has not moved. She must have heard the man rushing past her, his rapid breath when he stopped, then his flapping departure, but her back is still straight in the loose green robe, her head still faces forward at the same upright angle. She seems detached from everything around her. If her hair were washed, brushed, and combed, if she were conventionally dressed and had a suitcase beside her, she would look exactly like a woman on a bench at the train station, waiting for the hour of departure.

So even before Jack sees Judy Marshall's face, before she speaks a single word, there is about her this sense of leave-taking, of journeys begun and begun again – this suggestion of travel, this hint of a possible elsewhere.

'I'll tell her we're here,' Fred whispers, and ducks around the end of the bench to kneel in front of his wife. The back of her head tilts forward over the erect spine as if to answer the tangled combination of heartbreak, love, and anxiety burning in her husband's handsome face. Dark blond hair mingled with gold lies flat against the girlish curve of Judy Marshall's skull. Behind her ear, dozens of varicolored strands clump together in a cobwebby knot.

'How you feeling, sweetie?' Fred softly asks his wife.

'I'm managing to enjoy myself,' she says. 'You know, honey, I should stay here for at least a little while. The head nurse is positive I'm absolutely crazy. Isn't that convenient?'

'Jack Sawyer's here. Would you like to see him?'

Judy reaches out and pats his upraised knee. 'Tell Mr Sawyer to come around in front, and you sit right here beside me, Fred.'

Jack is already coming forward, his eyes on Judy Marshall's once again upright head, which does not turn. Kneeling, Fred has taken her extended hand in both of his, as if he intends to kiss it. He looks like a lovelorn knight before a queen. When he presses her hand to his cheek, Jack sees the white gauze wrapped around the tips of her fingers. Judy's cheekbone comes into view, then the side of her gravely unsmiling mouth; then her entire profile is visible, as sharp as the crack of ice on the first day of spring. It is the regal, idealized profile on a cameo, or on a coin: the slight upward curve of the lips, the crisp, chiseled downstroke of the nose, the sweep of the jawline, every angle in perfect, tender, oddly familiar alignment with the whole.

It staggers him, this unexpected beauty; for a fraction of a second it slows him with the deep, grainy nostalgia of its fragmentary, not-quite evocation of another's face. Grace Kelly? Catherine Deneuve? No, neither of these; it comes to him that Judy's profile reminds him of someone he has still to meet.

Then the odd second passes: Fred Marshall gets to his feet, Judy's face in three-quarter profile loses its regal quality as she watches her husband sit beside her on the bench, and Jack rejects what has just occurred to him as an absurdity.

She does not raise her eyes until he stands before her. Her hair is dull and messy; beneath the hospital gown she is wearing an old blue lace-trimmed nightdress that looked dowdy when it was new. Despite these disadvantages, Judy Marshall claims him for her own at the moment her eyes meet his.

An electrical current beginning at his optic nerves seems to pulse downward through his body, and he helplessly concludes that she has to be the most stunningly beautiful woman he has ever seen. He fears that the force of his reaction to her will knock him off his feet, then – even worse! – that she will see what is going on and think him a fool. He desperately does not want to come off as a fool in her eyes. Brooke Greer, Claire Evinrude, Iliana Tedesco, gorgeous as each of them was in her own way, look like little girls in Halloween costumes next to her. Judy Marshall puts his former beloveds on the shelf; she exposes them as whims and fancies, riddled with false ego and a hundred crippling insecurities. Judy's beauty is not put on in front of a mirror but grows, with breathtaking simplicity, straight from her innermost being: what you see is only the small, visible portion of a far greater, more comprehensive, radiant, and formal quality within.

Jack can scarcely believe that agreeable, good-hearted Fred Marshall actually had the fantastic luck to marry this woman. Does he know how great, how literally *marvelous*, she is? Jack would marry her in an instant, if she were single. It seems to him that he fell in love with her as soon as he saw the back of her head.

But he cannot be in love with her. She is Fred Marshall's wife and the mother of their son, and he will simply have to live without her.

She utters a short sentence that passes through him in a vibrating wave of sound. Jack bends forward muttering an apology, and Judy smilingly offers him a sweep of her hand that invites him to sit before her. He folds to the floor and crosses his ankles in front of him, still reverberating from the shock of having first seen her.

Her face fills beautifully with feeling. She has seen exactly what just happened to him, and it is all right. She does not think less of him for it. Jack opens his mouth to ask a question. Although he does not know what the question is to be, he must ask it. The nature of the question is unimportant. The most idiotic query will serve; he cannot sit here staring at that wondrous face.

Before he speaks, one version of reality snaps soundlessly into another, and without transition Judy Marshall becomes a tired-looking woman in her mid-thirties with tangled hair and smudges under her eyes who regards him steadily from a bench in a locked mental ward. It should seem like a restoration of his sanity, but it feels instead like a kind of trick, as though Judy Marshall has done this herself, to make their encounter easier on him.

The words that escape him are as banal as he feared they might be. Jack listens to himself say that it is nice to meet her.

'It's nice to meet you, too, Mr Sawyer. I've heard so many wonderful things about you.'

He looks for a sign that she acknowledges the enormity of the moment that has just passed, but he sees only her smiling warmth. Under the circumstances, that seems like acknowledgment enough. 'How are you getting on in here?' he asks, and the balance shifts even more in his direction.

'The company takes some getting used to, but the people here got lost and couldn't find their way back, that's all. Some of them are very intelligent. I've had conversations in here that were a lot more interesting than the ones in my church group or the PTA. Maybe I should have come to Ward D sooner! Being here has helped me learn some things.'

'Like what?'

'Like there are many different ways to get lost, for one, and getting lost is easier to do than anyone ever admits. The people in here can't hide how they feel, and most of them never found out how to deal with their fear.'

'How are you supposed to deal with that?'

'Why, you deal with it by taking it on, that's how! You don't just say, I'm lost and I don't know how to get back – you keep on going in the same direction. You put one foot in front of the other until you get *more* lost. Everybody should know that. Especially you, Jack Sawyer.'

'Especial—' Before he can finish the question, an elderly

woman with a lined, sweet face appears beside him and touches his shoulder.

'Excuse me.' She tucks her chin toward her throat with the shyness of a child. 'I want to ask you a question. Are you my father?'

Jack smiles at her. 'Let me ask you a question first. Is your name Estelle Packard?'

Eyes shining, the old woman nods.

'Then yes, I am your father.'

Estelle Packard clasps her hands in front of her mouth, dips her head in a bow, and shuffles backward, glowing with pleasure. When she is nine or ten feet away, she gives Jack a little bye-bye wave of one hand and twirls away.

When Jack looks again at Judy Marshall, it is as if she has parted her veil of ordinariness just wide enough to reveal a small portion of her enormous soul. 'You're a very nice man, aren't you, Jack Sawyer? I wouldn't have known that right away. You're a good man, too. Of course, you're also charming, but charm and decency don't always go together. Should I tell you a few other things about yourself?'

Jack looks up at Fred, who is holding his wife's hand and beaming. 'I want you to say whatever you feel like saying.'

'There are things I can't say, no matter how I feel, but you might hear them anyhow. I can say this, however: your good looks haven't made you vain. You're not shallow, and that might have something to do with it. Mainly, though, you had the gift of a good upbringing. I'd say you had a wonderful mother. I'm right, aren't I?'

Jack laughs, touched by this unexpected insight. 'I didn't know it showed.'

'You know one way it shows? In the way you treat other people. I'm pretty sure you come from a background people around here only know from the movies, but it hasn't gone to your head. You see us as people, not hicks, and that's why I know I can trust you. It's obvious that your mother did a great job. I was a good mother, too, or at least I tried to be, and I know what I'm talking about. I can *see*.'

'You say you *were* a good mother? Why use—'

'The past tense? Because I was talking about before.'

Fred's smile fades into an expression of ill-concealed concern. 'What do you mean, "before"?'

'Mr Sawyer might know,' she says, giving Jack what he thinks is a look of encouragement.

'Sorry, I don't think I do,' he says.

'I mean, before I wound up here and finally started to think a little bit. Before the things that were happening to me stopped scaring me out of my mind – before I realized I could look inside myself and examine these feelings I've had over and over all my life. Before I had time to travel. I think I'm still a good mother, but I'm not exactly the *same* mother.'

'Honey, please,' says Fred. 'You are the same, you just had a kind of breakdown. We ought to talk about Tyler.'

'We are talking about Tyler. Mr Sawyer, do you know that lookout point on Highway 93, right where it reaches the top of the big hill about a mile south of Arden?'

'I saw it today,' Jack says. 'Fred showed it to me.'

'You saw all those farms that keep going and going? And the hills off in the distance?'

'Yes. Fred told me you loved the view from up there.'

'I always want to stop and get out of the car. I love everything about that view. You can see for miles and miles, and then – whoops! – it stops, and you can't see any farther. But the sky keeps going, doesn't it? The sky proves that there's a world on the other side of those hills. If you travel, you can get there.'

'Yes, you can.' Suddenly, there are goose bumps on Jack's forearms, and the back of his neck is tingling.

'Me? I can only travel in my mind, Mr Sawyer, and I only remembered how to do that because I landed in the loony bin. But it came to me that *you* can get there – to the other side of the hills.'

His mouth is dry. He registers Fred Marshall's growing distress without being able to reduce it. Wanting to ask her a thousand questions, he begins with the simplest one:

'How did it come to you? What do you mean by that?'

Judy Marshall takes her hand from her husband and holds it out to Jack, and he holds it in both of his. If she ever looked like an ordinary woman, now is not the time. She is blazing away like a lighthouse, like a bonfire on a distant cliff.

'Let's say . . . late at night, or if I was alone for a long time, someone used to whisper to me. It wasn't that concrete, but let's say it was as if a person were whispering on the other side of a thick wall. A girl like me, a girl my age. And if I fell asleep then, I would almost always dream about the place where that girl lived. I called it Faraway, and it was like this world, the Coulee Country, only brighter and cleaner and more magical. In Faraway, people rode in carriages and lived in great white tents. In Faraway, there were men who could fly.'

'You're right,' he says. Fred looks from his wife to Jack in painful uncertainty, and Jack says, 'It sounds crazy, but she's right.'

'By the time these bad things started to happen in French Landing, I had pretty much forgotten about Faraway. I hadn't thought about it since I was about twelve or thirteen.

But the closer the bad things came, to Fred and Ty and me, I mean, the worse my dreams got, and the less and less real my life seemed to be. I wrote words without knowing I was doing it, I said crazy things, I was falling apart. I didn't understand that Faraway was trying to tell me something. The girl was whispering to me from the other side of the wall again, only now she was grown up and scared half to death.'

'What made you think I could help?'

'It was just a feeling I had, back when you arrested that Kinderling man and your picture was in the paper. The first thing I thought when I looked at your picture was, *He knows about Faraway*. I didn't wonder how, or how I could tell from looking at a picture; I simply understood that you knew. And then, when Ty disappeared and I lost my mind and woke up in this place, I thought if you could see into some of these people's heads, Ward D wouldn't be all that different from Faraway, and I remembered seeing your picture. And that's when I started to understand about traveling. All this morning, I have been walking through Faraway in my head. Seeing it, touching it. Smelling that unbelievable air. Did you know, Mr Sawyer, that over there they have jackrabbits the size of kangaroos? It makes you laugh just to look at them.'

Jack breaks into a wide grin, and he bends to kiss her hand, in a gesture much like her husband's.

Gently, she takes her hand from his grasp. 'When Fred told me he had met you, and that you were helping the police, I knew that you were here for a reason.'

What this woman has done astonishes Jack. At the worst moment of her life, with her son lost and her sanity crumbling, she used a monumental feat of memory to summon all of her strength and, in effect, accomplish a miracle. She found within herself the capacity to *travel*. From a locked ward, she moved halfway out of this world and into another known only from childhood dreams. Nothing but the immense courage her husband had described could have enabled her to have taken this mysterious step.

'You *did* something once, didn't you?' Judy asks him. 'You were there, in Faraway, and you *did* something – something tremendous. You don't have to say yes, because I can see it in you; it's as plain as day. But you have to say yes, so I can hear it, so say it, say yes.'

'Yes.'

'Did what?' Fred asks. 'In this dream country? How can you say yes?'

'Wait,' Jack tells him, 'I have something to show you later,' and returns to the extraordinary woman seated before him. Judy Marshall is aflame with insight, courage, and faith and, although she is forbidden to him, now seems to be the only woman in this world or any other whom he could love for the rest of his life.

'You were like me,' she says. 'You forgot all about that world. And you went out and became a policeman, a detective. In fact, you became one of the best detectives that ever lived. Do you know why you did that?'

'I guess the work appealed to me.'

'What about it appealed to you in particular?'

'Helping the community. Protecting innocent people. Putting away the bad guys. It was interesting work.'

'And you thought it would never stop being interesting. Because there would always be a new problem to solve, a new question in need of an answer.'

She has struck a bull's-eye that, until this moment, he did not know existed. 'That's right.'

'You were a great detective because, even though you

didn't know it, there was something – something vital – you needed to detect.'

I am a coppiceman, Jack remembers. His own little voice in the night, speaking to him from the other side of a thick, thick wall.

'Something you had to find, for the sake of your own soul.'

'Yes,' Jack says. Her words have penetrated straight into the center of his being, and tears spring to his eyes. 'I always wanted to find what was missing. My whole life was about the search for a secret explanation.'

In memory as vivid as a strip of film, he sees a great tented pavilion, a white room where a beautiful and wasted queen lay dying, and a little girl two or three years younger than his twelve-year-old self amid her attendants.

'Did you call it Faraway?' Judy asks.

'I called it the Territories.' Speaking the words aloud feels like the opening of a chest filled with a treasure he can share at last.

'That's a good name. Fred won't understand this, but when I was on my long walk this morning, I felt that my son was somewhere in Faraway – in your Territories. Somewhere out of sight, and hidden away. In grave danger, but still alive and unharmed. In a cell. Sleeping on the floor. But alive. Unharmed. Do you think that could be true, Mr Sawyer?'

'Wait a second,' Fred says. 'I know you feel that way, and I want to believe it, too, but this is the real world we're talking about here.'

'I think there are lots of real worlds,' Jack says. 'And yes, I believe Tyler is somewhere in Faraway.'

'Can you rescue him, Mr Sawyer? Can you bring him back?'

'It's like you said before, Mrs Marshall,' Jack says. 'I must be here for a reason.'

'Sawyer, I hope whatever you're going to show me makes more sense than the two of you do,' says Fred. 'We're through for now, anyhow. Here comes the warden.'

Driving out of the hospital parking lot, Fred Marshall glances at the briefcase lying flat on Jack's lap but says nothing. He holds his silence until he turns back onto 93, when he says, 'I'm glad you came with me.'

'Thank you,' Jack says. 'I am, too.'

'I feel sort of out of my depth here, you know, but I'd like to get your impressions of what went on in there. Do you think it went pretty well?'

'I think it went better than that. Your wife is . . . I hardly know how to describe her. I don't have the vocabulary to tell you how great I think she is.'

Fred nods and sneaks a glance at Jack. 'So you don't think she's out of her head, I guess.'

'If that's crazy, I'd like to be crazy right along with her.'

The two-lane blacktop highway that stretches before them lifts up along the steep angle of the hillside and, at its top, seems to extend into the dimensionless blue of the enormous sky.

Another wary glance from Fred. 'And you say you've seen this, this *place* she calls Faraway.'

'I have, yes. As hard as that is to believe.'

'No crap. No b.s. On your mother's grave.'

'On my mother's grave.'

'You've been there. And not just in a dream, really *been* there.'

'The summer I was twelve.'

'Could I go there, too?'

'Probably not,' Jack says. This is not the truth, since Fred could go to the Territories if Jack took him there, but Jack wants to shut this door as firmly as possible. He can imagine bringing Judy Marshall into that other world; Fred is another matter. Judy has more than earned a journey into the Territories, while Fred is still incapable of believing in its existence. Judy would feel at home over there, but her husband would be like an anchor Jack had to drag along with him, like Richard Sloat.

'I didn't think so,' says Fred. 'If you don't mind, I'd like to pull over again when we get to the top.'

'I'd like that,' Jack says.

Fred drives to the crest of the hill and crosses the narrow highway to park in the gravel turnout. Instead of getting out of the car, he points at the briefcase lying flat on Jack's knees. 'Is what you're going to show me in there?'

'Yes,' Jack says. 'I was going to show it to you earlier, but after we stopped here the first time, I wanted to wait until I heard what Judy had to say. And I'm glad I did. It might make more sense to you, now that you've heard at least part of the explanation of how I found it.'

Jack snaps open the briefcase, raises the top, and from its pale, leather-lined interior removes the Brewers cap he had found that morning. 'Take a look,' he says, and hands over the cap.

'Ohmygod,' Fred Marshall says in a startled rush of words. 'Is this . . . is it . . .?' He looks inside the cap and exhales hugely at the sight of his son's name. His eyes leap to Jack's. 'It's Tyler's. Good Lord, it's Tyler's. Oh, Lordy.' He crushes the cap to his chest and takes two deep breaths, still holding Jack's gaze. 'Where did you find this? How long ago was it?'

'I found it on the road this morning,' Jack says. 'In the place your wife calls Faraway.'

With a long moan, Fred Marshall opens his door and jumps out of the car. By the time Jack catches up with him, he is at the far edge of the lookout, holding the cap to his chest and staring at the blue-green hills beyond the long quilt of farmland. He whirls to stare at Jack. 'Do you think he's still alive?'

'I think he's alive,' Jack says.

'In that world.' Fred points to the hills. Tears leap from his eyes, and his mouth softens. 'The world that's over there somewhere, Judy says.'

'In that world.'

'Then you go there and find him!' Fred shouts. His face shining with tears, he gestures wildly toward the horizon with the baseball cap. 'Go there and bring him back, damn you! *I* can't do it, so *you* have to.' He steps forward as if to throw a punch, then wraps his arms around Jack Sawyer and sobs.

When Fred's shoulders stop trembling and his breath comes in gasps, Jack says, 'I'll do everything I can.'

'I know you will.' He steps away and wipes his face. 'I'm sorry I yelled at you like that. I know you're going to help us.'

The two men turn around to walk back to the car. Far off to the west, a loose, woolly smudge of pale gray blankets the land beside the river.

'What's that?' Jack asks. 'Rain?'

'No, fog,' Fred says. 'Coming in off the Mississippi.'

Part Three

NIGHT'S PLUTONIAN SHORE

15

By evening, the temperature has dropped fifteen degrees as a minor cold front pushes through our little patch of the Coulee Country. There are no thunderstorms, but as the sky tinges toward violet, the fog arrives. It's born out of the river and rises up the inclined ramp of Chase Street, first obscuring the gutters, then the sidewalks, then blurring the buildings themselves. It cannot completely hide them, as the fogs of spring and winter sometimes do, but the blurring is somehow worse: it steals colors and softens shapes. The fog makes the ordinary look alien. And there's the smell, the ancient, seagully odor that works deep into your nose and awakens the back part of your brain, the part that is perfectly capable of believing in monsters when the sight lines shorten and the heart is uneasy.

On Sumner Street, Debbi Anderson is still working dispatch. Arnold 'the Mad Hungarian' Hrabowski has been sent home without his badge – in fact, suspended – and feels he must ask his wife a few pointed questions (his belief that he already knows the answers makes him even more heartsick). Debbi is now standing at the window, a cup of coffee in her hand and a puckery little frown on her face.

'Don't like this,' she says to Bobby Dulac, who is glumly and silently writing reports. 'It reminds me of the Hammer pictures I used to watch on TV back when I was in junior high.'

'Hammer pictures?' Bobby asks, looking up.

'Horror pictures,' she says, looking out into the deepening fog. 'A lot of them were about Dracula. Also Jack the Ripper.'

'I don't want to hear nothing about Jack the Ripper,' Bobby says. 'You mind me, Debster.' And resumes writing.

In the parking lot of the 7-Eleven, Mr Rajan Patel stands beside his telephone (still crisscrossed by yellow police tape, and when it will be all right again for using, this Mr Patel could not be telling us). He looks toward downtown, which now seems to rise from a vast bowl of cream. The buildings on Chase Street descend into this bowl. Those at Chase's lowest point are visible only from the second story up.

'If he is down there,' Mr Patel says softly, and to no one but himself, 'tonight he will be doing whatever he wants.'

He crosses his arms over his chest and shivers.

Dale Gilbertson is at home, for a wonder. He plans to have a sit-down dinner with his wife and child even if the world ends because of it. He comes out of his den (where he has spent twenty minutes talking with WSP officer Jeff Black, a conversation in which he has had to exercise all his discipline to keep from shouting), and sees his wife standing at the window and looking out. Her posture is almost exactly the same as Debbi Anderson's, only she's got a glass of wine in her hand instead of a cup of coffee. The puckery little frown is identical.

'River fog,' Sarah says dismally. 'Isn't that ducky. If he's out there—'

Dale points at her. 'Don't say it. Don't even think it.'

But he knows that neither of them can help thinking about it. The streets of French Landing – the *foggy* streets of French Landing – will be deserted right now: no one shopping in the stores, no one idling along the sidewalks, no one in the parks. Especially no children. The parents will be keeping them in. Even on Nailhouse Row, where good parenting is the exception rather than the rule, the parents will be keeping their kids inside.

'I won't say it,' she allows. 'That much I can do.'

'What's for dinner?'

'How does chicken pot pie sound?'

Ordinarily such a hot dish on a July evening would strike him as an awful choice, but tonight, with the fog coming in, it sounds like just the thing. He steps up behind her, gives her a brief squeeze, and says, 'Great. And earlier would be better.'

She turns, disappointed. 'Going back in?'

'I shouldn't have to, not with Brown and Black rolling the ball—'

'Those pricks,' she says. 'I *never* liked them.'

Dale smiles. He knows that the former Sarah Asbury has never cared much for the way he earns his living, and this makes her furious loyalty all the more touching. And tonight it feels vital, as well. It's been the most painful day of his career in law enforcement, ending with the suspension of Arnold Hrabowski. Arnie, Dale knows, believes he will be back on duty before long. And the shitty truth is that Arnie may be right. Based on the way things are going, Dale may need even such an exquisite example of ineptitude as the Mad Hungarian.

'Anyway, I shouldn't *have* to go back in, but . . .'

'You have a feeling.'

'I do.'

'Good or bad?' She has come to respect her husband's intuitions, not in the least because of Dale's intense desire to see Jack Sawyer settled close enough to reach with seven keystrokes instead of eleven. Tonight that looks to her like – pardon the pun – a pretty good call.

'Both,' Dale says, and then, without explaining or giving Sarah a chance to question further: 'Where's Dave?'

'At the kitchen table with his crayons.'

At six, young David Gilbertson is enjoying a violent love affair with Crayolas, has gone through two boxes since school let out. Dale and Sarah's strong hope, expressed even to each other only at night, lying side by side before sleep, is that they may be raising a real artist. The next Norman Rockwell, Sarah said once. Dale – who helped Jack Sawyer hang his strange and wonderful pictures – has higher hopes for the boy. Too high to express, really, even in the marriage bed after the lights are out.

With his own glass of wine in hand, Dale ambles out to the kitchen. 'What you drawing, Dave? What—'

He stops. The crayons have been abandoned. The picture – a half-finished drawing of what might be either a flying saucer or perhaps just a round coffee table – has also been abandoned.

The back door is open.

Looking out at the whiteness that hides David's swing and jungle gym, Dale feels a terrible fear leap up his throat, choking him. All at once he can smell Irma Freneau again, that terrible smell of raw spoiled meat. Any sense that his family lives in a protected, magic circle – *it may happen to others, but it can never, never happen to us* – is gone now. What has replaced it is stark certainty: David is gone. The Fisherman has enticed him out of the house and spirited him away into the fog. Dale can see the grin on the Fisherman's face. He can see the gloved hand – it's yellow – covering his son's mouth but not the bulging, terrified child's eyes.

Into the fog and out of the known world.

David.

He moves forward across the kitchen on legs that feel boneless as well as nerveless. He puts his wineglass down on the table, the stem landing a-tilt on a crayon, not noticing when it spills and covers David's half-finished drawing with something that looks horribly like venous blood. He's out the door, and although he means to yell, his voice comes out in a weak and almost strengthless sigh: 'David? . . . Dave?'

For a moment that seems to last a thousand years, there is nothing. Then he hears the soft thud of running feet on damp grass. Blue jeans and a red-striped rugby shirt materialize out of the thickening soup. A moment later he sees his son's dear, grinning face and mop of yellow hair.

'Dad! Daddy! I was swinging in the fog! It was like being in a cloud!'

Dale snatches him up. There is a bad, blinding impulse to slap the kid across the face, to hurt him for scaring his father so. It passes as quickly as it came. He kisses David instead.

'I know,' he says. 'That must have been fun, but it's time to come in now.'

'Why, Daddy?'

'Because sometimes little boys get lost in the fog,' he says, looking out into the white yard. He can see the patio table, but it is only a ghost; he wouldn't know what he was looking at if he hadn't seen it a thousand times. He kisses his son again. 'Sometimes little boys get lost,' he repeats.

*

Oh, we could check in with any number of friends, both old and new. Jack and Fred Marshall have returned from Arden (neither suggested stopping at Gertie's Kitchen in Centralia when they passed it), and both are now in their otherwise deserted houses. For the balance of the ride back to French Landing, Fred never once let go of his son's baseball cap, and he has a hand on it even now, as he eats a microwaved TV dinner in his too empty living room and watches Action News Five.

Tonight's news is mostly about Irma Freneau, of course. Fred picks up the remote when they switch from shakycam footage of Ed's Eats to a taped report from the Holiday Trailer Park. The cameraman has focused on one shabby trailer in particular. A few flowers, brave but doomed, straggle in the dust by the stoop, which consists of three boards laid across two cement blocks. 'Here, on the outskirts of French Landing, Irma Freneau's grieving mother is in seclusion,' says the on-scene correspondent. 'One can only imagine this single mother's feelings tonight.' The reporter is prettier than Wendell Green but exudes much the same aura of glittering, unhealthy excitement.

Fred hits the OFF button on the remote and growls, 'Why can't you leave the poor woman alone?' He looks down at his chipped beef on toast, but he has lost his appetite.

Slowly, he raises Tyler's hat and puts it on his own head. It doesn't fit, and Fred for a moment thinks of letting out the plastic band at the back. The idea shocks him. Suppose that was all it took to kill his son? That one simple, deadly modification? The idea strikes him as both ridiculous and utterly inarguable. He supposes that if this keeps up, he'll soon be as mad as his wife . . . or Sawyer. Trusting Sawyer is as crazy as thinking he might kill his son by changing the size of the boy's hat . . . and yet he believes in both things. He picks up his fork and begins to eat again, Ty's Brewers cap sitting on his head like Spanky's beanie in an old *Our Gang* one-reeler.

Beezer St Pierre is sitting on his sofa in his underwear, a book open on his lap (it is, in fact, a book of William Blake's poems) but unread. Bear Girl's asleep in the other room, and he's fighting the urge to bop on down to the Sand Bar and score some crank, his old vice, untouched for going on five years now. Since Amy died, he fights this urge every single day, and lately he wins only by reminding himself that he won't be able to find the Fisherman – and punish him as he deserves to be punished – if he's fucked up on devil dust.

Henry Leyden is in his studio with a huge pair of Akai headphones on his head, listening to Warren Vaché, John Bunch, and Phil Flanigan dreamboat their way through 'I Remember April.' He can smell the fog even through the walls, and to him it smells like the air at Ed's Eats. Like bad death, in other words. He's wondering how Jack made out in good old Ward D at French County Lutheran. And he's thinking about his wife, who lately (especially since the record hop at Maxton's, although he doesn't consciously realize this) seems closer than ever. And unquiet.

Yes indeed, all sorts of friends are available for our inspection, but at least one seems to have dropped out of sight. Charles Burnside isn't in the common room at Maxton's (where an old episode of *Family Ties* is currently running on the ancient color TV bolted to the wall), nor in the dining hall, where snacks are available in the early evening, nor in his own room, where the sheets are currently clean (but where the air still smells vaguely of old shit). What about the bathroom? Nope. Thorvald Thorvaldson has stopped in to have a pee and a handwash, but otherwise the place is empty. One oddity: there's a fuzzy slipper lying on its side in one of the stalls. With its bright black and yellow stripes, it looks like the corpse of a huge dead bumblebee. And yes, it's the stall second from the left. Burny's favorite.

Should we look for him? Maybe we should. Maybe not knowing exactly where that rascal is makes us uneasy. Let us slip through the fog, then, silent as a dream, down to lower Chase Street. Here is the Nelson Hotel, its ground floor now submerged in river fog, the ocher stripe marking high water of that ancient flood no more than a whisper of color in the fading light. On one side of it is Wisconsin Shoe, now closed for the day. On the other is Lucky's Tavern, where an old woman with bowlegs (her name is Bertha Van Dusen, if you care) is currently bent over with her hands planted on her large knees, yarking a bellyful of Kingsland Old-Time Lager into the gutter. She makes sounds like a bad driver grinding a manual transmission. In the doorway of the Nelson Hotel itself sits a patient old mongrel, who will wait until Bertha has gone back into the tavern, then slink over to eat the half-digested cocktail franks floating in the beer. From Lucky's comes the tired, twanging voice of the late Dick Curless, Ole Country One-Eye, singing about those Hainesville Woods, where there's a tombstone every mile.

The dog gives a single disinterested growl as we pass him and slip into the Nelson's lobby, where moth-eaten heads – a wolf, a bear, an elk, and an ancient half-bald bison with a single glass eye – look at empty sofas, empty chairs, the elevator that hasn't worked since 1994 or so, and the empty registration desk. (Morty Fine, the clerk, is in the office with his feet propped up on an empty file-cabinet drawer, reading *People* and picking his nose.) The lobby of the Nelson Hotel always smells of the river – it's in the pores of the place – but this evening the smell is heavier than usual. It's a smell that makes us think of bad ideas, blown investments, forged checks, deteriorating health, stolen office supplies, unpaid alimony, empty promises, skin tumors, lost ambition, abandoned sample cases filled with cheap novelties, dead hope, dead skin, and fallen arches. This is the kind of place you don't come to unless you've been here before and all your other options are pretty much foreclosed. It's a place where men who left their families two decades before now lie on narrow beds with pee-stained mattresses, coughing and smoking cigarettes. The scuzzy old lounge (where scuzzy old Hoover Dalrymple once held court and knocked heads most every Friday and Saturday night) has been closed by unanimous vote of the town council since early June, when Dale Gilbertson scandalized the local political elite by showing them a video of three traveling strippers who billed themselves as the Anal University Trio, performing a synchronized cucumber routine on the tiny stage (FLPD cameraman: Officer Tom Lund, let's give him a hand), but the Nelson's residents still have only to go next door to get a beer; it's convenient. You pay by the week at the Nelson. You can keep a hot plate in your room, but only by permission and after the cord has been inspected. You can die on a fixed income at the Nelson, and the last sound you hear could well be the creaking of bedsprings over your head as some other helpless old loser jacks off.

Let us rise up the first flight, past the old canvas firehose in its glass box. Turn right at the second-floor landing (past the pay phone with its yellowing OUT OF ORDER sign) and continue to rise. When we reach the third floor, the smell of river fog is joined by the smell of chicken soup warming on someone's hot plate (the cord duly approved either by Morty Fine or George Smith, the day manager).

The smell is coming from 307. If we slip through the keyhole (there have never been keycards at the Nelson and never will be), we'll be in the presence of Andrew Railsback, seventy, balding, scrawny, good-humored. He once sold vacuum cleaners for Electrolux and appliances for Sylvania, but those days are behind him now. These are his golden years.

A candidate for Maxton's, we might think, but Andy Railsback knows that place, and places like it. Not for him, thanks. He's sociable enough, but he doesn't want people telling him when to go to bed, when to get up, and when he can have a little nip of Early Times. He has friends in Maxton's, visits them often, and has from time to time met the sparkling, shallow, predatory eye of our pal Chipper. He has thought on more than one such occasion that Mr Maxton looks like the sort of fellow who would happily turn the corpses of his graduates into soap if he thought he could turn a buck on it.

No, for Andy Railsback, the third floor of the Nelson Hotel is good enough. He has his hot plate; he has his bottle of hooch; he's got four packs of Bicycles and plays big-picture solitaire on nights when the sandman loses his way.

This evening he has made three Lipton Cup-A-Soups, thinking he'll invite Irving Throneberry in for a bowl and a chat. Maybe afterward they'll go next door to Lucky's and grab a beer. He checks the soup, sees it has attained a nice simmer, sniffs the fragrant steam, and nods. He also has saltines, which go well with soup. He leaves the room to make his way upstairs and knock on Irv's door, but what he sees in the hallway stops him cold.

It's an old man in a shapeless blue robe, walking away from him with suspicious quickness. Beneath the hem of the robe, the stranger's legs are as white as a carp's belly and marked with blue snarls of varicose veins. On his left foot is a fuzzy black-and-yellow slipper. His right foot is bare. Although our new friend can't tell for sure – not with the guy's back to him – he doesn't look like anyone Andy knows.

Also, he's trying doorknobs as he wends his way along the main third-floor hall. He gives each one a single hard, quick shake. Like a turnkey. Or a thief. A fucking thief.

Yeah. Although the man is obviously old – older than Andy, it looks like – and dressed as if for bed, the idea of thievery resonates in Andy's mind with queer certainty. Even the one bare foot, arguing that the fellow probably didn't come in off the street, has no power over this strong intuition.

Andy opens his mouth to call out – something like *Can I help you?* or *Looking for someone?* – and then changes his mind. He just has this feeling about the guy. It has to do with the fleet way the stranger scurries along as he tries the knobs, but that's not all of it. Not all of it by any means. It's a feeling of darkness and danger. There are pockets in the geezer's robe, Andy can see them, and there might be a weapon in one of them. Thieves don't *always* have weapons, but . . .

The old guy turns the corner and is gone. Andy stands where he is, considering. If he had a phone in his room, he might call downstairs and alert Morty Fine, but he doesn't. So, what to do?

After a brief interior debate, he tiptoes down the hall to the corner and peeps around. Here is a cul-de-sac with three doors: 312, 313, and, at the very end, 314, the only room in that little appendix which is currently occupied. The man in 314 has been there since the spring, but almost all Andy knows about him is his name: George Potter. Andy has asked both Irv and Hoover Dalrymple about Potter, but

Hoover doesn't know jack-shit and Irv has learned only a little more.

'You must,' Andy objected – this conversation took place in late May or early June, around the time the Buckhead Lounge downstairs went dark. 'I seen you in Lucky's with him, havin' a beer.'

Irv had lifted one bushy eyebrow in that cynical way of his. 'Seen me havin' a beer with him. What are you?' he'd rasped. 'My fuckin' wife?'

'I'm just saying. You drink a beer with a man, you have a little conversation—'

'Usually, maybe. Not with him. I sat down, bought a pitcher, and mostly got the dubious pleasure of listenin' to myself think. I say, "What do you think about the Brewers this year?" and he says, "They'll suck, same as last year. I can get the Cubs at night on my rah-dio—"'

'That the way he said it? *Rah*-dio?'

'Well, it ain't the way *I* say it, is it? You ever heard me say rah-dio? I say radio, same as any normal person. You want to hear this or not?'

'Don't sound like there's much to hear.'

'You got that right, buddy. He says, "I can get the Cubs at night on my rah-dio, and that's enough for me. I always went to Wrigley with my dad when I was a kid." So I found out he was from Chi, but otherwise, *bupkes*.'

The first thought to pop into Andy's mind upon glimpsing the fucking thief in the third-floor corridor had been Potter, but Mr George I-Keep-to-Myself Potter is a tall drink of water, maybe six-four, still with a pretty good head of salt-and-pepper hair. Mr One-Slipper was shorter than that, hunched over like a toad. (*A* poison *toad, at that* is the thought that immediately rises in Andy's mind.)

He's in there, Andy thinks. *Fucking thief's in Potter's room, maybe going through Potter's drawers, looking for a little stash. Fifty or sixty rolled up in the toe of a sock, like I used to do. Or stealing Potter's radio. His fucking* rah-*dio.*

Well, and what was that to him? You passed Potter in the hallway, gave him a civil good morning or good afternoon, and what you got back was an uncivil grunt. *Bupkes*, in other words. You saw him in Lucky's, he was drinking alone, far side of the jukebox. Andy guessed you could sit down with him and he'd split a pitcher with you – Irv's little tête-à-tête with the man proved that much – but what good was that without a little chin-jaw to go along with it? Why should he, Andrew Railsback, risk the wrath of some poison toad in a bathrobe for the sake of an old grump who wouldn't give you a yes, no, or maybe?

Well . . .

Because this is his home, cheesy as it might be, that's why. Because when you saw some crazy old one-slipper fuck in search of loose cash or the easily lifted rah-dio, you didn't just turn your back and shuffle away. Because the bad feeling he got from the scurrying old elf (*the bad vibe*, his grandchildren would have said) was probably nothing but a case of the chickenshits. Because—

Suddenly Andy Railsback has an intuition that, while not a direct hit, is at least adjacent to the truth. Suppose it *is* a guy from off the street? Suppose it's one of the old guys from Maxton Elder Care? It's not that far away, and he knows for a fact that from time to time an old feller (or old gal) will get mixed up in his (or her) head and wander off the reservation. Under ordinary circumstances that person would be spotted and hauled back long before getting this far downtown – kind of hard to miss on the street in an institutional robe and single slipper – but this evening the fog has come in and the streets are all but deserted.

Look at you, Andy berates himself. *Scared half to death of a feller that's probably got ten years on you and peanut butter for brains. Wandered in here past the empty desk – not a chance in the goddamn world Fine's out front; he'll be in back reading a magazine or a stroke book – and now he's looking for his room back at Maxton's, trying every knob on the goddamn corridor, no more idea of where he is than a squirrel on a freeway ramp. Potter's probably having a beer next door* (this, at least, turns out to be true) *and left his door unlocked* (this, we may be assured, is not).

And although he's still frightened, Andy comes all the way around the corner and walks slowly toward the open door. His heart is beating fast, because half his mind is still convinced the old man is maybe dangerous. There was, after all, that bad feeling he got just from looking at the stranger's *back*—

But he goes. God help him, he does.

'Mister?' he calls when he reaches the open door. 'Hey, mister, I think you got the wrong room. That's Mr Potter's room. Don't you—'

He stops. No sense talking, because the room is empty. How is that possible?

Andy steps back and tries the knobs of 312 and 313. Both locked up tight, as he knew they would be. With that ascertained, he steps into George Potter's room and has a good look around – curiosity killed the cat, satisfaction brought him back. Potter's digs are a little larger than his, but otherwise not much different: it's a box with a high ceiling (they made places a man could stand up in back in the old days, you had to say that much for them). The single bed is sagging in the middle but neatly made. On the night table is a bottle of pills (these turn out to be an antidepressant called Zoloft) and a single framed picture of a woman. Andy thinks she took a pretty good whopping with the ugly stick, but Potter must see her differently. He has, after all, put the picture in a place where it's the first thing he looks at in the morning and the last thing he sees at night.

'Potter?' Andy asks. 'Anyone? Hello?'

He is suddenly overcome with a sense of someone standing behind him and whirls around, lips drawn back from his dentures in a grinning snarl that is half a cringe. One hand comes up to shield his face from the blow he is suddenly certain will fall . . . only there's no one there. Is he lurking behind the corner at the end of this short addendum to the main corridor? No. Andy *saw* the stranger go scurrying around that corner. No way he could have gotten behind him again . . . unless he crawled along the ceiling like some kind of fly . . .

Andy looks up there, knowing he's being absurd, giving in to the whim-whams big time, but there's no one here to see him, so what the hey? And nothing for him to see overhead, either. Just an ordinary tin ceiling, now yellowed by age and decades of cigar and cigarette smoke.

The radio – oh, excuse me all to hell, *rah*-dio – is sitting on the windowsill, unmolested. Damn fine one, too, a Bose, the kind Paul Harvey always talks about on his noon show.

Beyond it, on the other side of the dirty glass, is the fire escape.

Ah-hah! Andy thinks, and hurries across to the window. One look at the turned thumb lock and his triumphant expression fades. He peers out just the same, and sees a short stretch of wet black iron descending into the fog. No blue robe, no scaly bald pate. Of course not. The knob shaker didn't go out that way unless he had some magic trick to move the window's inside thumb lock back into place once he was on the fire escape landing.

Andy turns, stands where he is a moment, thinking, then drops to his knees and looks under the bed. What he sees is an old tin ashtray with an unopened pack of Pall Malls and a Kingsland Old-Time Lager disposable lighter in it. Nothing else except dust kittens. He puts his hand on the coverlet preparatory to standing up, and his eyes fix on the closet door. It's standing ajar.

'There,' Andy breathes, almost too low for his own ears to hear.

He gets up and crosses to the closet door. The fog may or may not come in on little cat feet, as Carl Sandburg said, but that is certainly how Andy Railsback moves across George Potter's room. His heart is beating hard again, hard enough to start the prominent vein in the center of his forehead pulsing. The man he saw is in the closet. Logic demands it. Intuition screams it. And if the doorknob shaker's just a confused old soul who wandered into the Nelson Hotel out of the fog, why hasn't he spoken to Andy? Why has he concealed himself? Because he may be old but he's not confused, that's why. No more confused than Andy is himself. The doorknob shaker's a fucking thief, and he's in the closet. He's maybe holding a knife that he has taken from the pocket of his tatty old robe. Maybe a coat hanger that he's unwound and turned into a weapon. Maybe he's just standing there in the dark, eyes wide, fingers hooked into claws. Andy no longer cares. You can scare him, you bet – he's a retired salesman, not Superman – but if you load enough tension on top of fright you turn it into anger, same as enough pressure turns coal into a diamond. And right now Andy is more pissed off than scared. He closes his fingers around the cool glass knob of the closet door. He squeezes down on it. He takes one breath . . . a second . . . steeling himself, getting ready . . . *psyching himself up*, the grandkids would say . . . one more breath, just for good luck, and . . .

With a low, stressful sound – half growl and half howl – Andy yanks the closet door wide, setting off a chatter of hangers. He crouches, hands up in fists, looking like some ancient sparring partner from the Gym Time Forgot.

'Come outta there, you fucking—'

No one there. Four shirts, one jacket, two ties, and three pairs of pants hanging like dead skin. A battered old suitcase that looks as if it has been kicked through every Greyhound Bus terminal in North America. Nothing else. Not a goddamn th—

But there is. There's something on the floor beneath the shirts. Several somethings. Almost half a dozen somethings. At first Andy Railsback either doesn't understand what he's seeing or doesn't *want* to understand. Then it gets through to him, imprints itself on his mind and memory like a hoofprint, and he tries to scream. He can't. He tries again and nothing comes out but a rusty wheeze from lungs that feel no larger than old prune skins. He tries to turn around and can't do that, either. He is sure George Potter is coming, and if Potter finds him here, Andy's life will end. He has seen something George Potter can never allow him to talk about. But he can't turn. Can't scream. Can't take his eyes from the secret in George Potter's closet.

Can't move.

Because of the fog, nearly full dark has arrived in French Landing unnaturally early; it's barely six-thirty. The blurry yellow lights of Maxton Elder Care look like the lights of a cruise ship lying becalmed at sea. In Daisy wing, home of the wonderful Alice Weathers and the far less wonderful Charles Burnside, Pete Wexler and Butch Yerxa have both gone home for the day. A broad-shouldered, peroxide blonde named Vera Hutchinson is now on the desk. In front of her is a book entitled *E-Z Minute Crosswords*. She is currently puzzling over 6 Across: *Garfield, for example*. Six letters, first is F, third is L, sixth is E. She hates these tricky ones.

There's the swoosh of a bathroom door opening. She looks up and sees Charles Burnside come shuffling out of the men's in his blue robe and a pair of yellow-and-black striped slippers that look like great fuzzy bumblebees. She recognizes them at once.

'Charlie?' she asks, putting her pencil in her crossword book and closing it.

Charlie just goes shuffling along, jaw hanging down, a long runner of drool also hanging down. But he has an unpleasant half grin on his face that Vera doesn't care for. This one may have lost most of his marbles, but the few left in his head are *mean* marbles. Sometimes she knows that Charlie Burnside genuinely doesn't hear her when she speaks (or doesn't understand her), but she's positive that sometimes he just *pretends* not to understand. She has an idea this is one of the latter times.

'Charlie, what are you doing wearing Elmer's bee slippers? You know his great-granddaughter gave those to him.'

The old man – Burny to us, Charlie to Vera – just goes shuffling along, in a direction that will eventually take him back to D18. Assuming he stays on course, that is.

'Charlie, stop.'

Charlie stops. He stands at the head of Daisy's corridor like a machine that has been turned off. His jaw hangs. The string of drool snaps, and all at once there's a little wet spot on the linoleum beside one of those absurd but amusing slippers.

Vera gets up, goes to him, kneels down before him. If she knew what we know, she'd probably be a lot less willing to put her defenseless white neck within reach of those hanging hands, which are twisted by arthritis but still powerful. But of course she does not.

She grasps the left bee slipper. 'Lift,' she says.

Charles Burnside lifts his right foot.

'Oh, quit being such a turkey,' she says. 'Other one.'

Burny lifts his left foot a little, just enough for her to get the slipper off.

'*Now* the right one.'

Unseen by Vera, who is looking at his feet, Burny pulls his penis from the fly of his loose pajama pants and pretends to piss on Vera's bowed head. His grin widens. At the same time, he lifts his right foot and she removes the other slipper. When she looks back up, Burny's wrinkled old tool is back where it belongs. He considered baptizing her, he really did, but he has created almost enough mischief for one evening. One more little chore and he'll be off to the land of dreamy dreams. He's an old monster now. He needs his rest.

'All right,' Vera says. 'Want to tell me why one of these is dirtier than the other?' No answer. She hasn't really expected one. 'Okay, beautiful. Back to your room or down to the common room, if you want. There's microwave popcorn and Jell-O pops tonight, I think. They're showing *The Sound of Music*. I'll see that these slippers get back to where they belong, and you taking them will be our little secret. Take them again and I'll have to report you, though. *Capisce?*'

Burny just stands there, vacant . . . but with that nasty

little grin lifting his wrinkled old chops. And that light in his eyes. He *capisces*, all right.

'Go on,' Vera says. 'And you better not have dropped a load on the floor in there, you old buzzard.'

Again she expects no reply, but this time she gets one. Burny's voice is low but perfectly clear. 'Keep a civil tongue, you fat bitch, or I'll eat it right out of your head.'

She recoils as if slapped. Burny stands there with his hands dangling and that little grin on his face.

'Get out of here,' she says. 'Or I really *will* report you.' And a great lot of good that would do. Charlie is one of Maxton's cash cows, and Vera knows it.

Charlie recommences his slow walk (Pete Wexler has dubbed this particular gait the Old Fucks' Shuffle), now in his bare feet. Then he turns back. The bleary lamps of his eyes regard her. 'The word you're looking for is *feline*. Garfield's a *feline*. Got it? Stupid cow.'

With that he continues his trip down the corridor. Vera stands where she is, looking at him with her own jaw hanging. She has forgotten all about her crossword puzzle.

In his room, Burny lies down on his bed and slips his hands into the small of his back. From there down he aches like a bugger. Later he will buzz for the fat old bitch, get her to bring him an ibuprofen. For now, though, he has to stay sharp. One more little trick still to do.

'Found you, Potter,' he murmurs. 'Good . . . old . . . Potsie.'

Burny hadn't been shaking doorknobs at all (not that Andy Railsback will ever know this). He had been feeling for the fellow who diddled him out of a sweet little Chicago housing deal back in the late seventies. South Side, home of the White Sox. Blacktown, in other words. Lots of federal money in that one, and several bushels of Illinois dough as well. Enough skim available to last for years, more angles than on a baseball field, but George 'Go Fuck Your Mother' Potter had gotten there first, cash had changed hands beneath the proverbial table, and Charles Burnside (or perhaps then he'd still been Carl Bierstone; it's hard to remember) had been out in the cold.

But Burny has kept track of the thief for lo these many years. (Well, not Burny himself, actually, but as we must by now have realized, this is a man with powerful friends.) Old Potsie – what his friends called him in the days when he still had a few – declared bankruptcy in La Riviere back in the nineties, and lost most of what he still had hidden away during the Great Dot-Com Wreck of Double Aught. But that's not good enough for Burny. Potsie requires further punishment, and the coincidence of that particular fuckhead washing up in this particular fuckhole of a town is just too good to pass up. Burny's principal motive – a brainless desire to keep stirring the pot, to make sure bad goes to worse – hasn't changed, but this will serve that purpose, too.

So he traveled to the Nelson, doing so in a way Jack understands and Judy Marshall has intuited, homing in on Potsie's room like some ancient bat. And when he sensed Andy Railsback behind him, he was of course delighted. Railsback will save him having to make another anonymous call, and Burny is, in truth, getting tired of doing *all* their work for them.

Now, back in his room, all comfy-cozy (except for the arthritis, that is), he turns his mind away from George Potter, and begins to Summon.

Looking up into the dark, Charles Burnside's eyes begin

to glow in a distinctly unsettling way. '*Gorg*,' he says. '*Gorg t'eelee. Dinnit a abbalah. Samman Tansy. Samman a montah a Irma. Dinnit a abbalah, Gorg. Dinnit a Ram Abbalah*.'

Gorg. Gorg, come. Serve the abbalah. Find Tansy. Find the mother of Irma. Serve the abbalah, Gorg.

Serve the Crimson King.

Burny's eyes slip closed. He goes to sleep with a smile on his face. And beneath their wrinkled lids, his eyes continue to glow like hooded lamps.

Morty Fine, the night manager of the Nelson Hotel, is half-asleep over his magazine when Andy Railsback comes bursting in, startling him so badly that Morty almost tumbles out of his chair. His magazine falls to the floor with a flat slap.

'Jesus Christ, Andy, you almost gave me a heart attack!' Morty cries. 'You ever hear of knocking, or at least clearing your goddam *throat*?'

Andy takes no notice, and Morty realizes the old fella is as white as a sheet. Maybe *he's* the one having the heart attack. It wouldn't be the first time one occurred in the Nelson.

'You gotta call the police,' Andy says. 'They're *horrible*. Dear Jesus, Morty, they're the most horrible pictures I ever saw . . . Polaroids . . . and oh man, I thought he was going to come back in . . . come back in any second . . . but at first I was just *froze*, and I . . . I . . .'

'Slow down,' Morty says, concerned. 'What are you talking about?'

Andy takes a deep breath and makes a visible effort to get himself under control. 'Have you seen Potter?' he asks. 'The guy in 314?'

'Nope,' Morty says, 'but most nights he's in Lucky's

around this time, having a few beers and maybe a hamburger. Although why anybody would eat anything in that place, I don't know.' Then, perhaps associating one ptomaine palace with another: 'Hey, have you heard what the cops found out at Ed's Eats? Trevor Gordon was by and he said—'

'Never mind.' Andy sits in the chair on the other side of the desk and stares at Morty with wet, terrified eyes. 'Call the police. Do it right now. Tell them that the Fisherman is a man named George Potter, and he lives on the third floor of the Nelson Hotel.' Andy's face tightens in a hard grimace, then relaxes again. 'Right down the hall from yours truly.'

'*Potter?* You're dreaming, Andy. That guy's nothing but a retired builder. Wouldn't hurt a fly.'

'I don't know about flies, but he hurt the *hell* out of some little kids. I seen the Polaroids he took of them. They're in his closet. They're the worst things you ever saw.'

Then Andy does something that amazes Morty and convinces him that this isn't a joke, and probably not just a mistake, either: Andy Railsback begins to cry.

Tansy Freneau, a.k.a. Irma Freneau's grieving mother, is not actually grieving yet. She knows she should be, but grief has been deferred. Right now she feels as if she is floating in a cloud of warm bright wool. The doctor (Pat Skarda's associate, Norma Whitestone) gave her five milligrams of lorazepam four or five hours ago, but that's only the start. The Holiday Trailer Park, where Tansy and Irma have lived since Cubby Freneau took off for Green Bay in ninety-eight, is handy to the Sand Bar, and she has a part-time 'thing' going with Lester Moon, one of the bartenders. The Thunder Five has dubbed Lester Moon 'Stinky Cheese' for some reason, but Tansy unfailingly calls him Lester, which he appreciates almost as much as the occasional boozy grapple in Tansy's bedroom or out back of the Bar, where there's a mattress (and a black light) in the storeroom. Around five this evening, Lester ran over with a quart of coffee brandy and four hundred milligrams of OxyContin, all considerately crushed and ready for snorting. Tansy has done half a dozen lines already, and she is cruising. Looking over old pictures of Irma and just . . . you know . . . cruising.

What a pretty baby she was, Tansy thinks, unaware that not far away, a horrified hotel clerk is looking at a very different picture of her pretty baby, a nightmare Polaroid he will never be able to forget. It is a picture Tansy herself will never have to look at, suggesting that perhaps there *is* a God in heaven.

She turns a page (GOLDEN MEMORIES has been stamped on the front of her scrapbook), and here are Tansy and Irma at the Mississippi Electrix company picnic, back when Irma was four and Mississippi Electrix was still a year away from bankruptcy and everything was more or less all right. In the photo, Irma is wading with a bunch of other tykes, her laughing face smeared with chocolate ice cream.

Looking fixedly at this snapshot, Tansy reaches for her glass of coffee brandy and takes a small sip. And suddenly, from nowhere (or the place from which all our more ominous and unconnected thoughts float out into the light of our regard), she finds herself remembering that stupid Edgar Allan Poe poem they had to memorize in the ninth grade. She hasn't thought of it in years and has no reason to now, but the words of the opening stanza rise effortlessly and perfectly in her mind. Looking at Irma, she recites them aloud in a toneless, pauseless voice that no doubt would have caused Mrs Normandie to clutch her stringy white hair and groan.

Tansy's recitation doesn't affect us that way; instead it gives us a deep and abiding chill. It is like listening to a poetry reading given by a corpse.

'Once upon a mih'nigh' dreary while I ponnered weak 'n' weary over many a quaint 'n' curris volume of forgotten lore while I nodded nearly nappin' sun'ly there came a tappin' as of someone gen'ly rappin' rappin' at my chamber door—'

At this precise moment there comes a soft rapping at the cheap fiberboard door of Tansy Freneau's Airstream. She looks up, eyes floating, lips pursed and glossed with coffee brandy.

'Les'ser? Is that you?'

It might be, she supposes. Not the TV people, at least she hopes not. She wouldn't talk to the TV people, sent them packing. She knows, in some deep and sadly cunning part of her mind, that they would lull her and comfort her only to make her look stupid in the glare of their lights, the way that the people on the *Jerry Springer Show* always end up looking stupid.

No answer . . . and then it comes again. Tap. Tap-tap.

''Tis some visitor,' she says, getting up. It's like getting up in a dream. ''Tis some visitor, I murmured, tappin' at my chamber door, only this 'n' nothin' more.'

Tap. Tap-tap.

Not like curled knuckles. It's a thinner sound than that. A sound like a single fingernail.

Or a beak.

She crosses the room in her haze of drugs and brandy, bare feet whispering on carpet that was once nubbly and is now balding: the ex-mother. She opens the door onto this foggy summer evening and sees nothing, because she's looking too high. Then something on the welcome mat rustles.

Something, some black *thing*, is looking up at her with bright, inquiring eyes. It's a raven, omigod it's Poe's *raven*, come to pay her a visit.

'Jesus, I'm trippin',' Tansy says, and runs her hands through her thin hair.

'Jesus!' repeats the crow on the welcome mat. And then, chipper as a chickadee: 'Gorg!'

If asked, Tansy would have said she was too stoned to be frightened, but this is apparently not so, because she gives out a disconcerted little cry and takes a step backward.

The crow hops briskly across the doorsill and strides onto the faded purple carpet, still looking up at her with its bright eyes. Its feathers glisten with condensed drops of mist. It bops on past her, then pauses to preen and fluff. It looks around as if to ask, *How'm I doin', sweetheart?*

'Go away,' Tansy says. 'I don't know what the fuck you are, or if you're here at all, but—'

'Gorg!' the crow insists, then spreads its wings and fleets across the trailer's living room, a charred fleck burnt off the back of the night. Tansy screams and cringes, instinctively shielding her face, but Gorg doesn't come near her. It alights on the table beside her bottle, there not being any bust of Pallas handy.

Tansy thinks: *It got disoriented in the fog, that's all. It could even be rabid, or have that Key Lime disease, whatever you call it. I ought to go in the kitchen and get the broom. Shoo it out before it shits around . . .*

But the kitchen is too far. In her current state, the kitchen seems hundreds of miles away, somewhere in the vicinity of Colorado Springs. And there's probably no crow here at all. Thinking of that goddamn poem has caused her to hallucinate, that's all . . . that, and losing her daughter.

For the first time the pain gets through the haze, and Tansy winces from its cruel and wiry heat. She remembers the little hands that sometimes pressed so tidily against the sides of her neck. The cries in the night, summoning her from sleep. The smell of her, fresh from the bath.

'Her name was Irma!' she suddenly shouts at the figment standing so boldly beside the brandy bottle. '*Irma*, not fucking Lenore, what kind of stupid name is Lenore? Let's hear you say *Irma!*'

'Irma!' the visitor croaks obediently, stunning her to silence. And its eyes. Ah! Its glittering eyes draw her, like the eyes of the Ancient Mariner in that other poem she was supposed to learn but never did. 'Irma-Irma-Irma-Irma—'

'*Stop it!*' She doesn't want to hear it after all. She was wrong. Her daughter's name out of that alien throat is foul, insupportable. She wants to put her hands over her ears and can't. They're too heavy. Her hands have joined the stove and the refrigerator (miserable half-busted thing) in Colorado Springs. All she can do is look into those glittering black eyes.

It preens for her, ruffling its ebony sateen feathers. They make a loathsome little scuttering noise all up and down its back and she thinks, *'Prophet!' said I, 'thing of evil! prophet still, if bird or devil!'*

Certainty fills her heart like cold water. 'What do you know?' she asks. 'Why did you come?'

'Know!' croaks the Crow Gorg, nodding its beak briskly up and down. 'Come!'

And does it wink? Good God, *does it wink at her?*

'Who killed her?' Tansy Freneau whispers. 'Who killed my pretty baby?'

The crow's eyes fix her, turn her into a bug on a pin. Slowly, feeling more in a dream than ever (but this *is* happening, on some level she understands that perfectly), she crosses to the table. Still the crow watches her, still the crow draws her on. *Night's Plutonian shore*, she thinks. *Night's Plutonian fuckin' shore.*

'Who? Tell me what you know!'

The crow looks up at her with its bright black eyes. Its beak opens and closes, revealing a wet red interior in tiny peeks.

'Tansy!' it croaks. 'Come!'

The strength runs out of her legs, and she drops to her knees, biting her tongue and making it bleed. Crimson drops splatter her U of W sweatshirt. Now her face is on a level with the bird's face. She can see one of its wings brushing up and down, sensuously, on the glass side of the coffee-brandy bottle. The smell of Gorg is dust and heaped dead flies and ancient urns of buried spice. Its eyes are shining black portholes looking into some other world. Hell, perhaps. Or Sheol.

'*Who?*' she whispers.

Gorg stretches its black and rustling neck until its black beak is actually in the cup of her ear. It begins to whisper, and eventually Tansy Freneau begins to nod. The light of sanity has left her eyes. And when will it return? Oh, I think we all know the answer to that one.

Can you say 'Nevermore'?

16

6:45 p.m. French Landing is fogged out, fagged out, and uneasy in its heart, but quiet. The quiet won't last. Once it has started, *slippage* never stops for long.

At Maxton's, Chipper has stayed late, and considering the leisurely (and really quite sensational) blow job being administered to him by Rebecca Vilas as he sits sprawled in his office chair, his decision to put in a little overtime isn't that surprising.

In the common room, the old folks sit transfixed by Julie Andrews and *The Sound of Music.* Alice Weathers is actually crying with happiness – *Music* is her all-time favorite movie. *Singin' in the Rain* comes close, but close never won the cigar. Among those MEC inmates who are ambulatory, only Burny is missing . . . except no one here misses him at all. Burny is deep in sleep. The spirit that now controls him – the demon, we might as well say – has its own agenda in French Landing, and it has used Burny roughly over these last few weeks (not that Burny's complaining; he is a very willing accomplice).

On Norway Valley Road, Jack Sawyer is just pulling his Dodge Ram into Henry Leyden's driveway. The fog out here is thinner, but it still turns the truck's headlamps into soft coronas.

Tonight he will recommence *Bleak House* at chapter 7 ('The Ghost's Walk') and hopefully reach the end of chapter 8 ('Covering a Multitude of Sins'). But before Dickens, he has promised to listen to the Wisconsin Rat's latest candidate for hot rotation, a number called 'Gimme Back My Dog' by Slobberbone.

'Every five years or so, another great rock-'n'-roll song comes break-dancing out of the woodwork,' Henry has told him over the phone, and Jack's damned if he can't hear the Rat screaming around the edges of his friend's voice, popping wheelies out there on the edge of darkness. 'This is a *great* rock-'n'-roll song.'

'If you say so,' Jack replies dubiously. His idea of a great rock-'n'-roll song is 'Runaround Sue,' by Dion.

At 16 Robin Hood Lane (that sweet little Cape Cod honey of a home), Fred Marshall is down on his hands and knees, wearing a pair of green rubber gloves and washing the floor. He's still got Tyler's baseball cap balanced on his head, and he's weeping.

Out at the Holiday Trailer Park, the Crow Gorg is dripping poison into the porches of Tansy Freneau's ears.

In the sturdy brick house on Herman Street where he lives with the beautiful Sarah and the equally beautiful David, Dale Gilbertson is just getting ready to head back to the office, his movements slightly slowed by two helpings of chicken pot pie and a dish of bread pudding. When the telephone rings, he is not terribly surprised. He's had that feeling, after all. His caller is Debbi Anderson, and from her first word he knows that something has popped.

He listens, nodding, asking an occasional question. His wife stands in the kitchen doorway, watching him with worried eyes. Dale bends and jots on the pad beside the phone. Sarah walks over and reads two names: Andy Railsback and M. Fine.

'You've still got Railsback on the line?' he asks.

'Yes, on hold—'

'Patch me in.'

'Dale, I don't know if I know how to do that.' Debbi sounds uncharacteristically flustered. Dale closes his eyes a moment, reminds himself that this isn't her usual job.

'Ernie's not there yet?'

'No.'

'Who is?'

'Bobby Dulac . . . I think Dit might be in the shower . . .'

'Put Bobby on,' Dale says, and is relieved when Bobby is able to patch him quickly and painlessly through to Andy Railsback in Morty Fine's office. The two men have been upstairs to room 314, and one look at the Polaroids scattered on the floor of George Potter's closet has been enough for Morty. He's now as pale as Andy himself. Maybe paler.

Outside the police station, Ernie Therriault and Reginald 'Doc' Amberson meet in the parking lot. Doc has just arrived on his old (but perfectly maintained) Harley Fat Boy. They exchange amiable greetings in the fog. Ernie Therriault is another cop – sort of – but relax: he's the last one we'll have to meet (well, there *is* an FBI agent running around here someplace, but never mind him right now; he's in Madison, and he's a fool).

Ernie is a trim sixty-five, retired from full-time police duty for almost twelve years, and still four times the cop Arnold Hrabowski will ever be. He supplements his pension by doing night dispatch at the FLPD (he doesn't sleep so well these days, thanks to a cranky prostate) and pulling private security time at First Bank of Wisconsin on Fridays, when the Wells Fargo people come at two and the Brinks people at four.

Doc looks every inch the Hells Angel, with his long

black-and-gray beard (which he sometimes braids with ribbons in the style of the pirate Edward Teach), and he brews beer for a living, but the two men get along very well. For one thing, they recognize each other's intelligence. Ernie doesn't know if Doc really *is* a doctor, but he could be. Maybe at one point he was.

'Anything changed?' Doc asks.

'Not that I know of, my friend,' Ernie says. One of the Five comes by every night, in turn, to check. Tonight Doc's got the duty.

'Mind if I walk in with you?'

'Nope,' Ernie said. 'Just as long as you respect the rule.'

Doc nods. Some of the other Fives can be pissy about the rule (especially Sonny, who's pissy about lots of stuff), but Doc abides by it: one cup of coffee or five minutes, whichever comes first, then down the road you go. Ernie, who saw plenty of *real* Hells Angels when he was a cop in Phoenix back in the seventies, appreciates how deeply patient Beezer St Pierre and his crew have been. But of course, they are *not* Hells Angels, or Pagans, or Beasts on Bikes, or any of that nonsense. Ernie doesn't know exactly *what* they are, but he knows that they listen to Beezer, and he suspects that Beezer's patience is growing thin. Ernie knows his would be by now.

'Well, then, come on in,' Ernie says, clapping the big man on the shoulder. 'Let's see what's shaking.'

Quite a lot, as it turns out.

Dale finds he is able to think quickly and clearly. His earlier fear has left him, partly because the fuckup has already happened and the case – the *official* case, anyway – has been taken away from him. Mostly because he knows he can now call on Jack if he needs to, and Jack will answer. Jack's his safety net.

He listens to Railsback's description of the Polaroids – mostly letting the old fella vent and settle a bit – and then asks a single question about the two photos of the boy.

'Yellow,' Railsback replies with no hesitation. 'The shirt was yellow. I could read the word *Kiwanis* on it. Nothing else. The . . . the blood . . .'

Dale says he understands, and tells Railsback an officer will join them shortly.

There is the sound of the phone shifting hands, and then Fine is in his ear – a fellow Dale knows and doesn't much care for. 'What if he comes back, Chief? What if Potter comes back here to the hotel?'

'Can you see the lobby from where you are?'

'No.' Petulant. 'We're in the office. I told you that.'

'Then go out front. Look busy. If he comes in—'

'I don't want to do that. If you'd seen those pitchers, you wouldn't want to do it, either.'

'You don't have to say boo to him,' Dale says. 'Just call if he goes by.'

'But—'

'Hang up the telephone, sir. I've got a lot to do.'

Sarah has put her hand on her husband's shoulder. Dale puts his free one over hers. There is a click in his ear, loud enough to sound disgruntled.

'Bobby, are you on?'

'Right here, Chief. Debbi, too, and Dit. Oh, and Ernie just walked in.' He lowers his voice. 'He's got one of those motorcycle boys with him. The one who calls himself Doc.'

Dale thinks furiously. Ernie, Debbi, Dit, and Bobby: all in uniform. Not good for what he wants. He comes to a sudden decision and says, 'Put the hogger on.'

'What?'

'You heard me.'

A moment later he's talking to Doc Amberson. 'You want to help bust the fucker who killed Armand St Pierre's little girl?'

'Hell, yes.' No hesitation.

'All right: don't ask questions and don't make me repeat myself.'

'I'm listening,' Doc says crisply.

'Tell Officer Dulac to give you the blue cell phone in evidence storage, the one we took off the doper who skipped. He'll know the one I mean.' If anyone tries to star-69 a call originating from that phone, Dale knows, they won't be able to trace it back to his shop, and that's just as well. He is, after all, supposed to be off the case.

'Blue cell phone.'

'Then walk down to Lucky's Tavern, next to the Nelson Hotel.'

'I got my bike—'

'No. *Walk.* Go inside. Buy a lottery ticket. You'll be looking for a tall man, skinny, salt-and-pepper hair, about seventy, khaki pants, maybe a khaki shirt, too. Most likely alone. His favorite roost is between the jukebox and the little hall that goes to the johns. If he's there, call the station. Just hit 911. Got all that?'

'Yeah.'

'Go. Really shuck your buns, Doctor.'

Doc doesn't even bother to say good-bye. A moment later, Bobby's back on the phone. 'What are we gonna do, Dale?'

'If he's there, we're gonna take the son of a bitch,' Dale says. He's still under control, but he can feel his heartbeat accelerating, really starting to crank. The world stands out before him with a brilliance that hasn't been there since the first murder. He can feel every finger of his wife's hand on his shoulder. He can smell her makeup and her hairspray. 'Get Tom Lund. And lay out three of the Kevlar vests.' He thinks that over, then says: 'Make it four.'

'You're going to call Hollywood?'

'Yeah,' he says, 'but we're not gonna wait for him.' On that he hangs up. Because he wants to bolt, he makes himself stand still for a moment. Takes a deep breath. Lets it out, then takes another.

Sarah grasps his hands. 'Be careful.'

'Oh yeah,' Dale says. 'You can take that to the bank.' He starts for the door.

'What about Jack?' she calls.

'I'll get him from the car,' he says without slowing. 'If God's on our side, we'll have the guy in lockup before he makes it halfway to the station.'

Five minutes later, Doc is standing at the bar in Lucky's, listening to Trace Adkins sing 'I Left Something Turned On at Home' and scratching a Wisconsin instant-winner ticket. It actually *is* a winner – ten bucks – but most of Doc's attention is focused in the direction of the juke. He bops his shaggy head a little bit, as if he's really getting off on this particular example of Shitkicker Deluxe.

Sitting at the table in the corner with a plate of spaghetti in front of him (the sauce as red as a nosebleed) and a pitcher of beer close at hand is the man he's looking for: tall even sitting down, skinny, lines grooving his tanned hound dog's face, salt-and-pepper hair neatly combed back. Doc can't really see the shirt, because the guy's got a napkin tucked into the collar, but the long leg sticking out from under the table is dressed in khaki.

If Doc was entirely sure this was the baby-killing puke who did Amy, he'd make a citizen's arrest right now – an extremely rough one. Fuck the cops and their Miranda shit. But maybe the guy's only a witness, or an accomplice, or something.

He takes his ten-spot from the bartender, turns down the suggestion that he stay for a beer, and strolls back out into the fog. Ten steps up the hill, he takes the blue cell phone from his pocket and dials 911. This time it's Debbi who answers.

'He's there,' Doc says. 'What next?'

'Bring the phone back,' she says, and hangs up.

'Well, fuck you very much,' Doc says mildly. But he'll be a good boy. He'll play by their rules. Only first—

He dials another number on the blue phone (which has one more chore to do before it passes out of our tale forever) and Bear Girl answers. 'Put him on, sweetness,' he says, hoping she won't tell him that Beezer's gone down to the Sand Bar. If the Beez ever goes down there alone, it'll be because he's after one thing. A bad thing.

But a moment later Beezer's voice is in his ear – rough, as if he's been crying. 'Yeah? What?'

'Round 'em up and get your heavyset ass down to the police station parking lot,' Doc tells him. 'I'm not a hunnert percent certain, but I think they might be getting ready to nail the motherfucker done it. I might even have seen—'

Beezer is gone before Doc can get the phone off his ear and push the OFF button. He stands in the fog, looking up at the bleary lights of the French Landing cop shop, wondering why he didn't tell Beezer and the boys to meet him outside of Lucky's. He supposes he knows the answer. If Beezer got to that old guy before the cops, spaghetti might turn out to be the old guy's last meal.

Better to wait, maybe.

Wait and see.

There's nothing but a fine mist on Herman Street, but the soup thickens almost as soon as Dale turns toward downtown. He turns on his parking lights, but they're not enough. He goes to low beams, then calls Jack's. He hears the recorded announcement start, kills the call, and dials Uncle Henry's. And Uncle Henry answers. In the background, Dale can hear a howling fuzz-tone guitar and someone growling 'Gimme back my *dog*!' over and over.

'Yes, he's just arrived,' Henry allows. 'We're currently in the Musical Appreciation phase of our evening. Literature to follow. We've reached a critical juncture in *Bleak House* – Chesney Wold, the Ghost's Walk, Mrs Rouncewell, all of that – and so unless your need is actually *urgent*—'

'It is. Put him on *now*, Unc.'

Henry sighs. '*Oui, mon capitaine*.'

A moment later he's talking to Jack, who of course agrees to come at once. This is good, but French Landing's police chief finds some of his friend's reactions a trifle puzzling. No, Jack doesn't want Dale to hold the arrest until he arrives. Very considerate of him to ask, also very considerate of Dale to have saved him a Kevlar vest (part of the law enforcement booty showered on the FLPD and thousands of other small police departments during the Reagan years), but Jack believes Dale and his men can nab George Potter without much trouble.

The truth is, Jack Sawyer seems only slightly interested in George Potter. Ditto the horrific photos, although they must certainly be authentic; Railsback has ID'd Johnny Irkenham's yellow Kiwanis Little League shirt, a detail never given to the press. Even the loathsome Wendell Green never ferreted out that particular fact.

What Jack asks about – not once but several times – is the guy Andy Railsback saw in the hallway.

'Blue robe, one slipper, and that's all I know!' Dale is finally forced to admit. 'Jesus, Jack, what does it matter? Listen, I have to get off the telephone.'

'Ding-dong,' Jack replies, equably enough, and rings off.

Dale turns into the foggy parking lot. He sees Ernie Therriault and the biker-brewer called Doc standing outside the back door, talking. They are little more than shadows in the drifting fog.

Dale's conversation with Jack has left him feeling very uneasy, as if there are huge clues and signposts that he (dullard that he is) has entirely missed. But what clues? For Christ's sake, *what* signposts? And now a dash of resentment flavors his unease. Perhaps a high-powered Lucas Davenport type like Jack Sawyer just can't believe in the obvious. Perhaps guys like him are always more interested in the dog that *doesn't* bark.

Sound travels well in the fog, and halfway to the station's back door, Dale hears motorcycle engines explode into life down by the river. Down on Nailhouse Row.

'Dale,' Ernie says. He nods a greeting as if this were any ordinary evening.

'Hey, Chief,' Doc chips in. He's smoking an unfiltered cigarette, looks to Dale like a Pall Mall or a Chesterfield. *Some doctor*, Dale thinks. 'If I may egregiously misquote Misterogers,' Doc goes on, 'it's a beautiful night in the neighborhood. Wouldn't you say?'

'You called them,' Dale says, jerking his head in the direction of the revving motorcycles. Two pairs of headlights swing into the parking lot. Dale sees Tom Lund behind the wheel of the first car. The second vehicle is almost certainly Danny Tcheda's personal. The troops are gathering once more. Hopefully this time they can avoid any cataclysmic fuckups. They better. This time they could be playing for all the marbles.

'Well, I couldn't comment on that directly,' Doc says, 'but I could ask, If they were your friends, what would you do?'

'Same damn thing,' Dale says, and goes inside.

Henry Leyden once more sits primly in the passenger seat of the Ram pickup. Tonight he's dressed in an open-collared white shirt and a pair of trim blue khakis. Slim as a male model, silvering hair combed back. Did Sydney Carton look any cooler going to the guillotine? Even in Charles Dickens's mind? Jack doubts it.

'Henry—'

'I know,' Henry says. 'Sit here in the truck like a good little boy until I'm called.'

'With the doors locked. And don't say *Oui, mon capitaine*. That one's wore out.'

'Will *affirmative* do?'

'Nicely.'

The fog thickens as they near town, and Jack dips his headlights – high beams are no good in this shit. He looks at the dashboard clock. 7:03 p.m. Things are speeding up. He's glad. Do more, think less, Jack Sawyer's recipe for E-Z care sanity.

'I'll whisk you inside as soon as they've got Potter jugged.'

'You don't expect them to have a problem with that, do you?'

'No,' Jack says, then changes the subject. 'You know, you surprised me with that Slobberbone record.' He can't really call it a song, not when the lead vocalist simply shrieked most of the lyrics at the top of his lungs. 'That was good.'

'It's the lead guitar that makes the record,' Henry says, picking up on Jack's careful use of the word. 'Surprisingly sophisticated. Usually the best you can hope for is in tune.' He unrolls his window, sticks his head out like a dog, then pulls it back in. Speaking in that same conversational voice, he says: 'The whole town reeks.'

'It's the fog. It pulls up the river's stinkiest essence.'

'No,' Henry replies matter-of-factly, 'it's death. I smell it, and I think you do, too. Only maybe not with your nose.'

'I smell it,' Jack admits.

'Potter's the wrong man.'

'I think so.'

'The man Railsback saw was a Judas goat.'

'The man Railsback saw was almost certainly the Fisherman.'

They drive in silence for a while.

'Henry?'

'Affirmative.'

'What's the best record? The best record and the best song?'

Henry thinks about it. 'Do you realize what a dreadfully personal question that is?'

'Yes.'

Henry thinks some more, then says: '"Stardust," maybe. Hoagy Carmichael. For you?'

The man behind the wheel thinks back, all the way back to when Jacky was six. His father and Uncle Morgan had been the jazz fiends; his mother had had simpler tastes. He remembers her playing the same song over and over one endless LA summer, sitting and looking out the window and smoking. *Who is that lady, Mom?* Jacky asks, and his mother says, *Patsy Cline. She died in an airplane crash.*

'"Crazy Arms,"' Jack says. 'The Patsy Cline version. Written by Ralph Mooney and Chuck Seals. That's the best record. That's the best song.'

Henry says no more for the rest of the drive. Jack is crying.

Henry can smell his tears.

Let us now take the wider view, as some politician or other no doubt said. We almost have to, because things have begun to overlap. While Beezer and the rest of the Thunder Five are arriving in the FLPD parking lot just off Sumner Street, Dale and Tom Lund and Bobby Dulac – bulky in their Kevlar vests – are double-parking in front of Lucky's. They park in the street because Dale wants plenty of room to swing the back door of the cruiser wide, so that Potter can be bundled in as fast as possible. Next door, Dit Jesperson and Danny Tcheda are at the Nelson Hotel, where they will cordon off room 314 with yellow POLICE LINE tape. Once that's done, their orders are to bring Andy Railsback and Morty Fine to the police station. Inside the police station, Ernie Therriault is calling WSP officers Brown and Black, who will arrive after the fact . . . and if they're pissed about that, good deal. At the Sand Bar, a dead-eyed Tansy Freneau has just pulled the plug on the jukebox, killing the Wallflowers. '*Listen to me, everybody!*' she cries in a voice that's not her own. '*They've got him! They've got the baby-murdering son of a bitch! His name's Potter! They'll have him up in Madison by midnight, and unless we do something, some smart lawyer will have him back out on the street by next Monday! WHO WANTS TO HELP ME DO SOMETHING ABOUT IT?*' There is a moment of silence . . . and then a roar. The half-stoned, half-drunk habitués of the Sand Bar know *exactly* what they want to do about it. Jack and Henry, meanwhile, with no fog to slow them down until they hit town, swing into the police station parking lot just behind the Thunder Five, who park in a line around Doc's Fat Boy. The lot is filling up rapidly, mostly with cops' personal vehicles. Word of the impending arrest has spread like fire in dry grass. Inside, one of Dale's crew – we need not bother with exactly which one – spots the blue cell phone Doc used outside Lucky's. This cop grabs it and ducks into the closet-sized room marked EVIDENCE STORAGE.

At the Oak Tree Inn, where he has checked in for the duration of the Fisherman case, Wendell Green is getting sullenly drunk. In spite of three double whiskeys, his neck still aches from having his camera pulled off by the biker asshole, and his gut still aches from being sucker punched by the Hollywood asshole. The parts of him that hurt most of all, however, are his pride and his pocketbook. Sawyer concealed evidence just as sure as shit sticks to a blanket. Wendell is halfway to believing that Sawyer *himself* is the Fisherman . . . but how can he prove either thing with his film gone? When the bartender says he has a call, Wendell almost tells him to stick the call up his ass. But he's a professional, goddamnit, a *professional news hawk*, and so he goes over to the bar and takes the phone.

'Green,' he growls.

'Hello, asshole,' says the cop with the blue cell phone. Wendell doesn't yet know his caller is a cop, only that it's some cheery ghoul poaching on his valuable drinking time. 'You want to print some good news for a change?'

'Good news doesn't sell papers, my pal.'

'This will. We caught the guy.'

'*What?*' In spite of the three doubles, Wendell Green is suddenly the most undrunk man on the planet.

'Did I stutter?' The caller is positively gloating, but Wendell Green no longer cares. 'We caught the Fisherman. Not the staties, not the Feebs, *us*. Name's George Potter. Early seventies. Retired builder. Had Polaroids of all three dead kids. If you hustle, you can maybe be here to snap the picture when Dale takes him inside.'

This thought – this *shining possibility* – explodes in Wendell Green's head like a firework. Such a photo could be worth five times as much as one of little Irma's corpse, because the reputable mags would want it. And TV! Also, think of this: What if someone shot the bastard as Marshal Dillon was taking him in? Given the town's mood, it's far from impossible. Wendell has a brief and brilliant memory of Lee Harvey Oswald clutching his stomach, mouth open in his dying yawp.

'Who is this?' he blurts.

'Officer Fucking Friendly,' the voice on the other end says, and clicks off.

In Lucky's Tavern, Patty Loveless is now informing those assembled (older than the Sand Bar crowd, and a good deal less interested in nonalcoholic substances) that she can't get no satisfaction and her tractor can't get no traction. George Potter has finished his spaghetti, neatly folded his napkin (which in the end had to catch only a single drop of red-sauce), and turned seriously to his beer. Sitting close to the juke as he is, he doesn't notice that the room has quieted with the entrance of three men, only one in uniform but all three armed and wearing what look too much like bulletproof vests to be anything else.

'George Potter?' someone says, and George looks up. With his glass in one hand and his pitcher of suds in the other, he is a sitting duck.

'Yeah, what about it?' he asks, and then he is snatched by the arms and shoulders and yanked from his spot. His knees connect with the bottom of the table, overturning it. The spaghetti plate and the pitcher hit the floor. The plate shatters. The pitcher, made of sterner stuff, does not. A woman screams. A man says, 'Yow!' in a low and respectful voice.

Potter holds on to his partly filled glass for a moment, and then Tom Lund plucks this potential weapon from his hand. A second later, Dale Gilbertson is snapping on the cuffs, and Dale has time to think that it's the most satisfying sound he's ever heard in his life. *His* tractor has finally gotten some traction, by God.

This deal is light-years from the snafu at Ed's; this is slick and tidy. Less than ten seconds after Dale asked the only question – 'George Potter?' – the suspect is out the door and into the fog. Tom has one elbow, Bobby the other. Dale is still rattling off the Miranda warning, sounding like an auctioneer on amphetamines, and George Potter's feet never touch the sidewalk.

Jack Sawyer is fully alive for the first time since he was twelve years old, riding back from California in a Cadillac Eldorado driven by a werewolf. He has an idea that later on he will pay a high price for this regained vividness, but he hopes he will just button his lip and fork over when the time comes. Because the rest of his adult life now seems so *gray*.

He stands outside his truck, looking in the window at Henry. The air is dank and already charged with excitement. He can hear the blue-white parking lot lights sizzling, like something frying in hot juices.

'Henry.'

'Affirmative.'

'Do you know the hymn "Amazing Grace"?'

'Of course I do. Everyone knows "Amazing Grace."'

Jack says, '"Was blind but now I see." I understand that now.'

Henry turns his blind, fearfully intelligent face toward Jack. He is smiling. It is the second-sweetest smile Jack has ever seen. The blue ribbon still goes to Wolf, that dear friend of his wandering twelfth autumn. Good old Wolf, who liked everything right here and now.

'You're back, aren't you?'

Standing in the parking lot, our old friend grins. 'Jack's back, that's affirmative.'

'Then go do what you came back to do,' Henry says.

'I want you to roll up the windows.'

'And not be able to hear? I think not,' Henry tells him, pleasantly enough.

More cops are coming, and this time the blue lights of the lead car are flashing and the siren is blurping. Jack detects a celebratory note to those little blurps and decides he doesn't have time to stand here arguing with Henry about the Ram's windows.

He heads for the back door of the police station, and two of the blue-white arcs cast his shadow double on the fog, one dark head north and one south.

Part-time officers Holtz and Nestler pull in behind the car bearing Gilbertson, Lund, Dulac, and Potter. We don't care much about Holtz and Nestler. Next in line is Jesperson and Tcheda, with Railsback and Morton Fine in the back seat (Morty is complaining about the lack of knee room). We care about Railsback, but he can wait. Next into the lot – oh, this is interesting, if not entirely unexpected: Wendell Green's beat-up red Toyota, with the man himself behind the wheel. Around his neck is his backup camera, a Minolta that'll keep taking pictures as long as Wendell keeps pressing the button. No one from the Sand Bar – not yet – but there *is* one more car waiting to turn into the already crowded lot. It's a discreet green Saab with a POLICE POWER sticker on the left side of the bumper and one reading HUGS NOT DRUGS on the right. Behind the wheel of the Saab, looking stunned but determined to do the right thing (whatever the right thing might be), is Arnold 'the Mad Hungarian' Hrabowski.

Standing in a line against the brick wall of the police station are the Thunder Five. They wear identical denim vests with gold **5**'s on the left breast. Five sets of meaty arms are crossed on five broad chests. Doc, Kaiser Bill, and Sonny wear their hair in thick ponytails. Mouse's is cornrowed tonight. And Beezer's floods down over his shoulders, making him look to Jack a little like Bob Seger in his prime. Earrings twinkle. Tats flex on huge biceps.

'Armand St Pierre,' Jack says to the one closest the door. 'Jack Sawyer. From Ed's?' He holds out his hand and isn't exactly surprised when Beezer only looks at it. Jack smiles pleasantly. 'You helped big-time out there. Thanks.'

Nothing from the Beez.

'Is there going to be trouble with the intake of the prisoner, do you think?' Jack asks. He might be asking if Beezer thinks it will shower after midnight.

Beezer watches over Jack's shoulder as Dale, Bobby, and Tom help George Potter from the back of the cruiser and begin walking him briskly toward the back door. Wendell Green raises his camera, then is nearly knocked off his feet by Danny Tcheda, who doesn't even have the pleasure of seeing which asshole he's bumped. 'Watch it, dickweed,' Wendell squawks.

Beezer, meanwhile, favors Jack – if that is the word – with

a brief, cold glance. 'Well now,' he says. 'We'll have to see how it shakes out, won't we?'

'Indeed we will,' Jack agrees. He sounds almost happy. He pushes in between Mouse and Kaiser Bill, making himself a place: the Thunder Five Plus One. And perhaps because they sense he doesn't fear them, the two wide-boys make room. Jack crosses his own arms over his chest. If he had a vest, an earring, and a tattoo, he really would fit right in.

The prisoner and his custodians kill the distance between the car and the building quickly. Just before they reach it, Beezer St Pierre, spiritual leader of the Thunder Five and father of Amy, whose liver and tongue were eaten, steps in front of the door. His arms are still folded. In the heartless glare of the parking lot lights, his massive biceps are blue.

Bobby and Tom suddenly look like guys with a moderate case of the flu. Dale looks stony. And Jack continues to smile gently, arms placidly crossed, seeming to gaze everywhere and nowhere at once.

'Get out of the way, Beezer,' Dale says. 'I want to book this man.'

And what of George Potter? Is he stunned? Resigned? Both? It's hard to tell. But when Beezer's bloodshot blue eyes meet Potter's brown ones, Potter does not drop his gaze. Behind him, the lookie-loos in the parking lot fall silent. Standing between Danny Tcheda and Dit Jesperson, Andy Railsback and Morty Fine are gawking. Wendell Green raises his camera and then holds his breath like a sniper who's lucked into a shot – just one, mind you – at the commanding general.

'Did you kill my daughter?' Beezer asks. The gentle inquiry is somehow more terrible than any raw yell could have been, and the world seems to hold its breath. Dale makes no move. In that moment he seems as frozen as the rest of them. The world waits, and the only sound is a low, mournful hoot from some fogbound boat on the river.

'Sir, I never killed no one,' Potter says. He speaks softly and without emphasis. Although he has expected nothing else, the words still box Jack's heart. There is an unexpected painful dignity in them. It's as if George Potter is speaking for all the lost good men of the world.

'Stand aside, Beezer,' Jack says gently. 'You don't want to hurt this guy.'

And Beezer, looking suddenly not at all sure of himself, does stand aside.

Before Dale can get his prisoner moving again, a raucously cheerful voice – it can only be Wendell's – yells out: 'Hey! Hey, Fisherman! Smile for the camera!'

They all look around, not just Potter. They have to; that cry is as insistent as fingernails dragged slowly down a slate blackboard. White light strobes the foggy parking lot – one! two! three! four! – and Dale snarls. 'Aw, fuck me till I cry! Come on, you guys! Jack! Jack, I want you!'

From behind them, one of the other cops calls, 'Dale! You want me to grab this creep?'

'Leave him alone!' Dale shouts, and bulls his way inside. It's not until the door is closed behind him and he's in the lower hall with Jack, Tom, and Bobby that Dale realizes how certain he was that Beezer would simply snatch the old man away from him. And then crack his neck like a chicken bone.

'Dale?' Debbi Anderson calls uncertainly from halfway down the stairs. 'Is everything all right?'

Dale looks at Jack, who still has his arms crossed over his chest and is still smiling his little smile. 'I think it is,' Dale says. 'For now.'

★

Twenty minutes later, Jack and Henry (the latter gentleman retrieved from the truck and still reet-petite) sit in Dale's office. Beyond the closed door, the ready room roars with conversation and laughter: almost every cop on the FLPD force is out there, and it sounds like a goddamn New Year's Eve party. There are occasional shouts and smacking sounds that can only be relieved boys (and girls) in blue high-fiving each other. In a little while Dale will put a stop to that shit, but for now he's content to let them go ahead. He understands how they feel, even though he no longer feels that way himself.

George Potter has been printed and stuck in a cell upstairs to think things over. Brown and Black of the State Police are on their way. For now, that is enough. As for triumph . . . well, something about his friend's smile and his faraway eyes have put triumph on hold.

'I didn't think you were going to give Beezer his moment,' Jack says. 'It's a good thing you did. There might have been trouble right here in River City if you'd tried to face him down.'

'I suppose I have a better idea tonight of how he feels,' Dale replies. 'I lost track of my own kid tonight, and it scared the living shit out of me.'

'David?' Henry cries, leaning forward. 'Is David okay?'

'Yeah, Uncle Henry, Dave's fine.'

Dale returns his gaze to the man who now lives in his father's house. He's remembering the first time Jack ever laid eyes on Thornberg Kinderling. Dale had at that point known Jack only nine days – long enough to form some favorable opinions, but not long enough to realize how really extraordinary Jack Sawyer was. That was the day Janna Massengale at the Taproom told Jack about the trick Kinderling did when he was getting squiffy, that little trick of pinching his nostrils shut with his palm turned out to the world.

They had just arrived back at the police station from interviewing Janna, Dale in his personal unit that day, and he'd touched Jack on the shoulder just as Jack was about to get out of the car. 'Speak a name, see the face it belongs to before suppertime, that's what my mother used to say.' He pointed down to Second Street, where a broad-shouldered bald fellow had just come out of News 'n Notions, a newspaper under his arm and a fresh deck of smokes in his hand. 'That's Thornberg Kinderling, his very own self.'

Jack had bent forward without speaking, looking with the sharpest (and perhaps the most merciless) eyes Dale had ever seen in his life.

'Do you want to approach him?' Dale had asked.

'No. Hush.'

And Jack simply sat with one leg in Dale's car and one out of it, not moving, eyes narrowed. So far as Dale could tell, he didn't even breathe. Jack watched Kinderling open his cigarettes, tap one out, put it in his mouth, and light it. He watched Kinderling glance at the headline of the *Herald* and then saunter to his own car, an all-wheel-drive Subaru. Watched him get in. Watched him drive away. And by that time, Dale realized he was holding his own breath.

'Well?' he'd asked when the Kinderling-mobile was gone. 'What do you think?'

And Jack had said, 'I think he's the guy.'

Only Dale had known better. Even then he had known better. Jack was saying *I think* only because he and Chief Dale Gilbertson of French Landing, Wisconsin, were still on short terms, getting-to-know-you, getting-to-work-with-you terms. What he had meant was *I know*. And although that was impossible, Dale had quite believed him.

Now, sitting in his office with Jack directly across the

desk from him – his reluctant but scarily gifted deputy – Dale asks, 'What do you think? Did he do it?'

'Come on, Dale, how can I—'

'Don't waste my time, Jack, because those assholes from WSP are going to be here any minute and they'll take Potter heigh-ho over the hills. You knew it was Kinderling the second you looked at him, and you were halfway down the block. You were close enough to Potter when I brought him in to count the hairs in his nose. So what do you think?'

Jack is quick, at least; spares him the suspense and just administers the chop. 'No,' he says. 'Not Potter. Potter's not the Fisherman.'

Dale has known that Jack believes this – knew it from his face outside – but hearing it is still an unhappy thump. He sits back, disappointed.

'Deduction or intuition?' Henry asks.

'Both,' Jack says. 'And stop looking like I plugged your mother, Dale. You may still have the key to this thing.'

'Railsback?'

Jack makes a seesawing gesture with one hand – maybe, maybe not, it says. 'Railsback probably saw what the Fisherman wanted him to see . . . although the single slipper is intriguing, and I want to ask Railsback about it. But if Mr One-Slipper *was* the Fisherman, why would he lead Railsback – and us – to Potter?'

'To get us off his trail,' Dale says.

'Oh, have we been on it?' Jack asks politely, and when neither of them answers: 'But say he *thinks* we're on his trail. I can almost buy that, especially if he just remembered some goof he might have made.'

'Nothing back yet on the 7-Eleven phone one way or the other, if that's what you're thinking of,' Dale tells him.

Jack appears to ignore this. His eyes gaze off into the middle distance. That little smile is back on his face. Dale looks at Henry and sees Henry looking at Jack. Unc's smile is easier to read: relief and delight. *Look at that*, Dale thinks. *He's doing what he was built to do. By God, even a blind man can see it.*

'Why Potter?' Jack finally repeats. 'Why not one of the Thunder Five, or the Hindu at the 7-Eleven, or Ardis Walker down at the bait shop? Why not Reverend Hovdahl? What motive usually surfaces when you uncover a frame job?'

Dale thinks it over. 'Payback,' he says at last. 'Revenge.'

In the ready room, a phone rings. 'Shut up, shut up!' Ernie bellows to the others. 'Let's try to act professional here for thirty seconds or so!'

Jack, meanwhile, is nodding at Dale. 'I think I need to question Potter, and rather closely.'

Dale looks alarmed. 'Then you better get on it right away, before Brown and Black—' He comes to a halt, frowning, with his head cocked. A rumbling sound has impinged on his attention. It's low, but rising. 'Uncle Henry, what's that?'

'Motors,' Henry says promptly. 'A lot of them. They're east of here, but coming this way. Edge of town. And I don't know if you've noticed this, but it sounds like the party next door is like, over, dude.'

As if this were a cue, Ernie Therriault's distressed cry comes through the door. 'Ohhhh, *shit*.'

Dit Jesperson: 'What's—'

Ernie: 'Get the chief. Aw, never mind, I'll—' There is a single perfunctory knock and then Ernie's looking in at the brain trust. He's as collected and soldierly as ever, but his cheeks have paled considerably beneath his summer tan, and a vein is pulsing in the middle of his forehead.

'Chief, I just took a call on the 911, twenty was the Sand Bar?'

'*That* hole,' Dale mutters.

'Caller was the bartender. Says about fifty to seventy people are on their way.' By now the sound of approaching engines is very loud. It sounds to Henry like the Indy 500 just before the pace car runs for dear life and the checkered flag drops.

'Don't tell me,' Dale says. 'What do I need to make my day complete? Let me think. They're coming to take my prisoner.'

'Umm, yes, sir, that's what the caller said,' Ernie agrees. Behind him, the other cops are silent. In that moment they don't look like cops at all to Dale. They look like nothing but dismayed faces crudely drawn on a dozen or so white balloons (also two black ones – can't forget Pam Stevens and Bob Holtz). The sound of the engines continues to grow. 'Also might want to know one other thing the caller said?'

'Christ, *what?*'

'Said the, um . . .' Ernie searches for a word that isn't *mob*. 'The protest group was being led by the Freneau girl's mom?'

'Oh . . . my . . . *Christ*,' Dale says. He gives Jack a look of sick panic and utter frustration – the look of a man who knows he is dreaming but can't seem to wake up no matter how hard he tries. 'If I lose Potter, Jack, French Landing is going to be the lead story on CNN tomorrow morning.'

Jack opens his mouth to reply, and the cell phone in his pocket picks that moment to start up its annoying tweet.

Henry Leyden immediately crosses his arms and tucks his hands into his armpits. 'Don't hand it to me,' he says. 'Cell phones give you cancer. We agreed on that.'

Dale, meanwhile, has left the room. As Jack digs for the cell phone (thinking someone has picked a cataclysmically shitty time to ask him about his network television preferences), Henry follows his nephew, walking briskly with his hands now held slightly out, fingers gently fluttering the air, seeming to read the currents for obstacles. Jack hears Dale saying that if he sees *a single drawn weapon*, the person who drew it will join Arnie Hrabowski on the suspension list. Jack is thinking exactly one thing: no one is taking Potter anywhere until Jack Sawyer has had time to put a few pointed questions. No way.

He flicks the cell phone open and says, 'Not now, whoever you are. We've got—'

'Hidey-ho, Travelin' Jack,' says the voice from the phone, and for Jack Sawyer the years once more roll away.

'Speedy?'

'The very one,' Speedy says. Then the drawl is gone. The voice becomes brisk and businesslike. 'And as one coppiceman to another, son, I think you ought to visit Chief Gilbertson's private bathroom. Right now.'

Outside, there are enough vehicles arriving to shake the building. Jack has a bad feeling about this; has since he heard Ernie say who was leading the fools' parade.

'Speedy, I don't exactly have the time to visit the facilities right n—'

'You haven't got time to visit anyplace else,' Speedy replies coldly. Only now he's the other one. The hard boy named Parkus. 'What you're gonna find there you can use twice. But if you don't use it almighty quick the first time, you won't need it the second time. Because that man is gonna be up a lamppost.'

And just like that, Speedy is gone.

⋆

When Tansy leads the willing patrons into the Sand Bar's parking lot, there is none of the carnival raucousness that was the keynote of the cluster fuck at Ed's Eats & Dawgs. Although most of the folks we met at Ed's have been spending the evening in the Bar, getting moderately to seriously tanked, they are quiet, even funereal, as they follow Tansy out and fire up their cars and pickups. But it's a savage funereality. She has taken something in from Gorg – some stone powerful poison – and passed it along to them.

In the belt of her slacks is a single crow feather.

Doodles Sanger takes her arm and guides her sweetly to Teddy Runkleman's International Harvester pickup. When Tansy heads for the truck bed (which already holds two men and one hefty female in a white rayon waitress's uniform), Doodles steers her toward the cab. 'No, honey,' Doodles says, 'you sit up there. Be comfy.'

Doodles wants that last place in the truck bed. She's spotted something, and knows just what to do with it. Doodles is quick with her hands, always has been.

The fog isn't thick this far from the river, but after two dozen cars and trucks have spun out of the Bar's dirt parking lot, following Teddy Runkleman's dented, one-taillight I.H., you can barely see the tavern. Inside, only half a dozen people are left – these were somehow immune to Tansy's eerily powerful voice. One of them is Stinky Cheese, the bartender. Stinky has a lot of liquid assets to protect out here and isn't going anywhere. When he calls 911 and speaks to Ernie Therriault, it will be mostly in the spirit of petulance. If he can't go along and enjoy the fun, by God, at least he can spoil it for the rest of those monkeys.

Twenty vehicles leave the Sand Bar. By the time the caravan passes Ed's Eats (the lane leading to it cordoned off by yellow tape) and the NO TRESPASSING sign alongside the overgrown lane to that queer forgotten house (not cordoned off; not even noticed, for that matter), the caravan has grown to thirty. There are fifty cars and trucks rolling down both lanes of Highway 35 by the time the mob reaches Goltz's, and by the time it passes the 7-Eleven, there must be eighty vehicles or more, and maybe two hundred and fifty people. Credit this unnaturally rapid swelling to the ubiquitous cell phone.

Teddy Runkleman, oddly silent (he is, in fact, afraid of the pallid woman sitting beside him – her snarling mouth and her wide, unblinking eyes), brings his old truck to a halt in front of the FLPD parking lot entrance. Sumner Street is steep here, and he sets the parking brake. The other vehicles halt behind him, filling the street from side to side, rumbling through rusty mufflers and blatting through broken exhaust pipes. Misaligned headlights stab the fog like searchlight beams at a movie premiere. The night's dank wet-fish smell has been overlaid with odors of burning gas, boiling oil, and cooking clutch lining. After a moment, doors begin to open and then clap shut. But there is no conversation. No yelling. No indecorous *yee-haw* whooping. Not tonight. The newcomers stand in clusters around the vehicles that brought them, watching as the people in the back of Teddy's truck either jump over the sides or slip off the end of the tailgate, watching as Teddy crosses to the passenger door, at this moment as attentive as a young man arriving with his date at the junior prom, watching as he helps down the slim young woman who has lost her daughter. The mist seems to outline her somehow, and give her a bizarre electric aura, the same blue of the sodium lights on Beezer's upper arms. The crowd gives out a collective (and weirdly amorous) sigh when it sees her. She is what connects them. All her life, Tansy Freneau has been the forgotten one – even Cubby Freneau forgot her eventually, running off to Green Bay and leaving her here to work odd jobs and collect the ADC. Only Irma remembered her, only Irma cared, and now Irma is dead. Not here to see (unless she's looking down from heaven, Tansy thinks in some distant and ever-receding part of her mind) her mother suddenly idolized. Tansy Freneau has tonight become the dearest subject of French Landing's eye and heart. Not its mind, because its mind is temporarily gone (perhaps in search of its conscience), but certainly of its eye and heart, yes. And now, as delicately as the girl she once was, Doodles Sanger approaches this woman of the hour. What Doodles spotted lying on the floor of Teddy's truck bed was an old length of rope, dirty and oily but thick enough to do the trick. Below Doodles's petite fist hangs the noose that her clever hands have fashioned on the ride into town. She hands it to Tansy, who holds it up in the misty light.

The crowd lets out another sigh.

Noose raised, looking like a female Diogenes in search of an honest man rather than of a cannibal in need of lynching, Tansy walks – delicate herself in her jeans and bloodstained sweatshirt – into the parking lot. Teddy, Doodles, and Freddy Saknessum walk behind her, and behind them come the rest. They move toward the police station like the tide.

The Thunder Five are still standing with their backs to the brick wall and their arms folded. 'What the fuck do we do?' Mouse asks.

'I don't know about you,' Beezer says, 'but I'm gonna stand here until they grab me, which they probably will.' He's looking at the woman with the upraised noose. He's a big boy and he's been in a lot of hard corners, but this chick frightens him with her blank, wide eyes, like the eyes of a statue. And there's something stuck in her belt. Something black. Is it a knife? Some kind of dagger? 'And I'm not gonna fight, because it won't work.'

'They'll lock the door, right?' Doc asks nervously. 'I mean, the cops'll lock the door.'

'I imagine,' Beezer says, never taking his eyes from Tansy Freneau. 'But if these folks want Potter, they'll have him on the half shell. *Look* at 'em, for Christ's sake. There's a couple of hundred.'

Tansy stops, the noose still held up. 'Bring him out,' she says. Her voice is louder than it should be, as if some doctor has cunningly hidden an amplifying gadget in her throat. 'Bring him out. Give us the killer!'

Doodles joins in. 'Bring him out!'

And Teddy. '*Give us the killer!*'

And Freddy. '*Bring him out! Give us the killer!*'

And then the rest. It could almost be the sound track of George Rathbun's *Badger Barrage*, only instead of '*Block that kick!*' or '*On Wisconsin!*' they are screaming, *'BRING HIM OUT! GIVE US THE KILLER!'*

'They're gonna take him,' Beezer murmurs. He turns to his troops, his eyes both fierce and frightened. Sweat stands out on his broad forehead in large perfect drops. 'When she's got 'em pumped up to high, she'll come and they'll be right on her ass. Don't run, don't even unfold your arms. And when they grab you, let it happen. If you want to see daylight tomorrow, *let it happen.*'

The crowd stands knee-deep in fog like spoiled skim milk, chanting, *'BRING HIM OUT! GIVE US THE KILLER!'*

Wendell Green is chanting right along with them, but that doesn't keep him from continuing to take pictures.

Because shit, this is the story of a lifetime.

From the door behind Beezer, there's a click. *Yeah, they locked it*, he thinks. *Thanks, you whores.*

But it's the latch, not the lock. The door opens. Jack Sawyer steps out. He walks past Beezer without looking or reacting as Beez mutters, 'Hey, man, I wouldn't go near her.'

Jack advances slowly but not hesitantly into the no-man's-land between the building and the mob with the woman standing at its head, Lady Liberty with the upraised hangman's noose instead of a torch in her hand. In his simple gray collarless shirt and dark pants, Jack looks like a cavalier from some old romantic tale advancing to propose marriage. The flowers he holds in his own hand add to this impression. These tiny white blooms are what Speedy left for him beside the sink in Dale's bathroom, a cluster of impossibly fragrant white blossoms.

They are lilies of the vale, and they are from the Territories. Speedy left him no explanation about how to use them, but Jack needs none.

The crowd falls silent. Only Tansy, lost in the world Gorg has made for her, continues to chant: *'Bring him out! Give us the killer!'* She doesn't stop until Jack is directly in front of her, and he doesn't kid himself that it's his handsome face or dashing figure that ends the too loud repetition. It is the smell of the flowers, their sweet and vibrant smell the exact opposite of the meaty stench that hung over Ed's Eats.

Her eyes clear . . . a little, at least.

'Bring him out,' she says to Jack. Almost a question.

'No,' he says, and the word is filled with heartbreaking tenderness. 'No, dear.'

Behind them, Doodles Sanger suddenly thinks of her father for the first time in maybe twenty years and begins to weep.

'Bring him out,' Tansy pleads. Now her own eyes are filling. 'Bring out the monster who killed my pretty baby.'

'If I had him, maybe I would,' Jack says. 'Maybe I would at that.' Although he knows better. 'But the guy we've got's not the guy you want. He's not the one.'

'But Gorg said—'

Here is a word he knows. One of the words Judy Marshall tried to eat. Jack, not in the Territories but not entirely in this world right now either, reaches forward and plucks the feather from her belt. 'Did Gorg give you this?'

'Yes—'

Jack lets it drop, then steps on it. For a moment he thinks – *knows* – that he feels it buzzing angrily beneath the sole of his shoe, like a half-crushed wasp. Then it stills. 'Gorg lies, Tansy. Whatever Gorg is, he lies. The man in there is not the one.'

Tansy lets out a great wail and drops the rope. Behind her, the crowd sighs.

Jack puts his arm around her and again he thinks of George Potter's painful dignity; he thinks of all the lost, struggling along without a single clean Territories dawn to light their way. He hugs her to him, smelling sweat and grief and madness and coffee brandy.

In her ear, Jack whispers: 'I'll catch him for you, Tansy.'

She stiffens. 'You . . .'

'Yes.'

'You . . . promise?'

'Yes.'

'He's not the one?'

'No, dear.'

'You swear?'

Jack hands her the lilies and says, 'On my mother's name.'

She lowers her nose to the flowers and inhales deeply. When her head comes up again, Jack sees that the danger has left her, but not the insanity. She's one of the lost ones now. Something has gotten to her. Maybe if the Fisherman is caught, it will leave her. Jack would like to believe that.

'Someone needs to take this lady home,' Jack says. He speaks in a mild, conversational voice, but it still carries to the crowd. 'She's very tired and full of sadness.'

'I'll do it,' Doodles says. Her cheeks gleam with tears. 'I'll take her in Teddy's truck, and if he don't give me the keys, I'll knock him down. I—'

And that's when the chant starts again, this time from back in the crowd: '*Bring him out! Give us the killer! Give us the Fisherman! Bring out the Fisherman!*' For a moment it's a solo job, and then a few other hesitant voices begin to join in and lend harmony.

Still standing with his back against the bricks, Beezer St Pierre says: 'Ah, shit. Here we go again.'

Jack forbade Dale to come out into the parking lot with him, saying that the sight of Dale's uniform might set off the crowd. He didn't mention the little bouquet of flowers he was holding, and Dale barely noticed them; he was too terrified of losing Potter to Wisconsin's first lynching of the new millennium. He followed Jack downstairs, however, and has now commandeered the peephole in the door by right of seniority.

The rest of the FLPD is still upstairs, looking out of the ready-room windows. Henry has ordered Bobby Dulac to give him a running play-by-play. Even in his current state of worry about Jack (Henry thinks there's at least a 40 percent chance the mob will either trample him or tear him apart), Henry is amused and flattered to realize that Bobby is doing George Rathbun without even realizing it.

'Okay, Hollywood's out there . . . he approaches the woman . . . no sign of fear . . . the rest of them are quiet . . . Jack and the woman appear to be talking . . . and holy jeezum, he's givin' her a bouquet of flowers! What a ploy!'

'Ploy' is one of George Rathbun's favorite sports terms, as in *The Brew Crew's hit-and-run ploy failed yet again last night at Miller Park.*

'She's *turnin' away!*' Bobby yells jubilantly. He grabs Henry's shoulder and shakes it. 'Hot damn, I think it's over! *I think Jack turned her off!*'

'Even a blind man could see he turned her off,' Henry says.

'Just in time, too,' Bobby says. 'Here's Channel Five and there's another truck with one of those big orange poles on it . . . Fox-Milwaukee, I think . . . and—'

'*Bring him out!*' a voice outside begins yelling. It sounds cheated and indignant. '*Give us the killer! Give us the Fisherman!*'

'Oh nooo!' Bobby says, even now sounding like George Rathbun, telling his morning-after audience how another Badger rally had started to fizzle. 'Not nowwww, not with the TV here! That's—'

'Bring out the Fisherman!'

Henry already knows who that is. Even through two layers of chicken-wire-reinforced glass, that high, yapping cry is impossible to mistake.

Wendell Green understands his job – don't ever make the mistake of thinking he doesn't. His job is to *report* the news, to *analyze* the news, to sometimes *photojournalize* the news. His job is not to *make* the news. But tonight he can't help it. This is the second time in the last twelve hours that a career maker of a story has been extended to his grasping, pleading hands, only to be snatched away at the last second.

'Bring him out!' Wendell bawls. The raw strength in his voice surprises, then thrills him. *'Give us the killer! Give us the Fisherman!'*

The sound of other voices joining in with his provides an incredible rush. It is, as his old college roommate used to say, a real zipper buster. Wendell takes a step forward, his chest swelling, his cheeks reddening, his confidence building. He's vaguely aware that the Action News Five truck is rolling slowly toward him through the crowd. Soon there will be 10-k's and 5-k's shining through the fog; soon there will be TV cameras rolling tape by their harsh light. So what? If the woman in the blood-spattered sweatshirt was in the end too chicken to stand up for her own kid, Wendell will do it for her! Wendell Green, shining exemplar of civic responsibility! Wendell Green, *leader of the people!*

He begins to pump his camera up and down. It's exhilarating. Like being back in college! At a Skynyrd concert! Stoned! It's like—

There is a huge flash in front of Wendell Green's eyes. Then the lights go out. All of them.

'*ARNIE HIT HIM WITH HIS FLASHLIGHT!*' Bobby is screaming.

He grabs Dale's blind uncle by the shoulders and whirls him in a delirious circle. A thick aroma of Aqua Velva descends toward Henry, who knows Bobby's going to kiss him on both cheeks, French style, a second before Bobby actually does this.

And when Bobby's narration resumes, he sounds as transported as George Rathbun on those rare occasions when the local sports teams actually buck the odds and grab the gold.

'Can you believe it, the Mad Hungarian hit him with his ever-lovin' flashlight and . . . GREEN'S DOWN! THE FUCKIN' HUNGARIAN HAS PUT EVERYONE'S FAVORITE ASSHOLE REPORTER ON THE MAT! WAY TO GO, HRABOWSKI!'

All around them, cops are cheering at the tops of their lungs. Debbi Anderson starts chanting 'We Are the Champions,' and other voices quickly lend support.

These are strange days in French Landing, Henry thinks. He stands with his hands in his pockets, smiling, listening to the bedlam. There's no lie in the smile; he's happy. But he's also uneasy in his heart. Afraid for Jack.

Afraid for all of them, really.

'That was good work, man,' Beezer tells Jack. 'I mean, balls to the wall.'

Jack nods. 'Thanks.'

'I'm not going to ask you again if that was the guy. You say he's not, he's not. But anything we can do to help you find the right one, you just call us.'

The other members of the Thunder Five rumble assent; Kaiser Bill gives Jack a friendly bop on the shoulder. It will probably leave a bruise.

'Thanks,' Jack says again.

Before he can knock on the door, it's opened. Dale grabs him and gives him a crushing embrace. When their chests touch, Jack can feel Dale's heart beating hard and fast.

'You saved my ass,' Dale says into his ear. 'Anything I can do—'

'You can do something, all right,' Jack says, pulling him inside. 'I saw another cop car behind the news trucks. Couldn't tell for sure, but I think this one was blue.'

'Oh-oh,' Dale says.

'Oh-oh is right. I need at least twenty minutes with Potter. It might not get us anything, but it might get us a lot. Can you hold off Brown and Black for twenty minutes?'

Dale gives his friend a grim little smile. 'I'll see you get half an hour. Minimum.'

'That's great. And the 911 tape of the Fisherman's call, do you still have that?'

'It went with the rest of the evidence we were holding after Brown and Black took the case. A trooper picked it up this afternoon.'

'Dale, *no!*'

'Easy, big boy. I've got a cassette copy, safe in my desk.'

Jack pats his chest. 'Don't scare me that way.'

'Sorry,' Dale says, thinking, *Seeing you out there, I wouldn't have guessed you were afraid of anything.*

Halfway up the stairs, Jack remembers Speedy telling him he could use what had been left in the bathroom twice . . . but he has given the flowers to Tansy Freneau. Shit. Then he cups his hands over his nose, inhales, and smiles.

Maybe he still has them after all.

17

George Potter is sitting on the bunk in the third holding cell down a short corridor that smells of piss and disinfectant. He's looking out the window at the parking lot, which has lately been the scene of so much excitement and which is still full of milling people. He doesn't turn at the sound of Jack's approaching footfalls.

As he walks, Jack passes two signs. ONE CALL MEANS ONE CALL, reads the first. AA MEETINGS MON. AT 7 P.M., NA MEETINGS THURS. AT 8 P.M., reads the second. There's a dusty drinking fountain and an ancient fire extinguisher, which some wit has labeled LAUGHING GAS.

Jack reaches the bars of the cell and raps on one with his house key. Potter at last turns away from the window. Jack, still in that state of hyperawareness that he now recognizes as a kind of Territorial residue, knows the essential truth of the man at a single look. It's in the sunken eyes and the dark hollows beneath them; it's in the sallow cheeks and the slightly hollowed temples with their delicate nestles of veins; it's in the too sharp prominence of the nose.

'Hello, Mr Potter,' he says. 'I want to talk to you, and we have to make it fast.'

'They wanted me,' Potter remarks.

'Yes.'

'Maybe you should have let 'em take me. Another three-four months, I'm out of the race anyway.'

In his breast pocket is the Mag-card Dale has given him, and Jack uses it to unlock the cell door. There's a harsh buzzing as it trundles back on its short track. When Jack removes the key, the buzzing stops. Downstairs in the ready room, an amber light marked H.C. 3 will now be glowing.

Jack comes in and sits down on the end of the bunk. He has put his key ring away, not wanting the metallic smell to corrupt the scent of lilies. 'Where have you got it?'

Without asking how Jack knows, Potter raises one large gnarled hand – a carpenter's hand – and touches his midsection. Then he lets it drop. 'Started in the gut. That was five years ago. I took the pills and the shots like a good boy. La Riviere, that was. That stuff . . . man, I was throwing up ever'where. Corners and just about ever'where. Once I threw up in my own bed and didn't even know it. Woke up the next morning with puke drying on my chest. You know anything about that, son?'

'My mother had cancer,' Jack says quietly. 'When I was twelve. Then it went away.'

'She get five years?'

'More.'

'Lucky,' Potter says. 'Got her in the end, though, didn't it?'

Jack nods.

Potter nods back. They're not quite friends yet, but it's edging that way. It's how Jack works, always has been.

'That shit gets in and waits,' Potter tells him. 'My theory is that it *never* goes away, not really. Anyway, shots is done. Pills is done, too. Except for the ones that kill the pain. I come here for the finish.'

'Why?' This is not a thing Jack needs to know, and time is short, but it's his technique, and he won't abandon what works just because there are a couple of State Police jarheads downstairs waiting to take his boy. Dale will have to hold them off, that's all.

'Seems like a nice enough little town. And I like the river. I go down ever' day. Like to watch the sun on the water. Sometimes I think of all the jobs I did – Wisconsin, Minnesota, Illinois – and then sometimes I don't think about much of anything. Sometimes I just sit there on the bank and feel at peace.'

'What was your line of work, Mr Potter?'

'Started out as a carpenter, just like Jesus. Progressed to builder, then got too big for my britches. When that happens to a builder, he usually goes around calling himself a contractor. I made three-four million dollars, had a Cadillac, had a young woman who hauled my ashes Friday nights. Nice young woman. No trouble. Then I lost it all. Only thing I missed was the Cadillac. It had a smoother ride than the woman. Then I got my bad news and come here.'

He looks at Jack.

'You know what I think sometimes? That French Landing's close to a better world, one where things look and smell better. Maybe where people *act* better. I don't go around with folks – I'm not a friendly type person – but that doesn't mean I don't feel things. I got this idea in my head that it's not too late to be decent. You think I'm crazy?'

'No,' Jack tells him. 'That's pretty much why I came here

myself. I'll tell you how it is for me. You know how if you put a thin blanket over a window, the sun will still shine through?'

George Potter looks at him with eyes that are suddenly alight. Jack doesn't even have to finish the thought, which is good. He has found the wavelength – he almost always does, it's his gift – and now it's time to get down to business.

'You *do* know,' Potter says simply.

Jack nods. 'You know why you're here?'

'They think I killed that lady's kid.' Potter nods toward the window. 'The one out there that was holdin' up the noose. I didn't. That's what I know.'

'Okay, that's a start. Listen to me, now.'

Very quickly, Jack lays out the chain of events that has brought Potter to this cell. Potter's brow furrows as Jack speaks, and his big hands knot together.

'Railsback!' he says at last. 'I shoulda known! Nosy goddamn old man, always askin' questions, always askin' do you want to play cards or maybe shoot some pool or, I dunno, play *Parcheesi*, for Christ's sake! All so he can ask questions. Goddamn nosey parker . . .'

There's more in this vein, and Jack lets him go on with it for a while. Cancer or no cancer, this old fellow has been ripped out of his ordinary routine without much mercy, and needs to vent a little. If Jack cuts him off to save time, he'll lose it instead. It's hard to be patient (how is Dale holding those two assholes off? Jack doesn't even want to know), but patience is necessary. When Potter begins to widen the scope of his attack, however (Morty Fine comes in for some abuse, as does Andy Railsback's pal Irv Throneberry), Jack steps in.

'The point is, Mr Potter, that Railsback followed someone to your room. No, that's the wrong way to put it. Railsback was *led* to your room.'

Potter doesn't reply, just sits looking at his hands. But he nods. He's old, he's sick and getting sicker, but he's four counties over from stupid.

'The person who led Railsback was almost certainly the same person who left the Polaroids of the dead children in your closet.'

'Yar, makes sense. And if he had pictures of the dead kiddies, he was prob'ly the one who made 'em dead.'

'Right. So I have to wonder—'

Potter waves an impatient hand. 'I guess I know what you got to wonder. Who there is around these parts who'd like to see Chicago Potsie strung up by the neck. Or the balls.'

'Exactly.'

'Don't want to put a stick in your spokes, sonny, but I can't think of nobody.'

'No?' Jack raises his eyebrows. 'Never did business around here, built a house or laid out a golf course?'

Potter raises his head and gives Jack a grin. 'Course I did. How else d'you think I knew how nice it is? Specially in the summer? You know the part of town they call Libertyville? Got all those "ye olde" streets like Camelot and Avalon?'

Jack nods.

'I built half of those. Back in the seventies. There was a fella around then . . . some moke I knew from Chicago . . . or thought I knew. . . . Was he in the business?' This last seems to be Potter addressing Potter. In any case, he gives his head a brief shake. 'Can't remember. Doesn't matter, anyway. How could it? Fella was gettin' on then, must be dead now. It was a long time ago.'

But Jack, who interrogates as Jerry Lee Lewis once played the piano, thinks it *does* matter. In the usually dim section of his mind where intuition keeps its headquarters, lights are coming on. Not a lot yet, but maybe more than just a few.

'A moke,' he says, as if he has never heard the word before. 'What's that?'

Potter gives him a brief, irritated look. 'A citizen who . . . well, not exactly a *citizen.* Someone who knows people who are connected. Or maybe sometimes connected people call him. Maybe they do each other favors. A moke. It's not the world's best thing to be.'

No, Jack thinks, *but moking can get you a Cadillac with that nice smooth ride.*

'Were you ever a moke, George?' Got to get a little more intimate now. This is not a question Jack can address to a Mr Potter.

'Maybe,' Potter says after a grudging, considering pause. 'Maybe I was. Back in Chi. In Chi, you had to scratch backs and wet beaks if you wanted to land the big contracts. I don't know how it is there now, but in those days, a clean contractor was a poor contractor. You know?'

Jack nods.

'The biggest deal I ever made was a housing development on the South Side of Chicago. Just like in that song about bad, bad Leroy Brown.' Potter chuckles rustily. For a moment he's not thinking about cancer, or false accusations, or almost being lynched. He's living in the past, and it may be a little sleazy, but it's better than the present – the bunk chained to the wall, the steel toilet, the cancer spreading through his guts.

'Man, that one was *big*, I kid you not. Lots of federal money, but the local hotshots decided where the dough went home at night. And me and this other guy, this moke, we were in a horse race—'

He breaks off, looking at Jack with wide eyes.

'Holy shit, what are you, magic?'

'I don't know what you mean. I'm just sitting here.'

'*That* guy was the guy who showed up here. That was the moke!'

'I'm not following you, George.' But Jack thinks he is. And although he's starting to get excited, he shows it no more than he did when the bartender told him about Kinderling's little nose-pinching trick.

'It's probably nothing,' Potter says. 'Guy had plenty of reasons not to like yours truly, but he's got to be dead. He'd be in his eighties, for Christ's sake.'

'Tell me about him,' Jack says.

'He was a moke,' Potter repeats, as if this explains everything. 'And he must have got in trouble in Chicago or somewhere around Chicago, because when he showed up here, I'm pretty sure he was using a different name.'

'When did you swink him on the housing-development deal, George?'

Potter smiles, and something about the size of his teeth and the way they seem to jut from the gums allows Jack to see how fast death is rushing toward this man. He feels a little shiver of gooseflesh, but he returns the smile easily enough. This is also how he works.

'If we're gonna talk about mokin' and swinkin', you better call me Potsie.'

'All right, Potsie. When did you swink this guy in Chicago?'

'That much is easy,' Potter says. 'It was summer when the bids went out, but the hotshots were still bellerin' about how the hippies came to town the year before and gave the cops and the mayor a black eye. So I'd say 1969. What happened was I'd done the building commissioner a big favor, and I'd done another for this old woman who swung weight on this special Equal Opportunity Housing Commission that Mayor Daley had set up. So when the bids went out, mine got special consideration. This other guy – the moke – I have no doubt that his bid was lower. He knew his way around, and he musta had his own contacts, but that time I had the inside track.'

He smiles. The gruesome teeth appear, then disappear again.

'Moke's bid? Somehow gets lost. Comes in too late. Bad luck. Chicago Potsie nails the job. Then, four years later, the moke shows up here, bidding on the Libertyville job. Only that time when I beat him, everything was square-john. I pulled no strings. I met him in the bar at the Nelson Hotel the night after the contract was awarded, just by accident. And he says, "You were that guy in Chicago." And I say, "There are lots of guys in Chicago." Now this guy was a moke, but he was a *scary* moke. He had a kind of smell about him. I can't put it any better than that. Anyway, I was big and strong in those days, I could be mean, but I was pretty meek that time. Even after a drink or two, I was pretty meek.

'"Yeah," he says, "there are a lot of guys in Chicago, but only one who diddled me. I still got a sore ass from that, Potsie, and I got a long memory."

'Any other time, any other *guy*, I might have asked how good his memory stayed after he got his head knocked on the floor, but with him I just took it. No more words passed between us. He walked out. I don't think I ever saw him again, but I heard about him from time to time while I was working the Libertyville job. Mostly from my subs. Seems like the moke was building a house of his own in French Landing. For his retirement. Not that he was old enough to retire back then, but he was gettin' up a little. Fifties, I'd say . . . and that was in '72.'

'He was building a house here in town,' Jack muses.

'Yeah. It had a name, too, like one of those English houses. The Birches, Lake House, Beardsley Manor, you know.'

'What name?'

'Shit, I can't even remember the *moke's* name, how do you expect me to remember the name of the house he built? But one thing I *do* remember: none of the subs liked it. It got a reputation.'

'Bad?'

'The worst. There were accidents. One guy cut his hand clean off on a band saw, almost bled to death before they got him to the hospital. Another guy fell off a scaffolding and ended up paralyzed . . . what they call a quad. You know what that is?'

Jack nods.

'Only house I ever heard of people were calling haunted even before it was all the way built. I got the idea that he had to finish most of it himself.'

'What else did they say about this place?' Jack puts the question idly, as if he doesn't care much one way or the other, but he cares a lot. He has never heard of a so-called haunted house in French Landing. He knows he hasn't been here anywhere near long enough to hear all the tales and legends, but something like this . . . you'd think something like this would pop out of the deck early.

'Ah, man, I can't remember. Just that . . .' He pauses, eyes distant. Outside the building, the crowd is finally beginning to disperse. Jack wonders how Dale is doing with Brown and Black. The time seems to be racing, and he hasn't gotten what he needs from Potter. What he's gotten so far is just enough to tantalize.

'One guy told me the sun never shone there even when it shone,' Potter says abruptly. 'He said the house was a little way off the road, in a clearing, and it should have gotten sun at least five hours a day in the summer, but it somehow . . . didn't. He said the guys lost their shadows, just like in a fairy tale, and they didn't like it. And sometimes they heard a dog growling in the woods. Sounded like a big one. A mean one. But they never saw it. You know how it is, I imagine. Stories get started, and then they just kinda feed on themselves . . .'

Potter's shoulders suddenly slump. His head lowers.

'Man, that's all I can remember.'

'What was the moke's name when he was in Chicago?'

'Can't remember.'

Jack suddenly thrusts his open hands under Potter's nose. With his head lowered, Potter doesn't see them until they're right there, and he recoils, gasping. He gets a noseful of the dying smell on Jack's skin.

'What . . .? Jesus, what's that?' Potter seizes one of Jack's hands and sniffs again, greedily. 'Boy, that's nice. What is it?'

'Lilies,' Jack says, but it's not what he thinks. What he thinks is *The memory of my mother*. 'What was the moke's name when he was in Chicago?'

'It . . . something like beer stein. That's not it, but it's close. Best I can do.'

'Beer stein,' Jack says. 'And what was his name when he got to French Landing three years later?'

Suddenly there are loud, arguing voices on the stairs. 'I don't care!' someone shouts. Jack thinks it's Black, the more officious one. 'It's our case, he's our prisoner, and we're taking him out! *Now!*'

Dale: 'I'm not arguing. I'm just saying that the paperwork—'

Brown: 'Aw, fuck the paperwork. We'll take it with us.'

'What was his name in French Landing, Potsie?'

'I can't—' Potsie takes Jack's hands again. Potsie's own hands are dry and cold. He smells Jack's palms, eyes closed. On the long exhale of his breath he says: 'Burnside. Chummy Burnside. Not that he was chummy. The nickname was a joke. I think his real handle might have been Charlie.'

Jack takes his hands back. Charles 'Chummy' Burnside. Once known as Beer Stein. Or something like Beer Stein.

'And the house? What was the name of the house?'

Brown and Black are coming down the corridor now, with Dale scurrying after them. *There's no time*, Jack thinks. *Damnit all, if I had even five minutes more—*

And then Potsie says, 'Black House. I don't know if that's what he called it or what the subs workin' the job got to calling it, but that was the name, all right.'

Jack's eyes widen. The image of Henry Leyden's cozy living room crosses his mind: sitting with a drink at his elbow and reading about Jarndyce and Jarndyce. 'Did you say *Bleak* House?'

'*Black*,' Potsie reiterates impatiently. 'Because it really *was*. It was—'

'Oh dear to Christ,' one of the state troopers says in a snotty look-what-the-cat-dragged-in voice that makes Jack feel like rearranging his face. It's Brown, but when Jack glances up, it's Brown's partner he looks at. The coincidence of the other trooper's name makes Jack smile.

'Hello, boys,' Jack says, getting up from the bunk.

'What are you doing here, Hollywood?' Black asks.

'Just batting the breeze and waiting for you,' Jack says, and smiles brilliantly. 'I suppose you want this guy.'

'You're goddamn right,' Brown growls. 'And if you fucked up our case—'

'Gosh, I don't think so,' Jack says. It's a struggle, but he manages to achieve a tone of amiability. Then, to Potsie: 'You'll be safer with them than here in French Landing, sir.'

George Potter looks vacant again. Resigned. 'Don't matter much either way,' he says, then smiles as a thought occurs to him. 'If old Chummy's still alive, and you run across him, you might ask him if his ass still hurts from that diddling I gave him back in '69. And tell him old Chicago Potsie says hello.'

'What the hell are you talking about?' Brown asks, glowering. He has his cuffs out, and is clearly itching to snap them on George Potter's wrists.

'Old times,' Jack says. He stuffs his fragrant hands in his pockets and leaves the cell. He smiles at Brown and Black. 'Nothing to concern you boys.'

Trooper Black turns to Dale. 'You're out of this case,' he says. 'Those are words of one syllable. I can't make it any simpler. So tell me once and mean it forever, Chief: Do you understand?'

'Of course I do,' Dale said. 'Take the case and welcome. But get off the tall white horse, willya? If you expected me to simply stand by and let a crowd of drunks from the Sand Bar take this man out of Lucky's and lynch him—'

'Don't make yourself look any stupider than you already are,' Brown snaps. 'They picked his name up off your police calls.'

'I doubt that,' Dale says quietly, thinking of the doper's cell phone borrowed out of evidence storage.

Black grabs Potter's narrow shoulder, gives it a vicious twist, then thrusts him so hard toward the door at the end of the corridor that the man almost falls down. Potter recovers, his haggard face full of pain and dignity.

'Troopers,' Jack says.

He doesn't speak loudly or angrily, but they both turn.

'Abuse that prisoner one more time in my sight, and I'll be on the phone to the Madison shoofly-pies the minute you leave, and believe me, Troopers, they will listen to me. Your attitude is arrogant, coercive, and counter-productive to the resolution of this case. Your interdepartmental cooperation skills are nonexistent. Your demeanor is unprofessional and reflects badly upon the state of Wisconsin. You will either behave yourselves or I guarantee you that by next Friday you will be looking for security jobs.'

Although his voice remains even throughout, Black and Brown seem to shrink as he speaks. By the time he finishes, they look like a pair of chastened children. Dale is gazing at Jack with awe. Only Potter seems unaffected; he's gazing down at his cuffed hands with eyes that could be a thousand miles away.

'Go on, now,' Jack says. 'Take your prisoner, take your case records, and get lost.'

Black opens his mouth to speak, then shuts it again. They leave. When the door closes behind them, Dale looks at Jack and says, very softly: 'Wow.'

'What?'

'If you don't know,' Dale says, 'I'm not going to tell you.'

Jack shrugs. 'Potter will keep them occupied, which frees us up to do a little actual work. If there's a bright side to tonight, that's it.'

'What did you get from him? Anything?'

'A name. Might mean nothing. Charles Burnside. Nicknamed Chummy. Ever heard of him?'

Dale sticks out his lower lip and pulls it thoughtfully. Then he lets go and shakes his head. 'The name itself seems to ring a faint bell, but that might only be because it's so common. The nickname, no.'

'He was a builder, a contractor, a wheeler-dealer in Chicago over thirty years ago. According to Potsie, at least.'

'Potsie,' Dale says. The tape is peeling off a corner of the ONE CALL MEANS ONE CALL sign, and Dale smooths it back down with the air of a man who doesn't really know what he's doing. 'You and he got pretty chummy, didn't you?'

'No,' Jack says. '*Burnside's* Chummy. And Trooper Black doesn't own the Black House.'

'You've gone dotty. What black house?'

'First, it's a proper name. Black, capital *B*, house, capital *H*. Black House. You ever heard of a house named that around here?'

Dale laughs. 'God, no.'

Jack smiles back, but all at once it's his interrogation smile, not his I'm-discussing-things-with-my-friend smile. Because he's a coppiceman now. And he has seen a funny little flicker in Dale Gilbertson's eyes.

'Are you sure? Take a minute. Think about it.'

'Told you, no. People don't name their houses in these parts. Oh, I guess old Miss Graham and Miss Pentle call their place on the other side of the town library Honeysuckle, because of the honeysuckle bushes all over the fence in front, but that's the only one in these parts I ever heard named.'

Again, Jack sees that flicker. Potter is the one who will be charged for murder by the Wisconsin State Police, but Jack didn't see that deep flicker in Potter's eyes a single time during their interview. Because Potter was straight with him.

Dale isn't being straight.

But I have to be gentle with him, Jack tells himself. *Because he doesn't* know *he's not being straight. How is that possible?*

As if in answer, he hears Chicago Potsie's voice: *One guy told me the sun never shone there even when it shone . . . he said the guys lost their shadows, just like in a fairy tale.*

Memory is a shadow; any cop trying to reconstruct a crime or an accident from the conflicting accounts of eyewitnesses knows it well. Is Potsie's Black House like this? Something that casts no shadow? Dale's response (he has now turned full-face to the peeling poster, working on it as seriously as he might work on a heart attack victim in the street, administering CPR right out of the manual until the ambulance arrives) suggests to Jack that it might be something like *just* that. Three days ago he wouldn't have allowed himself to consider such an idea, but three days ago he hadn't returned to the Territories.

'According to Potsie, this place got a reputation as a haunted house even before it was completely built,' Jack says, pressing a little.

'Nope.' Dale moves on to the sign about the AA and NA meetings. He examines the tape studiously, not looking at Jack. 'Doesn't ring the old chimeroo.'

'Sure? One man almost bled to death. Another took a fall that paralyzed him. People complained – listen to this, Dale, it's good – according to Potsie, people complained about losing their shadows. Couldn't see them even at midday, with the sun shining full force. Isn't that something?'

'Sure is, but I don't remember any stories like that.' As Jack walks toward Dale, Dale moves away. Almost scutters away, although Chief Gilbertson is not ordinarily a scuttering man. It's a little funny, a little sad, a little horrible. He doesn't know he's doing it, Jack's sure of that. There *is* a shadow. Jack sees it, and on some level Dale *knows* he sees it. If Jack should force him too hard, Dale would have to see it, too . . . and Dale doesn't want that. Because it's a *bad* shadow. Is it worse than a monster who kills children and then eats selected portions of their bodies? Apparently part of Dale thinks so.

I could make him see that shadow, Jack thinks coldly. *Put my hands under his nose – my lily-scented hands – and make him see it. Part of him even* wants *to see it. The coppiceman part.*

Then another part of Jack's mind speaks up in the Speedy Parker drawl he now remembers from his childhood. *You could push him over the edge of a nervous breakdown, too, Jack. God knows he's close to one, after all the goin's-on since the Irkenham boy got took. You want to chance that? And for what? He didn't know the name, about that he* was *bein' straight.*

'Dale?'

Dale gives Jack a quick, bright glance, then looks away. The furtive quality in that quick peek sort of breaks Jack's heart. 'What?'

'Let's go get a cup of coffee.'

At this change of subject, Dale's face fills with glad relief. He claps Jack on the shoulder. 'Good idea!'

God-pounding good idea, right here and now, Jack thinks, then smiles. There's more than one way to skin a cat, and more than one way to find a Black House. It's been a long day. Best, maybe, to let this go. At least for tonight.

'What about Railsback?' Dale asks as they clatter down the stairs. 'You still want to talk to him?'

'You bet,' Jack replies, heartily enough, but he holds out little hope for Andy Railsback, a picked witness who saw exactly what the Fisherman wanted him to see. With one little exception . . . perhaps. The single slipper. Jack doesn't know if it will ever come to anything, but it might. In court, for instance . . . as an identifying link . . .

This is never going to court and you know it. It may not even finish in this w—

His thoughts are broken by a wave of cheerful sound as they step into the combination ready room and dispatch center. The members of the French Landing Police Department are standing and applauding. Henry Leyden is also standing and applauding. Dale joins in.

'Jesus, guys, quit it,' Jack says, laughing and blushing at the same time. But he won't lie to himself, try to tell himself he takes no pleasure in that round of applause. He feels the warmth of them; can see the light of their regard. Those things aren't important. But it feels like coming home, and that is.

When Jack and Henry step out of the police station an hour or so later, Beezer, Mouse, and Kaiser Bill are still there. The other two have gone back to the Row to fill in the various old ladies on tonight's events.

'Sawyer,' Beezer says.

'Yes,' Jack says.

'Anything we can do, man. Can you dig that? *Anything.*'

Jack looks at the biker thoughtfully, wondering what his story is . . . other than grief, that is. A father's grief. Beezer's eyes remain steady on his. A little off to one side, Henry Leyden stands with his head raised to smell the river fog, humming deep down in his throat.

'I'm going to look in on Irma's mom tomorrow around eleven,' Jack says. 'Do you suppose you and your friends could meet me in the Sand Bar around noon? She lives close to there, I understand. I'll buy youse a round of lemonade.'

Beezer doesn't smile, but his eyes warm up slightly. 'We'll be there.'

'That's good,' Jack says.

'Mind telling me why?'

'There's a place that needs finding.'

'Does it have to do with whoever killed Amy and the other kids?'

'Maybe.'

Beezer nods. 'Maybe's good enough.'

Jack drives back toward Norway Valley slowly, and not just because of the fog. Although it's still early in the evening, he is tired to the bone and has an idea that Henry feels the same way. Not because he's quiet; Jack has become used to Henry's occasional dormant stretches. No, it's the quiet in the truck itself. Under ordinary circumstances, Henry is a restless, compulsive radio tuner, running through the La Riviere stations, checking KDCU here in town, then ranging outward, hunting for Milwaukee, Chicago, maybe even Omaha, Denver, and St Louis, if conditions are right. An appetizer of bop here, a salad of spiritual music there, perhaps a dash of Perry Como way down at the foot of the dial: hot-diggity, dog-diggity, *boom* what-ya-do-to-me. Not tonight, though. Tonight Henry just sits quiet on his side of the truck with his hands folded in his lap. At last, when they're no more than two miles from his driveway, Henry says: 'No Dickens tonight, Jack. I'm going straight to bed.'

The weariness in Henry's voice startles Jack, makes him uneasy. Henry doesn't sound like himself or any of his radio personae; at this moment he just sounds old and tired, on the way to being used up.

'I am, too,' Jack agrees, trying not to let his concern show in his voice. Henry picks up on every vocal nuance. He's eerie that way.

'What do you have in mind for the Thunder Five, may I ask?'

'I'm not entirely sure,' Jack says, and perhaps because

he's tired, he gets this untruth past Henry. He intends to start Beezer and his buddies looking for the place Potsie told him about, the place where shadows had a way of disappearing. At least way back in the seventies they did. He had also intended to ask Henry if he's ever heard of a French Landing domicile called Black House. Not now, though. Not after hearing how beat Henry sounds. Tomorrow, maybe. Almost certainly, in fact, because Henry is too good a resource not to use. Best to let him recycle a little first, though.

'You have the tape, right?'

Henry pulls the cassette with the Fisherman's 911 call on it partway out of his breast pocket, then puts it back. 'Yes, Mother. But I don't think I can listen to a killer of small children tonight, Jack. Not even if you come in and listen with me.'

'Tomorrow will be fine,' Jack says, hoping he isn't condemning another of French Landing's children to death by saying this.

'You're not entirely sure of that.'

'No,' Jack agrees, 'but you listening to that tape with dull ears could do more harm than good. I *am* sure of that.'

'First thing in the morning. I promise.'

Henry's house is up ahead now. It looks lonely with only the one light on over the garage, but of course Henry doesn't need lights inside to find his way.

'Henry, are you going to be all right?'

'Yes,' Henry says, but to Jack he doesn't seem entirely sure.

'No Rat tonight,' Jack tells him firmly.

'No.'

'Ditto the Shake, the Shook, the Sheik.'

Henry's lips lift in a small smile. 'Not even a George

Rathbun promo for French Landing Chevrolet, where price is king and you never pay a dime of interest for the first six months with approved credit. Straight to bed.'

'Me too,' Jack says.

But an hour after lying down and putting out the lamp on his bedside table, Jack is still unable to sleep. Faces and voices revolve in his mind like crazy clock hands. Or a carousel on a deserted midway.

Tansy Freneau: *Bring out the monster who killed my pretty baby.*

Beezer St Pierre: *We'll have to see how it shakes out, won't we?*

George Potter: *That shit gets in and waits. My theory is that it* never *goes away, not really.*

Speedy, a voice from the distant past on the sort of telephone that was science fiction when Jack first met him: *Hidey-ho, Travelin' Jack . . . as one coppiceman to another, son, I think you ought to visit Chief Gilbertson's private bathroom. Right now.*

As one coppiceman to another, right.

And most of all, over and over again, Judy Marshall: *You don't just say, I'm lost and I don't know how to get back – you keep on going . . .*

Yes, but keep on going where? *Where?*

At last he gets up and goes out onto the porch with his pillow under his arm. The night is warm; in Norway Valley, where the fog was thin to begin with, the last remnants have now disappeared, blown away by a soft east wind. Jack hesitates, then goes on down the steps, naked except for his underwear. The porch is no good to him, though. It's where he found that hellish box with the sugar-packet stamps.

He walks past his truck, past the bird hotel, and into the north field. Above him are a billion stars. Crickets hum softly in the grass. His fleeing path through the hay and timothy has disappeared, or maybe now he's entering the field in a different place.

A little way in, he lies down on his back, puts the pillow under his head, and looks up at the stars. *Just for a little while*, he thinks. *Just until all those ghost voices empty out of my head. Just for a little while.*

Thinking this, he begins to drowse.

Thinking this, he goes over.

Above his head, the pattern of the stars changes. He *sees* the new constellations form. What is that one, where the Big Dipper was a moment before? Is it the Sacred Opopanax? Perhaps it is. He hears a low, pleasant creaking sound and knows it's the windmill he saw when he flipped just this morning, a thousand years ago. He doesn't need to look at it to be sure, any more than he needs to look at where his house was and see that it has once more become a barn.

Creak . . . creak . . . creak: vast wooden vanes turning in that same east wind. Only now the wind is infinitely sweeter, infinitely purer. Jack touches the waistband of his underpants and feels some rough weave. No Jockey shorts in this world. His pillow has changed, too. Foam has become goosedown, but it's still comfortable. More comfortable than ever, in truth. Sweet under his head.

'I'll catch him, Speedy,' Jack Sawyer whispers up at the new shapes in the new stars. 'At least I'll try.'

He sleeps.

When he awakens, it's early morning. The breeze is gone. In the direction from which it came, there's a bright orange line on the horizon – the sun is on its way. He's stiff and his ass hurts and he's damp with dew, but he's rested. The steady, rhythmic creaking is gone, but that doesn't surprise him. He knew from the moment he opened his eyes that he's in Wisconsin again. And he knows something else: he can go back. Any time he wants. The real Coulee Country, the *deep* Coulee Country, is just a wish and a motion away. This fills him with joy and dread in equal parts.

Jack gets up and barefoots back to the house with his pillow under his arm. He guesses it's about five in the morning. Another three hours' sleep will make him ready for anything. On the porch steps, he touches the cotton of his Jockey shorts. Although his skin is damp, the shorts are almost dry. Of course they are. For most of the hours he spent sleeping rough (as he spent so many nights that autumn when he was twelve), they weren't on him at all. They were somewhere else.

'In the Land of Opopanax,' Jack says, and goes inside. Three minutes later he's asleep again, in his own bed. When he wakes at eight, with the sensible sun streaming in through his window, he could almost believe that his latest journey was a dream.

But in his heart, he knows better.

18

Remember those news vans that drove into the parking lot behind the police station? And Wendell Green's contribution to the excitement, before Officer Hrabowski's giant flashlight knocked him into the Land of Nod? Once the crews inside the vans took in the seeming inevitability of a riot, we can be sure they rose to the occasion, for the next morning their footage of the wild night dominates television screens across the state. By nine o'clock, people in Racine and Milwaukee, people in Madison and Delafield, and people who live so far north in the state that they need satellite dishes to get any television at all are looking up from their pancakes, their bowls of Special K, their fried eggs, and their buttered English muffins to watch a small, nervous-looking policeman finishing off a large, florid reporter's budding career as a demagogue by clocking him with a blunt instrument. And we may also be sure of one other matter: that nowhere is this footage watched as widely and compulsively as in French Landing and the neighboring communities of Centralia and Arden.

Thinking about several matters at once, Jack Sawyer watches it all on a little portable TV placed on his kitchen counter. He hopes that Dale Gilbertson will not revoke Arnold Hrabowski's suspension, although he strongly suspects that the Mad Hungarian will soon be back in uniform. Dale only *thinks* he wants him off the force for good: he is too softhearted to listen to Arnie's pleas – and after last night, even a blind man can see that Arnie is going to plead – without relenting. Jack also hopes that the awful Wendell Green will get fired or move away in disgrace. Reporters are not supposed to thrust themselves into their stories, and here is good old loudmouth Wendell, baying for blood like a werewolf. However, Jack has the depressing feeling that Wendell Green will talk his way out of his present difficulties (that is, *lie* his way out of them) and go on being a powerful nuisance. And Jack is pondering Andy Railsback's description of the creepy old man trying the doorknobs on the third floor of the Nelson Hotel.

There he was, *the Fisherman*, given form at last. An old man in a blue robe and one slipper striped black and yellow, like a bumblebee. Andy Railsback had wondered if this unpleasant-looking old party had wandered away from the Maxton Elder Care Facility. That was an interesting notion, Jack thought. If 'Chummy' Burnside is the man who planted the photographs in George Potter's room, Maxton's would be a perfect hidey-hole for him.

Wendell Green is watching the news on the Sony in his hotel room. He cannot take his eyes off the screen, although what he sees there afflicts him with a mixture of feelings – anger, shame, and humiliation – that makes his stomach boil. The knot on his head throbs, and every time he witnesses that poor excuse for a cop sneaking up behind him with his flashlight raised, he pushes his fingers into the thick, curly hair at the back of his head and gently palpates it. The damn thing feels about the size of a ripe tomato and just as ready to burst.

He's lucky not to have a concussion. That pipsqueak could have killed him!

Okay, maybe he went a little bit over the edge, maybe he took a tiny step across a professional boundary; he never claimed to be perfect. The local news guys, they piss him off, all that guff about Jack Sawyer. Who is the top guy covering the Fisherman story? Who has been all over it from day one, telling the citizens what they need to know? Who's been putting himself on the line, day after crummy goddamn day? Who *gave the guy his name?* Not those blow-dried airheads Bucky and Stacey, those wanna-be news reporters and local anchors who smile into the camera to show off their capped teeth, that's for sure. Wendell Green is a legend around here, a star, the closest thing to a giant of journalism ever to come out of western Wisconsin. Even over in Madison, the name Wendell Green stands for . . . well, unquestioned excellence. And if the name Wendell Green is like the gold standard now, just wait until he rides the Fisherman's blood-spattered shoulders all the way to a Pulitzer Prize.

So Monday morning he has to go into the office and pacify his editor. Big deal. It isn't the first time, and it won't be the last. Good reporters make waves; nobody admits it, but that's the deal, that's the fine print nobody reads until it's too late. When he walks into his editor's office, he knows what he's going to say: *Biggest story of the day, and did you see any other reporters there?* And when he has the editor eating out of his hand again, which will take about ten minutes flat, he intends to drop in on a Goltz's salesman named Fred Marshall. One of Wendell's most valuable sources has suggested that Mr Marshall has some interesting information about his special, special baby, the Fisherman case.

Arnold Hrabowski, now a hero to his darling wife, Paula,

is watching the news in a postcoital glow and thinking that she is right: he really should call Chief Gilbertson and ask to be taken off suspension.

Wondering with half his mind where he might look for George Potter's old adversary, Dale Gilbertson watches Bucky and Stacey cut away yet again to the spectacle of the Mad Hungarian taking care of Wendell Green and thinks that he really should reinstate the little guy. Would you look at the beautiful swing Arnie took? Dale can't help it – that swing really brightens up his day. It's like watching Mark McGwire, like watching Tiger Woods.

Alone in her dark little house off the highway, Wanda Kinderling, to whom we have made passing mention from time to time, is listening to the radio. Why is she listening to the radio? Some months ago, she had to decide between paying her cable bill and buying another half gallon of Aristocrat vodka, and sorry, Bucky and Stacey, but Wanda followed her bliss, she went with her heart. Without cable service, her television set brings in little more than snow and a heavy dark line that scrolls up over her screen in an endless loop. Wanda always hated Bucky and Stacey anyhow, along with almost everyone else on television, especially if they looked content and well groomed. (She has a special loathing for the hosts of morning news programs and network anchors.) Wanda has not been content or well groomed since her husband, Thorny, was accused of terrible crimes he could never ever have committed by that high and mighty show-off Jack Sawyer. Jack Sawyer ruined her life, and Wanda is not about to forgive or forget.

That man trapped her husband. He *set him up*. He smeared Thorny's innocent name and packed him off to jail just to make himself look good. Wanda hopes they never catch the Fisherman, because the Fisherman is exactly what they deserve, those dirty bastards. *Play* dirty, you *are* dirty, and people like that can go straight to the deepest bowels of hell – that's what Wanda Kinderling thinks. The Fisherman is *retribution* – that's what Wanda thinks. Let him kill a hundred brats, let him kill a thousand, and after that he can start in on their parents. Thorny could not have killed those sluts down there in Los Angeles. Those were sex murders, and Thorny had no interest in sex, thank the Lord. The rest of him grew up, but his man-part never did; his thingie was about the size of his little finger. It was impossible for him to care about nasty women and sex things. But Jack Sawyer lived in Los Angeles, didn't he? So why couldn't *he* have killed those sluts, those whores, and blamed it all on Thorny?

The newscaster describes former Lieutenant Sawyer's actions of the previous night, and Wanda Kinderling spits up bile, grabs the glass from her bedside table, and douses the fire in her guts with three inches of vodka.

Gorg, who would seem a natural visitor to the likes of Wanda, pays no attention to the news, for he is far away in Faraway.

In his bed at Maxton's, Charles Burnside is enjoying dreams not precisely his, for they emanate from another being, from elsewhere, and depict a world he has never seen on his own. Ragged, enslaved children plod on their bleeding foodzies past leaping flames, turning giant wheels that turn yet larger wheels oho aha that power the beyoodiful engynes of destruction mounting mounting to the black-and-red sky. The Big Combination! An acrid stink of molten metal and something truly vile, something like dragon urine, perfumes the air, as does the leaden stench of despair. Lizard demons with thick, flickering tails whip the children along. A din of clattering and banging, of crashing and enormous thuds punishes the ears.

These are the dreams of Burny's dearest friend and loving master, Mr Munshun, a being of endless and perverse delight.

Down past the end of Daisy wing, across the handsome lobby, and through Rebecca Vilas's little cubicle, Chipper Maxton is concerned with matters considerably more mundane. The little TV on a shelf over the safe broadcasts the wondrous image of Mad Hungarian Hrabowski clobbering Wendell Green with a nice, clean sweep of his heavy-duty flashlight, but Chipper barely notices the splendid moment. He has to come up with the thirteen thousand dollars he owes his bookie, and he has only about half of that sum. Yesterday, lovely Rebecca drove to Miller to withdraw most of what he had stashed there, and he can use about two thousand dollars from his own account, as long as he replaces it before the end of the month. That leaves about six grand, an amount that will call for some seriously creative bookkeeping. Fortunately, creative bookkeeping is a speciality of Chipper's, and when he begins to think of his options, he sees his current difficulty as an opportunity.

After all, he went into business in the first place to steal as much money as possible, didn't he? Apart from being serviced by Ms Vilas, stealing is about the only activity that makes him truly happy. The amount is almost irrelevant: as we have seen, Chipper derives as much pleasure from conning chump change out of the visiting relatives after the Strawberry Fest as from screwing the government out of ten or fifteen thousand dollars. The thrill lies in *getting away with it*. So he needs six thousand; why not take ten thousand? That way, he can leave his own account untouched and still have an extra two grand to play with. He has two sets of books on his computer, and he can easily draw the money from the company's bank account without setting off bells during his next state audit, which is coming up in about a month. Unless the auditors demand the bank records, and even then there are a couple of tricks he can use. It's too bad about the audit, though – Chipper would like to have a little more time to paper over the cracks. Losing the thirteen thousand wasn't the problem, he thinks. The problem was that he lost it at *the wrong time.*

In order to keep everything clear in his head, Chipper pulls his keyboard toward him and tells the computer to print out complete statements of both sets of books for the past month. By the time the auditors show up, baby, those pages will have been fed into the shredder and come out as macaroni.

Let us move from one form of insanity to another. After the owner of the Holiday Trailer Park has extended a trembling index finger to point out the Freneau residence, Jack drives toward it on the dusty path with gathering doubts. Tansy's Airstream is the last and least maintained of a row of four. Two of the others have flowers in a bright border around them, and the third has been dressed up with striped green awnings that make it look more like a house. The fourth trailer displays no signs of decoration or improvement. Dying flowers and skimpy weeds straggle in the beaten earth surrounding it. The shades are pulled down. An air of misery and waste hangs about it, along with a quality Jack might define, if he stopped to consider it, as *slippage*. In no obvious way, the trailer looks wrong. Unhappiness has distorted it, as it can distort a person, and when Jack gets out of his truck and walks toward the cinder blocks placed before the entrance, his doubts increase. He can no longer be sure why he has come to this place. It occurs to Jack that he can give Tansy Freneau nothing but his pity, and this thought makes him uneasy.

Then it occurs to him that these doubts mask his real feelings, which have to do with the discomfort the trailer arouses in him. He does not want to enter that thing. Everything else is a rationalization; he has no choice but to keep moving forward. His eyes find the welcome mat, a reassuring touch of the ordinary world he can feel already disappearing around him, and he steps up onto the topmost board and knocks on the door. Nothing happens. Maybe she really is still asleep and would prefer to stay that way. If he were Tansy, he would stay in bed as long as possible. If he were Tansy, he'd stay in bed for *weeks.* Once more pushing away his reluctance, Jack raps on the door again and says, 'Tansy? Are you up?'

A little voice from within says, 'Up where?'

Uh-oh, Jack thinks, and says, 'Out of bed. I'm Jack Sawyer, Tansy. We met last night. I'm helping the police, and I told you I'd come over today.'

He hears footsteps moving toward the door. 'Are you the man who gave me the flowers? He was a nice man.'

'That was me.'

A lock clicks, and the knob revolves. The door cracks open. A sliver of a faintly olive-skinned face and a single eye shine out of the inner darkness. 'It is you. Come in, fast. *Fast.*' She steps back, opening the door just wide enough for him to pass through. As soon as he is inside, she slams it shut and locks it again.

The molten light burning at the edges of the curtains and the window shades deepens the darkness of the long trailer's interior. One soft lamp burns above the sink, and another, just as low, illuminates a little table otherwise occupied by a bottle of coffee brandy, a smeary glass decorated with a picture of a cartoon character, and a scrapbook. The circle of light cast by the lamp extends to take in half of a low, fabric-covered chair next to the table. Tansy Freneau pushes herself off the door and takes two light, delicate steps toward him. She tilts her head and folds her hands together beneath her chin. The eager, slightly glazed expression in her eyes dismays Jack. By even the widest, most comprehensive definition of sanity, this woman is not sane. He has no idea what to say to her.

'Would you care to . . . sit down?' With a hostessy wave of her hand, she indicates a high-backed wooden chair.

'If it's all right with you.'

'Why wouldn't it be all right? I'm going to sit down in *my* chair, why shouldn't you sit down in that one?'

'Thank you,' Jack says, and sits down, watching her glide back to the door to check the lock. Satisfied, Tansy gives him a brilliant smile and pads back to her chair, moving almost with the duck-waddle grace of a ballerina. When she lowers herself to the chair, he says, 'Are you afraid of someone who might come here, Tansy? Is there someone you want to keep locked out?'

'Oh, yes,' she says, and leans forward, pulling her eyebrows together in an exaggerated display of little-girl seriousness. 'But it isn't a *someone*, it's a *thing*. And I'm never, never going to let him in my house again, not ever. But I'll let you in, because you're a very nice man and you gave me those beautiful flowers. And you're very handsome, too.'

'Is Gorg the thing you want to keep out, Tansy? Are you afraid of Gorg?'

'Yes,' she says, primly. 'Would you care for a cup of tea?'

'No, thank you.'

'Well, *I'm* going to have some. It's very, very good tea. It tastes sort of like coffee.' She raises her eyebrows and gives him a bright, questioning look. He shakes his head. Without moving from her chair, Tansy pours two fingers of the brandy into her glass and sets the bottle back down on the table. The figure on her glass, Jack sees, is Scooby-Doo. Tansy sips from the glass.

'Yummy. Do you have a girlfriend? I could be your girlfriend, you know, especially if you gave me more of those lovely flowers. I put them in a vase.' She pronounces the word like a parody of a Boston matron: *vahhhz*. 'See?'

On the kitchen counter, the lilies of the vale droop in a mason jar half-filled with water. Removed from the Territories, they do not have long to live. This world, Jack supposes, is poisoning them faster than they are able to deal with. Every ounce of goodness they yield to their surroundings subtracts from their essence. Tansy, he realizes, has been kept afloat on the residue of the Territories remaining in the lilies – when they die, her protective little-girl persona will crumble into dust, and her madness may engulf her. That madness came from Gorg; he'd bet his life on it.

'I *do* have a boyfriend, but he doesn't count. His name is Lester Moon. Beezer and his friends call him Stinky Cheese, but I don't know why. Lester isn't all that stinky, at least not when he's sober.'

'Tell me about Gorg,' Jack says.

Extending her little finger away from the Scooby-Doo glass, Tansy takes another sip of coffee brandy. She frowns. 'Oh, that's a real icky thing to talk about.'

'I want to know about him, Tansy. If you help me, I can make sure he never bothers you again.'

'Really?'

'And you'd be helping me find the man who killed your daughter.'

'I can't talk about that now. It's too upsetting.' Tansy flutters her free hand over her lap as if sweeping off a crumb. Her face contracts, and a new expression moves into her eyes. For a second, the desperate, unprotected Tansy rises to the surface, threatening to explode in a madness of grief and rage.

'Does Gorg look like a person, or like something else?'

Tansy shakes her head from side to side with great slowness. She is composing herself again, reinstating a personality that can ignore her real emotions. 'Gorg does *not* look like a person. Not at all.'

'You said he gave you the feather you were wearing. Does he look like a bird?'

'Gorg doesn't look like a bird, he *is* a bird. And do you know what kind?' She leans forward again, and her face takes on the expression of a six-year-old girl about to tell the worst thing she knows. 'A *raven*. That's what he is, a big, old *raven*. All black. But not shiny black.' Her eyes widen with the seriousness of what she has to say. 'He came from Night's Plutonian shore. That's from a poem Mrs Normandie taught us in the sixth grade. "The Raven," by Edgar Allan Poe.'

Tansy straightens up, having passed on this nugget of literary history. Jack guesses that Mrs Normandie probably wore the same satisfied, pedagogic expression that is now on Tansy's face, but without the bright, unhealthy glaze in Tansy's eyes.

'Night's Plutonian shore is not part of this world,' Tansy continues. 'Did you know that? It's *alongside* this world, and *outside* it. You need to find a door, if you want to go there.'

This is like talking to Judy Marshall, Jack abruptly realizes, but a Judy without the depth of soul and the unbelievable courage that rescued her from madness. The instant that Judy Marshall comes into his mind, he wants to see her again, so strongly that Judy feels like the one essential key to the puzzle all around him. And if she is the key, she is also the door the key opens. Jack wants to be out of the dark, warped atmosphere of Tansy's Airstream; he wants to put off the Thunder Five and speed up the highway and over the hill to Arden and the gloomy hospital where radiant Judy Marshall has found freedom in a locked mental ward.

'But I don't ever want to find that door, because I don't want to go there,' Tansy says in a singsong voice. 'Night's Plutonian shore is a *bad* world. Everything's on *fire* there.'

'How do you know that?'

'Gorg told me,' she whispers. Tansy's gaze skitters away from him and fastens on the Scooby-Doo glass. 'Gorg likes fire. But not because it makes him warm. Because it burns things up, and that makes him happy. Gorg said . . .' She shakes her head and lifts the glass to her mouth. Instead of drinking from it, she tilts the liquid toward the lip of the glass and laps at it with her tongue. Her eyes slide up to meet his again. 'I think my tea is magic.'

I bet you do, Jack thinks, and his heart nearly bursts for delicate lost Tansy.

'You can't cry in here,' she tells him. 'You looked like you wanted to cry, but you can't. Mrs Normandie doesn't allow it. You can kiss me, though. Do you want to kiss me?'

'Of course I do,' he says. 'But Mrs Normandie doesn't allow kissing, either.'

'Oh, well.' Tansy laps again at her drink. 'We can do it later, when she leaves the room. And you can put your arms around me, like Lester Moon. And everything Lester does, you can do. With me.'

'Thank you,' Jack says. 'Tansy, can you tell me some of the other things Gorg said?'

She cants her head and pushes her lips in and out. 'He said he came here through a burning hole. With folded-back edges. And he said I was a mother, and I had to help my daughter. In the poem, her name is Lenore, but her real name is Irma. And he said . . . he said a mean old man ate her leg, but there were worse things that could have happened to my Irma.'

For a couple of seconds, Tansy seems to recede into herself, to vanish behind her stationary surface. Her mouth remains half open; she does not even blink. When she returns from where she has gone, it is like watching a statue slowly come to life. Her voice is almost too soft to be heard. 'I was supposed to *fix* that old man, fix him but good. Only you gave me my beautiful lilies, and he wasn't the right man, was he?'

Jack feels like screaming.

'He said there were worse things,' Tansy says in a whisper of disbelief. 'But he didn't say what they were. He showed me, instead. And when I saw, I thought my eyes burned up. Even though I could still see.'

'What did you see?'

'A big, big place all made of fire,' Tansy says. 'Going way high up.' She falls silent, and an internal temblor runs through her, beginning in her face and moving down and out through her fingers. '*Irma* isn't there. No, she isn't. She got dead, and a mean old man ate her leg. He sent me a letter, but I never got it. So Gorg read it to me. I don't want to think about that letter.' She sounds like a little girl describing something she has heard about third-hand, or has invented. A thick curtain lies between Tansy and what she has seen and heard, and that curtain allows her to function. Jack again wonders what will happen to her when the lilies die.

'And now,' she says, 'if you're not going to kiss me, it's time you left. I want to be alone for a while.'

Surprised by her decisiveness, Jack stands up and begins to say something polite and meaningless. Tansy waves him toward the door.

★

Outside, the air seems heavy with bad odors and unseen chemicals. The lilies from the Territories retained more power than Jack had imagined, enough to sweeten and purify Tansy's air. The ground beneath Jack's feet has been baked dry, and a parched sourness hangs in the atmosphere. Jack has nearly to force himself to breathe as he walks toward his truck, but the more he breathes, the more quickly he will readjust to the ordinary world. *His* world, though now it feels poisoned. He wants to do one thing only: drive up Highway 93 to Judy Marshall's lookout point and keep on going, through Arden and into the parking lot, past the hospital doors, past the barriers of Dr Spiegleman and Warden Jane Bond, until he can find himself once again in the life-giving presence of Judy Marshall herself.

He almost thinks he loves Judy Marshall. Maybe he does love her. He knows he needs her: Judy is his door and his key. His *door*, his *key*. Whatever that means, it is the truth. All right, the woman he needs is married to the extremely nice Fred Marshall, but he doesn't want to marry her; in fact, he doesn't even want to sleep with her, not exactly – he just wants to stand before her and see what happens. *Something* will happen, that's for sure, but when he tries to picture it, all he sees is an explosion of tiny red feathers, hardly the image he was hoping for.

Feeling unsteady, Jack props himself on the cab of his truck with one hand while he grabs the door handle with the other. Both surfaces sear his hands, and he waves them in the air for a little while. When he gets into the cab, the seat is hot, too. He rolls down his window and, with a twinge of loss, notices that the world smells normal to him again. It smells fine. It smells like summer. Where is he going to go? That is an interesting question, he thinks, but after he gets back on the road and travels no more than a hundred feet, the low, gray wooden shape of the Sand Bar appears on his left, and without hesitating he turns into the absurdly extensive parking lot, as if he knew where he was going all along. Looking for a shady spot, Jack cruises around to the back of the building and sees the Bar's single hint of landscaping, a broad maple tree that rises out of the asphalt at the far end of the lot. He guides the Ram into the maple's shadow and gets out, leaving the windows cranked down. Waves of heat ripple upward from the only other two cars in the lot.

It is 11:20 a.m. He is getting hungry, too, since his breakfast consisted of a cup of coffee and a slice of toast smeared with marmalade, and that was three hours ago. Jack has the feeling that the afternoon is going to be a long one. He might as well have something to eat while he waits for the bikers.

The back door of the Sand Bar opens onto a narrow rest-room alcove that leads into a long, rectangular space with a gleaming bar at one side and a row of substantial wooden booths on the other. Two big pool tables occupy the middle of the room, and a jukebox stands set back against the wall between them. At the front of the room, a big television screen hangs where it can be seen by everyone, suspended eight or nine feet above the clean wooden floor. The sound has been muted on a commercial that never quite identifies the purpose of its product. After the glare of the parking lot, the Bar seems pleasantly dark, and while Jack's eyes adjust, the few low lamps appear to send out hazy beams of light.

The bartender, whom Jack takes to be the famous Lester 'Stinky Cheese' Moon, looks up once as Jack enters, then returns to the copy of the *Herald* folded open on the bar. When Jack takes a stool a few feet to his right, he looks up again. Stinky Cheese is not as awful as Jack had expected. He is wearing a clean shirt only a few shades whiter than his round, small-featured face and his shaven head. Moon has the unmistakable air, half professional and half resentful, of someone who has taken over the family business and suspects he could have done better elsewhere. Jack's intuition tells him that this sense of weary frustration is the source of his nickname among the bikers, because it gives him the look of one who expects to encounter a nasty smell any minute now.

'Can I get something to eat here?' Jack asks him.

'It's all listed on the board.' The bartender turns sideways and indicates a white board with movable letters that spell out the menu. Hamburger, cheeseburger, hot dog, bratwurst, kielbasa, sandwiches, french fries, onion rings. The man's gesture is intended to make Jack feel unobservant, and it works.

'Sorry, I didn't see the sign.'

The bartender shrugs.

'Cheeseburger, medium, with fries, please.'

'Lunch don't start until eleven-thirty, which it says on the board. See?' Another half-mocking gesture toward the sign. 'But Mom is setting up in back. I could give her the order now, and she'll start in on it when she's ready.'

Jack thanks him, and the bartender glances up at the television screen and walks down to the end of the bar and disappears around a corner. A few seconds later, he returns, looks up at the screen, and asks Jack what he would like to drink.

'Ginger ale,' Jack says.

Watching the screen, Lester Moon squirts ginger ale from a nozzle into a beer glass and pushes the glass toward Jack. Then he slides his hand down the bar to pick up the remote control and says, 'Hope you don't mind, but I was watching this old movie. Pretty funny.' He punches a button on the remote, and from over his left shoulder Jack hears his mother's voice say, *Looks like Smoky's coming in late today. I wish that little rascal would learn how to handle his liquor.*

Before he can turn sideways to face the screen, Lester Moon is asking him if he remembers Lily Cavanaugh.

'Oh, yes.'

'I always liked her when I was a kid.'

'Same here,' Jack says.

As Jack had known instantly, the movie is *The Terror of Deadwood Gulch*, a 1950 comic Western in which the then-famous and still fondly remembered Bill Towns, a sort of poor man's Bob Hope, played a cowardly gambler and cardsharp who arrives in the little Potemkin community of Deadwood Gulch, Arizona, and is soon mistaken for a notorious gunfighter. As the beautiful, quick-witted owner of a saloon called the Lazy 8, the lively center of village social life, Lily Cavanaugh is much appreciated by the crowd of cowpokes, loungers, ranchers, merchants, lawmen, and riffraff who fill her place every night. She makes her patrons check their revolvers at the door and mind their manners, which tend toward the opopanax. In the scene playing now, which is about half an hour into the movie, Lily is alone in her saloon, trying to get rid of a persistent bee.

A bee for the Queen of the B's, Jack thinks, and smiles.

At the buzzing nuisance, Lily flaps a cleaning rag, a flyswatter, a mop, a broom, a gun belt. The bee eludes her every effort, zooming here and there, from the bar to a card table, to the top of a whiskey bottle, the tops of three other bottles all in a row, the lid of the upright piano, often waiting while its adversary comes sneaking up by subtle indirection, then taking off a second before the latest weapon slams down. It is a lovely little sequence that verges on slapstick, and when Jacky was six,

six, six, or maybe seven, half hysterical with laughter at the sight of his competent mother failing repeatedly to vanquish this flying annoyance and suddenly curious as to how the movie guys had made the insect *do* all these things, his mother had explained that it was not a real bee but an enchanted one produced by the special-effects department.

Lester Moon says, 'I could never figure out how they got the bee to go where they wanted. Like, what did they do, *train* it?'

'First they filmed her alone on the set,' Jack says, having concluded that, after all, Stinky Cheese is a pretty decent fellow with great taste in actresses. 'Special effects put the bee in later. It isn't a real bee, it's a drawing – an animation. You really can't tell, can you?'

'No way. Are you sure? How do you know that, anyhow?'

'I read it in a book somewhere,' Jack says, using his all-purpose response to such questions.

Resplendent in fancy cardsharp getup, Bill Towns saunters through the Lazy 8's swinging doors and leers at its proprietress without noticing that she is edging toward the bee now once again installed upon the shiny bar. He has romance in mind, and he swaggers when he walks.

I see you came back for more, hotshot, Lily says. *You must like the place.*

Baby, this is the sweetest joint west of the wide Missouri. Reminds me of the place where I beat Black Jack McGurk to the draw. Poor Black Jack. He never did know when to fold 'em.

With a noise like the revving of a B-52, the enchanted bee, a creature of fiction inside the fiction, launches itself at Bill Towns's slickly behatted head. The comedian's face turns rubbery with comic terror. He waves his arms, he jigs, he screeches. The enchanted bee performs aeronautic stunts around the panicky pseudogunfighter. Towns's splendid hat falls off; his hair disarranges itself. He edges toward a table and, with a final flurry of hand waving, dives under it and begs for help.

Eye fixed on the ambling bee, Lily walks to the bar and picks up a glass and a folded newspaper. She approaches the table, watching the bee walking around in circles. She jumps forward and lowers the glass, trapping the bee. It flies up and bumps the bottom of the glass. Lily tilts the glass, slides the folded paper underneath it, and raises her hands, holding the newspaper against the top of the glass.

The camera pulls back, and we see the cowardly gambler peeking out from under the table as Lily pushes the doors open and releases the bee.

Behind him, Lester Moon says, 'Cheeseburger's ready, mister.'

For the next half hour, Jack eats his burger and tries to lose himself in the movie. The burger is great, world-class, with that juicy taste you can get only from a greased-up griddle, and the fries are perfect, golden and crunchy on the outside, but his concentration keeps wandering from *The Terror of Deadwood Gulch*. The problem is not that he has seen the movie perhaps a dozen times; the problem is Tansy Freneau. Certain things she said trouble him. The more he thinks about them, the less he understands what is going on.

According to Tansy, the crow – the *raven* – named Gorg came from a world alongside and outside the world we know. She had to be talking about the Territories. Using a phrase from Poe's 'The Raven,' she called this other world 'Night's Plutonian shore,' which was pretty good for someone like Tansy, but did not seem in any way applicable to the magical Territories. Gorg had told Tansy that everything in his world was *on fire*, and not even the Blasted Lands met that description. Jack could remember the Blasted Lands and the odd train that had taken him and Rational Richard, then a sick, wasted Rational Richard, across that vast red desert. Strange creatures had lived there, alligator-men and birds with the faces of bearded monkeys, but it had certainly not been on fire. The Blasted Lands were the product of some past disaster, not the site of a present conflagration. What had Tansy said? *A big, big place made all of fire . . . going way high up*. What had she seen, to what landscape had Gorg opened her eyes? It sounded like a great burning tower, or a tall building consumed by fire. A burning tower, a burning building in a burning world – how could that world be the Territories?

Jack has been in the Territories twice in the past forty-eight hours, and what he has seen has been beautiful. More than beautiful – cleansing. The deepest truth Jack knows about the Territories is that they contain a kind of sacred magic: the magic he saw in Judy Marshall. Because of that magic, the Territories can confer a wondrous blessing on human beings. The life of that extraordinary tough beloved woman making fun of Bill Towns on the big screen before him was saved by an object from the Territories. Because Jack had been in the Territories – and maybe because he had held the Talisman – almost every horse he bets on comes in first, every stock he buys triples in value, every poker hand he holds takes the pot.

So what world is Tansy talking about? And what's all this stuff about Gorg coming here through a burning hole?

When Jack flipped over yesterday, he had sensed something unhappy, something unhealthy, far off to the southwest, and he suspected that was where he would find the Fisherman's Twinner. Kill the Fisherman, kill the Twinner; it didn't matter which he did first, the other one would weaken. But . . .

It still didn't make sense. When you travel between worlds,

you just *flip* – you don't set a fire at the world's edge and run through it into another one.

A few minutes before twelve, the rumble of motorcycles drowns the voices on the screen. 'Um, mister, you might want to take off,' says Moon. 'That's the—'

'The Thunder Five,' Jack says. 'I know.'

'Okay. It's just, they scare the shit out of some of my customers. But as long as you treat 'em right, they act okay.'

'I know. There's nothing to worry about.'

'I mean, if you buy 'em a beer or something, they'll think you're all right.'

Jack gets off his stool and faces the bartender. 'Lester, there is no reason to be nervous. They're coming here to meet me.'

Lester blinks. For the first time, Jack notices that his eyebrows are thin, curved wisps, like those of a 1920s vamp. 'I'd better start pourin' a pitcher of Kingsland.' He grabs a pitcher from beneath the bar, sets it under the Kingsland Ale tap, and opens the valve. A thick stream of amber liquid rushes into the pitcher and turns to foam.

The sound of the motorcycles builds to an uproar at the front of the building, then cuts off. Beezer St Pierre bangs through the door, closely followed by Doc, Mouse, Sonny, and Kaiser Bill. They look like Vikings, and Jack is overjoyed to see them.

'Stinky, turn that TV the fuck off,' Beezer roars. 'And we didn't come here to drink, so empty that pitcher into the drain. The way you pour, it's all head anyhow. And when you're done, get back in the kitchen with your momma. Our business with this man's got nothin' to do with you.'

'Okay, Beezer,' Moon says in a shaky voice. 'All I need is a second.'

'Then that's what you got,' Beezer says.

Beezer and the others line up in front of the bar, some of them staring at Stinky Cheese, some, more kindly, at Jack. Mouse is still wearing his cornrows, and he has daubed some black antiglare substance beneath his eyes, like a football player. Kaiser Bill and Sonny have pulled their manes back into ponytails again. Ale and foam slide out of the pitcher and seep into the drain. 'Okay, guys,' Moon says. His footsteps retreat along the back of the bar. A door closes.

The members of the Thunder Five separate and spread out in front of Jack. Most of them have crossed their arms on their chests, and muscles bulge.

Jack pushes his plate to the back of the bar, stands up, and says, 'Before last night, had any of you guys ever heard of George Potter?'

From his perch on the edge of the pool table nearest to the front door, Jack faces Beezer and Doc, who lean forward on their bar stools. Kaiser Bill, one finger against his lips and his head bowed, stands beside Beezer. Mouse lies stretched out on the second pool table, propping his head up with one hand. Banging his fists together and scowling, Sonny is pacing back and forth between the bar and the jukebox.

'You sure he didn't say "Bleak House," like the Dickens novel?' Mouse says.

'I'm sure,' says Jack, reminding himself that he should not be surprised every time one of these guys demonstrates that he went to college. 'It was "Black House."'

'Jeez, I almost think I . . .' Mouse shakes his head.

'What was the builder's name again?' asks Beezer.

'Burnside. First name probably Charles, sometimes known as "Chummy." A long time ago, he changed it from something like "Beer Stein."'

'Beerstein? Bernstein?'

'You got me,' Jack says.

'And you think he's the Fisherman.'

Jack nods. Beezer is staring at him as if trying to see the back of his head.

'How sure are you?'

'Ninety-nine percent. He planted the Polaroids in Potter's room.'

'Damn.' Beezer pushes himself off his stool and walks around to the back of the bar. 'I want to make sure nobody forgets the obvious.' He bends down and straightens up with a telephone book in one hand. 'Know what I mean?' Beezer opens the directory on the bar, flips a few pages, flips back, and runs his thick finger down a column of names. 'No Burnside. Too bad.'

'Good idea, though,' Jack says. 'This morning, I tried the same thing myself.'

Sonny pauses on his return journey from the jukebox and jabs a finger at Jack. 'How long ago was this damn house built?'

'Nearly thirty years ago. During the seventies.'

'Hell, we were all kids then, back in Illinois. How are we supposed to know about that house?'

'You guys get around. I thought there was a pretty good chance you might have seen it. And the place is spooky. People tend to talk about houses like that.' They did in normal cases, at least, Jack thought. In normal cases, spooky houses got that way because they had been empty for a couple of years, or because something terrible had happened in them. In this case, he thought, the house itself was terrible, and the people who otherwise would have talked about it could barely remember seeing it. Judging by Dale's response, Black House had vanished into its own nonexistent shadow.

He says, 'Think about this. Try to remember. In the years you've been living in French Landing, have you ever heard of a house that seemed to have a curse on it? Black House caused injuries to the people who built it. The workmen hated the place; they were afraid of it. They said you couldn't see your shadow when you got near it. They were claiming it was haunted while they worked on it! Eventually, they all quit, and Burnside had to finish the job himself.'

'It's off by itself somewhere,' Doc says. 'Obviously, this thing isn't sitting around in plain view. It's not in some development like Libertyville. You're not going to find it on Robin Hood Lane.'

'Right,' Jack says. 'I should have mentioned that before. Potter told me it was built a little way off what he called "the road," in a kind of clearing. So it's in the woods, Doc, you're right. It's isolated.'

'Hey, hey, hey,' Mouse says, swinging his legs over the side of the pool table and grunting himself upright.

His eyes are screwed shut, and he claps one meaty hand on his forehead. 'If I could only remember . . .' He lets out a howl of frustration.

'*What?*' Beezer's voice is at twice its normal volume, and the word sounds like a paving stone hitting a cement sidewalk.

'I *know* I saw that fucking place,' he says. 'As soon as you started talking about it, I had this feeling it sounded kinda familiar. It kept hanging at the back of my mind, but it wouldn't come out. When I tried to think about it – you know, make myself remember – I kept seeing these sparkly lights. When Jack said it was back in the woods, I knew what he was talking about. I had a clear picture of the place. Surrounded by all these sparkling lights.'

'That doesn't sound much like Black House,' Jack says.

'Sure it does. The lights weren't really there, I just *saw* them.' Mouse offers this observation as though it is completely rational.

Sonny utters a bark of laughter, and Beezer shakes his head and says, 'Shit.'

'I don't get it,' Jack says.

Beezer looks at Jack, holds up one finger, and asks Mouse, 'Are we talking about July, August, two years ago?'

'Naturally,' Mouse says. 'The summer of the Ultimate Acid.' He looks at Jack and smiles. 'Two years ago, we got this amazing, amazing acid. Drop a tab, you're in for five or six hours of the most *unbelievable* head games. Nobody ever had a bad experience with the stuff. It was all *groove*, know what I mean?'

'I suppose I can guess,' Jack says.

'You could even do your job behind it. For sure, you could *drive*, man. Get on your hog, go anywhere you could think of. Doing anything normal was a piece of cake. You weren't fucked up, you were operating way beyond your max.'

'Timothy Leary wasn't *all* wrong,' Doc says.

'God, that was great stuff,' Mouse says. 'We did it until there was no more to do, and then the whole thing was over. The *whole* acid thing. If you couldn't get that stuff, there was no point in taking anything else. I never knew where it came from.'

'You don't want to know where it came from,' says Beezer. 'Trust me.'

'So you were doing this acid when you saw Black House,' Jack says.

'Sure. That's why I saw the lights.'

Very slowly, Beezer asks, 'Where is it, Mouse?'

'I don't exactly know. But hold on, Beezer, let me talk. That was the summer I was tight with Little Nancy Hale, remember?'

'Sure,' Beezer says. 'That was a damn shame.' He glances at Jack. 'Little Nancy died right after that summer.'

'Tore me apart,' Mouse says. 'It was like she turned allergic to air and sunlight, all of a sudden. Sick all the time. Rashes all over her body. She couldn't stand being outside, because the light hurt her eyes. Doc couldn't figure out what was wrong with her, so we took her to the big hospital in La Riviere, but they couldn't find what was wrong, either. We talked to a couple of guys at Mayo, but they weren't any help. She died *hard*, man. Broke your heart to see it happen. Broke mine, for sure.'

He falls silent for a long moment, during which he stares down at his gut and his knees and no one else says a word. 'All right,' Mouse finally says, raising his head. 'Here's what I remember. On this Saturday, Little Nancy and I were tripping on the Ultimate, just riding around to some places we liked. We went to the riverfront park in La Riviere, drove over to Dog Island and Lookout Point. We came back this direction and went up on the bluff – beautiful, man. After that, we didn't feel like going home, so we just wheeled around. Little Nancy noticed this NO TRESPASSING sign I must have passed about a thousand times before without seeing it.'

He looks at Jack Sawyer. 'I can't say for certain, but I think it was on 35.'

Jack nods.

'If we hadn't been on the Ultimate, I don't think she ever would have seen that sign, either. Oh man, it's all coming back to me. "What's that?" she says, and I swear, I had to look two or three times before I saw that sign – it was all beat-up and bent, with a couple rusty bullet holes in it. Sort of leaning back into the trees. "Somebody wants to keep us off that road," Little Nancy says. "What are they hiding up there, anyhow?" Something like that. "What road?" I ask, and then I see it. It's hardly even what you could call a road. About wide enough for a car to fit in, if you have a compact. Thick trees on both sides. Hell, I didn't think anything interesting was hidden up there, unless it was an old shack. Besides that, I didn't like the way it looked.' He glances at Beezer.

'What do you mean, you didn't like the way it looked?' Beezer asks. 'I've seen you go into places you damn well knew were no good. Or are you getting *mystical* on me, Mouse?'

'Call it what you fucking want, I'm telling you how it was. It was like that sign was saying KEEP OUT IF YOU KNOW WHAT'S GOOD FOR YOU. Gave me a bad feeling.'

'On account of it was a bad place,' Sonny interrupts. 'I've seen some bad places. They don't want you there, and they let you know.'

Beezer shoots him a measured look and says, 'I don't care how evil this *bad* place is, if it's where the Fisherman lives, I'm going there.'

'And I'm going with you,' says Mouse, 'but just listen. I wanted to bag it and get some fried chicken or something, which combined with the Ultimate would have been like eating the food of Paradise, or whatever Coleridge said, but Little Nancy wanted to go in *because* she had the same feeling I did. She was a game broad, man. Ornery, too. So I turned in, and Little Nancy's hanging on in back of me, and she's saying, "Don't be a pussy, Mouse, let's haul ass," so I gun it a little bit, and everything feels all weird and shit, but all I can see's this track curving away into the trees and the shit I *know* isn't there.'

'Like what?' asks Sonny, in what sounds like the spirit of scientific inquiry.

'These dark shapes coming up to the edge of the road and looking out through the trees. A couple of them ran toward me, but I rolled right through them like smoke. I don't know, maybe they *were* smoke.'

'Fuck that, it was the acid,' Beezer says.

'Maybe, but it didn't feel that way. Besides, the Ultimate never turned on you, remember? It wasn't about *darkness*. Anyhow, right before the shit hit the fan, all of a sudden I was thinking about Kiz Martin. I can remember that, all right. It was like I could practically see her, right in front of me – the way she looked when they loaded her in the ambulance.'

'Kiz Martin,' Beezer says.

Mouse turns to Jack. 'Kiz was a girl I went out with when we were all at the university. She used to beg us to let her ride with us, and one day the Kaiser said, okay, she could borrow his bike. Kiz was having a *ball*, man, she's diggin' it. And then she rolls over some damn little twig, I think it was—'

'Bigger than a twig,' Doc says. 'Little branch. Maybe two inches in diameter.'

'Which is just enough to test your balance, especially if you're not used to hogs,' Mouse says. 'She rolls over this little branch, and the bike flops over, and Kiz flies off and hits the road. My heart damn near stopped, man.'

'I knew she was gone the second I came up close enough to see the angle of her head,' says Doc. 'There wasn't even any point in trying CPR. We covered her with our jackets, and I rode off to call an ambulance. Ten minutes later, they were loading her in. One of the guys recognized me from my stint in the ER, or they might have given us some trouble.'

'I wondered if you were really a doctor,' Jack says.

'Completed my residency in surgery at UI, walked away from the whole deal right there.' Doc smiles at him. 'Hanging around with these guys, getting into beer brewing, sounded like more fun than spending all day cutting people up.'

'Mouse,' Beezer says.

'Yeah. I was just getting to the curve in the little road, and it was like Kiz was standing right in front of me, it was so vivid. Her eyes closed, and her head hanging like a leaf about to fall. *Oh man*, I said to myself, *this is not what I want to see at this particular moment.* I could feel it all over again – the way I felt when Kiz hit the road. Sick dread. That's the word for it, sick dread.

'And we come around the curve, and I hear this dog growling somewhere off in the woods. Not just growling, *growling.* Like twenty big dogs are out there, and they're all mad as hell. My head starts feeling like it wants to explode. And I look up ahead of me to see if a pack of wolves or something is running toward us, and it takes me a while to realize that the weird shadowy stuff I see up ahead is a house. A black house.

'Little Nancy is hitting me on the back and rapping my head, screaming at me to stop. Believe me, I can get with the program, because the last thing I want to do is get any closer to that place. I stop the bike, and Little Nancy jumps off and pukes on the side of the road. She holds her head and she pukes some more. I'm feeling like my legs turned to rubber, like something heavy is pressing on my chest. That *thing*, whatever it is, is still going nuts in the woods, and it's getting closer. I take another look up at the end of the road, and that ugly damn house is stretching back into the woods, like it's crawling into them, only it's standing still. It gets bigger the more you look at it! Then I see the sparkly lights floating around it, and they look dangerous – *Stay away*, they're telling me, *get out of here, Mouse.* There's another NO TRESPASSING sign leaning against the porch, and that sign, man . . . that sign kind of flashed, like it was saying THIS TIME I MEAN IT, BUDDY.

'My head is splitting in half, but I get Little Nancy on

the bike, and she sags against me, like pure dead weight except she's hanging on, and I kick the hog on and spin around and take off. When we get back to my place, she goes to bed and stays there for three days. To me, it seemed like I could hardly remember what happened. The whole thing went kind of *dark.* In my mind. I hardly had time to think about it anyhow, because Little Nancy got sick and I had to take care of her whenever I wasn't at work. Doc gave her some stuff to get her temperature down, and she got better, so we could drink beer and smoke shit and ride around, like before, but she was never really the same. End of August, she started getting bad again, and I had to put her in the hospital. Second week of September, hard as she was fighting, Little Nancy passed away.'

'How big was Little Nancy?' Jack asks, picturing a woman roughly the size of Mouse.

'Little Nancy Hale was about the size and shape of Tansy Freneau,' Mouse says, looking surprised by the question. 'If she stood on my hand, I could lift her up with one arm.'

'And you never talked about this with anyone,' Jack says.

'How could I talk about it?' Mouse asks. 'First, I was crazy with worry about Little Nancy, and then it went clean out of my head. Weird shit will do that to you, man. Instead of sticking in your head, it erases itself.'

'I know exactly what you mean,' Jack says.

'I guess I do, too,' says Beezer, 'but I'd say that the Ultimate kicked the shit out of your reality there for a while. You did see the place, though – Black House.'

'Damn straight,' says Mouse.

Beezer focuses on Jack. 'And you say the Fisherman, this creep Burnside, built it.'

Jack nods.

'So maybe he's living there, and he rigged up a bunch of gadgets to scare people away.'

'Could be.'

'Then I think we're gonna let Mouse take us over on Highway 35 and see if he can find that little road he was talking about. Are you coming with us?'

'I can't,' Jack says. 'I have to see someone in Arden first, someone who I think can also help us. She has another piece of the puzzle, but I can't explain it to you until I see her.'

'This woman knows something?'

'Oh, yes,' Jack says. 'She knows something.'

'All right,' Beezer says, and stands up from his stool. 'Your choice. We'll have to talk to you afterward.'

'Beezer, I want to be with you when you go inside Black House. Whatever we have to do in there, whatever we see . . .' Jack pauses, trying to find the right words. Beezer is rocking on his heels, practically jumping out of his skin in his eagerness to hunt down the Fisherman's lair. 'You're going to want me there. There's more to this business than you can imagine, Beezer. You're going to know what I'm talking about in a little while, and you'll be able to stand up to it – I think all of you will – but if I tried to describe it now, you wouldn't believe me. When the time comes, you'll need me to see you through, if we get through. You'll be glad I was there. We're at a dangerous point here, and none of us wants to mess it up.'

'What makes you think I'll mess it up?' Beezer asks, with deceptive mildness.

'Anyone would mess it up, if they didn't have the last piece of the puzzle. Go out there. See if Mouse can find the house he saw two years ago. Check it out. Don't go in – to do that, you need me. After you check it out, come back here, and I'll see you as soon as I can. I should be back before two-thirty, three at the latest.'

'Where are you going in Arden? Maybe I'll want to call you.'

'French County Lutheran Hospital. Ward D. If you can't get me, leave a message with a Dr Spiegleman.'

'Ward D, huh?' Beezer says. 'Okay, I guess everybody's crazy today. And I guess I can be satisfied with only a look at this house, as long as I know that sometime this afternoon, I can count on you to explain all these pieces I'm too stupid to understand.'

'It'll be soon, Beezer. We're closing in. And the last thing I'd call you is stupid.'

'I guess you must have been one hell of a cop,' Beezer says. 'Even though I think half the stuff you say is crap, I can't help but believe it.' He turns around and brings his fists down on the bar. 'Stinky Cheese! It's safe now. Drag your pale ass out of the kitchen.'

19

Jack follows the Thunder Five out of the parking lot, and for the moment we will let him go alone on his northward way on Highway 93 toward Judy Marshall's lookout and Judy Marshall's locked ward. Like Jack, the bikers are headed toward the unknown, but their unknown lies westward on Highway 35, into the land of the steadily accumulating past, and we want to know what they will find there. These men do not appear to be nervous; they still project the massive confidence with which they burst into the Sand Bar. In truth, they never really display nervousness, for situations that would make other people worried or anxious generally make them get physical. Fear affects them differently than it does other people, too: in the rare moments when they have experienced fear, they've tended on the whole to enjoy it. In their eyes, fear represents a God-given opportunity for focusing their collective concentration. Due to their remarkable solidarity, that concentration is formidable. For those of us who are not members of a biker gang or the Marine Corps, solidarity means little more than the compassionate impulse that leads us to comfort a bereft friend; for Beezer and his merry band, solidarity is the assurance that someone's always got your back. They are on each other's hands, and they know it. For the Thunder Five, safety really is in numbers.

Yet the encounter toward which they are flying has no precedents or analogues in their experience. Black House is something new, and its newness – the sheer *strangeness* of Mouse's story – sinks tendrils down into their guts, one and all.

Eight miles west of Centralia, where the flatland around Potsie's thirty-year-old development yields to the long stretch of woods that runs all the way to Maxton's, Mouse and Beezer ride side by side in front of the others. Beezer occasionally looks to his friend, asking a wordless question. The third time that Mouse shakes his head, he follows the gesture with a backward wave of his hand that says *Stop bugging me, I'll tell you when we're there.* Beezer drops back; Sonny, Kaiser Bill, and Doc automatically assume Beezer is giving them a signal, and they string out in a single line.

At the head of the column, Mouse keeps taking his eyes off the highway to inspect the right-hand side of the road. The little road is hard to see, Mouse knows, and by now it will be more overgrown than it was two years ago. He is trying to spot the white of the battered NO TRESPASSING sign. It, too, may be partially hidden by new growth. He slows down to thirty-five. The four men behind him match his change in pace with the smoothness of long practice.

Alone of the Thunder Five, Mouse has already seen their destination, and in the deepest places of his soul he can scarcely believe that he is going there again. At first, the ease and rapidity with which his memories had flown out of their dark vault had pleased him; now, instead of feeling that he has effortlessly reclaimed a lost part of his life, he has the sense of being at the mercy of that lost afternoon. A grave danger then – and he does not doubt that some great and dangerous *force* had brushed him with a warning hand – is an increased danger now. Memory has returned a miserable conclusion he thrust away long ago: that the hideous structure Jack Sawyer called Black House had killed Little Nancy Hale as surely as if its rafters had fallen in on her. Moral more than physical, Black House's ugliness exhaled toxic fumes. Little Nancy had been killed by the invisible poisons carried on the warning hand; now Mouse had to look at that knowledge without blinking. He can feel her hands on his shoulders, and their thin bones are covered with rotting flesh.

If I'd been five foot three and weighed one hundred and five pounds instead of being six-two and two hundred and ninety, by now I'd be rotting, too, he thinks.

Mouse may look for the narrow road and the sign beside it with the eyes of a fighter pilot, but someone else has to see them, because he never will. His unconscious has taken a vote, and the decision was unanimous.

Each of the other men, Sonny, Doc, the Kaiser, and even Beezer, have also connected Little Nancy's death with Black House, and the same speculations about comparative size and weight have passed through their minds. However, Sonny Cantinaro, Doc Amberson, Kaiser Bill Strassner, and especially Beezer St Pierre assume that whatever poison surrounded Black House had been concocted in a laboratory by human beings who knew what they were doing. These four men derive the old, primitive reassurance from one another's company that they have enjoyed since college; if anything makes them feel a touch uneasy, it is that Mouse Baumann, not Beezer, leads their column. Even though Beezer let Mouse wave him back, Mouse's position contains a hint of insurrection, of mutiny: the universe has been subtly disordered.

Twenty yards from the back end of the Maxton property, Sonny decides to put an end to this farce, guns his Softail, roars past his friends, and moves up parallel to Mouse. Mouse glances at him with a trace of worry, and Sonny motions to the side of the road.

When they have all pulled over, Mouse says, 'What's your problem, Sonny?'

'You are,' Sonny says. 'Either you missed the turnoff, or your whole story's all fucked up.'

'I *said* I wasn't sure where it is.' He notices with nearly immeasurable relief that Little Nancy's dead hands no longer grip his shoulders.

'Of course not. You were ripped on acid!'

'*Good* acid.'

'Well, there's no road up ahead, I know that much. It's just trees all the way to the old fucks' home.'

Mouse ponders the stretch of road ahead as if the road just might be up there, after all, although he knows it is not.

'Shit, Mouse, we're practically in town. I can see *Queen Street* from here.'

'Yeah,' Mouse says. 'Okay.' If he can get to Queen Street, he thinks, those hands will never fasten on him again.

Beezer walks his Electra Glide up to them and says, 'Okay what, Mouse? You agree it's farther back, or is the road somewhere else?'

Frowning, Mouse turns his head to look back down the highway. 'Goddamn. I *think* it's along here somewhere, unless I got totally turned around that day.'

'Gee, how could that have happened?' says Sonny. 'I looked at every inch of ground we passed, and I sure as hell didn't see a road. Did you, Beezer? How about a NO TRESPASSING sign, you happen to see one of those?'

'You don't get it,' Mouse says. 'This shit doesn't want to be seen.'

'Maybe you shoulda gone to Ward D with Sawyer,' Sonny says. 'People in there appreciate visionaries.'

'Can it, Sonny,' Beezer says.

'I was there before, and you weren't,' Mouse says. 'Which one of us knows what he's talking about?'

'I've heard enough out of both of you guys,' Beezer says. 'Do you still think it's along here somewhere, Mouse?'

'As far as I can recollect, yeah.'

'Then we missed it. We'll go back and check again, and if we don't find it, we'll look somewhere else. If it's not here, it's between two of the valleys along 93, or in the woods on the hill leading up to the lookout. We have plenty of time.'

'What makes you so sure?' Sonny asks. Mild anxiety about what they might come across is making him belligerent. He would just as soon go back to the Sand Bar and down a pitcher of Kingsland while messing with Stinky's head as waste his time goofing along the highways.

Beezer looks at him, and his eyes crackle. 'You know anywhere else there's enough trees to call it a woods?'

Sonny backs down immediately. Beezer is never going to give up and go back to the Sand Bar. Beezer is in this for keeps. Most of that has to do with Amy, but some of it relates to Jack Sawyer. Sawyer impressed the shit out of Beezer the other night, that's what happened, and now Beezer thinks everything the guy says is golden. To Sonny, this makes no sense at all, but Beezer's the one who calls the shots, so for now, Sonny guesses, they will all run around like junior G-men for a while. If this adopt-a-cop program goes on for more than a couple of days, Sonny plans to have a little chat with Mouse and the Kaiser. Doc will always side with Beezer no matter what, but the other two are capable of listening to reason.

'All right, then,' Beezer says. 'Scratch from here to Queen Street. We *know* there's no fuckin' road along that stretch. We'll go back the way we came, give it one more shot. Single file the whole way. Mouse, you're point man again.'

Mouse nods and prepares himself to feel those hands on his shoulders again. Gunning his Fat Boy, he rolls forward and takes his place at the head of the line. Beezer moves in behind him, and Sonny follows Beezer, with Doc and the Kaiser in the last two slots.

Five pairs of eyes, Sonny thinks. *If we don't see it this time, we never will. And we won't, because that damned road is halfway across the state. When Mouse and his old lady got buzzed on the Ultimate, they could go for hundreds of miles and think they'd taken a spin around the block.*

Everybody scans the opposite side of the road and the edge of the woods. Five pairs of eyes, as Sonny puts it, register an unbroken line of oaks and pine trees. Mouse has set a pace somewhere between a fast walk and a medium jog, and the trees crawl by. At this speed, they can notice the moss blistering the trunks of the oaks and the bright smears of sunlight on the forest's floor, which is brownish gray and resembles a layer of rumpled felt. A hidden world of upright trees, shafts of light, and deadfalls extends backward from the first, sentinel row. Within that world, paths that are not paths wind mazelike between the thick trunks and lead to mysterious clearings. Sonny becomes suddenly aware of a tribe of squirrels doing squirrel gymnastics in the map of branches that lace into an intermittent canopy. And with the squirrels, an aviary of birds pops into view.

All of this reminds him of the deep Pennsylvania woods

he had explored as a boy, before his parents sold their house and moved to Illinois. Those woods had contained a rapture he had found nowhere else. Sonny's conviction that Mouse got things wrong and they are looking in the wrong place takes on greater inner density. Earlier, Sonny had spoken about bad places, of which he has seen at least one he was absolutely certain about. In Sonny's experience, *bad* places, the ones that let you know you were not welcome, tended to be on or near borders.

During the summer after his high school graduation, he and his two best buddies, all of them motorcycle freaks, had taken their bikes to Rice Lake, Wisconsin, where he had two cousins cute enough to show off to his friends. Sal and Harry were thrilled with the girls, and the girls thought the bikers were sexy and exotic. After a couple of days spent as a literal fifth wheel (or fifth *and* sixth wheel, depending on what you are counting), Sonny proposed extending their trip by a week and, in the interest of expanding their educations, ballin' the jack down to Chicago and spending the rest of their money on beer and hookers until they had to go home. Sal and Harry loved the whole idea, and on their third evening in Rice Lake, they packed their rolls on their bikes and roared south, making as much noise as possible. By 10:00 they had managed to get completely lost.

It might have been the beer, it might have been inattention, but for one reason or another they had wandered off the highway and, in the deep black of a rural night, found themselves on the edge of an almost nonexistent town named Harko. Harko could not be found on their gas-station road map, but it had to be close to the Illinois border, on either one side or the other. Harko seemed to consist of an abandoned motel, a collapsing general store, and an empty grain mill. When the boys reached the mill, Sal and Harry groused about being exhausted and hungry and wanted to turn back to spend the night in the motel.

Sonny, who was no less worn out, rode back with them; the second they rolled into the dark forecourt of the motel, he had a bad feeling about the place. The air seemed heavier, the darkness darker than they should have been. To Sonny, it seemed that malign, invisible presences haunted the place. He could all but make them out as they flitted between the cabins. Sal and Harry jeered at his reservations: he was a coward, a fairy, a *girl*. They broke down a door and unrolled their sleeping bags in a bare, dusty rectangular room. He carried his across the street and slept in a field.

Dawn awakened him, and his face was wet with dew. He jumped up, pissed into the high grass, and checked for the motorcycles on the other side of the road. There they were, all three of them, listing over their stands outside a broken door. The dead neon sign at the entrance of the forecourt read HONEYMOONER'S BOWER. He walked across the narrow road and swept a hand over the moisture shining black on the seats of the motorcycles. A funny sound came from the room where his friends were sleeping. Already tasting dread, Sonny pushed open the broken door. If he had not initially refused to make sense of what was before him, what he saw in the room would have made him pass out.

His face streaked with blood and tears, Sal Turso was sitting on the floor. Harry Reilly's severed head rested in his lap, and an ocean of blood soaked the floor and daubed the walls. Harry's body lay loose and disjointed on top of his blood-soaked sleeping bag. The body was naked; Sal wore only a blood-red T-shirt. Sal raised both his hands – the one holding his prize long-bladed knife and the one holding only a palmful of blood – and lifted his contorted face to Sonny's frozen gaze. *I don't know what happened.* His voice was high and screechy, not his. *I don't remember doing this, how could I have done this? Help me, Sonny. I don't know what happened.*

Unable to speak, Sonny had backed out and flown away on his cycle. He'd had no clear idea of where he was going except that it was out of Harko. Two miles down the road, he came to a little town, a real one, with people in it, and someone finally took him to the sheriff's office.

Harko: *there* was a bad place. In a way, both of his high school friends had died there, because Sal Turso hanged himself six months after being committed to a state penitentiary for life on a second-degree murder charge. In Harko, you saw no red-winged blackbirds or woodpeckers. Even sparrows steered clear of Harko.

This little stretch of 35? Nothing but a nice, comfortable woodland. Let me tell you, Senator, Sonny Cantinaro has seen Harko, and this ain't no Harko. This don't even come close. It might as well be in another world. What meets Sonny's appraising eye and increasingly impatient spirit is about a mile and a quarter of beautiful wooded landscape. You could call it a mini-forest. He thinks it would be cool to come out here by himself one day, tuck the Harley out of sight, and just walk around through the great oaks and pines, that big pad of felt beneath his feet, digging the birds and the crazy squirrels.

Sonny gazes at and through the sentinel trees on the far side of the road, enjoying his anticipation of the pleasure to come, and a flash of white jumps out at him from the darkness beside a huge oak tree. Caught up in the vision of walking alone under that green canopy, he almost dismisses it as a trick of the light, a brief illusion. Then he remembers what he is supposed to be looking for, and he slows down and leans sideways and sees, emerging from the tangle of underbrush at the base of the oak, a rusty bullet hole and a large, black letter N. Sonny swerves across the road, and the N expands into NO. He doesn't believe it, but there it is, Mouse's goddamn sign. He rolls ahead another foot, and the entire phrase comes into view.

Sonny puts the bike in neutral and plants one foot on the ground. The darkness next to the oak stretches like a web to the next tree at the side of the road, which is also an oak, though not as huge. Behind him, Doc and the Kaiser cross the road and come to a halt. He ignores them and looks at Beezer and Mouse, who are already some thirty feet up the road, intently scanning the trees.

'Hey,' he shouts. Beezer and Mouse do not hear him. '*Hey! Stop!*'

'You got it?' Doc calls out.

'Go up to those assholes and bring them back,' Sonny says.

'It's here?' Doc asks, peering into the trees.

'What, you think I found a body? Of course it's here.'

Doc speeds up, stops just behind Sonny, and stares at the woods.

'Doc, you see it?' Kaiser Bill shouts, and he speeds up, too.

'Nope,' Doc says.

'You can't see it from there,' Sonny tells him. 'Will you please get your ass in gear and tell Beezer to come back here?'

'Why don't you do it, instead?' Doc says.

'Because if I leave this spot, I might not ever be able to fucking find it again,' Sonny says.

Mouse and Beezer, now about sixty feet up the road, continue blithely on their way.

'Well, I still don't see it,' Doc says.

Sonny sighs. 'Come up alongside me.' Doc walks his Fat Boy to a point parallel with Sonny's bike, then moves a couple of inches ahead. 'There,' Sonny says, pointing at the sign.

Doc squints and leans over, putting his head above Sonny's handlebars. 'Where? Oh, I see it now. It's all beat to hell.'

The top half of the sign curls over and shades the bottom half. Some antisocial lad has happened along and creased the sign with his baseball bat. His older brothers, more advanced in the ways of crime, had tried to kill it with their .22 rifles, and he was just delivering the coup de grâce.

'Where's the road supposed to be?' Doc asks.

Sonny, who is a little troubled about this point, indicates the flat sheet of darkness to the right of the sign and extending to the next, smaller oak tree. As he looks at it, the darkness loses its two-dimensionality and deepens backward like a cave, or a black hole softly punched through the air. The cave, the black hole, melts and widens into the earthen road, about five and a half feet wide, that it must have been all along.

'That sure as hell is it,' says Kaiser Bill. 'I don't know how all of us could have missed it the first time.'

Sonny and Doc glance at each other, realizing that the Kaiser came along too late to watch the road seem to materialize out of a black wall with the thickness of a sheet of paper.

'It's kind of tricky,' Sonny says.

'Your eyes have to adjust,' Doc says.

'Okay,' says Kaiser Bill, 'but if you two want to argue about who tells Mouse and the Beeze, let me put you out of your misery.' He jams his bike into gear and tears off like a World War I messenger with a hot dispatch from the front. By now a long way up the road, Mouse and Beezer come to a halt and look back, having apparently heard the sound of his bike.

'I guess that's it,' Sonny says, with an uneasy glance at Doc. 'Our eyes had to adjust.'

'Couldn't be anything else.'

Less convinced than they would like to be, both men let it drop in favor of watching Kaiser Bill conversing with Beezer and Mouse. The Kaiser points at Sonny and Doc, Beezer points. Then Mouse points at them, and the Kaiser points again. It looks like a discussion in an extremely unevolved version of sign language. When everybody has gotten the point, Kaiser Bill spins his bike around and comes roaring back down the road with Beezer and Mouse on his tail.

There is always that feeling of disorder, of misrule, when Beezer is not in the lead.

The Kaiser stops on the side of the narrow road. Beezer and Mouse halt beside him, and Mouse winds up stationed directly in front of the opening in the woods.

'Shouldn't have been *that* hard to see,' Beezer says. 'But there she is, anyhow. I was beginning to have my doubts, Mousie.'

'Uh-huh,' says Mouse. His customary manner, that of an intellectual roughneck with a playful take on the world, has lost all of its buoyancy. Beneath his biker's fair-weather sunburn, his skin looks pale and curdlike.

'I want to tell you guys the truth,' Beezer says. 'If Sawyer is right about this place, the creepy fuck who built it could have set up booby traps and all sorts of surprises. It was a long time ago, but if he really is the Fisherman, he has more reason than ever to keep people away from his crib. So we gotta watch our backs. The best way to do that is to go in strong, and go in ready. Put your weapons where you can reach them in a hurry, all right?'

Beezer opens one of his saddlebags and draws out a Colt

9mm pistol with ivory grips and a blue-steel barrel. He chambers a round and unlocks the safety. Under his gaze, Sonny pulls his massive .357 Magnum from his bag, Doc a Colt identical to Beezer's, and Kaiser Bill an old S&W .38 Special he has owned since the late seventies. They shove the weapons, which until this moment have seen use only on firing ranges, into the pockets of their leather jackets. Mouse, who does not own a gun, pats the various knives he has secreted in the small of his back, in the hip and front pockets of his jeans, and sheathed within both of his boots.

'Okay,' Beezer says. 'Anybody in there is going to hear us coming no matter what we do, and maybe already *has* heard us, so there's no point in being sneaky about this. I want a fast, aggressive entrance – just what you guys are good at. We can use speed to our advantage. Depending on what happens, we get as close to the house as possible.'

'What if nothing happens?' asks the Kaiser. 'Like, if we roll on in there and just keep going until we get to the house? I mean, I don't see any particular reason to be spooked here. Okay, something bad happened to Mouse, but . . . you know. Doesn't mean it's going to happen all over again.'

'Then we enjoy the ride,' Beezer says.

'Don't you want to take a look inside?' the Kaiser asks. 'He might have kids in there.'

'*He* might be in there,' Beezer tells him. 'If he is, no matter what I said to Sawyer, we're bringing him out. Alive would be better than dead, but I wouldn't mind putting him in a serious state of bad health.'

He gets a rumble of approval. Mouse does not contribute to this wordless, but otherwise universal agreement; he lowers his head and tightens his hands on the grips of his bike.

'Because Mouse has been here before, he goes in on

point. Doc and I'll be right behind him, with Sonny and the Kaiser covering our asses.' Beezer glances at them and says, 'Stay about six, eight feet back, all right?'

Don't put Mouse on point; you have to go in first, speaks in Sonny's mind, but he says, 'All right, Beeze.'

'Line up,' Beezer says.

They move their bikes into the positions Beezer has specified. Anyone driving fast along Highway 35 would have to hit his brakes to avoid running into at least two beefy men on motorcycles, but the road stays empty. Everyone, including Mouse, guns his engine and prepares to move. Sonny slaps his fist against the Kaiser's and looks back at that dark tunnel into the woods.

A big crow flaps onto a low-hanging branch, cocks its head, and seems to fix Sonny's eyes with its own. The crow must be looking at all of them, Sonny knows, but he cannot shake the illusion that the crow is staring directly at him, and that its black insatiable eyes are dancing with malice. The uncomfortable feeling that the crow is amused by the sight of him bent over his bike makes Sonny think of his Magnum.

Turn you into a mess of bloody feathers, baby.

Without unfolding its wings, the crow hops backward and disappears into the oak leaves.

'GO!' Beezer shouts.

The moment Mouse charges in, Little Nancy's rotting hands clamp down on his shoulders. Her thin bones press down on the leather hard enough to leave bruises on his skin. Although he knows this is impossible – you cannot get rid of what does not exist – the sudden flare of pain causes him to try to shake her off. He twitches his shoulders and wiggles the handlebars, and the bike wobbles. As the bike dips, Little Nancy digs in harder. When Mouse rights himself, she pulls herself forward, wraps her bony arms around his chest, and flattens her body against his back. Her skull grinds against the nape of his neck; her teeth bite down on his skin.

It is *too much*. Mouse had known she would reappear, but not that she would put him in a vise. And despite his speed, he has the feeling that he is traveling through a substance heavier and more viscous than air, a kind of syrup that slows him down, holds him back. Both he and the bike seem unnaturally dense, as if gravity exerts a stronger pull on the little road than anywhere else. His head pounds, and already he can hear that dog growling in the woods off to his right. He could take all of that, he supposes, if it were not for what stopped him the last time he drove up this path: a dead woman. Then she was Kiz Martin; now the dead woman is Little Nancy, and she is riding him like a dervish, slapping his head, punching him in the side, battering his ears. He feels her teeth leave his neck and sink into the left shoulder of his jacket. One of her arms whips in front of him, and he enters a deeper level of shock and horror when he realizes that this arm is visible. Rags of skin flutter over long bones; he glimpses white maggots wriggling into the few remaining knots of flesh.

A hand that feels both spongelike and bony flaps onto his cheek and crawls up his face. Mouse cannot keep it together anymore: his mind fills with white panic, and he loses control of the bike. When he heads into the curve that leads to Black House, the wheels are already tilting dangerously, and Mouse's sideways jerk of revulsion pushes them over beyond the possibility of correction.

As the bike topples, he hears the dog snarling from only a few yards away. The Harley smashes down on his left leg, then skids ahead, and he and his ghastly passenger slide after it. When Mouse sees Black House looming from its dark bower amid the trees, a rotting hand flattens over his eyes. His scream is a bright, thin thread of sound against the fury of the dog.

A few seconds after going in, Beezer feels the air thicken and congeal around him. It's some *trick*, he tells himself, an illusion produced by the Fisherman's mind-fuck toxins. Trusting that the others will not be suckered by this illusion, he raises his head and looks over Mouse's broad back and cornrowed head to see the road curve to the left about fifty feet ahead. The thick air seems to weigh down on his arms and shoulders, and he feels the onset of the mother and father of all headaches, a dull, insistent pain that begins as a sharp twinge behind his eyes and moves thudding deeper into his brain. Beezer gives Doc a half second of attention, and from what he sees, Doc is taking care of business. A glance at the speedometer tells him that he is traveling at thirty-five miles per hour and gathering steam, so they should be doing sixty by the time they come into the curve.

Off to his left, a dog growls. Beezer hauls his pistol out of his pocket and listens to the growling keep pace with them as they speed toward the curve. The band of pain in his head widens and intensifies; it seems to push at his eyes from the inside, making them bulge in their sockets. The big dog – it has to be a dog, what else could it be? – is getting closer, and the fury of its noises makes Beezer see a giant, tossing head with blazing red eyes and ropes of slather whipping from a gaping mouth filled with shark's teeth.

Two separate things destroy his concentration: the first is that he sees Mouse slamming himself back and forth on his bike as he goes into the curve, as if he is trying to scratch his back on the thickening air; the second is that the pressure behind his eyes triples in force, and immediately after he sees Mouse going into what is surely a fall, the blood vessels in his eyes explode. From deep red, his vision shifts rapidly to absolute black. An ugly voice starts up in his head, saying, *Amy zadt in my lap an huggedt mee. I made opp my mindt to eed hurr. How she dud, dud, dud kick an scrutch. I chokked hurr do deff—*

'No!' Beezer shouts, and the voice that is pushing at his eyes drops into a rasping chuckle. For less than a second, he gets a vision of a tall, shadowy creature and a single eye, a flash of teeth beneath a hat or a hood –

– and the world abruptly revolves around him, and he ends up flat on his back with the bike weighing on his chest. Everything he sees is stained a dark, seething red. Mouse is screaming, and when Beezer turns his head in the direction of the screams, he sees a red Mouse lying on a red road with a huge red dog barreling toward him. Beezer cannot find his pistol; it went sailing into the woods. Shouts, screams, and the roar of motorcycles fill his ears. He scrambles out from under the bike yelling he knows not what. A red Doc flashes by on his red bike and almost knocks him down again. He hears a gunshot, then another.

Doc sees Beezer glance at him and tries not to show how sick he feels. Dishwater boils in his stomach, and his guts are writhing. It feels like he is going about five miles an hour, the air is so thick and rancid. For some reason, his head weighs thirty or forty pounds, damnedest thing; it would almost be interesting if he could stop the disaster happening inside him. The air seems to *concentrate* itself, to *solidify*, and then *boom*, his head turns into a super-heavyweight bowling ball that wants to drop onto his chest. A giant growling sound comes from out of the woods beside him, and Doc almost yields to the impulse to puke. He is dimly aware that Beezer is pulling out his gun, and he supposes he should do the same, but part of his problem is that the memory of a child named Daisy Temperly has moved into his mind, and the memory of Daisy Temperly paralyzes his will.

As a resident in surgery at the university hospital in Urbana, Doc had performed, under supervision, nearly a hundred operations of every sort and assisted at as many. Until Daisy Temperly was wheeled into the OR, all of them had gone well. Complicated but not especially difficult or life-threatening, her case involved bone grafts and other repair work. Daisy was being put back together again after a serious auto accident, and she had already endured two previous surgeries. Two hours after the start of the procedure, the head of the department, Doc's supervisor, was called away for an emergency operation, and Doc was left in charge. Partly because he had been sleep-deprived for forty-eight hours, partly because in his exhaustion he had pictured himself cruising along the highway with Beezer, Mouse, and his other new friends, he made a mistake – not during the operation, but after it. While writing a prescription for medication, he miscalculated the dosage, and two hours later, Daisy Temperly was dead. There were things he could have done to rescue his career, but he did none of them. He was allowed to finish his residency, and then he left medicine for good. Talking to Jack Sawyer, he had vastly simplified his motives.

The uproar in the middle of his body can no longer be contained. Doc turns his head and vomits as he races forward. It is not the first time he has puked while riding, but it is the messiest and the most painful. The weight of his bowling-ball head means that he cannot extend his neck, so vomit spatters against his right shoulder and right arm; and what comes leaping out of him feels alive and equipped with teeth and claws. He is not surprised to see blood mixed with the vomit erupting from his mouth. His stomach doubles in on itself with pain.

Without meaning to, Doc has slowed down, and when he accelerates and faces forward again, he sees Mouse topple over sideways and skid behind his bike into the curve up ahead. His ears report a rushing sound, like that of a distant waterfall. Dimly, Mouse screams; equally dimly, Beezer shouts 'No!' Right after that, the Beeze runs headlong into a big rock or some other obstruction, because his Electra Glide leaves the ground, flips completely over in the compacted air, and comes down on top of him. It occurs to Doc that this mission is totally FUBAR. The whole world has hung a left, and now they are in deep shit. He does the only sensible thing: he yanks his trusty 9mm out of his pocket and tries to figure out what to shoot first.

His ears pop, and the sounds around him surge into life. Mouse is still screeching. Doc cannot figure out how he missed hearing the noise of the dog before, because even with the roaring of the cycles and Mouse's screams, that moving growl is the loudest sound in the woods. The fucking Hound of the Baskervilles is racing toward them, and both Mouse and Beezer are out of commission. From the noise it makes, the thing must be the size of a bear. Doc aims the pistol straight ahead and steers with one hand as he blasts by Beezer, who is wriggling out from beneath his bike. That enormous sound – Doc imagines a bear-sized dog widening its chops around Mouse's head, and instantly erases the image. Things are happening too fast, and if he doesn't pay attention, those jaws could close on *him*.

He has just time enough to think, *That's no ordinary dog, not even a huge one –*

– when something enormous and black comes charging

out of the woods to his right and cuts on a diagonal toward Mouse. Doc pulls the trigger, and at the sound of the pistol the animal whirls halfway around and snarls at him. All Doc can see clearly are two red eyes and an open red mouth with a long tongue and a lot of sharp canine teeth. Everything else is smudgy and indistinct, with no more definition than if it were covered in a swirling cape. A lightning bolt of pure terror that tastes as clean and sharp as cheap vodka pierces Doc from gullet to testicles, and his bike slews its rear end around and comes to a halt – he has stopped it out of sheer reflex. Suddenly it feels like deep night. Of course he can't see it – how could you see a black dog in the middle of the night?

The creature whirls around again and streaks toward Mouse.

It doesn't want to charge me because of the gun and because the other two guys are right behind me, Doc thinks. His head and arms seem to have gained another forty pounds apiece, but he fights against the weight of his muscles and straightens his arms and fires again. This time he *knows* he hits that thing, but its only reaction is to shudder off-course for a moment. The big smudge of its head swings toward Doc. The growling gets even louder, and long, silvery streamers of dog drool fly from its open mouth. Something that suggests a tail switches back and forth.

When Doc looks into the open red gash, his resolve weakens, his arms get heavier, and he is scarcely capable of holding his head upright. He feels as though he is falling down into that red maw; his pistol dangles from his limp hand. In a moment suspended throughout eternity, the same hand scribbles a post-op prescription for Daisy Temperly. The creature trots toward Mouse. Doc can hear Sonny's voice, cursing furiously. A loud explosion on his right side seals both of his ears, and the world falls perfectly silent. *Here we are*, Doc says to himself. *Darkness at noon.*

For Sonny, the darkness strikes at the same time as the searing pain in his head and his stomach. A single band of agony rips right down through his body, a phenomenon so unparalleled and extreme that he assumes it has also erased the daylight. He and Kaiser Bill are eight feet behind Beezer and Doc, and about fifteen feet up the narrow dirt road. The Kaiser lets go of his handlebars and grips the sides of his head. Sonny understands exactly how he feels: a four-foot section of red-hot iron pipe has been thrust through the top of his head and pushed down into his guts, burning everything it touches. 'Hey, man,' he says, in his misery noticing that the air has turned sludgy, as though individual atoms of oxygen and carbon dioxide are gummy enough to stick to his skin. Then Sonny notices that the Kaiser's eyes are swimming up toward the back of his head, and he realizes that the man is passing out right next to him. Sick as he is, he has to do something to protect the Kaiser. Sonny reaches out for the other man's bike, watching as well as he can the disappearance of the Kaiser's irises beneath his upper eyelids. Blood explodes out of his nostrils, and his body slumps backward on the seat and rolls over the side. For a couple of seconds, he is dragged along by a boot caught in the handlebars, but the boot slips off, and the cycle drifts to a halt.

The red-hot iron bar seems to rupture his stomach, and Sonny has no choice; he lets the other bike fall and utters a groan and bends sideways and vomits out what feels like every meal he has ever eaten. When nothing is left inside him, his stomach feels better, but John Henry has decided to drive giant rail spikes through his skull. His arms and legs are made of rubber. Sonny focuses on his bike. It seems to be standing still.

He does not understand how he can go forward, but he watches a blood-spattered hand gun his bike and manages to stay upright when it takes off. *Is that my blood?* he wonders, and remembers two long red flags unfurling from the Kaiser's nose.

A noise that had been gathering strength in the background turns into the sound of a 747 coming in for a landing. Sonny thinks that the last thing he wants to do today is get a look at the animal capable of making that sound. Mouse was right on the money: this is a bad, bad place, right up there with the charming town of Harko, Illinois. Sonny wishes to encounter no more Harkos, okay? One was enough. So why is he moving forward instead of turning around and running for the sunny peace of Highway 35? Why is he pulling that massive gun out of his pocket? It's simple. He is not about to let that jet-airplane-dog mess up his homeys, no matter how much his head hurts.

John Henry keeps pounding in those five-dollar spikes while Sonny picks up speed and squints at the road ahead, trying to figure out what is going on. Someone screams, he cannot identify who. Through the growling, he hears the unmistakable sound of a motorcycle hitting the ground after a flip, and his heart shivers. *Beezer should always be point man,* he thinks, *otherwise we're asking for punishment.* A gun goes off with a loud explosion. Sonny forces himself to press through the gluey atoms in the air, and after another five or six seconds he spots Beezer, who is painfully pushing himself upward beside his toppled bike. A few feet beyond Beezer, Doc's bulky figure comes into view, sitting astride his bike and aiming his 9 at something in the road ahead of him. Doc fires, and red flame bursts from the barrel of his pistol.

Feeling more beat-up and useless than ever before in his life, Sonny jumps from his moving bike and runs toward Doc, trying to look past him. The first thing he sees is a flash of light off Mouse's bike, which comes into view flat on its side about twenty feet down the road, at the top of the curve. Then he finds Mouse, on his ass and scrambling backward from some animal Sonny can barely make out, except for its eyes and teeth. Unconscious of the stream of obscenities that pour from his mouth, Sonny levels his pistol at the creature and fires just as he runs past Doc.

Doc just stands there; Doc is out for the count. The weird animal up on the road closes its jaws on Mouse's leg. It is going to rip away a hamburger-sized chunk of muscle, but Sonny hits it with a fucking hollow-point *missile* from his Magnum, a bit show-offy for target practice but under the circumstances no more than prudent, thank you very much. Contrary to all expectations and the laws of physics, Sonny's amazing wonder-bullet does not knock a hole the size of a football in the creature's hide. The wonderbullet pushes the animal sideways and distracts it from Mouse's leg; it does not even knock it down. Mouse sends up a howl of pain.

The dog whips around and glares at Sonny with red eyes the size of baseballs. Its mouth opens on jagged white teeth, and it snaps the air. Ropes of slime shoot out of its jaws. The creature lowers its shoulders and steps forward. Amazingly, its snarling grows in volume and ferocity. Sonny is being warned: if he does not turn and run, he is next on the menu.

'Fuck that,' Sonny says, and fires straight at the animal's mouth. Its whole head should fly apart in bloody rags, but for a second after the Magnum goes off, nothing changes.

Oh, shit, Sonny thinks.

The dog-thing's eyes blaze, and its feral, wedge-shaped head seems to assemble itself out of the darkness in the air and emerge into view. As though an inky robe had been partially twitched aside, Sonny can see a thick neck descending to meaty shoulders and strong front legs. Maybe the tide is turning here, maybe this monster will turn out to be vulnerable after all. Sonny braces his right wrist with his left hand, aims at the dog-thing's chest, and squeezes off another round. The explosion seems to stuff his ears with cotton. All the railroad spikes in his head heat up like electric coils, and bright pain sings between his temples.

Dark blood gouts from the creature's brisket. At the center of Sonny Cantinaro's being, a pure, primitive triumph bursts into life. More of the monster melts into visibility, the wide back and a suggestion of its rear legs. Of no recognizable breed and four and a half feet high, the dog-thing is approximately the size of a gigantic wolf. When it moves toward him, Sonny fires again. Like an echo, the sound of his gun repeats from somewhere close behind; a bullet like a supercharged wasp zings past his chest.

The creature staggers back, limping on an injured leg. Its enraged eyes bore into Sonny's. He risks glancing over his shoulder and sees Beezer braced in the middle of the narrow road.

'Don't look at me, shoot!' Beezer yells.

His voice seems to awaken Doc, who raises his arm and takes aim. Then all three of them are pulling their triggers, and the little road sounds like the firing range on a busy day. The dog-thing (*hell hound*, Sonny thinks) limps back a step and opens wide its terrible mouth to howl in rage and frustration. Before the howl ends, the creature gathers its rear legs beneath its body, springs across the road, and vanishes into the woods.

Sonny fights off the impulse to collapse under a wave of relief and fatigue. Doc swivels his body and keeps firing into the darkness behind the trees until Beezer puts a hand on his arm and orders him to stop. The air stinks of cordite and some animal odor that is musky and disgustingly sweet. Pale gray smoke shimmers almost white as it filters upward through the darker air.

Beezer's haggard face turns to Sonny, and the whites of his eyes are crimson. 'You hit that fucking animal, didn't you?' Through the wads of cotton in his ears, Beezer's voice sounds small and tinny.

'Shit, yes. At least twice, probably three times.'

'And Doc and I hit it once apiece. What the hell is that thing?'

'"What the hell" is right,' Sonny says.

Weeping with pain, Mouse a third time repeats his cry of 'Help me!' and the others hear him at last. Moving slowly and pressing their hands over whatever parts of their bodies hurt the most, they hobble up the road and kneel in front of Mouse. The right leg of his jeans is ripped and soaked with blood, and his face is contorted.

'Are you assholes deaf?'

'Pretty near,' Doc says. 'Tell me you didn't take a bullet in your leg.'

'No, but it must be some kind of miracle.' He winces and inhales sharply. Air hisses between his teeth. 'Way you guys were shooting. Too bad you couldn't draw a bead before it bit my leg.'

'I did,' Sonny says. 'Reason you still *got* a leg.'

Mouse peers at him, then shakes his head. 'What happened to the Kaiser?'

'He lost about a liter of blood through his nose and passed out,' Sonny tells him.

Mouse sighs as if at the frailty of the human species. 'I believe we might try to get out of this crazy shithole.'

'Is your leg all right?' Beezer asks.

'It's not broken, if that's what you mean. But it's not all right, either.'

'What?' Doc asks.

'I can't say,' Mouse tells him. 'I don't answer medical questions from guys all covered in puke.'

'Can you ride?'

'Fuck yes, Beezer – you ever know me when I couldn't *ride*?'

Beezer and Sonny each take a side and, with excruciating effort, lift Mouse to his feet. When they release his arms, Mouse lumbers sideways a few steps. 'This is not right,' he says.

'That's brilliant,' says Beezer.

'Beeze, old buddy, you know your eyes are, like, bright red? You look like fuckin' Dracula.'

To the extent that hurry is possible, they are hurrying. Doc wants to get a look at Mouse's leg; Beezer wants to make sure that Kaiser Bill is still alive; and all of them want to get out of this place and back into normal air and sunlight. Their heads pound, and their muscles ache from strain. None of them can be sure that the dog-thing is not preparing for another charge.

As they speak, Sonny has been picking up Mouse's Fat Boy and rolling it toward its owner. Mouse takes the handles and pushes his machine forward, wincing as he goes. Beezer and Doc rescue their bikes, and six feet along Sonny pulls his upright out of a snarl of weeds.

Beezer realizes that when he was at the curve in the road, he failed to look for Black House. He remembers Mouse saying, *This shit doesn't want to be seen*, and he thinks Mouse got it just about right: the Fisherman did not want them there, and the Fisherman did not want his house to be seen. Everything else was spinning around in his head the way his Electra Glide had spun over after that ugly voice spoke up in his mind. Beezer is certain of one thing, however: Jack Sawyer is not going to hold out on him any longer.

Then a terrible thought strikes him, and he asks, 'Did anything funny – anything really *strange* – happen to you guys before the dog from hell jumped out of the woods? Besides the physical stuff, I mean.'

He looks at Doc, and Doc blushes. *Hello?* Beezer thinks.

Mouse says, 'Go fuck yourself. I'm not gonna talk about that.'

'I'm with Mouse,' Sonny says.

'I guess the answer is yes,' Beezer says.

Kaiser Bill is lying by the side of the road with his eyes closed and the front of his body wet with blood from mouth to waist. The air is still gray and sticky; their bodies seem to weigh a thousand pounds, the bikes to roll on leaden wheels. Sonny walks his bike up beside the Kaiser's supine body and kicks him, not all that gently, in the ribs.

The Kaiser opens his eyes and groans. 'Fuck, Sonny,' he says. 'You kicked me.' His eyelids flutter, and he lifts his head off the ground and notices the blood soaking into his clothing. 'What happened? Am I shot?'

'You conducted yourself like a hero,' Sonny says. 'How do you feel?'

'Lousy. Where was I hit?'

'How am I supposed to know?' Sonny says. 'Come on, we're getting out of here.'

The others file past. Kaiser Bill manages to get to his feet and, after another epic struggle, hauls his bike upright beside him. He pushes it down the track after the others, marveling at the pain in his head and the quantity of blood on his body.

When he comes out through the last of the trees and joins his friends on Highway 35, the sudden brightness stabs his eyes, his body feels light enough to float away, and he nearly passes out all over again. 'I don't think I did get shot,' he says.

No one pays any attention to the Kaiser. Doc is asking Mouse if he wants to go to the hospital.

'No hospital, man. Hospitals kill people.'

'At least let me take a look at your leg.'

'Fine, look.'

Doc kneels at the side of the road and tugs the cuff of Mouse's jeans up to the bottom of his knee. He probes with surprisingly delicate fingers, and Mouse winces.

'Mouse,' he says, 'I've never seen a dog bite like this before.'

'Never saw a dog like that before, either.'

The Kaiser says, 'What dog?'

'There's something funny about this wound,' Doc says. 'You need antibiotics, and you need them right away.'

'Don't you have antibiotics?'

'Sure, I do.'

'Then let's go back to Beezer's place, and you can stick me full of needles.'

'Whatever you say,' says Doc.

20

Around the time Mouse and Beezer first fail to see the little road and the NO TRESPASSING sign beside it, Jack Sawyer answers the annoying signal of his cell phone, hoping that his caller will turn out to be Henry Leyden with information about the voice on the 911 tape. Although an identification would be wonderful, he does not expect Henry to ID the voice; the Fisherman – Burnside – is Potsie's age, and Jack does not suppose the old villain has much of a social life, here or in the Territories. What Henry *can* do, however, is to apply his finely tuned ears to the nuances of Burnside's voice and describe what he hears in it. If we did not know that Jack's faith in his friend's capacity to hear distinctions and patterns inaudible to other people was justified, that faith would seem as irrational as the belief in magic: Jack trusts that a refreshed, invigorated Henry Leyden will pick up at least one or two crucial details of history or character that will narrow the search. Anything that Henry picks up will interest Jack.

If someone else is calling him, he intends to get rid of whoever it is, fast.

The voice that answers his greeting revises his plans. Fred

Marshall wants to talk to him, and Fred is so wound up and incoherent that Jack must ask him to slow down and start over.

'Judy's flipping out again,' Fred says. 'Just . . . babbling and raving, and getting crazy like before, trying to rip through the walls – oh God, they put her in restraints and she hates that, she wants to help Ty, it's all because of that tape. Christ, it's getting to be too much to handle, Jack, Mr Sawyer, I mean it, and I know I'm running off at the mouth, but I'm really worried.'

'Don't tell me someone sent her the 911 tape,' Jack says.

'No, not . . . what 911 tape? I'm talking about the one that was delivered to the hospital today. Addressed to Judy. Can you believe they let her *listen* to that thing? I want to strangle Dr Spiegleman and that nurse, Jane Bond. What's the matter with these people? The tape comes in, they say, oh goody, here's a nice tape for you to listen to, Mrs Marshall, hold on, I'll be right back with a cassette player. On a *mental ward*? They don't even bother to listen to it first? Look, whatever you're doing, I'd be eternally grateful if you'd let me pick you up, so I could drive you over there. You could talk to her. You're the only person who can calm her down.'

'You don't have to pick me up, because I'm already on the way. What was on the tape?'

'I don't get it.' Fred Marshall has become considerably more lucid. 'Why are you going there without me?'

After a second of thought, Jack tells him an outright lie. 'I thought you would probably be there already. It's a pity you weren't.'

'I would have had the sense to screen that tape before letting *her* hear it. Do you know what was on that thing?'

'The Fisherman,' Jack says.

'How did you know?'

'He's a great communicator,' Jack says. 'How bad was it?'

'You tell me, and then we'll both know. I'm piecing it together from what I gathered from Judy and what Dr Spiegleman told me later.' Fred Marshall's voice begins to waver. 'The Fisherman was taunting her. Can you believe that? He said, *Your little boy is very lonely*. Then he said something like, *He's been begging and begging to call home and say hello to his mommy*. Except Judy says he had a weird foreign accent, or a speech impediment, or something, so he wasn't easy to understand right away. Then he says, *Say hello to your mommy, Tyler*, and Tyler . . .' Fred's voice breaks, and Jack can hear him stifling his agony before he begins again. 'Tyler, ah, Tyler was apparently too distressed to do much but scream for help.' A long, uncertain inhalation comes over the phone. 'And he *cried*, Jack, he *cried*.' Unable to contain his feelings any longer, Fred weeps openly, unguardedly. His breath rattles in his throat; Jack listens to all the wet, undignified, helpless noises people make when grief and sorrow cancel every other feeling, and his heart moves for Fred Marshall.

The sobbing relents. 'Sorry. Sometimes I think they'll have to put *me* in restraints.'

'Was that the end of the tape?'

'*He* got on again.' Fred breathes noisily for a moment, clearing his head. 'Boasting about what he was going to do. *Dere vill be morrr mur-derts, and morrr afder dat, Choo-dee, we are all goink zu haff sotch fun* – Spiegleman quoted this junk to me! The children of French Landing will be harvested like wheat. *Havv-uz-ted like wheed.* Who talks like that? What kind of person is this?'

'I wish I knew,' Jack says. 'Maybe he was putting on an accent to sound even scarier. Or to disguise his voice.' *He'd never disguise his voice*, Jack thinks, *he's too delighted with himself to hide behind an accent.* 'I'll have to get the tape from the hospital and listen to it myself. And I'll call you as soon as I have some information.'

'There's one more thing,' Marshall says. 'I probably made a mistake. Wendell Green came over about an hour ago.'

'Anything involving Wendell Green is automatically a mistake. So what happened?'

'It was like he knew all about Tyler and just needed me to confirm it. I thought he must have heard from Dale, or the state troopers. But Dale hasn't made us public yet, has he?'

'Wendell has a network of little weasels that feed him information. If he knows anything, that's how he heard about it. What did you tell him?'

'More or less everything,' Marshall says. 'Including the tape. Oh, God, I'm such a dope. But I thought it'd be all right – I thought it would all get out anyhow.'

'Fred, did you tell him anything about me?'

'Only that Judy trusts you and that we're both grateful for your help. And I think I said that you would probably be going in to see her this afternoon.'

'Did you mention Ty's baseball cap?'

'Do you think I'm *nuts*? As far as I'm concerned, that stuff is between you and Judy. If I don't get it, I'm not going to talk about it to Wendell Green. At least I got him to promise to stay away from Judy. He has a great reputation, but I got the feeling he isn't everything he's cracked up to be.'

'You said a mouthful,' Jack says. 'I'll be in touch.'

When Fred Marshall hangs up, Jack punches in Henry's number.

'I may be a little late, Henry. I'm on my way to French County Lutheran. Judy Marshall got a tape from the Fisherman, and if they'll let me have it, I'll bring it over. There's something strange going on here – on Judy's tape, I guess he has some kind of foreign accent.'

Henry tells Jack there is no rush. He has not listened to the first tape yet, and now will wait until Jack comes over with the second one. He might hear something useful if he plays them in sequence. At least, he could tell Jack if they were made by the same man. 'And don't worry about me, Jack. In a little while, Mrs Morton is coming by to take me over to KDCU. George Rathbun butters my bread today, baby – six or seven radio ads. "Even a *blind man* knows you want to treat your honey, your sweetheart, your lovey-dovey, your wife, your best friend through thick and thin, to a mm-mmm fine dinner tonight, and there's no better place to show your appreciation to the old ball and chain than to take her to Cousin Buddy's Rib Crib on South Wabash Street in beautiful downtown La Riviere!"'

'"The old ball and chain"?'

'You pay for George Rathbun, you get George Rathbun, warts and all.'

Laughing, Jack tells Henry he will see him later that day, and pushes the Ram up to seventy. What is Dale going to do, give him a speeding ticket?

He parks in front of the hospital instead of driving around to the parking lot, and trots across the concrete with his mind filled with the Territories and Judy Marshall. Things are hurtling forward, picking up pace, and Jack has the sense that everything converges on Judy – no, on Judy and *him*. The Fisherman has chosen them more purposefully than he did his first three victims: Amy St Pierre, Johnny Irkenham, and Irma Freneau were simply the right age – any three children would have done – but Tyler was Judy Marshall's son, and that set him apart. Judy has glimpsed the Territories, Jack has traveled through them, and the Fisherman lives there the way a cancer cell lives in a healthy organism. The Fisherman sent Judy a tape, Jack a grisly present. At Tansy Freneau's, he had seen Judy as his key and the door it opened, and where did that door lead but into Judy's Faraway?

Faraway. God, that's pretty. Beautiful, in fact.

Aaah . . . the word evokes Judy Marshall's face, and when he sees that face, a door in his mind, a door that is his and his alone, flies open, and for a moment Jack Sawyer stops moving altogether, and in shock, dread, and joyous expectation, freezes on the concrete six feet from the hospital's entrance.

Through the door in his mind pours a stream of disconnected images: a stalled Ferris wheel, Santa Monica cops milling behind a strip of yellow crime-scene tape, light reflected off a black man's bald head. Yes, a bald man's black head, that which he really and truly, in fact most desperately, had not wished to see, so take a good look, kiddo, here it is again. There had been a guitar, but the guitar was elsewhere; the guitar belonged to the magnificent demanding comforting comfortless Speedy Parker, God bless him God damn his eyes God love him Speedy, who touched its strings and sang

Travelin' Jack, ole Travelin' Jack,
Got a far long way to go,
Longer way to come back.

Worlds spin around him, worlds within worlds and other worlds alongside them, separated by a thin membrane composed of a thousand thousand doors, if only you know how to find them. A thousand thousand red feathers, tiny ones, feathers from a robin redbreast, hundreds of robin redbreasts, flew through one of those doors, Speedy's. *Robin*, as in *robin's-egg blue*, thank you, Speedy, and a song that said *Wake up, wake up, you sleepyhead.*

Or: *Wake up, wake up, you DUNDERHEAD!*

Crazily, Jack hears George Rathbun's now-not-so genial roar: *Eeeven a BLIIIND MAAAN coulda seen THIS one coming, you KNOTHEAD!*

'Oh, yeah?' Jack says out loud. It is a good thing Head Nurse Jane Bond, Warden Bond, Agent OO Zero, cannot hear him. She's tough, but on the other hand, she's unfair, and if she were to appear beside him now, she would probably clap him in irons, sedate him, and drag him back to her domain. 'Well, I know something you don't know, old buddy: Judy Marshall has a Twinner, and the Twinner has been whispering through the wall for a considerable old time now. It's no surprise she finally started to shout.'

A red-haired teenager in an ARDEN H.S. BASEBALL T-shirt shoves open the literal door six feet from Jack and gives him a wary, disconcerted look. *Man, grown-ups are weird*, the look says; *aren't I glad I'm a kid?* Since he is a high school student and not a mental-health professional, he does not clap our hero in irons and drag him sedated away to the padded room. He simply takes care to steer a wide course around the madman and keeps walking, albeit with a touch of self-conscious stiffness in his gait.

It is all about Twinners, of course. Rebuking his stupidity, Jack raps his knuckles against the side of his head. He should have seen it before; he should have understood *immediately*. If he has any excuse, it is that at first he refused to think about the case despite Speedy's efforts to wake him up, then became so caught up in concentrating on the Fisherman that until this morning, while watching his mother on the Sand Bar's big TV, he had neglected to consider the monster's Twinner. In Judy

Marshall's childhood, her Twinner had spoken to her through that membrane between the two worlds; growing more and more alarmed over the past month, the Twinner had all but thrust her arms through the membrane and shaken Judy senseless. Because Jack is single-natured and has no Twinner, the corresponding task fell to Speedy. Now that everything seems to make sense, Jack cannot believe it has taken him so long to see the pattern.

And *this* is why he has resented everything that kept him from standing before Judy Marshall: Judy is the doorway to her Twinner, to Tyler, and to the destruction of both the Fisherman and his opposite number in the Territories, the builder of the satanic, fiery structure a crow named Gorg showed Tansy Freneau. Whatever happens on Ward D today, it is going to be world-altering.

Heart thrumming in anticipation, Jack passes from intense sunlight into the vast ocher space of the lobby. The same bathrobed patients seem to occupy the many chairs; in a distant corner, the same doctors discuss a troublesome case or, who knows, that tricky tenth hole at Arden Country Club; the same golden lilies raise their luxuriant, attentive heads outside the gift shop. This repetition reassures Jack, it hastens his step, for it surrounds and cushions the unforeseeable events awaiting him on the fifth floor.

The same bored clerk responds to the proffer of the same password with an identical, if not the same, green card stamped VISITOR. The elevator surprisingly similar to one in the Ritz Hôtel on the Place Vendôme obediently trembles upward past floors two, three, and four, in its dowager-like progress pausing to admit a gaunt young doctor who summons the memory of Roderick Usher, then releases Jack on five, where the beautiful ocher light seems a shade or two darker than down there in the huge lobby. From the elevator Jack retraces the steps he took with his guide Fred Marshall down the corridor, through the two sets of double doors and past the way stations of Gerontology and Ambulatory Ophthalmology and Records Annex, getting closer and closer to the unforeseen unforeseeable as the corridors grow narrower and darker, and emerges as before into the century-old room with high, skinny windows and a lot of walnut-colored wood.

And there the spell breaks, for the attendant seated behind the polished counter, the person currently the guardian of this realm, is taller, younger, and considerably more sullen than his counterpart of the day before. When Jack asks to see Mrs Marshall, the young person glances in disdain at his VISITOR card and inquires if he should happen to be a relative or – another glance at the card – a medical professional. Neither, Jack admits, but if the young person could trouble himself to inform Nurse Bond that Mr Sawyer wishes to speak to Mrs Marshall, Nurse Bond is practically guaranteed to swing open the forbidding metal doors and wave him inward, since that is more or less what she did yesterday.

That is all well and good, if it happens to be true, the young person allows, but Nurse Bond is not going to be doing any door opening and waving in today, for today Nurse Bond is off duty. Could it be that when Mr Sawyer showed up to see Mrs Marshall yesterday he was accompanied by a family member, say Mr Marshall?

Yes. And if Mr Marshall were to be consulted, say via the telephone, he would urge the young fellow presently discussing the matter in a commendably responsible fashion with Mr Sawyer to admit the gentleman promptly.

That may be the case, the young person grants, but hospital regulations require that nonmedical personnel in positions such as the young person's obtain authorization for any outside telephone calls.

And from whom, Jack wishes to know, would this authorization be obtained?

From the acting head nurse, Nurse Rack.

Jack, who is growing a little hot, as they say, under the collar, suggests in that case that the young person seek out the excellent Nurse Rack and obtain the required authorization, so that things might progress in the manner Mr Marshall, the patient's husband, would wish.

No, the young person sees no reason to pursue such a course, the reason being that doing so would represent a pitiful waste of time and effort. Mr Sawyer is not a member of Mrs Marshall's family; therefore the excellent Nurse Rack would under no circumstances grant the authorization.

'Okay,' Jack says, wishing he could strangle this irritating pip-squeak, 'let's move a step up the administrative ladder, shall we? Is Dr Spiegleman somewhere on the premises?'

'Could be,' the young person says. 'How'm I supposed to know? Dr Spiegleman doesn't tell me everything he does.'

Jack points to the telephone at the end of the counter. 'I don't expect you to know, I expect you to find out. Get on that phone *now*.'

The young man slouches down the counter to the telephone, rolls his eyes, punches two numbered keys, and leans against the counter with his back to the room. Jack hears him muttering about Spiegleman, sigh, then say, 'All right, transfer me, whatever.' Transferred, he mutters something that includes Jack's name. Whatever he hears in response causes him to jerk himself upright and sneak a wide-eyed look over his shoulder at Jack. 'Yes, sir. He's here now, yes. I'll tell him.'

He replaces the receiver. 'Dr Spiegleman'll be here right

away.' The boy – he is no more than twenty – steps back and shoves his hands in his pockets. 'You're that cop, huh?'

'What cop?' Jack says, still irritated.

'The one from California that came here and arrested Mr Kinderling.'

'Yes, that's me.'

'I'm from French Landing, and boy, that was some shock. To the whole town. Nobody would have guessed. Mr *Kinderling*? Are you kidding? You'd never believe that someone like that would . . . you know, kill people.'

'Did you know him?'

'Well, in a town like French Landing, everybody sort of knows everybody, but I didn't really know Mr Kinderling, except to say hi. The one I knew was his wife. She used to be my Sunday school teacher at Mount Hebron Lutheran.'

Jack cannot help it; he laughs at the incongruity of the murderer's wife teaching Sunday school classes. The memory of Wanda Kinderling radiating hatred at him during her husband's sentencing stops his laughter, but it is too late. He sees that he has offended the young man. 'What was she like?' he asks. 'As a teacher.'

'Just a teacher,' the boy says. His voice is uninflected, resentful. 'She made us memorize all the books of the Bible.' He turns away and mutters, 'Some people think he didn't do it.'

'What did you say?'

The boy half-turns toward Jack but looks at the brown wall in front of him. 'I said, Some people think he didn't do it. Mr Kinderling. They think he got put in jail because he was a small-town guy who didn't know anybody out there.'

'That's too bad,' Jack says. 'Do you want to know the real reason Mr Kinderling went to prison?'

The boy turns the rest of the way and looks at Jack.

'Because he was guilty of murder, and he confessed. That's it, that's all. Two witnesses put him at the scene, and two other people saw him on a plane to LA when he told everyone he was flying to Denver. After that, he said, Okay, I did it. I always wanted to know what it was like to kill a girl, and one day I couldn't stand it anymore, so I went out and killed two whores. His lawyer tried to get him off on an insanity plea, but the jury at his hearing found him sane, and he went to prison.'

The boy lowers his head and mumbles something.

'I couldn't hear that,' Jack says.

'Lots of ways to make a guy confess.' The boy repeats the sentence just loud enough to be heard.

Then footsteps ring in the hallway, and a plump, white-coated man with steel-rimmed glasses and a goatee comes striding toward Jack with his hand out. The boy has turned away. The opportunity to convince the attendant that he did not beat a confession out of Thornberg Kinderling has slipped away. The smiling man with the white jacket and the goatee seizes Jack's hand, introduces himself as Dr Spiegleman, and declares it a pleasure to meet such a famous personage. (*Personage, persiflage*, Jack thinks.) From one step behind the doctor, a man unnoticed until this moment steps fully into view and says, 'Hey, Doctor, do you know what would be perfect? If Mr Famous and I interview the lady together. Twice the information in half the time – perfect.'

Jack's stomach turns sour. Wendell Green has joined the party.

After greeting the doctor, Jack turns to the other man. 'What are you doing here, Wendell? You promised Fred Marshall you'd stay away from his wife.'

Wendell Green holds up his hands and dances back on the balls of his feet. 'Are we calmer today, Lieutenant Sawyer? Not inclined to use a sucker punch on the hard-working press, are we? I have to say, I'm getting a little tired of being assaulted by the police.'

Dr Spiegleman frowns at him. 'What are you saying, Mr Green?'

'Yesterday, before that cop knocked me out with his flashlight, Lieutenant Sawyer here punched me in the stomach for no real reason at all. It's a good thing I'm a reasonable man, or I'd have filed lawsuits already. But, Doctor, you know what? I don't do things that way. I believe everything works out better if we cooperate with each other.'

Halfway through this self-serving speech, Jack thinks, *Oh hell*, and glances at the young attendant. The boy's eyes burn with loathing. A lost cause: now Jack will never persuade the boy that he did not mistreat Kinderling. By the time Wendell Green finishes congratulating himself, Jack has had a bellyful of his specious, smarmy affability.

'Mr Green offered to give me a percentage of his take, if I let him sell photographs of Irma Freneau's corpse,' he tells the doctor. 'What he is asking now is equally unthinkable. Mr Marshall urged me to come here and see his wife, and he made Mr Green promise *not* to come.'

'Technically, that may be true,' Green says. 'As an experienced journalist, I know that people often say things they don't mean and will eventually regret. Fred Marshall understands that his wife's story is going to come out sooner or later.'

'Does he?'

'Especially in the light of the Fisherman's latest communication,' Green says. 'This tape proves that Tyler Marshall is his fourth victim, and that, miraculously, he is still alive. How long do you think that can be kept from the public? And wouldn't you agree that the boy's mother should be able to explain the situation in her own words?'

'I refuse to be badgered like this.' The doctor scowls at Green and gives Jack a look of warning. 'Mr Green, I am very close to ordering you out of this hospital. I wish to discuss several matters with Lieutenant Sawyer, in private. If you and the lieutenant can work out some agreement between the two of you, that is your affair. I am certainly not going to permit a joint interview with my patient. I am in no way certain that she should talk to Lieutenant Sawyer, either. She is calmer than she was this morning, but she is still fragile.'

'The best way to deal with her problem is to let her express herself,' Green says.

'You will be quiet *now*, Mr Green,' Dr Spiegleman says. The double chins that fold under his goatee turn a warm pink. He glares at Jack. 'What specifically is it that you request, Lieutenant?'

'Do you have an office in this hospital, Doctor?'

'I do.'

'Ideally, I'd like to spend about half an hour, maybe less, talking to Mrs Marshall in a safe, quiet environment where our conversation would be completely confidential. Your office would probably be perfect. There are too many people on the ward, and you can't talk without being interrupted or having other patients listen in.'

'My office,' Spiegleman says.

'If you're willing.'

'Come with me,' the doctor says. 'Mr Green, you will please stand back next to the counter while Lieutenant Sawyer and I step into the hallway.'

'Anything you say.' Green executes a mocking bow and

moves lightly, with a suggestion of dance steps, to the counter. 'In your absence, I'm sure this handsome young man and I will find something to talk about.'

Smiling, Wendell Green props his elbows on the counter and watches Jack and Dr Spiegleman leave the room. Their footsteps click against the floor tiles until it sounds as though they have gone more than halfway down the corridor. Then there is silence. Still smiling, Wendell about-faces and finds the attendant openly staring at him.

'I read you all the time,' the boy says. 'You write real good.'

Wendell's smile becomes beatific. 'Handsome *and* intelligent. What a stunning combination. Tell me your name.'

'Ethan Evans.'

'Ethan, we do not have much time here, so let's make this snappy. Do you think responsible members of the press should have access to information the public needs?'

'You bet.'

'And wouldn't you agree that an informed press is one of our best weapons against monsters like the Fisherman?'

A single, vertical wrinkle appears between Ethan Evans's eyebrows. 'Weapons?'

'Let me put it this way. Isn't it true that the more we know about the Fisherman, the better chance we have of stopping him?'

The boy nods, and the wrinkle disappears.

'Tell me, do you think the doctor is going to let Sawyer use his office?'

'Prob'ly, yeah,' Evans says. 'But I don't like the way that Sawyer guy works. He's a police brutality. Like when they hit people to make them confess. That's brutality.'

'I have another question for you. Two questions, really. Is

there a closet in Dr Spiegleman's office? And is there some way you could take me there without going through that corridor?'

'Oh.' Evans's dim eyes momentarily shine with understanding. 'You want to *listen*.'

'Listen and record.' Wendell Green taps the pocket that contains his cassette recorder. 'For the good of the public at large, God bless 'em one and all.'

'Well, maybe, yeah,' the boy says. 'But Dr Spiegleman, he . . .'

A twenty-dollar bill has magically appeared folded around the second finger of Wendell Green's right hand. 'Act fast, and Dr Spiegleman will never know a thing. Right, Ethan?'

Ethan Evans snatches the bill from Wendell's hand and motions him back behind the counter, where he opens a door and says, 'Come on, hurry.'

Low lights burn at both ends of the dark corridor. Dr Spiegleman says, 'I gather that my patient's husband told you about the tape she received this morning.'

'He did. How did it get here, do you know?'

'Believe me, Lieutenant, after I saw the effect that tape had on Mrs Marshall and listened to it myself, I tried to learn how it reached my patient. All of our mail goes through the hospital's mailroom before being delivered, *all* of it, whether to patients, medical staff, or administrative offices. From there, a couple of volunteers deliver it to the addressees. I gather that the package containing the tape was in the hospital mailroom when a volunteer looked in there this morning. Because the package was addressed only with my patient's name, the volunteer went to our general information office. One of the girls brought it up.'

'Shouldn't someone have consulted you before giving the tape and a cassette player to Judy?'

'Of course. Nurse Bond would have done so immediately, but she is not on duty today. Nurse Rack, who is on duty, assumed that the address referred to a childhood nickname and thought that one of Mrs Marshall's old friends had sent her some music to cheer her up. And there is a cassette player in the nurses' station, so she put the tape in the player and gave it to Mrs Marshall.'

In the gloom of the corridor, the doctor's eyes take on a sardonic glint. 'Then, as you might imagine, all hell broke loose. Mrs Marshall reverted to the condition in which she was first hospitalized, which takes in a range of alarming behaviors. Fortunately, I happened to be in the hospital, and when I heard what had happened, I ordered her sedated and placed in a secure room. A secure room, Lieutenant, has padded walls – Mrs Marshall had reopened the wounds to her fingers, and I did not want her to do any more damage to herself. Once the sedative had taken effect, I went in and talked to her. I listened to the tape. Perhaps I should have called the police immediately, but my first responsibility is to my patient, and I called Mr Marshall instead.'

'From where?'

'From the secure room, with my cell phone. Mr Marshall of course insisted on speaking to his wife, and she wanted to speak to him. She became very distraught during their conversation, and I had to give her another mild sedative. When she calmed down, I went out of the room and called Mr Marshall again, to tell him more specifically about the contents of the tape. Do you want to hear it?'

'Not now, Doctor, thanks. But I do want to ask you about one aspect of it.'

'Then ask.'

'Fred Marshall tried to imitate the way you had

reproduced the accent of the man who made the tape. Did it sound like any recognizable accent to you? German, maybe?'

'I've been thinking about that. It was sort of like a Germanic pronunciation of English, but not really. If it sounded like anything recognizable, it was English spoken by a Frenchman trying to put on a German accent, if that makes sense to you. But really, I've never heard anything like it.'

From the start of this conversation, Dr Spiegleman has been measuring Jack, assessing him according to standards Jack cannot even begin to guess. His expression remains as neutral and impersonal as that of a traffic cop. 'Mr Marshall informed me that he intended to call you. It seems that you and Mrs Marshall have formed a rather extraordinary bond. She respects your skill at what you do, which is to be expected, but she also seems to trust you. Mr Marshall asks that you be allowed to interview his wife, and his wife tells me that she must talk to you.'

'Then you should have no problems with letting me see her in private for half an hour.'

Dr Spiegleman's smile is gone as soon as it appears. 'My patient and her husband have demonstrated their trust in you, Lieutenant Sawyer, but that is not the issue. The issue is whether or not I can trust you.'

'Trust me to do what?'

'A number of things. Primarily, to act in the best interest of my patient. To refrain from unduly distressing her, also from giving her false hopes. My patient has developed a number of delusions centered on the existence of another world somehow contiguous to ours. She thinks her son is being held captive in this other world. I must tell you, Lieutenant, that both my patient and her husband believe you are familiar with this fantasy-world – that is, my patient accepts this belief wholly, and her husband accepts it only provisionally, on the grounds that it comforts his wife.'

'I understand that.' There is only one thing Jack can tell the doctor now, and he says it. 'And what you should understand is that in all of my conversations with the Marshalls, I have been acting in my unofficial capacity as a consultant to the French Landing Police Department and its chief, Dale Gilbertson.'

'Your unofficial capacity.'

'Chief Gilbertson has been asking me to advise him on his conduct of the Fisherman investigation, and two days ago, after the disappearance of Tyler Marshall, I finally agreed to do what I could. I have no official status whatsoever. I'm just giving the chief and his officers the benefit of my experience.'

'Let me get this straight, Lieutenant. You have been misleading the Marshalls as to your familiarity with Mrs Marshall's delusional fantasy-world?'

'I'll answer you this way, Doctor. We know from the tape that the Fisherman really is holding Tyler Marshall captive. We could say that he is no longer in this world, but in the Fisherman's.'

Dr Spiegleman raises his eyebrows.

'Do you think this monster inhabits the same universe that we do?' asks Jack. 'I don't, and neither do you. The Fisherman lives in a world all his own, one that operates according to fantastically detailed rules he has made up or invented over the years. With all due respect, my experience has made me far more familiar with structures like this than the Marshalls, the police, and, unless you have done a great deal of work with psychopathic criminals, even you. I'm sorry if that sounds arrogant, because I don't mean it that way.'

'You're talking about profiling? Something like that?'

'Years ago, I was invited into a special VICAP profiling unit run by the FBI, and I learned a lot there, but what I'm talking about now goes beyond profiling.' *And that's the understatement of the year,* Jack says to himself. *Now it's in your court, Doctor.*

Spiegleman nods, slowly. The distant glow flashes in the lenses of his glasses. 'I think I see, yes.' He ponders. He sighs, crosses his arms over his chest, and ponders some more. Then he raises his eyes to Jack's. 'All right. I'll let you see her. Alone. In my office. For thirty minutes. I wouldn't want to stand in the way of advanced investigative procedure.'

'Thank you,' Jack says. 'This will be extremely helpful, I promise you.'

'I have been a psychiatrist too long to believe in promises like that, Lieutenant Sawyer, but I hope you succeed in rescuing Tyler Marshall. Let me take you to my office. You can wait there while I get my patient and bring her there by another hallway. It's a little quicker.'

Dr Spiegleman marches to the end of the dark corridor and turns left, then left again, pulls a fat ball of keys from his pocket, and opens an unmarked door. Jack follows him into a room that looks as though it had been created by combining two small offices into one. Half of the room is taken up by a long wooden desk, a chair, a glass-topped coffee table stacked with journals, and filing cabinets; the other half is dominated by a couch and the leather recliner placed at its head. Georgia O'Keeffe posters decorate the walls. Behind the desk stands a door Jack assumes opens into a small closet; the door directly opposite, behind the recliner and at the midpoint between the two halves of the office, looks as though it leads into an adjoining room.

'As you see,' Dr Spiegleman says, 'I use this space as both

an office and a supplementary consulting room. Most of my patients come in through the waiting room, and I'll bring Mrs Marshall in that way. Give me two or three minutes.'

Jack thanks him, and the doctor hurries out through the door to the waiting room.

In the little closet, Wendell Green slides his cassette recorder from the pocket of his jacket and presses both it and his ear to the door. His thumb rests on the RECORD button, and his heart is racing. Once again, western Wisconsin's most distinguished journalist is doing his duty for the man in the street. Too bad it's so blasted dark in that closet, but being stuffed into a black hole is not the first sacrifice Wendell has made for his sacred calling; besides, all he really needs to see is the little red light on his tape recorder.

Then, a surprise: although Doctor Spiegleman has left the room, here is his voice, asking for Lieutenant Sawyer. How did that Freudian quack get back in without opening or closing a door, and what happened to Judy Marshall?

Lieutenant Sawyer, I must speak to you. Pick up the receiver. You have a call, and it sounds urgent.

Of course – he is on the intercom. Who can be calling Jack Sawyer, and why the urgency? Wendell hopes that Golden Boy will push the telephone's SPEAKER button, but alas Golden Boy does not, and Wendell must be content with hearing only one side of the conversation.

'A call?' Jack says. 'Who's it from?'

'He refused to identify himself,' the doctor says. 'Someone you told you'd be visiting Ward D.'

Beezer, with news of Black House. 'How do I take the call?'

'Just punch the flashing button,' the doctor says. 'Line one. I'll bring in Mrs Marshall when I see you're off the line.'

Jack hits the button and says, 'Jack Sawyer.'

'Thank God,' says Beezer St Pierre's honey-and-tobacco voice. 'Hey man, you gotta get over to my place, the sooner the better. Everything got messed up.'

'Did you find it?'

'Oh yeah, we found Black House, all right. It didn't exactly welcome us. That place wants to stay *hidden*, and it lets you know. Some of the guys are hurting. Most of us will be okay, but Mouse, I don't know. He got something terrible from a dog bite, if it was a dog, which I doubt. Doc did what he could, but . . . Hell, the guy is out of his mind, and he won't let us take him to the hospital.'

'Beezer, why don't you take him anyway, if that's what he needs?'

'We don't do things that way. Mouse hasn't stepped inside a hospital since his old man croaked in one. He's twice as scared of hospitals as of what's happening to his leg. If we took him to La Riviere General, he'd probably drop dead in the ER.'

'And if he didn't, he'd never forgive you.'

'You got it. How soon can you be here?'

'I still have to see the woman I told you about. Maybe an hour – not much longer than that, anyhow.'

'Didn't you hear me? Mouse is dying on us. We got a whole lot of things to say to each other.'

'I agree,' Jack says. 'Work with me on this, Beez.' He hangs up, turns to the door near the consulting-room chair, and waits for his world to change.

What the hell was that all about? Wendell wonders. He has squandered two minutes' worth of tape on a conversation between Jack Sawyer and the dumb SOB who spoiled the film that should have paid for a nice car and a fancy house on a bluff above the river, and all he got was worthless crap. Wendell deserves the nice car and the fancy house, has earned them thrice over, and his sense of deprivation makes him seethe with resentment. Golden Boys get everything handed to them on diamond-studded salvers, people fall all over themselves to give them stuff they don't even need, but a legendary, selfless working stiff and gentleman of the press like Wendell Green? It costs Wendell Green *twenty bucks* to hide in a dark, crowded little closet just to do his job!

His ears tingle when he hears the door open. The red light burns, the faithful recorder passes the ready tape from spool to spool, and whatever happens now is going to change everything: Wendell's gut, that infallible organ, his best friend, warms with the assurance that justice will soon be his.

Dr Spiegleman's voice filters through the closet door and registers on the spooling tape: 'I'll leave you two alone now.'

Golden Boy: 'Thank you, Doctor. I'm very grateful.'

Dr Spiegleman: 'Thirty minutes, right? That means I'll be back at, umm, ten past two.'

Golden Boy: 'Fine.'

The soft closing of the door, the click of the latch. Then long seconds of silence. *Why aren't they talking to each other?* But of course . . . the question answers itself. *They're waiting for fat-ass Spiegleman to move out of hearing range.*

Oh, this is just delicious, that's what this is! The whisper of Golden Boy's footsteps moving toward that door all but confirms the sterling reporter's intuition. O gut of Wendell Green, O Instrument Marvelous and Trustworthy, once more you come through with the journalistic goods! Wendell hears, the machine records, the inevitable next sound: the click of the lock.

Judy Marshall: 'Don't forget the door behind you.'

Golden Boy: 'How are you?'

Judy Marshall: 'Much, much better, now that you're here. The door, Jack.'

Another set of footsteps, another unmistakable sliding into place of a metal bolt.

Soon-To-Be-Ruined Boy: 'I've been thinking about you all day. I've been thinking about *this*.'

The Harlot, the Whore, the Slut: 'Is half an hour long enough?'

Him With Foot In Bear Trap: 'If it isn't, he'll just have to bang on the doors.'

Wendell barely restrains himself from crowing with delight. These two people are actually going to have sex together, they are going to rip off their clothes and have at it like animals. Man, talk about your paybacks! When Wendell Green is done with him, Jack Sawyer's reputation will be lower than the Fisherman's.

Judy's eyes look tired, her hair is limp, and her fingertips wear the startling white of fresh gauze, but besides registering the depth of her feeling, her face glows with the clear, hard-won beauty of the imaginative strength she called upon to earn what she has seen. To Jack, Judy Marshall looks like a queen falsely imprisoned. Instead of disguising her innate nobility of spirit, the hospital gown and the faded nightdress make it all the more apparent. Jack takes his eyes from her long enough to lock the second door, then takes a step toward her.

He sees that he cannot tell her anything she does not already know. Judy completes the movement he has begun; she moves before him and holds out her hands to be grasped.

'I've been thinking about you all day,' he says, taking her hands. 'I've been thinking about *this*.'

Her response takes in everything she has come to see, everything they must do. 'Is half an hour long enough?'

'If it isn't, he'll just have to bang on the doors.'

They smile; she increases the pressure on his hands. 'Then let him bang.' With the smallest, slightest tug, she pulls him forward, and Jack's heart pounds with the expectation of an embrace.

What she does is far more extraordinary than a mere embrace: she lowers her head and, with two light, dry brushes of her lips, kisses his hands. Then she presses the back of his right hand against her cheek, and steps back. Her eyes kindle. 'You know about the tape.'

He nods.

'I went mad when I heard it, but sending it to me was a mistake. He pushed me too hard. Because I fell right back into being that child who listened to another child whispering through a wall. I went crazy and I tried to rip the wall apart. I heard my son screaming for my help. And he was there – on the other side of the wall. Where you have to go.'

'Where *we* have to go.'

'Where we have to go. Yes. But I can't get through the wall, and you can. So you have work to do, the most important work there could be. You have to find Ty, and you have to stop the abbalah. I don't know what that is, exactly, but stopping it is your *job*. Am I saying this right: you are a coppiceman?'

'You're saying it right,' Jack says. 'I am a coppiceman. That's why it's my job.'

'Then this is right, too. You have to get *rid* of Gorg and his master, Mr Munshun. That's not what his name really *is*, but it's what it sounds like: Mr Munshun. When I went mad, and I tried to rip through the world, she told me, and she could whisper straight into my ear. I was so close!'

What does Wendell Green, ear and whirling tape recorder pressed to the door, make of this conversation? It is hardly what he expected to hear: the animal grunts and moans of desire busily being satisfied. Wendell Green grinds his teeth, he stretches his face into a grimace of frustration.

'I love that you've let yourself see,' says Jack. 'You're an amazing human being. There isn't a person in a thousand who could even understand what that means, much less do it.'

'You talk too much,' Judy says.

'I mean, I love you.'

'In your way, you love me. But you know what? Just by coming here, you made me more than I was. There's this sort of *beam* that comes out of you, and I just locked on to that beam. Jack, you *lived* there, and all I could do was peek at it for a little while. That's enough, though. I'm satisfied. You and Ward D, you let me travel.'

'What you have inside you lets you travel.'

'Okay, three cheers for a well-examined spell of craziness. Now it's time. You have to be a coppiceman. I can only come halfway, but you'll need all your strength.'

'I think your strength is going to surprise you.'

'Take my hands and do it, Jack. Go over. She's waiting, and I have to give you to her. You know her name, don't you?'

He opens his mouth, but cannot speak. A force that seems to come from the center of the earth surges into his body, rolling electricity through his bloodstream, tightening his scalp, sealing his trembling fingers to Judy Marshall's, which also tremble. A feeling of tremendous lightness and mobility gathers within all the hollow spaces of his body; at the same time he has never been so aware of his body's obduracy, its resistance to flight. When they leave, he thinks, it'll be like a rocket launch. The floor seems to vibrate beneath his feet.

He manages to look down the length of his arms to Judy Marshall, who leans back with her head parallel to the shaking floor, eyes closed, smiling in a trance of accomplishment. A band of shivery white light surrounds her. Her beautiful knees, her legs shining beneath the hem of the old blue garment, her bare feet planted. That light shivers around him, too. *All of this comes from her,* Jack thinks, *and from—*

A rushing sound fills the air, and the Georgia O'Keeffe prints fly off the walls. The low couch dances away from the wall; papers swirl up from the jittering desk. A skinny halogen lamp crashes to the ground. All through the hospital, on every floor, in every room and ward, beds vibrate, television sets go black, instruments rattle in their rattling trays, lights flicker. Toys drop from the gift-shop shelves, and the tall lilies skid across the marble in their vases. On the fifth floor, light bulbs detonate into showers of golden sparks.

The hurricane noise builds, builds, and with a great whooshing sound becomes a wide, white sheet of light, which immediately vanishes into a pinpoint and is gone. Gone, too, is Jack Sawyer; and gone from the closet is Wendell Green.

Sucked *into the Territories, blown out of one world and* sucked *into another, blasted and dragged, man, we're a hundred levels up from the simple, well-known flip.* Jack is lying down, looking up at a ripped white sheet that flaps like a torn sail. A quarter of a second ago, he saw another white sheet, one made of pure light and not literal, like this one. The soft, fragrant air blesses him. At first, he is conscious only that his right hand is being held, then that an astonishing woman lies beside him. Judy Marshall. No, not Judy Marshall, whom he does love, in his way, but another astonishing woman, who once whispered to Judy through a wall of night and has lately drawn a great deal closer. He had been about to speak her name when—

Into his field of vision moves a lovely face both like and unlike Judy's. It was turned on the same lathe, baked in the same kiln, chiseled by the same besotted sculptor, but more delicately, with a lighter, more caressing touch. Jack cannot move for wonder. He is barely capable of breathing. This woman whose face is above him now, smiling down with a tender impatience, has never borne a child, never traveled beyond her native Territories, never flown in an airplane, driven a car, switched on a television, scooped ice ready-made from the freezer, or used a microwave: and she is radiant with spirit and inner grace. She is, he sees, lit from within.

Humor, tenderness, compassion, intelligence, strength, glow in her eyes and speak from the curves of her mouth, from the very molding of her face. He knows her name, and her name is perfect for her. It seems to Jack that he has fallen in love with this woman in an instant, that he enlisted in her cause on the spot, and at last he finds he can speak her perfect name:

Sophie.

21

'Sophie.'

Still holding her hand, he gets to his feet, pulling her up with him. His legs are trembling. His eyes feel hot and too large for their sockets. He is terrified and exalted in equal, perfectly equal, measure. His heart is hammering, but oh the beats are sweet. The second time he tries, he manages to say her name a little louder, but there's still not much to his voice, and his lips are so numb they might have been rubbed with ice. He sounds like a man just coming back from a hard punch in the gut.

'Yes.'

'Sophie.'

'Yes.'

'Sophie.'

'Yes.'

There's something weirdly familiar about this, him saying the name over and over and her giving back that simple affirmation. Familiar and funny. And it comes to him: there's a scene almost identical to this in *The Terror of Deadwood Gulch*, after one of the Lazy 8 Saloon's patrons has knocked Bill Towns unconscious with a whiskey bottle. Lily, in her role as sweet Nancy

O'Neal, tosses a bucket of water in his face, and when he sits up, they—

'This is funny,' Jack says. 'It's a good bit. We should be laughing.'

With the slightest of smiles, Sophie says, 'Yes.'

'Laughing our fool heads off.'

'Yes.'

'Our *tarnal* heads off.'

'Yes.'

'I'm not speaking English anymore, am I?'

'No.'

He sees two things in her blue eyes. The first is that she doesn't know the word *English*. The second is that she knows exactly what he means.

'Sophie.'

'Yes.'

'Sophie-Sophie-Sophie.'

Trying to get the reality of it. Trying to pound it home like a nail.

A smile lights her face and enriches her mouth. Jack thinks of how it would be to kiss that mouth, and his knees feel weak. All at once he is fourteen again, and wondering if he dares give his date a peck good-night after he walks her home.

'Yes-yes-yes,' she says, the smile strengthening. And then: 'Have you got it yet? Do you understand that you're here and how you got here?'

Above and around him, billows of gauzy white cloth flap and sigh like living breath. Half a dozen conflicting drafts gently touch his face and make him aware that he carried a coat of sweat from the other world, and that it stinks. He arms it off his brow and cheeks in quick gestures, not wanting to lose sight of her for longer than a moment at a time.

They are in a tent of some kind. It's huge – many-chambered – and Jack thinks briefly of the pavilion in which the Queen of the Territories, his mother's Twinner, lay dying. That place had been rich with many colors, filled with many rooms, redolent of incense and sorrow (for the Queen's death had seemed inevitable, sure – only a matter of time). This one is ramshackle and ragged. The walls and the ceiling are full of holes, and where the white material remains whole, it's so thin that Jack can actually see the slope of land outside, and the trees that dress it. Rags flutter from the edges of some of the holes when the wind blows. Directly over his head he can see a shadowy maroon shape. Some sort of cross.

'Jack, do you understand how you—'

'Yes. I flipped.' Although that isn't the word that comes out of his mouth. The literal meaning of the word that comes out seems to be *horizon road*. 'And it seems that I sucked a fair number of Spiegleman's accessories with me.' He bends and picks up a flat stone with a flower carved on it. 'I believe that in my world, this was a Georgia O'Keeffe print. And that –' He points to a blackened, fireless torch leaning against one of the pavilion's fragile walls. 'I think that was a –' But there are no words for it in this world, and what comes out of his mouth sounds as ugly as a curse in German: '– halogen lamp.'

She frowns. 'Hal-do-jen . . . limp? Lemp?'

He feels his numb lips rise in a little grin. 'Never mind.'

'But you are all right.'

He understands that she needs him to be all right, and so he'll say that he is, but he's not. He is sick and glad to be sick. He is one lovestruck daddy, and wouldn't have it any other way. If you discount how he felt about his mother – a very different kind of love, despite what the Freudians might think – it's the first time for him. Oh, he certainly *thought* he had been in and out of love, but that was before today. Before the cool blue of her eyes, her smile, and even the way the shadows thrown by the decaying tent fleet across her face like schools of fish. At this moment he would try to fly off a mountain for her if she asked, or walk through a forest fire, or bring her polar ice to cool her tea, and those things do *not* constitute being all right.

But she needs him to be.

Tyler needs him to be.

I am a coppiceman, he thinks. At first the concept seems insubstantial compared to her beauty – to her simple *reality* – but then it begins to take hold. As it always has. What else brought him here, after all? Brought him against his will and all his best intentions?

'Jack?'

'Yes, I'm all right. I've flipped before.' *But never into the presence of such beauty*, he thinks. *That's the problem*. You're *the problem, my lady*.

'Yes. To come and go is your talent. *One* of your talents. So I have been told.'

'By whom?'

'Shortly,' she says. 'Shortly. There's a great deal to do, and yet I think I need a moment. You . . . rather take my breath away.'

Jack is fiercely glad to know it. He sees he is still holding her hand, and he kisses it, as Judy kissed his hands in the world on the other side of the wall from this one, and when he does, he sees the fine mesh of bandage on the tips of three of her fingers. He wishes he dared to take her in his arms, but she daunts him: her beauty and her presence. She is slightly taller than Judy – a matter of two inches, surely no more – and her hair is lighter, the golden shade of unrefined honey spilling from a broken comb. She is wearing a simple cotton robe, white trimmed with a blue that matches her eyes. The narrow V-neck frames her throat. The hem falls to just below her knees. Her legs are bare but she's wearing a silver anklet on one of them, so slim it's almost invisible. She is fuller-breasted than Judy, her hips a bit wider. *Sisters*, you might think, except that they have the same spray of freckles across the nose and the same white line of scar across the back of the left hand. Different mishaps caused that scar, Jack has no doubt, but he also has no doubt that those mishaps occurred at the same hour of the same day.

'You're her Twinner. Judy Marshall's Twinner.' Only the word that comes out of his mouth isn't *Twinner*; incredibly, dopily, it seems to be *harp*. Later he will think of how the strings of a harp lie close together, only a finger's touch apart, and he will decide that word isn't so foolish after all.

She looks down, her mouth drooping, then raises her head again and tries to smile. '*Judy*. On the other side of the wall. When we were children, Jack, we spoke together often. Even when we grew up, although then we spoke in each other's dreams.' He is alarmed to see tears forming in her eyes and then slipping down her cheeks. 'Have I driven her mad? Run her to lunacy? Please say I haven't.'

'Nah,' Jack says. 'She's on a tightrope, but she hasn't fallen off yet. She's tough, that one.'

'You have to bring her Tyler back to her,' Sophie tells him. 'For both of us. I've never had a child. I *cannot* have a child. I was . . . mistreated, you see. When I was young. Mistreated by one you knew well.'

A terrible certainty forms in Jack's mind. Around them, the ruined pavilion flaps and sighs in the wonderfully fragrant breeze.

'Was it Morgan? Morgan of Orris?'

She bows her head, and perhaps this is just as well. Jack's

face is, at that moment, pulled into an ugly snarl. In that moment he wishes he could kill Morgan Sloat's Twinner all over again. He thinks to ask her how she was mistreated, and then realizes he doesn't have to.

'How old were you?'

'Twelve,' she says . . . as Jack has known she would say. It happened that same year, the year when Jacky was twelve and came here to save his mother. Or *did* he come here? Is this really the Territories? Somehow it doesn't feel the same. Almost . . . but not quite.

It doesn't surprise him that Morgan would rape a child of twelve, and do it in a way that would keep her from ever having children. Not at all. Morgan Sloat, sometimes known as Morgan of Orris, wanted to rule not just one world or two, but the entire universe. What are a few raped children to a man with such ambitions?

She gently slips her thumbs across the skin beneath his eyes. It's like being brushed with feathers. She's looking at him with something like wonder. 'Why do you weep, Jack?'

'The past,' he says. 'Isn't that always what does it?' And thinks of his mother, sitting by the window, smoking a cigarette, and listening while the radio plays 'Crazy Arms.' Yes, it's always the past. That's where the hurt is, all you can't get over.

'Perhaps so,' she allows. 'But there's no time to think about the past today. It's the future we must think about today.'

'Yes, but if I could ask just a few questions . . .?'

'All right, but only a few.'

Jack opens his mouth, tries to speak, and makes a comical little gaping expression when nothing comes out. Then he laughs. 'You take my breath away, too,' he tells her. 'I have to be honest about that.'

A faint tinge of color rises in Sophie's cheeks, and she

looks down. She opens her lips to say something . . . then presses them together again. Jack wishes she had spoken and is glad she hasn't, both at the same time. He squeezes her hands gently, and she looks up at him, blue eyes wide.

'Did I know you? When you were twelve?'

She shakes her head.

'But I saw you.'

'Perhaps. In the great pavilion. My mother was one of the Good Queen's handmaidens. I was another . . . the youngest. You could have seen me then. I think you *did* see me.'

Jack takes a moment to digest the wonder of this, then goes on. Time is short. They both know this. He can almost feel it fleeting.

'You and Judy are Twinners, but neither of you travel – she's never been in your head over here and you've never been in *her* head, over there. You . . . talk through a wall.'

'Yes.'

'When she wrote things, that was you, whispering through the wall.'

'Yes. I knew how hard I was pushing her, but I had to. *Had* to! It's not just a question of restoring her child to her, important as that may be. There are larger considerations.'

'Such as?'

She shakes her head. 'I am not the one to tell you. The one who will is much greater than I.'

He studies the tiny dressings that cover the tips of her fingers, and muses on how hard Sophie and Judy have tried to get through that wall to each other. Morgan Sloat could apparently become Morgan of Orris at will. As a boy of twelve, Jack had met others with that same talent. Not him; he was single-natured and had always been Jack in both worlds. Judy and Sophie, however, have proved incapable of flipping back and forth in any fashion. Something's been left out of them, and they could only whisper through the wall between the worlds. There must be sadder things, but at this moment he can't think of a single one.

Jack looks around at the ruined tent, which seems to breathe with sunshine and shadow. Rags flap. In the next room, through a hole in the gauzy cloth wall, he sees a few overturned cots. 'What *is* this place?' he asks.

She smiles. 'To some, a hospital.'

'Oh?' He looks up and once more takes note of the cross. Maroon now, but undoubtedly once red. *A red cross, stupid*, he thinks. 'Oh! But isn't it a little . . . well . . . old?'

Sophie's smile widens, and Jack realizes it's ironic. Whatever sort of hospital this is, or was, he's guessing it bears little or no resemblance to the ones on *General Hospital* or *ER*. 'Yes, Jack. *Very* old. Once there were a dozen or more of these tents in the Territories, On-World, and Mid-World; now there are only a few. Mayhap just this one. Today it's here. Tomorrow . . .' Sophie raises her hands, then lowers them. 'Anywhere! Perhaps even on Judy's side of the wall.'

'Sort of like a traveling medicine show.'

This is supposed to be a joke, and he's startled when she first nods, then laughs and claps her hands. 'Yes! Yes, indeed! Although you wouldn't want to be treated here.'

What exactly is she trying to say? 'I suppose not,' he agrees, looking at the rotting walls, tattered ceiling panels, and ancient support posts. 'Doesn't exactly look sterile.'

Seriously (but her eyes are sparkling), Sophie says: 'Yet if you were a patient, you would think it beautiful out of all measure. And you would think your nurses, the Little Sisters, the most beautiful any poor patient ever had.'

Jack looks around. 'Where are they?'

'The Little Sisters don't come out when the sun shines. And if we wish to continue our lives with the blessing, Jack, we'll be gone our separate ways from here long before dark.'

It pains him to hear her talk of separate ways, even though he knows it's inevitable. The pain doesn't dampen his curiosity, however; once a coppiceman, it seems, always a coppiceman.

'Why?'

'Because the Little Sisters are vampires, and their patients never get well.'

Startled, uneasy, Jack looks around for signs of them. Certainly disbelief doesn't cross his mind – a world that can spawn werewolves can spawn anything, he supposes.

She touches his wrist. A little tremble of desire goes through him.

'Don't fear, Jack – they also serve the Beam. *All* things serve the Beam.'

'What beam?'

'Never mind.' The hand on his wrist tightens. 'The one who can answer your questions will be here soon, if he's not already.' She gives him a sideways look that contains a glimmer of a smile. 'And after you hear him, you'll be more apt to ask questions that matter.'

Jack realizes that he has been neatly rebuked, but coming from her, it doesn't sting. He allows himself to be led through room after room of the great and ancient hospital. As they go, he gets a sense of how really huge this place is. He also realizes that, in spite of the fresh breezes, he can detect a faint, unpleasant undersmell, something that might be a mixture of fermented wine and spoiled meat. As to what sort of meat, Jack is afraid he can guess pretty well. After visiting over a hundred homicide crime scenes, he *should* be able to.

★

It would have been impolite to break away while Jack was meeting the love of his life (not to mention bad narrative business), so we didn't. Now, however, let us slip through the thin walls of the hospital tent. Outside is a dry but not unpleasant landscape of red rocks, broom sage, desert flowers that look a bit like sego lilies, stunted pines, and a few barrel cacti. Somewhere not too far distant is the steady cool sigh of a river. The hospital pavilion rustles and flaps as dreamily as the sails of a ship riding down the sweet chute of the trade winds. As we float along the great ruined tent's east side in our effortless and peculiarly pleasant way, we notice a strew of litter. There are more rocks with drawings etched on them, there is a beautifully made copper rose that has been twisted out of shape as if by some great heat, there is a small rag rug that looks as if it has been chopped in two by a meat cleaver. There's other stuff as well, stuff that has resisted any change in its cyclonic passage from one world to the other. We see the blackened husk of a television picture tube lying in a scatter of broken glass, several Duracell AA batteries, a comb, and – perhaps oddest – a pair of white nylon panties with the word *Sunday* written on one side in demure pink script. There has been a collision of worlds; here, along the east side of the hospital pavilion, is an intermingled detritus that attests to how hard that collision was.

At the end of that littery plume of exhaust – the head of the comet, we might say – sits a man we recognize. We're not used to seeing him in such an ugly brown robe (and he clearly doesn't know how to wear such a garment, because if we look at him from the wrong angle, we can see *much* more than we want to), or wearing sandals instead of wing tips, or with his hair pulled back into a rough horsetail and secured with a hank of rawhide, but this is undoubtedly Wendell Green. He is muttering to himself. Drool drizzles from the corners of his mouth. He is looking fixedly at an untidy crumple of foolscap in his right hand. He ignores all the more cataclysmic changes that have occurred around him and focuses on just this one. If he can figure out how his Panasonic mini-corder turned into a little pile of ancient paper, perhaps he'll move on to the other stuff. Not until then.

Wendell (we'll continue to call him Wendell, shall we, and not worry about any name he might or might not have in this little corner of existence, since *he* doesn't know it or want to) spies the Duracell AA batteries. He crawls to them, picks them up, and begins trying to stick them into the little pile of foolscap. It doesn't work, of course, but that doesn't keep Wendell from trying. As George Rathbun might say, 'Give that boy a flyswatter and he'd try to catch dinner with it.'

'Geh,' says the Coulee Country's favorite investigative reporter, repeatedly poking the batteries at the foolscap. 'Geh . . . in. Geh . . . in! Gah-damnit, geh in th—'

A sound – the approaching jingle of what can only be, God help us, spurs – breaks into Wendell's concentration, and he looks up with wide, bulging eyes. His sanity may not be gone forever, but it's certainly taken the wife and kids and gone to Disney World. Nor is the current vision before his eyes apt to coax it back anytime soon.

Once in our world there was a fine black actor named Woody Strode. (Lily knew him; acted with him, as a matter of fact, in a late-sixties American International stinkeroo called *Execution Express*.) The man now approaching the place where Wendell Green crouches with his batteries and his handful of foolscap looks remarkably like that actor. He is wearing faded jeans, a blue chambray shirt, a neck scarf, and a heavy revolver on a wide leather gun belt in which four dozen or so shells twinkle. His head is bald, his eyes deep-set. Slung over one shoulder by a strap of intricate design is a guitar. Sitting on the other is what appears to be a parrot. The parrot has two heads.

'No, no,' says Wendell in a mildly scolding voice. 'Don't. Don't see. Don't see. That.' He lowers his head and once more begins trying to cram the batteries into the handful of paper.

The shadow of the newcomer falls over Wendell, who resolutely refuses to look up.

'Howdy, stranger,' says the newcomer.

Wendell carries on not looking up.

'My name's Parkus. I'm the law 'round these parts. What's your handle?'

Wendell refuses to respond, unless we can call the low grunts issuing from his drool-slicked mouth a response.

'I asked your name.'

'Wen,' says our old acquaintance (we can't really call him a friend) without looking up. 'Wen. Dell. Gree . . . *Green.* I . . . I . . . I . . .'

'Take your time,' Parkus says (not without sympathy). 'I can wait till your branding iron gets hot.'

'I . . . *news hawk!*'

'Oh? That what you are?' Parkus hunkers; Wendell cringes back against the fragile wall of the pavilion. 'Well, don't that just beat the bass drum at the front of the parade? Tell you what, I've seen *fish* hawks, and I've seen *red* hawks, and I've seen goshawks, but you're my first *news* hawk.'

Wendell looks up, blinking rapidly.

On Parkus's left shoulder, one head of the parrot says: 'God is love.'

'Go fuck your mother,' replies the other head.

'All must seek the river of life,' says the first head.

'Suck my tool,' says the second.

'We grow toward God,' responds the first.

'Piss up a rope,' invites the second.

Although both heads speak equably – even in tones of reasonable discourse – Wendell cringes backward even farther, then looks down and furiously resumes his futile work with the batteries and the handful of paper, which is now disappearing into the sweat-grimy tube of his fist.

'Don't mind 'em,' Parkus says. '*I* sure don't. Hardly hear 'em anymore, and that's the truth. Shut up, boys.'

The parrot falls silent.

'One head's Sacred, the other's Profane,' Parkus says. 'I keep 'em around just to remind me that—'

He is interrupted by the sound of approaching footsteps, and stands up again in a single lithe and easy movement. Jack and Sophie are approaching, holding hands with the perfect unconsciousness of children on their way to school.

'Speedy!' Jack cries, his face breaking into a grin.

'Why, Travelin' Jack!' Parkus says, with a grin of his own. 'Well-met! Look at you, sir – you're all grown up.'

Jack rushes forward and throws his arms around Parkus, who hugs him back, and heartily. After a moment, Jack holds Parkus at arm's length and studies him. 'You were older – you looked older to *me*, at least. In both worlds.'

Still smiling, Parkus nods. And when he speaks again, it is in Speedy Parker's drawl. 'Reckon I did look older, Jack. You were just a child, remember.'

'But—'

Parkus waves one hand. 'Sometimes I look older, sometimes not so old. It all depends on—'

'Age is wisdom,' one head of the parrot says piously, to which the other responds, 'You senile old fuck.'

'—depends on the place and the circumstances,' Parkus concludes, then says: 'And I told you boys to shut up. You keep on, I'm apt to wring your scrawny neck.' He turns his attention to Sophie, who is looking at him with wide, wondering eyes, as shy as a doe. 'Sophie,' he says. 'It's wonderful to see you, darling. Didn't I say he'd come? And here he is. Took a little longer than I expected, is all.'

She drops him a deep curtsey, all the way down to one knee, her head bowed. '*Thankee-sai*,' she says. 'Come in peace, gunslinger, and go your course along the Beam with my love.'

At this, Jack feels an odd, deep chill, as if many worlds had spoken in a harmonic tone, low but resonant.

Speedy – so Jack still thinks of him – takes her hand and urges her to her feet. 'Stand up, girl, and look me in the eye. I'm no gunslinger here, not in the borderlands, even if I do still carry the old iron from time to time. In any case, we have a lot to talk about. This's no time for ceremony. Come over the rise with me, you two. We got to make palaver, as the gunslingers say. Or used to say, before the world moved on. I shot a good brace of grouse, and think they'll cook up just fine.'

'What about—' Jack gestures toward the muttering, crouched heap that is Wendell Green.

'Why, he looks right busy,' Parkus says. 'Told me he's a news hawk.'

'I'm afraid he's a little above himself,' Jack replies. 'Old Wendell here's a news *vulture*.'

Wendell turns his head a bit. He refuses to lift his eyes, but his lip curls in a sneer that may be more reflexive than real. 'Heard. That.' He struggles. The lip curls again, and this time the sneer seems less reflexive. It is, in fact, a snarl. 'Gol. *Gol*. *Gol*-den boy. Holly. Wood.'

'He's managed to retain at least some of his charm and his joi de vivre,' Jack says. 'Will he be okay here?'

'Not much with ary brain in its head comes near the Little

Sisters' tent,' Parkus says. 'He'll be okay. And if he smells somethin' tasty on the breeze and comes for a look-see, why, I guess we can feed him.' He turns toward Wendell. 'We're going just over yonder. If you want to come and visit, why, you just up and do her. Understand me, Mr News Hawk?'

'Wen. Dell. *Green*.'

'Wendell Green, yessir.' Parkus looks at the others. 'Come on. Let's mosey.'

'We mustn't forget him,' Sophie murmurs, with a look back. 'It will be dark in a few hours.'

'No,' Parkus agrees as they top the nearest rise. 'Wouldn't do to leave him beside that tent after dark. That wouldn't do at all.'

There's more foliage in the declivity on the far side of the rise – even a little ribbon of creek, presumably on its way to the river Jack can hear in the distance – but it still looks more like northern Nevada than western Wisconsin. Yet in a way, Jack thinks, that makes sense. The last one had been no ordinary flip. He feels like a stone that has been skipped all the way across a lake, and as for poor Wendell—

To the right of where they descend the far side of the draw, a horse has been tethered in the shade of what Jack thinks is a Joshua tree. About twenty yards down the draw to the left is a circle of eroded stones. Inside it a fire, not yet lit, has been carefully laid. Jack doesn't like the look of the place much – the stones remind him of ancient teeth. Nor is he alone in his dislike. Sophie stops, her grip on his fingers tightening.

'Parkus, do we have to go in there? Please say we don't.'

Parkus turns to her with a kindly smile Jack knows well: a Speedy Parker smile for sure.

'The Speaking Demon's been gone from this circle many

the long age, darling,' he says. 'And you know that such as yon are best for stories.'

'Yet—'

'Now's no time to give in to the willies,' Parkus tells her. He speaks with a trace of impatience, and 'willies' isn't precisely the word he uses, but only how Jack's mind translates it. 'You waited for him to come in the Little Sisters' hospital tent—'

'Only because *she* was there on the other side—'

'—and now I want you to come along.' All at once he seems taller to Jack. His eyes flash. Jack thinks: *A gunslinger. Yes, I suppose he* could *be a gunslinger. Like in one of Mom's old movies, only for real.*

'All right,' she says, low. 'If we must.' Then she looks at Jack. 'I wonder if you'd put your arm around me?'

Jack, we may be sure, is happy to oblige.

As they step between two of the stones, Jack seems to hear an ugly twist of whispered words. Among them, one voice is momentarily clear, seeming to leave a trail of slime behind it as it enters his ear: *Drudge drudge drudge, oho the bledding foodzies, soon he cummz, my good friend Munshun, and such a prize I have for him, oho, oho—*

Jack looks at his old friend as Parkus hunkers by a tow sack and loosens the drawstring at the top. 'He's close, isn't he? The Fisherman. And Black House, that's close, too.'

'Yep,' Parkus says, and from the sack he spills the gutted corpses of a dozen plump dead birds.

Thoughts of Irma Freneau reenter Jack's head at the sight of the grouse, and he thinks he won't be able to eat. Watching as Parkus and Sophie skewer the birds on green-sticks reinforces this idea. But after the fire is lit and the birds begin to brown, his stomach weighs in, insisting that the grouse smell wonderful and will probably taste even better. Over here, he remembers, everything always does.

'And here we are, in the speaking circle,' Parkus says. His smiles have been put away for the nonce. He looks at Jack and Sophie, who sit side by side and still holding hands, with somber gravity. His guitar has been propped against a nearby rock. Beside it, Sacred and Profane sleeps with its two heads tucked into its feathers, dreaming its no doubt bifurcated dreams. 'The Demon may be long gone, but the legends say such things leave a residue that may lighten the tongue.'

'Like kissing the Blarney Stone, maybe,' Jack suggests.

Parkus shakes his head. 'No blarney today.'

Jack says, 'If only we were dealing with an ordinary scumbag. That I could handle.'

Sophie looks at him, puzzled.

'He means a dust-off artist,' Parkus tells her. 'A hard-case.' He looks at Jack. 'And in one way, that *is* what you're dealing with. Carl Bierstone isn't much – an ordinary monster, let's say. Which is *not* to say he couldn't do with a spot of killing. But as for what's going on in French Landing, he has been used. Possessed, you'd say in your world, Jack. Taken by the spirits, we'd say in the Territories—'

'Or brought low by pigs,' Sophie adds.

'Yes.' Parkus is nodding. 'In the world just beyond this borderland – Mid-World – they would say he has been infested by a demon. But a demon far greater than the poor, tattered spirit that once lived in this circle of stones.'

Jack hardly hears that. His eyes are glowing. *It sounded something like beer stein,* George Potter told him last night, a thousand years ago. *That's not it, but it's close.*

'Carl Bierstone,' he says. He raises a clenched fist, then shakes it in triumph. 'That was his name in Chicago. Burnside here in French Landing. Case closed, game over, zip up your fly. Where is he, Speedy? Save me some time h—'

'*Shut . . . up*,' Parkus says.

The tone is low and almost deadly. Jack can feel Sophie shrink against him. He does a little shrinking himself. This sounds nothing like his old friend, nothing at all. *You have to stop thinking of him as Speedy*, Jack tells himself. *That's not who he is or ever was. That was just a character he played, someone who could both soothe and charm a scared kid on the run with his mother.*

Parkus turns the birds, which are now browned nicely on one side and spitting juice into the fire.

'I'm sorry to speak harsh to you, Jack, but you have to realize that your Fisherman is pretty small fry compared to what's really going on.'

Why don't you tell Tansy Freneau he's small fry? Why don't you tell Beezer St Pierre?

Jack thinks these things, but doesn't say them out loud. He's more than a little afraid of the light he saw in Parkus's eyes.

'Nor is it about Twinners,' Parkus says. 'You got to get that idea out of your mind. That's just something that has to do with your world and the world of the Territories – a link. You can't kill some hardcase over here and end the career of your cannibal over there. And if you kill him over there, in Wisconsin, the thing inside will just jump to another host.'

'The thing—?'

'When it was in Albert Fish, Fish called it the Monday Man. Fellow you're after calls it Mr Munshun. Both are only ways of trying to say something that can't be pronounced by any earthly tongue on any earthly world.'

'How many worlds are there, Speedy?'

'Many,' Parkus says, looking into the fire. 'And this business concerns every one of them. Why else do you think I've been after you like I have? Sending you feathers, sending you robins' eggs, doing every damned thing I could to make you wake up.'

Jack thinks of Judy, scratching on walls until the tips of her fingers were bloody, and feels ashamed. Speedy has been doing much the same thing, it seems. 'Wake up, wake up, you dunderhead,' he says.

Parkus seems caught between reproof and a smile. 'For sure you must have seen me in the case that sent you running out of LA.'

'Ah, man – why do you think I went?'

'You ran like Jonah, when God told him to go preach against the wickedness in Nineveh. Thought I was gonna have to send a whale to come and swallow you up.'

'I *feel* swallowed,' Jack tells him.

In a small voice, Sophie says: 'I do, too.'

'We've all been swallowed,' says the man with the gun on his hip. 'We're in the belly of the beast, like it or not. It's *ka*, which is destiny and fate. Your Fisherman, Jack, is now your *ka*. *Our ka*. This is more than murder. Much more.'

And Jack sees something that frankly scares the shit out of him. Lester Parker, a.k.a. Speedy, a.k.a. Parkus, is himself scared almost to death.

'This business concerns the Dark Tower,' he says.

Beside Jack, Sophie gives a low, desperate cry of terror and lowers her head. At the same time she raises one hand and forks the sign of the Evil Eye at Parkus, over and over.

That gentleman doesn't seem to take it amiss. He simply sets to work turning the birds again on their sticks. 'Listen to me, now,' he says. 'Listen, and ask as few questions as you can.

We still have a chance to get Judy Marshall's son back, but time is blowing in our teeth.'

'Talk,' Jack says.

Parkus talks. At some point in his tale he judges the birds done and serves them out on flat stones. The meat is tender, almost falling off the small bones. Jack eats hungrily, drinking deep of the sweet water from Parkus's waterskin each time it comes around to him. He wastes no more time comparing dead children to dead grouse. The furnace needs to be stoked, and he stokes it with a will. So does Sophie, eating with her fingers and licking them clean without the slightest reserve or embarrassment. So, in the end, does Wendell Green, although he refuses to enter the circle of old stones. When Parkus tosses him a golden-brown grouse, however, Wendell catches it with remarkable adroitness and buries his face in the moist meat.

'You asked how many worlds,' Parkus begins. 'The answer, in the High Speech, is *da fan:* worlds beyond telling.' With one of the blackened sticks he draws a figure eight on its side, which Jack recognizes as the Greek symbol for infinity.

'There is a Tower that binds them in place. Think of it as an axle upon which many wheels spin, if you like. And there is an entity that would bring this Tower down. Ram Abbalah.'

At these words, the flames of the fire seem to momentarily darken and turn red. Jack wishes he could believe that this is only a trick of his overstrained mind, but cannot. 'The Crimson King,' he says.

'Yes. His physical being is pent in a cell at the top of the Tower, but he has another manifestation, every bit as real, and this lives in Can-tah Abbalah – the Court of the Crimson King.'

'Two places at once.' Given his journeying between the

world of America and the world of the Territories, Jack has little trouble swallowing this concept.

'Yes.'

'If he – or it – destroys the Tower, won't that defeat his purpose? Won't he destroy his physical being in the process?'

'Just the opposite: he'll set it free to wander what will then be chaos . . . *din-tah* . . . the furnace. Some parts of Mid-World have fallen into that furnace already.'

'How much of this do I actually need to know?' Jack asks. He is aware that time is fleeting by on his side of the wall, as well.

'Hard telling what you need to know and what you don't,' Parkus says. 'If I leave out the wrong piece of information, maybe all the stars go dark. Not just here, but in a thousand thousand universes. That's the pure hell of it. Listen, Jack – the King has been trying to destroy the Tower and set himself free for time out of mind. Forever, mayhap. It's slow work, because the Tower is bound in place by crisscrossing force beams that act on it like guy wires. The Beams have held for millennia, and would hold for millennia to come, but in the last two hundred years – that's speaking of time as you count it, Jack; to you, Sophie, it would be Full-Earth almost five hundred times over—'

'So long,' she says. It's almost a sigh. 'So very long.'

'In the great sweep of things, it's as short as the gleam of a single match in a dark room. But while good things usually take a long time to develop, evil has a way of popping up full-blown and ready-made, like Jack out of his box. Ka is a friend to evil as well as to good. It embraces both. And, speaking of Jack . . .' Parkus turns to him. 'You've heard of the Iron Age and the Bronze Age, of course?'

Jack nods.

'On the upper levels of the Tower, there are those who

call the last two hundred or so years in your world the Age of Poisoned Thought. That means—'

'You don't have to explain it to me,' Jack says. 'I knew Morgan Sloat, remember? I knew what he planned for *Sophie's* world.' Yes, indeed. The basic plan had been to turn one of the universe's sweetest honeycombs into first a vacation spot for the rich, then a source of unskilled labor, and finally a waste pit, probably radioactive. If that wasn't an example of poisoned thought, Jack doesn't know what is.

Parkus says, 'Rational beings have always harbored telepaths among their number; that's true in all the worlds. But they're ordinarily rare creatures. Prodigies, you might say. But since the Age of Poisoned Thought came on your world, Jack – infested it like a demon – such beings have become much more common. Not as common as slow mutants in the Blasted Lands, but common, yes.'

'You speak of mind readers,' Sophie says, as if wanting to be sure.

'Yes,' Parkus agrees, 'but not *just* mind readers. Precognates. Teleports – world jumpers like old Travelin' Jack here, in other words – and telekinetics. Mind readers are the most common, telekinetics the rarest . . . and the most valuable.'

'To *him*, you mean,' Jack says. 'To the Crimson King.'

'Yes. Over the last two hundred years or so, the abbalah has spent a good part of his time gathering a crew of telepathic slaves. Most of them come from Earth and the Territories. *All* of the telekinetics come from Earth. This collection of slaves – this gulag – is his crowning achievement. We call them Breakers. They . . .' He trails off, thinking. Then: 'Do you know how a galley travels?'

Sophie nods, but Jack at first has no idea what Parkus is

talking about. He has a brief, lunatic vision of a fully equipped kitchen traveling down Route 66.

'Many oarsmen,' Sophie says, then makes a rowing motion that throws her breasts into charming relief.

Parkus is nodding. 'Usually slaves chained together. They—'

From outside the circle, Wendell suddenly sticks his own oar in. 'Spart. Cus.' He pauses, frowning, then tries it again. '*Spart-a-cus*.'

'What's he on about?' Parkus asks, frowning. 'Any idea, Jack?'

'A movie called *Spartacus*,' Jack says, 'and you're wrong as usual, Wendell. I believe you're thinking about *Ben-Hur*.'

Looking sulky, Wendell holds out his greasy hands. 'More. Meat.'

Parkus pulls the last grouse from its sizzling stick and tosses it between two of the stones, where Wendell sits with his pallid, greasy face peering from between his knees. 'Fresh prey for the news hawk,' he says. 'Now do us a favor and shut up.'

'Or. What.' The old defiant gleam is rising in Wendell's eyes.

Parkus draws his shooting iron partway from its holster. The grip, made of sandalwood, is worn, but the barrel gleams murder-bright. He has to say no more; holding his second bird in one hand, Wendell Green hitches up his robe and hies himself back over the rise. Jack is extremely relieved to see him go. Spartacus *indeed*, he thinks, and snorts.

'So the Crimson King wants to use these Breakers to destroy the Beams,' Jack says. 'That's it, isn't it? That's his plan.'

'You speak as though of the future,' Parkus says mildly. 'This is happening *now*, Jack. Only look at your own world if you want to see the ongoing disintegration. Of the six Beams, only one still holds true. Two others still generate some holding power. The other three are dead. One of these went out thousands of years ago, in the ordinary course of things. The others . . . killed by the Breakers. All in two centuries or less.'

'Christ,' Jack says. He is beginning to understand how Speedy could call the Fisherman small-fry.

'The job of protecting the Tower and the Beams has always belonged to the ancient war guild of Gilead, called gunslingers in this world and many others. They also generated a powerful psychic force, Jack, one fully capable of countering the Crimson King's Breakers, but—'

'The gunslingers are all gone save for one,' Sophie says, looking at the big pistol on Parkus's hip. And, with timid hope: 'Unless you really *are* one, too, Parkus.'

'Not I, darling,' he says, 'but there's more than one.'

'I thought Roland was the last. So the stories say.'

'He has made at least three others,' Parkus tells her. 'I've no idea how that can be possible, but I believe it to be true. If Roland were still alone, the Breakers would have toppled the Tower long since. But with the force of these others added to his—'

'I have no clue what you're talking about,' Jack says. 'I *did*, sort of, but you lost me about two turns back.'

'There's no need for you to understand it all in order to do your job,' Parkus says.

'Thank God for that.'

'As for what you *do* need to understand, leave galleys and oarsmen and think in terms of the Western movies your mother used to make. To begin with, imagine a fort in the desert.'

'This Dark Tower you keep talking about. That's the fort.'

'Yes. And surrounding the fort, instead of wild Indians—'

'The Breakers. Led by Big Chief Abbalah.'

Sophie murmurs: 'The King is in his Tower, eating bread and honey. The Breakers in the basement, making all the money.'

Jack feels a light but singularly unpleasant chill shake up his spine: he thinks of rat paws scuttering over broken glass. 'What? Why do you say that?'

Sophie looks at him, flushes, shakes her head, looks down. 'It's what *she* says, sometimes. Judy. It's how I hear her, sometimes.'

Parkus seizes one of the charred greensticks and draws in the rocky dust beside the figure-eight shape. 'Fort here. Marauding Indians here, led by their merciless, evil – and most likely insane – chief. But over here—' Off to the left, he draws a harsh arrow in the dirt. It points at the rudimentary shapes indicating the fort and the besieging Indians. 'What always arrives at the last moment in all the best Lily Cavanaugh Westerns?'

'The cavalry,' Jack says. 'That's us, I suppose.'

'No,' Parkus says. His tone is patient, but Jack suspects it is costing him a great effort to maintain that tone. 'The cavalry is Roland of Gilead and his new gunslingers. Or so those of us who want the Tower to stand – or to fall in its own time – dare hope. The Crimson King hopes to hold Roland back, and to finish the job of destroying the Tower while he and his band are still at a distance. That means gathering all the Breakers he can, especially the telekinetics.'

'Is Tyler Marshall—'

'Stop interrupting. This is difficult enough without that.'

'You used to be a hell of a lot cheerier, Speedy,' Jack says reproachfully. For a moment he thinks his old friend is going to give him another tongue-lashing – or perhaps even lose his temper completely and turn him into a frog – but Parkus relaxes a little, and utters a laugh.

Sophie looks up, relieved, and gives Jack's hand a squeeze.

'Oh, well, maybe you're right to yank on my cord a little,' Parkus says. 'Gettin' all wound up won't help anything, will it?' He touches the big iron on his hip. 'I wouldn't be surprised if wearin' this thing has given me a few delusions of grandeur.'

'It's a step or two up from amusement-park janitor,' Jack allows.

'In both the Bible – your world, Jack – and the Book of Good Farming – *yours*, Sophie dear – there's a scripture that goes something like "For in my kingdom there are many mansions." Well, in the Court of the Crimson King there are many *monsters*.'

Jack hears a short, hard laugh bolt out of his mouth. His old friend has made a typically tasteless policeman's joke, it seems.

'They are the King's courtiers . . . his knights-errant. They have all sorts of tasks, I imagine, but in these last years their chief job has been to find talented Breakers. The more talented the Breaker, the greater the reward.'

'They're headhunters,' Jack murmurs, and doesn't realize the resonance of the term until it's out of his mouth. He has used it in the business sense, but of course there is another, more literal meaning. Headhunters are cannibals.

'Yes,' Parkus agrees. 'And they have mortal subcontractors, who work for . . . one doesn't like to say for the joy of it, but what else could we call it?'

Jack has a nightmarish vision then: a cartoon Albert Fish standing on a New York sidewalk with a sign reading WILL WORK FOR FOOD. He tightens his arm around Sophie. Her blue eyes turn to him, and he looks into them gladly. They soothe him.

'How many Breakers did Albert Fish send his pal Mr Monday?' Jack wants to know. 'Two? Four? A dozen? And do they die off, at least, so the abbalah has to replace them?'

'They don't,' Parkus replies gravely. 'They are kept in a place – a basement, yes, or a cavern – where there is essentially no time.'

'*Purgatory*. Christ.'

'And it doesn't matter. Albert Fish is long gone. Mr Monday is now Mr Munshun. The deal Mr Munshun has with your killer is a simple one: this Burnside can kill and eat all the children he wants, as long as they are *untalented* children. If he should find any who *are* talented – any Breakers – they are to be turned over to Mr Munshun at once.'

'Who will take them to the abbalah,' Sophie murmurs.

'That's right,' Parkus says.

Jack feels that he's back on relatively solid ground, and is extremely glad to be there. 'Since Tyler hasn't been killed, he must be talented.'

'"Talented" is hardly the word. Tyler Marshall is, potentially, one of the two most powerful Breakers in all the history of all the worlds. If I can briefly return to the analogy of the fort surrounded by Indians, then we could say that the Breakers are like fire arrows shot over the walls . . . a new kind of warfare. But Tyler Marshall is no simple fire arrow. He's more like a guided missile.

'Or a nuclear weapon.'

Sophie says, 'I don't know what that is.'

'You don't want to,' Jack replies. 'Believe me.'

He looks down at the scribble of drawings in the dirt. Is he surprised that Tyler should be so powerful? No, not really. Not after experiencing the aura of strength surrounding the boy's mother. Not after meeting Judy's Twinner, whose plain dress and manner can't conceal a character that strikes him as almost regal. She's beautiful, but he senses that beauty is one of the least important things about her.

'Jack?' Parkus asks him. 'You all right?' *There's no time to be anythin' else*, his tone suggests.

'Give me a minute,' Jack says.

'We don't have much t—'

'That has been made perfectly clear to me,' Jack says, biting off the words, and he feels Sophie shift in surprise at his tone of voice. 'Now give me a minute. Let me do my job.'

From beneath a ruffle of green feathers, one of the parrot's heads mutters: 'God loves the poor laborer.' The other replies: 'Is that why he made so fucking many of them?'

'All right, Jack,' Parkus says, and cocks his head up at the sky.

Okay, what have we got here? Jack thinks. *We've got a valuable little boy, and the Fisherman* knows *he's valuable. But this Mr Munshun doesn't have him yet, or Speedy wouldn't be here. Deduction?*

Sophie, looking at him anxiously. Parkus, still looking up into the blameless blue sky above this borderland between the Territories – what Judy Marshall calls Faraway – and the Whatever Comes Next. Jack's mind is ticking faster now, picking up speed like an express train leaving the station. He is aware that the black man with the bald head is watching the sky for a certain malevolent crow. He is aware that the fair-skinned woman beside him is looking at him with the sort of fascination that could become love, given world enough and time. Mostly, though, he's lost in his own thoughts. They are the thoughts of a coppiceman.

Now Bierstone's Burnside, and he's old. Old and not doing so well in the cognition department these days. I think maybe he's gotten caught between what he wants, which is to keep Tyler for himself, and what he's promised this Munshun guy. Somewhere there's a fuddled, creaky, dangerous mind trying to make itself up. If he decides to kill Tyler and stick him in the stewpot like the witch in 'Hansel and Gretel,' *that's bad for Judy and Fred. Not to mention Tyler, who may already have seen things that would drive a Marine combat vet insane. If the Fisherman turns the boy over to Mr Munshun, it's bad for everyone in creation. No wonder Speedy said time was blowing in our teeth.*

'You knew this was coming, didn't you?' he says. 'Both of you. You must have. Because *Judy* knew. She's been weird for months, long before the murders started.'

Parkus shifts and looks away, uncomfortable. 'I knew something was coming, yes – there have been great disruptions on this side – but I was on other business. And Sophie can't cross. She came here with the flying men and will go back the same way when our palaver's done.'

Jack turns to her. 'You are who my mother once was. I'm sure of it.' He supposes he isn't being entirely clear about this, but he can't help it; his mind is trying to go in too many directions at once. 'You're Laura DeLoessian's successor. The Queen of this world.'

Now Sophie is the one who looks uncomfortable. 'I was nobody in the great scheme of things, really I wasn't, and that was the way I liked it. What I did mostly was write letters of commendation and thank people for coming to see me . . . only in my official capacity, I always said "us." I enjoyed walking, and sketching flowers, and cataloging them. I enjoyed hunting. Then, due to bad luck, bad times, and bad behavior, I found myself the last of the royal line. Queen of this world, as you say. Married once, to a good and simple man, but my Fred Marshall died and left me alone. Sophie the Barren.'

'Don't,' Jack says. He is surprised at how deeply it hurts him to hear her refer to herself in this bitter, joking way.

'Were you not single-natured, Jack, your Twinner would be my cousin.'

She turns her slim fingers so that now she is gripping him instead of the other way around. When she speaks again, her voice is low and passionate. 'Put all the great matters aside. All *I* know is that Tyler Marshall is Judy's child, that I love her, that I'd not see her hurt for all the worlds that are. He's the closest thing to a child of my own that I'll ever have. These things I know, and one other: that you're the only one who can save him.'

'Why?' He has sensed this, of course – why else in God's name is he here? – but that doesn't lessen his bewilderment. 'Why me?'

'Because you touched the Talisman. And although some of its power has left you over the years, much still remains.'

Jack thinks of the lilies Speedy left for him in Dale's bathroom. How the smell lingered on his hands even after he had given the bouquet itself to Tansy. And he remembers how the Talisman looked in the murmuring darkness of the Queen's Pavilion, rising brightly, changing everything before it finally vanished.

He thinks: *It's* still *changing everything*.

'Parkus.' Is it the first time he's called the other man – the other coppiceman – by that name? He doesn't know for sure, but he thinks it may be.

'Yes, Jack.'

'What's left of the Talisman – is it enough? Enough for me to take on this Crimson King?'

Parkus looks shocked in spite of himself. 'Never in your life, Jack. Never in *any* life. The abbalah would blow you out like a candle. But it *may* be enough for you to take on Mr Munshun – to go into the furnace-lands and bring Tyler out.'

'There are machines,' Sophie says. She looks caught in some dark and unhappy dream. 'Red machines and black machines, all lost in smoke. There are great belts and children without number upon them. They trudge and trudge, turning the belts that turn the machines. Down in the foxholes. Down in the ratholes where the sun never shines. Down in the great caverns where the furnace-lands lie.'

Jack is shaken to the bottom of his mind and spirit. He

finds himself thinking of Dickens – not *Bleak House* but *Oliver Twist.* And, of course he thinks of his conversation with Tansy Freneau. *At least Irma's not there,* he thinks. *Not in the furnace-lands, not she. She got dead, and a mean old man ate her leg. Tyler, though . . . Tyler . . .*

'They trudge until their feet bleed,' he mutters. 'And the way there . . .?'

'I think you know it,' Parkus says. 'When you find Black House, you'll find your way to the furnace-lands . . . the machines . . . Mr Munshun . . . and Tyler.'

'The boy is alive. You're sure of that.'

'Yes.' Parkus and Sophie speak together.

'And where is Burnside now? That information might speed things up a bit.'

'I don't know,' Parkus says.

'Christ, if you know who he *was*—'

'That was the fingerprints,' Parkus says. 'The fingerprints on the telephone. Your first real idea about the case. The Wisconsin State Police got the Bierstone name back from the FBI's VICAP database. You have the Burnside name. That should be enough.'

Wisconsin State Police, FBI, VICAP, database: these terms come out in good old American English, and in this place they sound unpleasant and foreign to Jack's ear.

'How do you know all that?'

'I have my sources in your world; I keep my ear to the ground. As you know from personal experience. And surely you're cop enough to do the rest on your own.'

'Judy thinks you have a friend who can help,' Sophie says unexpectedly.

'Dale? Dale Gilbertson?' Jack finds this a little hard to believe, but he supposes Dale may have uncovered something.

'I don't know the name. Judy thinks he's like many here

in Faraway. A man who sees much because he sees nothing.'

Not Dale, after all. It's Henry she's talking about.

Parkus rises to his feet. The heads of the parrot come up, revealing four bright eyes. Sacred and Profane flutters up to his shoulder and settles there. 'I think our palaver is done,' Parkus says. 'It *must* be done. Are you ready to go back, my friend?'

'Yes. And I suppose I better take Green, little as I want to. I don't think he'd last long here.'

'As you say.'

Jack and Sophie, still holding hands, are halfway up the rise when Jack realizes Parkus is still standing in the speaking circle with his parrot on his shoulder. 'Aren't you coming?'

Parkus shakes his head. 'We go different ways now, Jack. I may see you again.'

If I survive, Jack thinks. *If* any *of us survive.*

'Meantime, go your course. And be true.'

Sophie drops another deep curtsey. *'Sai.'*

Parkus nods to her and gives Jack Sawyer a little salute. Jack turns and leads Sophie back to the ruined hospital tent, wondering if he will ever see Speedy Parker again.

Wendell Green – ace reporter, fearless investigator, explicator of good and evil to the great unwashed – sits in his former place, holding the crumpled foolscap in one hand and the batteries in the other. He has resumed muttering, and barely looks up when Sophie and Jack approach.

'You'll do your best, won't you?' Sophie asks. 'For her.'

'And for you,' Jack says. 'Listen to me, now. If this were to end with all of us still standing . . . and if I were to come back here . . .' He finds he can say no more. He's appalled at his temerity. This is a queen, after all. A *queen*. And he's . . . what? Trying to ask her for a date?

'Perhaps,' she says, looking at him with her steady blue eyes. 'Perhaps.'

'Is it a perhaps you want?' he asks softly.

'Yes.'

He bends and brushes his lips over hers. It's brief, barely a kiss at all. It is also the best kiss of his life.

'I feel like fainting,' she tells him when he straightens up again.

'Don't joke with me, Sophie.'

She takes his hand and presses it against the under-swell of her left breast. He can feel her heart pounding. 'Is this a joke? If she were to run faster, she'd catch her feet and fall.' She lets him go, but he holds his hand where it is a moment longer, palm curved against that springing warmth.

'I'd come with you if I could,' she says.

'I know that.'

He looks at her, knowing if he doesn't get moving now, right away, he never will. It's wanting not to leave her, but that's not all. The truth is that he's never been more frightened in his life. He searches for something mundane to bring him back to earth – to slow the pounding of his own heart – and finds the perfect object in the muttering creature that is Wendell Green. He drops to one knee. 'Are you ready, big boy? Want to take a trip on the mighty Mississip'?'

'Don't. Touch. Me.' And then, in a nearly poetic rush: 'Fucking Hollywood asshole!'

'Believe me, if I didn't have to, I wouldn't. And I plan to wash my hands just as soon as I get the chance.'

He looks up at Sophie and sees all the Judy in her. All the *beauty* in her. 'I love you,' he says.

Before she can reply, he seizes Wendell's hand, closes his eyes, and flips.

22

This time there's something that isn't quite silence: a lovely white rushing he has heard once before. In the summer of 1997, Jack went up way north to Vacaville with an LAPD skydiving club called the P.F. Flyers. It was a dare, one of those stupid things you got yourself into as a result of too many beers too late at night and then couldn't get yourself out of again. Not with any grace. Which was to say, not without looking like a chickenshit. He expected to be frightened; instead, he was exalted. Yet he had never done it again, and now he knows why: he had come too close to remembering, and some frightened part of him must have known it. It was the sound before you pulled the ripcord – that lonely white rushing of the wind past your ears. Nothing else to hear but the soft, rapid beat of your heart and – maybe – the click in your ears as you swallowed saliva that was in free fall, just like the rest of you.

Pull the ripcord, Jack, he thinks. *Time to pull the ripcord, or the landing's going to be awfully damn hard.*

Now there's a new sound, low at first but quickly swelling to a tooth-rattling bray. *Fire alarm*, he thinks, and then: *No, it's a* symphony *of fire alarms*. At the same moment, Wendell Green's hand is snatched out of his grip. He hears a faint, squawking cry as his fellow sky diver is swept away, and then there's a smell –

Honeysuckle –

No, it's her hair –

– and Jack gasps against a weight on his chest and his diaphragm, a feeling that the wind has been knocked out of him. There are hands on him, one on his shoulder, the other at the small of his back. Hair tickling his cheek. The sound of alarms. The sound of people yelling in confusion. Running footfalls that clack and echo.

'jack jack jack are you all right'

'Ask a queen for a date, get knocked into the middle of next week,' he mutters. Why is it so dark? Has he been blinded? Is he ready for that intellectually rewarding and financially remunerative job as an ump at Miller Park?

'*Jack!*' A palm smacks his cheek. Hard.

No, not blind. His eyes are just shut. He pops them open and Judy is bending over him, her face inches from his. Without thinking, he closes his left hand in the hair at the nape of her neck, brings her face down to his, and kisses her. She exhales into his mouth – a surprised reverse gasp that inflates his lungs with her electricity – and then kisses him back. He has never been kissed with such intensity in his entire life. His hand goes to the breast beneath her nightdress, and he feels the frenzied gallop of her heart – *If she were to run faster, she'd catch her feet and fall*, Jack thinks – beneath its firm rise. At the same moment her hand slips inside his shirt, which has somehow come unbuttoned, and tweaks his nipple. It's as hard and hot as the slap. As she does it, her tongue darts into his mouth in one quick plunge, there and gone, like a bee into a flower. He tightens his grip on the nape of her neck and God knows what would have happened next, but at that moment something falls over in the corridor with a huge crash of glass and someone screams. The voice is high and almost sexless with panic, but Jack believes it's Ethan Evans, the sullen young person from the hall. '*Get back here! Stop running, goldarnit!*' Of course it's Ethan; only a graduate of Mount Hebron Lutheran Sunday school would use *goldarnit*, even in extremis.

Jack pulls away from Judy. She pulls away from him. They are on the floor. Judy's nightdress is all the way up to her waist, exposing plain white nylon underwear. Jack's shirt is open, and so are his pants. His shoes are still on, but on the wrong feet, from the feel of them. Nearby, the glass-topped coffee table is overturned and the journals that were on it are scattered. Some seem to have been literally blown out of their bindings.

More screams from the corridor, plus a few cackles and mad ululations. Ethan Evans continues to yell at stampeding mental patients, and now a woman is yelling as well – Head Nurse Rack, perhaps. The alarms bray on and on.

All at once a door bursts open and Wendell Green gallops into the room. Behind him is a closet with clothes scattered everywhere, the spare items of Dr Spiegleman's wardrobe all ahoo. In one hand Wendell's holding his Panasonic minicorder. In the other he has several gleaming tubular objects. Jack is willing to bet they're double-A Duracells.

Jack's clothes have been unbuttoned (or perhaps blown open), but Wendell has fared much worse. His shirt is in tatters. His belly hangs over a pair of white boxer shorts, severely pee-stained in front. He is dragging his brown gabardine slacks by one foot. They slide across the carpet like a shed snakeskin.

And although his socks are on, the left one appears to have been turned inside out.

'*What did you do?*' Wendell blares. '*Oh you Hollywood son of a bitch, WHAT DID YOU DO TO M—*'

He stops. His mouth drops open. His eyes widen. Jack notes that the reporter's hair appears to be standing out like the quills on a porcupine.

Wendell, meanwhile, is noting Jack Sawyer and Judy Marshall, embracing on the glass- and paper-littered floor, with their clothes disarranged. They aren't quite in flagrante delicious, but if Wendell ever saw two people on the verge, dese are dem. His mind is whirling and filled with impossible memories, his balance is shot, his stomach is chugging like a washing machine that has been overloaded with clothes and suds; he desperately needs something to hold on to. He needs news. Even better, he needs *scandal*. And here, lying in front of him on the floor, are both.

'*RAPE!*' Wendell bellows at the top of his lungs. A mad, relieved grin twists up the corners of his mouth. '*SAWYER BEAT ME UP AND NOW HE'S RAPING A MENTAL PATIENT!*' It doesn't look much like rape to Wendell, in all truth, but who ever yelled *CONSENSUAL SEX!* at the top of his lungs and attracted any attention?

'Shut that idiot up,' Judy says. She yanks down the hem of her nightgown and prepares to stand.

'Watch out,' Jack says. 'Broken glass everywhere.'

'I'm okay,' she snaps. Then, turning to Wendell with that perfect fearlessness Fred knew so well: 'Shut up! I don't know who you are, but quit that bellowing! Nobody's being—'

Wendell backs away from Hollywood Sawyer, dragging his pants along with him. *Why doesn't someone come?* he thinks. *Why doesn't someone come before he shoots me, or something?* In his frenzy and near hysteria, Wendell has either not registered the alarms and general outcry or believes them to be going on inside his head, just a little more false information to go with his absurd 'memories' of a black gunslinger, a beautiful woman in a robe, and Wendell Green himself crouching in the dust and eating a half-cooked bird like a caveman.

'Keep away from me, Sawyer,' he says, backing up with his hands held out in front of him. 'I have an extremely hungry lawyer. Caveet-emporer, you asshole, lay one finger on me and he and I will strip you of everything you – OW! *OW!*'

Wendell has stepped on a piece of broken glass, Jack sees – probably from one of the prints that formerly decorated the walls and are now decorating the floor. He takes one more off-balance lurch backward, this time steps on his own trailing slacks, and goes sprawling into the leather recliner where Dr Spiegleman presumably sits while quizzing his patients on their troubled childhoods.

La Riviere's premier muckraker stares at the approaching Neanderthal with wide, horrified eyes, then throws the mini-corder at him. Jack sees that it's covered with scratches. He bats it away.

'*RAPE!*' Wendell squeals. '*HE'S RAPING ONE OF THE LOONIES! HE'S—*'

Jack pops him on the point of the chin, pulling the punch just a little at the last moment, delivering it with almost scientific force. Wendell flops back in Dr Spiegleman's recliner, eyes rolling up, feet twitching as if to some tasty beat that only the semiconscious can truly appreciate.

'The Mad Hungarian couldn't have done better,' Jack murmurs. It occurs to him that Wendell ought to treat himself to a complete neurological workup in the not too distant future. His head has put in a hard couple of days.

The door to the hall bursts open. Jack steps in front of the recliner to hide Wendell, stuffing his shirt into his pants (at some point he's zipped his fly, thank God). A candy striper pokes her fluffy head into Dr Spiegleman's office. Although she's probably eighteen, her panic makes her look about twelve.

'Who's yelling in here?' she asks. 'Who's hurt?'

Jack has no idea what to say, but Judy manages like a pro. 'It was a patient,' she says. 'Mr Lackley, I think. He came in, yelled that we were all going to be raped, and then ran out again.'

'You have to leave at once,' the candy striper tells them. 'Don't listen to that idiot Ethan. And don't use the elevator. We think it was an earthquake.'

'Right away,' Jack says crisply, and although he doesn't move, it's good enough for the candy striper; she heads out. Judy crosses quickly to the door. It closes but won't latch. The frame has been subtly twisted out of true.

There was a clock on the wall. Jack looks toward it, but it's fallen face-down to the floor. He goes to Judy and takes her by the arms. 'How long was I over there?'

'Not long,' she says, 'but what an exit you made! Ka-*pow!* Did you get anything?' Her eyes plead with him.

'Enough to know I have to go back to French Landing right away,' he tells her. *Enough to know that I love you – that I'll always love you, in this world or any other.*

'Tyler . . . is he alive?' She reverses his grip so she is holding him. Sophie did exactly the same thing in Faraway, Jack remembers. '*Is my son alive?*'

'Yes. And I'm going to get him for you.'

His eye happens on Spiegleman's desk, which has danced its way into the room and stands with all its drawers open. He sees something interesting in one of those drawers and hurries across the carpet, crunching on broken glass and kicking aside one of the prints.

In the top drawer to the left of the desk's kneehole is a tape recorder, considerably bigger than Wendell Green's trusty Panasonic, and a torn piece of brown wrapping paper. Jack snatches up the paper first. Scrawled across the front in draggling letters he's seen at both Ed's Eats and on his own front porch is this:

Deliver to JUDY MARSHALL
also known as SOPHIE

There are what appear to be stamps in the upper corner of the torn sheet. Jack doesn't need to examine them closely to know that they are really cut from sugar packets, and that they were affixed by a dangerous old dodderer named Charles Burnside. But the Fisherman's identity no longer matters much, and Speedy knew it. Neither does his location, because Jack has an idea Chummy Burnside can flip to a new one pretty much at will.

But he can't take the real doorway with him. The doorway to the furnace-lands, to Mr Munshun, to Ty. If Beezer and his pals found that—

Jack drops the wrapping paper back into the drawer, hits the EJECT button on the tape recorder, and pops out the cassette tape inside. He sticks it in his pocket and heads for the door.

'Jack.'

He looks back at her. Beyond them, fire alarms honk and blat, lunatics scream and laugh, staff run to and fro. Their eyes meet. In the clear blue light of Judy's regard, Jack can almost touch that other world with its sweet smells and strange constellations.

'Is it wonderful over there? As wonderful as in my dreams?'

'It's wonderful,' he tells her. 'And you are, too. Hang in there, okay?'

Halfway down the hallway, Jack comes upon a nasty sight: Ethan Evans, the young man who once had Wanda Kinderling as his Sunday school teacher, has laid hold of a disoriented old woman by her fat upper arms and is shaking her back and forth. The old woman's frizzy hair flies around her head.

'*Shut up!*' young Mr Evans is shouting at her. '*Shut up, you crazy old cow! You're not going anywhere except back to your dadblame room!*'

Something about his sneer makes it obvious that even now, with the world turned upside down, young Mr Evans is enjoying both his power to command and his Christian duty to brutalize. This is only enough to make Jack angry. What infuriates him is the look of terrified incomprehension on the old woman's face. It makes him think of boys he once lived with long ago, in a place called the Sunlight Home.

It makes him think of Wolf.

Without pausing or so much as breaking stride (they have entered the endgame phase of the festivities now, and somehow he knows it), Jack drives his fist into young Mr Evans's temple. That worthy lets go of his plump and squawking victim, strikes the wall, then slides down it, his eyes wide and dazed.

'Either you didn't listen in Sunday school or Kinderling's wife taught you the wrong lessons,' Jack says.

'You . . . hit . . . me . . .' young Mr Evans whispers. He finishes his slow dive splay-legged on the hallway floor halfway between the Records Annex and Ambulatory Ophthalmology.

'Abuse another patient – this one, the one I was just talking to, *any* of them – and I'll do a lot more than that,' Jack promises young Mr Evans. Then he's down the stairs, taking them two at a time, not noticing a handful of johnny-clad patients who stare at him with expressions of puzzled, half-fearful wonder. They look at him as if at a vision who passes them in an envelope of light, some wonder as brilliant as it is mysterious.

Ten minutes later (long after Judy Marshall has walked composedly back to her room without professional help of any kind), the alarms cut off. An amplified voice – perhaps even Dr Spiegleman's own mother wouldn't have recognized it as her boy's – begins to blare from the overhead speakers. At this unexpected roar, patients who had pretty much calmed down begin to shriek and cry all over again. The old woman whose mistreatment so angered Jack Sawyer is crouched below the admissions counter with her hands over her head, muttering something about the Russians and Civil Defense.

'THE EMERGENCY IS OVER!' Spiegleman assures his cast and crew. 'THERE IS NO FIRE! PLEASE REPORT TO THE COMMON ROOMS ON EACH FLOOR! THIS IS DR SPIEGLEMAN, AND I REPEAT THAT THE EMERGENCY IS *OVER*!'

Here comes Wendell Green, weaving his way slowly toward the stairwell, rubbing his chin gently with one hand. He sees young Mr Evans and offers him a helping hand. For a moment it looks as though Wendell may be pulled over himself, but then young Mr Evans gets his buttocks against the wall and manages to gain his feet.

'THE EMERGENCY IS OVER! I REPEAT, THE EMERGENCY IS *OVER*! NURSES, ORDERLIES, AND DOCTORS, PLEASE ESCORT ALL PATIENTS TO THE COMMON ROOMS ON EACH FLOOR!'

Young Mr Evans eyes the purple bruise rising on Wendell's chin.

Wendell eyes the purple bruise rising on the temple of young Mr Evans.

'Sawyer?' young Mr Evans asks.

'Sawyer,' Wendell confirms.

'Bastard sucker punched me,' young Mr Evans confides.

'Son of a bitch came up behind *me*,' Wendell says. 'The Marshall woman. He had her down.' He lowers his voice. 'He was getting ready to *rape* her.'

Young Mr Evans's whole manner says he is sorrowful but not surprised.

'Something ought to be done,' Wendell says.

'You got that right.'

'People ought to be told.' Gradually, the old fire returns to Wendell's eyes. People *will* be told. By him! Because that is what he does, by God! He *tells* people!

'Yeah,' young Mr Evans says. He doesn't care as much as Wendell does – he lacks Wendell's burning commitment – but there's one person he *will* tell. One person who deserves to be comforted in her lonely hours, who has been left on her own Mount of Olives. One person who will drink up the knowledge of Jack Sawyer's evil like the very waters of life.

'This kind of behavior cannot just be swept under the rug,' Wendell says.

'No way,' young Mr Evans agrees. 'No way, José.'

Jack has barely cleared the gates of French County Lutheran when his cell phone tweets. He thinks of pulling over to take the call, hears the sound of approaching fire engines, and decides for once to risk driving and talking at the same time.

He wants to be out of the area before the local fire brigade shows up and slows him down.

He flips the little Nokia open. 'Sawyer.'

'Where the fuck *are* you?' Beezer St Pierre bellows. 'Man, I been hittin' redial so hard I damn near punched it off the phone!'

'I've been . . .' But there's no way he can finish that, not and stay within shouting distance of the truth, that is. Or maybe there is. 'I guess I got into one of those dead zones where the cell phone just doesn't pick up—'

'Never mind the science lesson, chum. Get your ass over here right *now*. The actual address is 1 Nailhouse Row – it's County Road Double-O just south of Chase. It's the babyshit brown two-story on the corner.'

'I can find it,' Jack says, and steps down a little harder on the Ram's gas pedal. 'I'm on my way now.'

'What's your twenty, man?'

'Still Arden, but I'm rolling. I can be there in maybe half an hour.'

'*Fuck!*' There is an alarming crash-rattle in Jack's ear as somewhere on Nailhouse Row Beezer slams his fist against something. Probably the nearest wall. 'The fuck's *wrong* with you, man? Mouse is goin' down, I mean *fast*. We're doin' our best – those of us who're still here – but he is goin' *down*.' Beezer is panting, and Jack thinks he's trying not to cry. The thought of Armand St Pierre in that particular state is alarming. Jack looks at the Ram's speedometer, sees it's touching seventy, and eases off a tad. He won't help anybody by getting himself greased in a road wreck between Arden and Centralia.

'What do you mean "those of us who are still here"?'

'Never mind, just get your butt down here, if you want to talk to Mouse. And he sure wants to talk to you, because he keeps sayin' your name.' Beezer lowers his voice. 'When he ain't just ravin' his ass off, that is. Doc's doing his best – me and Bear Girl, too – but we're shovelin' shit against the tide here.'

'Tell him to hold on,' Jack says.

'Fuck that, man – tell him yourself.'

There's a rattling sound in Jack's ear, the faint murmuring of voices. Then another voice, one which hardly sounds human, speaks in his ear. 'Got to hurry . . . got to get over here, man. Thing . . . bit me. I can feel it in there. Like acid.'

'Hold on, Mouse,' Jack says. His fingers are dead white on the telephone. He wonders that the case doesn't simply crack in his grip. 'I'll be there fast as I can.'

'Better be. Others . . . already forgot. Not me.' Mouse chuckles. The sound is ghastly beyond belief, a whiff straight out of an open grave. 'I got . . . the memory serum, you know? It's eatin' me up . . . eatin' me alive . . . but I got it.'

There's the rustling sound of the phone changing hands again, then a new voice. A woman's. Jack assumes it's Bear Girl.

'You got them moving,' she says. 'You brought it to this. Don't let it be for nothing.'

There is a click in his ear. Jack tosses the cell phone onto the seat and decides that maybe seventy isn't too fast, after all.

A few minutes later (they seem like very long minutes to Jack), he's squinting against the glare of the sun on Tamarack Creek. From here he can almost see his house, and Henry's.

Henry.

Jack thumps the side of his thumb lightly against his breast pocket and hears the rattle of the cassette tape he took from the machine in Spiegleman's office. There's not much reason to turn it over to Henry now; given what Potter told him last night and what Mouse is holding on to tell him today, this tape and the 911 tape have been rendered more or less redundant. Besides, he's got to hurry to Nailhouse Row. There's a train getting ready to leave the station, and Mouse Baumann is very likely going to be on it.

And yet . . .

'I'm worried about him,' Jack says softly. 'Even a blind man could see I'm worried about Henry.'

The brilliant summer sun, now sliding down the afternoon side of the sky, reflects off the creek and sends shimmers of light dancing across his face. Each time this light crosses his eyes, they seem to burn.

Henry isn't the only one Jack's worried about, either. He's got a bad feeling about all of his new French Landing friends and acquaintances, from Dale Gilbertson and Fred Marshall right down to such bit players as old Steamy McKay, an elderly gent who makes his living shining shoes outside the public library, and Ardis Walker, who runs the ramshackle bait shop down by the river. In his imagination, all these people now seem made of glass. If the Fisherman decides to sing high C, they'll vibrate and then shatter to powder. Only it's not really the Fisherman he's worried about anymore.

This is a case, he reminds himself. *Even with all the Territories weirdness thrown in, it's still a case, and it's not the first one you've ever been on where everything suddenly started to seem too big. Where all the shadows seemed to be too long.*

True enough, but usually that funhouse sense of false perspective fades away once he starts to get a handle on things. This time it's worse, and worse by far. He knows why, too. The Fisherman's long shadow is a thing called Mr Munshun, an immortal talent scout from some other plane of existence. Nor is even that the end, because Mr Munshun also casts a shadow. A *red* one.

'Abbalah,' Jack mutters. 'Abbalah-doon and Mr Munshun and the Crow Gorg, just three old pals walking together on night's Plutonian shore.' For some reason this makes him think of the Walrus and the Carpenter from *Alice.* What was it they took for a walk in the moonlight? Clams? Mussels? Jack's damned if he can remember, although one line surfaces and resonates in his mind, spoken in his mother's voice: '*The time has come,' the Walrus said, 'to talk of many things.*'

The abbalah is presumably hanging out in his court (the part of him that isn't imprisoned in Speedy's Dark Tower, that is), but the Fisherman and Mr Munshun could be anywhere. Do they know Jack Sawyer has been meddling? Of course they do. By today, that is common knowledge. Might they try to slow him down by doing something nasty to one of his friends? A certain blind sportscaster-headbanger-bebopper, for instance?

Yes indeed. And now, perhaps because he's been sensitized to it, he can once more feel that nasty pulse coming out of the southwestern landscape, the one he sensed when he flipped over for the first time in his adult life. When the road curves southeast, he almost loses it. Then, when the Ram points its nose southwest again, the poisonous throb regains strength, beating into his head like the onset of a migraine headache.

That's Black House you feel, only it's not a house, not really. It's a wormhole in the apple of existence, leading all the way down into the furnace-lands. It's a door. Maybe it was only standing ajar before today, before Beezer and his pals turned up there, but now it's wide open and letting in one hell of a draft. Ty needs to be brought back, yes . . . but that door needs to be shut, as well. Before God knows what awful things come snarling through.

Jack abruptly swings the Ram onto Tamarack Road. The tires scream. His seat belt locks, and for a moment he thinks the truck may overturn. It stays up, though, and he goes flying toward Norway Valley Road. Mouse will just have to hang on a little bit longer; he's not going to leave Henry way out here on his own. His pal doesn't know it, but he's going on a little field trip to Nailhouse Row. Until this situation stabilizes, it seems to Jack that the buddy system is very much in order.

Which would have been all well and good if Henry had been at home, but he's not. Elvena Morton, dust mop in hand, comes in response to Jack's repeated jabbing at the doorbell.

'He's been over at KDCU, doing commercials,' Elvena says. 'Dropped him off myself. I don't know why he doesn't just do them in his studio here, something about the sound effects, I think he might have said. I'm surprised he didn't tell you that.'

The bitch of it is, Henry did. Cousin Buddy's Rib Crib. The old ball and chain. Beautiful downtown La Riviere. All that. He even told Jack that Elvena Morton was going to drive him. A few things have happened to Jack since that conversation – he's reencountered his old childhood friend, he's fallen in love with Judy Marshall's Twinner, and just by the way he's been filled in on your basic Secret of All Existence – but none of that keeps him from turning his left hand into a fist and then slamming himself directly between the eyes with it. Given how fast things are now moving, making this needless detour strikes him as an almost unforgivable lapse.

Mrs Morton is regarding him with wide-eyed alarm.

'Are you going to be picking him up, Mrs Morton?'

'No, he's going for a drink with someone from ESPN. Henry said the fellow would bring him back afterward.' She lowers her voice to the timbre of confidentiality at which secrets are somehow best communicated. 'Henry didn't come right out and say so, but I think there may be big things ahead for George Rathbun. Ver-ry big things.'

Badger Barrage going national? Jack wouldn't be entirely surprised, but he has no time to be delighted for Henry now. He hands Mrs Morton the cassette tape, mostly so he won't feel this was an *entirely* wasted trip. 'Leave this for him where . . .'

He stops. Mrs Morton is looking at him with knowing amusement. *Where he'll be sure to see it* is what Jack almost said. Another mental miscue. Big-city detective, indeed.

'I'll leave it by the soundboard in his studio,' she says. 'He'll find it there. Jack, maybe it's none of my business, but you don't look all right. You're very pale, and I'd swear you've lost ten pounds since last week. Also . . .' She looks a bit embarrassed. 'Your shoes are on the wrong feet.'

So they are. He makes the necessary change, standing first on one foot and then the other. 'It's been a tough forty-eight hours, but I'm hanging in there, Mrs M.'

'It's the Fisherman business, isn't it?'

He nods. 'And I have to go. The fat, as they say, is in the fire.' He turns, reconsiders, turns back. 'Leave him a message on the kitchen tape recorder, would you? Tell him to call me on my cell. Just as soon as he gets in.' Then, one thought leading to another, he points to the unmarked cassette tape in her hand. 'Don't play that, all right?'

Mrs Morton looks shocked. 'I'd never do such a thing! It would be like opening someone else's mail!'

Jack nods and gives her a scrap of a smile. 'Good.'

'Is it . . . him on the tape? Is it the Fisherman?'

'Yes,' Jack says. 'It's him.' *And there are worse things waiting*, he thinks but doesn't say. *Worse things by far.*

He hurries back to his truck, not quite running.

Twenty minutes later Jack parks in front of the babyshit brown two-story at 1 Nailhouse Row. Nailhouse Row and the dirty snarl of streets around it strike him as unnaturally silent under the sun of this hot summer afternoon. A mongrel dog (it is, in fact, the old fellow we saw in the doorway of the Nelson Hotel just last night) goes limping across the intersection of Ames and County Road Oo, but that's about the extent of the traffic. Jack has an unpleasant vision of the Walrus and the Carpenter toddling along the east bank of the Mississippi with the hypnotized residents of Nailhouse Row following along behind them. Toddling along toward the fire. And the cooking pot.

He takes two or three deep breaths, trying to steady himself. Not far out of town – close to the road leading to Ed's Eats, in fact – that nasty buzzing in his head peaked, turning into something like a dark scream. For a few moments there it was so strong Jack wondered if he was perhaps going to drive right off the road, and he slowed the Ram to forty. Then, blessedly, it began to move around toward the back of his head and fade. He didn't see the NO TRESPASSING sign that marks the overgrown road leading to Black House, didn't even look for it, but he knew it was there. The question is whether or not he'll be able to approach it when the time comes without simply exploding.

'Come on,' he tells himself. 'No time for this shit.'

He gets out of the truck and starts up the cracked cement

walk. There's a fading hopscotch diagram there, and Jack swerves to avoid it without even thinking, knowing it's one of the few remaining artifacts which testify that a little person named Amy St Pierre once briefly trod the boards of existence. The porch steps are dry and splintery. He's vilely thirsty and thinks, *Man, I'd kill for a glass of water, or a nice cold—*

The door flies open, cracking against the side of the house like a pistol shot in the sunny silence, and Beezer comes running out.

'Christ almighty, I didn't think you were *ever* gonna get here!'

Looking into Beezer's alarmed, agonized eyes, Jack realizes that he will never tell this guy that he might be able to find Black House without Mouse's help, that thanks to his time in the Territories he has a kind of range finder in his head. No, not even if they live the rest of their lives as close friends, the kind who usually tell each other everything. The Beez has suffered like Job, and he doesn't need to find out that his friend's agony may have been in vain.

'Is he still alive, Beezer?'

'By an inch. Maybe an inch and a quarter. It's just me and Doc and Bear Girl now. Sonny and Kaiser Bill got scared, ran off like a couple of whipped dogs. March your boots in here, sunshine.' Not that Beezer gives Jack any choice; he grabs him by the shoulder and hauls him into the little two-story on Nailhouse Row like luggage.

23

'One more!' says the guy from ESPN.

It sounds more like an order than a request, and although Henry can't see the fellow, he knows this particular homeboy never played a sport in his life, pro or otherwise. He has the lardy, slightly oily aroma of someone who has been overweight almost from the jump. Sports is perhaps his compensation, with the power to still memories of clothes bought in the Husky section at Sears and all those childhood rhymes like 'Fatty-fatty, two-by-four, had to do it on the floor, couldn't get through the bathroom door.'

His name is Penniman. 'Just like Little Richard!' he told Henry when they shook hands at the radio station. 'Famous rock 'n' roller from back in the fifties? Maybe you remember him.'

'Vaguely,' Henry said, as if he hadn't at one time owned every single Little Richard had ever put out. 'I believe he was one of the Founding Fathers.' Penniman laughed uproariously, and in that laugh Henry glimpsed a possible future for himself. But was it a future he wanted? People laughed at Howard Stern, too, and Howard Stern was a dork.

'One more drink!' Penniman repeats now. They are in the bar of the Oak Tree Inn, where Penniman has tipped the bartender five bucks to switch the TV from bowling on ABC to ESPN, even though there's nothing on at this hour of the day except golf tips and bass fishing. 'One more drink, just to seal the deal!'

But they *don't* have a deal, and Henry isn't sure he wants to make one. Going national with George Rathbun as part of the ESPN radio package should be attractive, and he doesn't have any serious problem with changing the name of the show from *Badger Barrage* to *ESPN Sports Barrage* – it would still focus primarily on the central and northern areas of the country – but . . .

But what?

Before he can even get to work on the question, he smells it again: My Sin, the perfume his wife used to wear on certain evenings, when she wanted to send a certain signal. Lark was what he used to call her on those certain evenings, when the room was dark and they were both blind to everything but scents and textures and each other.

Lark.

'You know, I think I'm going to pass on that drink,' Henry says. 'Got some work to do at home. But I'm going to think over your offer. And I mean seriously.'

'Ah-ah-ah,' Penniman says, and Henry can tell from certain minute disturbances in the air that the man is shaking a finger beneath his nose. Henry wonders how Penniman would react if Henry suddenly darted his head forward and bit off the offending digit at the second knuckle. If Henry showed him a little Coulee Country hospitality Fisherman-style. How loud would Penniman yell? As loud as Little Richard before the instrumental break of 'Tutti Frutti,' perhaps? Or not quite as loud as that?

'Can't go till I'm ready to take you,' Mr I'm Fat But It No Longer Matters tells him. 'I'm your ride, y'know.' He's on his fourth gimlet, and his words are slightly slurred. *My friend*, Henry thinks, *I'd poke a ferret up my ass before I'd get into a car with you at the wheel.*

'Actually, I can,' Henry says pleasantly. Nick Avery, the bartender, is having a kick-ass afternoon: the fat guy slipped him five to change the TV channel, and the blind guy slipped him five to call Skeeter's Taxi while the fat guy was in the bathroom, making a little room.

'Huh?'

'I said, "Actually, I can." Bartender?'

'He's outside, sir,' Avery tells him. 'Pulled up two minutes ago.'

There is a hefty creak as Penniman turns on his bar stool. Henry can't see the man's frown as he takes in the taxi now idling in the hotel turnaround, but he can sense it.

'Listen, Henry,' Penniman says. 'I think you may lack a certain understanding of your current situation. There are stars in the firmament of sports radio, damned right there are – people like the Fabulous Sports Babe and Tony Kornheiser make six figures a year just in speaking fees, six figures *easy* – but you ain't there yet. That door is currently closed to you. But I, my friend, am one helluva doorman. The upshot is that if I say we ought to have one more drink, then—'

'Bartender,' Henry says quietly, then shakes his head. 'I can't just call you bartender; it might work for Humphrey Bogart but it doesn't work for me. What's your name?'

'Nick Avery, sir.' The last word comes out automatically, but Avery never would have used it when speaking to the other one, never in a million years. Both guys tipped him five, but the one in the dark glasses is the gent. It's got nothing to do with him being blind, it's just something he *is*.

'Nick, who else is at the bar?'

Avery looks around. In one of the back booths, two men are drinking beer. In the hall, a bellman is on the phone. At the bar itself, no one at all except for these two guys – one slim, cool, and blind, the other fat, sweaty, and starting to be pissed off.

'No one, sir.'

'There's not a . . . lady?' *Lark*, he's almost said. *There's not a lark?*

'No.'

'Listen here,' Penniman says, and Henry thinks he's never heard anyone so unlike 'Little Richard' Penniman in his entire life. This guy is whiter than Moby Dick . . . and probably about the same size. 'We've got a lot more to discuss here.' *Loh more t'dishcush* is how it comes out. 'Unless, that is' – *Unlesh* – 'you're trying to let me know you're not interested.' *Never in a million years*, Penniman's voice says to Henry Leyden's educated ears. *We're talking about putting a money machine in your living room, sweetheart, your very own private ATM, and there ain't no way in hell you're going to turn that down.*

'Nick, you don't smell perfume? Something very light and old-fashioned? My Sin, perhaps?'

A flabby hand falls on Henry's shoulder like a hot-water bottle. 'The sin, old buddy, would be for you to *refuse* to have another drink with me. Even a blindman could see th—'

'Suggest you get your hand off him,' Avery says, and perhaps Penniman's ears aren't *entirely* deaf to nuance, because the hand leaves Henry's shoulder at once.

Then another hand comes in its place, higher up. It touches the back of Henry's neck in a cold caress that's there and then gone. Henry draws in breath. The smell of perfume comes with it. Usually scents fade after a period of exposure, as the receptors that caught them temporarily deaden. Not this time, though. Not this smell.

'No perfume?' Henry almost pleads. The touch of her hand on his neck he can dismiss as a tactile hallucination. But his nose never betrays him.

Never until now, anyway.

'I'm sorry,' Avery says. 'I can smell beer . . . peanuts . . . this man's gin and his aftershave . . .'

Henry nods. The lights above the backbar slide across the dark lenses of his shades as he slips gracefully off his stool.

'I think you want another drink, my friend,' Penniman says in what he no doubt believes to be a tone of polite menace. 'One more drink, just to celebrate, and then I'll take you home in my Lexus.'

Henry smells his wife's perfume. He's sure of it. And he seemed to feel the touch of his wife's hand on the back of his neck. Yet suddenly it's skinny little Morris Rosen he finds himself thinking about – Morris, who wanted him to listen to 'Where Did Our Love Go' as done by Dirtysperm. And of course for Henry to play it in his Wisconsin Rat persona. Morris Rosen, who has more integrity in one of his nail-chewed little fingers than this bozo has got in his entire body.

He puts a hand on Penniman's forearm. He smiles into Penniman's unseen face, and feels the muscles beneath his palm relax. Penniman has decided he's going to get his way. Again.

'You take my drink,' Henry says pleasantly, 'add it to *your* drink, and then stick them both up your fat and bepimpled ass. If you need something to hold them in place, why, you can stick your job up there right after them.'

Henry turns and walks briskly toward the door, orienting

himself with his usual neat precision and holding one hand out in front of him as an insurance policy. Nick Avery has broken into spontaneous applause, but Henry barely hears this and Penniman he has already dismissed from his mind. What occupies him is the smell of My Sin perfume. It fades a little as he steps out into the afternoon heat . . . but is that not an amorous sigh he hears beside his left ear? The sort of sigh his wife sometimes made just before falling asleep after love? His Rhoda? His Lark?

'Hello, the taxi!' he calls from the curb beneath the awning.

'Right here, buddy – what're you, blind?'

'As a bat,' Henry agrees, and walks toward the sound of the voice. He'll go home, he'll put his feet up, he'll have a glass of tea, and then he'll listen to the damned 911 tape. That as yet unperformed chore may be what's causing his current case of the heebie-jeebies and shaky-shivers, knowing that he must sit in darkness and listen to the voice of a child-killing cannibal. Surely that must be it, because there's no reason to be afraid of his Lark, is there? If she were to return – to return and haunt him – she would surely haunt with love.

Wouldn't she?

Yes, he thinks, and lowers himself into the taxi's stifling back seat.

'Where to, buddy?'

'Norway Valley Road,' Henry says. 'It's a white house with blue trim, standing back from the road. You'll see it not long after you cross the creek.'

Henry settles back in the seat and turns his troubled face toward the open window. French Landing feels strange to him today . . . *fraught*. Like something that has slipped and slipped until it is now on the verge of simply falling off the table and smashing to pieces on the floor.

Say that she has *come back. Say that she* has. *If it's love she's come with, why does the smell of her perfume make me so uneasy? So almost revolted? And why was her touch (her* imagined *touch, he assures himself) so unpleasant?*

Why was her touch so cold?

After the dazzle of the day, the living room of Beezer's crib is so dark that at first Jack can't make out anything. Then, when his eyes adjust a little, he sees why: blankets – a double thickness, from the look – have been hung over both of the living-room windows, and the door to the other downstairs room, almost certainly the kitchen, has been closed.

'He can't stand the light,' Beezer says. He keeps his voice low so it won't carry across to the far side of the room, where the shape of a man lies on a couch. Another man is kneeling beside him.

'Maybe the dog that bit him was rabid,' Jack says. He doesn't believe it.

Beezer shakes his head decisively. 'It isn't a phobic reaction. Doc says it's physiological. Where light falls on him, his skin starts to melt. You ever hear of anything like that?'

'No.' And Jack has never smelled anything like the stench in this room, either. There's the buzz of not one but two table fans, and he can feel the cross-draft, but that stink is too gluey to move. There's the reek of spoiled meat – of gangrene in torn flesh – but Jack has smelled that before. It's the other smell that's getting to him, something like blood and funeral flowers and feces all mixed up together. He makes a gagging noise, can't help it, and Beezer looks at him with a certain impatient sympathy.

'Bad, yeah, I know. But it's like the monkey house at the zoo, man – you get used to it after a while.'

The swing door to the other room opens, and a trim little woman with shoulder-length blond hair comes through. She's carrying a bowl. When the light strikes the figure lying on the couch, Mouse screams. It's a horribly thick sound, as if the man's lungs have begun to liquefy. Something – maybe smoke, maybe steam – starts to rise up from the skin of his forehead.

'Hold on, Mouse,' the kneeling man says. It's Doc. Before the kitchen door swings all the way shut again, Jack is able to read what's pasted to his battered black bag. Somewhere in America there may be another medical man sporting a STEPPENWOLF RULES bumper sticker on the side of his physician's bag, but probably not in Wisconsin.

The woman kneels beside Doc, who takes a cloth from the basin, wrings it out, and places it on Mouse's forehead. Mouse gives a shaky groan and begins to shiver all over. Water runs down his cheeks and into his beard. The beard seems to be coming out in mangy patches.

Jack steps forward, telling himself he will get used to the smell, sure he will. Maybe it's even true. In the meantime he wishes for a little of the Vicks VapoRub most LAPD homicide detectives carry in their glove compartments as a matter of course. A dab under each nostril would be very welcome right now.

There's a sound system (scruffy) and a pair of speakers in the corners of the room (huge), but no television. Stacked wooden crates filled with books line every wall without a door or a window in it, making the space seem even smaller than it is, almost cryptlike. Jack has a touch of claustrophobia in his makeup, and now this circuit warms up, increasing his discomfort. Most of the books seem to deal with religion and philosophy – he sees Descartes, C. S. Lewis, the Bhagavad-Gita, Steven Avery's *Tenets of Existence* – but there's also a lot of fiction, books on beer making, and (on top of one giant speaker) Albert Goldman's trash tome about Elvis Presley. On the other speaker is a photograph of a young girl with a splendid smile, freckles, and oceans of reddish-blond hair. Seeing the child who drew the hopscotch grid out front makes Jack Sawyer feel sick with anger and sorrow. Otherworldly beings and causes there may be, but there's also a sick old fuck prowling around who needs to be stopped. He'd do well to remember that.

Bear Girl makes a space for Jack in front of the couch, moving gracefully even though she's on her knees and still holding the bowl. Jack sees that in it are two more wet cloths and a heap of melting ice cubes. The sight of them makes him thirstier than ever. He takes one and pops it into his mouth. Then he turns his attention to Mouse.

A plaid blanket has been pulled up to his neck. His forehead and upper cheeks – the places not covered by his decaying beard – are pasty. His eyes are closed. His lips are drawn back to show teeth of startling whiteness.

'Is he—' Jack begins, and then Mouse's eyes open. Whatever Jack meant to ask leaves his head entirely. Around the hazel irises, Mouse's eyes have gone an uneasy, shifting scarlet. It's as if the man is looking into a terrible radioactive sunset. From the inner corners of his eyes, some sort of black scum is oozing.

'*The Book of Philosophical Transformation* addresses most current dialectics,' Mouse says, speaking mellowly and lucidly, 'and Machiavelli also speaks to these questions.' Jack can almost picture him in a lecture hall. Until his teeth begin to chatter, that is.

'Mouse, it's Jack Sawyer.' No recognition in those weird red-and-hazel eyes. The black gunk at the corners of them seems to twitch, however, as if it is somehow sentient. Listening to him.

'It's Hollywood,' Beezer murmurs. 'The cop. Remember?'

One of Mouse's hands lies on the plaid blanket. Jack takes it, and stifles a cry of surprise when it closes over his with amazing strength. It's hot, too. As hot as a biscuit just out of the oven. Mouse lets out a long, gasping sigh, and the stench is fetid – bad meat, decayed flowers. *He's rotting,* Jack thinks. *Rotting from the inside out. Oh Christ, help me through this.*

Christ may not, but the memory of Sophie might. Jack tries to fix her eyes in his memory, that lovely, level, clear blue gaze.

'Listen,' Mouse says.

'I'm listening.'

Mouse seems to gather himself. Beneath the blanket, his body shivers in a loose, uncoordinated way that Jack guesses is next door to a seizure. Somewhere a clock is ticking. Somewhere a dog is barking. A boat hoots on the Mississippi. Other than these sounds, all is silence. Jack can remember only one other such suspension of the world's business in his entire life, and that was when he was in a Beverly Hills hospital, waiting for his mother to finish the long business of dying. Somewhere Ty Marshall is waiting to be rescued. Hoping to be rescued, at least. Somewhere there are Breakers hard at work, trying to destroy the axle upon which all existence spins. Here is only this eternal room with its feeble fans and noxious vapors.

Mouse's eyes close, then open again. They fix upon the newcomer, and Jack is suddenly sure some great truth is going to be confided. The ice cube is gone from his mouth; Jack supposes he crunched it up and swallowed it without even realizing, but he doesn't dare take another.

'Go on, buddy,' Doc says. 'You get it out and then I'll load you up with another hypo of dope. The good stuff. Maybe you'll sleep.'

Mouse pays no heed. His mutating eyes hold Jack's. His hand holds Jack's, tightening still more. Jack can almost feel the bones of his fingers grinding together.

'Don't . . . go out and buy top-of-the-line equipment,' Mouse says, and sighs out another excruciatingly foul breath from his rotting lungs.

'Don't . . .?'

'Most people give up brewing after . . . a year or two. Even dedicated . . . dedicated hobbyists. Making beer is not . . . is not for pussies.'

Jack looks around at Beezer, who looks back impassively. 'He's in and out. Be patient. Wait on him.'

Mouse's grip tightens yet more, then loosens just as Jack is deciding he can take it no longer.

'Get a big pot,' Mouse advises him. His eyes bulge. The reddish shadows come and go, come and go, fleeting across the curved landscape of his corneas, and Jack thinks, *That's* its *shadow. The shadow of the Crimson King. Mouse has already got one foot in its court.* 'Five gallons . . . at least. You find the best ones are in . . . sea-food supply stores. And for a fermentation vessel . . . plastic water-cooler jugs are good . . . they're lighter than glass, and *. . . I'm burning up. Christ, Beez, I'm burning up!*'

'Fuck this, I'm going to shoot it to him,' Doc says, and snaps open his bag.

Beezer grabs his arm. 'Not yet.'

Bloody tears begin to slip out of Mouse's eyes. The black goo seems to be forming into tiny tendrils. These reach greedily downward, as if trying to catch the moisture and drink it.

'Fermentation lock and stopper,' Mouse whispers. 'Thomas Merton is shit, never let anyone tell you different. No real thought there. You have to let the gases escape while keeping dust out. Jerry Garcia wasn't God. Kurt Cobain wasn't God.

The perfume he smells is not that of his dead wife. He's caught the eye of the King. *Gorg-ten-abbalah, ee-lee-lee.* The opopanax is dead, long live the opopanax.'

Jack leans more deeply into Mouse's smell. 'Who's smelling perfume? Who's caught the eye of the King?'

'The mad King, the bad King, the sad King. Ring-a-ding-ding, all hail the King.'

'Mouse, *who's* caught the eye of the King?'

Doc says, 'I thought you wanted to know about—'

'*Who?*' Jack has no idea why this seems important to him, but it does. Is it something someone has said to him recently? Was it Dale? Tansy? Was it, God save us, Wendell Green?

'Racking cane and hose,' Mouse says confidentially. 'That's what you need when the fermentation's done! And you can't put beer in screw-top bottles! You—'

Mouse turns his head away from Jack, nestles it cozily in the hollow of his shoulder, opens his mouth, and vomits. Bear Girl screams. The vomit is pus-yellow and speckled with moving black bits like the crud in the corners of Mouse's eyes. It is alive.

Beezer leaves the room in a hurry, not quite running, and Jack shades Mouse from the brief glare of kitchen sunlight as best he can. The hand clamped on Jack's loosens a little more.

Jack turns to Doc. 'Do you think he's going?'

Doc shakes his head. 'Passed out again. Poor old Mousie ain't getting off that easy.' He gives Jack a grim, haunted look. 'This better be worth it, Mr Policeman. 'Cause if it ain't, I'm gonna replumb your sink.'

Beezer comes back with a huge bundle of rags, and he's put on a pair of green kitchen gloves. Not speaking, he mops up the pool of vomit between Mouse's shoulder and the back-rest of the couch. The black specks have ceased moving, and that's good. To have not seen them moving in the first place would have been even better. The vomit, Jack notices with dismay, has eaten into the couch's worn fabric like acid.

'I'm going to pull the blanket down for a second or two,' Doc says, and Bear Girl gets up at once, still holding the bowl with the melting ice. She goes to one of the bookshelves and stands there with her back turned, trembling.

'Doc, is this something I really need to see?'

'I think maybe it is. I don't think you know what you're dealing with, even now.' Doc takes hold of the blanket and eases it out from beneath Mouse's limp hand. Jack sees that more of the black stuff has begun to ooze from beneath the dying man's fingernails. 'Remember that this happened only a couple of hours ago, Mr Policeman.'

He pulls the blanket down. Standing with her back to them, Susan 'Bear Girl' Osgood faces the great works of Western philosophy and begins to cry silently. Jack tries to hold back his scream and cannot.

Henry pays off the taxi, goes into his house, takes a deep and soothing breath of the air-conditioned cool. There is a faint aroma – sweet – and he tells himself it's just fresh-cut flowers, one of Mrs Morton's specialties. He knows better, but wants no more to do with ghosts just now. He is actually feeling better, and he supposes he knows why: it was telling the ESPN guy to take his job and shove it. Nothing more apt to make a fellow's day, especially when the fellow in question is gainfully employed, possessed of two credit cards that are nowhere near the max-out point, and has a pitcher of cold iced tea in the fridge.

Henry heads kitchenward now, making his way down the hall with one hand held out before him, testing the air for obstacles and displacements. There's no sound but the whisper of the air conditioner, the hum of the fridge, the clack of his heels on the hardwood . . .

. . . and a sigh.

An amorous sigh.

Henry stands where he is for a moment, then turns cautiously. Is the sweet aroma a little stronger now, especially facing back in this direction, toward the living room and the front door? He thinks yes. And it's not flowers; no sense fooling himself about that. As always, the nose knows. That's the aroma of My Sin.

'Rhoda?' he says, and then, lower: 'Lark?'

No answer. Of course not. He's just having the heebie-jeebies, that's all; those world-famous shaky-shivers, and why not?

'Because I'm the sheik, baby,' Henry says. 'The Sheik, the Shake, the Shook.'

No smells. No sexy sighs. And yet he's haunted by the idea of his wife back in the living room, standing there in perfumed cerements of the grave, watching him silently as he came in and passed blindly before her. His Lark, come back from Noggin Mound Cemetery for a little visit. Maybe to listen to the latest Slobberbone CD.

'Quit it,' he says softly. 'Quit it, you dope.'

He goes into his big, well-organized kitchen. On his way through the door he slaps a button on the panel there without even thinking about it. Mrs Morton's voice comes from the overhead speaker, which is so high-tech she might almost be in the room.

'Jack Sawyer was by, and he dropped off another tape he wants you to listen to. He said it was . . . you know, that man. That bad man.'

'Bad man, right,' Henry murmurs, opening the refrigerator and enjoying the blast of cold air. His hand goes unerringly to one of three cans of Kingsland Lager stored inside the door. Never mind the iced tea.

'Both of the tapes are in your studio, by the soundboard. Also, Jack wanted you to call him on his cell phone.' Mrs Morton's voice takes on a faintly lecturing tone. 'If you do speak to him, I hope you tell him to be careful. And be careful yourself.' A pause. '*Also*, don't forget to eat supper. It's all ready to go. Second shelf of the fridge, on your left.'

'Nag, nag, nag,' Henry says, but he's smiling as he opens his beer. He goes to the telephone and dials Jack's number.

On the seat of the Dodge Ram parked in front of 1 Nailhouse Row, Jack's cell phone comes to life. This time there's no one in the cab to be annoyed by its tiny but penetrating tweet.

'The cellular customer you are trying to reach is currently not answering. Please try your call again later.'

Henry hangs up, goes back to the doorway, and pushes another button on the panel there. The voices that deliver the time and temperature are all versions of his own, but he's programmed a random shuffle pattern into the gadget, so he never knows which one he's going to get. This time it's the Wisconsin Rat, screaming crazily into the sunny air-conditioned silence of his house, which has never felt so far from town as it does today:

'Time's four twenty-two p.m.! Outside temperature's eighty-two! Inside temperature's seventy! What the hell do you care? What the hell does *anyone* care? Chew it up, eat it up, wash it down, *it aaall*—'

—comes out the same place. Right. Henry thumbs the

button again, silencing the Rat's trademark cry. How did it get late so fast? God, wasn't it just noon? For that matter, wasn't he just young, twenty years old and so full of spunk it was practically coming out of his ears? What—

That sigh comes again, derailing his mostly self-mocking train of thought. A sigh? Really? More likely just the air conditioner's compressor, cutting off. He can tell himself that, anyway.

He can tell himself that if he wants to.

'Is anyone here?' Henry asks. There is a tremble in his voice that he hates, an old man's palsied quaver. 'Is anyone in the house with me?'

For a terrible second he is almost afraid something will answer. Nothing does – of *course* nothing does – and he swallows half the can of beer in three long gulps. He decides he'll go back into the living room and read for a little while. Maybe Jack will call. Maybe he'll get himself a little more under control once he has a little fresh alcohol in his system.

And maybe the world will end in the next five minutes, he thinks. *That way you'll never have to deal with the voice on those damned tapes waiting in the studio. Those damned tapes lying there on the soundboard like unexploded bombs.*

Henry walks slowly back down the hall to the living room with one hand held out before him, telling himself he's not afraid, not a bit afraid of touching his wife's dead face.

Jack Sawyer has seen a lot, he's traveled to places where you can't rent from Avis and the water tastes like wine, but he's never encountered anything like Mouse Baumann's leg. Or, rather, the pestilential, apocalyptic horror show that *was* Mouse Baumann's leg. Jack's first impulse once he's got himself back under something like control is to upbraid Doc for taking off Mouse's pants. Jack keeps thinking of sausages, and how the casing forces them to keep their shape even after the fry pan's sizzling on a red-hot burner. This is an undoubtedly stupid comparison, *primo stupido*, but the human mind under pressure puts on some pretty odd jinks and jumps.

There's still the *shape* of a leg there – sort of – but the flesh has spread away from the bone. The skin is almost completely gone, melted to a runny substance that looks like a mixture of milk and bacon fat. The interwoven mat of muscle beneath what remains of the skin is sagging and undergoing the same cataclysmic metamorphosis. The infected leg is in a kind of undisciplined motion as the solid becomes liquid and the liquid sizzles relentlessly into the couch upon which Mouse is lying. Along with the almost insupportable stench of decay, Jack can smell scorching cloth and melting fabric.

Poking out of this spreading, vaguely leglike mess is a foot that looks remarkably undamaged. *If I wanted to, I could pull it right off . . . just like a squash off a vine.* The thought gets to him in a way the sight of the grievously wounded leg hasn't quite been able to, and for a moment Jack can only bow his head, gagging and trying not to vomit down the front of his shirt.

What perhaps saves him is a hand on his back. It's Beezer, offering what comfort he can. The rowdy color has completely left the Beez's face. He looks like a motorcyclist come back from the grave in an urban myth.

'You see?' Doc is asking, and his voice seems to come from a great distance. 'This ain't the chicken pox, my friend, although it looked a little like that while it was still getting cranked up. He's already exhibiting red spots on his left leg . . . his belly . . . his balls. That's pretty much what the skin around the bite looked like when we first got him back here, just some redness and swelling. I thought, "Shit, ain't nothin' to this, I got enough Zithromax to put this on the run before sundown." Well, you see what good the Zithro did. You see what good *anything* did. It's eating through the couch, and I'm guessing that when it finishes with the couch, it'll go right to work on the floor. This shit is *hungry*. So was it worth it, Hollywood? I guess only you and Mouse know the answer to that.'

'He still knows where the house is,' Beezer says. 'Me, I don't have a clue, even though we just *came* from there. You, either. Do you?'

Doc shakes his head.

'But Mouse, *he* knows.'

'Susie, honey,' Doc says to Bear Girl. 'Bring another blanket, would you? This one's damn near et through.'

Bear Girl goes willingly enough. Jack gets to his feet. His legs are rubbery, but they hold him. 'Shield him,' he tells Doc. 'I'm going out to the kitchen. If I don't get a drink, I'm going to die.'

Jack takes on water directly from the sink, swallowing until a spike plants itself in the center of his forehead and he belches like a horse. Then he just stands there, looking out into Beezer and Bear Girl's backyard. A neat little swing set has been planted there in the weedy desolation. It hurts Jack to look at it, but he looks anyway. After the lunacy of Mouse's leg, it seems important to remind himself that he's here for a reason. If the reminder hurts, so much the better.

The sun, now turning gold as it eases itself down toward the Mississippi, glares in his eyes. Time hasn't been standing still after all, it seems. Not outside this little house, anyway. Outside 1 Nailhouse Row, time actually seems to have sped up. He's haunted by the idea that coming here was as pointless as detouring to Henry's house; tormented by the thought that

Mr Munshun and his boss, the abbalah, are running him around like a windup toy with a key in its back while they do their work. He can follow that buzz in his head to Black House, so why the hell doesn't he just get back in his truck and *do* it?

The perfume he smells is not that of his dead wife.

What does that mean? Why does the idea of someone smelling perfume make him so crazy and afraid?

Beezer knocks on the kitchen door, making him jump. Jack's eye fixes on a sampler hung over the kitchen table. Instead of GOD BLESS OUR HOME, it reads HEAVY METAL THUNDER. With a carefully stitched HARLEY-DAVIDSON beneath.

'Get back in here, man,' the Beez says. 'He's awake again.'

Henry's on a path in the woods – or maybe it's a lane – and something is behind him. Each time he turns to see – in this dream he can see, but seeing is no blessing – there's a little more of that something back there. It appears to be a man in evening dress, but the man is frightfully elongated, with spike teeth that jut over a smiling red lower lip. And he seems – is it possible? – to have only one eye.

The first time Henry looks back, the shape is only a milky blur amid the trees. The next time he can make out the uneasy dark swim of its coat and a floating red blotch that might be a tie or an ascot. Up ahead of him is this thing's den, a stinking hole that only coincidentally looks like a house. Its presence buzzes in Henry's head. Instead of pine, the woods pressing in on either side smell of heavy, cloying perfume: My Sin.

It's driving me, he thinks with dismay. *Whatever that thing back there is, it's driving me like a steer toward the slaughterhouse.*

He thinks of cutting off the lane to his left or right, of using the miracle of his new sight to escape through the woods. Only there are things there, too. Dark, floating shapes like sooty scarves. He can almost see the closest. It's some sort of gigantic dog with a long tongue as red as the apparition's tie and bulging eyes.

Can't let it drive me to the house, he thinks. *I have to get out of this before it can get me there . . . but how? How?*

It comes to him with startling simplicity. All he has to do is wake up. Because this is a dream. This is just a—

'*It's a dream!*' Henry cries out, and jerks forward. He's not walking, he's *sitting*, sitting in his very own easy chair, and pretty soon he's going to have a very wet crotch because he fell asleep with a can of Kingsland Lager balanced there, and—

But there's no spill, because there's no can of beer. He feels cautiously to his right and yep, there it is, on the table with his book, a braille edition of *Reflections in a Golden Eye*. He must have put it there before first falling asleep and then falling into that horrible nightmare.

Except Henry's pretty sure he didn't do any such thing. He was holding the book and the beer was between his legs, freeing his hands to touch the little upraised dots that tell the story. Something very considerately took both the book and the can after he dropped off, and put them on the table. Something that smells of My Sin perfume.

The air *reeks* of it.

Henry takes a long, slow breath with his nostrils flared and mouth tightly sealed shut.

'No,' he says, speaking very clearly. 'I can smell flowers . . . and rug shampoo . . . and fried onions from last night. Very faint but still there. The nose knows.'

All true enough. But the smell *had* been there. It's gone now because *she's* gone, but she will be back. And suddenly he wants her to come. If he's frightened, surely it's the unknown he's frightened of, right? Only that and nothing more. He doesn't want to be alone here, with nothing for company but the memory of that rancid dream.

And the tapes.

He has to listen to the tapes. He promised Jack.

Henry gets shakily to his feet and makes his way to the living-room control panel. This time he's greeted by the voice of Henry Shake, a mellow fellow if ever there was one.

'Hey there, all you hoppin' cats and boppin' kitties, at the tone it's seven-fourteen p.m., Bulova Watch Time. Outside the temp is a very cool seventy-five degrees, and here in the Make-Believe Ballroom it's a very nifty seventy degrees. So why not get off your money, grab your honey, and make a little magic?'

Seven-fourteen! When was the last time he fell asleep for almost three hours in the daytime? For that matter, when was the last time he had a dream in which he could see? The answer to that second question, so far as he can remember, is never.

Where was that lane?

What was the thing behind him?

What was the place ahead of him, for that matter?

'Doesn't matter,' Henry tells the empty room – if it *is* empty. 'It was a dream, that's all. The tapes, on the other hand . . .'

He doesn't want to listen to them, has never wanted to listen to anything any less in his life (with the possible exception of Chicago singing 'Does Anybody Really Know What Time It Is?'), but he has to. If it might save Ty Marshall's life, or the life of even one other child, he must.

Slowly, dreading every step, Henry Leyden makes his blind way to his studio, where two cassettes wait for him on the soundboard.

★

'In heaven there is no beer,' Mouse sings in a toneless, droning voice.

His cheeks are now covered with ugly red patches, and his nose seems to be sinking sideways into his face, like an atoll after an undersea earthquake.

'That's why we drink it here. And when . . . we're gone . . . from here . . . our friends will be drinking all the beer.'

It's been like this for hours now: philosophical nuggets, instructions for the beginning beer-making enthusiast, snatches of song. The light coming through the blankets over the windows has dimmed appreciably.

Mouse pauses, his eyes closed. Then he starts another ditty.

'Hundred bottles of beer on the wall, one *hun*dred *bot*tles of *beer* . . . if one of those bottles should happen to fall . . .'

'I have to go,' Jack says. He's hung in there as well as he can, convinced that Mouse is going to give him something, but he can wait no longer. Somewhere, Ty Marshall is waiting for *him*.

'Hold on,' Doc says. He rummages in his bag and comes out with a hypodermic needle. He raises it in the dimness and taps the glass barrel with a fingernail.

'What's that?'

Doc gives Jack and Beezer a brief, grim smile. 'Speed,' he says, and injects it into Mouse's arm.

For a moment there's nothing. Then, as Jack is opening his mouth again to tell them he has to go, Mouse's eyes snap wide. They are now entirely red – a bright and bleeding red. Yet when they turn in his direction, Jack knows that Mouse is seeing him. Maybe really seeing him for the first time since he got here.

Bear Girl flees the room, trailing a single diminishing phrase behind her: 'No more no more no more no more—'

'Fuck,' Mouse says in a rusty voice. 'Fuck, I'm fucked. Ain't I?'

Beezer touches the top of his friend's head briefly but tenderly. 'Yeah, man. I think you are. Can you help us out?'

'Bit me once. Just once, and now . . . now . . .' His hideous red gaze turns to Doc. 'Can barely see you. Fuckin' eyes are all weird.'

'You're going down,' Doc says. 'Ain't gonna lie to you, man.'

'Not yet I ain't,' Mouse says. 'Gimme something to write on. To draw a map on. Quick. Dunno what you shot me with, Doc, but the stuff from the dog's stronger. I ain't gonna be *compos* long. Quick!'

Beezer feels around at the foot of the couch and comes up with a trade-sized paperback. Given the heavy shit on the bookcases, Jack could almost laugh – the book is *The 7 Habits of Highly Effective People*. Beezer tears off the back cover and hands it to Mouse with the blank side up.

'Pencil,' Mouse croaks. 'Hurry up. I got it all, man. I got it . . . up here.' He touches his forehead. A patch of skin the size of a quarter sloughs off at his touch. Mouse wipes it on the blanket as if it were a booger.

Beezer pulls a gnawed stub of pencil from an inside pocket of his vest. Mouse takes it and makes a pathetic effort to smile. The black stuff oozing from the corners of his eyes has continued to build up, and now it lies on his cheeks like smears of decayed jelly. More of it is springing out of the pores on his forehead in minute black dots that remind Jack of Henry's braille books. When Mouse bites his lower lip in concentration, the tender flesh splits open at once. Blood begins dribbling into his beard. Jack supposes the rotted-meat smell is still there, but Beezer had been right: he's gotten used to it.

Mouse turns the book cover sideways, then draws a series of quick squiggles. 'Lookit,' he says to Jack. 'This the Mississippi, right?'

'Right,' Jack says. When he leans in, he starts getting the smell again. Up close it's not even a stench; it's a miasma trying to crawl down his throat. But Jack doesn't move away. He knows what an effort Mouse is making. The least he can do is play his part.

'Here's downtown – the Nelson, Lucky's, the Agincourt Theater, the Taproom . . . here's where Chase Street turns into Lyall Road, then Route 35 . . . here's Libertyville . . . the VFW . . . Goltz's . . . *ah, Christ—*'

Mouse begins to thrash on the couch. Sores on his face and upper body burst open and begin leaking. He screams with pain. The hand not holding the pencil goes to his face and paws at it ineffectually.

Something inside Jack speaks up, then – speaks in a shining, imperative voice he remembers from his time on the road all those years ago. He supposes it's the voice of the Talisman, or whatever remains of it in his mind and soul.

It doesn't want him to talk, it's trying to kill him before he can talk, it's in the black stuff, maybe it is *the black stuff, you've got to get rid of it—*

Some things can only be done without the mind's prudish interference; when the work is nasty, instinct is often best. So it is without thinking that Jack reaches out, grasps the black slime oozing from Mouse's eyes between his fingers, and pulls. At first the stuff only stretches, as if made of rubber. At the same time Jack can feel it squirming and writhing in his grip, perhaps trying to pinch or bite him. Then it lets go with a *twang* sound. Jack throws the convulsing black tissue onto the floor with a cry.

The stuff tries to slither beneath the couch – Jack sees this even as he wipes his hands on his shirt, frantic with revulsion. Doc slams his bag down on one piece. Beezer squashes the other with the heel of a motorcycle boot. It makes a squittering sound.

'What the fuck is that shit?' Doc asks. His voice, ordinarily husky, has gone up into a near-falsetto range. 'What the *fuck*—'

'Nothing from here,' Jack says, 'and never mind. Look at him! Look at Mouse!'

The red glare in Mouse's eyes has retreated; for the moment he looks almost normal. Certainly he's seeing *them*, and the pain seems gone. 'Thanks,' he breathes. 'I only wish you could get it all that way, but man, it's already coming back. Pay attention.'

'I'm listening,' Jack says.

'You better,' Mouse replies. 'You think you know. You think you can find the place again even if these two can't, and maybe you can, but maybe you don't know quite so much as you . . . ah, *fuck*.' From somewhere beneath the blanket there is a ghastly bursting sound as something gives way. Sweat runs down Mouse's face, mixing with the black poison venting from his pores and turning his beard a damp and dirty gray. His eyes roll up to Jack's, and Jack can see that red glare starting to haze over them again.

'This sucks,' Mouse pants. 'Never thought I'd go out this way. Lookit, Hollywood . . .' The dying man draws a small rectangle on his makeshift scribble of map. 'This—'

'Ed's Eats, where we found Irma,' Jack says. 'I know.'

'All right,' Mouse whispers. 'Good. Now look . . . over on the other side . . . the Schubert and Gale side . . . and to the west . . .'

Mouse draws a line going north from Highway 35. He

puts little circles on either side of it. Jack takes these to be representations of trees. And, across the front of the line like a gate: NO TRESPASSING.

'Yeah,' Doc breathes. 'That's where it was, all right. Black House.'

Mouse takes no notice. His dimming gaze is fixed solely on Jack. 'Listen to me, cop. Are you listening?'

'Yes.'

'Christ, you better be,' Mouse tells him.

As it always has, the work captures Henry, absorbs him, takes him away. Boredom and sorrow have never been able to stand against this old captivation with sound from the sighted world. Apparently fear can't stand against it, either. The hardest moment isn't listening to the tapes but mustering the courage to stick the first one in the big TEAC audio deck. In that moment of hesitation he's sure he can smell his wife's perfume even in the soundproofed and air-filtered environment of the studio. In that moment of hesitation he is positive he isn't alone, that someone (or some*thing*) is standing just outside the studio door, looking in at him through the glass upper half. And that is, in fact, the absolute truth. Blessed with sight as we are, we can see what Henry cannot. We want to tell him what's out there, to lock the studio door, for the love of God lock it *now*, but we can only watch.

Henry reaches for the PLAY button on the tape deck. Then his finger changes course and hits the intercom toggle instead.

'Hello? Is anyone out there?'

The figure standing in Henry's living room, looking in at him the way someone might look into an aquarium at a single exotic fish, makes no sound. The last of the sun's on the other side of the house and the living room is becoming quite dark, Henry being understandably forgetful when it comes to turning on the lights. Elmer Jesperson's amusing bee slippers (not that they amuse us much under these circumstances) are just about the brightest things out there.

'Hello? Anyone?'

The figure looking in through the glass half of the studio door is grinning. In one hand it is holding the hedge clippers from Henry's garage.

'Last chance,' Henry says, and when there's still no response, he becomes the Wisconsin Rat, shrieking into the intercom, trying to startle whatever's out there into revealing itself: *'Come on now, honey, come on now, you muthafukkah, talk to Ratty!'*

The figure peering in at Henry recoils – as a snake might recoil when its prey makes a feint – but it utters no sound. From between the grinning teeth comes a leathery old tongue, wagging and poking in derision. This creature has been into the perfume that Mrs Morton has never had the heart to remove from the vanity in the little powder room adjacent to the master bedroom, and now Henry's visitor reeks of My Sin.

Henry decides it's all just his imagination playing him up again – oy, such a mistake, Morris Rosen would have told him, had Morris been there – and hits PLAY with the tip of his finger.

He hears a throat-clearing sound, and then Arnold Hrabowski identifies himself. The Fisherman interrupts him before he can even finish: *Hello, asswipe.*

Henry rewinds, listens again: *Hello, asswipe.* Rewinds and listens yet again: *Hello, asswipe.* Yes, he has heard this voice before. He's sure of it. But where? The answer will come, answers of this sort always do – eventually – and getting there is half the fun. Henry listens, enrapt. His fingers dance back and forth over the tape deck's buttons like the fingers of a concert pianist over the keys of a Steinway. The feeling of being watched slips from him, although the figure outside the studio door – the thing wearing the bee slippers and holding the hedge clippers – never moves. Its smile has faded somewhat. A sulky expression is growing on its aged face. There is confusion in that look, and perhaps the first faint trace of fear. The old monster doesn't like it that the blind fish in the aquarium should have captured its voice. Of course it doesn't matter; maybe it's even part of the fun, but if it is, it's Mr Munshun's fun, not *its* fun. And their fun should be the same . . . shouldn't it?

You have an emergency. Not me. You.

'Not me, *you*,' Henry says. The mimicry is so good it's weird. 'A little bit of sauerkraut in your salad, *mein* friend, *ja?*'

Your worst nightmare . . . worst nightmare.

Abbalah.

I'm the Fisherman.

Henry listening, intent. He lets the tape run awhile, then listens to the same phrase four times over: *Kiss my scrote, you monkey . . . kiss my scrote, you monkey . . . you monkey . . . monkey . . .*

No, not *monkey*. The voice is actually saying *munggey. MUNG-ghee.*

'I don't know where you are now, but you grew up in Chicago,' Henry murmurs. 'South Side. And . . .'

Warmth on his face. Suddenly he remembers warmth on his face. Why is that, friends and neighbors? Why is that, O great wise ones?

You're no better'n a monkey on a stick.

Monkey on a stick.

Monkey—

'Monkey,' Henry says. He's rubbing his temples with the

tips of his fingers now. 'Monkey on a stick. MUNG-ghee on a stigg. Who said that?'

He plays the 911: *Kiss my scrote, you monkey.*

He plays his memory: *You're no better'n a monkey on a stick.*

Warmth on his face.

Heat? Light?

Both?

Henry pops out the 911 tape and sticks in the one Jack brought today.

Hello, Judy. Are you Judy today, or are you Sophie? The abbalah sends his best, and Gorg says 'Caw-caw-caw!' [Husky, phlegmy laughter.] *Ty says hello, too. Your little boy is very lonely* . . .

When Tyler Marshall's weeping, terrified voice booms through the speakers, Henry winces and fast-forwards.

Derr vill be morrr mur-derts.

The accent much thicker now, a burlesque, a joke, *Katzenjammer Kids Meet the Wolfman*, but somehow even more revealing because of that.

Der liddul chull-drun . . . havv-uz-ted like wheed. Like wheed. Havv-uz-ted like . . .

'Harvested like a monkey on a stick,' Henry says. 'MUNG-ghee. HAVV-us-ted. Who are you, you son of a bitch?'

Back to the 911 tape.

There are whips in hell and chains in Sheol. But it's almost *vips in hell*, almost *chenz in Shayol.*

Vips. Chenz. MUNG-ghee on a stick. A *stigg.*

'You're no better'n—' Henry begins, and then, all at once, another line comes to him.

'Lady Magowan's Nightmare.' That one's good.

A bad nightmare of what? Vips in hell? Chenz in Shayol? Mung-ghees on sticks?

'My God,' Henry says softly. 'Oh . . . my . . . God. The dance. *He was at the dance.*'

Now it all begins to fall into place. How stupid they have been! How criminally stupid! The boy's bike . . . it had been right there. *Right there*, for Christ's sake! They were all blind men, make them all umps.

'But he was so *old*,' Henry whispers. 'And senile! How were we supposed to guess such a man could be the Fisherman?'

Other questions follow this one. If the Fisherman is a resident at Maxton Elder Care, for instance, where in God's name could he have stashed Ty Marshall? And how is the bastard getting around French Landing? Does he have a car somewhere?

'Doesn't matter,' Henry murmurs. 'Not now, anyway. Who is he and *where* is he? Those are the things that matter.'

The warmth on his face – his mind's first effort to locate the Fisherman's voice in time and place – had been the spotlight, of course, Symphonic Stan's spotlight, the pink of ripening berries. And some woman, some nice old woman –

Mr Stan, yoo-hoo, Mr Stan?

– had asked him if he took requests. Only, before Stan could reply, a voice as flat and hard as two stones grinding together –

I was here first, old woman.

– had interrupted. Flat . . . and hard . . . and with that faint Germanic harshness that said South Side Chicago, probably second or even third generation. Not *vass* here first, not old *vumman*, but those telltale *v*'s had been lurking, hadn't they? Ah yes.

'Mung-ghee,' Henry says, looking straight ahead. Looking straight at Charles Burnside, had he only known it. 'Stigg. *Havv*-us-ted. *Hasta la vista* . . . baby.'

Was that what it came down to, in the end? A dotty old maniac who sounded a bit like Arnold Schwarzenegger?

Who was the woman? If he can remember her name, he can call Jack . . . or Dale, if Jack's still not answering his phone . . . and put an end to French Landing's bad dream.

Lady Magowan's Nightmare. That one's good.

'Nightmare,' Henry says, then adjusting his voice: '*Nahht-mare.*' Once again the mimicry is good. Certainly too good for the old codger standing outside the studio door. He is now scowling bitterly and gnashing the hedge clippers in front of the glass. How can the blindman in there sound so much like him? It's not right; it's *completely* improper. The old monster longs to cut the vocal cords right out of Henry Leyden's throat. Soon, he promises himself, he will do that.

And eat them.

Sitting in the swivel chair, drumming his fingers nervously on the gleaming oak in front of him, Henry recalls the brief encounter at the bandstand. Not long into the Strawberry Fest dance, this had been.

Tell me your name and what you'd like to hear.

I am Alice Weathers, and— 'Moonglow,' please. By Benny Goodman.

'Alice Weathers,' Henry says. 'That was her name, and if she doesn't know *your* name, my homicidal friend, then *I'm* a monkey on a stick.'

He starts to get up, and that is when someone – some*thing* – begins to knock, very softly, on the glass upper half of the door.

Bear Girl has drawn close, almost against her will, and now she, Jack, Doc, and the Beez are gathered around the sofa.

Mouse has sunk halfway into it. He looks like a person dying badly in quicksand.

Well, Jack thinks, *there's no quicksand, but he's dying badly, all right. Guess there's no question about that.*

'Listen up,' Mouse tells them. The black goo is forming at the corners of his eyes again. Worse, it's trickling from the corners of his mouth. The stench of decay is stronger than ever as Mouse's inner workings give up the struggle. Jack is frankly amazed that they've lasted as long as they have.

'You talk,' Beezer says. 'We'll listen.'

Mouse looks at Doc. 'When I finish, give me the fireworks. The Cadillac dope. Understand?'

'You want to get out ahead of whatever it is you've got.'

Mouse nods.

'I'm down with that,' Doc agrees. 'You'll go out with a smile on your face.'

'Doubt that, bro, but I'll give it a try.'

Mouse shifts his reddening gaze to Beezer. 'When it's done, wrap me up in one of the nylon tents that're in the garage. Stick me in the tub. I'm betting that by midnight, you'll be able to wash me down the drain like . . . like so much beer foam. I'd be careful, though. Don't . . . touch what's left.'

Bear Girl bursts into tears.

'Don't cry, darlin',' Mouse says. 'I'm gonna get out ahead. Doc promised. Beez?'

'Right here, buddy.'

'You have a little service for me. Okay? Read a poem . . . the one by Auden . . . the one that always used to frost your balls . . .'

'"Thou shalt not read the Bible for its prose,"' Beezer says. He's crying. 'You got it, Mousie.'

'Play some Dead . . . "Ripple," maybe . . . and make sure

you're full enough of Kingsland to christen me good and proper into the next life. Guess there won't . . . be any grave for you to piss on, but . . . do the best you can.'

Jack laughs at that. He can't help it. And this time it's his turn to catch the full force of Mouse's crimson eyes.

'Promise me you'll wait until tomorrow to go out there, cop.'

'Mouse, I'm not sure I can do that.'

'You *gotta*. Go out there tonight, you won't have to worry about the devil dog . . . the other things in the woods around that house . . . the other things . . .' The red eyes roll horribly. Black stuff trickles into Mouse's beard like tar. Then he somehow forces himself to go on. 'The other things in those woods will eat you like candy.'

'I think that's a chance I'll have to take,' Jack says, frowning. 'There's a little boy somewhere—'

'Safe,' Mouse whispers.

Jack raises his eyebrows, unsure if he's heard Mouse right. And even if he has, can he trust what he's heard? Mouse has some powerful, evil poison working in him. So far he's been able to withstand it, to communicate in spite of it, but—

'Safe for a little while,' Mouse says. 'Not from everything . . . there's things that might still get him, I suppose . . . but for the time being he's safe from Mr Munching. Is that his name? Munching?'

'Munshun, I think. How do you know it?'

Mouse favors Jack with a smile of surpassing eeriness. It is the smile of a dying sibyl. Once more he manages to touch his forehead, and Jack notes with horror that the man's fingers are now melting into one another and turning black from the nails down. 'Got it up here, man. Got it *alll* up here. Told you that. And listen: it's better the kid should get eaten by some giant bug or rock crab over there . . . where he is . . . than that you should die trying to rescue him. If you do that, the abbalah will wind up with the kid for sure. That's what your . . . your friend says.'

'What friend?' Doc asks suspiciously.

'Never mind,' Mouse says. '*Hollywood* knows. Don'tcha, Hollywood?'

Jack nods reluctantly. It's Speedy, of course. Or Parkus, if you prefer.

'Wait until tomorrow,' Mouse says. 'High noon, when the sun's strongest in both worlds. *Promise.*'

At first Jack can say nothing. He's torn, in something close to agony.

'It'd be almost full dark before you could get back out Highway 35 anyway,' Bear Girl says quietly.

'And there's bad shit in those woods, all right,' Doc says. 'Makes the stuff in that *Blair Witch Project* look fuckin' tame. I don't think you want to try it in the dark. Not unless you got a death wish, that is.'

'When you're done . . .' Mouse whispers. 'When you're done . . . if any of you are left . . . burn the place to the ground. That hole. That tomb. Burn it to the ground, do you hear me? *Close the door.*'

'Yeah,' Beezer says. 'Heard and understood, buddy.'

'Last thing,' Mouse says. He's speaking directly to Jack now. 'You may be able to find it . . . but I think I got something else you need. It's a word. It's powerful to you because of something you . . . you touched. Once a long time ago. I don't understand that part, but . . .'

'It's all right,' Jack tells him. 'I do. What's the word, Mouse?'

For a moment he doesn't think Mouse will, in the end, be able to tell him. Something is clearly struggling to keep him from saying the word, but in this struggle, Mouse comes out on top. It is, Jack thinks, very likely his life's last W.

'*D'yamba*,' Mouse says. 'Now you, Hollywood. You say it.'

'*D'yamba*,' Jack says, and a row of weighty paperbacks slides from one of the makeshift shelves at the foot of the couch. They hang there in the dimming air . . . hang . . . hang . . . and then drop to the floor with a crash.

Bear Girl voices a little scream.

'Don't forget it,' Mouse says. 'You're gonna need it.'

'How? *How* am I going to need it?'

Mouse shakes his head wearily. 'Don't . . . know.'

Beezer reaches over Jack's shoulder and takes the pitiful little scribble of map. 'You're going to meet us tomorrow morning at the Sand Bar,' he tells Jack. 'Get there by eleven-thirty, and we should be turning into that goddamned lane right around noon. In the meantime, maybe I'll just hold on to this. A little insurance policy to make sure you do things Mouse's way.'

'Okay,' Jack says. He doesn't need the map to find Chummy Burnside's Black House, but Mouse is almost certainly right: it's probably not the sort of place you want to tackle after dark. He hates to leave Ty Marshall in the furnace-lands – it feels wrong in a way that's almost sinful – but he has to remember that there's more at stake here than one little boy lost.

'Beezer, are you sure you want to go back there?'

'Hell no, I don't want to go back,' Beezer says, almost indignantly. 'But something killed my daughter – my *daughter!* – and it got *here* from *there!* You want to tell me you don't know that's true?'

Jack makes no reply. Of course it's true. And of course he wants Doc and the Beez with him when he turns up the lane to Black House. If they can bear to come, that is.

D'yamba, he thinks. *D'yamba. Don't forget.*

He turns back to the couch. 'Mouse, do you—'

'No,' Doc says. 'Guess he won't need the Cadillac dope, after all.'

'Huh?' Jack peers at the big brewer-biker stupidly. He *feels* stupid. Stupid and exhausted.

'Nothin' tickin' but his watch,' Doc says, and then he begins to sing. After a moment Beezer joins in, then Bear Girl. Jack steps away from the couch with a thought queerly similar to Henry's: How did it get late so early? Just how in hell did that happen?

'In heaven, there is no beer . . . that's why we drink it here . . . and when . . . we're gone . . . from here . . .'

Jack tiptoes across the room. On the far side, there's a lighted Kingsland Premium Golden Pale Ale bar clock. Our old friend – who is finally looking every year of his age and not quite so lucky – peers at the time with disbelief, not accepting it until he has compared it to his own watch. Almost eight. He has been here for *hours*.

Almost dark, and the Fisherman still out there someplace. Not to mention his otherworldly playmates.

D'yamba, he thinks again as he opens the door. And, as he steps out onto the splintery porch and closes the door behind him, he speaks aloud with great sincerity into the darkening day: 'Speedy, I'd like to wring your neck.'

24

D'yamba is a bright and powerful spell; powerful connections form a web that extends, ramifying, throughout infinity. When Jack Sawyer peels the living poison from Mouse's eyes, *d'yamba* first shines within the dying man's mind, and that mind momentarily expands into knowledge; down the filaments of the web flows some measure of its shining strength, and soon a touch of *d'yamba* reaches Henry Leyden. Along the way, the *d'yamba* brushes Tansy Freneau, who, seated in a windowed alcove of the Sand Bar, observes a wry, beautiful young woman take smiling shape in the pool of light at the far end of the parking lot and realizes, a moment before the young woman vanishes, that she has been given a glimpse of the person her Irma would have become; and it touches Dale Gilbertson, who while driving home from the station experiences a profound, sudden yearning for the presence of Jack Sawyer, a yearning like an ache in his heart, and vows to pursue the Fisherman case to the end with him, no matter what the obstacles; the *d'yamba* quivers flashing down a filament to Judy Marshall and opens a window into Faraway, where Ty sleeps in an iron-colored cell, awaiting rescue *and still alive*; within Charles Burnside, it touches the true

Fisherman, Mr Munshun, once known as the Monday Man, just as Burny's knuckles rap the glass. Mr Munshun feels a subtle drift of cold air infiltrate his chest like a warning, and freezes with rage and hatred at this violation; Charles Burnside, who knows nothing of *d'yamba* and cannot hate it, picks up his master's emotion and remembers the time when a boy supposed dead in Chicago crept out of a canvas sack and soaked the back seat of his car in incriminating blood. *Damnably* incriminating blood, a substance that continued to mock him long after he had washed away its visible traces. But Henry Leyden, with whom we began this chain, is visited not by grace or rage; what touches Henry is a kind of informed clarity.

Rhoda's visits, he realizes, were one and all produced by his loneliness. The only thing he heard climbing the steps was his unending need for his wife. And the being on the other side of his studio door is the horrible old man from Maxton's, who intends to do to Henry the same thing he has done to three children. Who else would appear at this hour and knock on the studio window? Not Dale, not Jack, and certainly not Elvena Morton. Everyone else would stay outside and ring the doorbell.

It takes Henry no more than a couple of seconds to consider his options and work out a rudimentary plan. He supposes himself both quicker and stronger than the Fisherman, who sounded like a man in his mid- to late eighties; and the Fisherman does not know that his would-be victim is aware of his identity. To take advantage of this situation, Henry has to appear puzzled but amiable, as if he is merely curious about his visitor. And once he opens the studio door, which unfortunately he has left unlocked, he will have to act with speed and decisiveness.

Are we up to this? Henry asks himself, and thinks, *We'd better be.*

Are the lights on? No; because he expected to be alone, he never bothered with the charade of switching them on. The question then becomes: How dark is it outside? Maybe not quite dark enough, Henry imagines – an hour later, he would be able to move through the house entirely unseen and escape through the back door. Now his odds are probably no better than fifty-fifty, but the sun is sinking at the back of his house, and every second he can delay buys him another fraction of darkness in the living room and kitchen.

Perhaps two seconds have passed since the lurking figure rapped on the window, and Henry, who has maintained the perfect composure of one who failed to hear the sound made by his visitor, can stall no longer. Pretending to be lost in thought, with one hand he grips the base of a heavy Excellence in Broadcasting award accepted in absentia by George Rathbun some years before and with the other scoops from a shallow tray before him a switchblade an admirer once left at the university radio station as a tribute to the Wisconsin Rat. Henry uses the knife to unwrap CD jewel boxes, and not long ago, in search of something to do with his hands, he taught himself how to sharpen it. With its blade retracted, the knife resembles an odd, flat fountain pen. Two weapons are twice as good as one, he thinks, especially if your adversary imagines the second weapon to be harmless.

Now it has been four seconds since the rapping came from the window by his side, and in their individual ways both Burny and Mr Munshun have grown considerably more restive. Mr Munshun recoils in loathing from the suggestion of *d'yamba* that has somehow contaminated this otherwise delightful scene. Its appearance can mean one thing only, that some person connected to the blind man managed to get close enough to Black House to have tasted the poisons of its ferocious guardian. And that in turn means that now the hateful Jack Sawyer undoubtedly knows of the existence of Black House and intends to breach its defenses. It is time to destroy the blind man and return home.

Burny registers only an inchoate mixture of hatred and an emotion surprisingly like fear from within his master. Burny feels rage at Henry Leyden's appropriation of his voice, for he knows it represents a threat; even more than this self-protective impulse, he feels a yearning for the simple but profound pleasure of bloodletting. When Henry has been butchered, Charles Burnside wishes to claim one more victim before flying to Black House and entering a realm he thinks of as Sheol.

His big, misshapen knuckles rap once more against the glass.

Henry turns his head to the window in a flawless imitation of mild surprise. 'I *thought* someone was out there. Who is it? . . . Come on, speak up.' He toggles a switch and speaks into the mike: 'If you're saying anything, I can't hear you. Give me a second or two to get organized in here, and I'll be right out.' He faces forward again and hunches over his desk. His left hand seems idly to touch his handsome award; his right hand is hidden from sight. Henry appears to be deep in concentration. In reality, he is listening as hard as he ever has in his life.

He hears the handle on the studio door revolve clockwise with a marvelous slowness. The door whispers open an inch, two inches, three. The floral, musky scent of My Sin invades the studio, seeming to coat a thin chemical film over the mike, the tape canisters, all the dials, and the back of Henry's deliberately exposed neck. The sole of what sounds like a carpet slipper hushes over the floor. Henry tightens his hands on his weapons and waits for the particular sound that will be his signal. He hears another nearly soundless step, then another, and knows the Fisherman has moved behind him. He carries some weapon of his own, something that cuts through the mist of perfume with the grassy smell of front yards and the smoothness of machine oil. Henry cannot imagine what this is, but the movement of the air tells him it is heavier than a knife. Even a blind man can see that. An awkwardness in the way the Fisherman takes his next oh-so-quiet step suggests to Henry that the old fellow holds this weapon with both of his hands.

An image has formed in Henry's mind, that of his adversary standing behind him poised to strike, and to this image he now adds extended, upraised arms. The hands hold an instrument like garden shears. Henry has his own weapons, the best of these being surprise, but the surprise must be well timed to be effective. In fact, if Henry is to avoid a quick and messy death, his timing has to be perfect. He lowers his neck farther over the desk and awaits the signal. His calm surprises him.

A man standing unobserved with an object like garden shears or a heavy pair of scissors in his hands behind a seated victim will, before delivering the blow, take a long second to arch his back and reach up, to get a maximum of strength into the downward stroke. As he extends his arms and arches his back, his clothing will shift on his body. Fabric will slide over flesh; one fabric may pull against another; a belt may creak. There will be an intake of breath. An ordinary person would hear few or none of these telltale disturbances, but Henry Leyden can be depended upon to hear them all.

Then at last he does. Cloth rubs against skin and rustles against itself; air hisses into Burny's nasal passages. Instantly, Henry shoves his chair backward and in the same movement spins around and swings the award toward his assailant as he stands upright. It works! He feels the force of the blow run down his arm and hears a grunt of shock and pain. The odor of My Sin fills his nostrils. The chair bumps the top of his knees. Henry pushes the button on the switchblade, feels the long blade leap out, and thrusts it forward. The knife punches into flesh. From eight inches before his face comes a scream of outrage. Again, Henry batters the award against his attacker, then yanks the knife free and shoves it home again. Skinny arms tangle around his neck and shoulders, filling him with revulsion, and foul breath washes into his face.

He becomes aware that he has been injured, for a pain that is sharp on the surface and dull beneath announces itself on the left side of his back. *The goddamn hedge clippers,* he thinks and jabs again with the knife. This time, he stabs only empty air. A rough hand closes on his elbow, and another grips his shoulder. The hands pull him forward, and to keep upright he rests his knee on the seat of the chair. A long nose bangs against the bridge of his own nose and jars his sunglasses. What follows fills him with disgust: two rows of teeth like broken clamshells fasten on his left cheek and saw through the skin. Blood sluices down his face. The rows of teeth come together and rip away an oval wedge of Henry's skin, and over the white jolt of pain, which is incredible, worse by far than the pain in his back, he can hear his blood spatter against the old monster's face. Fear and revulsion, along with an amazing amount of adrenaline, give him the strength to lash out with the knife as he spins away from the man's grip. The blade connects with some moving part of the Fisherman's body – an arm, he thinks.

Before he can feel anything like satisfaction, he hears the sound of the hedge clippers slicing the air before they bite into his knife hand. It happens almost before he can take it in: the hedge clippers' blades tear through his skin, snap the bones, and sever the last two fingers on his right hand.

And then, as if the hedge clippers were the Fisherman's last contact with him, he is free. Henry's foot finds the edge of the door, kicks it aside, and he propels his body through the open space. He lands on a floor so sticky his feet slide when he tries to get up. Can all of that blood be his?

The voice he had been studying in another age, another era, comes from the studio door. 'You stabbed me, you asswipe moke.'

Henry is not waiting around to listen; Henry is on the move, wishing he did not feel that he was leaving a clear, wide trail of blood behind him. Somehow, he seems to be drenched in the stuff, his shirt is sodden with it, and the backs of his legs are wet. Blood continues to gush down his face, and in spite of the adrenaline, Henry can feel his energy dissipating. How much time does he have before he bleeds to death – twenty minutes?

He slides down the hallway and runs into the living room.

I'm not going to get out of this, Henry thinks. *I've lost too much blood. But at least I can make it through the door and die outside, where the air is fresh.*

From the hallway, the Fisherman's voice reaches him. 'I ate part of your cheek, and now I'm going to eat your fingers. Are you listening to me, you moke of an asshole?'

Henry makes it to the door. His hand slips and slips on the knob; the knob resists him. He feels for the lock button, which has been depressed.

'I said, are you *listening*?' The Fisherman is coming closer, and his voice is full of rage.

All Henry has to do is push the button that unlocks the door and turn the knob. He could be out of the house in a second, but his remaining fingers will not obey orders. *All right, I'm going to die*, he says to himself. *I'll follow Rhoda, I'll follow my Lark, my beautiful Lark.*

A sound of chewing, complete with smacking lips and crunching noises. 'You taste like shit. I'm eating your fingers, and they taste like shit. You know what I like? Know my all-time favorite meal? The buttocks of a tender young child. Albert Fish liked that too, oh yes he did. *Mmmmmm!* BABY BUTT! That's GOOD EATIN'!'

Henry realizes that he has somehow slipped all the way down the unopenable door and is now resting, breathing far too heavily, on his hands and knees. He shoves himself forward and crawls behind the Mission-style sofa, from the comfort of which he had listened to Jack Sawyer reading a great many eloquent words written by Charles Dickens. Among the things he would now never be able to do, he realizes, is find out what finally happens in *Bleak House*. Another is seeing his friend Jack again.

The Fisherman's footsteps enter the living room and stop moving. 'All right, where the fuck are you, asshole? You can't hide from me.' The hedge clippers' blades go *snick-snick*.

Either the Fisherman has grown as blind as Henry, or the room is too dark for vision. A little bit of hope, a match flame, flares in Henry's soul. Maybe his adversary will not be able to see the light switches.

'Asshole!' *Ahzz-hill*. 'Damn it, where are you hiding?' *Dahmmut, vhey ah you high-dung?*

This is fascinating, Henry thinks. The more angry and frustrated the Fisherman gets, the more his accent melts into that weird non-German. It isn't the South Side of Chicago anymore, but neither is it anything else. It certainly isn't German, not really. If Henry had heard Dr Spiegleman's description of this accent as that of a Frenchman trying to speak English like a German, he would have nodded in smiling agreement. It's like some kind of *outer space* German accent, like something that mutated toward German without ever having heard it.

'You hurt me, you stinking pig!' *You huhht me, you steenk-ung peek!*

The Fisherman lurches toward the easy chair and shoves it over on its side. In his Chicago voice, he says, 'I'm gonna find you, buddy, and when I do, I'll cut your fucking head off.'

A lamp hits the floor. The slippered footsteps move heavily toward the right side of the room. 'A blind guy hides in the dark, huh? Oh, that's cute, that's really cute. Lemme tell you something. I haven't tasted a tongue in a while, but I think I'll try yours.' A small table and the lamp atop it clunk and crash to the floor. 'I got some information for you. Tongues are funny. An old guy's doesn't taste much different from a young fella's – though of course the tongue on a kid is twice as good as both. *Venn I vas Fridz Hahhmun I ade munny dungs, ha ha.*'

Strange – that extraterrestrial version of a German accent bursts out of the Fisherman like a second voice. A fist strikes the wall, and the footsteps plod nearer. Using his elbows, Henry crawls around the far end of the sofa and squirms toward the shelter of a long, low table. The footsteps squish in blood, and when Henry rests his head on his hands, warm blood pumps out against his face. The fiery agony in his fingers almost swallows the pain in his cheek and his back.

'You can't hide forever,' the Fisherman says. Immediately, he switches to the weird accent and replies, *'Eenuff ov dis, Burn-Burn. Vee huv murr impurdund vurk zu do.'*

'Hey, you're the one who called him an *abzz-hill*. He *hurt* me!'

'Fogzes down fogzhulls, oho, radz in radhulls, dey too ahh huhht. My boor loss babbies ahh huhht, aha, vurze vurze vurze dan uz.'

'But what about him?'

'Hee iz bledding zu deff, bledding zu deff, aha. Led hum dy.'

In the darkness, we can just make out what is happening. Charles Burnside appears to be performing an eerie imitation of the two heads of Parkus's parrot, Sacred and Profane. When he speaks in his own voice, he turns his head to the left; when speaking with the accent of an extraterrestrial, he looks to his right. Watching his head swivel back and forth, we might be watching a comic actor like Jim Carrey or Steve Martin pretending to be the two halves of a split personality – except that this man is not funny. Both of his personalities are awful, and their voices hurt our ears. The greatest difference between them is that right-head, the guttural extraterrestrial, runs the show: his hands hold the wheel of the other's vehicle, and left-head – our Burny – is essentially a slave. Since the difference between them has become so clear, we begin to get the impression that it will not be long before Mr Munshun peels off Charles Burnside and discards him like a worn-out sock.

'But I WANT to kill him!' Burny screeches.

'Hee iz alreddy dud, dud, dud. Chack Zawyuh's hardt iz go-ung do break. Chack Zawyuh vill nod know whud he iz do-ung. Vee go now du Muxtun'z and oho vee kull Chibbuh, yuzz? You vahhnd kull Chibbuh I ding, yuzz?'

Burny snickers. 'Yeah. I *vahhnd* to kill Chipper. I *vahhnd* to slice that asshole into little pieces and chew on his bones. And if his snippy bitch is there, I want to cut off her head and suck her juicy little tongue down my throat.'

To Henry Leyden, this conversation sounds like insanity, demonic possession, or both. Blood continues to stream out of his back and from the ends of his mutilated fingers, and he is powerless to stop the flow. The smell of all the blood beneath and around him makes him feel nauseated, but nausea is the least of his problems. A light-headed sense of drift, of pleasing numbness – that is his real problem, and his best weapon against it is his own pain. He must remain conscious. Somehow, he must leave a message for Jack.

'Zo vee go now, Burn-Burn, and vee hahhv ah bleshah vid

Chibbuh, yuzz? End denn . . . oho end denn, denn, denn vee go do de beeyoodiful beeyoodiful Blagg Huzz, my Burn-Burn, end in Blagg Huzz vee mayyg reddy for de Grimsunn Ging!'

'I *want* to meet the Crimson King,' Burny says. A rope of drool sags from his mouth, and for an instant his eyes gleam in the darkness. 'I'm gonna give the Marshall brat *to* the Crimson King, and the Crimson King is gonna love me, because all I'm gonna eat is like one little ass cheek, one little hand, something like that.'

'Hee vill lahhv you fuhr my zake, Burn-Burn, fuhr de Ging lahhvs mee bezzd, mee, mee, mee, Mizz-durr Munnshunn! End venn de Ging roolz sooprumm, fogzes down fogzhulls veep and veep, dey gryy, gryy, gryy dere liddul hardz utt, on-cuzz you end mee, mee, mee, vee vull eed end eed end eed, eed, eed undill de vurrldz on all zydes are nudding bahd embdy bee-nudd shillz!'

'Empty peanut shells.' Burny chuckles, and noisily retracts another rope of slobber. 'That's a hell of a lot of eatin'.'

Any second now, Henry thinks, horrible old Burn-Burn is going to fork over a substantial down payment on the Brooklyn Bridge.

'Gumm.'

'I'm coming,' says Burnside. 'First I want to leave a message.'

There is a silence.

The next thing Henry hears is a curious whooshing sound and the joined *smack-smacks* of sodden footwear parting from a sticky floor. The door to the closet beneath the stairs bangs open; the studio door bangs shut. A smell of ozone comes and goes. They have gone; Henry does not know how it happened, but he feels certain that he is alone. Who cares how it happened? Henry has more important matters to think about. '*Murr impurdund vurk,*' he says aloud. 'That guy's a German like I'm a speckled hen.'

He crawls out from beneath the long table and uses its surface to lever himself up on his feet. When he straightens his back, his mind wobbles and goes gray, and he grasps a lampstand to stay upright. 'Don't pass out,' he says. 'Passing out is not allowed, nope.'

Henry can walk, he is sure of it. He's been walking most of his life, after all. Come to that, he can drive a car, too; driving is even easier than walking, only no one ever had the *cojones* to let him demonstrate his talents behind the wheel. Hell, if Ray Charles could drive – and he *could*, he *can*, Ray Charles is probably spinning into a left turn off the highway *at this moment* – why not Henry Leyden? Well, Henry does not happen to have an automobile available to him right now, so Henry is going to have to settle for taking a brisk walk. Well, as brisk as possible anyhow.

And where is Henry going on this delightful stroll through the blood-soaked living room? 'Why,' he answers himself, 'the answer is obvious. I am going to my studio. I feel like taking a stroll into my lovely little studio.'

His mind slides into gray once more, and gray is to be avoided. We have an antidote for the gray feeling, don't we? Yes, we do: the antidote is a good sharp taste of pain. Henry slaps his good hand against the stumps of his severed fingers – whoo boy, yes indeed, whole arm sort of went up in flames there. Flaming arm, that will work. Sparks shooting white hot from burning fingers *will* get us to the studio.

Let those tears flow. Dead folks don't cry.

'The smell of blood is like laughter,' Henry says. 'Who said that? Somebody. It's in a book. "The smell of blood was like laughter." Great line. Now put one foot in front of the other.'

When he reaches the short hallway to the studio, he leans against the wall for a moment. A wave of luxurious weariness begins at the center of his chest and laps through his body. He snaps his head up, blood from his torn cheek spattering the wall. 'Keep talking, you dope. Talking to yourself isn't crazy. It's a wonderful thing to do. And guess what? It's how you make your living – you talk to yourself all day long!'

Henry pushes himself off the wall, steps forward, and George Rathbun speaks through his vocal cords. 'Friends, and you ARE my friends, let me be clear about that, we here at KDCU-AM seem to be experiencing some technical difficulties. The power levels are sinking, and brownouts have been recorded, yes they have. Fear not, my dear ones. Fear *not!* Even as I speak, we are but four paltry feet from the studio door, and in no time at all, we shall be up and running, yessir. No ancient cannibal and his space-alien sidekick can put this station out of business, uh-UHH, not before we make our last and final broadcast.'

It is as if George Rathbun gives life to Henry Leyden, instead of the other way around. His back is straighter, and he holds his head upright. Two steps bring him to the closed studio door. 'It's a tough catch, my friends, and if Pokey Reese is going to snag that ball, his mitt had better be clean as a whistle. What is he doing out there, folks? Can we believe our eyes? Can he be shoving one hand into his pants pocket? Is he pulling something out? Man oh man, it causes the mind to reel. . . . Pokey is using THE OLD HANDKERCHIEF PLOY! That's right! He is WIPING his mitt, WIPING his throwing hand, DROPPING the snotrag, GRABBING the handle . . . And the door is OPEN! Pokey Reese has done it again, he is IN THE STUDIO!'

Henry winds the handkerchief around the ends of his fingers and fumbles for the chair. 'And Rafael Furcal seems lost out there, the man is GROPING for the ball . . . Wait, wait, does he have it? Has he caught an edge? YES! He has the ARM of the ball, he has the BACK of the ball, and he pulls it UP, ladies and gents, the ball is UP on its WHEELS! Furcal sits down, he pushes himself toward the console. We're facing a lot of blood here, but baseball is a bloody game when they come at you with their CLEATS up.'

With the fingers of his left hand, from which most of the blood has been cleaned, Henry punches the ON switch for the big tape recorder and pulls the microphone close. He is sitting in the dark listening to the sound of tape hissing from reel to reel, and he feels oddly satisfied to be here, doing what he has done night after night for thousands of nights. Velvety exhaustion swims through his body and his mind, darkening whatever it touches. It is too early to yield. He will surrender soon, but first he must do his job. He must talk to Jack Sawyer by talking to himself, and to do that he calls upon the familiar spirits that give him voice.

George Rathbun: 'Bottom of the ninth, and the home team is headed for the showers, pal. But the game ain't OVER till the last BLIND man is DEAD!'

Henry Shake: 'I'm talking to *you*, Jack Sawyer, and I don't want you to flip out on me or nothin'. Keep cool and listen to your old friend Henry the Sheik the Shake the Shook, all right? The Fisherman paid me a visit, and when he left here he was on his way to Maxton's. He wants to kill Chipper, the guy who owns the place. Call the police, save him if you can. The Fisherman lives at Maxton's, did you know that? He's an old man with a demon inside him. He wanted to stop me from telling you that I recognized his voice. And he wanted to mess with your feelings – he thinks he can screw you up by killing me. Don't give him that satisfaction, all right?'

The Wisconsin Rat: '*BECAUSE THAT WOULD REALLY SUCK! FISH-BRAINS WILL BE WAITING FOR*

YOU IN A PLACE CALLED BLACK HOUSE, AND YOU HAVE TO BE READY FOR THE BASTARD! RIP HIS NUTS OFF!'

The Rat's buzz-saw voice ends in a fit of coughing.

Henry Shake, breathing hard: 'Our friend the Rat was suddenly called away. The boy has a tendency to get overexcited.'

George Rathbun: 'SON, are you trying to tell ME that—'

Henry Shake: 'Calm down. Yes, he has a right to be excited. But Jack doesn't want us to scream at him. Jack wants information.'

George Rathbun: 'I reckon you better hurry up and give it to him, then.'

Henry Shake: 'This is the deal, Jack. The Fisherman's not very bright, and neither is his whatever, his demon, who's called something like Mr Munching. He's incredibly vain, too.'

Henry Leyden folds back into the chair and stares at nothing for a second or two. He can feel nothing from the waist down, and blood from his right hand has pooled around the microphone. From the stumps of his fingers comes a steady, diminishing pulse.

George Rathbun: 'Not *now*, Chuckles!'

Henry Leyden shakes his head and says, 'Vain and stupid you can beat, my friend. I have to sign off now. Jack, you don't have to feel too bad about me. I had a goddamn wonderful life, and I'm going to be with my darling Rhoda now.' He smiles in the darkness; his smile widens. 'Ah, Lark. Hello.'

At times, it is possible for the smell of blood to be like laughter.

What is this, at the end of Nailhouse Row? A horde, a swarm of fat, buzzing things that circle and dart about Jack Sawyer, in the dying light seeming almost *illuminated*, like the radiant pages of a sacred text. Too small to be hummingbirds, they seem to carry their own individual, internal glow as they mesh through the air. If they are wasps, Jack Sawyer is going to be in serious trouble. Yet they do not sting; their round bodies brush his face and hands, blundering softly against his body as a cat will nudge its owner's leg, both giving and receiving comfort.

At present, they give much more comfort than they receive, and even Jack cannot explain why this should be so. The creatures surrounding him are not wasps, hummingbirds, or cats, but they *are* bees, honeybees, and ordinarily he would be frightened to be caught in a swarm of bees. Especially if they appeared to be members of a sort of master bee race, superbees, larger than any he has seen before, their golds more golden, their blacks vibrantly black. Yet Jack is not frightened. If they were going to sting him, they would already have done it. And from the first, he understood that they meant him no harm. The touch of their many bodies is surpassingly smooth and soft; their massed buzzing is low and harmonious, as peaceable as a Protestant hymn. After the first few seconds, Jack simply lets it happen.

The bees sift even closer, and their low noise pulses in his ears. It sounds like speech, or like song. For a moment, all he can see is a tightly woven network of bees moving this way and that; then the bees settle everywhere on his body but the oval of his face. They cover his head like a helmet. They blanket his arms, his chest, his back, his legs. Bees land on his shoes and obscure them from view. Despite their number, they are almost weightless. The exposed parts of Jack's body, his hands and neck, feel as though wrapped in cashmere. A dense, feather-light bee suit shimmers black and gold all over Jack Sawyer. He raises his arms, and the bees move with him.

Jack has seen photographs of beekeepers aswarm with bees, but this is no photograph and he is no beekeeper. His amazement – really, his sheer pleasure in the unexpectedness of this visitation – stuns him. For as long as the bees cling to him, he forgets Mouse's terrible death and the next day's fearsome task. What he does not forget is Sophie; he wishes Beezer and Doc would walk outside, so they could see what is happening, but more than that, he wishes Sophie could see it. Perhaps, by grace of *d'yamba*, she does. Someone is comforting Jack Sawyer, someone is wishing him well. A loving, invisible presence offers him support. It feels like a blessing, that support. Clothed in his glowing black-and-yellow bee suit, Jack has the idea that if he stepped toward the sky, he would be airborne. The bees would carry him over the valleys. They would carry him over the wrinkled hills. Like the winged men in the Territories who carried Sophie, he would fly. Instead of their two, he would have two thousand wings to bear him up.

In our world, Jack remembers, bees return to the hive before nightfall. As if reminded of their daily routine, the bees lift from Jack's head, his trunk, his arms and legs, not en masse, like a living carpet, but individually and in parties of five and six, wander a short distance above him, then swirl around, shoot like bullets eastward over the houses on the inland side of Nailhouse Row, and disappear one and all into the same dark infinity. Jack becomes aware of their sound only when it disappears with them.

In the seconds before he can once again begin moving toward his truck, he has the feeling that someone is watching over him. He has been . . . what? It comes to him as he turns his key in the Ram's ignition and flutters the gas pedal: he has been embraced.

Jack has no idea how much he will need the warmth of that embrace, nor of the manner in which it shall be returned to him, during the coming night.

★

First of all, he is exhausted. He has had the kind of day that *should* end in a surreal event like an embrace by a swarm of bees: Sophie, Wendell Green, Judy Marshall, Parkus – that cataclysm, that deluge! – and the strange death of Mouse Baumann, these things have stretched him taut, left him gasping. His body aches for rest. When he leaves French Landing and drives into the wide, dark countryside, he is tempted to pull over to the side of the road and catch a half-hour nap. The deepening night promises the refreshment of sleep, and that is the problem: he could wind up sleeping in the truck all night, which would leave him feeling bleary and arthritic on a day when he must be at his best.

Right now, he is not at his best – not by a longshot, as his father, Phil Sawyer, used to say. Right now he is running on fumes, another of Phil Sawyer's pet expressions, but he figures that he can stay awake long enough to visit Henry Leyden. Maybe Henry cut a deal with the guy from ESPN – maybe Henry will move into a wider market and make a lot more money. Henry in no way needs any more money than he has, for Henry's life seems flawless, but Jack likes the idea of his dear friend Henry suddenly flush with cash. A Henry with extra money to throw around is a Henry Jack would love to see. Imagine the wondrous clothes he could afford! Jack pictures going to New York with him, staying in a nice hotel like the Carlyle or the St Regis, walking him through half a dozen great men's stores, helping him pick out whatever he wants.

Just about everything looks good on Henry. He seems to improve all the clothes he wears, no matter what they are, but he has definite, particular tastes. Henry likes a certain classic, even old-fashioned, stylishness. He often dresses himself in pinstripes, windowpane plaids, herring-bone tweeds. He likes cotton, linen, and wool. He sometimes wears bow ties, ascots, and little handkerchiefs that puff out of his breast pocket. On his feet, he puts penny loafers, wing tips, cap toes, and low boots of soft, fine leather. He never wears sneakers or jeans, and Jack has never seen him in a T-shirt that has writing on it. The question was, how did a man blind from birth evolve such a specific taste in clothing?

Oh, Jack realizes, *it was his mother. Of course. He got his taste from his mother.*

For some reason, this recognition threatens to bring tears to Jack's eyes. *I get too emotional when I get this tired,* he says to himself. *Watch out, or you'll go overboard.* But diagnosing a problem is not the same as fixing it, and he cannot follow his own advice. That Henry Leyden all of his life should have held to his mother's ideas about men's clothing strikes Jack as beautiful and moving. It implies a kind of loyalty he admires – unspoken loyalty. Henry probably got a lot from his mother: his quick-wittedness, his love of music, his levelheadedness, his utter lack of self-pity. Levelheadedness and lack of self-pity are a great combination, Jack thinks; they go a long way toward defining courage.

For Henry *is* courageous, Jack reminds himself. Henry is damn near fearless. It's funny, how he talks about being able to drive a car, but Jack feels certain that, if allowed, his friend would unhesitatingly jump behind the wheel of the nearest Chrysler, start the engine, and take off for the highway. He would not exult or show off, such behavior being foreign to his nature; Henry would nod toward the windshield and say things like, 'Looks like the corn is nice and tall for this time of year,' and 'I'm glad Duane finally got around to painting his house.' And the corn would be tall, and Duane Updahl would have recently painted his house, information delivered to Henry by his mysterious sensory systems.

Jack decides that if he makes it out of Black House alive,

he will give Henry the opportunity to take the Ram out for a spin. They might wind up nose-down in a ditch, but it will be worth it for the expression on Henry's face. Some Saturday afternoon, he'll get Henry out on Highway 93 and let him drive to the Sand Bar. If Beezer and Doc do not get savaged by weredogs and survive their journey to Black House, they ought to have the chance to enjoy Henry's conversation, which, odd as it seems, is perfectly suited to theirs. Beezer and Doc *should* know Henry Leyden, they'd love the guy. After a couple of weeks, they'd have him up on a Harley, swooping toward Norway Valley from Centralia.

If only *Henry* could come with them to Black House. The thought pierces Jack with the sadness of an inspired idea that can never be put into practice. Henry would be brave and unfaltering, Jack knows, but what he most likes about the idea is that he and Henry would ever after be able to talk about what they had done. Those talks – the two of them, in one living room or another, snow piling on the roof – would be wonderful, but Jack cannot endanger Henry that way.

'That's a stupid thing to think about,' Jack says aloud, and realizes that he regrets not having been completely open and unguarded with Henry – that's where the stupid worry comes from, his stubborn silence. It isn't what he will be unable to say in the future; it's what he failed to say in the past. He should have been honest with Henry from the start. He should have told him about the red feathers and the robins' eggs and his gathering uneasiness. Henry would have helped him open his eyes; he would have helped Jack resolve his own blindness, which was more damaging than Henry's.

All of that is over, Jack decides. No more secrets. Since he is lucky enough to have Henry's friendship, he will demonstrate that he values it. From now on, he will tell Henry everything, including the background: the Territories, Speedy Parker, the dead man on the Santa Monica Pier, Tyler Marshall's baseball cap. Judy Marshall. Sophie. Yes, he has to tell Henry about Sophie – how can he not have done so already? Henry will rejoice with him, and Jack cannot wait to see how he does it. Henry's rejoicing will be unlike anyone else's; Henry will impart some delicate, cool, good-hearted topspin to the expression of his delight, thereby increasing Jack's own delight. What an incredible, *literally* incredible friend! If you were to describe Henry to someone who had never met him, he would sound unbelievable. Someone like *that*, living alone in an outback of the boonies? But there he was, all alone in the entirely obscure area of Norway Valley, French County, Wisconsin, waiting for the latest installment of *Bleak House*. By now, in anticipation of Jack's arrival, he would have turned on the lights in his kitchen and living room, as he had done for years in honor of his dead, much-loved wife.

Jack thinks: *I must not be so bad, if I have a friend like that.*

And he thinks: *I really adore Henry.*

Now, even in the darkness, everything seems beautiful to him. The Sand Bar, ablaze with neon lights in its vast expanse of parking lot; the spindly, intermittent trees picked out by his headlights after the turn onto 93; the long, invisible fields; the glowing light bulbs hung like Christmas decorations from the porch of Roy's Store. The rattle over the first bridge and the sharp turn into the depths of the valley. Set back from the left side of the road, the first of the farmhouses gleam in the darkness, the lights in their windows burning like sacramental candles. Everything seems touched by a higher meaning, everything seems to *speak*. He is traveling, within a hush of sacred silence, through a sacred grove. Jack remembers when Dale first drove him into this valley, and that memory is sacred, too.

Jack does not know it, but tears are coursing down his

cheeks. His blood sings in his veins. The pale farmhouses shine half-hidden by the darkness, and out of that darkness leans the stand of tiger lilies that greeted him on his first down-valley journey. The tiger lilies blaze in his headlights, then slip murmuring behind him. Their lost speech joins the speech of the tires rolling eagerly, gently toward Henry Leyden's warm house. Tomorrow he may die, Jack knows, and this may be the last night he will ever see. That he *must* win does not mean that he *will* win; proud empires and noble epochs have gone down in defeat, and the Crimson King may burst out of the Tower and rage through world after world, spreading chaos.

They could all die in Black House: he, Beezer, and Doc. If that happens, Tyler Marshall will be not only a Breaker, a slave chained to an oar in a timeless Purgatory, but a super-Breaker, a nuclear-powered Breaker the abbalah will use to turn all the worlds into furnaces filled with burning corpses. *Over my dead body*, Jack thinks, and laughs a little crazily – it's so literal!

What an extraordinary moment; he is laughing while he rubs tears off his face. The paradox suddenly makes him feel as though he is being torn in half. Beauty and terror, beauty and pain – there is no way out of the conundrum. Exhausted, strung out, Jack cannot hold off his awareness of the world's essential fragility, its constant, unstoppable movement toward death, or the deeper awareness that in that movement lies the source of all its meaning. Do you see all this heart-stopping beauty? Look closely, because in a moment your heart *will* stop.

In the next second, he remembers the swarm of golden bees that descended upon him: it was against this that they comforted him, exactly this, he tells himself. The blessing of blessings that vanish. What you love, you must love all the harder because someday it will be gone. It felt true, but it did not feel like all of the truth.

Against the vastness of the night, he sees the giant shape of the Crimson King holding aloft a small boy to use as a burning glass that will ignite the worlds into flaming waste. What Parkus said was right: he cannot destroy the giant, but he may find it possible to rescue the boy.

The bees said: *Save Ty Marshall.*

The bees said: *Love Henry Leyden.*

The bees said: *Love Sophie.*

That is close enough, right enough, for Jack. To the bees, these were all the same sentence. He supposes that the bees might well also have said, *Do your job, coppiceman*, and that sentence was only slightly different. Well, he would do his job, all right. After having been given such a miracle, he could do nothing else.

His heart warms as he turns up Henry's drive. What was Henry but another kind of miracle?

Tonight, Jack gleefully resolves, he is going to give the amazing Henry Leyden a thrill he will never forget. Tonight, he will tell Henry the whole story, the entire long tale of the journey he took in his twelfth year: the Blasted Lands, Rational Richard, the Agincourt, and the Talisman. He will not leave out the Oatley Tap and the Sunlight Home, for these travails will get Henry wonderfully worked up. And Wolf! Henry is going to be crazy about Wolf; Wolf will tickle him right down to the soles of his chocolate-brown suede loafers. As Jack speaks, every word he says will be an apology for having been silent for so long.

And when he has finished telling the whole story, telling it at least as well as he can, the world, this world, will have been transformed, for one person in it besides himself will know everything that happened. Jack can barely imagine what it will feel like to have the dam of his loneliness so *obliterated*, so *destroyed*, but the very thought of it floods him with the anticipation of relief.

Now, this is strange . . . Henry has not turned on his lights, and his house looks dark and empty. He must have fallen asleep.

Smiling, Jack turns off the engine and gets out of the pickup's cab. Experience tells him that he won't get more than three paces into the living room before Henry rouses himself and pretends that he has been awake all along. Once, when Jack found him in the dark like this, he said, 'I was just resting my eyes.' So what is it going to be tonight? He was planning his Lester Young–Charlie Parker birthday tribute, and he found it easier to concentrate this way? He was thinking about frying up some fish, and he wanted to see if food tasted different if you cooked it in the dark? Whatever it is, it'll be entertaining. And maybe they will celebrate Henry's new deal with ESPN!

'Henry?' Jack raps on the door, then opens it and leans in. 'Henry, you faker, are you asleep?'

Henry does not respond, and Jack's question falls into a soundless void. He can see nothing. The room is a two-dimensional pane of blackness. 'Hey, Henry, I'm here. And boy, do I have a story for you!'

More dead silence. 'Huh,' Jack says, and steps inside. Immediately, his instincts scream that he should *get out, take off, scram*. But why should he feel that? This is just Henry's house, that's all; he has been inside it hundreds of times before, and he knows Henry has either fallen asleep on his sofa or walked over to Jack's house, which come to think of it is probably exactly what happened. Henry got a terrific offer from the ESPN representative, and in his excitement – for even Henry Leyden can get excited, you just have to look a little closer than you do with most people – decided to surprise Jack at his house. When Jack failed to arrive by five or six, he decided to wait for him. And right now, he is probably sound asleep on Jack's sofa, instead of his own.

All of this is plausible, but it does not alter the message blasting from Jack's nerve endings. *Go! Leave! You don't want to be here!*

He calls Henry's name again, and his response is the silence he expects.

The transcendent mood that had carried him down the valley has already disappeared, but he never noted its passing, merely that it is a thing of the past. If he were still a homicide detective, this is the moment when he would unholster his weapon. Jack steps quietly into the living room. Two strong odors come to him. One is the scent of perfume, and the other . . .

He knows what the other one is. Its presence here means that Henry is dead. The part of Jack that is not a cop argues that the smell of blood means no such thing. Henry may have been wounded in a fight, and the Fisherman could have taken him across worlds, as he did with Tyler Marshall. Henry may be trussed up in some pocket of the Territories, salted away to be used as a bargaining chip, or as bait. He and Ty might be side by side, waiting for rescue.

Jack knows that none of this is true. Henry is dead, and the Fisherman killed him. It is his job now to find the body. He's a coppiceman; he has to act like one. That the last thing in the world he wants to do is look at Henry's corpse does not change the nature of his task. Sorrow comes in many forms, but the kind of sorrow that has been building within Jack Sawyer feels as if it is made of granite. It slows his step and clenches his jaw. When he moves to his left and reaches for the light switch, this stony sorrow directs his hand to the right spot on the wall as surely as if he were Henry.

Because he is looking at the wall when the lights go on, only his peripheral vision takes in the interior of the room, and the damage does not seem as extensive as he had feared. A lamp has been toppled, a chair knocked over. But when Jack turns his head, two aspects of Henry's living room sear themselves onto his retinas. The first is a red slogan on the cream-colored opposite wall; the second, the sheer amount of blood on the floor. The bloodstains are like a map of Henry's progress into and back out of the room. Gouts of blood like those left by a wounded animal begin at the hallway and trail, accompanied by many loops and spatters, to the back of the Mission sofa, where blood lies pooled. Another large pool covers the hardwood floor beneath the long, low table where Henry sometimes used to park his portable CD player and stack the evening's CDs. From the table, another series of splashes and gouts lead back into the hallway. To Jack, it looks as though Henry must have been very low on blood when he felt safe enough to crawl out from under the table. *If* that is the way it went.

While Henry lay dead or dying, the Fisherman had taken something made of cloth – his shirt? a handkerchief? – and used it like a fat, unwieldy paintbrush. He had dipped it in the blood behind the sofa, raised it dripping to the wall, and daubed a few letters. Then he'd repeated and repeated the action until he had wiped the last letter of his message onto the wall.

HELLO HOLLYWOOD CUM GET MEE
CK CK CK CK

But the Crimson King had not written the taunting initials, and neither had Charles Burnside. They had been daubed on the wall by the Fisherman's master, whose name, in our ears, sounds like *Mr Munshun.*

Don't worry, I'll come for you soon enough, Jack thinks.

At this point, he could not be criticized for walking outside, where the air does not reek of blood and perfume, and using his cell phone to call Sumner Street. Maybe Bobby Dulac is on duty. He might even find Dale still at the station. To fulfill all of his civic obligations, he need speak only eight or nine words. After that, he could pocket the cell phone and sit on Henry's front steps until the guardians of law and order come barreling up the long drive. There would be a lot of them, at least four cars, maybe five. Dale would have to call the troopers, and Brown and Black might feel obliged to call the FBI. In about forty-five minutes, Henry's living room would be crowded with men taking measurements, writing in their notebooks, setting down evidence tags, and photographing bloodstains. There would be the ME and the evidence wagon. And when the first stage of everybody's various jobs came to an end, two men in white jackets would carry a stretcher through the front door and load the stretcher into whatever the hell they were driving.

Jack does not consider this option for much longer than a couple of seconds. He wants to see what the Fisherman and Mr Munshun did to Henry – he has to see it, he has no choice. His grim sorrow demands it, and if he does not obey his sorrow's commands, he will never feel quite whole again.

His sorrow, which is closed like a steel vault around his love for Henry Leyden, drives him deeper into the room. Jack moves slowly, picking his way forward the way a man crossing a stream moves from rock to rock. He is looking for the bare places where he can set his feet. From across the room, dripping red letters eight inches high mock his progress.

HELLO HOLLYWOOD

It seems to wink on and off, like a neon sign. HELLO HOLLYWOOD HELLO HOLLYWOOD.

CUM GET MEE
CUM GET MEE

He wants to curse, but the weight of his sorrow will not permit him to utter the words that float into his mind. At the end of the hallway to the studio and the kitchen, Jack steps over a long smear of blood and turns his back on the living room and the distracting flashes of neon. The light penetrates only three or four feet into the hallway. The kitchen is solid, featureless darkness. The studio door hangs half open, and reflected light shines softly in its window.

Blood lies spattered and smeared everywhere on the floor of the hallway. He can no longer avoid stepping in it but moves down the hallway with his eyes on the gaping studio door. Henry Leyden never left this door yawning into the little corridor; he kept it closed. Henry was *neat.* He had to be: if he left the studio door hanging open, he would walk right into it the next time he went to the kitchen. The mess, the disorder left in his wake by Henry's murderer disturbs Jack more than he wishes to admit, maybe even more than he recognizes. This messiness represents a true violation, and, on his friend's behalf, Jack hugely resents it.

He reaches the door, touches it, opens it wider. A concentrated stench of perfume and blood hangs in the air. Nearly as dark as the kitchen, the studio offers Jack only the dim shape of the console and the murky rectangles of the speakers fixed to the wall. The window into the kitchen hovers like a black sheet, invisible. His hand still on the door, Jack moves nearer and sees, or thinks he sees, the back of a tall chair and a shape stretched over the desk in front of the console. Only then does he hear the *whup-whup-whup* of tape hitting the end of a reel.

'Ohmygod,' Jack says, all in one word, as if he had all along not been expecting something precisely like what is before him. With a terrible, insistent certainty, the sound of the tape drives home the fact that Henry is dead. Jack's sorrow overrides his chickenhearted desire to go outside and call every cop in the state of Wisconsin by compelling him to grope for the light switch. He cannot leave; he must witness, as he did with Irma Freneau.

His fingers brush against the down-ticked plastic switch and settle on it. Into the back of his throat rises a sour, brassy taste. He flicks the switch up, and light floods the studio.

Henry's body leans out of the tall leather chair and over the desk, his hands on either side of his prize microphone, his face flattened on its left side. He is still wearing his dark glasses, but one of the thin metal bows is bent. At first, everything seems to have been painted red, for the nearly uniform coat of blood covering the desk has been dripping onto Henry's lap and the tops of his thighs for some time, and all the equipment has been sprayed with red. Part of Henry's cheek has been bitten off. He is missing two fingers from his right hand. To Jack's eyes, which have been taking an inventory as they register all the details of the room, most of Henry's blood loss came from a wound in his back. Blood-soaked clothing conceals the injury, but as much blood lies pooled, dripping, at the back of the chair as covers the desk. Most of the blood on the floor came from the chair. The Fisherman must have sliced an internal organ, or severed an artery.

Very little blood, apart from a fine mist over the controls, has hit the tape recorder. Jack can hardly remember how these machines work, but he has seen Henry change reels often enough to have a sense of what to do. He turns the recorder off and threads the end of the tape into the empty reel. Then he turns the machine on and pushes REWIND. The tape glides smoothly over the heads, spooling from one reel to the other.

'Did you make a tape for me, Henry?' Jack asks. 'I bet you did, but I hope you didn't die telling me what I already know.'

The tape clicks to a stop. Jack pushes PLAY and holds his breath.

In all his bull-necked, red-faced glory, George Rathbun booms from the speakers. 'Bottom of the ninth, and the home team is headed for the showers, pal. But the game ain't OVER till the last BLIND man is DEAD!'

Jack sags against the wall.

Henry Shake enters the room and tells him to call Maxton's. The Wisconsin Rat sticks his head in and screams about Black House. The Sheik the Shake the Shook and George Rathbun have a short debate, which the Shake wins. It is too much for Jack; he cannot stop his tears, and he does not bother to try. He lets them come. Henry's last performance moves him enormously. It is so *bountiful*, so *pure* – so purely Henry. Henry Leyden kept himself alive by calling on his alternate selves, and they did the job. They were a faithful crew, George and the Shake and the Rat, and they went down with the ship, not that they had much choice. Henry Leyden reappears, and in a voice that grows fainter with each phrase, says that Jack can beat *vain and stupid*. Henry's dying voice says he had a wonderful life. His voice drops to a whisper and utters three words filled to the brim with gratified surprise: *Ah, Lark. Hello.* Jack can hear the smile in those words.

Weeping, Jack staggers out of the studio. He wants to collapse into a chair and cry until he has no more tears, but he cannot fail either himself or Henry so greatly. He moves down the hallway, wipes his eyes, and waits for the stony sorrow to help him deal with his grief. It will help him deal with Black House, too. The sorrow is not to be deterred or deflected; it works like steel in his spine.

The ghost of Henry Shake whispers: *Jack, this sorrow is never going to leave you. Are you down with that?*

– Wouldn't have it any other way.

Just as long as you know. Wherever you go, whatever you do. Through every door. With every woman. If you have children, with your children. You'll hear it in all the music you listen to, you'll see it in every book you read. It will be part of the food you eat. With you forever. In all the worlds. In Black House.

– I am it, and it is me.

George Rathbun's whisper is twice as loud as the Sheik the Shake the Shook's: *Well, damnit, son, can I hear you say D'YAMBA?*

– D'yamba.

I reckon now you know why the bees embraced you. Don't you have a telephone call to make?

Yes, he does. But he cannot bear to be in this bloodsoaked house any longer; he needs to be out in the warm summer night. Letting his feet land where they may, Jack walks across the ruined living room and passes through the doorway. His sorrow walks with him, for he is it and it is he. The enormous sky hangs far above him, pierced with stars. Out comes the trusty cell phone.

And who answers the telephone at the French Landing Police Station? Arnold 'Flashlight' Hrabowski, of course, with a new nickname and just reinstated as a member of the force. Jack's news puts Flashlight Hrabowski in a state of high agitation. What? Gosh! Oh, no. Oh, who woulda believed it? Gee. Yeah, yessir. I'll take care of that right away, you bet.

So while the former Mad Hungarian tries to keep both his hands and voice from trembling as he dials the chief's home number and passes on Jack's two-sided message, Jack himself wanders away from the house, away from the drive and his pickup truck, away from anything that reminds him of human beings, and into a meadow filled with high, yellow-green grasses. His sorrow leads him, for his sorrow knows better than he what he needs.

Above all, he needs rest. Sleep, if sleep is possible. A soft spot on level ground far from the coming uproar of red lights and sirens and furious, hyperactive policemen. Far from all that desperation. A place where a man can lay his head and get a representative view of the local heavens. Half a mile down the fields, Jack comes to such a place between a cornfield and the rocky beginnings of the wooded hills. His sorrowing mind tells his sorrowing, exhausted body to lie down and make itself comfortable, and his body obeys. Overhead, the stars seem to vibrate and blur, though of course real stars in the familiar, real heavens do not act that way, so it must be an optical illusion. Jack's body stretches out, and the pad of grass and topsoil beneath his body seems to adjust itself around him, although this, too, must be an illusion, for everyone knows that in real life, the actual ground tends to be obdurate, inflexible, and stony. Jack Sawyer's sorrowing mind tells his sorrowing ache of a body to fall asleep, and impossible as it may seem, fall asleep it does.

Within minutes, Jack Sawyer's sleeping body undergoes a subtle transformation. Its edges seem to soften, its colors – his wheaten hair, his light tan jacket, his soft brown shoes – grow paler. An odd translucency, a mistiness or cloudiness, enters the process. It is as if we can peer through the cloudy, indistinct mass of his slow-breathing body to see the soft, crushed blades of grass that form its mattress. The longer we peer, the more clearly we can take in the grass beneath him, for his body is getting vaguer and vaguer. At last it is only a shimmer over the grass, and by the time the Jack-shaped pad of green has again straightened itself, the body that shaped it is long gone.

25

Oh, forget about that. We know where Jack Sawyer went when he disappeared from the edge of the cornfield, and we know who he is likely to meet when he gets there. Enough of that stuff. We want fun, we want excitement! Luckily for us, that charming old party Charles Burnside, who can always be depended upon to slip a whoopee cushion under the governor's seat during a banquet, to pour a little hot sauce into the stew, to fart at the prayer meeting, is at this moment emerging from a toilet bowl and into a stall in the men's room on Daisy wing. We note that Ol' Burny, our Burn-Burn, hugs Henry Leyden's hedge clippers to his sunken chest with both arms, actually cradling them, as if he were holding a baby. On his bony right arm, blood slides out of a nasty gash and rolls down toward his elbow. When he gets one foot, clad in another resident's bee slipper, on the rim of the bowl, he pushes himself up and steps out, wobbling a bit. His mouth is twisted into a scowl, and his eyes look like bullet holes, but we do not suppose that he, too, carries a weight of heavy-duty sorrow. Blood soaks the bottoms of his trousers and the front of his shirt, which has darkened with the flow of blood from a knife wound to his abdomen.

Wincing, Burny opens the door of the stall and walks out into the empty men's room. Fluorescent lights on the ceiling reflect from the long mirror above the row of sinks; thanks to Butch Yerxa, who is working a double shift because the regular night man called in drunk, the white tiles of the floor gleam. In all this sparkling whiteness, the blood on Charles Burnside's clothes and body looks radiantly red. He peels off his shirt and tosses it into a sink before plodding down to the far end of the bathroom and a cabinet marked with a piece of tape on which someone has printed BANDAGES. Old men have a tendency to fall down in their bathrooms, and Chipper's father thoughtfully installed the cabinet where he thought it might be needed. Drops of blood lay spattered across the white tiles.

Burny rips a handful of paper towels from a dispenser, dampens them with cold water, and lays them on the side of the nearest sink. Then he opens the bandage cabinet, removes a wide roll of tape and a wad of gauze bandages, and tears off a six-inch strip of the tape. He wipes blood off the skin around the wound in his belly and presses the wet paper towels over the opening. He lifts away the towels and presses a pad of gauze to the cut. Awkwardly, he flattens the strip of tape over the gauze. He dresses the stab wound on his arm in the same fashion.

Now swirls and scoops of blood cover the white tiles.

He moves up the row of sinks and runs cold water over his shirt. The water turns red in the bowl. Burny keeps scrubbing the old shirt under cold running water until it has turned a pale rose only a few shades brighter than his skin. Satisfied, he wrings the shirt in his hands, flaps it once or twice, and puts it back on. That it clings to him bothers Burny not at all. His goal is a very basic version of acceptability, not elegance:

insofar as it is possible, he wants to pass unnoticed. His cuffs are soaked with blood, and Elmer Jesperson's slippers are dark red and wet, but he thinks most people will not bother to look at his feet.

Within him, a coarse voice keeps saying, *Fazzdur, BurnBurn, fazzdur!*

Burny's only mistake is that, while buttoning up his damp shirt, he looks at himself in the mirror. What he sees stops him cold with shock. Despite his ugliness, Charles Burnside has always approved of the image returned to him by mirrors. In his opinion, he looks like a guy who knows where to find the corners – sly, unpredictable, and foxy. The man staring at him from the other side of the mirror is nothing like the canny old operator Burny remembered. The man facing him looks dim-witted, worn-out, and seriously ill. Sunken, red-rimmed eyes, cheeks like craters, veins crawling across his bald, skull-like crown . . . even his nose looks bonier and more twisted than it once had. He is the sort of old man who frightens children.

You shud fry-den cheerun, Burn-Burn. Dime do ged moo-vuhn.

He couldn't really look that bad, could he? If he did, he would have noticed long before this. Nah, that wasn't how Charles Burnside faced the world. The bathroom's too damn white, that's all. A white like that makes you look bleached. Makes you look skinned, like a rabbit. The dying old horror in the mirror takes a step nearer, and the spotty discolorations on his skin seem to darken. The spectacle of his teeth makes him close his mouth.

Then his master is like a fishhook in his mind, pulling him toward the door and muttering, *Dime, dime.*

Burny knows why it's *dime:* Mr Munshun wants to get back to Black House. Mr Munshun comes from some place incredibly distant from French Landing, and certain parts of Black House, which they built together, feel like the world of his home – the deepest parts, which Charles Burnside seldom visits, and which make him feel hypnotized, weak with longing, and sick to his stomach when he does. When he tries to picture the world that gave birth to Mr Munshun, he envisions a dark, craggy landscape littered with skulls. On the bare slopes and peaks stand houses like castles that change size, or vanish, when you blink. From the flickering defiles comes an industrial cacophony mingled with the cries of tortured children.

Burnside is eager to return to Black House, too, but for the simpler pleasures of the first set of rooms, where he can rest, eat canned food, and read his scrapbooks. He relishes the particular smell that inhabits those rooms, an order of rot, sweat, dried blood, must, sewage. If he could distill that fragrance, he would wear it like cologne. Also, a sweet little morsel named Tyler Marshall sits locked in a chamber located in another layer of Black House – and another world – and Burny cannot wait to torment little Tyler, to run his wrinkled hands over the boy's beautiful skin. Tyler Marshall *thrills* Burny.

But there are pleasures yet to be reaped in this world, and it is *dime* to attend to them. Burny peeks out through a crack in the bathroom door and sees that Butch Yerxa has succumbed to weariness and the cafeteria's meat loaf. He occupies his chair like an oversized doll, his arms on the desk and his fat chin resting on what would be a neck on a normal person. That useful little painted rock stands a few inches away from Butch's right hand, but Burny has no need of the rock, for he has acquired an instrument far more versatile. He wishes he had discovered the potential of hedge clippers long ago. Instead of one blade, you get two. One up, one down, *snick-snick!* And sharp! He had not intended to amputate the blind man's fingers. Back then he thought of the clippers as a big, primitive variety of knife, but when he got stabbed in the arm, he jerked the clippers toward the blind man and they more or less bit off his fingers by themselves, as neatly and swiftly as the old-time butchers in Chicago used to slice bacon.

Chipper Maxton is going to be fun. He deserves what he is going to get, too. Burny figures that Chipper is responsible for the way he has deteriorated. The mirror told him that he is about twenty pounds less than he should be, maybe even thirty, and no wonder – look at the slop they serve in the cafeteria. Chipper has been chiseling on the food, Burny thinks, the same way he chisels on everything else. The state, the government, Medicaid, Medicare, Chipper steals from all of them. A couple of times when he thought Charles Burnside was too out of it to know what was happening, Maxton had told him to sign forms that indicated he'd had an operation, prostate surgery, lung surgery. The way Burny sees it, half of the Medicaid money that paid for the nonexistent operation should have been his. It was his name on the form, wasn't it?

Burnside eases into the hallway and pads toward the lobby, leaving bloody footprints from the squishing slippers. Because he will have to pass the nurses' station, he shoves the clippers under his waistband and covers them with his shirt. The flabby cheeks, gold-rimmed glasses, and lavender hair of a useless old bag named Georgette Porter are visible to Burnside above the counter of the nurses' station. Things could be worse, he thinks. Ever since she waltzed into D18 and caught him trying to masturbate stark naked in the middle of the room, Georgette Porter has been terrified of him.

She glances his way, seems to suppress a shudder, and

looks back down at whatever she is doing with her hands. Knitting, probably, or reading the kind of murder mystery in which a cat solves the crime. Burny slops nearer the station and considers using the clippers on Georgette's face, but decides it is not worth the waste of energy. When he reaches the counter, he looks over it and sees that she is holding a paperback book in her hands, just as he had imagined.

She looks up at him with profound suspicion in her eyes.

'We sure look yummy tonight, Georgie.'

She glances up the hallway, then at the lobby, and realizes that she must deal with him by herself. 'You should be in your room, Mr Burnside. It's late.'

'Mind your own business, Georgie. I got a right to take a walk.'

'Mr Maxton doesn't like the residents to go into the other wings, so please stay in Daisy.'

'Is the big boss here tonight?'

'I believe so, yes.'

'Good.'

He turns away and continues on toward the lobby, and she calls after him. 'Wait!'

He looks back. She is standing up, a sure sign of great concern.

'You aren't going to bother Mr Maxton, are you?'

'Say any more, and I'll bother *you*.'

She places a hand on her throat and finally notices the floor. Her chin drops, and her eyebrows shoot up. 'Mr Burnside, what do you have on your slippers? And your pants cuffs? You're tracking it everywhere!'

'Can't keep your mouth shut, can you?'

Grimly, he plods back to the nurses' station. Georgette Porter backs against the wall, and by the time she realizes that she could have tried to escape, Burny is already in front of her. She removes her hand from her throat and holds it out like a stop sign.

'Dumb bitch.'

Burnside yanks the clippers out of his belt, grips the handles, and clips off her fingers as easily as if they were twigs. 'Stupid.'

Georgette has entered a stage of shocked disbelief that holds her in paralysis. She stares at the blood spilling from the four stumps on her hand.

'Goddamn moron.'

He opens the clippers and rams one of the blades into her throat. Georgette makes a choked, gargling sound. She tries to get her hands on the clippers, but he pulls them from her neck and raises them to her head. Her hands flutter, scattering blood. The expression on Burny's face is that of a man who finally admits that he has to clean his cat's litter box. He levels the wet blade in front of her right eye and shoves it in, and Georgette is dead before her body slides down the wall and folds up on the floor.

Thirty feet up the hallway, Butch Yerxa mumbles in his sleep.

'They never listen,' Burny mutters to himself. 'You try and try, but they always ask for it in the end. Proves they want it – like those dumb little shits in Chicago.' He tugs the clippers' blade out of Georgette's head and wipes it clean on the shoulder of her blouse. The memory of one or two of those little shits in Chicago sends a tingle down the length of his member, which begins to stiffen in his baggy old pants. *Hel*-lo! Ah . . . the magic of tender memories. Though, as we have seen, Charles Burnside now and again enjoys erections in his sleep, in his waking hours they are so rare as to be nearly nonexistent, and he is tempted to pull down his pants and see what he could make it do. But what if Yerxa wakes up? He would assume that *Georgette Porter*, or at least her corpse, aroused Burny's long-smoldering lusts. That wouldn't do – not at all. Even a monster has his pride. Best to carry on to Chipper Maxton's office, and hope that his hammer doesn't go limp before it is time to pound the nail.

Burny tucks the clippers into the back of his waistband and yanks at his wet shirt, pulling it away from his body. Down the corridor of Daisy wing he shuffles, across the empty lobby, and up to the burnished door further distinguished by the brass nameplate reading WILLIAM MAXTON, DIRECTOR. This he reverentially opens, summoning to mind the image of a long-dead ten-year-old boy named Herman Flagler, otherwise known as 'Poochie,' one of his first conquests. Poochie! Tender Poochie! Those tears, those sobs of mingled pain and joy, that yielding to utter helplessness: the faint crust of dirt over Poochie's scabby knees and slender forearms. Hot tears; a jet of urine from his terrified little rosebud.

There will be no such bliss from Chipper, but we may be sure there will be *something*. Anyhow, Tyler Marshall lies bound and waiting in Black House, helpless as helpless could be.

Charles Burnside plods through Rebecca Vilas's windowless cubicle, Poochie Flagler's pallid, deeply dimpled backside blazing in his mind. He places a hand on the next doorknob, takes a moment to calm himself, and noiselessly revolves the knob. The door opens just wide enough to reveal Chipper Maxton, only monarch of this realm, leaning over his desk, his head propped on one fist, and using a yellow pencil to make notations on two sets of papers. The trace of a smile softens the tight purse of his mouth; his damp eyes betray the suggestion of a gleam; the busy pencil glides back and forth between the two stacks of papers, making tiny marks. So happily absorbed in his task is Chipper that he fails to notice he is no longer alone until his visitor steps inside and gives the door a backward kick with his foot.

When the door slams shut, Chipper glances up in irritated surprise and peers at the figure before him. His attitude almost immediately changes to a sly, unpleasant heartiness he takes to be disarming. 'Don't they knock on doors where you come from, Mr Burnside? Just barge right on in, do they?'

'Barge right on in,' says his visitor.

'Never mind. The truth is, I've been meaning to talk to you.'

'Talk to me?'

'Yes. Come on in, will you? Take a seat. I'm afraid we might have a little problem, and I want to explore some possibilities.'

'Oh,' Burny says. 'A problem.' He plucks his shirt away from his chest and trudges forward, leaving behind him progressively fainter footprints Maxton fails to see.

'Take a pew,' Chipper says, waving at the chair in front of his desk. 'Pull up a bollard and rest your bones.' This expression comes from Franky Shellbarger, the First Farmer's loan officer, who uses it all the time at the local Rotary meetings, and although Chipper Maxton has no idea what a bollard may be, he thinks it sounds cute as hell. 'Old-timer, you and me have to have a heart-to-heart discussion.'

'Ah,' Burny says, and sits down, his back rigidly straight, due to the clippers. *'Hardz zu hardz.'*

'Yeah, that's the idea. Hey, is that shirt wet? It is! We can't have that, old buddy – you might catch cold and die, and neither one of us would like that, would we? You need a dry shirt. Let me see what I can do for you.'

'Don't bother, you fucking monkey.'

Chipper Maxton is already on his feet and straightening his shirt, and the old man's words throw him momentarily off his stride. He recovers nicely, grins, and says, 'Stay right there, Chicago.'

Although the mention of his native city sends a prickling sensation down his spine, Burnside gives nothing away as Maxton moves around the side of his desk and walks across his office. He watches the director leave the room. *Chicago.* Where Poochie Flagler and Sammy Hooten and Ferd Brogan and all the others had lived and died, God bless 'em. Stalks of grain, blades of grass, so foul so beautiful so enticing. With their smiles and their screams. Like all Caucasian slum children, pure pale ivory white under the crust of dirt, the fishy white of the city's poor, the soon-to-be-lost. The slender bones of their shoulder blades, sticking out as if to break through the thin layer of flesh. Burny's old organ stirs and stiffens as if *it* remembers the frolics of yesteryear. *Tyler Marshall*, he croons to himself, *pretty little Ty, we will have ourselves some fun before we turn you over to the boss, yes we will yes indeedy yes yes.*

The door slams behind him, yanking him out of his erotic reverie. But his old mule, his old hoss, it stays awake and on its mettle, bold and brash as ever it was in the glory days.

'No one in the lobby,' Maxton complains. 'That old bag, what'shername, Porter, Georgette Porter, down in the kitchen stuffing her face, I bet, and Butch Yerxa sound asleep in his chair. What am I supposed to do, ransack the *rooms* to find a dry shirt?'

He strides past Burnside, throws up his hands, and drops

into his chair. It's all an act, but Burny has seen much better than this. Chipper cannot intimidate Burny, not even if he knows a few things about *Chicago*.

'I don't need a new shirt,' he says. 'Asswipe.'

Chipper leans back in his chair and clasps his hands behind his head. He grins – this patient amuses him, he's a real card. 'Now, now. There's no need for name-calling here. You don't fool me anymore, old man. I don't buy your Alzheimer's act. In fact, I don't buy any of it.'

He is nice and relaxed and he oozes the confidence of a gambler holding four aces. Burny figures he is being set up for some kind of con job or blackmail, which makes the moment all the more delicious.

'I gotta hand it to you, though,' Chipper goes on. 'You fooled everybody in sight, including me. It must take an *incredible* amount of discipline to fake late-stage Alzheimer's. All that slumping in your chair, being fed baby food, crapping in your pants. Pretending you don't understand what people are saying.'

'I wasn't faking, you jackass.'

'So it's no wonder you staged a comeback – when was that, about a year ago? I would have done the same. I mean, it's one thing to go undercover, but it's another to do it as a vegetable. So we have ourselves a little miracle, don't we? Our Alzheimer's gradually reverses itself, it comes and it goes, like the common cold. It's a good deal all around. You get to walk around and make a nuisance of yourself, and there's less work for the staff. You're still one of my favorite patients, Charlie. Or should I call you Carl?'

'I don't give a shit what you call me.'

'But Carl's your real name, isn't it?'

Burny does not even shrug. He hopes Chipper gets to

the point before Butch Yerxa wakes up, notices the bloody prints, and discovers Georgette Porter's body, because while he is interested in Maxton's tale, he wants to get to Black House without *too* much interference. And Butch Yerxa would probably put up a decent fight.

Under the illusion that he is playing a cat-and-mouse game in which he is the cat, Chipper smiles at the old man in the wet pink shirt and rolls on. 'A state detective called me today. Said ID on a local fingerprint had come back from the FBI. It belonged to a bad, bad man named Carl Bierstone who's been wanted for almost forty years. In 1964 he was sentenced to death for killing a couple of kids he molested, only he escaped from the car taking him to prison – killed two guards with his bare hands. No sign of him since then. He'd be eighty-five by now, and the detective thought Bierstone just might be one of our residents. What do you have to say, Charles?'

Nothing, evidently.

'Charles Burnside is pretty close to Carl Bierstone, isn't it? And we have no background information on you at all. That makes you a unique resident here. For everybody else, we damn near have a family tree, but you sort of come out of nowhere. The only information we have about you is your age. When you turned up at La Riviere General in 1996, you claimed to be seventy-eight. That would make you the same age as that fugitive.'

Burnside gives him a truly unsettling smile. 'I guess I must be the Fisherman, too, then.'

'You're eighty-five years old. I don't think you're capable of dragging a bunch of kids halfway across the county. But I do think you're this Carl Bierstone, and the cops are still eager to get their hands on you. Which brings me to this letter that came a few days ago. I've been meaning to discuss it with you, but you know how busy things get around here.' He opens his desk drawer and pulls out a single sheet torn from a yellow notepad. It bears a brief, neatly typed message. '"De Pere, Wisconsin," it says. No date. "To Whom It May Concern" is how it starts. "I regret to inform you that I am no longer able to continue monthly payments on behalf of my nephew, Charles Burnside." That's it. Instead of writing her signature, she typed her name. "Althea Burnside."'

Chipper places the yellow notepaper before him and folds his hands together on top of it. 'What's the deal here, Charles? There's no Althea Burnside living in De Pere, I know that much. And she can't be your aunt. How old would she be? At least a hundred. More like a hundred and ten. I don't believe it. But these checks have been coming in, regular as clockwork, since your first month here at Maxton's. Some buddy, some old partner of yours, has been looking out for you, my friend. And we want him to continue what he's been doing, don't we?'

'All the same to me, asswipe.' This is not precisely truthful. All Burny knows of the monthly payments is that Mr Munshun organized them long ago, and if these payments are to stop, well . . . what comes to an end with them? He and Mr Munshun are in this together, aren't they?

'Come on, kiddo,' Chipper says. 'You can do better than that. I'm looking for a little cooperation here. I'm sure you don't want to go through all the mess and trouble of being taken into custody, getting fingerprinted, plus whatever might happen after that. And me, speaking personally, I wouldn't want to put you through all of that. Because the real rat here is your friend. It sure looks to me like this guy, whoever he is, is forgetting that you probably have something on him from the old days, right? And he's thinking that he doesn't have to make sure that you have all your little comforts anymore. Only that's a mistake. I bet you could straighten the guy out, make him understand the situation.'

Burny's mule, his old hoss, has softened up and dwindled like a punctured balloon, which increases his gloom. Since entering this oily crook's office, he has lost something vital: a feeling of purpose, a sense of immunity, an edge. He wants to get back to Black House. Black House will restore him, for Black House is magic, *dark* magic. The bitterness of his soul went into its making; the darkness of his heart soaked through every beam and joist.

Mr Munshun helped Burny see the possibilities of Black House, and he contributed many and many a touch of his own devise. There are regions of Black House Charles Burnside has never truly understood, and that frighten him, badly: an underground wing seems to contain his secret career in Chicago, and when he drew near that part of the house, he could hear the pleading whimpers and pungent screams of a hundred doomed boys as well as his own rasps of command, his grunts of ecstasy. For some reason, the proximity of his earlier triumphs made him feel small and hunted, an outcast instead of a lord. Mr Munshun had helped him remember the scale of his achievement, but Mr Munshun had been of no use with another region of Black House, a small one, at best a room, more accurately a vault, which houses the whole of his childhood, and which he has never, ever visited. The merest hint of that room causes Burny to feel like an infant left outside to freeze to death.

The news of the fictitious Althea Burnside's defection has a lesser version of the same effect. This is intolerable, and he need not, in fact cannot, endure it.

'Yeah,' he says. 'Let's have some straightening out here. Let's have some understanding.'

He rises from the chair, and a sound from what seems to be the center of French Landing speeds him along. It is the wail of police sirens, at least two, maybe three. Burny doesn't know for sure, but he supposes that Jack Sawyer has discovered the body of his friend Henry, only Henry was less than perfectly dead and managed to say that he had recognized his killer's voice. So Jack called the cop shop and here we are.

His next step brings him to the front of the desk. He glances at the papers on the desk and instantly grasps their meaning.

'Cooking the books, hey? You aren't just an asswipe, you're a sneaky little numbers juggler.'

In an amazingly small number of seconds, Chipper Maxton's face registers a tremendous range of feeling states. Ire, surprise, confusion, wounded pride, anger, and disbelief chase across the landscape of his features as Burnside reaches back and produces the hedge clippers. In the office, they seem larger and more aggressive than they did in Henry Leyden's living room.

To Chipper, the blades look as long as scythes. And when Chipper tears his eyes away from them and raises them to the old man standing before him, he sees a face more demonic than human. Burnside's eyes gleam red, and his lips curl away from appalling, glistening teeth like shards of broken mirrors.

'Back off, buddy,' Chipper squeaks. 'The police are practically in the lobby.'

'I ain't deaf.' Burny rams one blade into Chipper's mouth and closes the clippers on his sweaty cheek. Blood shoots across the desk, and Chipper's eyes expand. Burny yanks on the clippers, and several teeth and a portion of Chipper's tongue fly from the yawning wound. He pushes himself upright and leans forward to grab the blades. Burnside steps back and lops off half of Chipper's right hand.

'*Damn*, that's sharp,' he says.

Then Maxton comes reeling around the side of the desk, spraying blood in all directions and bellowing like a moose. Burny dodges away, dodges back, and punches the blades into the bulge of the blue button-down shirt over Chipper's belly. When he tugs them out, Chipper sags, groans, drops to his knees. Blood pours out of him as if from an overturned jug. He falls forward on his elbows. There is no fun left in Chipper Maxton; he shakes his head and mutters something that is a plea to be left alone. A bloodshot, oxlike eye revolves toward Charles Burnside and silently expresses an oddly impersonal desire for mercy.

'Mother of Mercy,' Burny says, 'is this the end of Rico?' What a laugh – he hasn't thought of that movie in years. Chuckling at his own wit, he leans over, positions the blades on either side of Chipper's neck, and nearly succeeds in cutting off his head.

The sirens turn blaring on to Queen Street. Soon policemen will be running up the walk; soon they will burst into the lobby. Burnside drops the clippers onto Chipper's broad back and regrets that he does not have the time to piss on his body or take a dump on his head, but Mr Munshun is grumbling about *dime, dime, dime.*

'I ain't stupid, you don't have to tell me,' Burny says.

He pads out of the office and through Miss Vilas's cubicle. When he moves out into the lobby, he can see the flashing light bars on the tops of two police cars rolling down the far side of the hedge. They come to a halt not far from where he first put his hand around Tyler Marshall's slender boy-neck. Burny scoots along a little faster. When he reaches the beginning of the Daisy corridor, two baby-faced policemen burst through the opening in the hedge.

Down the hallway, Butch Yerxa is standing up and rubbing his face. He stares at Burnside and says, 'What happened?'

'Get out there,' Burny says. 'Take 'em to the office. Maxton's hurt.'

'Hurt?' Incapable of movement, Butch is gaping at Burnside's bloody clothes and dripping hands.

'Go!'

Butch stumbles forward, and the two young policemen charge in through the big glass door, from which Rebecca Vilas's poster has been removed. 'The office!' Butch yells, pointing to his right. 'The boss is hurt!'

While Yerxa indicates the office door by jabbing his hand at the wall, Charles Burnside scuttles past him. A moment later, he has entered the Daisy wing men's room and is hotfooting it toward one of the stalls.

And what of Jack Sawyer? We already know. That is, we know he fell asleep in a receptive place between the edge of a cornfield and a hill on the western side of Norway Valley. We know that his body grew lighter, less substantial, cloudy. That it grew vague and translucent. We can suppose that before his body attained transparency, Jack entered a certain nourishing dream. And in that dream, we may suppose, a sky of robin's-egg blue suggests an infinity of space to the inhabitants of a handsome residential property on Roxbury Drive, Beverly Hills, wherein Jacky is six, six, six, or twelve, twelve, twelve, or both at the same time, and Daddy played cool changes on his horn, horn, horn. ('Darn That Dream,' Henry Shake could tell you, is the last song on *Daddy Plays the Horn*, by Dexter Gordon – a daddy-o if there ever was.) In that dream, everyone went on a journey and no one went anywhere else, and a traveling boy captured a most marvelous prize, and Lily Cavanaugh Sawyer captured a bumblebee in a glass. Smiling, she carried it to the swinging doors and launched it into the upper air. So the bumblebee traveled far and away to Faraway, and as it journeyed worlds upon worlds on their mysterious courses trembled and swayed, and Jack, too, journeyed on his own mysterious course into the infinite robin's-egg blue and, in the bee's accurate wake, returned to the Territories, where he lay sleeping in a silent field. So in that same darned dream, Jack Sawyer, a person younger than twelve and older than thirty, stunned by both grief and love, is visited in his sleep by a certain woman of tender regard. And she lies down beside him on his bed of sweet grass and takes him in her arms and his grateful body knows the bliss of her touch, her kiss, her deep blessing. What they do, alone in the faraway Territories, is none of our business, but we compound Sophie's blessing with our own and leave them to what is after all, with the gentlest possible urgency, *their* business, which blesses this boy and this girl, this man and this woman, this dear couple, as nothing else can, certainly not us.

Return comes as it should, with the clean, rich smells of topsoil and corn, and a rooster's alarm-clock crowing from the Gilbertson cousins' farm. A spiderweb shining with dew stitches the loafer on Jack's left foot to a mossy rock. An ant trundling across Jack's right wrist carries a blade of grass bearing in the V of its central fold a bright and trembling drop of newly made water. Feeling as wondrously refreshed as if he, too, were newly created, Jack eases the hardworking ant off his wrist, separates his shoe from the spiderweb, and gets to his feet. Dew sparkles in his hair and his eyebrows. Half a mile back across the field, Henry's meadow curves around Henry's house. Tiger lilies shiver in the cool morning breeze.

Tiger lilies shiver . . .

When he sees the hood of his pickup nosing out from behind the house, everything comes back to him. Mouse, and the word given him by Mouse. Henry's house, Henry's studio, his dying message. By this time, all the police and investigators will have gone, and the house will be empty, echoing with bloodstains. Dale Gilbertson – and probably Troopers Brown and Black – will be looking for him. Jack has no interest in the troopers, but he does want to talk to Dale. It is time to let Dale in on some startling facts. What Jack has to say to Dale is going to peel his eyelids back, but we should remember what the Duke told Dean Martin about the whisking of eggs and the making of omelettes. In the words of Lily Cavanaugh, when the Duke spoke up, ever'-dang-body *lissened* up, and so must Dale Gilbertson, for Jack wants his faithful and resolute company on the journey through Black House.

Walking past the side of Henry's house, Jack puts the tips of his fingers to his lips and brushes them against the wood, transferring the kiss. *Henry. For all the worlds, for Tyler Marshall, for Judy, for Sophie, and for you, Henry Leyden.*

The cell phone in the cab of the Ram claims to have three saved messages, all from Dale, which he deletes unheard. At home, the answering machine's red light blinks 4–4–4, repeating itself with the ruthless insistence of a hungry infant. Jack pushes PLAYBACK. Four times, an increasingly unhappy Dale Gilbertson begs to know the whereabouts of his friend Jack Sawyer and communicates his great desire to converse with the same gentleman, largely in reference to the murder of his uncle and their friend, Henry, but it wouldn't hurt to talk about the goddamn *slaughter* at Maxton's, would it? And does the name Charles Burnside ring any bells?

Jack looks at his watch and, thinking that it cannot be correct, glances up at the clock in his kitchen. His watch was right after all. It is 5:42 a.m., and the rooster is still crowing behind Randy and Kent Gilbertson's barn. Tiredness suddenly washes through him, heavier than gravity. Someone is undoubtedly manning the telephone on Sumner Street, but Dale is just as certainly asleep in his bed, and Jack wishes to speak only to Dale. He yawns hugely, like a cat. The newspaper hasn't even been delivered yet!

He removes his jacket and tosses it onto a chair, then yawns again, even more widely than before. Maybe that cornfield was not so comfortable after all: Jack's neck feels pinched, and his back aches. He pulls himself up the staircase, shucks his clothes onto a love seat in his bedroom, and flops into bed. On the wall above the love seat hangs his sunny little Fairfield Porter painting, and Jack remembers how Dale responded to it, the night they uncrated and put up all the paintings. He had loved that picture the moment he saw it – it had probably been news to Dale that he could find such satisfaction in a painting. *All right,* Jack thinks, *if we manage to get out of Black House alive, I'll give it to him. And I'll make him take it: I'll threaten to chop it up and burn it in the woodstove if he doesn't. I'll tell him I'll give it to Wendell Green!*

His eyes are already closing; he sinks into the bedclothes and disappears, although this time not literally, from our world. He dreams.

He walks down a tricky, descending forest path toward a burning building. Beasts and monsters writhe and bellow on both sides, mostly unseen but now and then flicking out a gnarled hand, a spiky tail, a black, skeletal wing. These he severs with a heavy sword. His arm aches, and his entire body feels weary and sore. Somewhere he is bleeding, but he cannot see or feel the wound, merely the slow movement of blood running down the backs of his legs. The people who were with him at the start of his journey are all dead, and he is – he may be – dying. He wishes he were not so alone, for he is terrified.

The burning building grows taller and taller as he approaches. Screams and cries come from it, and around it lies a grotesque perimeter of dead, blackened trees and smoking ashes. This perimeter widens with every second, as if the building is devouring all of nature, one foot at a time. Everything is lost, and the burning building and the soulless creature who is both its master and its prisoner will triumph, blasted world without end, amen. Din-tah, the great furnace, eating all in its path.

The trees on his right side bend and contort their complaining branches, and a great stirring takes place in the dark, sharply pointed leaves. Groaning, the huge trunks bow, and the branches twine like snakes about one another, bringing into being a solid wall of gray, pointed leaves. From that wall emerges, with terrible slowness, the impression of a gaunt, bony face. Five feet tall from crown to chin, the face bulges out against the layer of leaves, weaving from side to side in search of Jack.

It is everything that has ever terrified him, injured him, wished him ill, either in this world or the Territories. The huge face vaguely resembles a human monster named Elroy who once tried to rape Jack in a wretched bar called the Oatley Tap, then it suggests Morgan of Orris, then Sunlight Gardener, then Charles Burnside, but as it continues its blind seeking from side to side, it suggests all of these malign faces layered on top of one another and melting into one. Utter fear turns Jack to stone.

The face bulging out of the massed leaves searches the downward path, then swings back and ceases its constant, flickering movement from side to side. It is pointed directly at him, The blind eyes see him, the nose without nostrils smells him. A quiver of pleasure runs through the leaves, and the face looms forward, getting larger and larger. Unable to move, Jack looks back over his shoulder to see a putrefying man prop himself up in a narrow bed. The man opens his mouth and shouts, '*D'YAMBA!*'

Heart thrashing in his chest, a shout dying before it leaves his throat, Jack vaults from his bed and lands on his feet before he quite realizes that he has awakened from a dream. His entire body seems to be trembling. Sweat runs down his forehead and dampens his chest. Gradually, the trembling ceases as he takes in what is really around him: not a giant face looming from an ugly wall of leaves but the familiar confines of his bedroom. Hanging on the wall opposite is a painting he intends to give to Dale Gilbertson. He wipes his face, he calms down. He needs a shower. His watch tells him that it is now 9:47 a.m. He has slept four hours, and it is time to get organized.

Forty-five minutes later, cleaned up, dressed, and fed, Jack calls the police station and asks to speak to Chief Gilbertson. At 11:25, he and a dubious, newly educated Dale – a Dale who badly wants to see some evidence of his friend's crazy tale – leave the chief's car parked beneath the single tree in the Sand Bar's lot and walk across the hot asphalt past two leaning Harleys and toward the rear entrance.

Part Four

BLACK HOUSE AND BEYOND

26

We have had our little conversation about *slippage*, and it's too late in the game to belabor the point more than a little, but wouldn't you say that most houses are an attempt to hold slippage back? To impose at least the illusion of normality and sanity on the world? Think of Libertyville, with its corny but endearing street names – Camelot and Avalon and Maid Marian Way. And think of that sweet little honey of a home in Libertyville where Fred, Judy, and Tyler Marshall once lived together. What else would you call 16 Robin Hood Lane but an ode to the everyday, a paean to the prosaic? We could say the same thing about Dale Gilbertson's home, or Jack's, or Henry's, couldn't we? Most of the homes in the vicinity of French Landing, really. The destructive hurricane that has blown through the town doesn't change the fact that the homes stand as brave bulwarks against slippage, as noble as they are humble. They are places of sanity.

Black House – like Shirley Jackson's Hill House, like the turn-of-the-century monstrosity in Seattle known as Rose Red – is *not* sane. It is not entirely of this world. It's hard to look at from the outside – the eyes play continual tricks – but if one *can* hold it steady for a few seconds, one sees a three-story dwelling of perfectly ordinary size. The color is unusual, yes – that dead black exterior, even the windows swabbed black – and it has a crouching, leaning aspect that would raise uneasy thoughts about its structural integrity, but if one could appraise it with the *glammer* of those other worlds stripped away, it would look almost as ordinary as Fred and Judy's place . . . if not so well maintained.

Inside, however, it is different.

Inside, Black House is *large*.

Black House is, in fact, almost infinite.

Certainly it is no place to get lost, although from time to time people have – hoboes and the occasional unfortunate runaway child, as well as Charles Burnside/Carl Bierstone's victims – and relics here and there mark their passing: bits of clothing, pitiful scratchings on the walls of gigantic rooms with strange dimensions, the occasional heap of bones. Here and there the visitor may see a skull, such as the ones that washed up on the banks of the Hanover River during Fritz Haarman's reign of terror in the early 1920s.

This is not a place where you want to get lost.

Let us pass through rooms and nooks and corridors and crannies, safe in the knowledge that we can return to the outside world, the sane antislippage world, anytime we want (and yet we are still uneasy as we pass down flights of stairs that seem all but endless and along corridors that dwindle to a point in the distance). We hear an eternal low humming and the faint clash of weird machinery. We hear the idiot whistle of a constant wind either outside or on the floors above and below us. Sometimes we hear a faint, houndly barking that is undoubtedly the abbalah's devil dog, the one that did for poor old Mouse.

Sometimes we hear the sardonic caw of a crow and understand that Gorg is here, too – somewhere.

We pass through rooms of ruin and rooms that are still furnished with a pale and rotten grandeur. Many of these are surely bigger than the whole house in which they hide. And eventually we come to a humble sitting room furnished with an elderly horsehair sofa and chairs of fading red velvet. There is a smell of noisome cooking in the air. (Somewhere close by is a kitchen we must never visit . . . not, that is, if we ever wish to sleep without nightmares again.) The electrical fixtures in here are at least seventy years old. How can that be, we ask, if Black House was built in the 1970s? The answer is simple: much of Black House – *most* of Black House – has been here much longer. The draperies in this room are heavy and faded. Except for the yellowed news clippings that have been taped to the ugly green wallpaper, it is a room that would not be out of place on the ground floor of the Nelson Hotel. It's a place that is simultaneously sinister and oddly banal, a fitting mirror for the imagination of the old monster who has gone to earth here, who lies sleeping on the horsehair sofa with the front of his shirt turning a sinister red. Black House is not his, although in his pathological grandiosity he believes differently (and Mr Munshun has not disabused him of this belief). This one room, however, is.

The clippings around him tell us all we need to know of Charles 'Chummy' Burnside's lethal fascinations.

YES, I ATE HER, FISH DECLARES: *New York Herald Tribune*

BILLY GAFFNEY PLAYMATE AVERS 'IT WAS THE GRAY MAN TOOK BILLY, IT WAS THE BOGEYMAN': New York *World Telegram*

GRACE BUDD HORROR CONTINUES: FISH CONFESSES!: *Long Island Star*

FISH ADMITS 'ROASTING, EATING' WM GAFFNEY: *New York American*

FRITZ HAARMAN, SO-CALLED 'BUTCHER OF HANOVER,' EXECUTED FOR MURDER OF 24: New York *World*

WEREWOLF DECLARES: 'I WAS DRIVEN BY LOVE, NOT LUST.' HAARMAN DIES UNREPENTANT: *The Guardian*

CANNIBAL OF HANOVER'S LAST LETTER: 'YOU CANNOT KILL ME, I SHALL BE AMONG YOU FOR ETERNITY': New York *World*

Wendell Green would *love* this stuff, would he not?

And there are more. God help us, there are so many more. Even Jeffrey Dahmer is here, declaring I WANTED ZOMBIES.

The figure on the couch begins to groan and stir.

'Way-gup, Burny!' This seems to come from thin air, not his mouth . . . although his lips move, like those of a second-rate ventriloquist.

Burny groans. His head turns to the left. 'No . . . need to sleep. Everything . . . hurts.'

The head turns to the right in a gesture of negation and Mr Munshun speaks again. *'Way-gup, dey vill be gummink. You must move der buuuoy.'*

The head switches back the other way. Sleeping, Burny thinks Mr Munshun is still safe inside his head. He has forgotten things are different here in Black House. Foolish Burny, now nearing the end of his usefulness! But not quite there yet.

'Can't . . . lea' me 'lone . . . stomach hurts . . . the blind man . . . fucking blind man hurt my stomach . . .'

But the head turns back the other way and the voice speaks again from the air beside Burny's right ear. Burny fights it, not wanting to wake and face the full ferocious impact of the pain. The blind man has hurt him *much* worse than he thought at the time, in the heat of the moment. Burny insists to the nagging voice that the boy is safe where he is, that they'll never find him even if they can gain access to Black House, that they will become lost in its unknown depth of rooms and hallways and wander until they first go mad and then die. Mr Munshun, however, knows that one of them is different from any of the others who have happened on this place. Jack Sawyer is acquainted with the infinite, and that makes him a problem. The boy must be taken out the back way and into End-World, into the very shadow of Din-tah, the great furnace. Mr Munshun tells Burny that he may still be able to have some of the boy before turning him over to the abbalah, but not here. Too dangerous. Sorry.

Burny continues to protest, but this is a battle he will not win, and we know it. Already the stale, cooked-meat air of the room has begun to shift and swirl as the owner of the voice arrives. We see first a whirlpool of black, then a splotch of red – an ascot – and then the beginnings of an impossibly long white face, which is dominated by a single black shark's eye. This is the *real* Mr Munshun, the creature who can only live in Burny's head outside of Black House and its enchanted environs. Soon he will be entirely here, he will pull Burny into wakefulness (torture him into wakefulness, if necessary), and he will put Burny to use while there is still use to be gotten from him. For Mr Munshun cannot move Ty from his cell in the Black House.

Once he is in End-World – Burny's Sheol – things will be different.

At last Burny's eyes open. His gnarled hands, which have spilled so much blood, now reach down to feel the dampness of his own blood seeping through his shirt. He looks, sees what has bloomed there, and lets out a scream of horror and cowardice. It does not strike him as just that, after murdering so many children, he should have been mortally wounded by a blind man; it strikes him as hideous, unfair.

For the first time he is visited by an *extremely* unpleasant idea: What if there's more to pay for the things he has done over the course of his long career? He has seen End-World; he has seen Conger Road, which winds through it to Din-tah. The blasted, burning landscape surrounding Conger Road is like hell, and surely An-tak, the Big Combination, is hell itself. What if such a place waits for him? What if—

There's a horrible, paralyzing pain in his guts. Mr Munshun, now almost fully materialized, has reached out and twisted one smoky, not-quite-transparent hand in the wound Henry inflicted with his switchblade knife.

Burny squeals. Tears run down the old child-murderer's cheeks. '*Don't hurt me!*'

'Zen do ass I zay.'

'I *can't*,' Burny snivels. 'I'm dying. Look at all the blood! Do you think I can get past something like this? *I'm eighty-five fucking years old!*'

'Duff brayyg, Burn-Burn . . . but dere are zose on z'osser zide who could hill you off your wunds.' Mr Munshun, like Black House itself, is hard to look at. He shivers in and out of focus. Sometimes that hideously long face (it obscures most of his body, like the bloated head of a caricature on some newspaper's op-ed page) has two eyes, sometimes just one. Sometimes there seem to be tufted snarls of orange hair leaping up from his distended skull, and sometimes Mr Munshun appears to be as bald as Yul Brynner. Only the red lips and the fangy pointed teeth that lurk inside them remain fairly constant.

Burny eyes his accomplice with a degree of hope. His hands, meanwhile, continue to explore his stomach, which is now hard and bloated with lumps. He suspects the lumps are clots. Oh, that someone should have hurt him so badly! That wasn't supposed to happen! That was *never* supposed to happen! He was supposed to be protected! He was supposed to—

'It iss not even peeyond ze realm of bossibility,' Mr Munshun says, 'zat ze yearz could be rawled avey vrum you jusst as ze stunn vas rawled avey from ze mouse of Cheezus Chrizze's doom.'

'To be young again,' Burny says, and exhales a low, harsh sigh. His breath stinks of blood and spoilage. 'Yes, I'd like that.'

'Of gorse! And soch zings are bossible,' Mr Munshun says, nodding his grotesquely unstable face. 'Soch gifts are ze abba-lah's to giff. But zey are not bromised, Charles, my liddle munching munchkin. But I *can* make you one bromise.'

The creature in the black evening suit and red ascot leaps forward with dreadful agility. His long-fingered hand darts again into Chummy Burnside's shirt, this time clenches into a fist, and produces a pain beyond any the old monster has ever dreamed of in his own life . . . although he has inflicted this and more on the innocent.

Mr Munshun's reeking countenance pushes up to Burny's. The single eye glares. 'Do you feel dat, Burny? Do you, you mizz-er-a-ble old bag of dirt and zorrow? Ho-ho, ha-ha, of *gorse* you do! It iss your in-*des*-tines I haff in my hand! Und if you do not mooff now, *schweinhund*, I vill rip dem from your bledding body, ho-ho, ha-ha, und *vrap* dem arund your neg! You vill die knowing you are choking on your own *gudz*! A trick I learned from Fritz himzelf, Fritz Haarman, who vas so yunk und loff-ly! Now! *Vat* do you say? Vill you brink him, or vill you *choke*?'

'*I'll bring him!*' Burny screams. '*I'll bring him, only stop, stop, you're tearing me apart!*'

'Brink him to ze station. Ze *station*, Burn-Burn. Dis one iz nodd for ze radhulls, de fogzhulls – not for ze Combin-*ay*-shun. No bledding foodzies for Dyler; he works for his abbalah vid *dis*.' A long finger tipped with a brutal black nail goes to the huge forehead and taps it above the eyes (for the moment Burny sees two of them, and then the second is once more gone). 'Understand?'

'*Yes! Yes!*' His guts are on fire. And still the hand in his shirt twists and twists.

The terrible highway of Mr Munshun's face hangs before him. 'Ze *station* – where you brought the other sbecial ones.'

'YES!'

Mr Munshun lets go. He steps back. Mercifully for Burny, he is beginning to grow insubstantial again, to discorporate. Yellowed clippings swim into view not behind him but *through* him. Yet the single eye hangs in the air above the paling blotch of the ascot.

'Mayg zure he vears za cab. Ziss one ezbeshully must wear za cab.'

Burnside nods eagerly. He still smells faintly of My Sin perfume. 'The cap, yes, I have the cap.'

'Be gare-ful, Burny. You are old und hurt. Ze bouy is young und desberate. Flitt of foot. If you let him get avey—'

In spite of the pain, Burny smiles. One of the children getting away from *him*! Even one of the special ones! What an idea! 'Don't worry,' he says. 'Just . . . if you speak to *him* . . . to Abbalah-doon . . . tell him I'm not past it yet. If he makes me better, he won't regret it. And if he makes me young again, I'll bring him a thousand young. A thousand *Breakers*.'

Fading and fading. Now Mr Munshun is again just a glow, a milky disturbance on the air of Burny's sitting room deep in the house he abandoned only when he realized he really did need someone to take care of him in his sunset years.

'Bring him just dis *vun*, Burn-Burn. Bring him just dis vun, und you vill be revarded.'

Mr Munshun is gone. Burny stands and bends over the horsehair sofa. Doing it squeezes his belly, and the resulting pain makes him scream, but he doesn't stop. He reaches into the darkness and pulls out a battered black leather sack. He grasps its top and leaves the room, limping and clutching at his bleeding, distended belly.

And what of Tyler Marshall, who has existed through most of these many pages as little more than a rumor? How badly has he been hurt? How frightened is he? Has he managed to retain his sanity?

As to his physical condition, he's got a concussion, but that's already healing. The Fisherman has otherwise done no more than stroke his arm and his buttocks (a creepy touch that made Tyler think of the witch in 'Hansel and Gretel'). Mentally . . . would you be shocked to hear that, while Mr Munshun is goading Burny onward, Fred and Judy's boy is *happy*?

He is. He is happy. And why not? He's at Miller Park.

The Milwaukee Brewers have confounded all the pundits this year, all the doomsayers who proclaimed they'd be in the cellar by July Fourth. Well, it's still relatively early, but the Fourth has come and gone and the Brew Crew has returned to Miller tied for first place with Cincinnati. They are in the hunt, in large part due to the bat of Richie Sexson, who came over to

Milwaukee from the Cleveland Indians and who has been 'really pickin' taters,' in the pungent terminology of George Rathbun.

They are in the hunt, and *Ty is at the game! EXCELLENT!* Not only is he there, he's got a front-row seat. Next to him – big, sweating, red-faced, a Kingsland beer in one hand and another tucked away beneath his seat for emergencies – is the Gorgeous George himself, bellowing at the top of his leather lungs. Jeromy Burnitz of the Crew has just been called out at first on a bang-bang play, and while there can be no doubt that the Cincinnati short-stop handled the ball well and got rid of it fast, there can also be no doubt (at least not in George Rathbun's mind) that Burnitz was safe! He rises in the twilight, his sweaty bald pate glowing beneath a sweetly lavender sky, a foamy rill of beer rolling up one cocked forearm, his blue eyes twinkling (you can tell he sees a lot with those eyes, just about everything), and Ty waits for it, they all wait for it, and here it is, that avatar of summer in the Coulee Country, that wonderful bray that means everything is okay, terror has been denied, and slippage has been canceled.

'COME ON, UMP, GIVE US A BREAK! GIVE US A FREEEEAKIN' BRAYYYYK! EVEN A BLIND MAN COULD SEE HE WAS SAFE!'

The crowd on the first-base side goes wild at the sound of that cry, none wilder than the fourteen or so people sitting behind the banner reading MILLER PARK WELCOMES GEORGE RATHBUN AND THE WINNERS OF THIS YEAR'S KDCU BREWER BASH. Ty is jumping up and down, laughing, waving his Brew Crew hat. What makes this doubly boss is that he thought he forgot to enter the contest this year. He guesses his father (or perhaps his mother) entered it for him . . . and he won! Not the grand prize, which was getting to be the Brew Crew's batboy for the entire Cincinnati series, but what he got (besides this excellent seat with the other winners, that is) is, in his opinion, even better. Of course Richie Sexson isn't Mark McGwire – *nobody* can hit the tar out of the ball like Big Mac – but Sexson has been awesome for the Brewers this year, just *awesome*, and Tyler Marshall has won—

Someone is shaking his foot.

Ty attempts to pull away, not wanting to lose this dream (this most excellent refuge from the horror that has befallen him), but the hand is relentless. It shakes. It shakes and shakes.

'Way-gup,' a voice snarls, and the dream begins to darken.

George Rathbun turns to Ty, and the boy sees an amazing thing: the eyes that were such a shrewd, sharp blue only a few seconds ago have gone dull and milky. *Cripe, he's* blind, Ty thinks. *George Rathbun really* is *a*—

'Way-gup,' the growling voice says. It's closer now. In a moment the dream will wink out entirely.

Before it does, George speaks to him. The voice is quiet, totally unlike the sportscaster's usual brash bellow. 'Help's on the way,' he says. 'So be cool, you little cat. Be—'

'Way-*GUP*, you shit!'

The grip on his ankle is crushing, paralyzing. With a cry of protest, Ty opens his eyes. This is how he rejoins the world, and our tale.

He remembers where he is immediately. It's a cell with reddish-gray iron bars halfway along a stone corridor lit with cobwebby electric bulbs. There's a dish of some sort of stew in one corner. In the other is a bucket in which he is supposed to pee (or take a dump if he has to – so far he hasn't, thank goodness). The only other thing in the room is a raggedy old futon from which Burny has just dragged him.

'All right,' Burny says. 'Awake at last. That's good. Now

get up. On your feet, asswipe. I don't have time to fuck with you.'

Tyler gets up. A wave of dizziness rolls through him and he puts his hand to the top of his head. There is a spongy, crusted place there. Touching it sends a bolt of pain all the way down to his jaws, which clench. But it also drives the dizziness away. He looks at his hand. There are flakes of scab and dried blood on his palm. *That's where he hit me with his damned rock. Any harder, and I would have been playing a harp.*

But the old man has been hurt somehow, too. His shirt is covered with blood; his wrinkled ogre's face is waxy and pallid. Behind him, the cell door is open. Ty measures the distance to the hallway, hoping he's not being too obvious about it. But Burny has been in this game a long time. He has had more than one liddle one dry to esscabe on hiz bledding foodzies, oh ho.

He reaches into his bag and brings out a black gadget with a pistol grip and a stainless steel nozzle at the tip.

'Know what this is, Tyler?' Burny asks.

'Taser,' Ty says. 'Isn't it?'

Burny grins, revealing the stumps of his teeth. 'Smart boy! A TV-watching boy, I'll be bound. It's a Taser, yes. But a special type – it'll drop a cow at thirty yards. Understand? You try to run, boy, I'll bring you down like a ton of bricks. Come out here.'

Ty steps out of the cell. He has no idea where this horrible old man means to take him, but there's a certain relief just in being free of the cell. The futon was the worst. He knows, somehow, that he hasn't been the only kid to cry himself to sleep on it with an aching heart and an aching, lumpy head, nor the tenth.

Nor, probably, the fiftieth.

'Turn to your left.'

Ty does. Now the old man is behind him. A moment later, he feels the bony fingers grip the right cheek of his bottom. It's not the first time the old man has done this (each time it happens he's reminded again of the witch in 'Hansel and Gretel,' asking the lost children to stick their arms out of their cage), but this time his touch is different. Weaker.

Die soon, Ty thinks, and the thought – its cold collectedness – is very, very Judy. *Die soon, old man, so I don't have to.*

'This one is mine,' the old man says . . . but he sounds out of breath, no longer quite sure of himself. 'I'll bake half, fry the rest. With bacon.'

'I don't think you'll be able to eat much,' Ty says, surprised at the calmness of his own voice. 'Looks like somebody ventilated your stomach pretty g—'

There is a crackling, accompanied by a hideous, jittery burning sensation in his left shoulder. Ty screams and staggers against the wall across the corridor from his cell, trying to clutch the wounded place, trying not to cry, trying to hold on to just a little of his beautiful dream about being at the game with George Rathbun and the other KDCU Brewer Bash winners. He knows he actually did forget to enter this year, but in dreams such things don't matter. That's what's so beautiful about them.

Oh, but it hurts so *bad*. And despite all his efforts – all the Judy Marshall in him – the tears begin to flow.

'You want another un?' the old man gasps. He sounds both sick and hysterical, and even a kid Ty's age knows that's a dangerous combination. 'You want another un, just for good luck?'

'No,' Ty gasps. 'Don't zap me again, please don't.'

'Then start walkin'! And no more smart goddamn remarks!'

Ty starts to walk. Somewhere he can hear water dripping. Somewhere, very faint, he can hear the laughing caw of a crow – probably the same one that tricked him, and how he'd like to have Ebbie's .22 and blow its evil shiny black feathers off. The outside world seems light-years away. But George Rathbun told him help was on the way, and sometimes the things you heard in dreams came true. His very own mother told him that once, and long before she started to go all wonky in the head, too.

They come to a stairway that seems to circle down forever. Up from the depths comes a smell of sulfur and a roast of heat. Faintly he can hear what might be screams and moans. The clank of machinery is louder. There are ominous creaking sounds that might be belts and chains.

Ty pauses, thinking the old guy won't zap him again unless he absolutely has to. Because Ty might fall down this long circular staircase. Might hit the place on his head the old guy already clipped with the rock, or break his neck, or tumble right off the side. And the old guy wants him alive, at least for now. Ty doesn't know why, but he knows this intuition is true.

'Where are we going, mister?'

'You'll find out,' Burny says in his tight, out-of-breath voice. 'And if you think I don't dare zap you while we're on the stairs, my little friend, you're very mistaken. Now get walking.'

Tyler Marshall starts down the stairs, descending past vast galleries and balconies, around and down, around and down. Sometimes the air smells of putrid cabbage. Sometimes it smells of burned candles. Sometimes of wet rot. He counts a hundred and fifty steps, then stops counting. His thighs are burning. Behind him, the old man is gasping, and twice he stumbles, cursing and holding the ancient banister.

Fall, old man, Ty chants inside his head. *Fall and die, fall and die.*

But at last they are at the bottom. They arrive in a circular room with a dirty glass ceiling. Above them, gray sky hangs down like a filthy bag. There are plants oozing out of broken pots, sending greedy feelers across a floor of broken orange bricks. Ahead of them, two doors – French doors, Ty thinks they are called – stand open. Beyond them is a crumbling patio surrounded by ancient trees. Some are palms. Some – the ones with the hanging, ropy vines – might be banyans. Others he doesn't know. One thing he's sure of: they are no longer in Wisconsin.

Standing on the patio is an object he knows very well. Something from his own world. Tyler Marshall's eyes well up again at the sight of it, which is almost like the sight of a face from home in a hopelessly foreign place.

'Stop, monkey-boy.' The old man sounds out of breath. 'Turn around.'

When Tyler does, he's pleased to see that the blotch on the old man's shirt has spread even farther. Fingers of blood now stretch all the way to his shoulders, and the waistband of his baggy old blue jeans has gone a muddy black. But the hand holding the Taser is rock-steady.

God damn you, Tyler thinks. *God damn you to hell.*

The old man has put his bag on a little table. He simply stands where he is for a moment, getting his breath. Then he rummages in the bag (something in there utters a faint metallic clink) and brings out a soft brown cap. It's the kind guys like Sean Connery sometimes wear in the movies. The old man holds it out.

'Put it on. And if you try to grab my hand, I'll zap you.'

Tyler takes the cap. His fingers, expecting the texture of

suede, are surprised by something metallic, almost like tinfoil. He feels an unpleasant buzzing in his hand, like a mild version of the Taser's jolt. He looks at the old man pleadingly. 'Do I have to?'

Burny raises the Taser and bares his teeth in a silent grin.

Reluctantly, Ty puts the cap on.

This time the buzzing fills his head. For a moment he can't think . . . and then the feeling passes, leaving him with an odd sense of weakness in his muscles and a throbbing at his temples.

'Special boys need special toys,' Burny says, and it comes out *sbecial boyz, sbecial toyz*. As always, Mr Munshun's ridiculous accent has rubbed off a little, thickening that touch of South Chicago Henry detected on the 911 tape. '*Now* we can go out.'

Because with the cap on, I'm safe, Ty thinks, but the idea breaks up and drifts away almost as soon as it comes. He tries to think of his middle name and realizes he can't. He tries to think of the bad crow's name and can't get that, either – was it something like Corgi? No, that's a kind of dog. The cap is messing him up, he realizes, and that's what it's *supposed* to do.

Now they pass through the open doors and onto the patio. The air is redolent with the smell of the trees and bushes that surround the back side of Black House, a smell that is heavy and cloying. *Fleshy*, somehow. The gray sky seems almost low enough to touch. Ty can smell sulfur and something bitter and electric and juicy. The sound of machinery is much louder out here.

The thing Ty recognized sitting on the broken bricks is an E-Z-Go golf cart. The Tiger Woods model.

'My dad sells these,' Ty says. 'At Goltz's, where he works.'

'Where do you think it came from, asswipe? Get in. Behind the wheel.'

Ty looks at him, amazed. His blue eyes, perhaps thanks to the effects of the cap, have grown bloodshot and rather confused. 'I'm not old enough to drive.'

'Oh, you'll be fine. A *baby* could drive this baby. Behind the wheel.'

Ty does as he is told. In truth, he has driven one of these in the lot at Goltz's, with his father sitting watchfully beside him in the passenger seat. Now the hideous old man is easing himself into that same place, groaning and holding his perforated midsection. The Taser is in the other hand, however, and the steel tip remains pointed at Ty.

The key is in the ignition. Ty turns it. There's a click from the battery beneath them. The dashboard light reading CHARGE glows bright green. Now all he has to do is push the accelerator pedal. And steer, of course.

'Good so far,' the old man says. He takes his right hand off his middle and points with a bloodstained finger. Ty sees a path of discolored gravel – once, before the trees and underbrush encroached, it was probably a driveway – leading away from the house. 'Now go. And go slow. Speed and I'll zap you. Try to crash us and I'll break your wrist for you. Then you can drive one-handed.'

Ty pushes down on the accelerator. The golf cart jerks forward. The old man lurches, curses, and waves the Taser threateningly.

'It would be easier if I could take off the cap,' Ty says. 'Please, I'm pretty sure that if you'd just let me—'

'No! Cap stays! *Drive!*'

Ty pushes down gently on the accelerator. The E-Z-Go rolls across the patio, its brand-new rubber tires crunching on broken shards of brick. There's a bump as they leave the pavement and go rolling up the driveway. Heavy fronds – they feel damp, sweaty – brush Tyler's arms. He cringes. The golf cart swerves. Burny jabs the Taser at the boy, snarling.

'Next time you get the juice! It's a promise!'

A snake goes writhing across the overgrown gravel up ahead, and Ty utters a little scream through his clenched teeth. He doesn't like snakes, didn't even want to touch the harmless little corn snake Mrs Locher brought to school, and this thing is the size of a python, with ruby eyes and fangs that prop its mouth open in a perpetual snarl.

'Go! Drive!' The Taser, waving in his face. The cap, buzzing faintly in his ears. *Behind* his ears.

The drive curves to the left. Some sort of tree burdened with what look like tentacles leans over them. The tips of the tentacles tickle across Ty's shoulders and the goose-prickled, hair-on-end nape of his neck.

Ourr boyy . . .

He hears this in his head in spite of the cap. It's faint, it's distant, but it's there.

Ourrrr boyyyyy . . . yesssss . . . ourrrs . . .

Burny is grinning. 'Hear 'em, don'tcha? They like you. So do I. We're all friends here, don't you see?' The grin becomes a grimace. He clutches his bloody middle again. 'Goddamned blind old fool!' he gasps.

Then, suddenly, the trees are gone. The golf cart rolls out onto a sullen, crumbling plain. The bushes dwindle and Ty sees that farther along they give way entirely to a crumbled, rocky scree: hills rise and fall beneath that sullen gray sky. A few birds of enormous size wheel lazily. A shaggy, slump-shouldered creature staggers down a narrow defile and is gone from sight before Ty can see exactly what it is . . . not that he wanted to. The thud and pound of machinery is stronger, shaking the earth. The crump of pile drivers; the clash of ancient gears; the squall of cogs. Tyler can feel the golf cart's steering wheel thrumming in his hands. Ahead of them the driveway ends in a wide road of beaten earth. Along the far side of it is a wall of round white stones.

'That thing you hear, that's the Crimson King's power plant,' Burny says. He speaks with pride, but there is more than a tinge of fear beneath it. 'The Big Combination. A million children have died on its belts, and a zillion more to come, for all I know. But that's not for you, Tyler. You might have a future after all. First, though, I'll have my piece of you. Yes indeed.'

His blood-streaked hand reaches out and caresses the top of Ty's buttock.

'A good agent's entitled to ten percent. Even an old buzzard like me knows that.'

The hand draws back. Good thing. Ty has been on the verge of screaming, holding the sound back only by thinking of sitting at Miller Park with good old George Rathbun. *If I'd really entered the Brewer Bash*, he thinks, *none of this would have happened.*

But he thinks that may not actually be true. Some things are meant to be, that's all. *Meant.*

He just hopes that what this horrible old creature wants is not one of them.

'Turn left,' Burny grunts, settling back. 'Three miles. Give or take.' And, as Tyler makes the turn, he realizes the ribbons of mist rising from the ground aren't mist at all. They're ribbons of smoke.

'Sheol,' Burny says, as if reading his mind. 'And this is the only way through it – Conger Road. Get off it and there are things out there that'd pull you to pieces just to hear you scream. My friend told me where to take you, but there might be just a *leedle* change of plan.' His painwracked face takes on a sulky cast. Ty thinks it makes him look extraordinarily stupid. 'He hurt me. Pulled my guts. I don't trust him.' And, in a horrible child's singsong: 'Carl Bierstone don't trust Mr Munshun! Not no more! Not no more!'

Ty says nothing. He concentrates on keeping the golf cart in the middle of Conger Road. He risks one look back, but the house, in its ephemeral wallow of tropical greenery, is gone, blocked from view by the first of the eroded hills.

'He'll have what's his, but I'll have what's mine. Do you hear me, boy?' When Ty says nothing, Burny brandishes the Taser. '*Do you hear me, you asswipe monkey?*'

'Yeah,' Ty says. 'Yeah, sure.' *Why don't you die? God, if You're there, why don't You just reach down and put Your finger on his rotten heart and stop it from beating?*

When Burny speaks again, his voice is sly. 'You looked at the wall on t'other side, but I don't think you looked close enough. Better take another gander.'

Tyler looks past the slumped old man. For a moment he doesn't understand . . . and then he does. The big white stones stretching endlessly away along the far side of Conger Road aren't stones at all. They're skulls.

What is this place? Oh God, how he wants his mother! How he wants to go *home*!

Beginning to cry again, his brain numbed and buzzing beneath the cap that looks like cloth but isn't, Ty pilots the golf cart deeper and deeper into the furnace-lands. Into Sheol.

Rescue – help of any kind – has never seemed so far away.

27

When Jack and Dale step into the air-conditioned cool, the Sand Bar is empty except for three people. Beezer and Doc are at the bar, with soft drinks in front of them – an End Times sign if there ever was one, Jack thinks. Far back in the shadows (any further and he'd be in the dive's primitive kitchen), Stinky Cheese is lurking. There is a vibe coming off the two bikers, a bad one, and Stinky wants no part of it. For one thing, he's never seen Beezer and Doc without Mouse, Sonny, and Kaiser Bill. For another . . . oh God, it's the California detective and the freakin' chief of police.

The jukebox is dark and dead, but the TV is on and Jack's not exactly surprised to see that today's Matinee Movie on AMC features his mother and Woody Strode. He fumbles for the name of the film, and after a moment it comes to him: *Execution Express*.

'You don't want to be in on this, Bea,' Woody says – in this film Lily plays a Boston heiress named Beatrice Lodge, who comes west and turns outlaw, mostly to spite her straitlaced father. 'This is looking like the gang's last ride.'

'Good,' Lily says. Her voice is stony, her eyes stonier. The picture is crap, but as always, she is dead on character. Jack has to smile a little.

'What?' Dale asks him. 'The whole world's gone crazy, so what's to smile about?'

On TV, Woody Strode says: 'What do you mean, *good*? The whole damn world's gone crazy.'

Jack Sawyer says, very softly: 'We're going to gun down as many as we can. Let them know we were here.'

On the screen, Lily says the same thing to Woody. The two of them are about to step aboard the Execution Express, and heads will roll – the good, the bad, and the ugly.

Dale looks at his friend, dazed.

'I know most of her lines,' Jack says, almost apologetically. 'She was my mother, you see.'

Before Dale can answer (supposing any answer came to mind), Jack joins Beezer and Doc at the bar. He looks up at the Kingsland Ale clock next to the television: 11:40. It should be high noon – in situations like this, it's always supposed to be high noon, isn't it?

'Jack,' Beezer says, and gives him a nod. 'How ya doin', buddy?'

'Not too bad. You boys carrying?'

Doc lifts his vest, disclosing the butt of a pistol. 'It's a Colt 9. Beez has got one of the same. Good iron, all registered and proper.' He glances at Dale. 'You along for the ride, are you?'

'It's my town,' Dale says, 'and the Fisherman just murdered my uncle. I don't understand very much of what Jack's been telling me, but I know that much. And if he says there's a chance we can get Judy Marshall's boy back, I think we'd better try it.' He glances at Jack. 'I brought you a service revolver. One of the Ruger automatics. It's out in the car.'

Jack nods absently. He doesn't care much about the guns, because once they're on the other side they'll almost certainly change into something else. Spears, possibly javelins. Maybe even slingshots. It's going to be the Execution Express, all right – the Sawyer Gang's last ride – but he doubts if it'll be much like the one in this old movie from the sixties. Although he'll take the Ruger. There might be work for it on this side. One never knows, does one?

'Ready to saddle up?' Beezer asks Jack. His eyes are deep-socketed, haunted. Jack guesses the Beez didn't get much sleep last night. He glances up at the clock again and decides – for no other reason than pure superstition – that he doesn't want to start for the Black House just yet, after all. They'll leave the Sand Bar when the hands on the Kingsland clock stand at straight-up noon, no sooner. The Gary Cooper witching hour.

'Almost,' he says. 'Have you got the map, Beez?'

'I got it, but I also got an idea you don't really need it, do you?'

'Maybe not,' Jack allows, 'but I'll take all the insurance I can get.'

Beezer nods. 'I'm down with that. I sent my old lady back to her ma's in Idaho. After what happened with poor old Mousie, I didn't have to argue too hard. Never sent her back before, man. Not even the time we had our bad rumble with the Pagans. But I got a terrible feeling about this.' He hesitates, then comes right out with it. 'Feel like none of us are coming back.'

Jack puts a hand on Beezer's meaty forearm. 'Not too late to back out. I won't think any less of you.'

Beezer mulls it over, then shakes his head. 'Amy comes to me in my dreams, sometimes. We talk. How am I gonna talk to her if I don't stand up for her? No, man, I'm in.'

Jack looks at Doc.

'I'm with Beez,' Doc says. 'Sometimes you just gotta stand up. Besides, after what happened to Mouse . . .' He shrugs. 'God knows what we might have caught from him. Or fucking around out there at that house. Future might be short after that, no matter what.'

'How'd it turn out with Mouse?' Jack inquires.

Doc gives a short laugh. 'Just like he said. Around three o'clock this morning, we just washed old Mousie down the tub drain. Nothing left but foam and hair.' He grimaces as if his stomach is trying to revolt, then quickly downs his glass of Coke.

'If we're going to do something,' Dale blurts, 'let's just do it.'

Jack glances up at the clock. It's 11:50 now. 'Soon.'

'I'm not afraid of dying,' Beezer says abruptly. 'I'm not even afraid of that devil dog. It can be hurt if you pour enough bullets into it, we found that out. It's how that fucking place makes you *feel*. The air gets thick. Your head aches and your muscles get weak.' And then, with a surprisingly good British accent: 'Hangovers ain't in it, old boy.'

'My gut was the worst,' Doc says. 'That and . . .' But he falls silent. He doesn't ever talk about Daisy Temperly, the girl he killed with an errant scratch of ink on a prescription pad, but he can see her now as clearly as the make-believe cowboys on the Sand Bar's TV. Blond, she was. With brown eyes. Sometimes he'd made her smile (even in her pain) by singing that song to her, the Van Morrison song about the brown-eyed girl.

'I'm going for Mouse,' Doc says. 'I *have* to. But that place . . . it's a sick place. You don't know, man. You may think you understand, but you don't.'

'I understand more than you think,' Jack says. Now it's his turn to stop, to consider. Do Beezer and Doc remember the word Mouse spoke before he died? Do they remember *d'yamba*? They should, they were right there, they saw the books slide off their shelf and hang in the air when Jack spoke that word . . . but Jack is almost sure that if he asked them right now, they'd give him looks that are puzzled, or maybe just blank. Partly because *d'yamba* is hard to remember, like the precise location of the lane that leads from sane antislippage Highway 35 to Black House. Mostly, however, because the word was for him, for Jack Sawyer, the son of Phil and Lily. He is the leader of the Sawyer Gang because he is different. He has traveled, and travel is broadening.

How much of this should he tell them? None of it, probably. But they must believe, and for that to happen he must use Mouse's word. He knows in his heart that he must be careful about using it – *d'yamba* is like a gun; you can only fire it so many times before it clicks empty – and he hates to use it here, so far from Black House, but he will. Because they must believe. If they don't, their brave quest to rescue Ty is apt to end with them all kneeling in Black House's front yard, noses bleeding, eyes bleeding, vomiting and spitting teeth into the poison air. Jack can tell them that most of the poison comes from their own minds, but talk is cheap. They must believe.

Besides, it's still only 11:53.

'Lester,' he says.

The bartender has been lurking, forgotten, by the swing door into the kitchen. Not eavesdropping – he's too far away for that – but not wanting to move and attract attention. Now it seems that he's attracted some anyway.

'Have you got honey?' Jack asks.

'H-honey?'

'Bees make it, Lester. Mokes make money and bees make honey.'

Something like comprehension dawns in Lester's eyes. 'Yeah, sure. I keep it to make Kentucky Getaways. Also—'

'Set it on the bar,' Jack tells him.

Dale stirs restively. 'If time's as short as you think, Jack—'

'This is important.' He watches Lester Moon put a small plastic squeeze bottle of honey on the bar and finds himself thinking of Henry. How Henry would have enjoyed the pocket miracle Jack is about to perform! But of course, he wouldn't have needed to perform such a trick for Henry. Wouldn't have needed to waste part of the precious word's power. Because Henry would have believed at once, just as he had believed he could drive from Trempealeau to French Landing – hell, to the fucking *moon* – if someone just dared to give him the chance and the car keys.

'I'll bring it to you,' Lester says bravely. 'I ain't afraid.'

'Just set it down on the far end of the bar,' Jack tells him. 'That'll be fine.'

He does as asked. The squeeze bottle is shaped like a bear. It sits there in a beam of six-minutes-to-noon sun. On the television, the gunplay has started. Jack ignores it. He ignores everything, focusing his mind as brightly as a point of light through a magnifying glass. For a moment he allows that tight focus to remain empty, and then he fills it with a single word:

(*D'YAMBA*)

At once he hears a low buzzing. It swells to a drone. Beezer, Doc, and Dale look around. For a moment nothing happens, and then the sunshiny doorway darkens. It's almost as if a very small rain cloud has floated into the Sand Bar—

Stinky Cheese lets out a strangled squawk and goes flailing backward. 'Wasps!' he shouts. 'Them are wasps! *Get clear!*'

But they are not wasps. Doc and Lester Moon might not recognize that, but both Beezer and Dale Gilbertson are country boys. They know bees when they see one. Jack, meanwhile, only looks at the swarm. Sweat has popped out on his forehead. He's concentrating with all his might on what he wants the bees to do.

They cloud around the squeeze bottle of honey so thickly it almost disappears. Then their humming deepens, and the bottle begins to rise, wobbling from side to side like a tiny missile with a really shitty guidance system. Then, slowly, it wavers its way toward the Sawyer Gang. The squeeze bottle is riding a cushion of bees six inches above the bar.

Jack holds his hand out and open. The squeeze bottle glides into it. Jack closes his fingers. Docking complete.

For a moment the bees rise around his head, their drone competing with Lily, who is shouting: 'Save the tall bastard for me! He's the one who raped Stella!'

Then they stream out the door and are gone.

The Kingsland Ale clock stands at 11:57.

'Holy Mary, mothera God,' Beezer whispers. His eyes are huge, almost popping out of their sockets.

'You've been hiding your light under a bushel, looks like to me,' Dale says. His voice is unsteady.

From the end of the bar there comes a soft thud. Lester 'Stinky Cheese' Moon has, for the first time in his life, fainted.

'We're going to go now,' Jack says. 'Beez, you and Doc lead. We'll be right behind you in Dale's car. When you get to the lane and the NO TRESPASSING sign, *don't go in.* Just park your scoots. We'll go the rest of the way in the car, but first we're going to put a little of this under our noses.' Jack holds up the squeeze bottle. It's a plastic version of Winnie-the-Pooh, grimy around the middle where Lester seizes it and squeezes it. 'We might even dab some *in* our nostrils. A little sticky, but better than projectile vomiting.'

Confirmation and approval are dawning in Dale's eyes. 'Like putting Vicks under your nose at a murder scene,' he says.

It's nothing like that at all, but Jack nods. Because this is about *believing*.

'Will it work?' Doc asks doubtfully.

'Yes,' Jack replies. 'You'll still feel some discomfort, I don't doubt that a bit, but it'll be mild. Then we're going to cross over to . . . well, to someplace else. After that, all bets are off.'

'I thought the kid was in the house,' Beez says.

'I think he's probably been moved. And the house . . . it's a kind of wormhole. It opens on another . . .' *World* is the first word to come into Jack's mind, but somehow he doesn't think it *is* a world, not in the Territories sense. 'On another place.'

On the TV, Lily has just taken the first of about six bullets. She dies in this one, and as a kid Jack always hated that, but at least she goes down shooting. She takes quite a few of the bastards with her, including the tall one who raped her friend, and that is good. Jack hopes he can do the same. More than anything, however, he hopes he can bring Tyler Marshall back to his mother and father.

Beside the television, the clock flicks from 11:59 to 12:00.

'Come on, boys,' Jack Sawyer says. 'Let's saddle up and ride.'

Beezer and Doc mount their iron horses. Jack and Dale stroll toward the chief of police's car, then stop as a Ford Explorer bolts into the Sand Bar's lot, skidding on the gravel and hurrying toward them, pulling a rooster tail of dust into the summer air.

'Oh Christ,' Dale murmurs. Jack can tell from the too

small baseball cap sitting ludicrously on the driver's head that it's Fred Marshall. But if Ty's father thinks he's going to join the rescue mission, he'd better think again.

'Thank God I caught you!' Fred shouts as he all but tumbles from his truck. 'Thank God!'

'Who next?' Dale asks softly. 'Wendell Green? Tom Cruise? George W. Bush, arm in arm with Miss Fucking Universe?'

Jack barely hears him. Fred is wrestling a long package from the bed of his truck, and all at once Jack is interested. The thing in that package could be a rifle, but somehow he doesn't think that's what it is. Jack suddenly feels like a squeeze bottle being levitated by bees, not so much acting as acted upon. He starts forward.

'Hey bro, let's roll!' Beezer yells. Beneath him, his Harley explodes into life. 'Let's—'

Then Beezer *cries out.* So does Doc, who jerks so hard he almost dumps the bike idling between his thighs. Jack feels something like a bolt of lightning go through his head and he reels forward into Fred, who is also shouting incoherently. For a moment the two of them appear to be either dancing with the long wrapped object Fred has brought them or wrestling over it.

Only Dale Gilbertson – who hasn't been to the Territories, hasn't been close to Black House, and who is not Ty Marshall's father – is unaffected. Yet even he feels something rise in his head, something like an interior shout. The world trembles. All at once there seems to be more color in it, more dimension.

'What was that?' he shouts. 'Good or bad? Good or bad? *What the hell is going on here?*'

For a moment none of them answer. They are too dazed to answer.

★

While a swarm of bees is floating a squeeze bottle of honey along the top of a bar in another world, Burny is telling Ty Marshall to face the wall, goddamnit, just face the wall.

They are in a foul little shack. The sounds of clashing machinery are much closer. Ty can also hear screams and sobs and harsh yells and what can only be the whistling crack of whips. They are very near the Big Combination now. Ty has seen it, a great crisscrossing confusion of metal rising into the clouds from a smoking pit about half a mile east. It looks like a madman's conception of a sky-scraper, a Rube Goldberg collection of chutes and cables and belts and platforms, everything run by the marching, staggering children who roll the belts and pull the great levers. Red-tinged smoke rises from it in stinking fumes.

Twice as the golf cart rolled slowly along, Ty at the wheel and Burny leaning askew in the passenger seat with the Taser pointed, squads of freakish green men passed them. Their features were scrambled, their skin plated and reptilian. They wore half-cured leather tunics from which tufts of fur still started in places. Most carried spears; several had whips.

Overseers, Burny said. *They keep the wheels of progress turning.* He began to laugh, but the laugh turned into a groan and the groan into a harsh and breathless shriek of pain.

Good, Ty thought coldly. And then, for the first time employing a favorite word of Ebbie Wexler's: *Die soon, you motherfucker.*

About two miles from the back of Black House, they came to a huge wooden platform on their left. A gantry-like thing jutted up from it. A long post projected out from the top, almost to the road. A number of frayed rope ends dangled from it, twitching in the hot and sulfurous breeze. Under the platform, on dead ground that never felt the sun, were litters of bones and ancient piles of white dust. To one side was a great mound of shoes. Why they'd take the clothes and leave the shoes was a question Ty probably couldn't have answered even had he not been wearing the cap (*sbecial toyz for sbecial boyz*), but a disjointed phrase popped into his head: custom of the country. He had an idea that was something his father sometimes said, but he couldn't be sure. He couldn't even remember his father's face, not clearly.

The gibbet was surrounded by crows. They jostled one another and turned to follow the humming progress of the E-Z-Go. None was the special crow, the one with the name Ty could no longer remember, but he knew why they were here. They were waiting for fresh flesh to pluck, that's what they were doing. Waiting for newly dead eyes to gobble. Not to mention the bare toesies of the shoe-deprived dead.

Beyond the pile of discarded, rotting footwear, a broken track led off to the north, over a fuming hill.

'Station House Road,' Burny said. He seemed to be talking more to himself than to Ty at that point, was perhaps edging into delirium. Yet still the Taser pointed at Ty's neck, never wavering. 'That's where I'm supposed to be taking the special boy.' *Taging the sbecial bouy*. 'That's where the special ones go. Mr Munshun's gone to get the mono. The End-World mono. Once there were two others. Patricia . . . and Blaine. They're gone. Went crazy. Committed suicide.'

Ty drove the cart and remained silent, but he had to believe old Burn-Burn was the one who had gone crazy (crazi*er*, he reminded himself). He knew about monorails, had even ridden one at Disney World in Orlando, but monorails named Blaine and Patricia? That was stupid.

Station House Road fell behind them. Ahead, the rusty red and iron gray of the Big Combination drew closer. Ty could see moving ants on cruelly inclined belts. Children. Some from other worlds, perhaps – worlds adjacent to this one – but many from his own. Kids whose faces appeared for a while on milk cartons and then disappeared forever. Kept a little longer in the hearts of their parents, of course, but eventually growing dusty even there, turning from vivid memories into old photographs. Kids presumed dead, buried somewhere in shallow graves by perverts who had used them and then discarded them. Instead, they were here. Some of them, anyway. *Many* of them. Struggling to yank the levers and turn the wheels and move the belts while the yellow-eyed, green-skinned overseers cracked their whips.

As Ty watched, one of the ant specks fell down the side of the convoluted, steam-wreathed building. He thought he could hear a faint scream. Or perhaps it was a cry of relief?

'Beautiful day,' Burny said faintly. 'I'll enjoy it more when I get something to eat. Having something to eat always . . . always perks me up.' His ancient eyes studied Ty, tightening a little at the corners with sudden warmth. 'Baby butt's the best eatin', but yours won't be bad. Nope, won't be bad at all. He said to take you to the station, but I ain't sure he'd give me my share. My . . . *commission*. Maybe he's honest . . . maybe he's still my friend . . . but I think I'll just take my share first, and make sure. Most agents take their ten percent off the top.' He reached out and poked Ty just below the belt-line. Even through his jeans, the boy could feel the tough, blunt edge of the old man's nail. 'I think I'll take mine off the *bottom*.' A wheezy, painful laugh, and Ty was not exactly displeased to see a bright bubble of blood appear between the old man's cracked lips. 'Off the *bottom*, get it?' The nail poked the side of Ty's buttock again.

'I get it,' Ty said.

'You'll be able to break just as well,' Burny said. 'It's just that when you fart, you'll have to do the old one-cheek sneak *every* time!' More wheezing laughter. Yes, he sounded delirious, all right – delirious or on the verge of it – yet still the tip of the Taser remained rock-steady. 'Keep on going, boy. 'Nother half a mile up the Conger Road. You'll see a little shack with a tin roof, down in a draw. It's on the right. It's a special place. Special to me. Turn in there.'

Ty, with no other choice, obeyed. And now—

'Do what I tell you! Face the fucking wall! Put your hands up and through those loops!'

Ty couldn't define the word *euphemism* on a bet, but he knows calling those metal circlets 'loops' is bullshit. What's hanging from the rear wall are shackles.

Panic flutters in his brain like a flock of small birds, threatening to obscure his thoughts. Ty fights to hold on – fights with grim intensity. If he gives in to panic, starts to holler and scream, he's going to be finished. Either the old man will kill him in the act of carving him up, or the old man's friend will take him away to some awful place Burny calls Din-tah. In either case, Ty will never see his mother and father again. Or French Landing. But if he can keep his head . . . wait for his chance . . .

Ah, but it's hard. The cap he's wearing actually helps a little in this respect – it has a dulling effect that helps hold the panic at bay – but it's still hard. Because he's not the first kid the old man has brought here, no more than he was the first to spend long, slow hours in that cell back at the old man's house. There's a blackened, grease-caked barbecue set up in the left corner of the shed, underneath a tin-plated smoke hole. The grill is hooked up to a couple of gas bottles with LA

RIVIERE PROPANE stenciled on the sides. Hung on the wall are oven mitts, spatulas, tongs, basting brushes, and meat forks. There are scissors and tenderizing hammers and at least four keen-bladed carving knives. One of the knives looks almost as long as a ceremonial sword.

Hanging beside that one is a filthy apron with YOU MAY KISS THE COOK printed on it.

The smell in the air reminds Ty of the VFW picnic his mom and dad took him to the previous Labor Day. Maui Wowie, it had been called, because the people who went were supposed to feel like they were spending the day in Hawaii. There had been a great big barbecue pit in the center of La Follette Park down by the river, tended by women in grass skirts and men wearing loud shirts covered with birds and tropical foliage. Whole pigs had been roasting over a glaring hole in the ground, and the odor had been like the one in this shed. Except the smell in here is stale . . . and old . . . and . . .

And not quite pork, Ty thinks. *It's*—

'I should stand here and jaw at you all day, you louse?'

The Taser gives off a crackling sizzle. Tingling, debilitating pain sinks into the side of Ty's neck. His bladder lets go and he wets his pants. He can't help it. Is hardly aware of it, in truth. Somewhere (in a galaxy far, far away) a hand that is trembling but still terribly strong thrusts Ty toward the back wall and the shackles that have been welded to steel plates about five and a half feet off the ground.

'There!' Burny cries, and gives a tired, hysterical laugh. 'Knew you'd get one for good luck eventually! Smart boy, ain'tcha? Little wisenheimer! Now put your hands through them loops and let's have no more foolishness about it!'

Ty has put out his hands in order to keep himself from crashing face-first into the shed's rear wall. His eyes are less than a foot from the wood, and he is getting a very good look at the old layers of blood that coat it. That *plate* it. The blood has an ancient metallic reek. Beneath his feet, the ground feels spongy. Jellylike. Nasty. This may be an illusion in the physical sense, but Ty knows that what he's feeling is nonetheless quite real. This is corpse ground. The old man may not prepare his terrible meals here every time – may not have that luxury – but this is the place he likes. As he said, it's special to him.

If I let him lock both of my hands into those shackles, Ty thinks, *I've had it. He'll cut me up. And once he starts cutting, he may not be able to stop himself – not for this Mr Munching, not for anyone. So get ready.*

That last is not like one of his own thoughts at all. It's like hearing his mother's voice in his head. His mother, or someone like her. Ty steadies. The flock of panic birds is suddenly gone, and he is as clearheaded as the cap will allow. He knows what he must do. Or try to do.

He feels the nozzle of the Taser slip between his legs and thinks of the snake wriggling across the overgrown driveway, carrying its mouthful of fangs. 'Put your hands through those loops right now, or I'm going to fry your balls like oysters.' *Ersters*, it sounds like.

'Okay,' Ty says. He speaks in a high, whiny voice. He hopes he sounds scared out of his mind. God knows it shouldn't be hard to sound that way. 'Okay, okay, just don't hurt me, I'm doing it now, see? See?'

He puts his hands through the loops. They are big and loose.

'Higher!' The growling voice is still in his ear, but the Taser is gone from between his legs, at least. 'Shove 'em in as far as you can!'

Ty does as he is told. The shackles slide to a point just

above his wrists. His hands are like starfish in the gloom. Behind him, he hears that soft clinking noise again as Burny rummages in his bag. Ty understands. The cap may be scrambling his thoughts a little, but this is too obvious to miss. The old bastard's got handcuffs in there. Handcuffs that have been used many, many times. He'll cuff Ty's wrists above the shackles, and here Ty will stand – or dangle, if he passes out – while the old monster carves him up.

'Now listen,' Burny says. He sounds out of breath, but he also sounds *lively* again. The prospect of a meal has refreshed him, brought back a certain amount of his vitality. 'I'm pointin' this shocker at you with one hand. I'm gonna slip a cuff around your left wrist with the other hand. If you move . . . if you so much as *twitch*, boy . . . you get the juice. Understand?'

Ty nods at the bloodstained wall. 'I won't move,' he gibbers. 'Honest I won't.'

'First one hand, then the other. That's how I do it.' There is a revolting complacency in his voice. The Taser presses between Ty's shoulder blades hard enough to hurt. Grunting with effort, the old man leans over Ty's left shoulder. Ty can smell sweat and blood and age. It *is* like 'Hansel and Gretel,' he thinks, only he has no oven to push his tormentor into.

You know what to do, Judy tells him coldly. *He may not give you a chance, and if he doesn't, he doesn't. But if he does . . .*

A handcuff slips around his left wrist. Burny is grunting softly, repulsively, in Ty's ear. The old man reaches . . . the Taser shifts . . . but not quite far enough. Ty holds still as Burny snaps the handcuff shut and tightens it down. Now Ty's left hand is secured to the shed wall. Dangling down from his left wrist by its steel chain is the cuff Burny intends to put on his right wrist.

The old man, still panting effortfully, moves to the right.

He reaches around Ty's front, groping for the dangling cuff. The Taser is once more digging into Ty's back. If the old man gets hold of the cuff, Ty's goose is probably cooked (in more ways than one). And he almost does. But the cuff slips out of his grip, and instead of waiting for it to pendulum back to where he can grab it, Burny leans farther forward. The bony side of his face is planted against Ty's right shoulder.

And when he leans to get the dangling handcuff, Ty feels the touch of the Taser first lighten, then disappear.

Now! Judy screams inside Ty's head. Or perhaps it is Sophie. Or maybe it's both of them together. *Now, Ty! It's your chance, there won't be another!*

Ty pistons his right arm downward, pulling free of the shackle. It would do him no good to try to shove Burny away from him – the old monster outweighs him by sixty pounds or more – and Ty doesn't try. He pulls away to his left instead, putting excruciating pressure on his shoulder and on his left wrist, which has been locked into the shackle holding it.

'What—' Burny begins, and then Ty's groping right hand has what it wants: the loose, dangling sac of the old man's balls. He squeezes with all the force in his body. He feels the monster's testicles squash toward each other; feels one of them rupture and deflate. Ty shouts, a sound of dismay and horror and savage triumph all mingled together.

Burny, caught entirely by surprise, howls. He tries to pull backward, but Ty has him in a harpy's grip. His hand – so small, so incapable (or so you would think) of any serious defense – has turned into a claw. If ever there was a time to use the Taser, this is it . . . but in his surprise, Burny's hand has sprung open. The Taser lies on the ancient, blood-impacted earth of the shed floor.

'Let go of me! That HURTS! That hurr—'

Before he can finish, Ty yanks forward on the spongy and deflating bag inside the old cotton pants; he yanks with all the force of panic, and something in there *rips*. Burny's words dissolve in a liquid howl of agony. This is more pain than he has ever imagined . . . certainly never in connection with *himself*.

But it is not enough. Judy's voice says it's not, and Ty might know it, anyway. He has hurt the old man – has given him what Ebbie Wexler would undoubtedly call 'a fuckin' rupture' – but it's not enough.

He lets go and turns to his left, pivoting on his shackled hand. He sees the old man swaying before him in the shadows. Beyond him, the golf cart stands in the open door, outlined against a sky filled with clouds and burning smoke. The old monster's eyes are huge and disbelieving, bulging with tears. He gapes at the little boy who has done this.

Soon comprehension will return. When it does, Burny is apt to seize one of the knives from the wall – or perhaps one of the meat forks – and stab his chained prisoner to death, screaming curses and oaths at him as he does so, calling him a monkey, a bastard, a fucking asswipe. Any thought of Ty's great talent will be gone. Any fear of what may happen to Burny himself if Mr Munshun – and the abbalah – is robbed of his prize will also be gone. In truth, Burny is nothing but a psychotic animal, and in another moment his essential nature will break loose and vent itself on this tethered child.

Tyler Marshall, son of Fred and the formidable Judy, does not give Burny this chance. During the last part of the drive he has thought repeatedly of what the old man said about Mr Munshun – *he hurt me, he pulled my guts* – and hoped he might get his own opportunity to do some pulling. Now it's come. Hanging from the shackle with his left arm pulled cruelly up, he shoots his right hand forward. Through the hole in Burny's shirt. Through the hole Henry has made with his switchblade knife. Suddenly Ty has hold of something ropy and wet. He seizes it and pulls a roll of Charles Burnside's intestines out through the rip in his shirt.

Burny's head turns up toward the shed's ceiling. His jaw snaps convulsively, the cords on his wrinkled old neck stand out, and he voices a great, agonized bray. He tries to pull away, which may be the worst thing a man can do when someone has him by the liver and lights. A blue-gray fold of gut, as plump as a sausage and perhaps still trying to digest Burny's last Maxton cafeteria meal, comes out with the audible pop of a champagne cork leaving the neck of its bottle.

Charles 'Chummy' Burnside's last words: *'LET GO, YOU LITTLE PIIIIG!'*

Tyler does not let go. Instead he shakes the loop of intestine furiously from side to side like a terrier with a rat in its jaws. Blood and yellowish fluid spray out of the hole in Burny's midsection. *'Die!'* Tyler hears himself screaming. *'Die, you old fuck, GO ON AND DIE!'*

Burny staggers back another step. His mouth drops open, and part of an upper plate tumbles out and onto the dirt. He is staring down at two loops of his own innards, stretching like gristle from the gaping red-black front of his shirt to the awful child's right hand. And he sees an even more terrible thing: a kind of white glow has surrounded the boy. It is feeding him more strength than he otherwise would have had. Feeding him the strength to pull Burny's living guts right out of his body and how it *hurt*, how it *hurt*, how it dud dud dud *hurrrrr*—

'Die!' the boy screams in a shrill and breaking voice. *'Oh please, WON'T YOU EVER DIE?'*

And at last – at long, long last – Burny collapses to his knees. His dimming gaze fixes on the Taser and he reaches one trembling hand toward it. Before it can get far, the light of consciousness leaves Burny's eyes. He hasn't endured enough pain to equal even the hundredth part of the suffering he has inflicted, but it's all his ancient body can take. He makes a harsh cawing sound deep in his throat, then tumbles over backward, more intestines pulling out of his lower abdomen as he does so. He is unaware of this or of anything else.

Carl Bierstone, also known as Charles Burnside, also known as 'Chummy' Burnside, is dead.

For over thirty seconds, nothing moves. Tyler Marshall is alive but at first only hangs from the axis of his shackled left arm, still clutching a loop of Burny's intestine in his right hand. Clutching it in a death grip. At last some sense of awareness informs his features. He gets his feet under him and scrambles upright, easing the all but intolerable pressure on the socket of his left shoulder. He suddenly becomes aware that his right arm is splashed with gore all the way to the biceps, and that he's got a handful of dead man's insides. He lets go of them and bolts for the door, not remembering that he's still chained to the wall until he is yanked back, the socket of his shoulder once more bellowing with pain.

You've done well, the voice of Judy-Sophie whispers. *But you have to get out of here, and quick.*

Tears start to roll down his dirty, pallid face again, and Ty begins to scream at the top of his voice.

'Help me! Somebody help me! I'm in the shed! I'M IN THE SHED!'

Out in front of the Sand Bar, Doc stays where he is, with his scoot rumbling between his legs, but Beezer turns his off, levers the stand into place with one booted heel, and walks over to Jack, Dale, and Fred. Jack has taken charge of the wrapped object Ty's father has brought them. Fred, meanwhile, has gotten hold of Jack's shirt. Dale tries to restrain the man, but as far as Fred Marshall's concerned, there are now only two people in the world: him and Hollywood Jack Sawyer.

'It was him, wasn't it? It was Ty. *That was my boy, I heard him!*'

'Yes,' Jack says. 'It certainly was and you certainly did.' He's gone rather pale, Beezer sees, but is otherwise calm. It's absolutely not bothering him that the missing boy's father has yanked his shirt out of his pants. No, all Jack's attention is on the wrapped package.

'What in God's name is going on here?' Dale asks plaintively. He looks at Beezer. 'Do *you* know?'

'The kid's in a shed somewhere,' Beezer says. 'Am I right about that?'

'Yes,' Jack says. Fred abruptly lets go of Jack's shirt and staggers backward, sobbing. Jack pays no attention to him and makes no effort to tuck in the tail of his crumpled shirt. He's still looking at the package. He half-expects sugar-packet stamps, but no, this is just a case of plain old metered mail. Whatever it is, it's been mailed Priority to Mr Tyler Marshall, 16 Robin Hood Lane, French Landing. The return address has been stamped in red: Mr George Rathbun, KDCU, 4 Peninsula Drive, French Landing. Below this, stamped in large black letters:

EVEN A BLIND MAN CAN SEE THAT COULEE COUNTRY LOVES THE BREWER BASH!

'Henry, you never quit, do you?' Jack murmurs. Tears sting his eyes. The idea of life without his old friend hits him all over again, leaves him feeling helpless and lost and stupid and hurt.

'What about Uncle Henry?' Dale asks. 'Jack, Uncle Henry's *dead*.'

Jack's no longer so sure of that, somehow.

'Let's go,' Beezer says. 'We got to get that kid. He's alive, but he ain't safe. I got that clear as a bell. Let's go for it. We can figure the rest out later.'

But Jack – who has not just heard Tyler's shout but has, for a moment, seen through Tyler's eyes – doesn't have much to figure out. In fact, figuring out now comes down to only one thing. Ignoring both Beezer and Dale, he steps toward Ty's weeping father.

'Fred.'

Fred goes on sobbing.

'Fred, if you ever want to see your boy again, you get hold of yourself right now and listen to me.'

Fred looks up, red eyes streaming. The ridiculously small baseball cap still perches on his head.

'What's in this, Fred?'

'It must be a prize in that contest George Rathbun runs every summer – the Brewer Bash. But I don't know how Ty could have won something in the first place. A couple of weeks ago he was pissing and moaning about how he forgot to enter. He even asked if maybe *I'd* entered the contest for him, and I kind of . . . well, I snapped at him.' Fresh tears begin running down Fred's stubbly cheeks at the memory. 'That was around the time Judy was getting . . . strange . . . I was worried about her and I just kind of . . . snapped at him. You know?' Fred's chest heaves. He makes a watery hitching sound and his Adam's apple bobs up and down. He wipes an arm across his eyes. 'And Ty . . . all he said was, "That's all right, Dad." He didn't get mad at me, didn't sulk or anything. Because that's just the kind of boy he was. That he *is*.'

'How did you know to bring it to me?'

'Your friend called,' Fred says. 'He told me the postman had brought something and I had to bring it to you here, right away. Before you left. He called you—'

'He called me Travelin' Jack.'

Fred Marshall looks at him wonderingly. 'That's right.'

'All right.' Jack speaks gently, almost absently. 'We're going to get your boy now.'

'I'll come. I've got my deer rifle in the truck—'

'And that's where it's going to stay. Go home. Make a place for him. Make a place for your wife. And let us do what we have to do.' Jack looks first at Dale, then at Beezer. 'Come on,' he says. 'Let's roll.'

Five minutes later, the FLPD chief's car is speeding west on Highway 35. Directly ahead, like an honor guard, Beezer and Doc are riding side by side, the sun gleaming on the chrome of their bikes. Trees in full summer leaf crowd close to the road on either side.

Jack can feel the buzzing that is Black House's signature starting to ramp up in his head. He has discovered he can wall that noise off if he has to, keep it from spreading and blanketing his entire thought process with static, but it's still damned unpleasant. Dale has given him one of the Ruger .357s that are the police department's service weapons; it's now stuck in the waistband of his blue jeans. He was surprised at how good the weight of it felt in his hand, almost like a homecoming. Guns may not be of much use in the world behind Black House, but they have to get there first, don't they? And according to Beezer and Doc, the approach is not exactly undefended.

'Dale, do you have a pocketknife?'

'Glove compartment,' Dale says. He glances at the long package on Jack's lap. 'I presume you want to open that.'

'You presume right.'

'Can you explain a few things while you do it? Like whether or not, once we get inside Black House, we can expect Charles Burnside to jump out of a secret door with an axe and start—'

'Chummy Burnside's days of jumping out at folks are all over,' Jack says. 'He's dead. Ty Marshall killed him. That's what hit us outside the Sand Bar.'

The chief's car swerves so extravagantly – all the way across to the left side of the road – that Beezer looks back for a moment, startled at what he's just seen in his rearview. Jack gives him a hard, quick wave – *Go on, don't worry about us* – and Beez faces forward again.

'*What?*' Dale gasps.

'The old bastard was hurt, but I have an idea that Ty still did one hell of a brave thing. Brave and crafty both.' Jack is thinking that Henry softened Burnside up and Ty *finished* him up. What George Rathbun would undoubtedly have called a honey of a double play.

'How—'

'Disemboweled him. With his bare hands. *Hand*. I'm pretty sure the other one's chained up somehow.'

Dale is silent for a moment, watching the motorcyclists ahead of him as they lean into a curve with their hair streaming out from beneath their token gestures at obeying Wisconsin's helmet law. Jack, meanwhile, is slitting open brown wrapping paper and revealing a long white carton beneath. Something rolls back and forth inside.

'You're telling me that a ten-year-old boy disemboweled a serial killer. A serial *cannibal*. You somehow know this.'

'Yes.'

'I find that extremely difficult to believe.'

'Based on the father, I guess I can understand that. Fred's . . .' *A wimp* is what comes to mind, but that is both unfair and untrue. 'Fred's tenderhearted,' Jack says. 'Judy, though . . .'

'Backbone,' Dale says. 'She *does* have that, I'm told.'

Jack gives his friend a humorless grin. He's got the buzzing confined to a small portion of his brain, but in that one small portion it's shrieking like a fire alarm. They're almost there. 'She certainly does,' he tells Dale. 'And so does the boy. He's . . . brave.' What Jack has almost said is *He's a prince*.

'*And* he's alive.'

'Yes.'

'Chained in a shed somewhere.'

'Right.'

'Behind Burnside's house.'

'Uh-huh.'

'If I've got the geography right, that places him somewhere in the woods near Schubert and Gale.'

Jack smiles and says nothing.

'All right,' Dale says heavily. 'What have I got wrong?'

'It doesn't matter. Which is good, because it's impossible to explain.' Jack just hopes Dale's mind is screwed down tightly, because it's apt to take one hell of a pounding in the next hour or so.

His fingernail slits the tape holding the box closed. He opens it. There's bubble wrap beneath. Jack pulls it out, tosses it into the footwell, and looks at Ty Marshall's Brewer Bash prize

– a prize he won even though he apparently never entered the contest.

Jack lets out a little sigh of awe. There's enough kid left in him to react to the object that he sees, even though he never played the game once he was too old for Little League. Because there's something about a bat, isn't there? Something that speaks to our primitive beliefs about the purity of struggle and the strength of our team. The home team. Of the right and the *white*. Surely Bernard Malamud knew it; Jack has read *The Natural* a score of times, always hoping for a different ending (and when the movie offered him one, he hated it), always loving the fact that Roy Hobbs named his cudgel Wonderboy. And never mind the critics with all their stuffy talk about the Arthurian legend and phallic symbols; sometimes a cigar is just a smoke and sometimes a bat is just a bat. A big stick. Something to hit home runs with.

'Holy wow,' Dale says, glancing over. And he looks *younger*. Boyish. Eyes wide. So Jack isn't the only one, it seems. 'Whose bat?'

Jack lifts it carefully from the box. Written up the barrel in black Magic Marker is this message:

To Tyler Marshall   Keep Slugging! Your pal, Richie Sexson

'Richie Sexson,' Jack says. 'Who's Richie Sexson?'

'Big slugger for the Brewers,' Dale says.

'Is he as good as Roy Hobbs?'

'Roy—' Then Dale grins. 'Oh, in that movie! Robert Redford, right? No I don't think—Hey, what are you doing?'

Still holding the bat (in fact he almost bashes Dale in the right cheekbone with the end of it), Jack reaches over and honks the horn. 'Pull over,' he says. 'This is it. Those dopes were out here only yesterday and they're going right past it.'

Dale pulls over on the shoulder, brings the cruiser to a jerky stop, and puts it in park. When he looks over at Jack, his face has gone remarkably pale. 'Oh man, Jack – I don't feel so good. Maybe it was breakfast. Christ, I hope I'm not going to start puking.'

'That buzzing you hear in your head, is that from breakfast?' Jack inquires.

Dale's eyes go wide. 'How do you—'

'Because I hear it, too. And feel it in my stomach. It's not your breakfast. It's Black House.' Jack holds out the squeeze bottle. 'Go on. Dab some more around your nostrils. Get some right up in. You'll feel better.' Projecting absolute confidence. Because it's not about secret weapons or secret formulas; it's certainly not about honey. It's about *belief*. They have left the realm of the rational and have entered the realm of slippage. Jack knows it for certain as soon as he opens the car door.

Ahead of him, the bikes swerve and come back. Beezer, an impatient look on his face, is shaking his head: *No, no, not here.*

Dale joins Jack at the front of the car. His face is still pale, but the skin around and below his nose is shiny with honey, and he looks steady enough on his feet. 'Thanks, Jack. This is *so* much better. I don't know how putting honey around my nose could affect my *ears*, but the buzzing's better, too. It's nothing but a low drone.'

'Wrong place!' Beezer bawls as he pulls his Harley up to the front of the cruiser.

'Nope,' Jack says calmly, looking at the unbroken woods. Sunlight on green leaves contrasting with crazy black zigzags of shadow. Everything trembling and unsteady, making mock of perspective. 'This is it. The hideout of Mr Munshun and the Black House Gang, as the Duke never said.'

Now Doc's bike adds to the din as he pulls up next to Beezer. 'Beez is right! We were just out here *yesterday*, y'damn fool! Don't you think we know what we're talking about?'

'This is just scrap woods on both sides,' Dale chimes in. He points across the road where, fifty yards or so southeast of their position, yellow police tape flutters from a pair of trees. 'That's the lane to Ed's Eats, there. The place we want is probably beyond it—'

Even though you know it's here, Jack thinks. Marvels, really. *Why else have you gone and smeared yourself with honey like Pooh-bear on a lucky day?*

He shifts his gaze to Beezer and Doc, who are also looking remarkably unwell. Jack opens his mouth to speak to them . . . and something flutters at the upper edge of his vision. He restrains his natural impulse to look up and define the source of that movement. Something – probably the old Travelin' Jack part of him – thinks it would be a very bad idea to do that. Something is watching them already. Better if it doesn't know it's been spotted.

He puts the Richie Sexson bat down, leaning it against the side of the idling cruiser. He takes the honey from Dale and holds it out to the Beez. 'Here you go,' he says, 'lather up.'

'There's no *point* in it, you goddamn fool!' Beezer cries in exasperation. *'This . . . ain't . . . the place!'*

'Your nose is bleeding,' Jack says mildly. 'Just a little. Yours too, Doc.'

Doc wipes a finger under his nose and looks at the red smear, startled. He starts, 'But I *know* this isn't—'

That flutter again, at the top of Jack's vision. He ignores it and points straight ahead. Beezer, Doc, and Dale all look, and Dale's the first one to see it. 'I'll be damned,' he says softly. 'A NO TRESPASSING sign. Was it there before?'

'Yep,' Jack says. 'Been there for thirty years or more, I'd guess.'

'Fuck,' Beez says, and begins rubbing honey around his nose. He pokes generous wads of the stuff up his nostrils; resinous drops gleam in his red-brown Viking's beard. 'We woulda gone right on, Doctor. All the way to town. Hell, maybe all the way to Rapid City, South Dakota.' He hands the honey to Doc and grimaces at Jack. 'I'm sorry, man. We should have known. No excuses.'

'Where's the driveway?' Dale's asking, and then: 'Oh. *There* it is. I could have *sworn*—'

'That there was nothing there, I know,' Jack says. He's smiling. Looking at his friends. At the Sawyer Gang. He is certainly *not* looking at the black rags fluttering restively at the upper periphery of his vision, nor down at his waist, where his hand is slowly drawing the Ruger .357 from his waistband. He was always one of the best out there. He'd only won badges a couple of times when it was shooting from a stand, but when it came to the draw-and-fire competition, he did quite well. Top five, usually. Jack has no idea if this is a skill he's retained, but he thinks he's going to find out right now.

Smiling at them, watching Doc swab his schnozz with honey, Jack says in a conversational voice: 'Something's watching us. Don't look up. I'm going to try and shoot it.'

'What is it?' Dale asks, smiling back. He doesn't look up, only straight ahead. Now he can quite clearly see the shadowy lane that must lead to Burnside's house. It wasn't there, he could have sworn it wasn't, but now it is.

'It's a pain in the ass,' Jack says, and suddenly swings the Ruger up, locking both hands around the stock. He's firing almost before he sees with his eyes, and he catches the great dark crow crouched on the overhanging branch of an oak tree entirely by surprise. It gives one loud, shocked cry – 'AWWWWK!' – and then it is torn apart on its roost. Blood flies against the faded blue summer sky. Feathers flutter down in clumps as dark as midnight shadows. And a body. It hits the shoulder in front of the lane with a heavy thud. One dark, glazing eye peers at Jack Sawyer with an expression of surprise.

'Did you fire five or six?' Beezer asks in a tone of deep awe. 'It was so fast I couldn't tell.'

'All of them,' Jack says. He guesses he's still not too bad at draw-and-fire after all.

'That's one big fucking crow,' Doc says.

'It's not just any crow,' Jack tells him. 'It's Gorg.' He advances to the blasted body lying on the dirt. 'How you doin', fella? How do you feel?' He spits on Gorg, a luscious thick lunger. 'That's for luring the kids,' he says. Then, suddenly, he boots the crow's corpse into the underbrush. It flies in a limp arc, the wings wrapping around the body like a shroud. 'And that's for fucking with Irma's mother.'

They are looking at him, all three of them, with identical expressions of stunned awe. Almost of fear. It's a look that makes Jack tired, although he supposes he must accept it. He can remember his old friend Richard Sloat looking at him the same way, once Richard realized that what he called 'Seabrook Island stuff' wasn't confined to Seabrook Island.

'Come on,' Jack says. 'Everybody in the car. Let's get it done.' Yes, and they must move quickly because a certain one-eyed gent will shortly be looking for Ty, too. Mr Munshun. *Eye of the King,* Jack thinks. *Eye of the abbalah. That's what Judy meant – Mr Munshun. Whoever or whatever he really is.*

'Don't like leaving the bikes out here by the side of the road, man,' Beezer says. 'Anybody could come along and—'

'Nobody will see them,' Jack tells him. 'Three or four cars have gone by since we parked, and no one's so much as looked over at us. And you know why.'

'We've already started to cross over, haven't we?' Doc asks. 'This is the edge of it. The border.'

'Opopanax,' Jack says. The word simply pops out.

'Huh?'

Jack picks up Ty's Richie Sexson bat and gets in on the passenger side of the cruiser. 'It means let's go,' he says. 'Let's get it done.'

And so the Sawyer Gang takes its last ride – up the wooded, poisonous lane that leads to Black House. The strong afternoon light quickly fades to the sullen glow of an overcast November evening. In the close-pressing trees on either side, dark shapes twine and crawl and sometimes fly. They don't matter, much, Jack reckons; they are only phantoms.

'You gonna reload that Roogalator?' Beezer asks from the back seat.

'Nope,' Jack says, looking at the Ruger without much interest. 'Think it's done its job.'

'What should we be ready for?' Dale asks in a thin voice.

'Anything,' Jack replies. He favors Dale Gilbertson with a humorless grin. Ahead of them is a house that won't keep its shape but whirls and wavers in the most distressing way. Sometimes it seems no bigger than a humble ranch house; a blink, and it seems to be a ragged monolith that blots out the entire sky; another blink and it appears to be a low, uneven construction stretching back under the forest canopy for what could be miles. It gives off a low hum that sounds like voices.

'Be ready for anything at all.'

28

But at first there is nothing.

The four of them get out and stand in front of Dale's cruiser, looking for all the world like men posing for the kind of group photo that will eventually show up on someone's den wall. Only the photographer would be on Black House's porch – that's the way they're facing – and the porch is empty except for the second NO TRESPASSING sign, which leans against a peeling newel post. Someone has drawn a skull on it with a Magic Marker or grease pencil. Burny? Some intrepid teenager who came all the way up to the house on a dare? Dale did some crazy things when he was seventeen, risked his life with a spray-paint can more than once, but he still finds that hard to believe.

The air is sullen and silent, as if before a thunderstorm. It stinks, too, but the honey seems to filter the worst of that out. In the woods, something makes a thick sound Dale has never heard before. *Groo-oooo.*

'What's that?' he asks Jack.

'I don't know,' Jack replies.

Doc says, 'I've heard bull gators. That's what they sound like when they're feeling horny.'

'This isn't the Everglades,' Dale says.

Doc gives him a thin smile. 'It ain't Wisconsin anymore, either, Toto. Or maybe you didn't notice.'

Dale has noticed plenty. There's the way the house won't hold its shape, for one thing – the way it sometimes seems *enormous*, as if it is many houses somehow all overlaid. A city perhaps the size of London folded under a single weird roof. And then there are the trees. There are old oaks and pines, there are birches like skinny ghosts, there are red maples – all of them indigenous to the area – but he also sees twisted, rooty growths that look like mutated banyan trees. And are these *moving*? Christ, Dale hopes not. But whether they are or not, they're *whispering*. He's almost sure of that. He can hear their words slithering through the buzzing in his head, and they're not encouraging words, not by a longshot.

Killyew . . . eatchew . . . hatechew . . .

'Where's the dog?' Beezer asks. He's holding his 9mm in one hand. 'Here, doggy! Got something yummy for you! Hurry and get it!'

Instead, that guttural growl drifts out of the woods again, this time closer: *GROO-OOOOO!* And the trees whisper. Dale looks up at the house, watches it suddenly stack floors into a sky that has gone white and cold, and vertigo rolls through his head like a wave of warm grease. He has a faint sensation of Jack grabbing his elbow to steady him. A little help there, but not enough; French Landing's chief of police twists to the left and vomits.

'Good,' Jack says. 'Get it out. Get rid of it. What about you, Doc? Beez?'

The Thunder Two tell him they're okay. For now it's true, but Beezer doesn't know how long equilibrium is going to last. His stomach is churning, low and slow. *Well, so what if I blow my groceries in there?* he thinks. *According to Jack, Burnside's dead, he won't mind.*

Jack leads them up the porch steps, pausing to boot the rusted NO TRESPASSING sign with its death's-head graffiti over the side and into a clutch of weeds that close over it at once, like a greedy hand. Dale is reminded of how Jack spit on the crow. His friend seems different now, younger and stronger. 'But we *are* going to trespass,' Jack says. 'We're going to trespass our *asses* off.'

At first, however, it seems they will not. The front door of Black House isn't just locked. There's no crack at all between the door and the jamb. In fact, once they're close up, the door looks painted on, a trompe l'oeil.

Behind them, in the woods, something screams. Dale jumps. The scream rises to an excruciating high note, breaks into a peal of maniacal laughter, and is suddenly gone.

'Natives are fuckin' restless,' Doc comments.

'Want to try a window?' Beezer asks Jack.

'Nope. We're going in the front way.'

Jack has been raising the Richie Sexson bat as he speaks. Now he lowers it, looking puzzled. There is a droning sound from behind them, quickly growing louder. And the daylight, thin already in this strange forest dell, seems to be weakening even further.

'What now?' Beezer asks, turning back toward the drive and the parked cruiser. He's holding the 9mm up by his right ear. 'What the—' And then he falls silent. The gun sags outward and downward. His mouth drops open.

'Holy shit,' Doc says quietly.

Dale, even more quietly: 'Is this your doing, Jack? If it is, you really *have* been hiding your light under a bushel.'

The light has dimmed because the clearing in front of

Black House has now acquired a canopy of bees. More are streaming in from the lane, a brownish-gold comet tail. They give off a sleepy, benevolent droning sound that drowns out the harsh fire-alarm buzz of the house entirely. The hoarse gator thing in the woods falls silent, and the flickering shapes in the trees disappear.

Jack's mind is suddenly filled with thoughts and images of his mother: Lily dancing, Lily pacing around behind one of the cameras before a big scene with a cigarette clamped between her teeth, Lily sitting at the living-room window and looking out as Patsy Cline sings 'Crazy Arms.'

In another world, of course, she'd been another kind of queen, and what is a queen without a loyal retinue?

Jack Sawyer looks at the vast cloud of bees – millions of them, perhaps billions; every hive in the Midwest must be empty this afternoon – and he smiles. This changes the shape of his eyes and the tears that have been growing there spill down his cheeks. *Hello,* he thinks. *Hello there, boys.*

The low pleasant hum of the bees seems to change slightly, as if in answer. Perhaps it's only his imagination.

'What are they *for,* Jack?' Beezer asks. His voice is resonant with awe.

'I don't exactly know,' Jack says. He turns back to the door, raises the bat, and knocks it once, hard, against the wood. '*Open!*' he cries. '*I demand it in the name of Queen Laura DeLoessian! And in the name of my mother!*'

There is a high-pitched crack, so loud and piercing that Dale and Beez both draw back, wincing. Beezer actually covers his ears. A gap appears at the top of the door and races along it left to right. At the door's upper right corner, the gap pivots and plunges straight down, creating a crack through which a musty draft blows. Jack catches a whiff of something both sour and familiar: the deathsmell they first encountered at Ed's Eats.

Jack reaches for the knob and tries it. It turns freely in his hand. He opens the way to Black House.

But before he can invite them in, Doc Amberson begins to scream.

Someone – maybe it's Ebbie, maybe T.J., maybe goofy old Ronnie Metzger – is yanking Ty's arm. It hurts like a son of a gun, but that's not the worst. The arm yanker is also making this weird humming noise that seems to vibrate deep inside his head. There's a clanking noise as well

(*the Big Combination, that's the Big Combination*) but that humming . . .! Man, that humming *hurts*.

'Quit it,' Ty mumbles. 'Quit it, Ebbie or I'll—'

Faint screams seep through that electric buzzing sound, and Ty Marshall opens his eyes. There's no merciful period of grace when he's unsure about where he is or what's happened to him. It all comes back with the force of some terrible picture – a car accident with dead people lying around, say – that is shoved into your face before you can look away.

He'd held on until the old man was dead; had obeyed the voice of his mother and kept his head. But once he started shouting for help, panic had come back and swallowed him. Or maybe it was shock. Or both. In any case, he'd passed out while still screaming for help. How long has he hung here by his shackled left arm, unconscious? It's impossible to tell from the light spilling through the shed door; that seems unchanged. So do the various clankings and groanings of the huge machine, and Ty understands that it goes on forever, along with the screams of the children and the crack of the whips as the unspeakable guards press the work ever onward. The Big Combination never shuts down. It runs on blood and terror and never takes a day off.

But that buzzing – that juicy electric buzzing, like the world's biggest Norelco razor – what the hell is that?

Mr Munshun's gone to get the mono. Burny's voice in his head. A vile whisper. *The End-World mono.*

A terrible dismay steals into Ty's heart. He has no doubt at all that what he hears is that very monorail, even now pulling under the canopy at the end of Station House Road. Mr Munshun will look for his boy, his sbecial bouy, and when he doesn't see him (nor Burn-Burn, either), will he come searching?

'Course he will,' Ty croaks. 'Oh boy. Suck an elf.'

He looks up at his left hand. It would be so easy to yank it back through the oversized shackle if not for the handcuff. He yanks downward several times anyway, but the cuff only clashes against the shackle. The other cuff, the one Burny was reaching for when Ty grabbed his balls, dangles and twitches, making the boy think of the gibbet at this end of Station House Road.

That eye-watering, tooth-rattling buzz suddenly cuts out.

He's shut it down. Now he's looking for me in the station, making sure I'm not there. And when he is *sure, what then? Does he know about this place? Sure he does.*

Ty's dismay is turning into an icy chill of horror. Burny would deny it. Burny would say that the shack down here in this dry wash was his secret, a place special to him. In his lunatic arrogance, it would never have occurred to him how well that mistaken idea might serve his supposed friend's purpose.

His mother speaks in Ty's head again, and this time he's reasonably sure it really *is* his mother. *You can't depend on anyone else. They might come in time, but they might not. You have to assume they won't. You have to get out of this yourself.*

But *how?*

Ty looks at the twisted body of the old man, lying on the bloody dirt with his head almost out the door. The thought of Mr Munshun tries to intrude, Burny's friend hurrying down Station House Road even now (or maybe driving in his own E-Z-Go golf cart), wanting to scoop him up and take him to the abbalah. Tyler pushes the image away. It will lead him back to panic, and he can't afford any more of that. He's all out of time.

'I can't reach him,' Ty says. 'If the key's in his pocket, I'm finished. Case closed, game over, zip up your f—'

His eye happens on something lying on the floor. It's the sack the old man was carrying. The one with the cap in it. And the handcuffs.

If the handcuffs were in it, maybe the key's in there, too.

Ty reaches forward with his left foot, stretching as far as he can. It's no good. He can't quite reach the bag. He's at least four inches short. Four inches short and Mr Munshun is coming, coming.

Ty can almost smell him.

Doc shrieks and shrieks, distantly aware that the others are shouting at him to stop, it's all right, there's nothing to be afraid of, distantly aware that he is hurting his throat, probably making it bleed. Those things don't matter. What matters is that when Hollywood swung open the front door of Black House, he exposed the official greeter.

The official greeter is Daisy Temperly, Doc's brown-eyed girl. She's wearing a pretty pink dress. Her skin is pale as paper, except on the right side of her forehead, where a flap of skin falls down, exposing the red skull beneath.

'Come in, Doc,' Daisy says. 'We can talk about how you killed me. And you can sing. You can sing to me.' She smiles. The smile becomes a grin. The grin exposes a mouthful of bulging vampire teeth. 'You can sing to me *forever*.'

Doc takes a blunder-step backward, turns to flee, and that is when Jack grabs him and shakes him. Doc Amberson is a hefty fellow – two-sixty out of the shower, more like two-eighty when dressed in full Road Warrior regalia as he is now – but Jack shakes him easily, snapping the big man's head back and forth. Doc's long hair flops and flies.

'They're all illusions,' Jack says. 'Picture-shows designed to keep out unwanted guests like us. I don't know what you saw, Doc, but it's not there.'

Doc looks cautiously past Jack's shoulder. For a moment he sees a pink, diminishing whirl – it's like the coming of the devil dog, only backward – and then it's gone. He looks up at Jack. Tears are rolling slowly down his sunburned face.

'I didn't mean to kill her,' he says. 'I *loved* her. But I was tired that night. Very tired. Do you know about being tired, Hollywood?'

'Yes,' Jack says. 'And if we get out of this, I intend to sleep for a week. But for now . . .' He looks from Doc to Beezer. From Beezer to Dale. 'We're going to see more stuff. The house will use your worst memories against you: the things you did wrong, the people you hurt. But on the whole, I'm encouraged. I think a lot of the poison went out of this place when Burny died. All we have to do is find our way through to the other side.'

'Jack,' Dale says. He is standing in the doorway, in the very spot where Daisy greeted her old physician. His eyes are very large.

'What?'

'Finding our way through . . . that might be easier said than done.'

They gather around him. Beyond the door is a gigantic circular foyer, a place so big it makes Jack think fleetingly of St Peter's Basilica. On the floor is an acre of poison-green carpet entwined with scenes of torture and blasphemy. Doors open off this room everywhere. In addition, Jack counts four sets of criss-crossing stairways. He blinks and there are six. Blinks again and there are a dozen, as bewildering to the eye as an Escher drawing.

He can hear the deep idiot drone that is the voice of Black House. He can hear something else, as well: laughter.

Come in, Black House is telling them. *Come in and wander these rooms forever.*

Jack blinks and sees a *thousand* stairways, some moving, bulging in and out. Doors stand open on galleries of paintings, galleries of sculpture, on whirling vortexes, on emptiness.

'What do we do now?' Dale asks bleakly. 'What the hell do we do now?'

Ty has never seen Burny's friend, but as he hangs from the shackle, he finds he can imagine him quite easily. In this world, Mr Munshun is a real creature . . . but not a human being. Ty sees a shuffling, busy figure in a black suit and a flowing red tie bustling down Station House Road. This creature has a vast white face dominated by a red mouth and a single blurry eye. The abbalah's emissary and chief deputy looks, in the gaze of Ty's imagination, like Humpty-Dumpty gone bad. It wears a vest buttoned with bones.

Got to get out of here. Got to get that bag . . . but how?

He looks at Burny again. At the hideous tangle of Burny's spilled guts. And suddenly the answer comes. He stretches his foot out again, but this time not toward the bag. He hooks the toe of his sneaker under a dirt-smeared loop of Burny's intestines, instead. He lifts it, pivots, and then kicks softly. The loop of gut leaves the toe of his sneaker.

And loops over the leather bag.

So far, so good. Now if he can only drag it close enough to get his foot on it.

Trying not to think of the stocky, hurrying figure with the grotesquely long face, Ty gropes out with his foot again. He gets it under the dirty snarl of intestine and begins to pull, slowly and with infinite care.

'It's impossible,' Beezer says flatly. 'Nothing can be this big. You know that, don't you?'

Jack takes a deep breath, lets it out, takes another, and speaks a single word in a low, firm voice.

'Dee-*yamber*?' Beez asks suspiciously. 'What the hell's dee-*yamber*?'

Jack doesn't bother answering. From the vast dark cloud of droning bees hanging over the clearing (Dale's cruiser is now nothing but a furry black-gold lump in front of the porch), a single bee emerges. It – *she*, for this is undoubtedly a queen bee – flies between Dale and Doc, pauses for a moment in front of Beezer, as if considering him (or considering the honey with which he has generously lathered himself), and then hovers in front of Jack. She is plump and aerodynamically unsound and ludicrous and somehow absolutely wonderful. Jack lifts a finger like a professor about to make a point or a bandleader about to deliver the downbeat. The bee lights on the end of it.

'Are you from her?' He asks this question in a low voice – too low for the others to hear, even Beezer, who is standing right next to him. Jack isn't quite sure who he means. His mother? Laura DeLoessian? Judy? Sophie? Or is there some other She, a counterbalancing force to the Crimson King? This somehow feels right, but he supposes he'll never know for sure.

In any case, the bee only looks at him with her wide black eyes, wings blurring. And Jack realizes that these are questions to which he needs no answer. He has been a sleepyhead, but now he's up, he's out of bed. This house is huge and deep, a place stacked with vileness and layered with secrets, but what of that? He has Ty's prize bat, he has friends, he has *d'yamba*, and here is the Queen of the Bees. Those things are enough. He's good to go. Better – perhaps best of all – he's *glad* to go.

Jack raises the tip of his finger to his mouth and blows the bee gently into Black House's foyer. She circles aimlessly for a moment, and then zips off to the left and through a door with an oddly bloated, obese shape.

'Come on,' Jack says. 'We're in business.'

The other three exchange uneasy glances, then follow him into what has clearly been their destiny all along.

It is impossible to say how long the Sawyer Gang spends in Black House, that hole which spewed the slippery stuff into French Landing and the surrounding towns. It is likewise impossible to say with any clarity what they see there. In a very real sense, touring Black House is like touring the brain of a deranged madman, and in such a mental framework we can expect to find no plan for the future or memory of the past. In the brain of a madman only the fuming present exists, with its endless shouting urges, paranoid speculations, and grandiose assumptions. So it is not surprising that the things they see in Black House should fade from their minds almost as soon as they are gone from their eyes, leaving behind only vague whispers of unease that might be the distant cry of the opopanax. This amnesia is merciful.

The queen bee leads them, and the other bees follow in a swarm that discolors the air with its vastness and shivers through rooms that have been silent for centuries (for surely we understand – intuitively if not logically – that Black House existed long before Burny built its most recent node in French Landing). At one point the quartet descends a staircase of green glass. In the abyss below the steps, they see circling birds like vultures with the white, screaming faces of lost babies. In a long, narrow room like a Pullman car, living cartoons – two rabbits, a fox, and a stoned-looking frog wearing white gloves – sit around a table catching and eating what appear to be fleas. They are *cartoons*, 1940s-era black-and-white *cartoons*, and it hurts Jack's eyes to look at them because they are also real. The rabbit tips him a knowing wink as the Sawyer Gang goes by, and in the eye that doesn't close Jack sees flat murder. There is an empty salon filled with voices shouting in some foreign language that sounds like French but isn't. There is a room filled with vomitous green jungle and lit by a sizzling tropical sun. Hanging from one of the trees is a vast cocoon that appears to hold a baby dragon still wrapped in its own wings. 'That can't be a dragon,' Doc Amberson says in a weirdly reasonable voice. 'They either come from eggs or the teeth of other dragons. Maybe both.' They walk down a long corridor that slowly rounds itself off, becomes a tunnel, and then drops them down a long and greasy slide as crazy percussion beats from unseen speakers. To Jack it sounds like Cozy Cole, or maybe Gene Krupa. The sides fall away, and for a moment they are sliding over a chasm that literally seems to have no bottom. 'Steer with your hands and feet!' Beezer shouts. 'If you don't want to go over the side, STEER!' They are finally spilled off in what Dale calls the Dirt Room. They struggle over vast piles of filth-smelling earth under a rusty tin ceiling festooned with bare light bulbs. Platoons of tiny greenish-white spiders school back and forth like fish. By the time they reach the far side, they're all panting and out of breath, their shoes muddy, their clothes filthy. There are three doors here. Their leader is buzzing and doing Immelmann turns in front of the one in the middle. 'No way,' Dale says. 'I want to trade for what's behind the curtain.'

Jack tells him he's got a future in stand-up comedy, no doubt about it, and then opens the door the bee has chosen for them. Behind it is a huge automated laundry, which Beezer immediately dubs the Hall of Cleanliness. Bunched together, they follow the bee down a humid corridor lined with sudsing washers and humming, shuddering dryers. The air smells like baked bread. The washers – each with a single glaring port-holed eye – are stacked up to a height of fifty feet or more. Above them, in an ocean of dusty air, pigeons flock in restless currents. Every now and then they pass piles of bones, or some other sign that human beings came (or were brought) this way. In a hallway they find a scooter overgrown with cobwebs. Farther on, a pair of girl's in-line skates, thick with dust. In a vast library room, the word LAUGH has been formed with human bones on a mahogany table. In a richly appointed (if obviously neglected) parlor through which the bee leads them in a no-nonsense straight line, Dale and Doc observe that the art on one wall appears to consist of human faces that have been cut off, cured, and then stretched on squares of wood. Huge bewildered eyes have been painted into the empty sockets. Dale thinks he recognizes at least one of the faces: Milton Wanderly, a schoolteacher who dropped out of sight three or four years back. Everyone had assumed that Don Wanderly's kid brother had simply left town. *Well*, Dale thinks, *he left, all right*. Halfway down a stone-throated corridor lined with cells, the bee darts into a squalid little chamber and circles above a ragged futon. At first none of them speak. They don't need to. Ty was here, and not that long ago. They can almost smell him – his fear. Then Beezer turns to Jack. The blue eyes above the lush red-brown beard are narrowed in fury.

'The old bastard burned him with something. Or zapped him.'

Jack nods. He can smell that, too, although whether he does so with his nose or his mind he neither knows nor cares. 'Burnside won't be zapping anyone else,' he says.

The queen bee zips between them and whirls impatiently in the corridor. To the left, back the way they came, the corridor is black with bees. They turn to the right instead, and soon the bee is leading them down another seemingly endless stairway. At one point they walk through a brief, drippy drizzle – somewhere above this part of the stairs, a pipe in Black House's unimaginable guts has perhaps let go. Half a dozen of the risers are wet, and they all see tracks there. They're too blurry to do a forensics team much good (both Jack and Dale have the same thought), but the Sawyer Gang is encouraged: there's a big set and a little set, and both sets are relatively fresh. Now they are getting somewhere, by God! They begin to move faster, and behind them the bees descend in a vast humming cloud, like some plague out of the Old Testament.

Time may have ceased to exist for the Sawyer Gang, but for Ty Marshall it has become an agonizing presence. He can't be sure if his sense of Mr Munshun's approach is imagination or precognition, but he's terribly afraid it's the latter. He has to get out of this shed, *has* to, but the damned bag keeps eluding him. He managed to pull it close to him with the loop of intestines; ironically, that was the easy part. The hard part is actually getting *hold* of the damned thing.

He can't reach it; no matter how he stretches or how cruelly he tests his left shoulder and shackled left wrist, he comes up at least two feet short. Tears of pain roll down his cheeks. Any moisture lost that way is quickly replaced by the sweat that runs stinging into his eyes from his greasy forehead.

'Foot it,' he says. 'Just like soccer.' He looks at the disfigured sprawl in the doorway – his erstwhile tormentor. 'Just like soccer, right, Burn-Burn?'

He gets the side of his foot against the bag, pushes it to the wall, and then begins to slide it up the bloodstained wood. At the same time he reaches down . . . now fourteen inches . . . now only a foot . . . reaching . . .

. . . and the leather bag tumbles off the toe of his sneaker and onto the dirt. Plop.

'You're watching out for him, aren't you, Burny?' Ty pants. 'You have to, you know, my back's turned. You're the lookout, right? You're—*Fuck!*' This time the bag has tumbled off his foot before he can even begin to raise it. Ty slams his free hand against the wall.

Why do you do that? a voice inquires coolly. This is the one who sounds like his mother but *isn't* his mother, not quite. *Will that help you?*

'No,' Ty says resentfully, 'but it makes me feel better.'

Getting free will make you feel better. Now try again.

Ty once more rolls the leather bag against the wall. He presses his foot against it, feeling for anything else that might be inside – a key, for instance – but he can't tell. Not through his sneaker. He begins to slide the bag up the wall again. Carefully . . . not too fast . . . like footing the ball toward the goal . . .

'Don't let him in, Burny,' he pants to the dead man behind him. 'You owe me that. I don't want to go on the mono. I don't want to go to End-World. And I don't want to be a Breaker.

Whatever it is, I don't want to be it. I want to be an explorer . . . maybe underwater, like Jacques Cousteau . . . or a flier in the Air Force . . . or maybe . . . *FUCK!*' This time it's not irritation when the bag falls off his foot but rage and near panic.

Mr Munshun, hustling and bustling. Getting closer. Meaning to take him away. *Din-tah. Abbalah-doon.* For ever and ever.

'Damn old key's probably not in there, anyway.' His voice wavering, close to a sob. 'Is it, Burny?'

'Chummy' Burnside offers no opinion.

'I bet there's nothing in there at all. Except maybe . . . I don't know . . . a roll of Tums, or something. Eating people's *got* to give you indigestion.'

Nonetheless, Ty captures the bag with his foot again, and again begins the laborious job of sliding it up the wall far enough so that perhaps his stretching fingers can grasp it.

Dale Gilbertson has lived in the Coulee Country his entire life, and he's used to greenery. To him trees and lawns and fields that roll all the way to the horizon are the norm. Perhaps this is why he looks at the charred and smoking lands that surround Conger Road with such distaste and growing dismay.

'What *is* this place?' he asks Jack. The words come out in little puffs. The Sawyer Gang has no golf cart and must hoof it. In fact, Jack has set a pace quite a bit faster than Ty drove the E-Z-Go.

'I don't exactly know,' Jack says. 'I saw a place *like* it a long time ago. It was called the Blasted Lands. It—'

A greenish man with plated skin suddenly leaps at them from behind a tumble of huge boulders. In one hand he holds a stumpy whip – what Jack believes is actually called a quirt. '*Bahhrrr!*' this apparition cries, sounding weirdly like Richard Sloat when Richard laughs.

Jack raises Ty's bat and looks at the apparition questioningly – *Did you want some of this?* Apparently the apparition does not. It stands where it is for a moment, then turns and flees. As it disappears back into the maze of boulders, Jack sees that twisted thorns grow in a ragged line down both of its Achilles tendons.

'They don't like Wonderboy,' Beezer says, looking appreciatively at the bat. It *is* still a bat, just as the 9mm's and .357 Rugers are still pistols and *they* are still *they*: Jack, Dale, Beezer, Doc. And Jack decides he isn't much surprised by that. Parkus *told* him that this wasn't about Twinners, told him that during their palaver near the hospital tent. This place may be adjacent to the Territories, but it's *not* the Territories. Jack had forgotten that.

Well, yes – but I've had a few other things on my mind.

'I don't know if you boys have taken a close look at the wall on the far side of this charming country lane,' Doc says, 'but those large white stones actually appear to be skulls.'

Beezer gives the wall of skulls a cursory glance, then looks ahead again. 'What worries me is *that* thing,' he says. Over the broken teeth of the horizon rises a great complication of steel, glass, and machinery. It disappears into the clouds. They can see the tiny figures who surge and struggle there, can hear the crack of the whips. From this distance they sound like the pop of .22 rifles. 'What's that, Jack?'

Jack's first thought is that he's looking at the Crimson King's Breakers, but no – there are too many of them. Yonder building is some sort of factory or power plant, powered by slaves. By children not talented enough to *qualify* as Breakers. A vast outrage rises in his heart. As if sensing it, the drone of the bees grows louder behind him.

Speedy's voice, whispering in his head: *Save your anger, Jack – your first job is that little boy. And time has grown very, very short.*

'Oh Christ,' Dale says, and points. 'Is that what I think it is?'

The gibbet hangs like a skeleton over the slanting road.

Doc says, 'If you're thinking gallows, I believe you win the stainless steel flatware and get to go on to the next round.'

'Look at all the shoes,' Dale says. 'Why would they pile the shoes up like that?'

'God knows,' Beezer says. 'Just the custom of the country, I guess. How close are we, Jack? Do you have any idea at all?'

Jack looks at the road ahead of them, then at the road leading away to the left, the one with the ancient gallows on its corner. 'Close,' he says. 'I think we're—'

Then, from ahead of them, the shrieks begin. They are the cries of a child who has been pushed to the edge of madness. Or perhaps over it.

Ty Marshall can hear the approaching drone of the bees but believes it is only in his head, that it is no more than the sound of his own growing anxiety. He doesn't know how many times he's tried to slide Burny's leather bag up the side of the shed; he's lost count. It does not occur to him that removing the odd cap – the one that looks like cloth and feels like metal – might improve his coordination, for he's forgotten all about the cap. All he knows is that he's tired and sweating and trembling, probably in shock, and if he doesn't manage to snag the bag this time, he'll probably just give up.

I'd probably go with Mr Munshun if he just promised me a glass of water, Ty thinks. But he *does* have Judy's toughness bred in his bones, and some of Sophie's regal insistence, as well. And, ignoring the ache in his thigh, he again begins sliding the bag up the wall, at the same time stretching down with his right hand.

Ten inches . . . eight . . . the closest he's gotten so far . . .

The bag slips to the left. It's going to fall off his foot. Again.

'No,' Ty says softly. 'Not this time.'

He presses his sneaker harder against the wood, then begins to raise it again.

Six inches . . . four inches . . . three and the bag starts to tilt farther and farther to the left, *it's going to fall off—*

'*No!*' Ty yells, and bends forward in a strenuous bow. His back creaks. So does his tortured left shoulder. But his fingers graze across the bag . . . and then snag it. He brings it toward him and then damned near drops it after all!

'No way, Burny,' he pants, first juggling the leather sack and then clutching it against his chest. 'You don't fool me with *that* old trick, no way in *hell* do you fool me with that one.' He bites the corner of the bag with his teeth. The stink of it is awful, rotten – eau de Burnside. He ignores it and pulls the bag open. At first he thinks it's empty, and lets out a low, sobbing cry. Then he sees a single silver gleam. Crying through his clenched teeth, Ty reaches into the dangling bag with his right hand and brings the key out.

Can't drop it, he thinks. *If I drop it, I'll lose my mind. I really will.*

He doesn't drop it. He raises it above his head, sticks it in the little hole on the side of the cuff holding his left wrist, and turns it. The cuff springs open.

Slowly, slowly, Ty draws his hand through the shackle. The handcuffs fall to the shed's dirt floor. As he stands there, a queerly persuasive idea occurs to Ty: he's really still back in Black House, asleep on the ragged futon with the slop bucket in one corner of his cell and the dish of reheated Dinty Moore beef stew in the other. This is just his exhausted mind giving him a little hope. A last vacation before he goes into the stewpot himself.

From outside comes the clank of the Big Combination and the screams of the children who march, march, march on their bleeding footsies, running it. Somewhere is Mr Munshun, who wants to take him someplace even worse than this.

It's no dream. Ty doesn't know where he'll go from here or how he'll ever get back to his own world, but the first step is getting out of this shed and this general vicinity. Moving on trembling legs, like an accident victim getting out of bed for the first time after a long stay, Ty Marshall steps over Burny's sprawled corpse and out of the shed. The day is overcast, the landscape sterile, and even here that rickety skyscraper of pain and toil dominates the view, but still Ty feels an immense gladness just to be in the light again. To be *free.* It is not until he stands with the shed behind him that he truly realizes how completely he expected to die there. For a moment Ty closes his eyes and turns his face up to the gray sky. Thus he never sees the figure that has been standing to one side of the shed, prudently waiting to make sure Ty is still wearing the cap when he comes out. Once he's sure he is, Lord Malshun – this is as close to his real name as we can come – steps forward. His grotesque face is like the bowl of a huge serving spoon upholstered in skin. The one eye bulges freakishly. The red lips grin. When he drops his arms around the boy, Ty begins to shriek – not just in fear and surprise, but in *outrage.* He has worked so hard to be free, so dreadfully hard.

'Hush,' Lord Malshun whispers, and when Ty continues to loose his wild screams (on the upper levels of the Big Combination, some of the children turn toward those cries until the brutish ogres who serve as foremen whip them back to business), the abbalah's lord speaks again, a single word in the Dark Speech. '*Pnung.*'

Ty goes limp. Had Lord Malshun not been hugging him

from behind, he would have fallen. Guttural moans of protest continue to issue from the child's drooling, slack mouth, but the screams have ceased. Lord Malshun cocks his long, spoon-shaped face toward the Big Combination, and grins. Life is good! Then he peers into the shed – briefly, but with great interest.

'Did for him,' Lord Malshun says. 'And with the cap on, too. Amazing boy! The King wants to meet you in person before you go to Din-tah, you know. He may give you cake and coffee. Imagine, young Tyler! Cake and coffee with the abbalah! Cake and coffee with the King!'

'. . . don't want go . . . want to go home . . . my maaaa . . .' These words spill out loose and low, like blood from a mortal wound.

Lord Malshun draws a finger across Ty's lips, and they press together behind his touch. 'Hush,' says the abbalah's talent scout again. 'Few things in life are more annoying than a noisy traveling companion. And we have a long trip ahead of us. Far from your home and friends and family . . . ah, but don't cry.' For Malshun has observed the tears that have begun to leak from the corners of the limp boy's eyes and roll down the planes of his cheeks. 'Don't cry, little Ty. You'll make new friends. The Chief Breaker, for instance. All the boys like the Chief Breaker. His name is Mr Brautigan. Perhaps he'll tell you tales of his many escapes. How funny they are! Perfectly *killing*! And now we must go! Cake and coffee with the King! Hold that thought!'

Lord Malshun is stout and rather bowlegged (his legs are, in fact, a good deal shorter than his grotesquely long face), but he is strong. He tucks Ty under his arm as if the boy weighed no more than two or three sheets bundled together. He looks back at Burny one last time, without much regret – there's a young fellow in upstate New York who shows great promise, and Burny was pretty well played out, anyway.

Lord Malshun cocks his head sideways and utters his almost soundless chuffing laugh. Then he sets out, not neglecting to give the boy's cap a good hard yank. The boy is not just a Breaker; he's perhaps the most powerful one to ever live. Luckily, he doesn't realize his own powers yet. Probably nothing would happen if the cap *did* fall off, yet it's best not to take chances.

Bustling – even humming a bit under his breath – Lord Malshun reaches the end of the draw, turns left onto Conger Road for the half-mile stroll back to Station House Road, and stops dead in his tracks. Standing in his way are four men from what Lord Malshun thinks of as Tertah. This is a slang term, and not a flattering one. In the Book of Good Farming, Ter is that period of Full-Earth in which breeding stock is serviced. Lord Malshun sees the world beyond the front door of Black House as a kind of vast *caldo largo*, a living soup into which he may dip his ladle – always on the abbalah's behalf, of course! – whenever he likes.

Four men from the Ter? Malshun's lip twists in contempt, causing upheavals all along the length of his face. What are they doing here? Whatever can they hope to *accomplish* here?

The smile begins to falter when he sees the stick one of them carries. It's glowing with a shifting light that is many colors but somehow always white at its core. A blinding light. Lord Malshun knows only one thing that has ever glowed with such light and that is the Globe of Forever, known by at least one small, wandering boy as the Talisman. That boy once touched it, and as Laura DeLoessian could have told him – as Jack himself now knows – the touch of the Talisman never completely fades.

The smile drops away entirely when Lord Malshun realizes that the man with the club *was that boy.* He has come again to annoy them, but if he thinks he will take back the prize of prizes, he's quite mistaken. It's only a stick, after all, not the Globe itself; perhaps a little of the Globe's residual power still lives within the man, but surely not much. Surely there can be no more than dust, after all the intervening years.

And dust is what my life would be worth if I let them take this boy from me, Lord Malshun thinks. *I must—*

His single eye is drawn to the black thunderhead hanging behind the men from the Ter. It gives off a vast, sleepy drone. Bees? Bees with stingers? Bees with stingers between him and Station House Road?

Well, he will deal with them. In time. First is the business of these annoying men.

'Good day, gentlemen,' Lord Malshun says in his most pleasant voice. The bogus German accent is gone; now he sounds like a bogus English aristocrat in a West End stage comedy from the 1950s. Or perhaps the World War II Nazi propagandist Lord Haw-Haw. 'It's wonderful that you should come so far to visit, perfectly *wonderful*, and on such a rotten day, too. Yet I'm afraid most days *are* rotten here, the Dins of End-World were simply *made* for the pathetic fallacy, you know, and – dash it all – I can't stay. I'm afraid these are time-delivery goods, here.'

Lord Malshun raises Ty and shakes him. Although Ty's eyes are open and he's obviously aware, his arms and legs flop as bonelessly as those of a rag doll.

'Put him down, Munshun,' says the one with the club, and Lord Malshun realizes with growing dismay that he *could* have trouble with this one. He really could. Yet his smile widens, exposing the full, ghoulish range of his teeth. They are pointed and tip inward. Anything bitten by them would tear itself to shreds trying to pull free of that bony trap.

'Munshun? *Munshun?* No one here by that name. Or Mr Monday either, for that matter. All gone, cheerio, tata, toodle-oo.

As for putting down the lad, couldn't do that, dear boy, simply *couldn't*. I've made commitments, you know. And really, you fellows should count yourselves fortunate. Your local reign of terror is over! Huzzah! The Fisherman is dead – dispatched by this boy right here, in fact, this perfectly admirable boy.' He gives Ty another shake, always being careful to keep the head raised. Wouldn't want that cap falling off, oh no.

The bees trouble him.

Who has sent the bees?

'The boy's mother is in an insane asylum,' says the man with the stick. That stick is glowing more fiercely than ever, Lord Malshun realizes with deepening fear. He now feels *very* afraid, and with fear comes anger. Is it possible they could take him? Really take the boy? 'She's in an asylum, and she wants her son back.'

If so, it's a corpse they'll have for their trouble.

Afraid or not, Lord Malshun's grin widens even further. (Dale Gilbertson has a sudden, nightmarish vision: William F. Buckley, Jr, with one eye and a face five feet long.) He lifts Ty's limp body close to his mouth and bites a series of needly little nips in the air less than an inch from the exposed neck.

'Have her husband stick his prick in her and make another 'un, old son – I'm sure he can do it. They live in Ter-tah, after all. Women get pregnant in Ter-tah just walking down the street.'

One of the bearded men says, 'She's partial to this one.'

'But so am *I*, dear boy. So am *I*.' Lord Malshun actually nips Ty's skin this time and blood flows, as if from a shaving cut. Behind them, the Big Combination grinds on and on, but the screams have ceased. It's as if the children driving the machine realize that something has changed or might change; that the world has come to a balancing point.

The man with the glowing stick takes a step forward. Lord

Malshun cringes back in spite of himself. It's a mistake to show weakness and fear, he knows this but can't help it. For this is no ordinary tah. This is someone like one of the old gunslingers, those warriors of the High.

'Take another step and I'll tear his throat open, dear boy. I'd hate doing that, would hate it awfully, but never doubt that I'll do it.'

'You'd be dead yourself two seconds later,' the man with the stick says. He seems completely unafraid, either for himself or for Ty. 'Is that what you want?'

Actually, given the choice between dying and going back to the Crimson King empty-handed, death is what Lord Malshun would choose, yes. But it may not come to that. The quieting word worked on the boy, and it will work on at least three of these – the ordinary three. With them lying open-eyed and insensible on the road, Lord Malshun can deal with the fourth. It's Sawyer, of course. That's his name. As for the bees, surely he has enough protective words to get him up Station House Road to the mono. And if he's stung a few times, what of that?

'*Is* it what you want?' Sawyer asks.

Lord Malshun smiles. '*Pnung!*' he cries, and behind Jack Sawyer, Dale, Beezer, and Doc fall still.

Lord Malshun's smile widens into a grin. 'Now what are you going to do, my meddling friend? What are you going to do with no friends to back you u—'

Armand 'Beezer' St Pierre steps forward. The first step is an effort, but after that it's easy. His own cold little smile exposes the teeth inside his beard. 'You're responsible for the death of my daughter,' he says. 'Maybe you didn't do it yourself, but you egged Burnside on to it. Didn't you? I'm her *father*, asshole. You think you can stop me with a single word?'

Doc lurches to his friend's side.

'You fucked up my town,' Dale Gilbertson growls. He also moves forward.

Lord Malshun stares at them in disbelief. The Dark Speech hasn't stopped them. Not *any* of them. They are blocking the road! They dare to block his proposed route of progress!

'I'll kill him!' he growls at Jack. 'I'll kill him. So what do you say, sunshine? What's it going to be?'

And so here it is, at long last: the showdown. We cannot watch it from above, alas, as the crow with whom we have hitched so many rides (all unknown by Gorg, we assure you) is dead, but even standing off to one side, we recognize this archetypal scene from ten thousand movies – at least a dozen of them starring Lily Cavanaugh.

Jack levels the bat, the one even Beezer has recognized as Wonderboy. He holds it with the knob pressing into the underside of his forearm and the barrel pointing directly at Lord Malshun's head.

'Put him down,' he says. 'Last chance, my friend.'

Lord Malshun lifts the boy higher. 'Go on!' he shouts. 'Shoot a bolt of energy out of that thing! I know you can do it! But you'll hit the boy, too! You'll hit the boy, t—'

A line of pure white fire jumps from the head of the Richie Sexson bat; it is as thin as the lead of a pencil. It strikes Lord Malshun's single eye and cooks it in its socket. The thing utters a shriek – it never thought Jack would call its bluff, not a creature from the *ter*, no matter how temporarily elevated – and it jerks forward, opening its jaws to bite, even in death.

Before it can, *another* bolt of white light, this one from the beaten silver commitment ring on Beezer St Pierre's left hand, shoots out and strikes the abbalah's emissary square in the mouth. The red plush of Lord Malshun's red lips bursts into flame . . . and still he staggers upright in the road, the Big Combination a skeletal skyscraper behind him, trying to bite, trying to end the life of Judy Marshall's gifted son.

Dale leaps forward, grabs the boy around the waist and the shoulders, and yanks him away, reeling toward the side of the road. His honest face is pale and grim and set. '*Finish him, Jack!*' Dale bawls. '*Finish the sonofabitch!*'

Jack steps forward to where the blinded, howling, charred thing reels back and forth in the Conger Road, his bony vest smoking, his long white hands groping. Jack cocks the bat back on his right shoulder and sets his grip all the way down to the knob. No choking up this afternoon; this afternoon he's wielding a bat that blazes with glowing white fire, and he'd be a fool not to swing for the fences.

'Batter up, sweetheart,' he says, and uncoils a swing that would have done credit to Richie Sexson himself. Or Big Mac. There is a punky, fleshy sound as the bat, still accelerating, connects with the side of Lord Malshun's huge head. It caves in like the rind of a rotted watermelon, and a spray of bright crimson flies out. A moment later the head simply explodes, spattering them all with its gore.

'Looks like the King's gonna have to find a new boy,' Beezer says softly. He wipes his face, looks at a handful of blood and shriveling tissue, then wipes it casually on his faded jeans. 'Home run, Jack. Even a blind man could see that.'

Dale, cradling Tyler, says: 'Game over, case closed, zip up your fly.'

French Landing's police chief sets Ty carefully on his feet. The boy looks up at him, then at Jack. A bleary sort of light is dawning in his eyes. It might be relief; it might be actual comprehension.

'Bat,' he says. His voice is husky and hoarse, almost impossible for them to understand. He clears his throat and tries again. 'Bat. Dreamed about it.'

'Did you?' Jack kneels in front of the boy and holds the bat out. Ty shows no inclination to actually take possession of the Richie Sexson wonder bat, but he touches it with one hand. Strokes the bat's gore-spattered barrel. His eyes look only at Jack. It's as if he's trying to get the sense of him. The *truth* of him. To understand that he has, after all, been rescued.

'George,' the boy says. 'George. Rathbun. Really is blind.'

'Yes,' Jack says. 'But sometimes blind isn't blind. Do you know that, Tyler?'

The boy nods. Jack has never in his life seen anyone who looks so fundamentally exhausted, so shocked and lost, so completely worn out.

'Want,' the boy says. He licks his lips and clears his throat again. 'Want . . . drink. Water. Want mother. See my mother.'

'Sounds like a plan to me,' Doc says. He is looking uneasily at the splattered remains of the creature they still think of as Mr Munshun. 'Let's get this young fellow back to Wisconsin before some of Old One Eye's friends show up.'

'Right,' Beezer says. 'Burning Black House to the ground is also on my personal agenda. I'll throw the first match. Or maybe I can shoot fire out of my ring again. I'd like that. First thing, though, is to make tracks.'

'I couldn't agree more,' Dale says. 'I don't think Ty's going to be able to walk either very far or very fast, but we can take turns giving him piggyb—'

'No,' Jack says.

They look at him with varying degrees of surprise and consternation.

'Jack,' Beezer says. He speaks with an odd gentleness. 'There's such a thing as overstaying your welcome, man.'

'We aren't finished,' Jack tells him. Then he shakes his head and corrects himself. '*Ty's* not finished.'

Jack Sawyer kneels in Conger Road, thinking: *I wasn't much older than this kid when I took off across America – and the Territories – to save my mother's life.* He knows this is true and at the same time absolutely can't believe it. Can't remember what it was to be twelve and never anything else, to be small and terrified, mostly below the world's notice and running just ahead of all the world's shadows. It *should* be over; Ty has been through nine kinds of hell, and he deserves to go home.

Unfortunately, it's *not* over. There's one more thing to do.

'Ty.'

'Want. Home.'

If there was light in the boy's eyes, it has gone out now. He wears the dull shockface of refugees at border checkpoints and the gates of deathcamps. His is the emptied visage of someone who has spent too long in the slippery opopanax landscape of slippage. And he is a child, damnit, only a *child*. He deserves better than what Jack Sawyer is about to serve out. But then, Jack Sawyer once deserved better than what he got and lived to tell the tale. That justifies nothing, of course, but it *does* give him the courage to be a bastard.

'Ty.' He grasps the boy's shoulder.

'Water. Mother. Home.'

'No,' Jack says. 'Not yet.' He pivots the boy. The spatters of Lord Malshun's blood on his face are very bright. Jack can sense the men he came with – men who have risked their lives and sanity for him – beginning to frown. Never mind. He has a job to do. He is a coppiceman, and there's still a crime in progress here.

'Ty.'

Nothing. The boy stands slumped. He's trying to turn himself into meat that does nothing but breathe.

Jack points at the ugly complication of struts and belts and girders and smoking chimneys. He points at the straining ants. The Big Combination disappears up into the clouds and down into the dead ground. How far in each direction? A mile? Two? Are there children above the clouds, shivering in oxygen masks as they trudge the treadmills and yank the levers and turn the cranks? Children below who bake in the heat of underground fires? Down there in the foxholes and the ratholes where the sun never shines?

'What is it?' Jack asks him. 'What do you call it? What did *Burny* call it?'

Nothing from Ty.

Jack gives the boy a shake. Not a gentle one, either. 'What do you *call* it?'

'Hey, man,' Doc says. His voice is heavy with disapproval. 'There's no need of that.'

'Shut up,' Jack says without looking at him. He's looking at Ty. Trying to see anything in those blue eyes but shocked vacancy. He needs for Ty to see the gigantic, groaning machine that stands yonder. To really see it. For until he does, how can he abominate it? 'What is it?'

After a long pause, Ty says: 'Big. The Big. The Big Combination.' The words come out slowly and dreamily, as if he's talking in his sleep.

'The Big Combination, yes,' Jack says. 'Now stop it.'

Beezer gasps. Dale says, 'Jack, have you gone—' and then falls silent.

'I. Can't.' Ty gives him a wounded look, as if to say Jack should know that.

'You can,' Jack says. 'You can and you will. What do you think, Ty? That we're going to just turn our backs on them and take you back to your mother and she'll make you Ovaltine and put you to bed and everyone will live happily ever after?' His voice is rising, and he makes no attempt to stop it, even when he sees that Tyler is crying. He shakes the boy again. Tyler cringes, but makes no actual attempt to get away. 'Do you think there's going to be any happily ever after for you while those children go on and on, until they drop and get replaced with new ones? You'll see their faces in your dreams, Tyler. You'll see their faces and their dirty little hands and their bleeding feet in your fucking *dreams*.'

'Stop it!' Beezer says sharply. 'Stop it right now or I'll kick your ass.'

Jack turns, and Beezer steps back from the ferocious blaze in his eyes. Looking at Jack Sawyer in this state is like looking into din-tah itself.

'Tyler.'

Tyler's mouth trembles. Tears roll down his dirty, bloody cheeks. 'Stop it. *I want to go home!*'

'Once you make the Big Combination quit. Then you go home. Not before.'

'I can't!'

'Yes, Tyler. You can.'

Tyler looks at the Big Combination, and Jack can feel the boy making some puny, faltering effort. Nothing happens. The belts continue to run; the whips continue to pop; the occasional screaming dot tumbles (or jumps) from the rust-ragged south side of the building.

Tyler looks back at him, and Jack hates the vacant stupidity in the kid's eyes, *loathes* it. 'I *caann't*,' Tyler whines, and Jack wonders how such a puler ever managed to survive over here in the first place. Did he use up all his ability in one mad, willful effort to escape? Is that it? He won't accept it. Anger blazes up in him and he slaps Tyler. Hard. Dale gasps. Ty's head rocks to the side, his eyes widening in surprise.

And the cap flies off his head.

Jack has been kneeling in front of the boy. Now he is knocked back, sprawling on his ass in the middle of Conger Road. The kid has . . . what?

Pushed me. Pushed me with his mind.

Yes. And Jack is suddenly aware of a new bright force in this dull place, a blazing bundle of light to rival the one that illuminated the Richie Sexson bat.

'Whoa, shit, what happened?' Doc cries.

The bees feel it too, perhaps more than the men. Their sleepy drone rises to a strident cry, and the cloud darkens as they pull together. Now it looks like a gigantic dark fist below the pendulous, swag-bellied clouds.

'*Why did you hit me?*' Ty shouts at Jack, and Jack is suddenly aware that the boy could kill him at a stroke, if he wanted to. In Wisconsin, this power has been hidden (except from eyes trained to see it). Here, though . . . *here* . . .

'*To wake you up!*' Jack shouts back. He pushes himself up. 'Was it that?' he points at the cap.

Ty looks at it, then nods. *Yes. The cap. But you didn't know,* couldn't *know, how much the cap was stealing from you until you took it off. Or someone knocked it off your forgetful head.* He returns his gaze to Jack. His eyes are wide and level. There is no shock in them now, no dullness. He doesn't glow, exactly, but he blazes with an inner light they all feel – with a power that dwarfs Lord Malshun's.

'What do you want me to do?' he asks. Tyler Marshall: the lioness's cub.

Once more Jack points at the Big Combination. 'You're what all this has been about, Ty. You're a Breaker.' He takes a deep breath and then whispers into the pink cup of the boy's ear.

'Break it.'

Tyler Marshall turns his head and gazes deep into Jack's eyes. He says, 'Break it?'

Jack nods his head, and Ty looks back at the Big Combination.

'Okay,' he says, speaking not to Jack but to himself. He blinks, settles his feet, clasps his hands in front of his waist. A tiny wrinkle appears between his eyebrows, and the corners of his mouth lift in the suggestion of a smile. 'Okay,' Ty whispers.

For a second, nothing happens.

Then a rumble emerges from the bowels of the Big Combination. Its upper portion wavers like a heat mirage. The guards hesitate, and the screams of tortured metal rip through the air. Visibly confused, the toiling children look up, look in all directions. The mechanical screaming intensifies, then divides into a hundred-different versions of torture. Gears reverse. Cogs jam smoking to a halt; cogs accelerate and strip their teeth. The whole of the Big Combination shivers and quakes. Deep in the earth, boilers detonate, and columns of fire and steam shoot upward, halting, sometimes shredding belts that have run for thousands of years, powered by billions of bleeding footsies.

It is as if an enormous metal jug has sprung a hundred leaks at once. Jack watches children leap from the lower levels and climb down the exterior of the structure in long, continuous lines. Children pour from the trembling building in dozens of unbroken streams.

Before the green-skinned whipslingers can make an organized attempt to stop their slaves from escaping, the bees assemble massively around the great foundry. When the guards begin to turn on the children, the bees descend in a furious tide of buzzing wings and needling stings. Some of Ty's power has passed into them, and their stings are fatal. Guards topple and fall from the unmoving belts and trembling girders. Others turn maddened on their own, whipping and being whipped until they tumble through the dark air.

The Sawyer Gang does not linger to see the end of the slaughter. The queen bee sails toward them out of the swarming chaos, floats above their upturned heads, and leads them back toward Black House.

In world upon world – in worlds strung side by side in multiple dimensions throughout infinity – evils shrivel and disperse: despots choke to death on chicken bones; tyrants fall before assassins' bullets, before the poisoned sweetmeats arrayed by their treacherous mistresses; hooded torturers collapse dying on bloody stone floors. Ty's deed reverberates through the great, numberless string of universes, revenging evil as it spreads. Three worlds over from ours and in the great city there known as Londinorium, Turner Topham, for two decades a respected member of Parliament and for three a sadistic pedophile, bursts abruptly into flame as he strides along the crowded avenue known as Pick-a-Derry. Two worlds down, a nice-looking young welder named Freddy Garver from the Isle of Irse, another, less seasoned member of Topham's clan, turns his torch upon his own left hand and incinerates every particle of flesh off his bones.

Up, up in his high, faraway confinement, the Crimson King feels a deep pain in his gut and drops into a chair, grimacing. Something, he knows, something fundamental, has changed in his dreary fiefdom.

In the wake of the queen bee, Tyler Marshall, his eyes alight and his face without fear, sits astride Jack's shoulders like a boy king. Behind Jack and his friends, hundreds upon hundreds of children who are fleeing from the disintegrating structure of the Big Combination come streaming on to Conger Road and the desolate fields beside it. Some of these children are from our world; many are not. Children move across the dark, empty plains in ragged armies, advancing toward the entrances to their own universes. Limping battalions of children stagger off like columns of drunken ants.

The children following the Sawyer Gang are no less ragged than the rest. Half of them are naked, or as good as naked. These children have faces we have seen on milk cartons and flyers headed MISSING and on child-find Web sites, faces from the dreams of heartbroken mothers and desolate fathers. Some of them are laughing, some are weeping, some are doing both. The stronger ones help the weaker ones along. They do not know where they are going, and they do not care. That they are going is enough for them. All they know is that they are free. The great machine that had stolen their strength and their joy and their hope is behind them, and a silken, protective canopy of bees is above them, and they are free.

At exactly 4:16 p.m., the Sawyer Gang steps out through the front door of Black House. Tyler is now riding on Beezer's burly shoulders. They descend the steps and stand in front of Dale Gilbertson's cruiser (there's a litter of dead bees on the hood and in the well where the windshield wipers hide).

'Look at the house, Hollywood,' Doc murmurs.

Jack does. It's *only* a house, now – a three-story job that might once have been a respectable ranch but has fallen into disrepair over the years. To make matters worse, someone has slopped it with black paint from top to bottom and stem to stern – even the windows have been blurred with swipes of that paint. The overall effect is sad and eccentric, but by no means sinister. The house's slippery shifting shape has solidified, and with the abbalah's glammer departed, what remains is only the abandoned home of an old fellow who was pretty crazy and *extremely* dangerous. An old fellow to put beside such human monsters as Dahmer, Haarman, and Albert Fish. The leering, rampant evil that once inhabited this building has been dissipated, blown away, and what remains is as mundane as an old man mumbling in a cell on Death Row. There is something Jack must do to this wretched place – something the dying Mouse made him promise to do.

'Doc,' Beezer says. 'Look yonder.'

A large dog – large but not monstrous – staggers slowly down the lane that leads back to Highway 35. It looks like a cross between a boxer and a Great Dane. The side of its head and one of its rear paws have been blown away.

'It's your devil dog,' the Beez says.

Doc gapes. 'What, *that*?'

'That,' Beezer confirms. He draws his 9mm, meaning to put the thing out of its misery, but before he can, it collapses on its side, takes a single deep, shuddering breath, and then lies still. Beezer turns to Jack and Dale. 'It's all a lot smaller with the machine turned off, isn't it?'

'I want to see my mother,' Ty says quietly. 'Please, may I?'

'Yes,' Jack says. 'Do you mind swinging by your house and picking up your father? I think he might like to go, too.'

Tyler breaks into a tired grin. 'Yes,' he says. 'Let's do that.'

'You got it,' Jack tells him.

Dale swings the car carefully around the yard and has

reached the beginning of the lane when Ty calls out, 'Look! Look, you guys! Here they come!'

Dale stops, peers in the rearview mirror, and whispers: 'Oh, Jack. Holy Mother of God.' He puts the cruiser in park and gets out. They all get out, looking back at Black House. Its shape remains ordinary, but it has not quite given up all of its magic after all, it seems. Somewhere a door – perhaps in the cellar or a bedroom or a dirty and neglected but otherwise perfectly ordinary kitchen – remains open. On this side is the Coulee Country; on the other is Conger Road, the smoking, newly stopped hulk of the Big Combination, and the Din-tah.

Bees are coming out onto the porch of Black House. Bees, and the children the bees are leading. They come in droves, laughing and crying and holding hands. Jack Sawyer has a brief, brilliant image of animals leaving Noah's Ark after the flood.

'Holy Mary, Mother of God,' Dale whispers again. The yard is filling with laughing, crying, murmuring children.

Jack walks up to Beezer, who turns to him with a brilliant smile.

'After all the children come through, we have to close the door,' Jack says. 'For good.'

'I know we do,' says Beezer.

'You happen to have any brilliant ideas?'

'Well,' Beezer says, 'let me put it this way. If you promise me, and I mean promise me, not to ask any awkward questions or say anything about it later, before midnight tonight I might find it possible to lay my hands on a substantial quantity of something pretty damn effective.'

'What? Dynamite?'

'Please,' Beezer says. 'Didn't I say effective?'

'You mean . . .?'

Beezer smiles, and his eyes become slits.

'I'm glad you're on my side,' Jack says. 'See you back on the road before midnight. We'll have to sneak in, but I don't think we'll have any trouble.'

'Sure won't have any on the way out,' Beezer says.

Doc claps Dale on the shoulder. 'I hope you've got some on-the-ball child-welfare organizations in this part of the world, Chiefy. I think you're going to need them.'

'Holy . . .' Dale turns stricken eyes to Jack. 'What am I going to *do*?'

Jack grins. 'I think you better make a call to . . . what does Sarah call them? The Color Posse?'

A gleam of hope dawns in Dale Gilbertson's eyes. Or maybe it's incipient triumph. John P. Redding of the FBI, officers Perry Brown and Jeffrey Black of the Wisconsin State Police. He imagines this trio of bungholes faced with the appearance of a medieval children's crusade in western Wisconsin. Imagines the Dickensian piles of paperwork such an unheard-of event must certainly generate. It will keep them occupied for months or years. It may generate nervous breakdowns. Certainly it will give them something to think about other than Chief Dale Gilbertson of French Landing.

'Jack,' he says. 'What exactly do you suggest?'

'In broad strokes,' Jack says, 'I suggest that they should get stuck with all the work and you should hog all the credit. How does that sound to you?'

Dale thinks about it. 'Very fair,' he says. 'What do you say we get this kiddo to his dad, then both of them up to Arden to see his mom?'

'Good,' Jack says. 'I only wish Henry was here, too.'

'That makes us a pair,' Dale says, and slides back behind the wheel. A moment later, they are rolling up the lane.

'What about all those kids?' Ty asks, looking out through the back window. 'Are you just going to *leave* them?'

'I'll call WSP as soon as we're back on the highway,' Dale says. 'I think they should get on this right away, don't you guys? And the Feebs, of course.'

'Right,' Beezer says.

'Fuckin' A,' Doc says.

'An excellent administrative call,' Jack says, and sits Tyler down on his lap. 'In the meantime they'll be fine,' he says in the boy's ear. 'They've seen a lot worse than Wisconsin.'

Let us slip now from the driver's window like the breeze we are and watch them go – four brave men and one brave child who will never be so young (or so innocent) again. Behind them, the now harmless and unmagicked yard of Black House is alive with children, their faces dirty, their eyes wide with wonder. English is a minority tongue here, and some of the languages being spoken will puzzle the world's best linguists in the years ahead. This is the beginning of a worldwide sensation (*Time*'s cover story the following week will be 'The Miracle Children from Nowhere') and, as Dale has already surmised, a bureaucratic nightmare.

Still, they are safe. And our guys are safe, too. All of them came back in one piece from the other side, and surely we did not expect that; most quests of this type usually demand at least one sacrifice (a relatively minor character like Doc, for instance). All's well that ends well. And this *can* be the end, if you want it to be; neither of the scribbling fellows who have brought you this far would deny you that. If you *do* choose to go on, never say you weren't warned: you're not going to like what happens next.

XXXXX DRUDGE REPORT XXXXX

FRENCH LANDING PD CHIEF REFUSES TO CANCEL PRESS CONFERENCE, CITES SUPPORT OF TOWN OFFICIALS; SOURCES CONFIRM CELEB LA COP WILL ATTEND; FBI, WISC SP EXPRESS STRONG DISAPPROVAL

Exclusive

One of them, Tyler Marshall, is from French Landing itself. Another, Josella Rakine, is from Bating, a small village in the south of England. A third is from Baghdad. All told, 17 of the so-called Miracle Children have been identified in the week since they were discovered walking along a rural highway (Rte 35) in western Wisconsin.

Yet these 17 are only the tip of the iceberg.

Sources close to the joint FBI/WSP (and now CIA?) investigation tell the Drudge Report that there are at least 750 children, far more than have been reported in the mainstream press. Who are they? Who took them, and to where? How did they get to the town of French Landing, which has been plagued by a serial killer (now reported deceased) in recent weeks? What part was played by Jack Sawyer, the Los Angeles detective who rose to stardom only to retire at age 31? And who was responsible for the massive explosion that destroyed a mysterious dwelling in the woods, reputedly central to the Fisherman case?

Some of these questions may be answered tomorrow in French Landing's La Follette Park, when PD Chief Dale Gilbertson holds a press conference. His longtime friend Jack Sawyer – reputed to have broken the Fisherman case single-handedly – will be standing next to him when he takes the podium. Also expected to be present are two deputies, Armand St Pierre and Reginald Amberson, who participated in last week's rescue mission.

The press conference will take place over the strong – almost strident – objections of an FBI/WSP task force headed by FBI agent John P. Redding and Wisconsin State Police Detective Jeffrey Black. 'They [task force leaders] believe this is nothing but a last-ditch effort on the part of Gilbertson to save his job,' a source said. 'He botched everything, but luckily has a friend who knows a lot about public relations.'

French Landing town officials sing a different tune. 'This summer has been a nightmare for the people of French Landing,' says town treasurer Beth Warren. 'Chief Gilbertson wants to assure the people that the nightmare is over. If he can give us some answers about the children in the process of doing that, so much the better.'

Interest focuses on Jack 'Hollywood' Sawyer, who got to know Chief Gilbertson and the town of French Landing during the case of Thornberg Kinderling, the so-called Prostitute Killer. Sawyer was urged by Gilbertson to take an active role in the Fisherman case, and apparently played a large part in the events that followed.

What events, exactly, were they? That is what the world is waiting to find out. The first answers may come tomorrow, in La Follette Park, on the banks of the mighty Mississippi.

Developing . . .

29

'You guys ready?' Dale asks.

'Aw, man, I don't know,' Doc says. This isn't the fifth time he's said it, maybe not even the fifteenth. He's pale, almost hyperventilating. The four of them are in a Winnebago – kind of a rolling green room – that has been set up on the edge of La Follette Park. Nearby is the podium on which they'll stand (always assuming Doc can keep his legs under him) and deliver their carefully crafted answers. On the slope running down to the broad river are gathered nearly four hundred newspeople, plus camera crews from six American networks and God knows how many foreign stations. The gentlemen of the press aren't in the world's best mood, because the prime space in front of the podium has been reserved for a representative sampling (drawn by lottery) of French Landing's residents. This was Dale's one ironclad demand for the press conference.

The idea for the press conference itself came from Jack Sawyer.

'Mellow out, Doc,' Beezer says. He looks bigger than ever in his gray linen slacks and open-collared white shirt – almost like a bear in a tuxedo. He has even made an effort to comb his acres of hair. 'And if you really think you're going to do one of the Three P's – piss, puke, or pass out – stay here.'

'Nah,' Doc says miserably. 'In for a penny, in for a fuckin' pound. If we're gonna give it a try, let's give it a try.'

Dale, resplendent in his dress uniform, looks at Jack. The latter is if anything more resplendent in his gray summerweight suit and dark blue silk tie. A matching blue handkerchief pokes from the breast pocket of his coat. 'You sure this is the right thing?'

Jack is completely sure. It's not a matter of refusing to allow Sarah Gilbertson's Color Posse to steal the limelight; it's a matter of making certain that his old friend is in an unassailable position. He can do this by telling a very simple story, which the three other men will back up. Ty will do the same, Jack is confident. The story is this: Jack's *other* old friend, the late Henry Leyden, figured out the Fisherman's identity from the 911 tape. This tape was supplied by Dale, his nephew. The Fisherman killed Henry, but not before the heroic Mr Leyden had mortally wounded him and passed his name to the police. (Jack's other interest in this press conference, understood perfectly and supported completely by Dale, is to make sure Henry gets the credit he deserves.) An examination of French Landing property records and plats uncovered the fact that Charles Burnside owned a house on Highway 35, not far out of town. Dale deputized Jack and two widebodies who just happened to be in the vicinity (that would be Messrs Amberson and St Pierre), and they went on out there.

'From that point on,' Jack told his friends repeatedly in the days leading up to the press conference, 'it's vital that you remember the three little words that lead to most acquittals in criminal trials. And what are those words?'

'"I can't remember,"' Dale said.

Jack nodded. 'Right. If you don't have a story to remember, the bastards can never trip you up. There was something in the air inside that place—'

'No lie,' Beezer rumbled, and grimaced.

'—and it messed us up. What we *do* remember is this: Ty Marshall was in the backyard, handcuffed to the clothesline whirligig.' Before Beezer St Pierre and Jack Sawyer slipped through the police barricades and vaporized Black House with plastic explosive, one reporter got out there and took numerous pictures. We know which reporter it was, of course; Wendell Green has finally realized his dreams of fame and fortune.

'And Burnside was dead at his feet,' Beezer said.

'Right. With the key to the handcuffs in his pocket. Dale, you found that and released the boy. There were a few other kids in the backyard, but as to how many—'

'We don't remember,' Doc said.

'As to their sexes—'

'A few boys, a few girls,' Dale said. 'We don't remember exactly how many of each.'

'And as for Ty, how he was taken, what happened to him—'

'He said he didn't remember,' Dale said, smiling.

'We left. We think we called to the other kids—'

'But don't exactly remember—' the Beez chips in.

'Right, and in any case they seemed safe enough where they were for the time being. It was when we were putting Ty into the cruiser that we saw them all streaming out.'

'And called the Wisconsin State Police for backup,' Dale said. 'I *do* remember *that*.'

'Of course you do,' Jack said benevolently.

'But we have no idea how that darn place got blasted all to hell, and we don't know who did it.'

'Some people,' Jack said, 'are all too eager to take justice into their own hands.'

'Lucky they didn't blow their heads clean off,' said Dale.

'All right,' Jack tells them now. They're standing at the door. Doc has produced half a joint, and four quick, deep tokes have calmed him visibly. 'Just remember why we're doing this. The message is that we were there first, we found Ty, we saw *only a few other children*, we deemed their situation secure due to the death of Charles Burnside, also known as Carl Bierstone, the South Side Monster, and the Fisherman. The message is that Dale behaved properly – that we all did – and he then handed the investigation off to the FBI and WSP, who are now holding the baby. *Babies*, I guess in this case. The message is that French Landing is okay again. Last but far from least, the message is that Henry Leyden's the real star. The heroic blind man who ID'd Charles Burnside and broke the Fisherman case, mortally wounding the monster and losing his own life in the process.'

'Amen,' Dale says. 'Sweet old Uncle Henry.'

Beyond the door of the Winnebago, he can hear the surf-like rumble of hundreds of people. Maybe even a thousand. He thinks, *This is what rock acts hear before they hit the stage.* A lump suddenly rises in his throat and he does his best to gulp it back down. He reckons that if he keeps thinking of Uncle Henry he will be okay.

'Anything else,' Jack says, 'questions that get too specific—'

'We can't remember,' Beezer says.

'Because the air was bad,' Doc agrees. 'Smelled like ether or chloro or something like that.'

Jack surveys them, nods, smiles. This will be a happy occasion, on the whole, he thinks. A love feast. Certainly the idea that he might be dying in a few minutes has not occurred to him.

'Okay,' he says, 'let's go out there and do it. We're politicians this afternoon, politicians at a press conference, and it's the politicians who stay on message who get elected.'

He opens the RV's door. The rumble of the crowd deepens in anticipation.

They cross to the jury-rigged platform this way: Beezer, Dale, Jack, and the good Doctor. They move in a warm white nova glare of exploding flashbulbs and 10-k TV lights. Jack has no idea why they need such things – the day is bright and warm, a Coulee Country charmer – but it seems they do. That they always do. Voices cry, 'Over here!' repeatedly. There are also thrown questions, which they ignore. When it comes time to answer questions they will – as best they can – but for now they are simply stunned by the crowd.

The noise begins with the two hundred or so French Landing residents sitting on folding chairs in a roped-off area directly in front of the podium. They rise to their feet, some clapping, others waving clenched fists in the air like winning boxers. The press picks it up from them, and as our four friends mount the steps to the podium, the roar becomes a thunder. We are with them, up on the platform with them, and God, we see so many faces we know looking up at us. There's Morris Rosen, who slipped Henry the Dirtysperm CD on our first day in town. Behind him is a contingent from the now defunct Maxton Elder Care: the lovely Alice Weathers is surrounded by Elmer Jesperson, Ada Meyerhoff (in a wheelchair), Flora Flostad, and the Boettcher brothers, Hermie and Tom Tom. Tansy Freneau, looking a bit spaced out but no longer outright insane, is standing next to Lester Moon, who has his arm around her. Arnold 'Flashlight' Hrabowski, Tom Lund, Bobby Dulac, and the other members of Dale's department are up on their feet, dancing around and cheering crazily. Look, over there – that's Enid Purvis, the neighbor who called Fred at work on the day Judy finally high-sided it. There's Rebecca Vilas, looking almost nunnish in a high-collared dress (but cry no tears for her, Argentina; Becky has stashed away quite a nice bundle, thank you very much). Butch Yerxa is with her. At the back of the crowd, lurking shamefully but unable to stay away from the triumph of their friends, are William Strassner and Hubert Cantinaro, better known to us as Kaiser Bill and Sonny. Look there! Herb Roeper, who cuts Jack's hair, standing beside Buck Evitz, who delivers his mail. So many others we know, and to whom we must say good-bye under less than happy circumstances. In the front row, Wendell Green is hopping around like a hen on a hot griddle (God knows how he got into the roped-off area, being from La Riviere instead of French Landing, but he's there), taking pictures. Twice he bumps into Elvena Morton, Henry's housekeeper. The third time he does it, she bats him a damned good one on top of the head. Wendell hardly seems to notice. His head has taken worse shots during the course of the Fisherman investigation. And off to one side, we see someone else we may or may not recognize. An elderly, dark-skinned gentleman wearing shades. He looks a little bit like an old blues singer. He also looks a little bit like a movie actor named Woody Strode.

The applause thunders and thunders. Folks cheer. Hats are thrown in the air and sail on the summer breeze. Their welcome becomes a kind of miracle in itself, an affirmation, perhaps even an acceptance of the children, who are widely supposed to have been held in some bizarre sexual bondage linked to the Internet. (Isn't all that weird stuff somehow linked to the Internet?) And of course they applaud because the nightmare is over. The boogeyman died in his own backyard, died at the foot of a prosaic, now vaporized aluminum clothes whirligig, and they are safe again.

Oh how the cheers ring in these few last moments of Jack Sawyer's life on planet Earth! Birds are startled up from the bank of the river and go squawking and veering into the sky, seeking quieter environs. On the river itself, a freighter responds to the cheers – or perhaps joins in – by blasting its air horn over and over. Other boats get the idea and add to the cacophony.

Without thinking about what he's doing, Jack takes Doc's right hand in his left, Dale's left hand in his right. Dale takes Beezer's hand, and the Sawyer Gang raises their arms together, facing the crowd.

Which, of course, goes nuts. If not for what is going to happen next, it would be the picture of the decade, perhaps of the century. They stand there in triumph, living symbols of victory with their linked hands in the sky, the crowd cheering, the videocams rolling, the Nikons flashing, and that is when the woman in the third row begins to make her move. This is someone else we know, but it takes us a second or two to recognize her, because she has had nothing at all to do with the case we have been following. She's just been . . . sort of lurking around. The two hundred seats up front have been awarded by random drawing from the French Landing voter rolls, the lucky lottery winners notified by Debbi Anderson, Pam Stevens, and Dit Jesperson. This woman was No. 199. Several people shrink from her as she passes them, although in their happy frenzy they are hardly aware of doing it; this pale woman with clumps of straw-colored hair sticking to her cheeks smells of sweat and sleeplessness and vodka. She's got a little purse. The little purse is open. She's reaching into it. And we who have lived through the second half of the twentieth century and have through the miracle of TV witnessed a dozen assassinations and near assassinations know exactly what she is reaching *for*. We want to scream a warning to the four men standing with their linked hands raised to the sky, but all we can do is watch.

Only the black man with the sunglasses sees what's happening. He turns and starts to move, aware that she has probably beaten him, that he is probably going to be too late.

No, Speedy Parker thinks. *It can't end like this, it can't.*

'*Jack, get down!*' he shouts, but no one hears him over the clapping, the cheering, the wild hurrahs. The crowd seems to block him on purpose, surging back and forth in front of him no matter which way he moves. For a moment Wendell Green, still bobbing around like a man in the throes of an epileptic seizure, is in the assassin's path. Then she heaves him aside with the strength of a madwoman. Why not? She *is* a madwoman.

'Folks—' Dale's got his mouth practically *on* the microphone, and the PA horns mounted to the nearby trees whine with feedback. He's still holding up Jack's hand on his left and Beezer's on his right. There's a small, dazed smile on his face. 'Thank you, folks, we sure do appreciate the support, but if you could just quiet down . . .'

That's when Jack sees her.

It's been a long time, years, but he recognizes her at once. He should; she spat in his face one day as he left the Los Angeles courthouse. Spat at him and called him a railroading bastard. *She's lost fifty pounds since then*, Jack thinks. *Maybe more*. Then he sees the hand in the purse, and even before it comes back out, he knows what's happening here.

The worst is that he can do nothing about it. Doc and Dale have his hands in a death grip. He drags in a deep breath and shouts as he has been taught to do in just such a situation as this – '*Gun!*' – and Dale Gilbertson nods as if to say, *Yes it* is, *it* is *fun*. Behind her, pushing through the clapping, cheering crowd, he sees Speedy Parker, but unless Speedy's got a particularly good magic trick up his sleeve—

He doesn't. Speedy Parker, known in the Territories as Parkus, is just fighting his way into the aisle when the woman standing below the platform brings out her gun. It's an ugly little thing, a bulldog .32 with its handle wrapped in black kitchen tape, and Jack has just half a second to think that maybe it will blow up in her hand.

'*Gun!*' Jack shouts again, and it's Doc Amberson who hears him and sees the snarling woman crouched just below them.

'Ohfuck,' Doc says.

'*Wanda, no!*' Jack cries. Doc has let go of his left hand (Dale has still got his right one hoisted high in the summer air) and Jack holds it out to her like a traffic cop. Wanda Kinderling's first bullet goes right through the palm, mushrooms slightly, begins to tumble, and punches into the hollow of Jack's left shoulder.

Wanda speaks to him. There's too much noise for Jack to hear her, but he knows what she's saying, just the same: *Here you go, you railroading son of a bitch – Thorny says hello.*

She empties the remaining five bullets into Jack Sawyer's chest and throat.

No one hears the insignificant popping sounds made by Wanda's bulldog .32, not over all that clapping and cheering, but Wendell Green has got his camera tilted up, and when the detective jerks backward, our favorite reporter's finger punches the Nikon's shutter-release button in simple reflex. It snaps off eight shots. The third is *the* picture, the one that will eventually become as well known as the photo of the Marines raising the flag on Iwo Jima and that of Lee Harvey Oswald clutching his belly in the parking garage of the Dallas police station. In Wendell's photo, Jack Sawyer looks calmly down toward the shooter (who is just a blur at the very bottom of the frame). The expression on his face might be one of forgiveness. Daylight is clearly visible through the hole in the palm of his outstretched hand. Droplets of blood, as red as rubies, hang frozen in the air beside his throat, which has been torn open.

The cheering and the applause stop as if amputated. There is a moment of awful, uncomprehending silence. Jack Sawyer, shot twice in the lungs and once in the heart, as well as in the hand and the throat, stands where he is, gazing at the hole below his spread fingers and above his wrist. Wanda Kinderling peers up at him with her dingy teeth bared. Speedy Parker is looking at Jack with an expression of naked horror that his wraparound sunglasses cannot conceal. To his left, up on one of four media towers surrounding the platform, a young cameraman faints and falls to the ground.

Then, suddenly, the freeze-frame that Wendell has captured without even knowing it bursts open and everything is in motion.

Wanda Kinderling screams '*See you in hell, Hollywood*' – several people will later verify this – and then puts the muzzle of her .32 to her temple. Her look of vicious satisfaction gives way to a more typical one of dazed incomprehension when the twitch of her finger produces nothing but a dry click. The bulldog .32 is empty.

A moment later she is pretty much obliterated – broken neck, broken left shoulder, four broken ribs – as Doc stage-dives onto her and drives her to the ground. His left shoe strikes the side of Wendell Green's head, but this time Wendell sustains no more than a bloody ear. Well, he was due to catch a break, wasn't he?

On the platform, Jack Sawyer looks unbelievingly at Dale,

tries to speak, and cannot. He staggers, remains upright a moment longer, then collapses.

Dale's face has gone from bemused delight to utter shock and dismay in a heartbeat. He seizes the microphone and screams, 'HE'S SHOT! WE NEED A DOCTOR!' The PA horns shriek with more feedback. No doctor comes forward. Many in the crowd panic and begin to run. The panic spreads.

Beezer is down on one knee, turning Jack over. Jack looks up at him, still trying to speak. Blood pours from the corners of his mouth.

'Ah fuck, it's bad, Dale, it's *really bad*,' Beezer cries, and then he is knocked sprawling. One wouldn't expect that the scrawny old black man who's vaulted up onto the stage could knock around a bruiser like Beezer, but this is no ordinary old man. As we well know. There is a thin but perfectly visible envelope of white light surrounding him. Beezer sees it. His eyes widen.

The crowd, meanwhile, flees to the four points of the compass. Panic infects some of the ladies and gentlemen of the press, as well. Not Wendell Green; he holds his ground like a hero, snapping pictures until his Nikon is as empty as Wanda Kinderling's gun. He snaps the black man as he stands with Jack Sawyer in his arms; snaps Dale Gilbertson putting a hand on the black man's shoulder; snaps the black man turning and speaking to Dale. When Wendell later asks French Landing's chief of police what the old fellow said, Dale tells him he doesn't remember – besides, in all that pandemonium, he could hardly make it out, anyway. All bullshit, of course, but we may be sure that if Jack Sawyer had heard Dale's response, he would have been proud. When in doubt, tell 'em you can't remember.

Wendell's last picture shows Dale and Beezer watching with identical dazed expressions as the old fellow mounts the steps to the Winnebago with Jack Sawyer still in his arms. Wendell has no idea how such an old party can carry such a big man – Sawyer is six-two and must go a hundred and ninety at least – but he supposes it's the same sort of deal that allows a distraught mother to lift up the car or truck beneath which her kid is pinned. And it doesn't matter. It's small beans compared to what happens next. Because when a group of men led by Dale, Beez, and Doc burst into the Winnebago (Wendell is at the rear of this group), they find nothing but a single overturned chair and several splashes of Jack Sawyer's blood in the kitchenette where Jack gave his little gang their final instructions. The trail of blood leads toward the rear, where there's a foldout bed and a toilet cubicle. And there the drops and splashes simply stop.

Jack and the old man who carried him in here have vanished.

Doc and Beezer are babbling, almost in hysterics. They bounce between questions of where Jack might have gone to distraught recollections of the final few moments on the platform before the shooting started. They can't seem to let that go, and Dale has an idea it will be quite a while before he can let go of it himself. He realizes now that Jack saw the woman coming, that he was trying to get his hand free of Dale's so he could respond.

Dale thinks it may be time to quit the chief's job after all, find some other line of work. Not right now, though. Right now he wants to get Beezer and Doc away from the Color Posse, get them calmed down. He has something to tell them that may help with that.

Tom Lund and Bobby Dulac join him, and the three of them escort Beez and Doc away from the Winnebago, where Special Agent Redding and WSP Detective Black are already establishing a CIP (crime investigation perimeter). Once they're behind the platform, Dale looks into the stunned faces of the two burly bikers.

'Listen to me,' Dale says.

'I should have stepped in front of him,' Doc says. 'I saw her coming, why didn't I step in front—'

'Shut up and *listen*!'

Doc shuts up. Tom and Bobby are also listening, their eyes wide.

'That black man said something to me.'

'What?' Beezer asks.

'He said, "Let me take him – there may still be a chance."'

Doc, who has treated his share of gunshot wounds, gives a forlorn little chuckle. 'And you *believed* him?'

'Not then, not exactly,' Dale says. 'But when we went in there and the place was empty—'

'No back door, either,' Beezer adds.

Doc's skepticism has faded a little. 'You really think . . .?'

'I do,' Dale Gilbertson says, and wipes his eyes. 'I have to hope. And you guys have to help me.'

'All right,' Beezer says. 'Then we will.'

And we think that here we must leave them for good, standing under a blue summer sky close to the Father of Waters, standing beside a platform with blood on the boards. Soon life will catch them up again and pull them back into its furious current, but for a few moments they are together, joined in hope for our mutual friend.

Let us leave them so, shall we?

Let us leave them hoping.

ONCE UPON A TIME IN
THE TERRITORIES . . .

Once upon a time (as all the best old stories used to begin when we all lived in the forest and nobody lived anywhere else), a scarred Captain of the Outer Guards named Farren led a frightened little boy named Jack Sawyer through the Queen's Pavilion. That small boy did not see the Queen's court, however; no, he was taken through a maze of corridors behind the scenes, secret and seldom-visited places where spiders spun in the high corners and the warm drafts were heavy with the smells of cooking from the kitchen.

Finally, Farren placed his hands in the boy's armpits and lifted him up. *There's a panel in front of you now*, he whispered – do you remember? I think you were there. I think we both were, although we were younger then, weren't we? *Slide it to the left.*

Jack did as he was bidden, and found himself peeking into the Queen's chamber; the room in which almost everyone expected her to die . . . just as Jack expected his mother to die in her room at the Alhambra Inn and Gardens in New Hampshire. It was a bright, airy room filled with bustling nurses who had assumed a busy and purposeful manner because they had no real idea of how to help their patient. The boy looked through the peephole into this room, at a woman he at first thought was his own mother somehow magically transported to this place, and we looked with him, none of us guessing that years later, grown to a man, Jack Sawyer would be lying in the same bed where he first saw his mother's Twinner.

Parkus, who has brought him from French Landing to the Inner Baronies, now stands at the panel through which Jack, hoisted by Captain Farren, once looked. Beside him is Sophie of Canna, now known in the Territories as both the Young Queen and Sophie the Good. There are no nurses in the sleeping chamber today; Jack lies silent beneath a slowly turning fan. Where he is not wrapped in bandages, his skin is pale. His closed eyelids are hazed with a delicate purple bruise-blush. The rise and fall of the fine linen sheet drawn up to his chin can hardly be seen . . . but it's there. He breathes.

For now, at least, he lives.

Speaking quietly, Sophie says, 'If he'd never touched the Talisman—'

'If he'd never touched the Talisman, actually held it in his arms, he would have been dead there on that platform before I could even get close to him,' Parkus says. 'But of course, if not for the Talisman, he never would have been there in the first place.'

'What chance has he?' She looks at him. Somewhere, in another world, Judy Marshall has already begun to subside back into her ordinary suburban life. There will be no such life for her Twinner, however – hard times have come again in this part of the universe – and her eyes gleam with an imperious, regal light. 'Tell me the truth, sir; I would not have a lie.'

'Nor would I give you one, my lady,' he tells her. 'I believe that, thanks to the residual protection of the Talisman, he will recover. You'll be sitting next to him one morning or evening and his eyes will open. Not today, and probably not this week, but soon.'

'And as for returning to his world? The world of his friends?'

Parkus has brought her to this place because the spirit of the boy Jack was still lingers, ghostly and child-sweet. He was here before the road of trials opened ahead of him, and in some ways hardened him. He was here with his innocence still intact. What has surprised him about Jack as a grown man – and touched him in a way Parkus never expected to be touched again – is how much of that innocence still remained in the man the boy has become.

That too is the Talisman's doing, of course.

'Parkus? Your mind wanders.'

'Not far, my lady; not far. You ask if he may return to his world after being mortally wounded three, perhaps even four times – after being heart-pierced, in fact. I brought him here because all the magic that has touched and changed his life is stronger here; for good or ill, the Territories have been Jack Sawyer's wellspring since he was a child. And it worked. He lives. But he will wake different. He'll be like . . .'

Parkus pauses, thinking hard. Sophie waits quietly beside him. Distantly, from the kitchen, comes the bellow of a cook lacing into one of the 'prentices.

'There are animals that live in the sea, breathing with gills,' Parkus says at last. 'And over time's long course, some of them develop lungs. Such creatures can live both under the water and on the land. Yes?'

'So I was taught as a girl,' Sophie agrees patiently.

'But some of these latter creatures lose their gills and can live only on the land. Jack Sawyer is that sort of creature now, I think. You or I could dive into the water and swim beneath the surface for a little while, and he may be able to go back and visit his own world for short periods . . . in time, of course. But if either you or I were to try *living* beneath the water—'

'We'd drown.'

'Indeed we would. And if Jack were to try living in his own world again, returning to his little house in Norway Valley, for instance, his wounds would return in a space of days or weeks. Perhaps in different forms – his death certificate might specify heart failure, for instance – but it would be Wanda Kinderling's bullet that killed him, all the same. Wanda Kinderling's heart shot.' Parkus bares his teeth. 'Hateful woman! I believe the abbalah was aware of her no more than I was, but look at the damage she's caused!'

Sophie ignores this. She is looking at the silent, sleeping man in the other room.

'Condemned to live in such a pleasant land as this . . .' She turns to him. 'It *is* a pleasant land, isn't it, sirrah? Still a pleasant land, in spite of all?'

Parkus smiles and bows. Around his neck, a shark's tooth swings at the end of a fine gold necklace. 'Indeed it is.'

She nods briskly. 'So living here might not be so terrible.'

He says nothing. After a moment or two, her assumed briskness departs, and her shoulders sag.

'I'd hate it,' she says in a small voice. 'To be barred from my own world except for occasional brief visits . . . paroles . . . to have to leave at the first cough or twinge in my chest . . . I'd hate it.'

Parkus shrugs. 'He'll have to accept what is. Like it or

not, his gills are gone. He's a creature of the Territories now. And God the Carpenter knows there's work for him over here. The business of the Tower is moving toward its climax. I believe Jack Sawyer may have a part to play in that, although I can't say for sure. In any case, when he heals, he won't want for work. He's a coppiceman, and there's always work for such.'

She looks through the slit in the wall, her lovely face troubled.

'You must help him, dear,' Parkus says.

'I love him,' she says, speaking very low.

'And he loves you. But what's coming will be difficult.'

'Why must that be, Parkus? Why must life always demand so much and give so little?'

He draws her into his arms and she goes willingly, her face pressed against his chest.

In the dark behind the chamber in which Jack Sawyer sleeps, Parkus answers her question with a single word:

Ka.

EPILOGUE

She sits by his bed on the first night of Full-Earth Moon, ten days after her conversation with Parkus in the secret passageway. Outside the pavilion, she can hear children singing 'The Green Corn A-Dayo.' On her lap is a scrap of embroidery. It is summer, still summer, and the air is sweet with summer's mystery.

And in this billowing room where his mother's Twinner once lay, Jack Sawyer opens his eyes.

Sophie lays aside her embroidery, leans forward, and puts her lips soft against the shell of his ear.

'Welcome back,' she says. 'My heart, my life, and my love: welcome back.'

April 14, 2001

DISCOVER THE WORLD OF THE TALISMAN
BY STEPHEN KING AND PETER STRAUB

To find out more about Stephen King,
please visit www.stephenkingbooks.co.uk
or www.facebook.com/stephenkingbooks